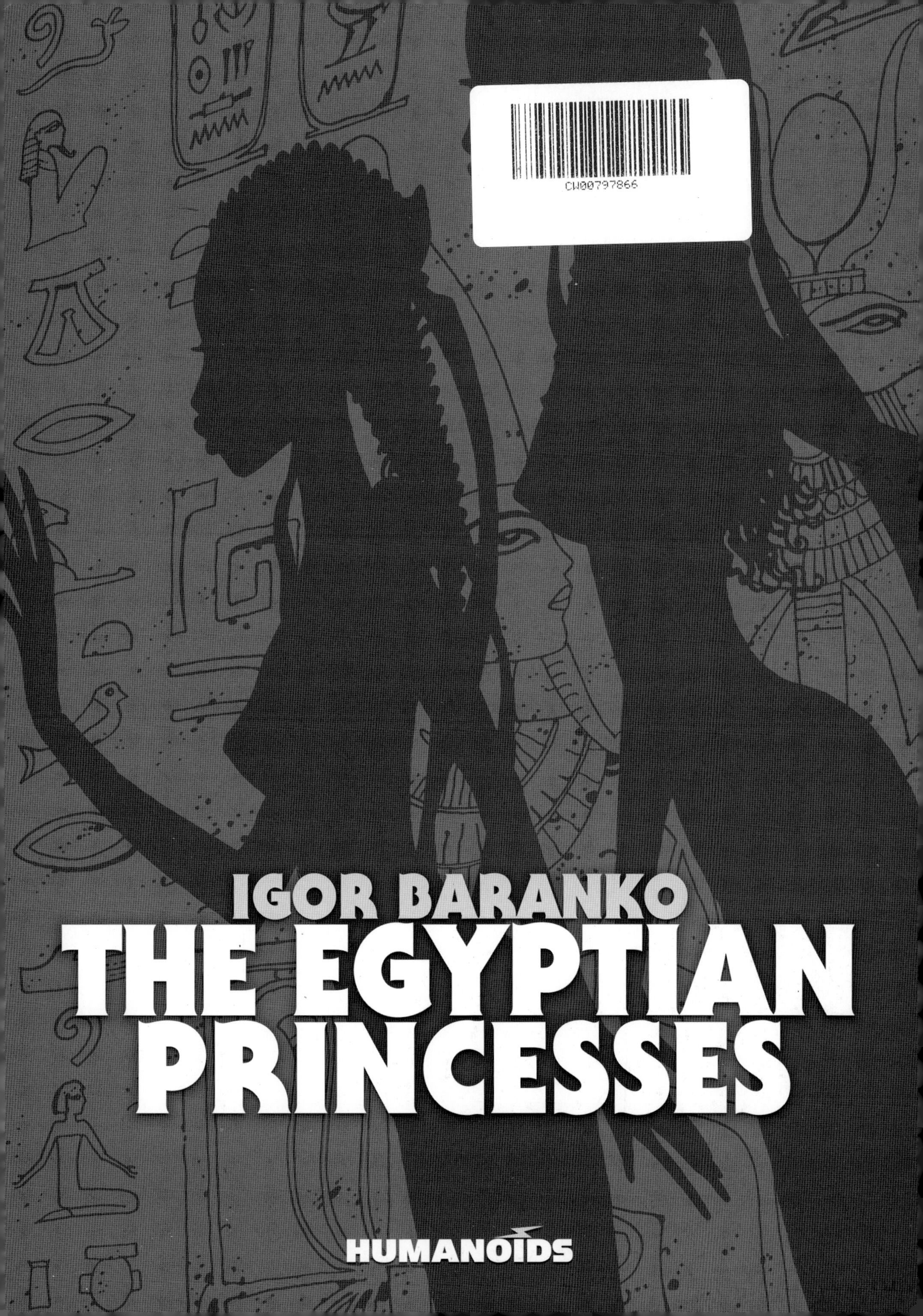

IGOR BARANKO

THE EGYPTIAN PRINCESSES

HUMANOIDS

IGOR BARANKO
Writer & Artist

QUINN & KATIA DONOGHUE
Translators

•

JERRY FRISSEN
Senior Art Director

TIM PILCHER
& ALEX DONOGHUE
U.S. Edition Editors

FABRICE GIGER
Publisher

Rights & Licensing - licensing@humanoids.com
Press and Social Media - pr@humanoids.com

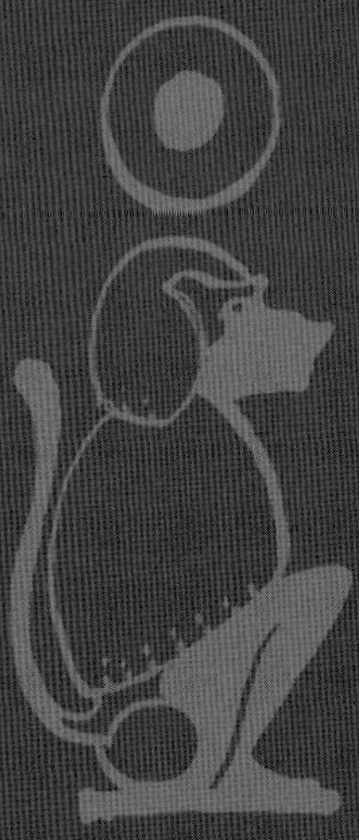

THE EGYPTIAN PRINCESSES
This title is a publication of Humanoids, Inc. 8033 Sunset Blvd. #628, Los Angeles, CA 90046.

Originally published in French by Les Humanoïdes Associés (Paris, France).

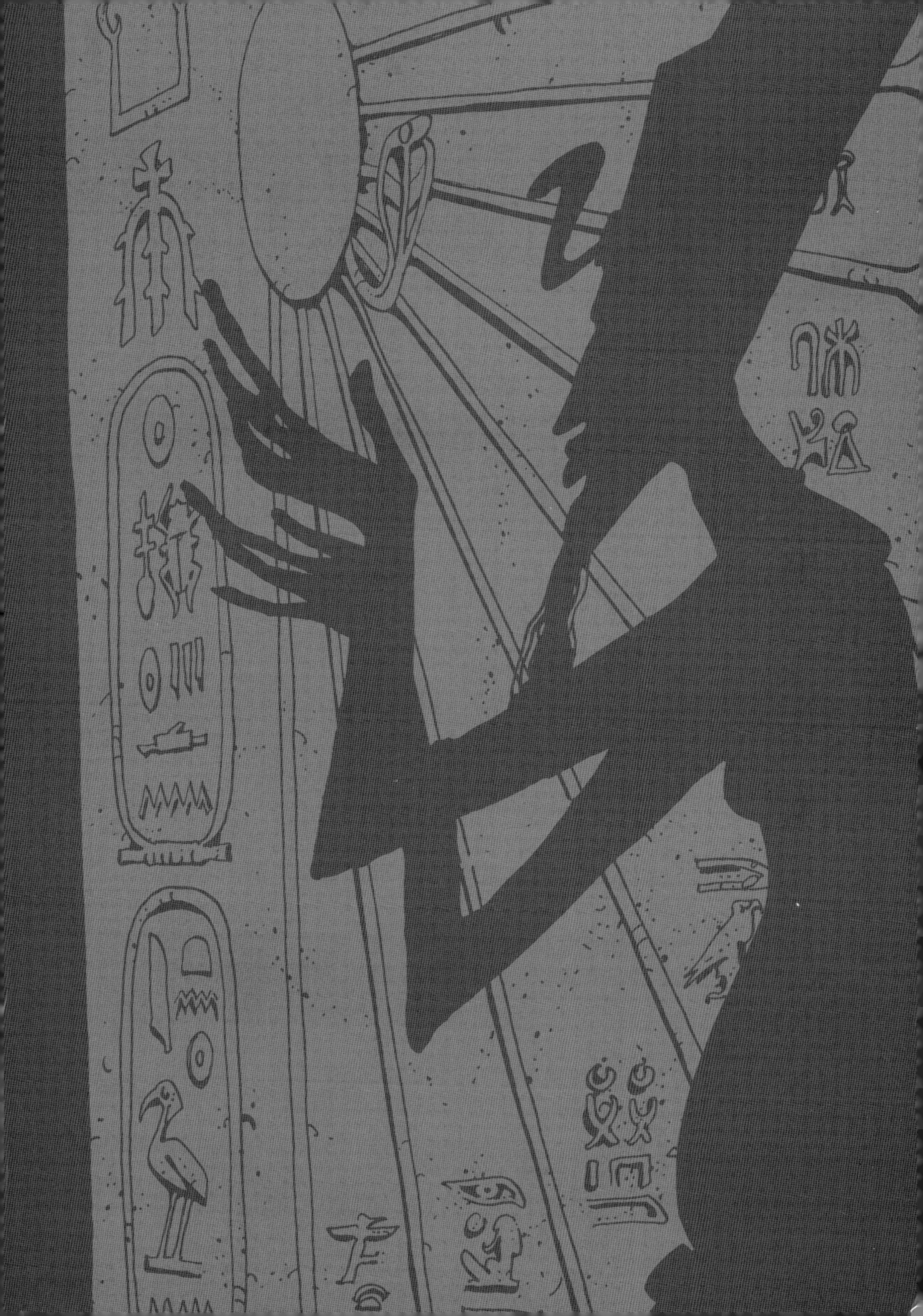

Other books by
IGOR BARANKO:

SHAMANISM
ISBN: 978-1-59465-095-6

JIHAD
ISBN: 978-1-59465-070-3

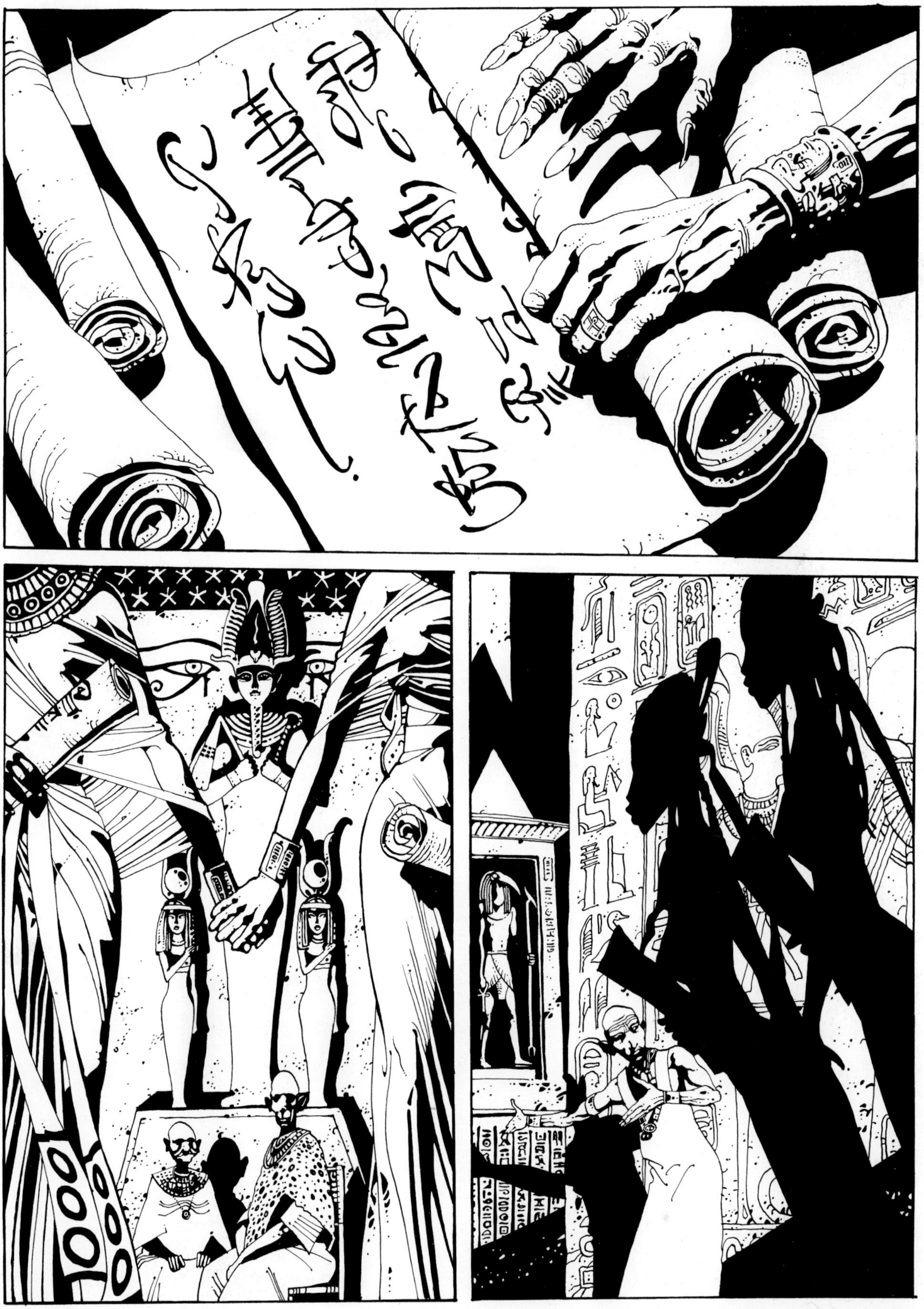

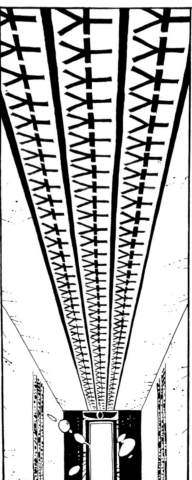

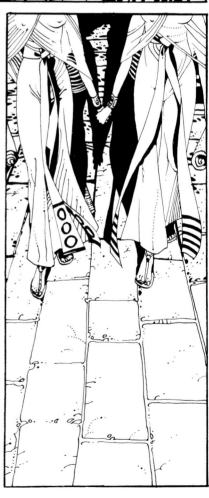

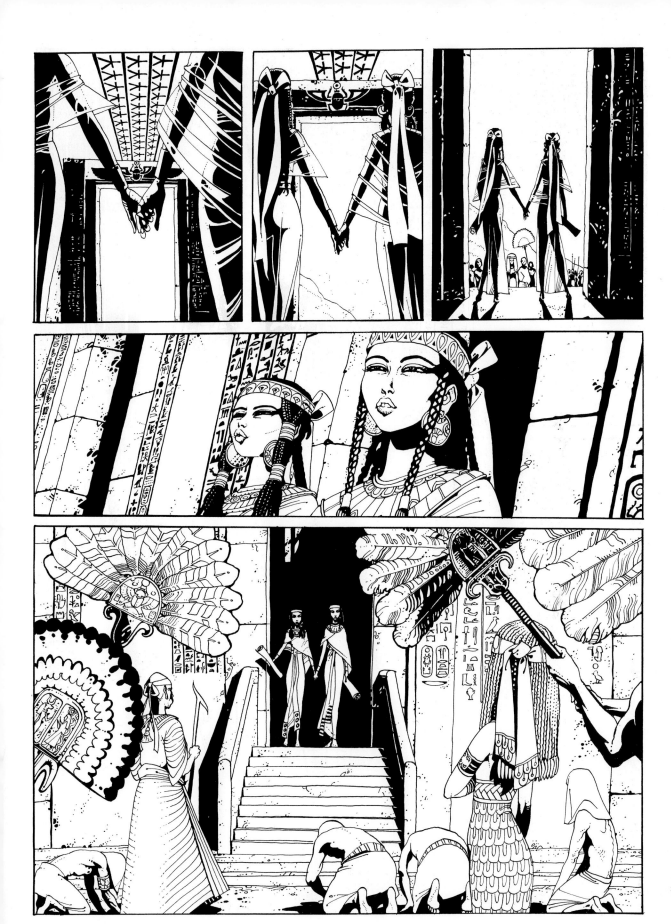

WE'RE FINALLY GOING TO KNOW EVERYTHING.

WHAT AN HONOR IT IS TO BE THE FIRST TO READ THE HOROSCOPE OF THE DAUGHTERS OF *PHARAOH RAMSES III* (MAY THE GODS GRANT HIM A LONG LIFE, HEALTH, AND STRENGTH).

SHOW ME YOURS, *TITI-NEFER SEHMETIKETH.*

IT'S EXCELLENT. A HAPPY DESTINY IS FORESEEN FOR YOU.

ISN'T THAT SO?

WHY, YES...

AND YOU, DEAR DAUGHTER OF THE PHARAOH'S FAVORITE CONCUBINE (MAY THE GODS GRANT HIM A LONG LIFE, HEALTH, AND STRENGTH), *KIKI-NEFER BASTIMERITH* ... WHAT IS YOUR DESTINY?

WELL?

YES...?

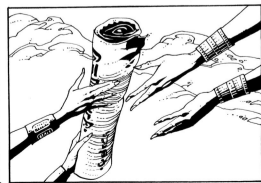

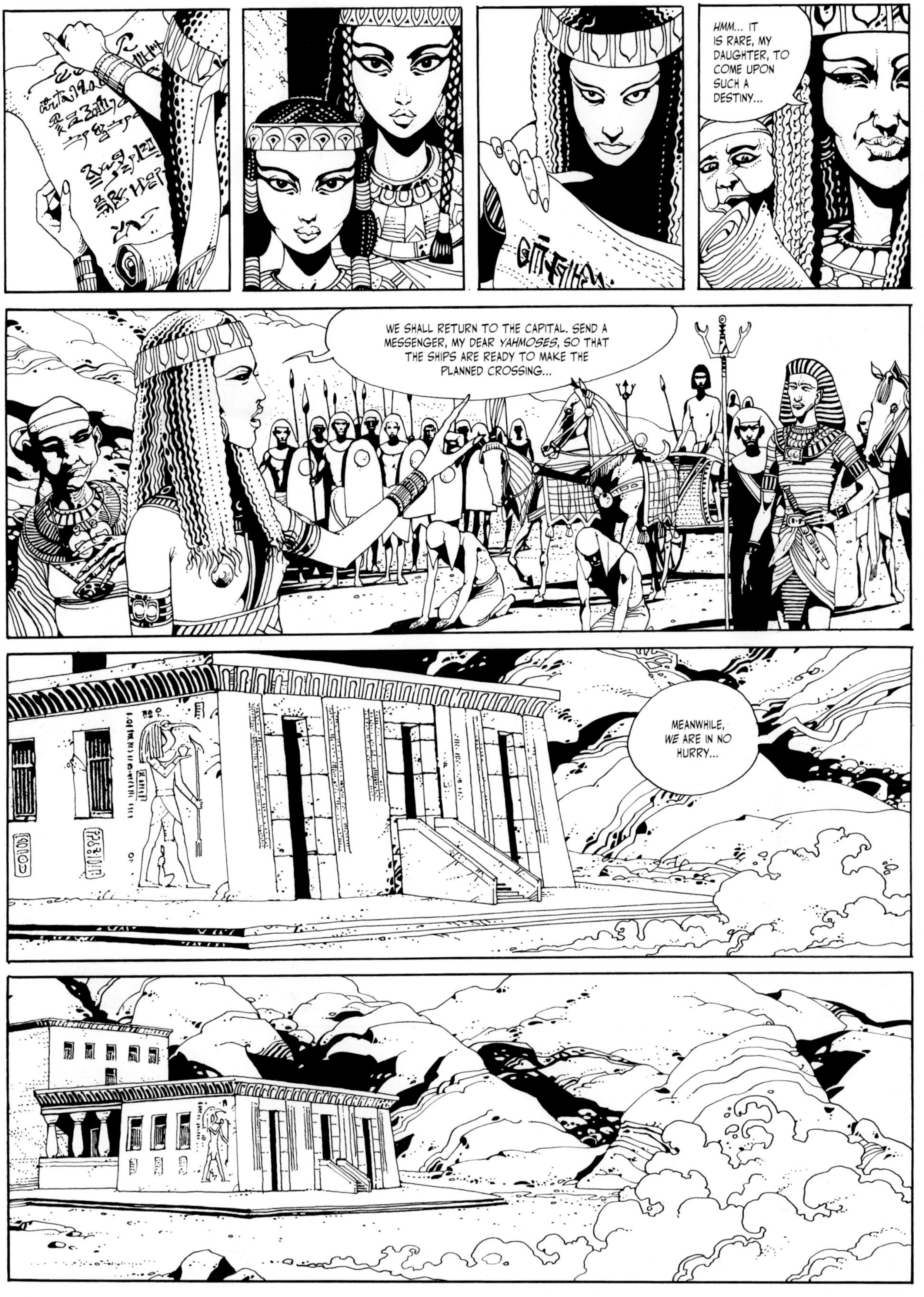
HMM... IT IS RARE, MY DAUGHTER, TO COME UPON SUCH A DESTINY...
WE SHALL RETURN TO THE CAPITAL. SEND A MESSENGER, MY DEAR *YAHMOSES*, SO THAT THE SHIPS ARE READY TO MAKE THE PLANNED CROSSING...
MEANWHILE, WE ARE IN NO HURRY...

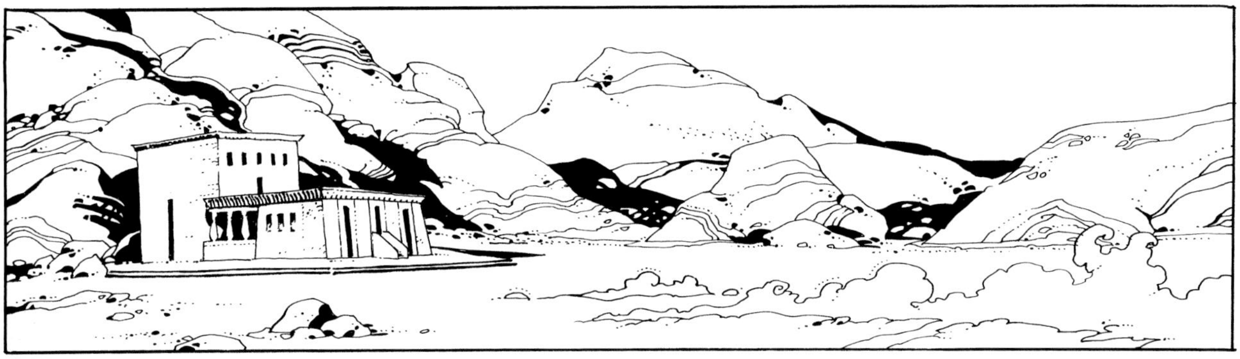

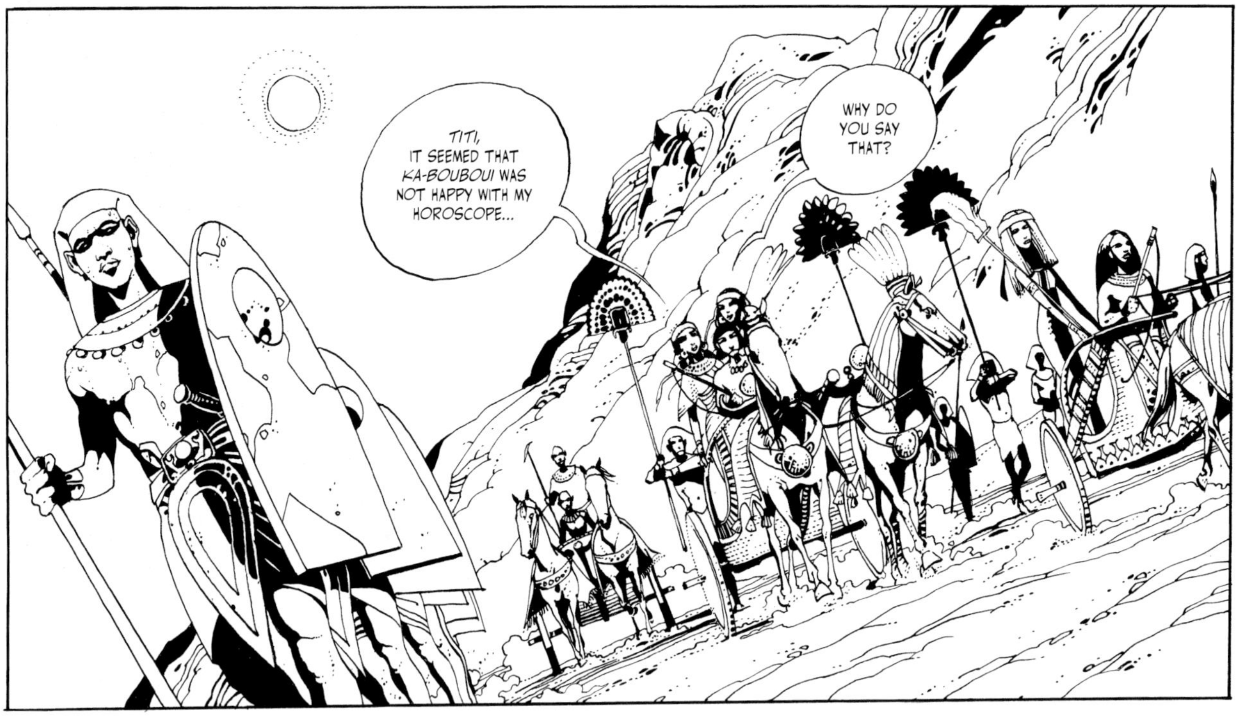
TITI, IT SEEMED THAT KA-BOUBOUI WAS NOT HAPPY WITH MY HOROSCOPE...
WHY DO YOU SAY THAT?

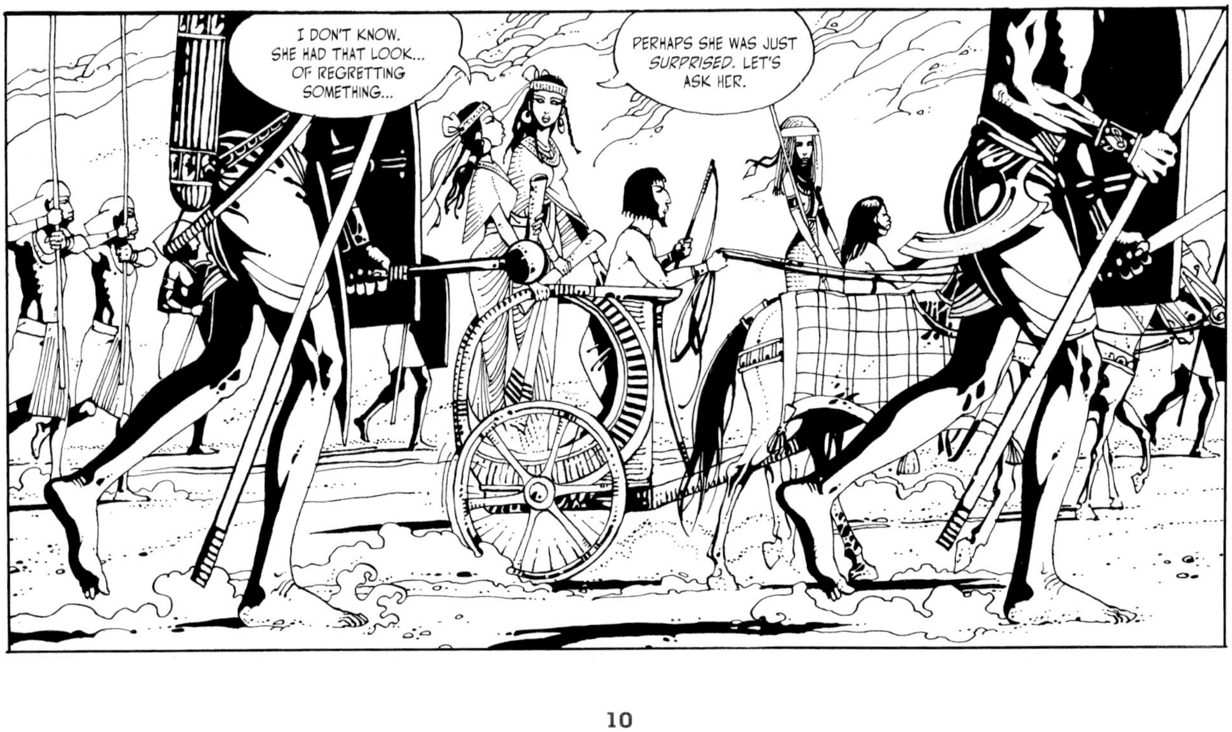
I DON'T KNOW. SHE HAD THAT LOOK... OF REGRETTING SOMETHING...
PERHAPS SHE WAS JUST SURPRISED. LET'S ASK HER.

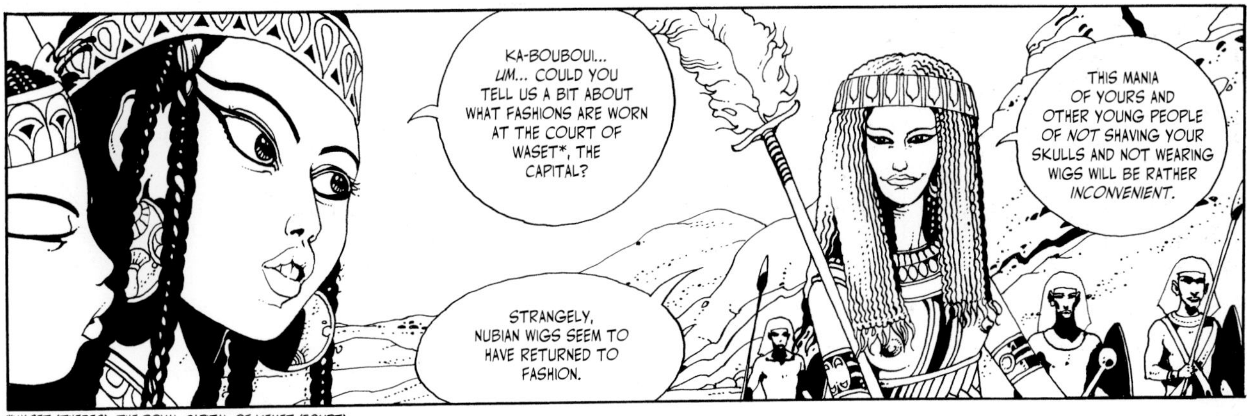
KA-BOUBOUI... UM... COULD YOU TELL US A BIT ABOUT WHAT FASHIONS ARE WORN AT THE COURT OF WASET*, THE CAPITAL?
STRANGELY, NUBIAN WIGS SEEM TO HAVE RETURNED TO FASHION.
THIS MANIA OF YOURS AND OTHER YOUNG PEOPLE OF NOT SHAVING YOUR SKULLS AND NOT WEARING WIGS WILL BE RATHER INCONVENIENT.

*WASET (THEBES): THE ROYAL CAPITAL OF KEMET (EGYPT).

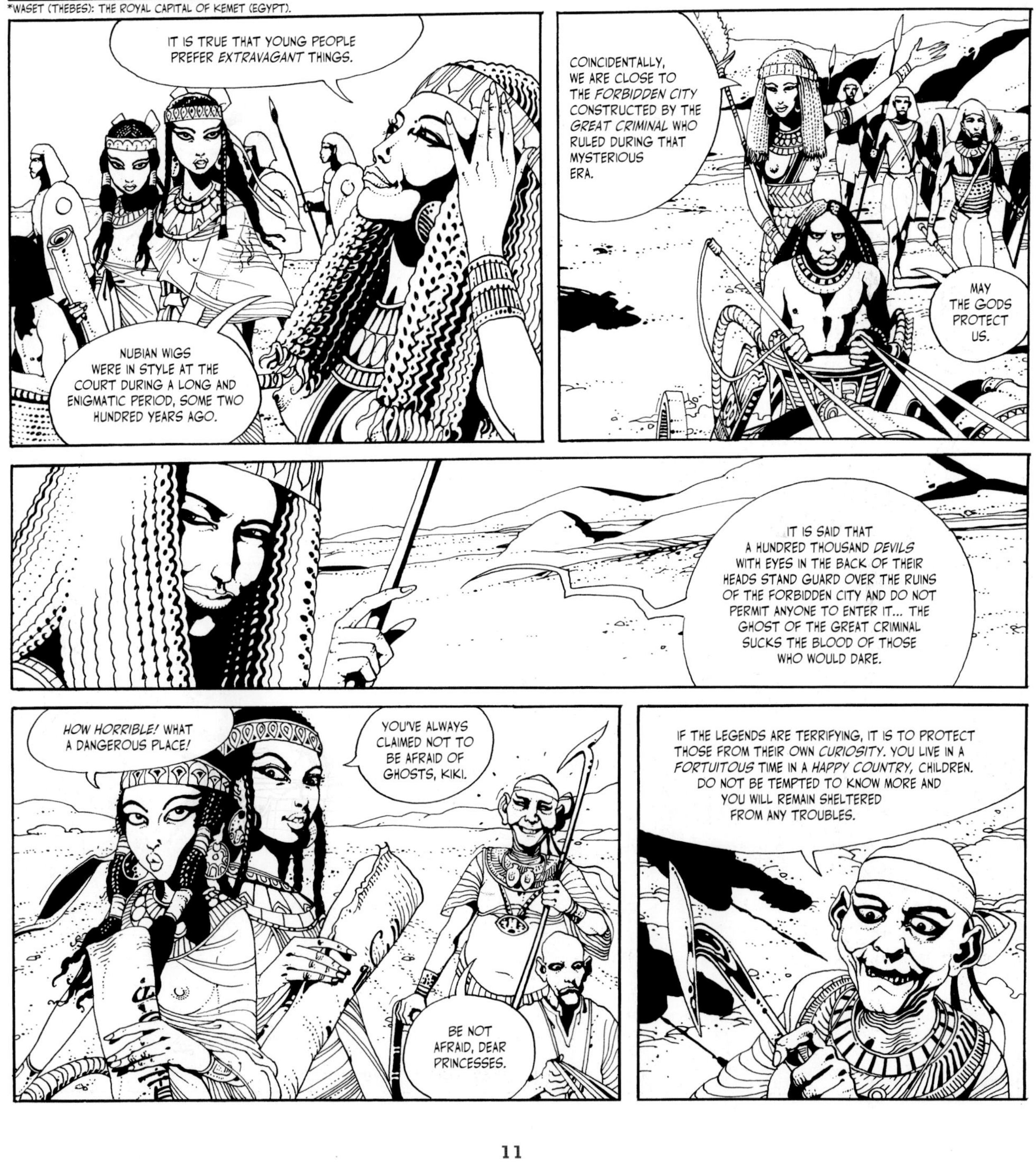
IT IS TRUE THAT YOUNG PEOPLE PREFER EXTRAVAGANT THINGS.
NUBIAN WIGS WERE IN STYLE AT THE COURT DURING A LONG AND ENIGMATIC PERIOD, SOME TWO HUNDRED YEARS AGO.
COINCIDENTALLY, WE ARE CLOSE TO THE FORBIDDEN CITY CONSTRUCTED BY THE GREAT CRIMINAL WHO RULED DURING THAT MYSTERIOUS ERA.
MAY THE GODS PROTECT US.
IT IS SAID THAT A HUNDRED THOUSAND DEVILS WITH EYES IN THE BACK OF THEIR HEADS STAND GUARD OVER THE RUINS OF THE FORBIDDEN CITY AND DO NOT PERMIT ANYONE TO ENTER IT... THE GHOST OF THE GREAT CRIMINAL SUCKS THE BLOOD OF THOSE WHO WOULD DARE.
HOW HORRIBLE! WHAT A DANGEROUS PLACE!
YOU'VE ALWAYS CLAIMED NOT TO BE AFRAID OF GHOSTS, KIKI.
BE NOT AFRAID, DEAR PRINCESSES.
IF THE LEGENDS ARE TERRIFYING, IT IS TO PROTECT THOSE FROM THEIR OWN CURIOSITY. YOU LIVE IN A FORTUITOUS TIME IN A HAPPY COUNTRY, CHILDREN. DO NOT BE TEMPTED TO KNOW MORE AND YOU WILL REMAIN SHELTERED FROM ANY TROUBLES.

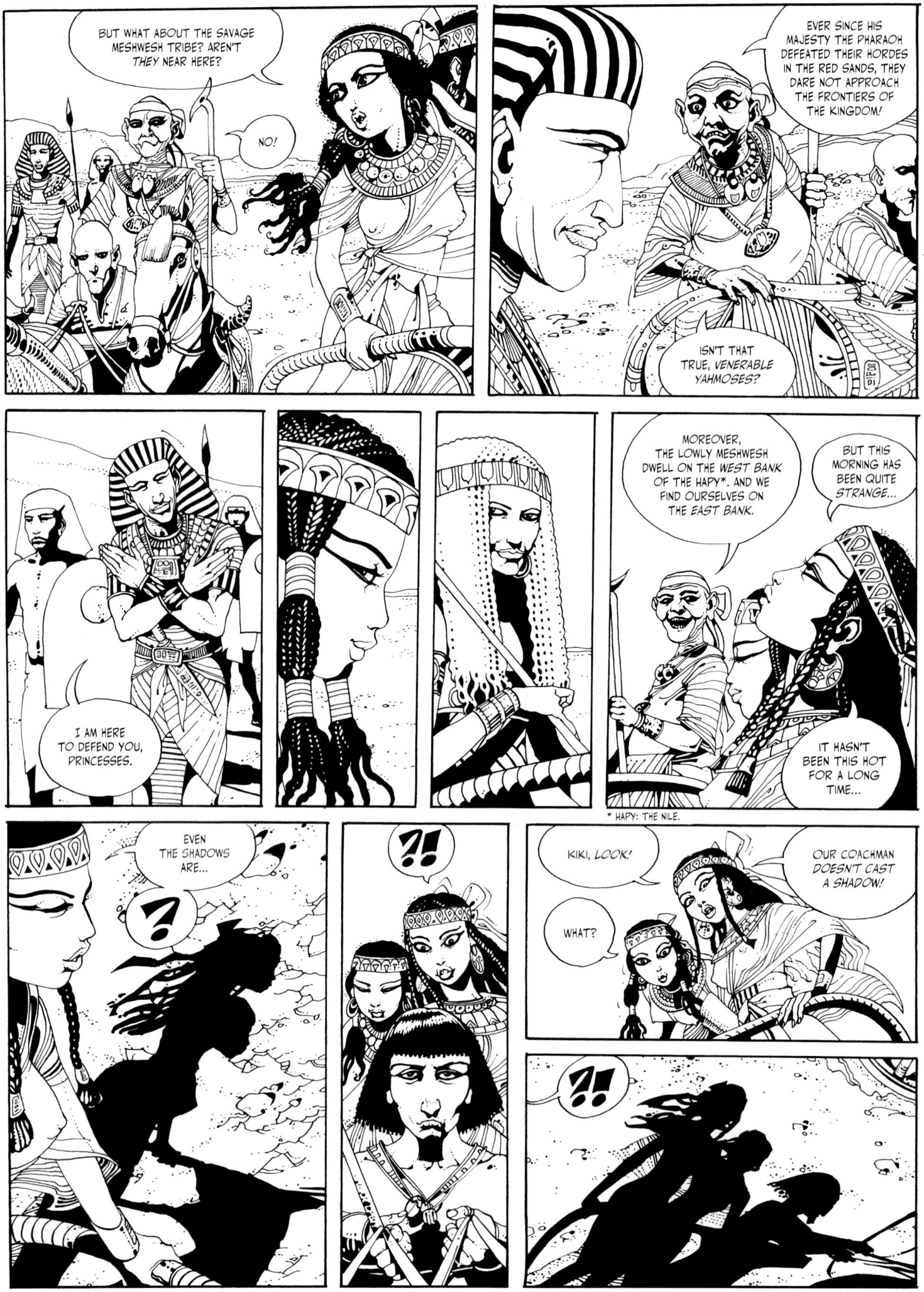

BUT WHAT ABOUT THE SAVAGE MESHWESH TRIBE? AREN'T *THEY* NEAR HERE?
NO!
EVER SINCE HIS MAJESTY THE PHARAOH DEFEATED THEIR HORDES IN THE RED SANDS, THEY DARE NOT APPROACH THE FRONTIERS OF THE KINGDOM!
ISN'T THAT TRUE, *VENERABLE YAHMOSES?*
I AM HERE TO DEFEND YOU, PRINCESSES.
MOREOVER, THE LOWLY MESHWESH DWELL ON THE *WEST BANK* OF THE HAPY*. AND WE FIND OURSELVES ON THE *EAST BANK.*
BUT THIS MORNING HAS BEEN QUITE *STRANGE...*
IT HASN'T BEEN THIS HOT FOR A LONG TIME...
* HAPY: THE NILE.
EVEN THE SHADOWS ARE...
?
?!
KIKI, *LOOK!*
WHAT?
OUR COACHMAN *DOESN'T CAST A SHADOW!*
?!

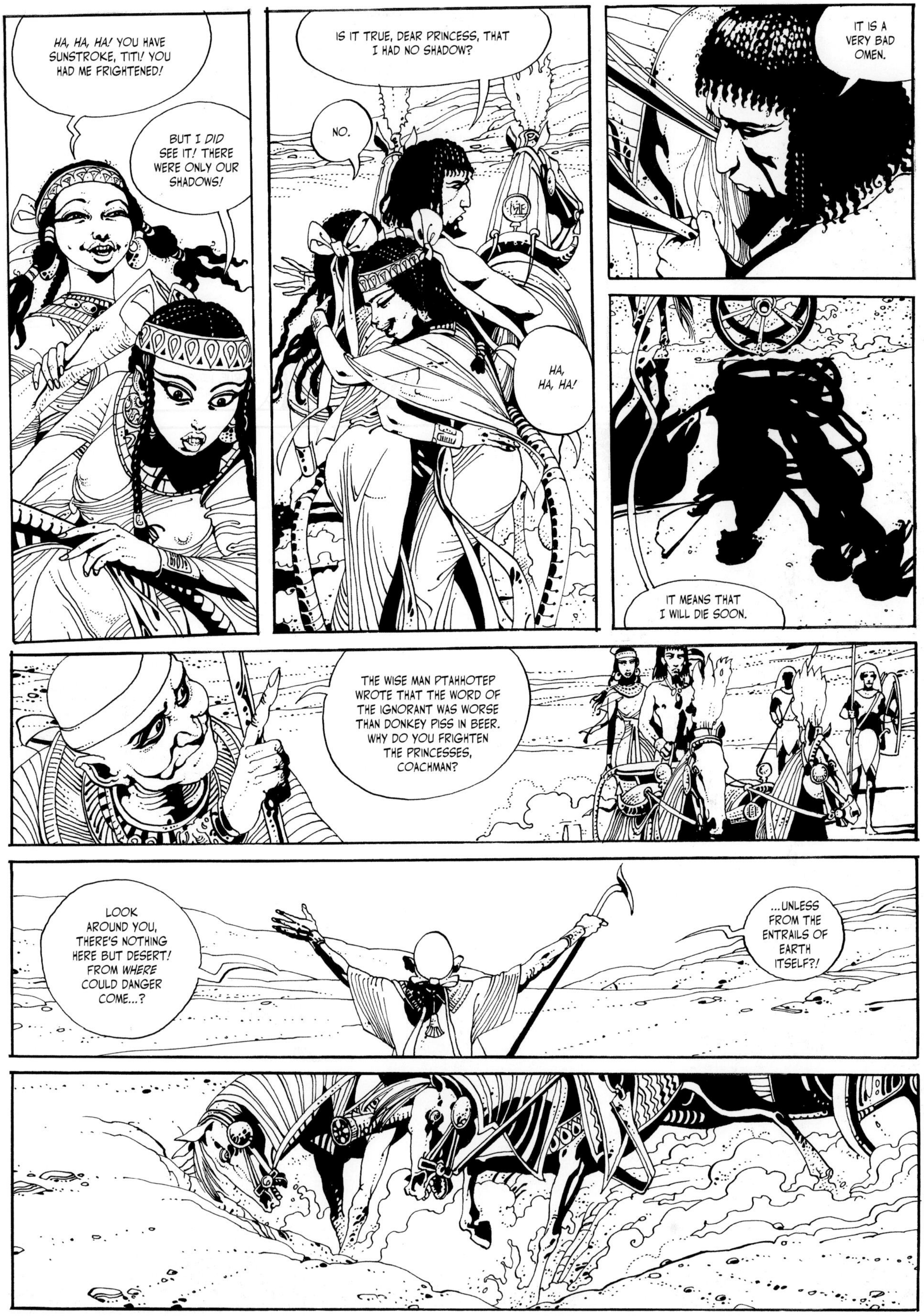
HA, HA, HA! YOU HAVE SUNSTROKE, TITI! YOU HAD ME FRIGHTENED!
BUT I DID SEE IT! THERE WERE ONLY OUR SHADOWS!
IS IT TRUE, DEAR PRINCESS, THAT I HAD NO SHADOW?
NO.
HA, HA, HA!
IT IS A VERY BAD OMEN.
IT MEANS THAT I WILL DIE SOON.
THE WISE MAN PTAHHOTEP WROTE THAT THE WORD OF THE IGNORANT WAS WORSE THAN DONKEY PISS IN BEER. WHY DO YOU FRIGHTEN THE PRINCESSES, COACHMAN?
LOOK AROUND YOU, THERE'S NOTHING HERE BUT DESERT! FROM WHERE COULD DANGER COME...?
...UNLESS FROM THE ENTRAILS OF EARTH ITSELF?!

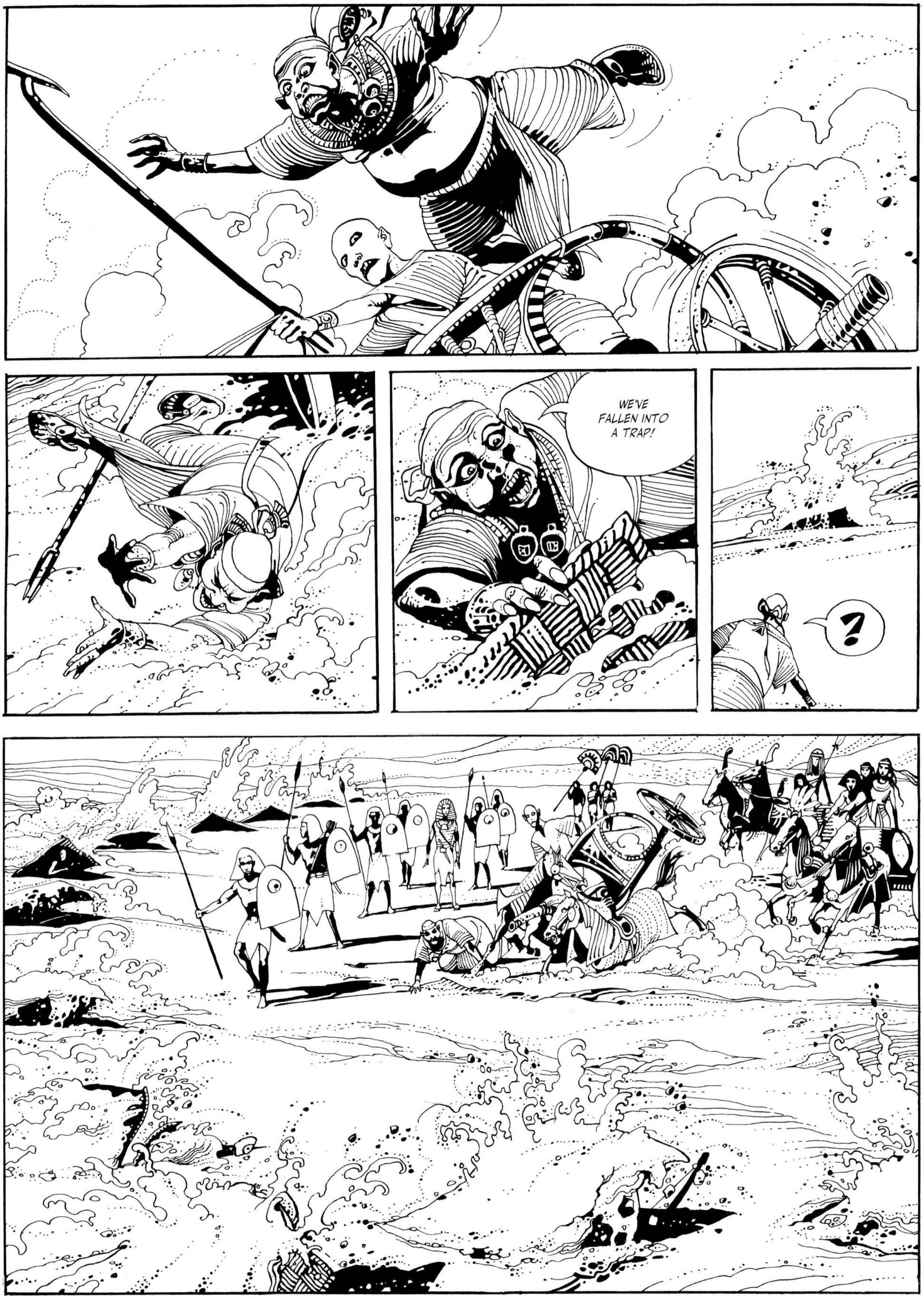
WE'VE FALLEN INTO A TRAP!
?

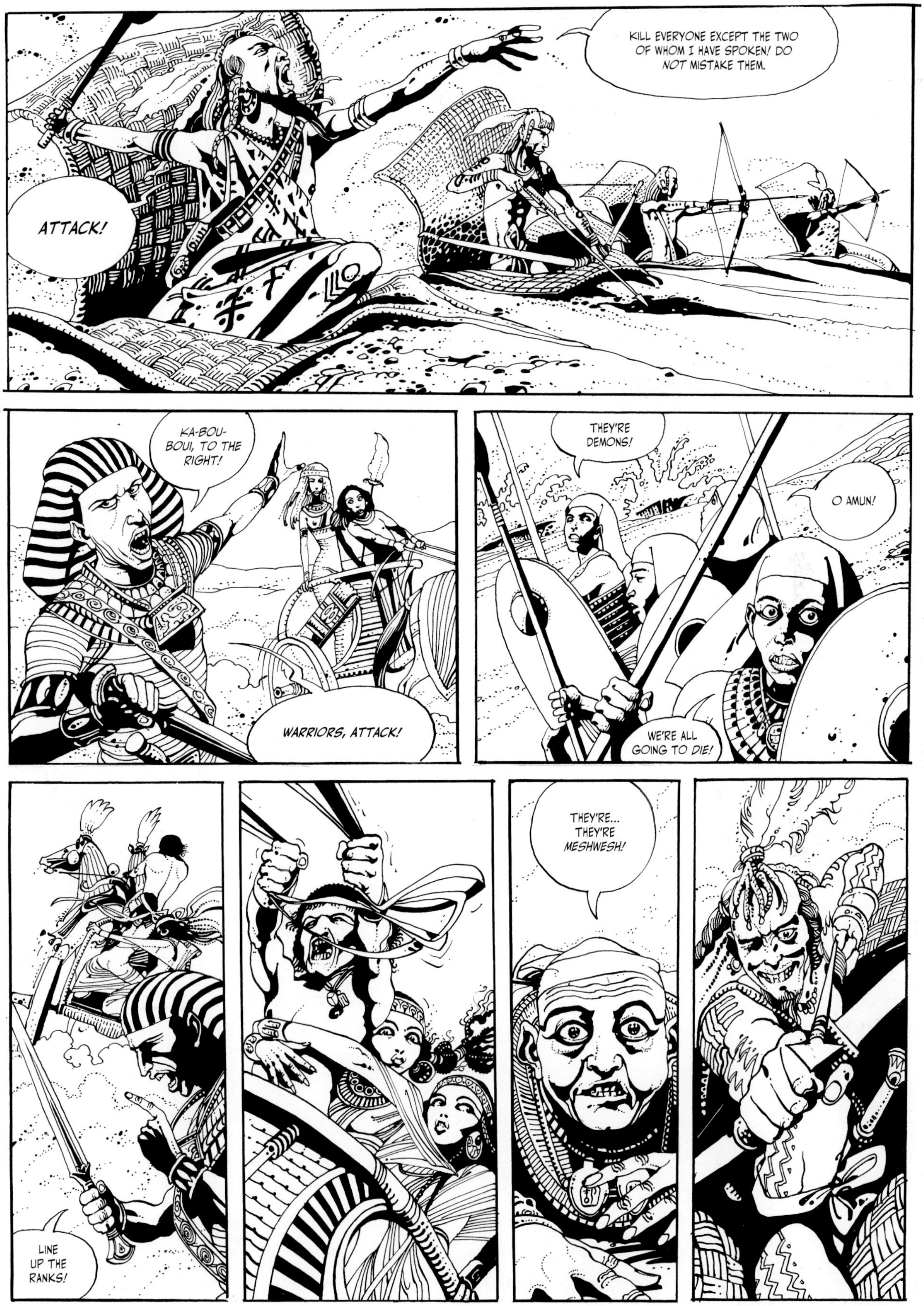
KILL EVERYONE EXCEPT THE TWO OF WHOM I HAVE SPOKEN! DO NOT MISTAKE THEM.
ATTACK!
KA-BOU-BOUI, TO THE RIGHT!
WARRIORS, ATTACK!
THEY'RE DEMONS!
O AMUN!
WE'RE ALL GOING TO DIE!
LINE UP THE RANKS!
THEY'RE... THEY'RE MESHWESH!

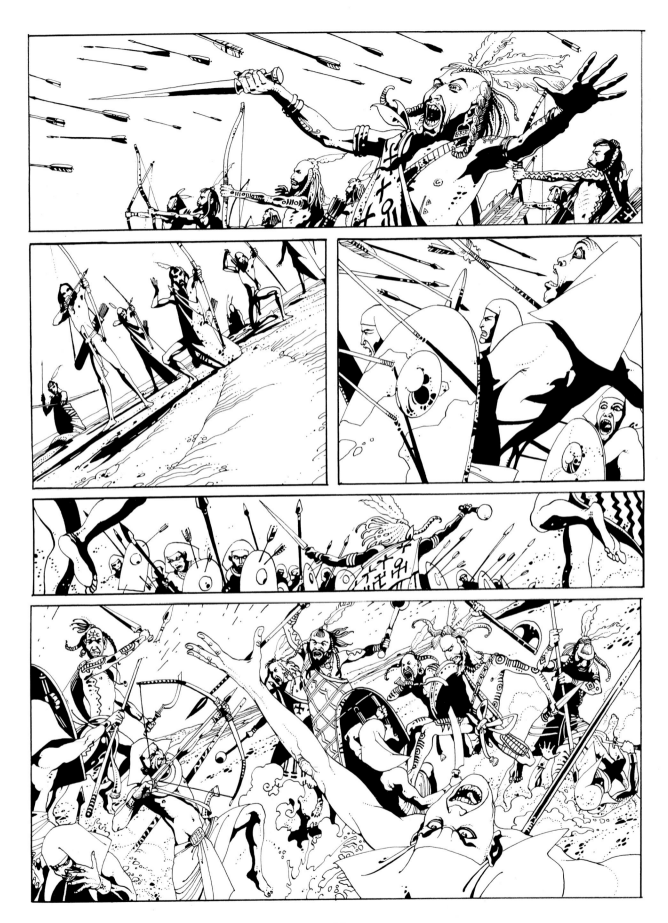

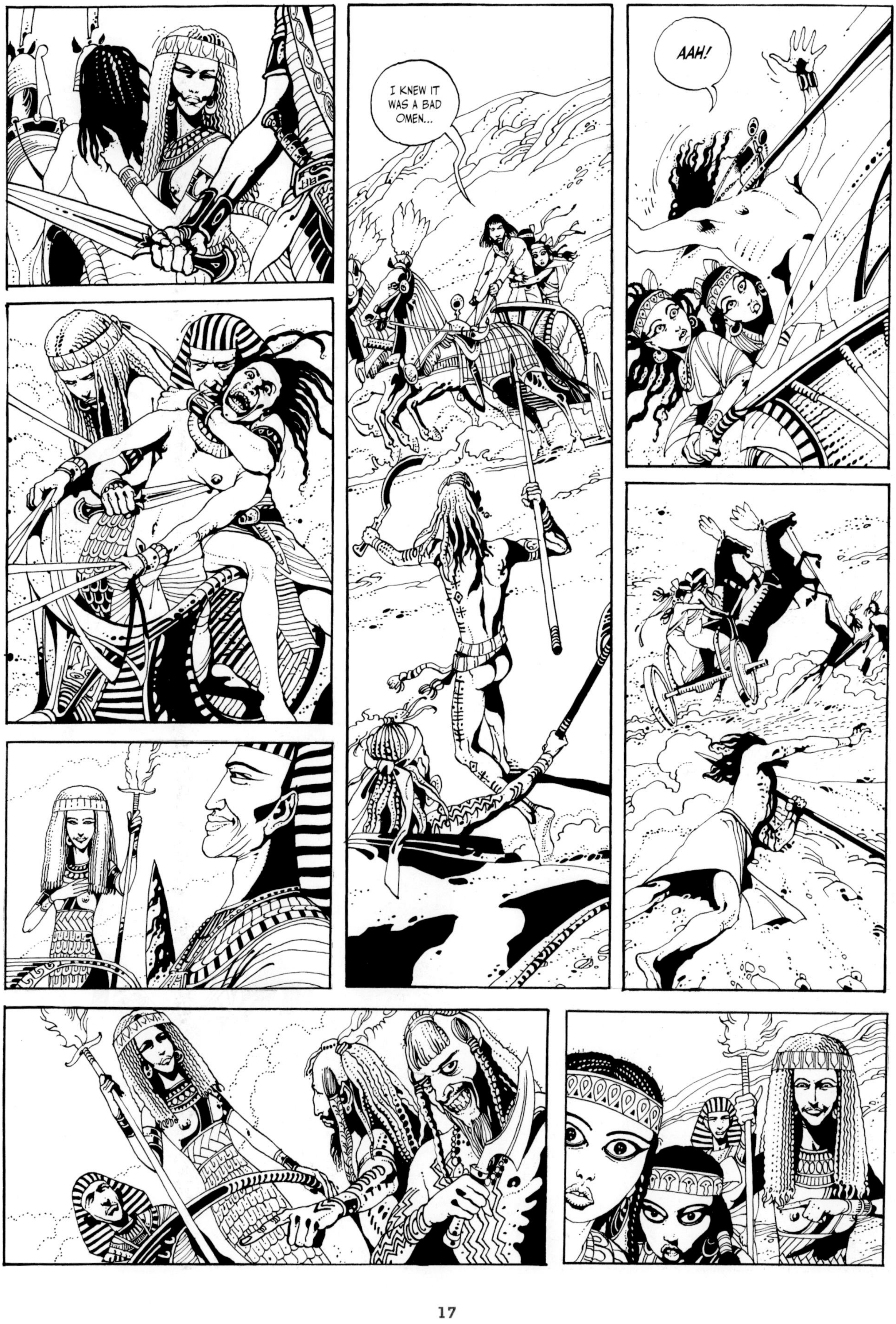
I KNEW IT WAS A BAD OMEN...
AAH!

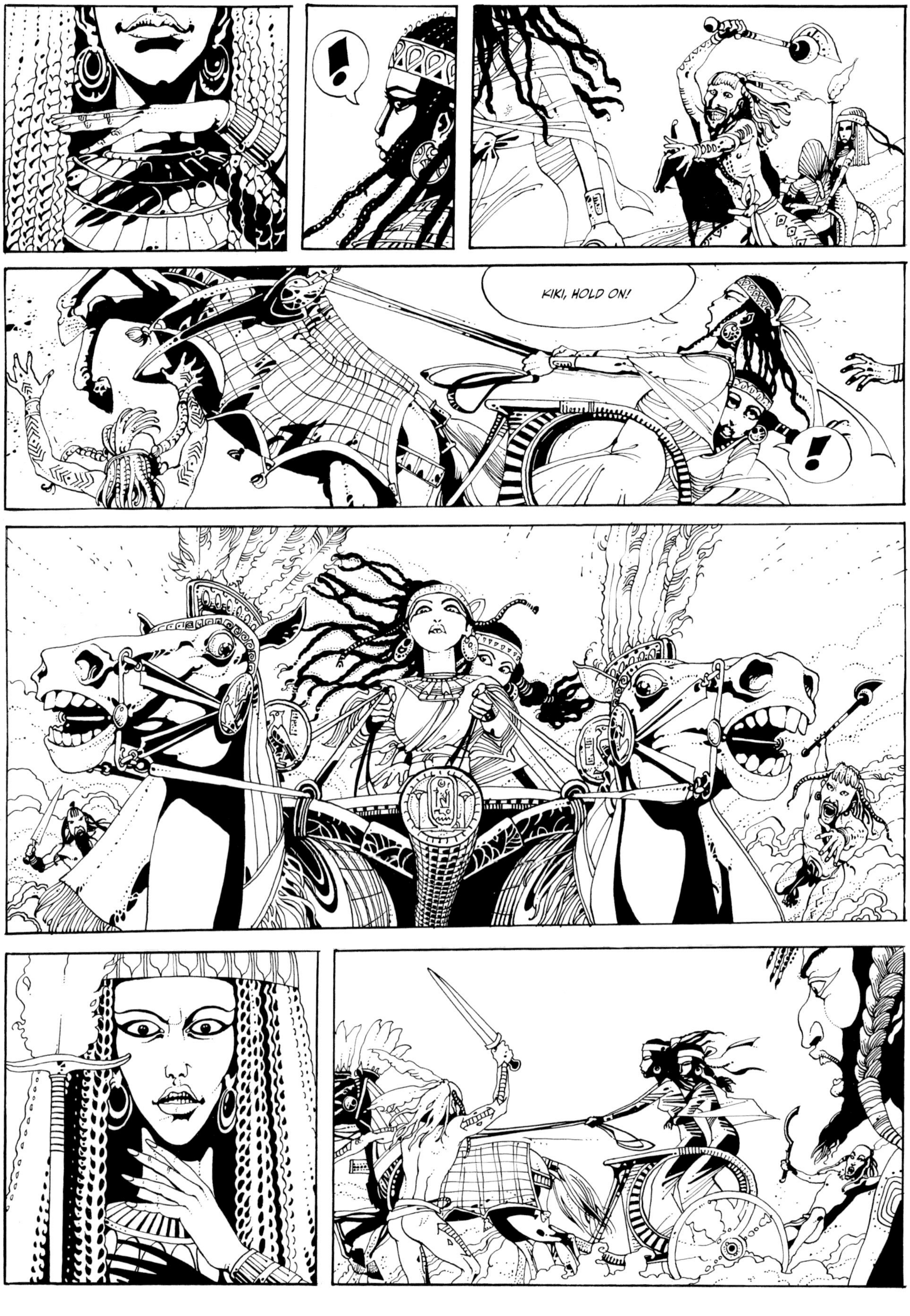
!
KIKI, HOLD ON!
!

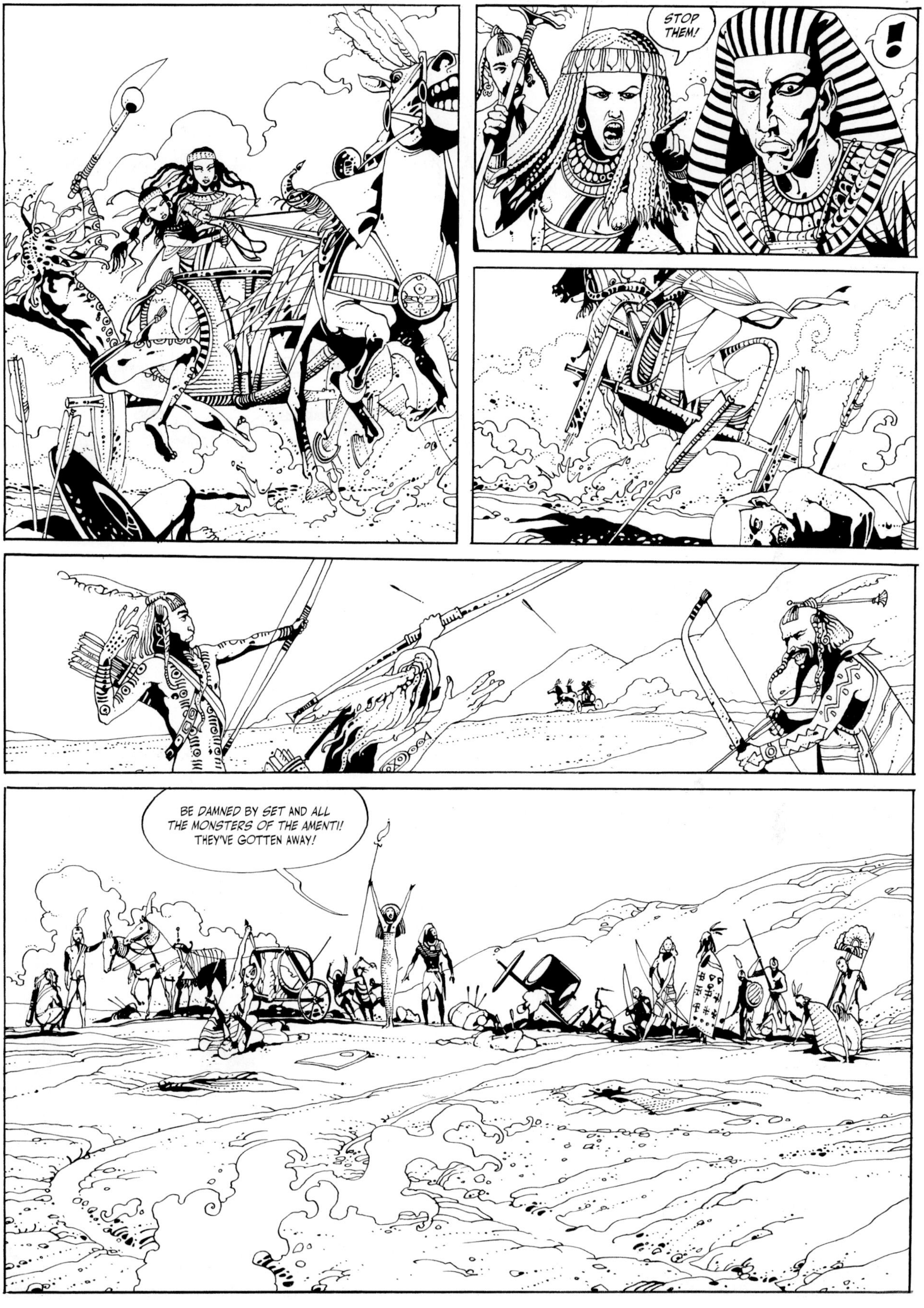
STOP THEM!
!
BE DAMNED BY SET AND ALL THE MONSTERS OF THE AMENTI! THEY'VE GOTTEN AWAY!

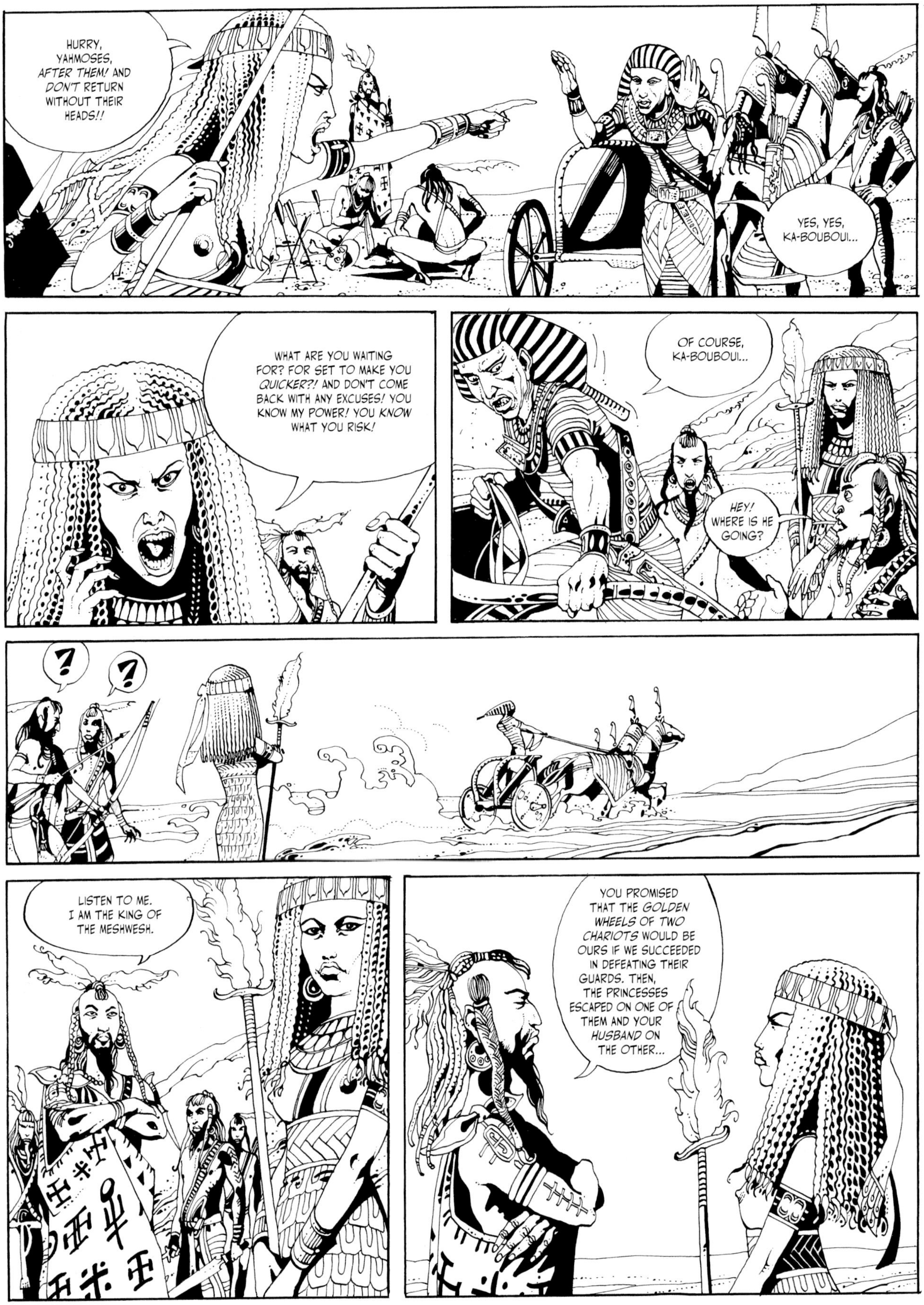
HURRY, YAHMOSES, AFTER THEM! AND DON'T RETURN WITHOUT THEIR HEADS!!
YES, YES, KA-BOUBOUI...
WHAT ARE YOU WAITING FOR? FOR SET TO MAKE YOU QUICKER?! AND DON'T COME BACK WITH ANY EXCUSES! YOU KNOW MY POWER! YOU KNOW WHAT YOU RISK!
OF COURSE, KA-BOUBOUI...
HEY! WHERE IS HE GOING?
?
?
LISTEN TO ME. I AM THE KING OF THE MESHWESH.
YOU PROMISED THAT THE GOLDEN WHEELS OF TWO CHARIOTS WOULD BE OURS IF WE SUCCEEDED IN DEFEATING THEIR GUARDS. THEN, THE PRINCESSES ESCAPED ON ONE OF THEM AND YOUR HUSBAND ON THE OTHER...

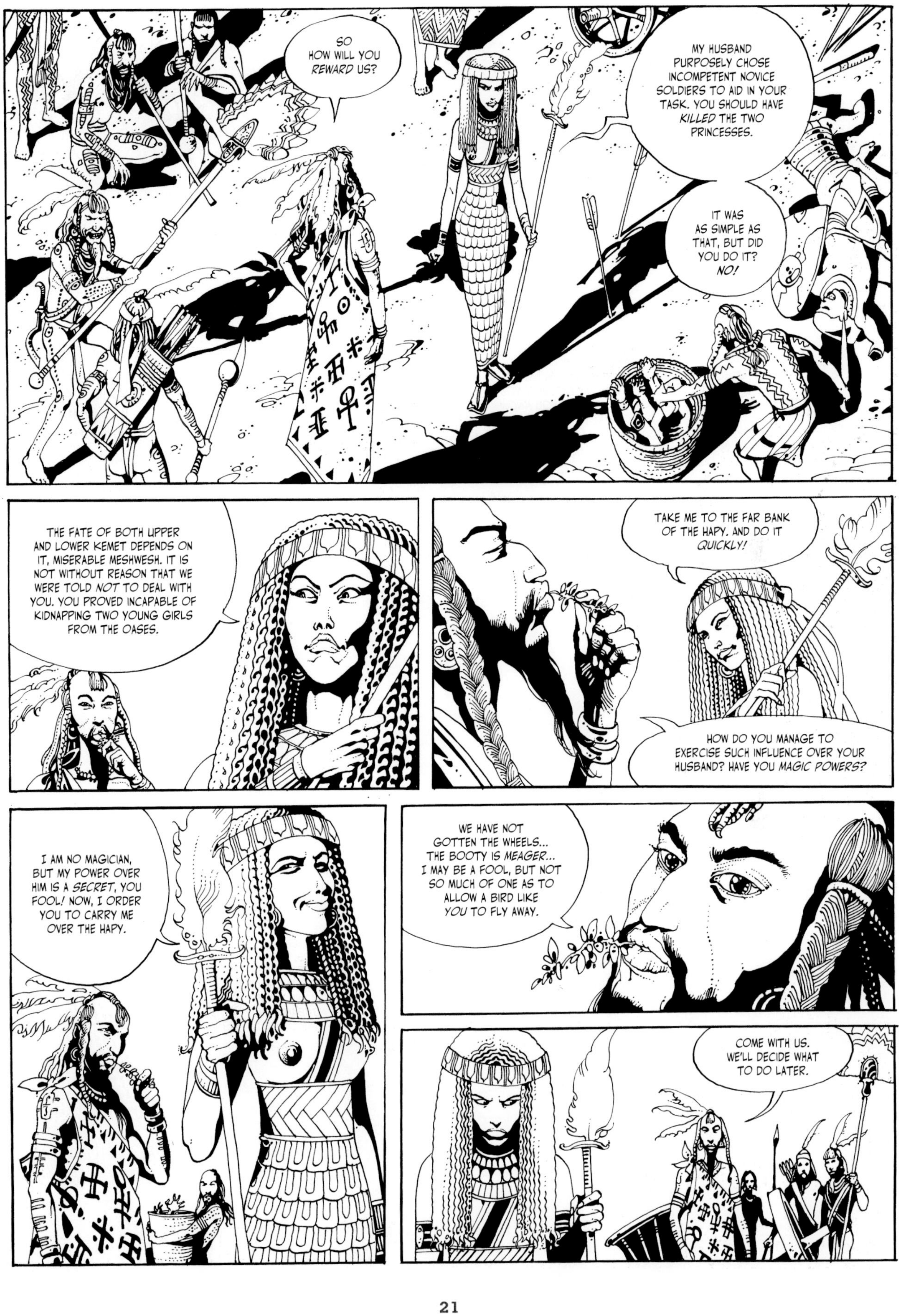

SO HOW WILL YOU *REWARD* US?
MY HUSBAND PURPOSELY CHOSE INCOMPETENT NOVICE SOLDIERS TO AID IN YOUR TASK. YOU SHOULD HAVE *KILLED* THE TWO PRINCESSES.
IT WAS AS SIMPLE AS THAT, BUT DID YOU DO IT? *NO!*
THE FATE OF BOTH UPPER AND LOWER KEMET DEPENDS ON IT, MISERABLE MESHWESH. IT IS NOT WITHOUT REASON THAT WE WERE TOLD *NOT* TO DEAL WITH YOU. YOU PROVED INCAPABLE OF KIDNAPPING TWO YOUNG GIRLS FROM THE OASES.
TAKE ME TO THE FAR BANK OF THE HAPY. AND DO IT *QUICKLY!*
HOW DO YOU MANAGE TO EXERCISE SUCH INFLUENCE OVER YOUR HUSBAND? HAVE YOU *MAGIC POWERS?*
I AM NO MAGICIAN, BUT MY POWER OVER HIM IS A *SECRET*, YOU FOOL! NOW, I ORDER YOU TO CARRY ME OVER THE HAPY.
WE HAVE NOT GOTTEN THE WHEELS... THE BOOTY IS *MEAGER*... I MAY BE A FOOL, BUT NOT SO MUCH OF ONE AS TO ALLOW A BIRD LIKE *YOU* TO FLY AWAY.
COME WITH US. WE'LL DECIDE WHAT TO DO LATER.

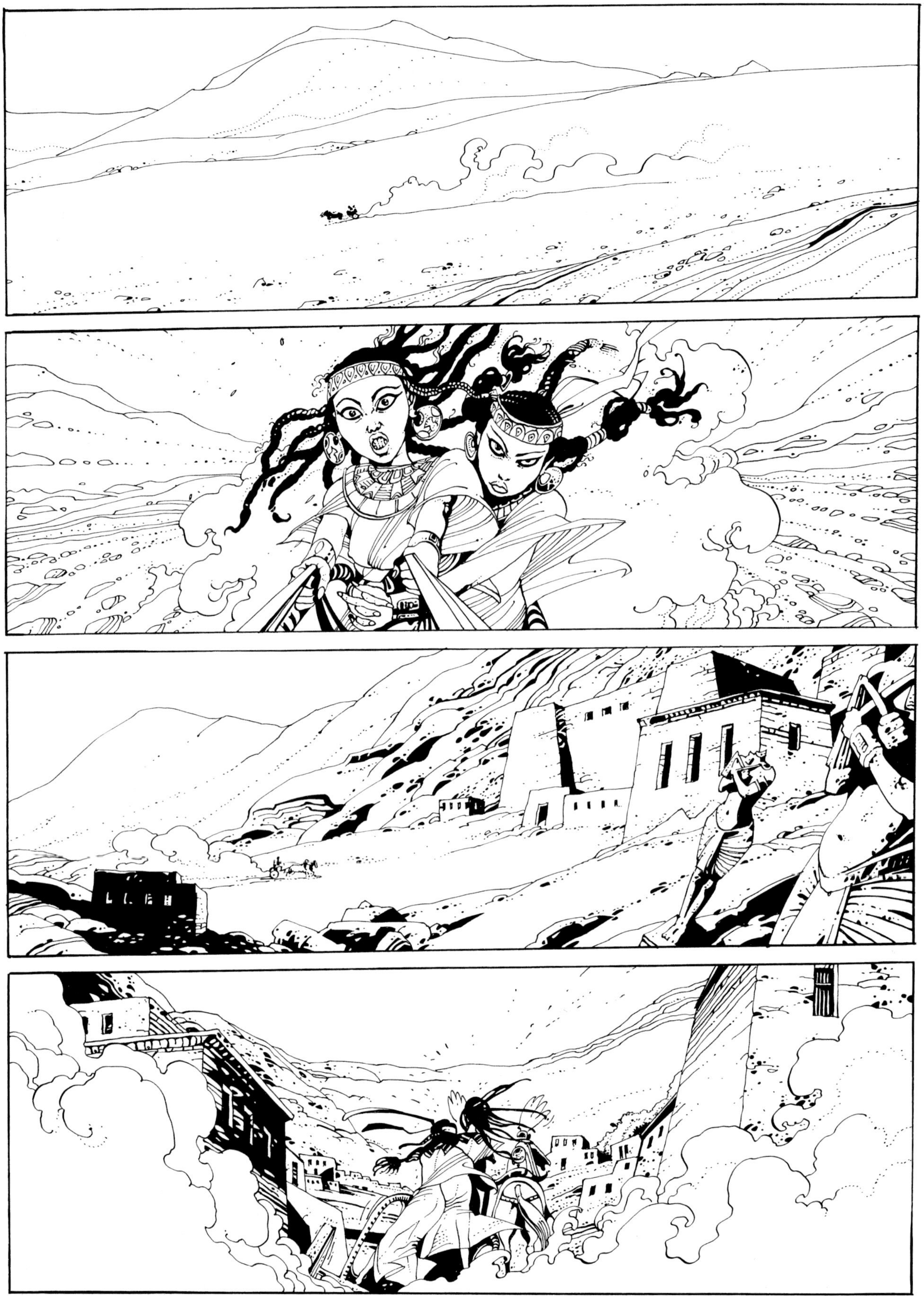

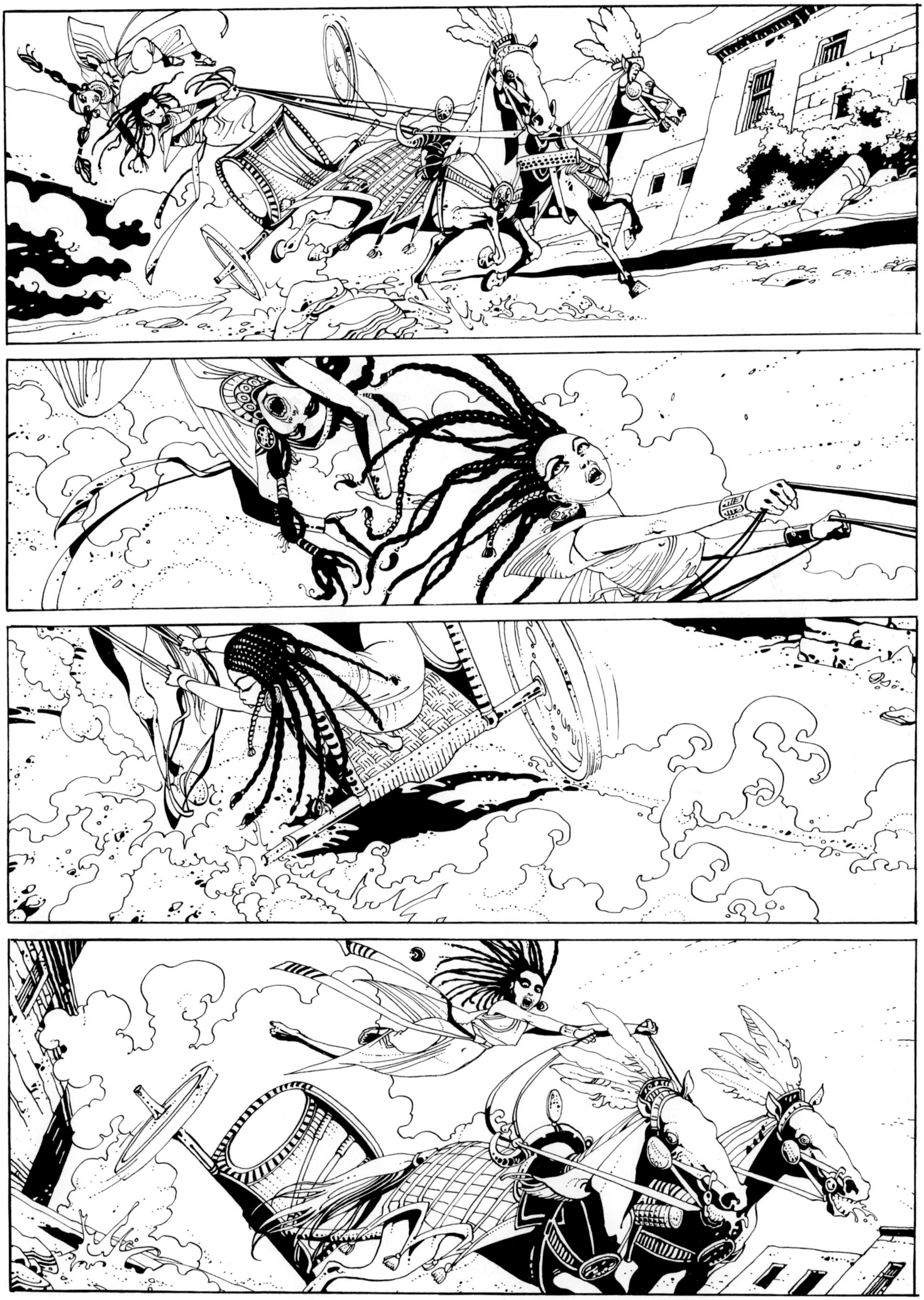

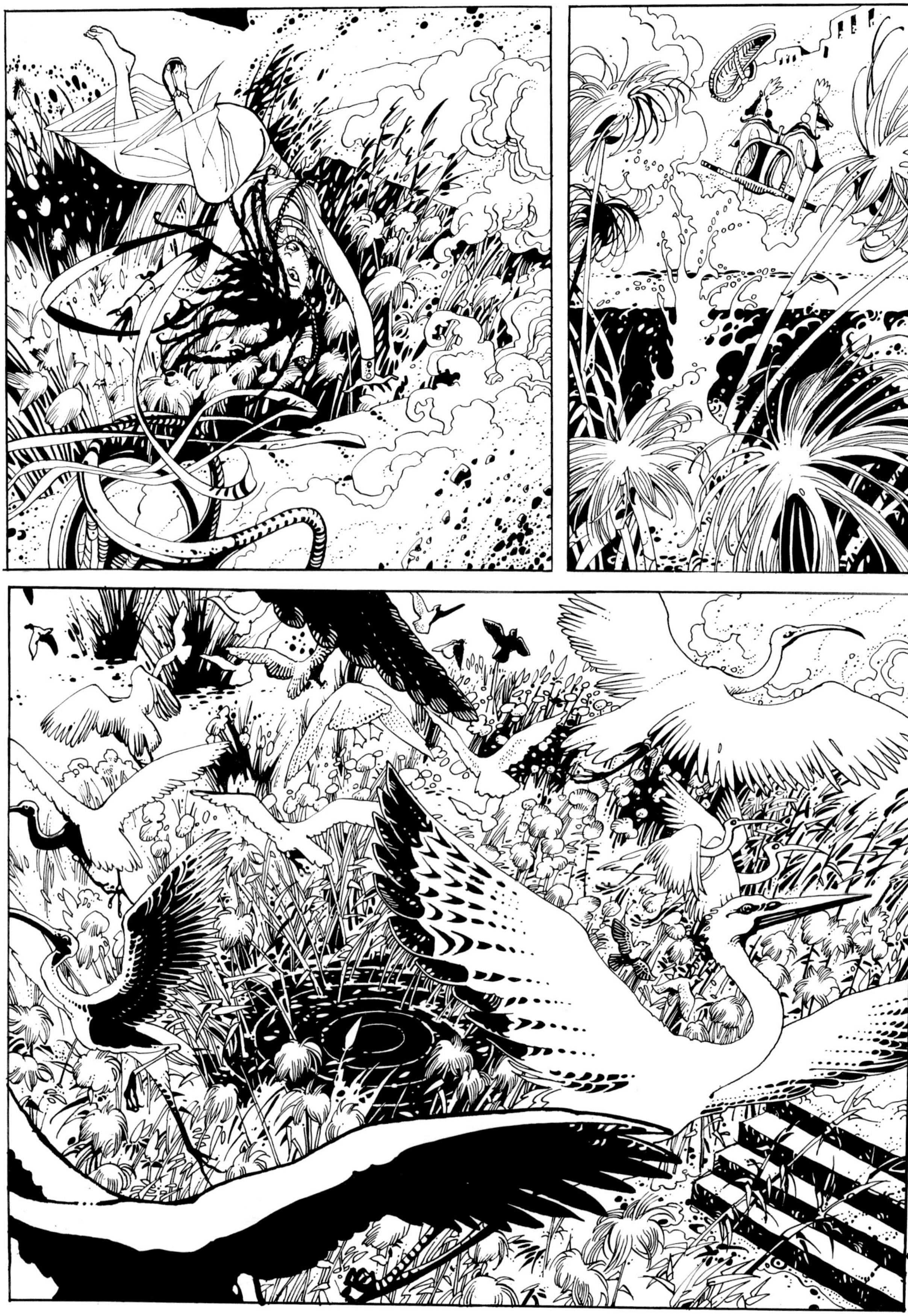

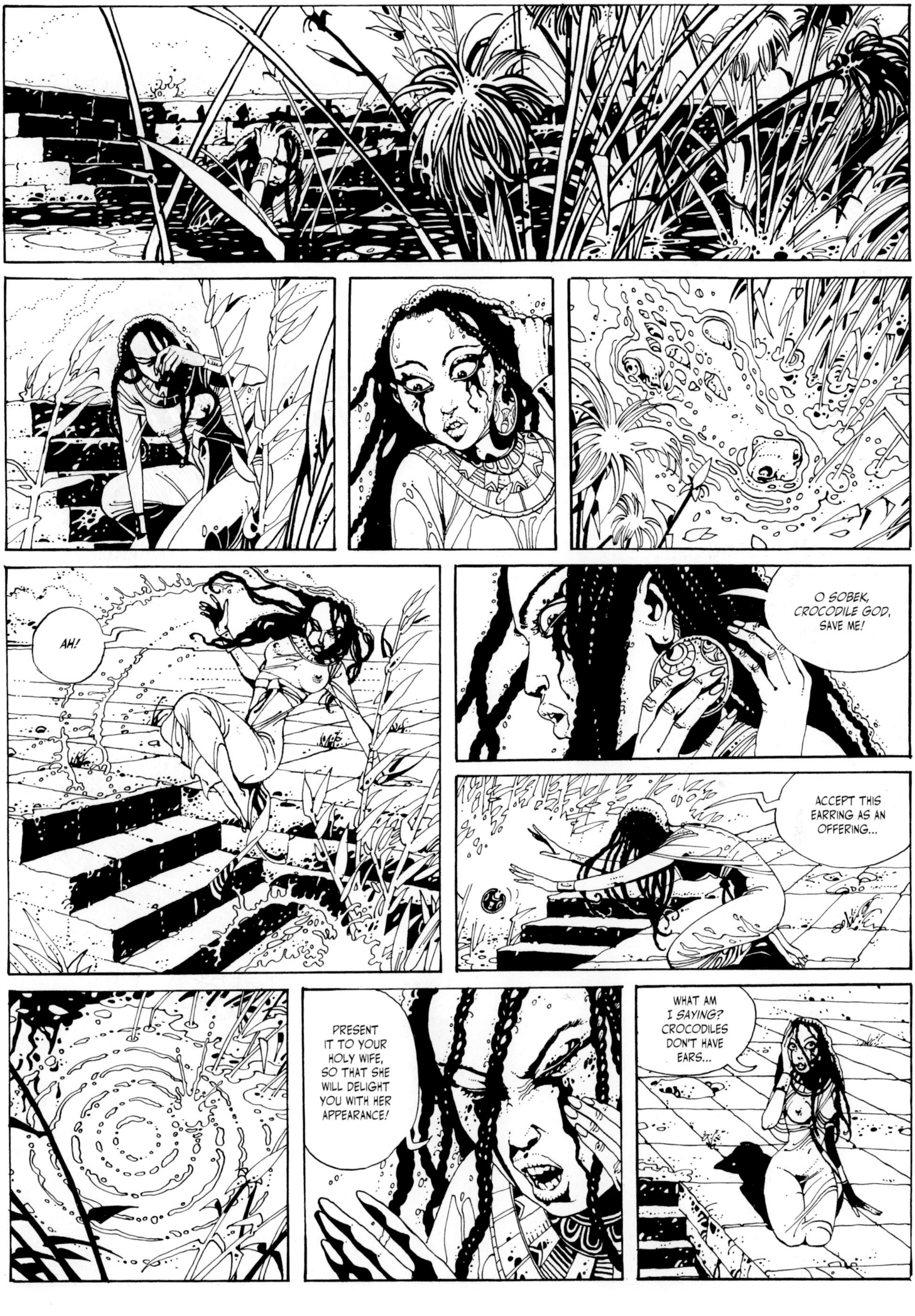
AH!
O SOBEK, CROCODILE GOD, SAVE ME!
ACCEPT THIS EARRING AS AN OFFERING...
PRESENT IT TO YOUR HOLY WIFE, SO THAT SHE WILL DELIGHT YOU WITH HER APPEARANCE!
WHAT AM I SAYING? CROCODILES DON'T HAVE EARS...

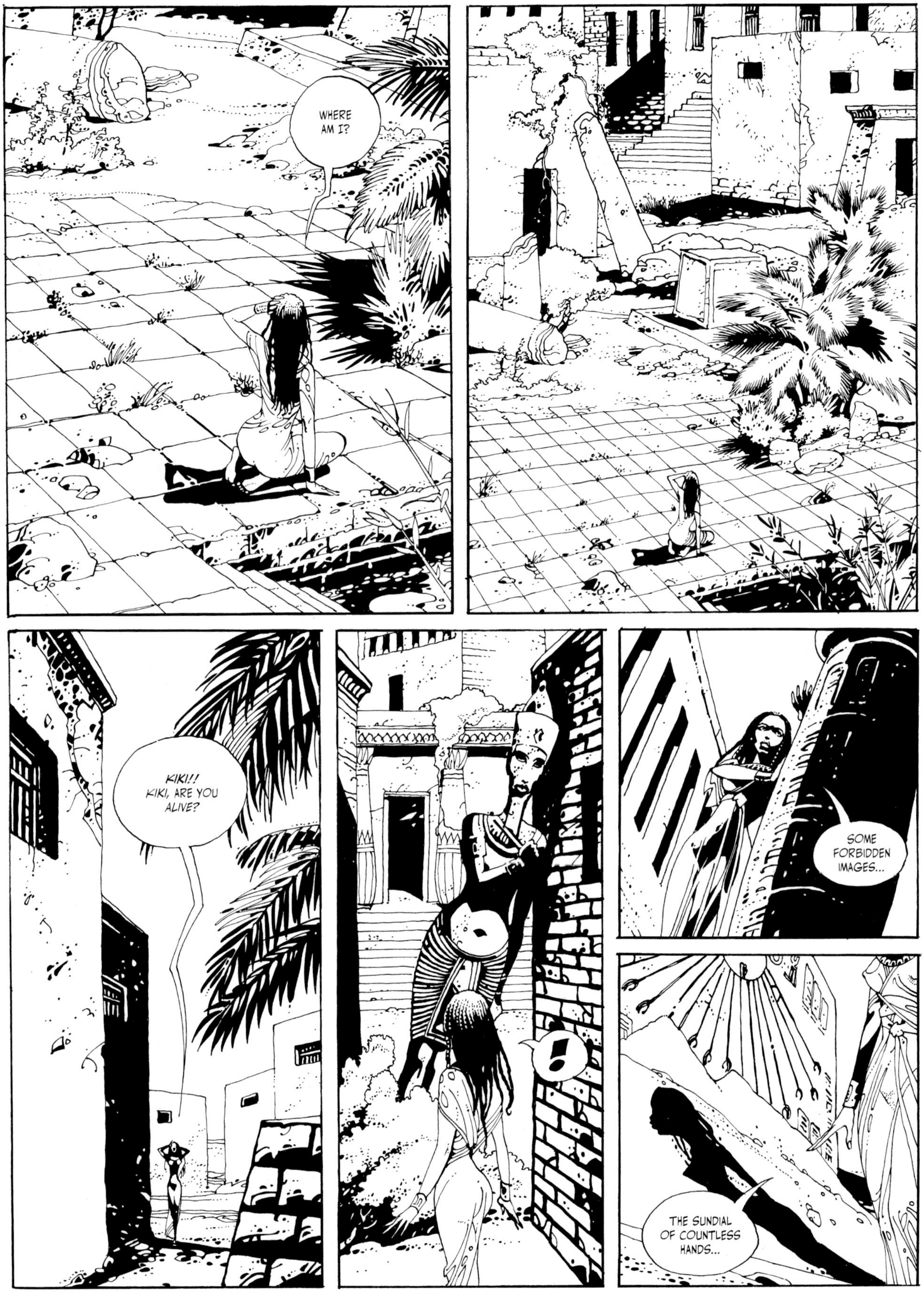
WHERE AM I?
KIKI!! KIKI, ARE YOU ALIVE?
!
SOME FORBIDDEN IMAGES...
THE SUNDIAL OF COUNTLESS HANDS...

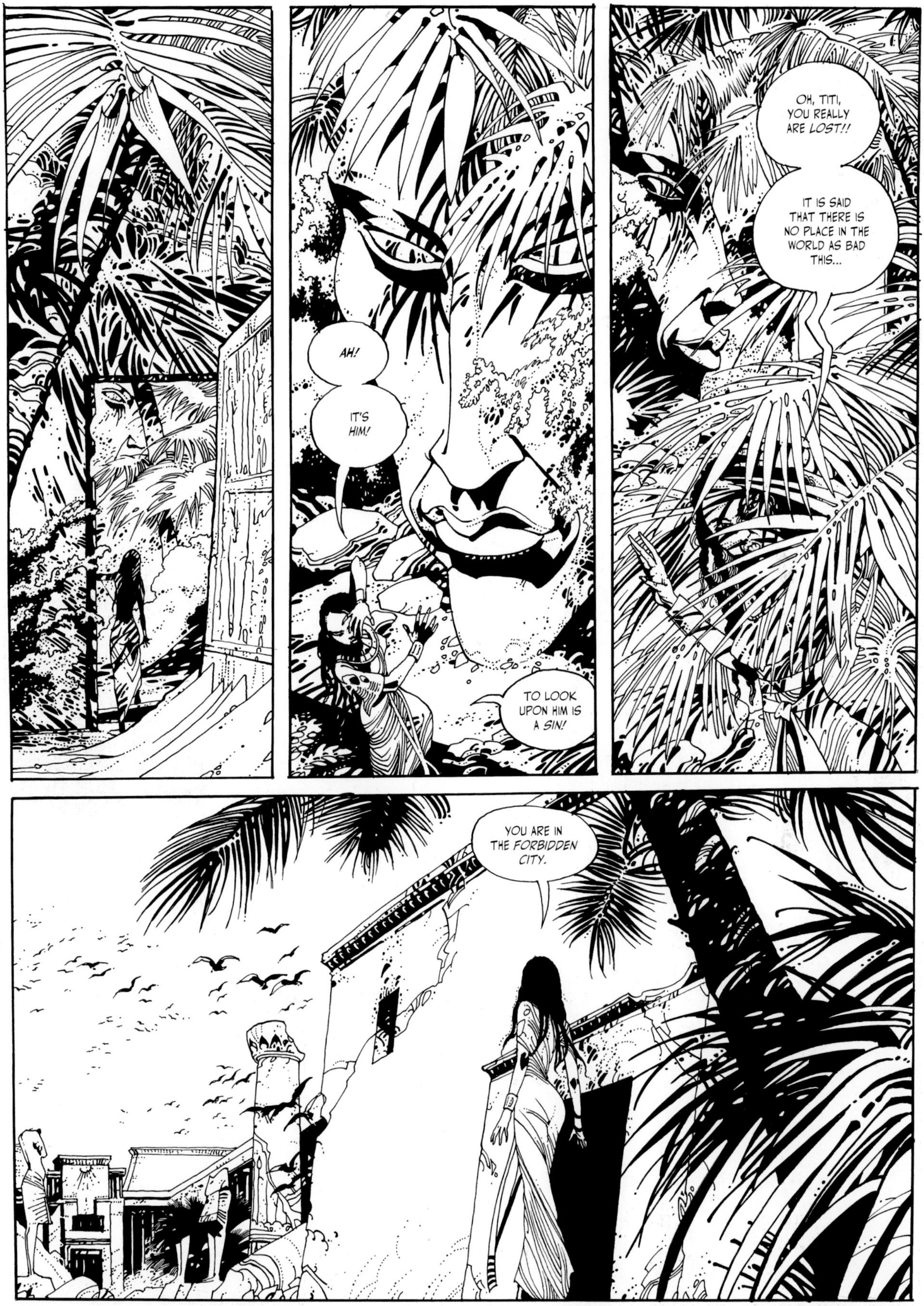
AH!
IT'S HIM!
TO LOOK UPON HIM IS A SIN!
OH, TITI, YOU REALLY ARE LOST!!
IT IS SAID THAT THERE IS NO PLACE IN THE WORLD AS BAD THIS...
YOU ARE IN THE FORBIDDEN CITY.

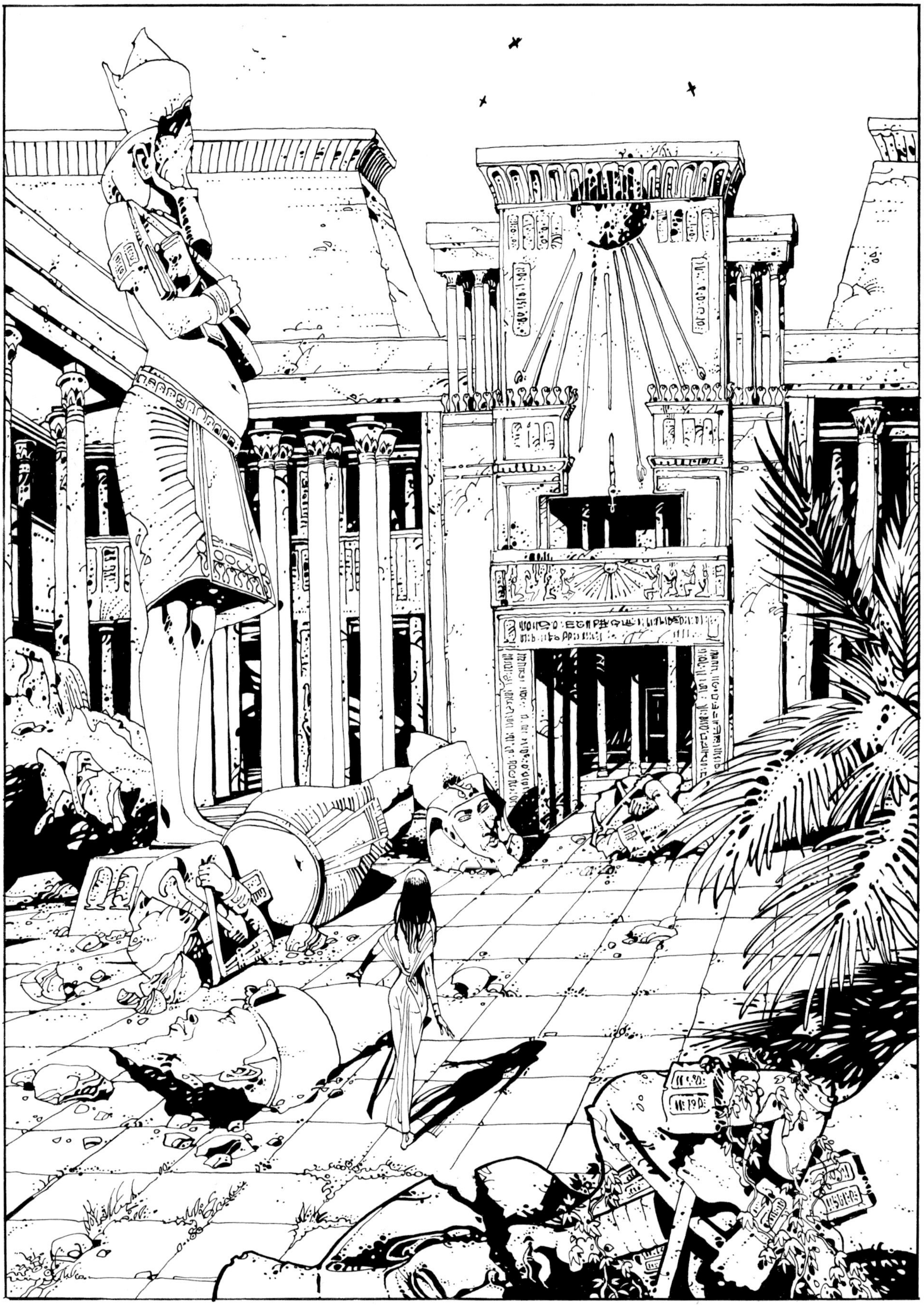

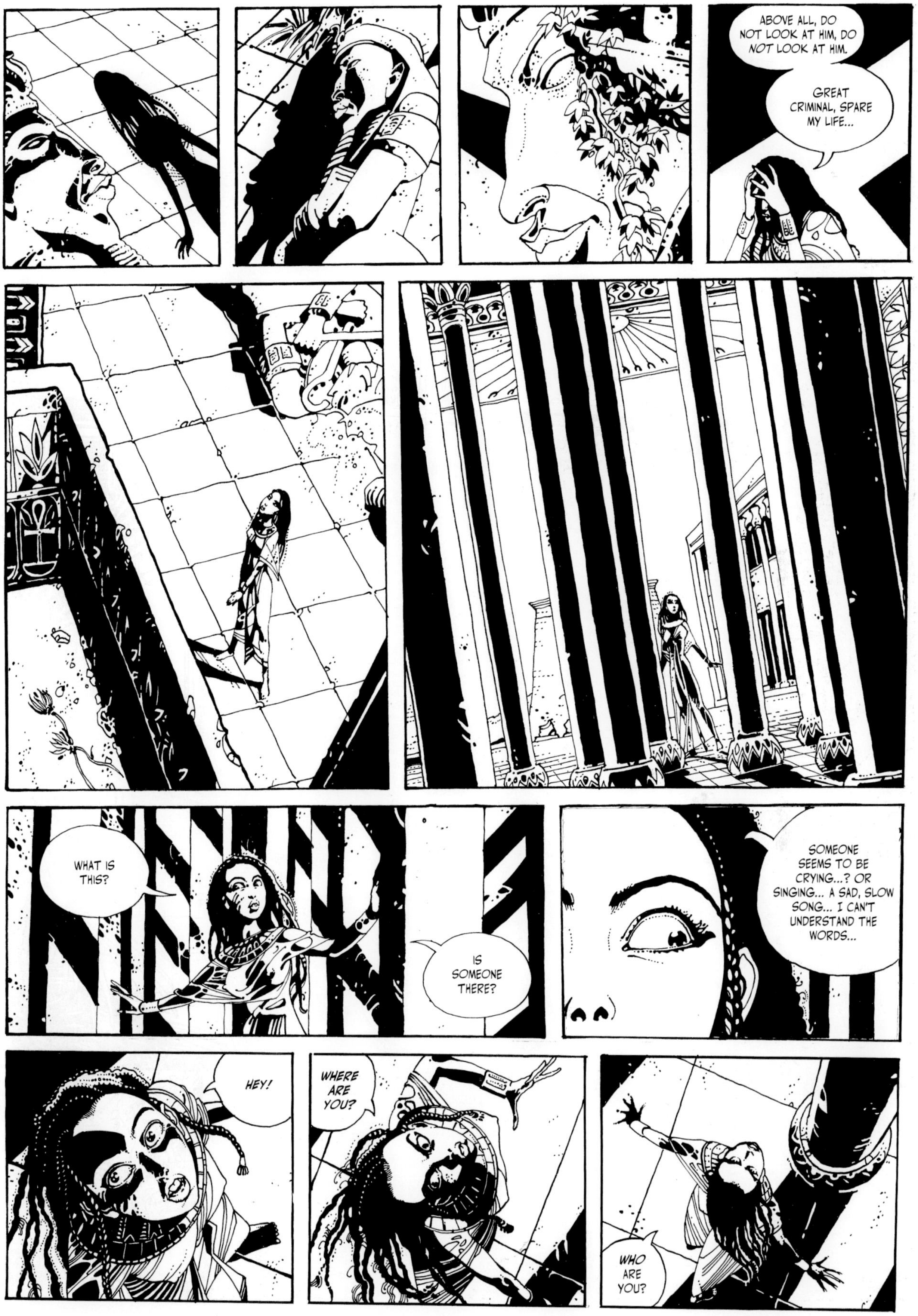
ABOVE ALL, DO NOT LOOK AT HIM, DO *NOT* LOOK AT HIM.
GREAT CRIMINAL, SPARE MY LIFE...
WHAT IS THIS?
IS SOMEONE THERE?
SOMEONE SEEMS TO BE CRYING...? OR SINGING... A SAD, SLOW SONG... I CAN'T UNDERSTAND THE WORDS...
HEY!
WHERE ARE YOU?
WHO ARE YOU?

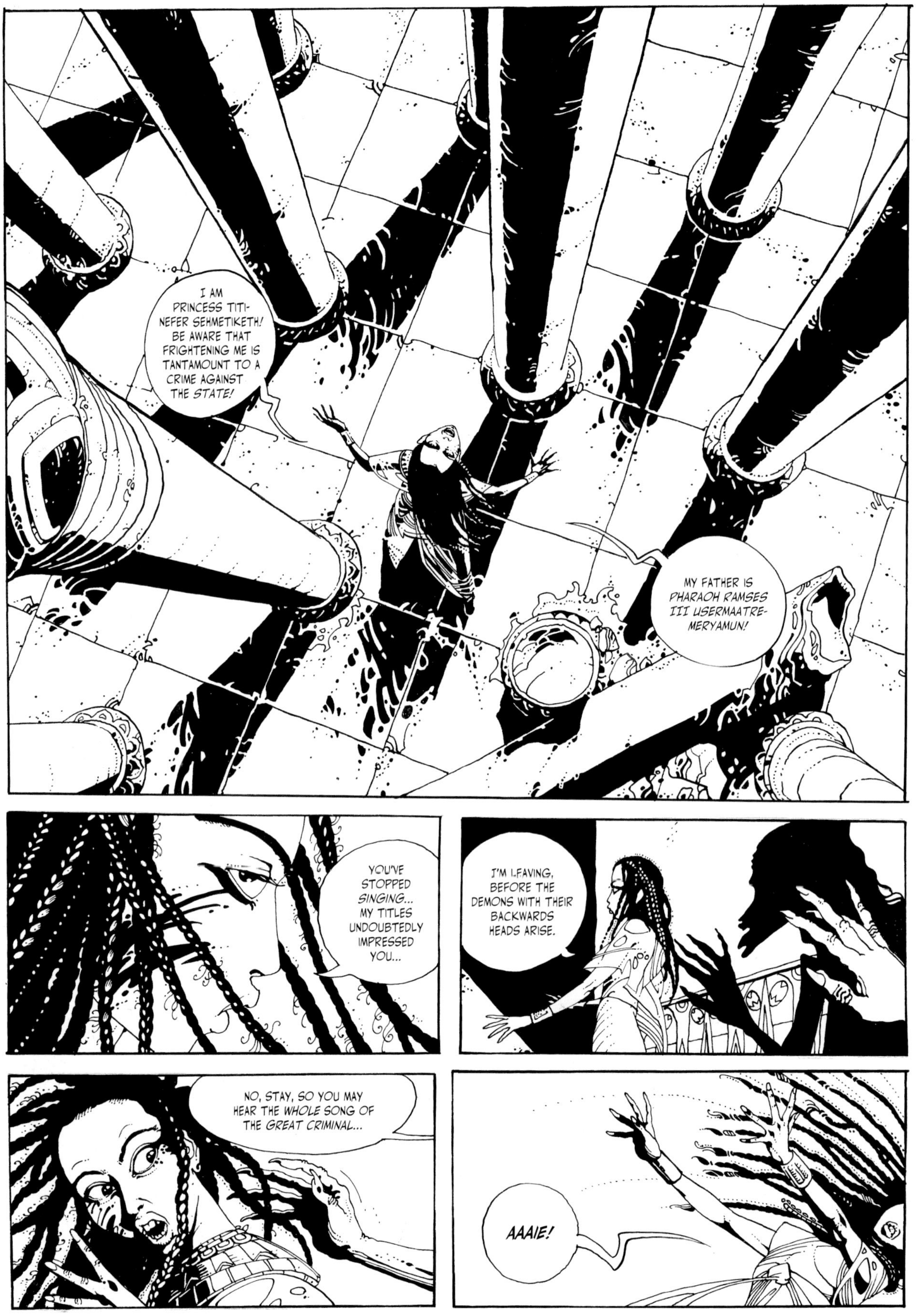
I AM PRINCESS TITI-NEFER SEHMETIKETH! BE AWARE THAT FRIGHTENING ME IS TANTAMOUNT TO A CRIME AGAINST THE STATE!
MY FATHER IS PHARAOH RAMSES III USERMAATRE-MERYAMUN!
YOU'VE STOPPED SINGING... MY TITLES UNDOUBTEDLY IMPRESSED YOU...
I'M LEAVING, BEFORE THE DEMONS WITH THEIR BACKWARDS HEADS ARISE.
NO, STAY, SO YOU MAY HEAR THE WHOLE SONG OF THE GREAT CRIMINAL...
AAAIE!

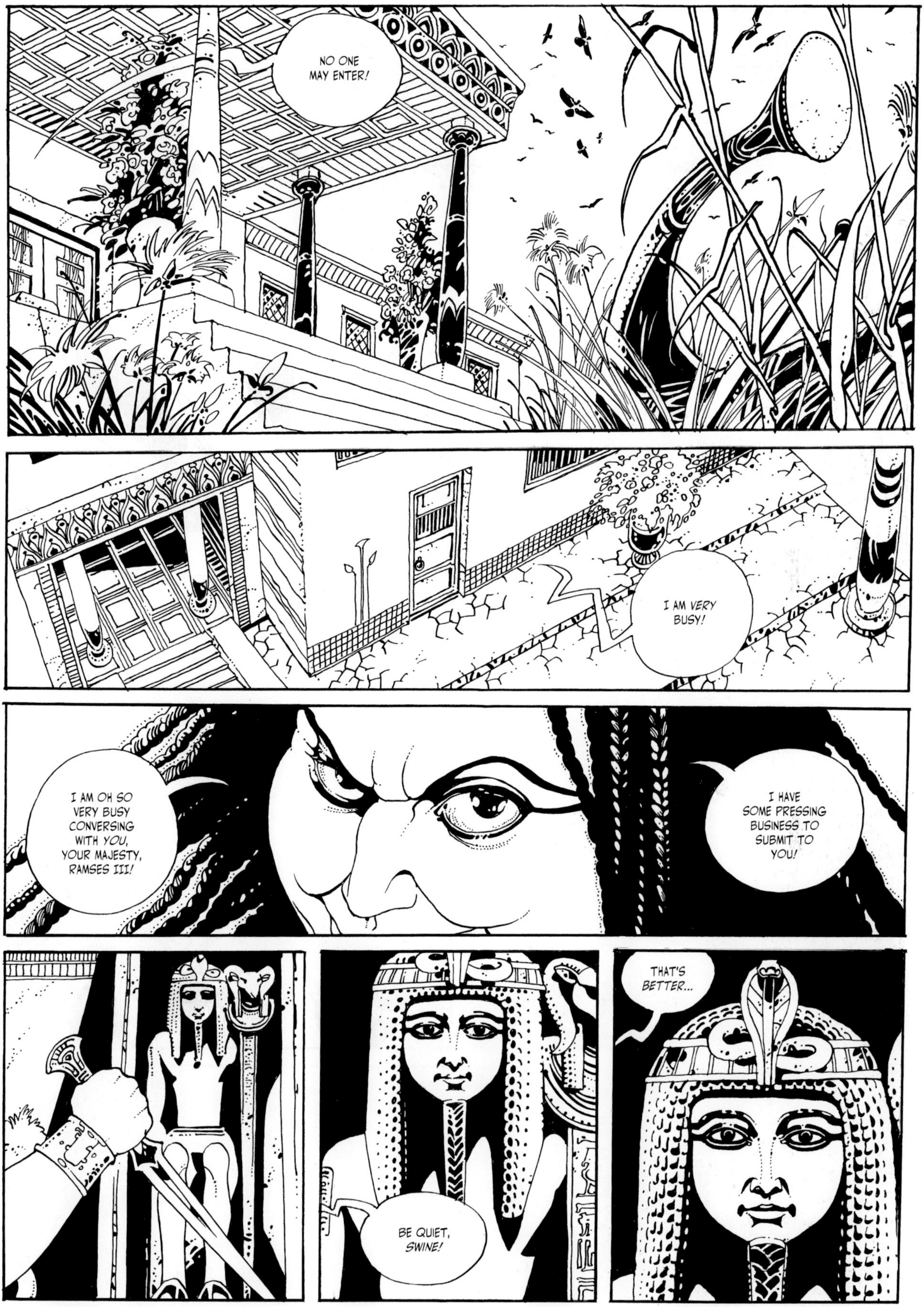
NO ONE MAY ENTER!
I AM VERY BUSY!
I AM OH SO VERY BUSY CONVERSING WITH YOU, YOUR MAJESTY, RAMSES III!
I HAVE SOME PRESSING BUSINESS TO SUBMIT TO YOU!
BE QUIET, SWINE!
THAT'S BETTER...

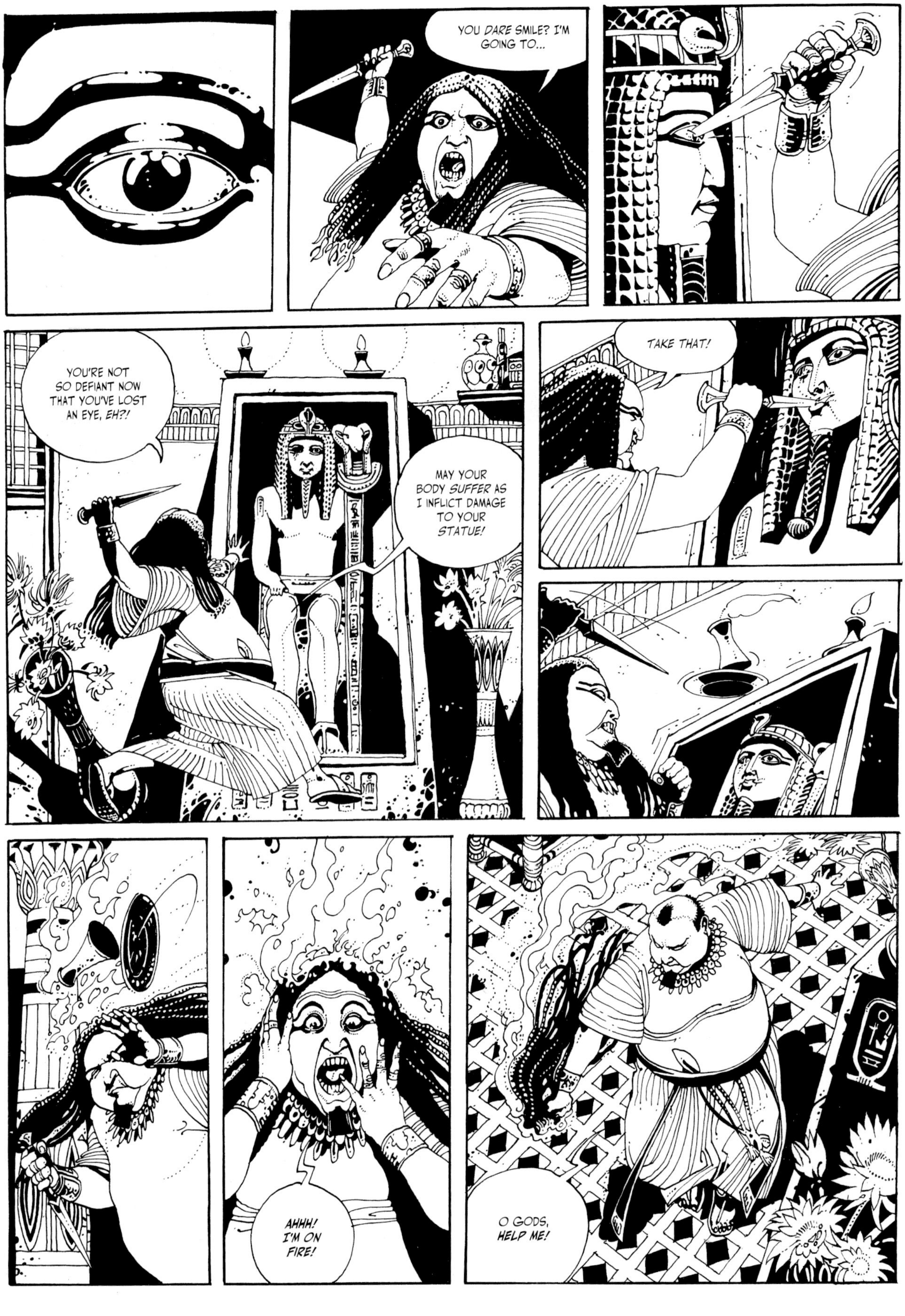
YOU DARE SMILE? I'M GOING TO...
YOU'RE NOT SO DEFIANT NOW THAT YOU'VE LOST AN EYE, EH?!
MAY YOUR BODY SUFFER AS I INFLICT DAMAGE TO YOUR STATUE!
TAKE THAT!
AHHH! I'M ON FIRE!
O GODS, HELP ME!

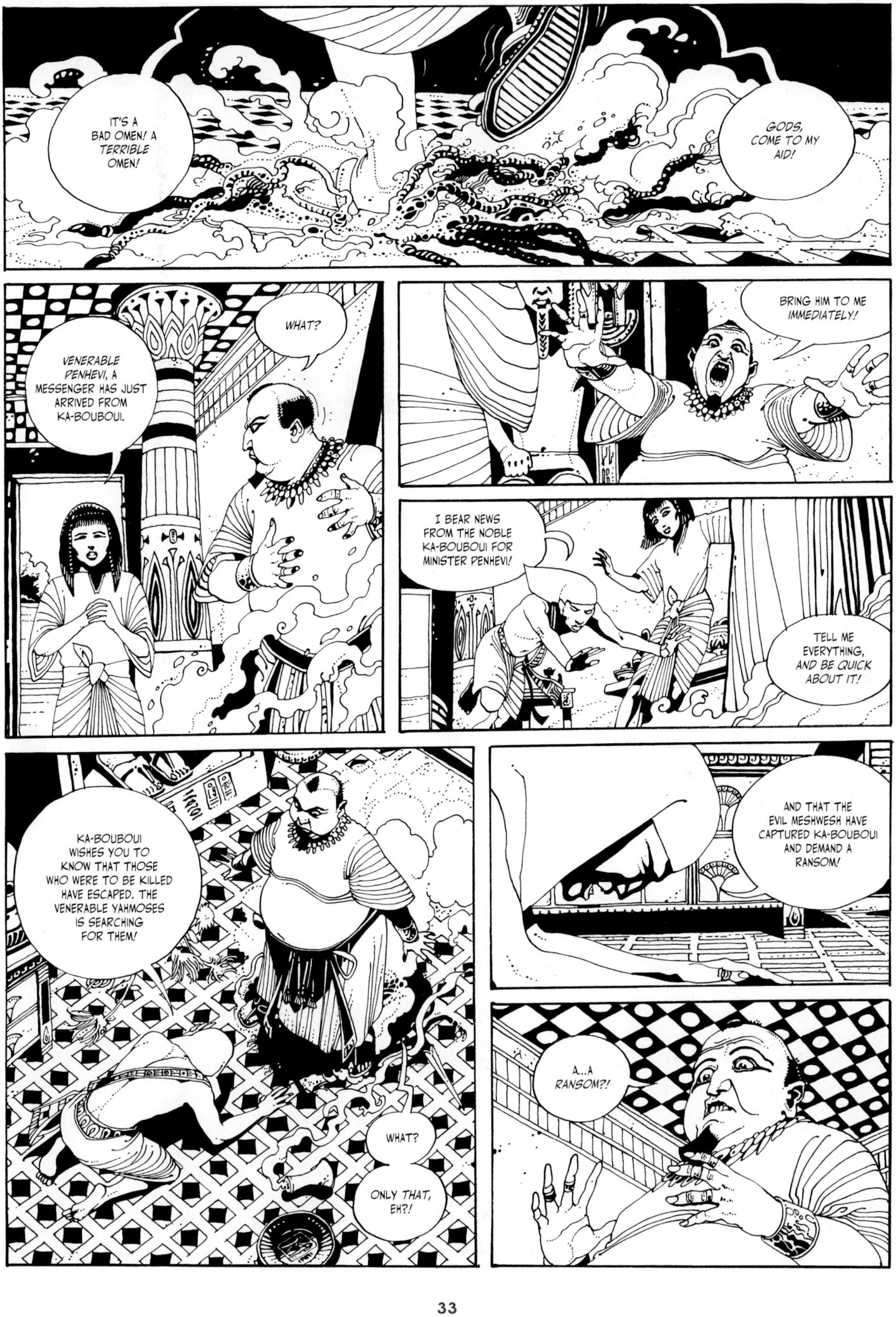
IT'S A BAD OMEN! A TERRIBLE OMEN!
GODS, COME TO MY AID!
VENERABLE PENHEVI, A MESSENGER HAS JUST ARRIVED FROM KA-BOUBOUI.
WHAT?
BRING HIM TO ME IMMEDIATELY!
I BEAR NEWS FROM THE NOBLE KA-BOUBOUI FOR MINISTER PENHEVI!
TELL ME EVERYTHING, AND BE QUICK ABOUT IT!
KA-BOUBOUI WISHES YOU TO KNOW THAT THOSE WHO WERE TO BE KILLED HAVE ESCAPED. THE VENERABLE YAHMOSES IS SEARCHING FOR THEM!
WHAT?
ONLY THAT, EH?!
AND THAT THE EVIL MESHWESH HAVE CAPTURED KA-BOUBOUI AND DEMAND A RANSOM!
A...A RANSOM?!

O GODS, HAVE PITY ON ME! QUICKLY!

VENERABLE PENHEVI... YOUR WIG! YOUR PALANQUIN!

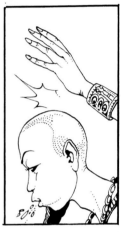

WHY HAVE YOU EATEN THE KHEPRI BEETLE? IT IS SACRED, AND HURTING IT IS A SIN!

MAMA, DON'T YOU REMEMBER THE TALE ABOUT THE ANCIENT PHARAOH LINAS WHO ATE THE SYMBOLS OF ALL THE GODS AND BECAME EVEN STRONGER THAN THEY WERE? I ATE THE KHEPRI BEETLE TO BECOME A GOD!

IT WAS SO I COULD HELP UNCLE KHEPRI, AUNT KA-BOUBOUI, AND YOU TO KILL PAPA!

AN INTRIGUING POINT OF VIEW, MY SON. YOU WILL BE A GREAT PHARAOH. BUT DO NOT TRY TO EAT MY SACRED CATS OR I WILL HAVE TO PUNISH YOU.

AND DON'T EAT THE BEETLES OR YOU'LL GET A STOMACH ACHE.

WHAT IS IT?

LET ME SEE THE NOBLE MAYA, IMBECILES!

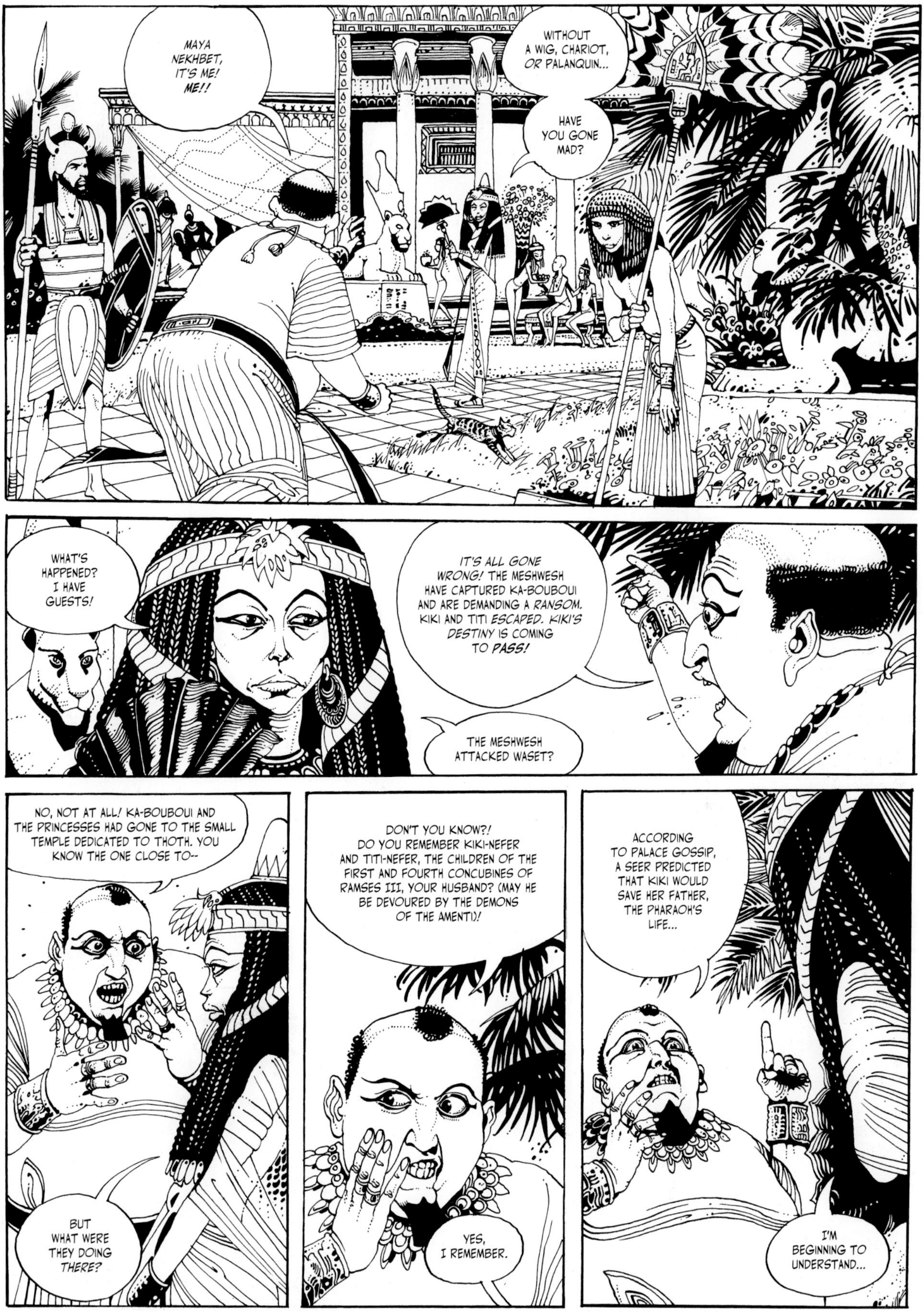
MAYA NEKHBET, IT'S ME! ME!!
WITHOUT A WIG, CHARIOT, OR PALANQUIN...
HAVE YOU GONE MAD?
WHAT'S HAPPENED? I HAVE GUESTS!
IT'S ALL GONE WRONG! THE MESHWESH HAVE CAPTURED KA-BOUBOUI AND ARE DEMANDING A RANSOM. KIKI AND TITI ESCAPED. KIKI'S DESTINY IS COMING TO PASS!
THE MESHWESH ATTACKED WASET?
NO, NOT AT ALL! KA-BOUBOUI AND THE PRINCESSES HAD GONE TO THE SMALL TEMPLE DEDICATED TO THOTH. YOU KNOW THE ONE CLOSE TO--
BUT WHAT WERE THEY DOING THERE?
DON'T YOU KNOW?! DO YOU REMEMBER KIKI-NEFER AND TITI-NEFER, THE CHILDREN OF THE FIRST AND FOURTH CONCUBINES OF RAMSES III, YOUR HUSBAND? (MAY HE BE DEVOURED BY THE DEMONS OF THE AMENTI)!
YES, I REMEMBER.
ACCORDING TO PALACE GOSSIP, A SEER PREDICTED THAT KIKI WOULD SAVE HER FATHER, THE PHARAOH'S LIFE...
I'M BEGINNING TO UNDERSTAND...

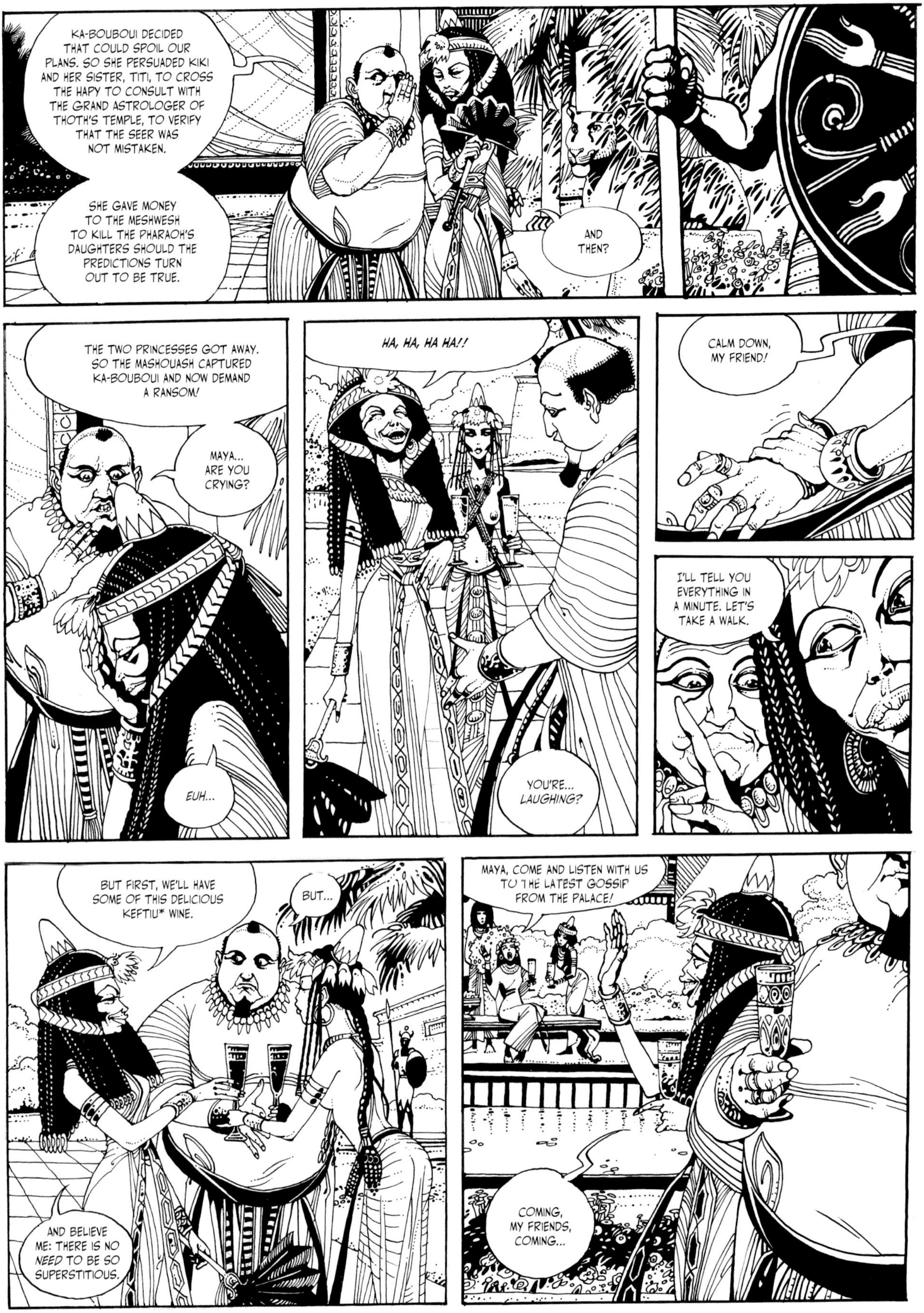
KA-BOUBOUI DECIDED THAT COULD SPOIL OUR PLANS. SO SHE PERSUADED KIKI AND HER SISTER, TITI, TO CROSS THE HAPY TO CONSULT WITH THE GRAND ASTROLOGER OF THOTH'S TEMPLE, TO VERIFY THAT THE SEER WAS NOT MISTAKEN.
SHE GAVE MONEY TO THE MESHWESH TO KILL THE PHARAOH'S DAUGHTERS SHOULD THE PREDICTIONS TURN OUT TO BE TRUE.
AND THEN?
THE TWO PRINCESSES GOT AWAY. SO THE MASHOUASH CAPTURED KA-BOUBOUI AND NOW DEMAND A RANSOM!
MAYA... ARE YOU CRYING?
EUH...
HA, HA, HA HA!!
YOU'RE... LAUGHING?
CALM DOWN, MY FRIEND!
I'LL TELL YOU EVERYTHING IN A MINUTE. LET'S TAKE A WALK.
BUT FIRST, WE'LL HAVE SOME OF THIS DELICIOUS KEFTIU* WINE.
BUT...
AND BELIEVE ME: THERE IS NO NEED TO BE SO SUPERSTITIOUS.
MAYA, COME AND LISTEN WITH US TO THE LATEST GOSSIP FROM THE PALACE!
COMING, MY FRIENDS, COMING...

*KEFTIU: CRETE

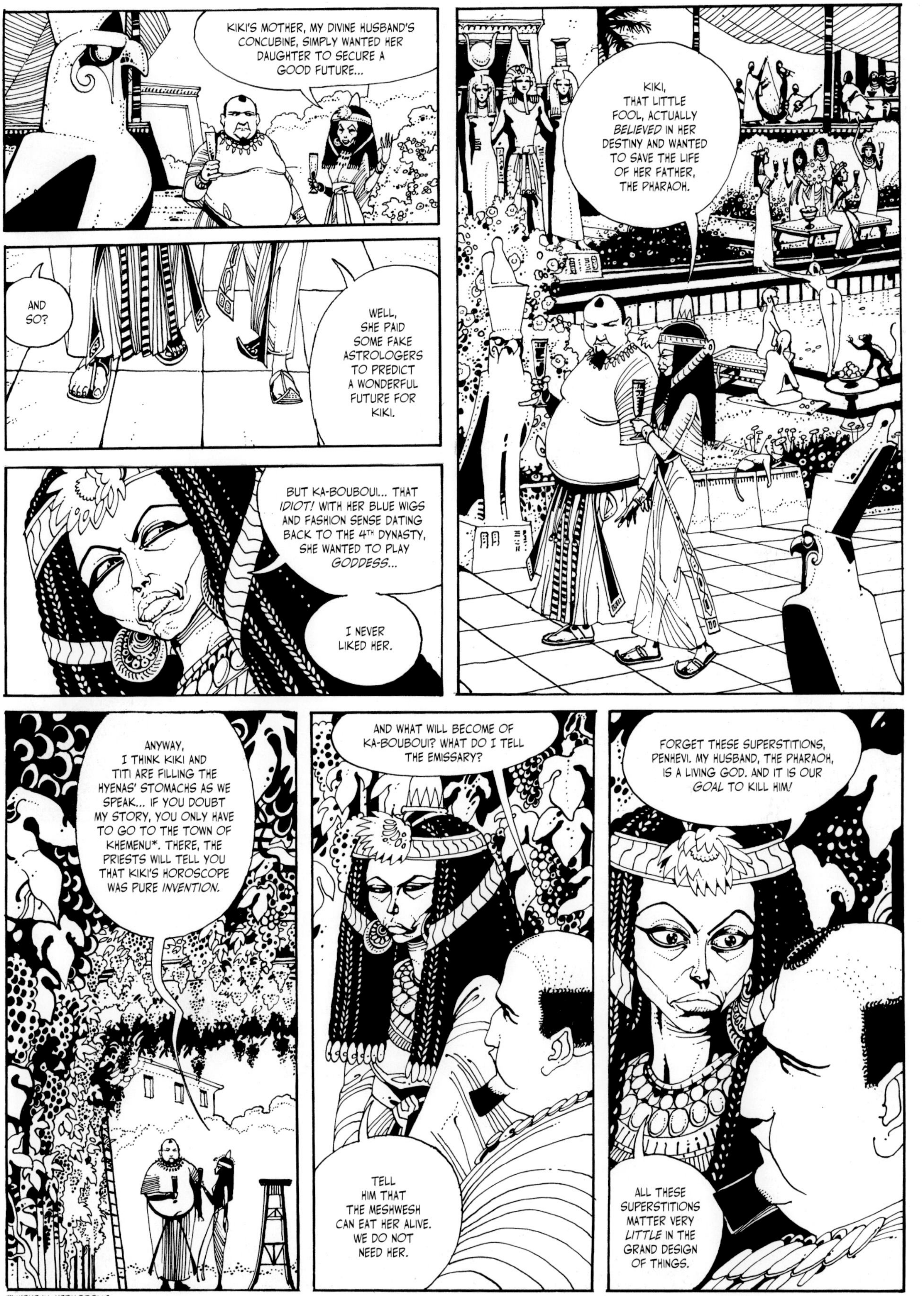
KIKI'S MOTHER, MY DIVINE HUSBAND'S CONCUBINE, SIMPLY WANTED HER DAUGHTER TO SECURE A GOOD FUTURE...
KIKI, THAT LITTLE FOOL, ACTUALLY BELIEVED IN HER DESTINY AND WANTED TO SAVE THE LIFE OF HER FATHER, THE PHARAOH.
AND SO?
WELL, SHE PAID SOME FAKE ASTROLOGERS TO PREDICT A WONDERFUL FUTURE FOR KIKI.
BUT KA-BOUBOUI... THAT IDIOT! WITH HER BLUE WIGS AND FASHION SENSE DATING BACK TO THE 4TH DYNASTY, SHE WANTED TO PLAY GODDESS...
I NEVER LIKED HER.
ANYWAY, I THINK KIKI AND TITI ARE FILLING THE HYENAS' STOMACHS AS WE SPEAK... IF YOU DOUBT MY STORY, YOU ONLY HAVE TO GO TO THE TOWN OF KHEMENU*. THERE, THE PRIESTS WILL TELL YOU THAT KIKI'S HOROSCOPE WAS PURE INVENTION.
AND WHAT WILL BECOME OF KA-BOUBOUI? WHAT DO I TELL THE EMISSARY?
TELL HIM THAT THE MESHWESH CAN EAT HER ALIVE. WE DO NOT NEED HER.
FORGET THESE SUPERSTITIONS, PENHEVI. MY HUSBAND, THE PHARAOH, IS A LIVING GOD. AND IT IS OUR GOAL TO KILL HIM!
ALL THESE SUPERSTITIONS MATTER VERY LITTLE IN THE GRAND DESIGN OF THINGS.

*KHEMENU: HERMOPOLIS

THE FORBIDDEN CITY...

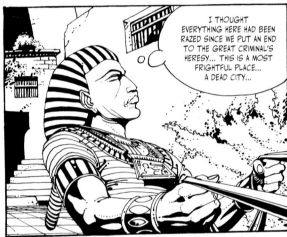

I THOUGHT EVERYTHING HERE HAD BEEN RAZED SINCE WE PUT AN END TO THE GREAT CRIMINAL'S HERESY... THIS IS A MOST FRIGHTFUL PLACE... A DEAD CITY...

...WITH NOT A SOUL AROUND.

ONLY GHOSTS!

KIKI-NEFER?

WE'VE CONQUERED THE MESHWESH. I'VE BEEN LOOKING FOR YOU.

FOLLOW ME!

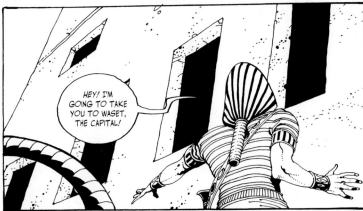

HEY! I'M GOING TO TAKE YOU TO WASET, THE CAPITAL!

I'VE COME TO SAVE YOU!

STOP!

WHY ARE YOU RUNNING, YOU FOOLISH GIRL?

I JUST FEEL LIKE PLAYING WITH YOU! HEE HEE!

BUT WHAT KIND OF GAME?! THIS IS A MATTER OF LIFE AND DEATH!

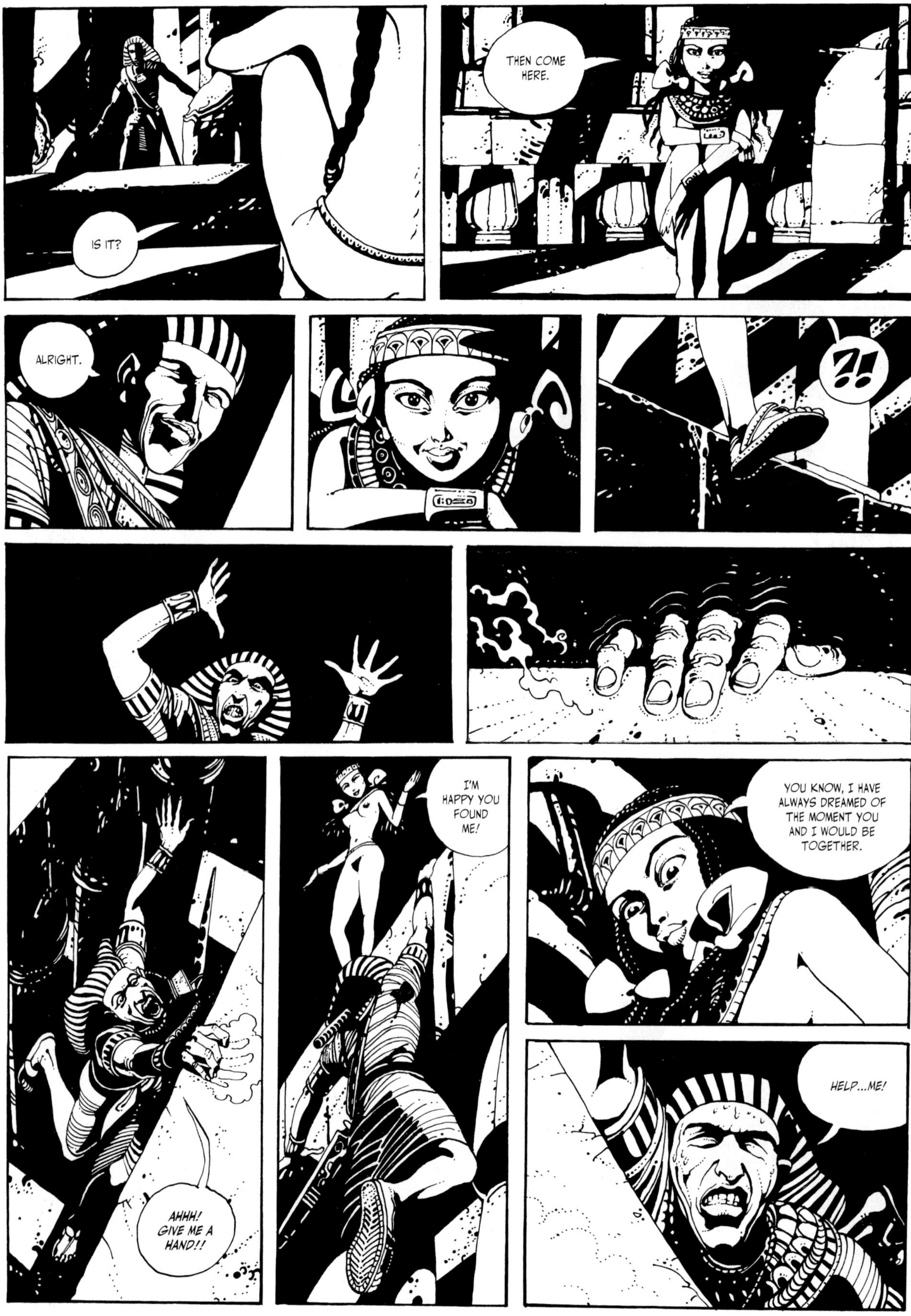
IS IT?
THEN COME HERE.
ALRIGHT.
?!
I'M HAPPY YOU FOUND ME!
AHHH! GIVE ME A HAND!!
YOU KNOW, I HAVE ALWAYS DREAMED OF THE MOMENT YOU AND I WOULD BE TOGETHER.
HELP...ME!

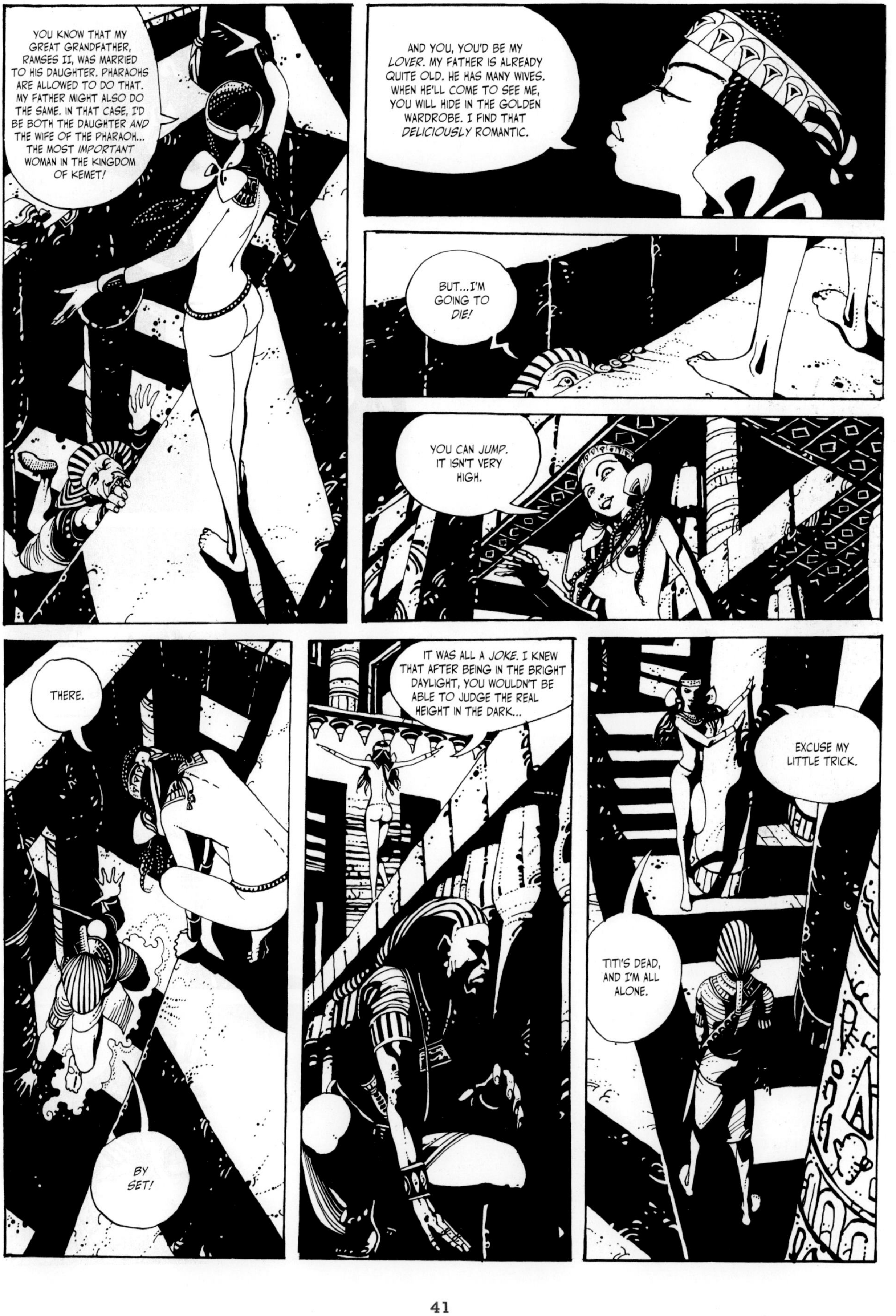

YOU KNOW THAT MY GREAT GRANDFATHER, RAMSES II, WAS MARRIED TO HIS DAUGHTER. PHARAOHS ARE ALLOWED TO DO THAT. MY FATHER MIGHT ALSO DO THE SAME. IN THAT CASE, I'D BE BOTH THE DAUGHTER AND THE WIFE OF THE PHARAOH... THE MOST IMPORTANT WOMAN IN THE KINGDOM OF KEMET!
AND YOU, YOU'D BE MY LOVER. MY FATHER IS ALREADY QUITE OLD. HE HAS MANY WIVES. WHEN HE'LL COME TO SEE ME, YOU WILL HIDE IN THE GOLDEN WARDROBE. I FIND THAT DELICIOUSLY ROMANTIC.
BUT...I'M GOING TO DIE!
YOU CAN JUMP. IT ISN'T VERY HIGH.
THERE.
BY SET!
IT WAS ALL A JOKE. I KNEW THAT AFTER BEING IN THE BRIGHT DAYLIGHT, YOU WOULDN'T BE ABLE TO JUDGE THE REAL HEIGHT IN THE DARK...
EXCUSE MY LITTLE TRICK.
TITI'S DEAD, AND I'M ALL ALONE.

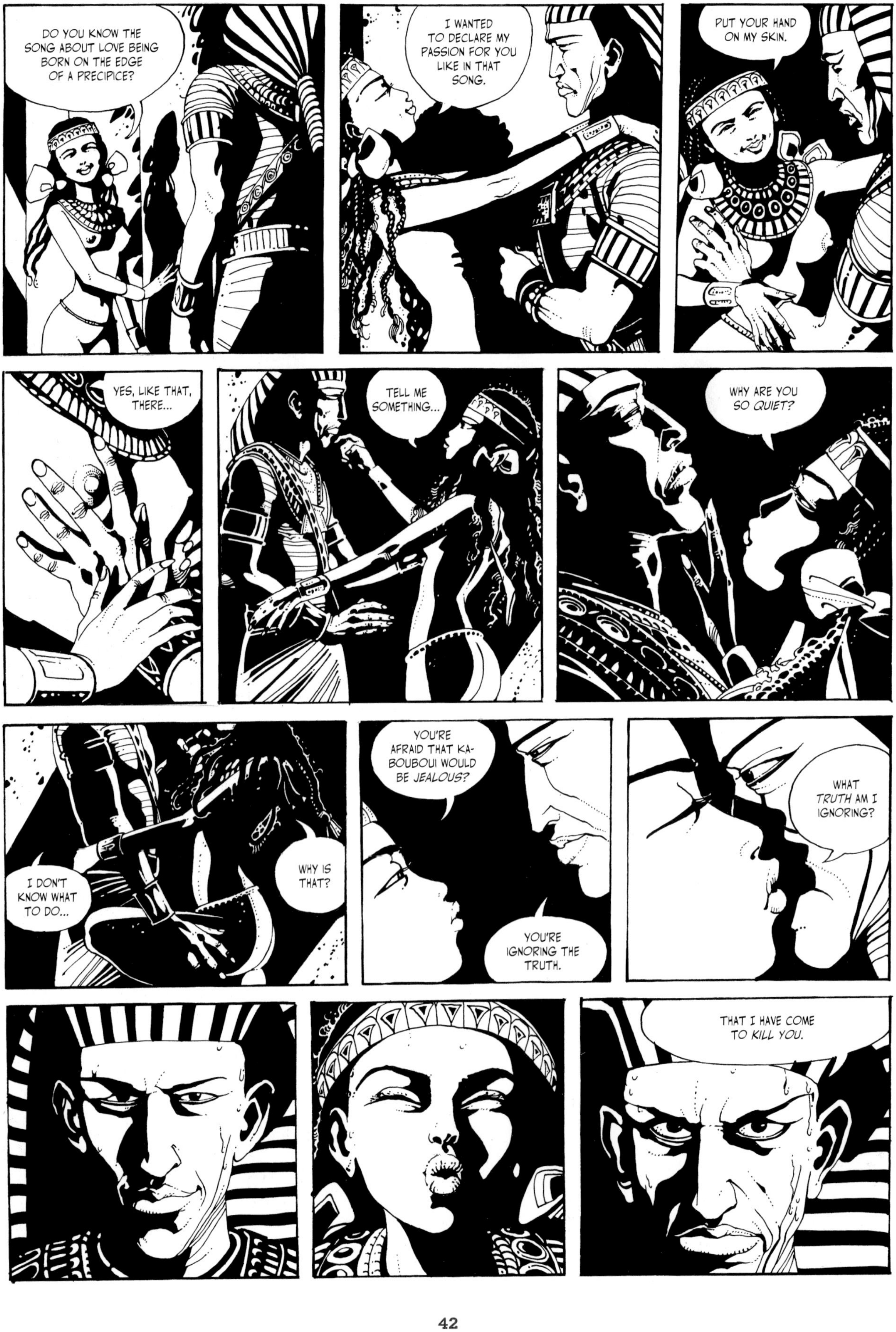
DO YOU KNOW THE SONG ABOUT LOVE BEING BORN ON THE EDGE OF A PRECIPICE?
I WANTED TO DECLARE MY PASSION FOR YOU LIKE IN THAT SONG.
PUT YOUR HAND ON MY SKIN.
YES, LIKE THAT, THERE...
TELL ME SOMETHING...
WHY ARE YOU SO QUIET?
I DON'T KNOW WHAT TO DO...
WHY IS THAT?
YOU'RE AFRAID THAT KA-BOUBOUI WOULD BE JEALOUS?
YOU'RE IGNORING THE TRUTH.
WHAT TRUTH AM I IGNORING?
THAT I HAVE COME TO KILL YOU.

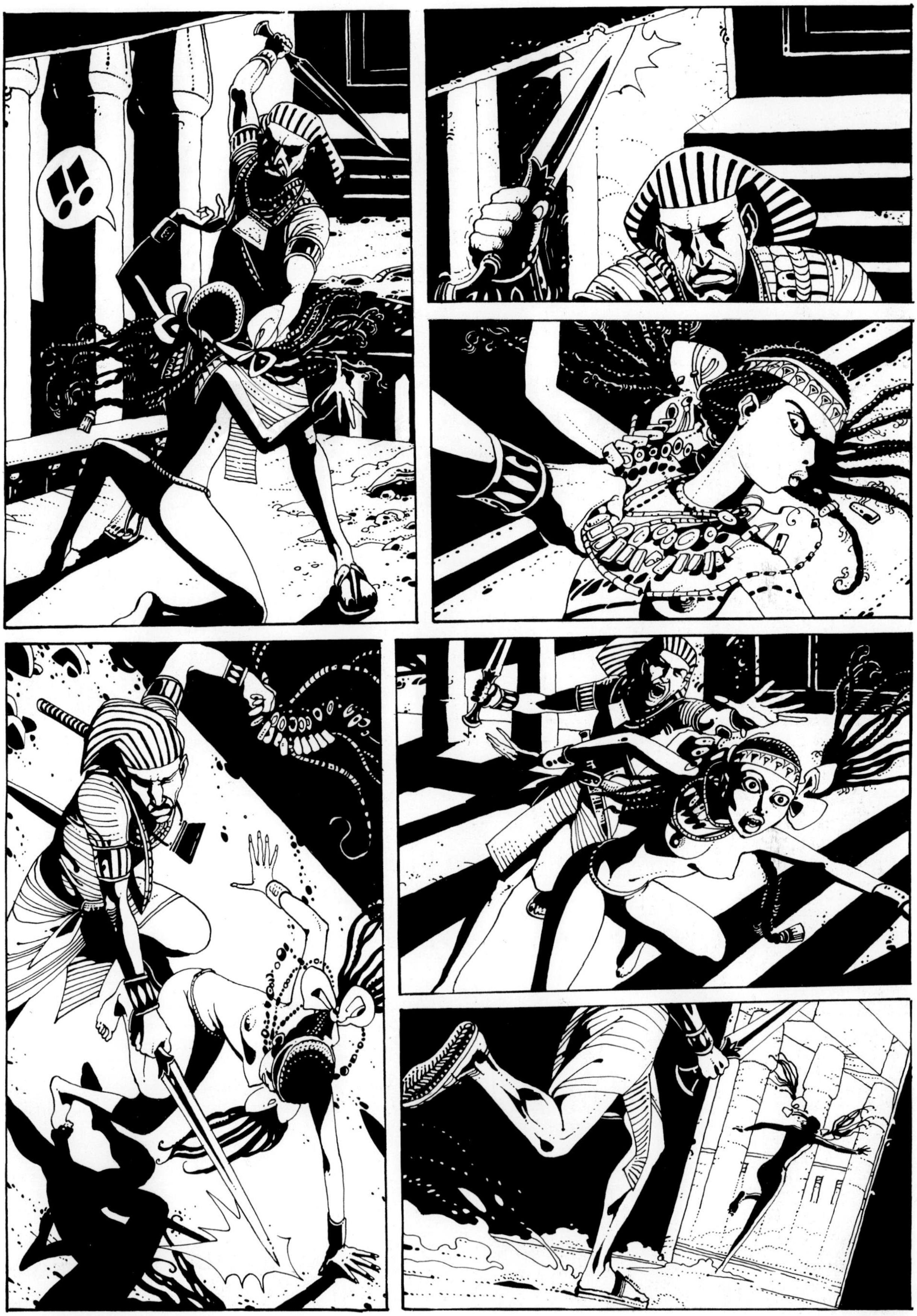
!!

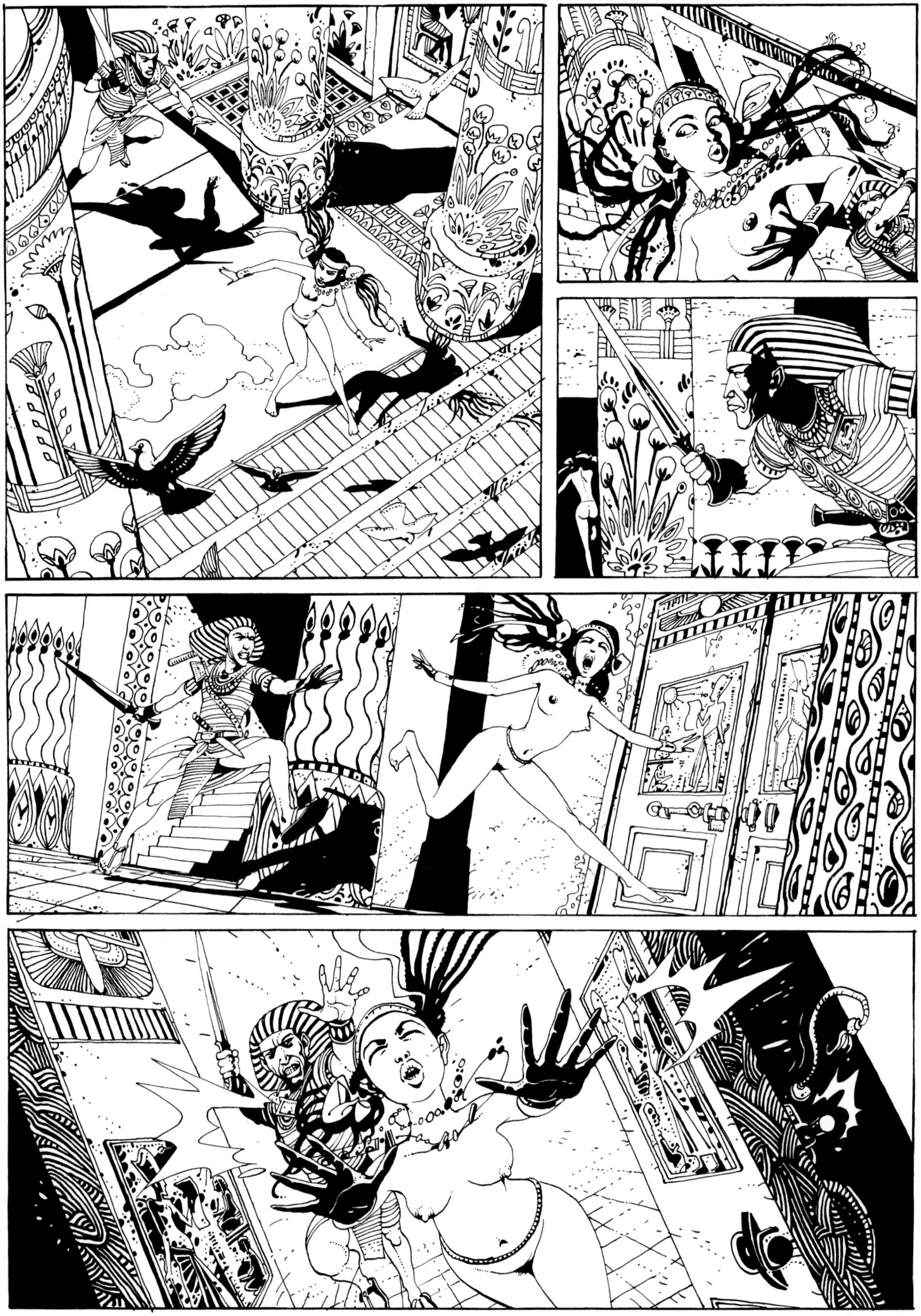

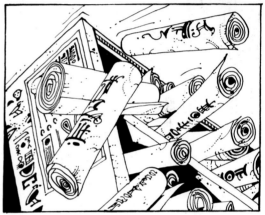

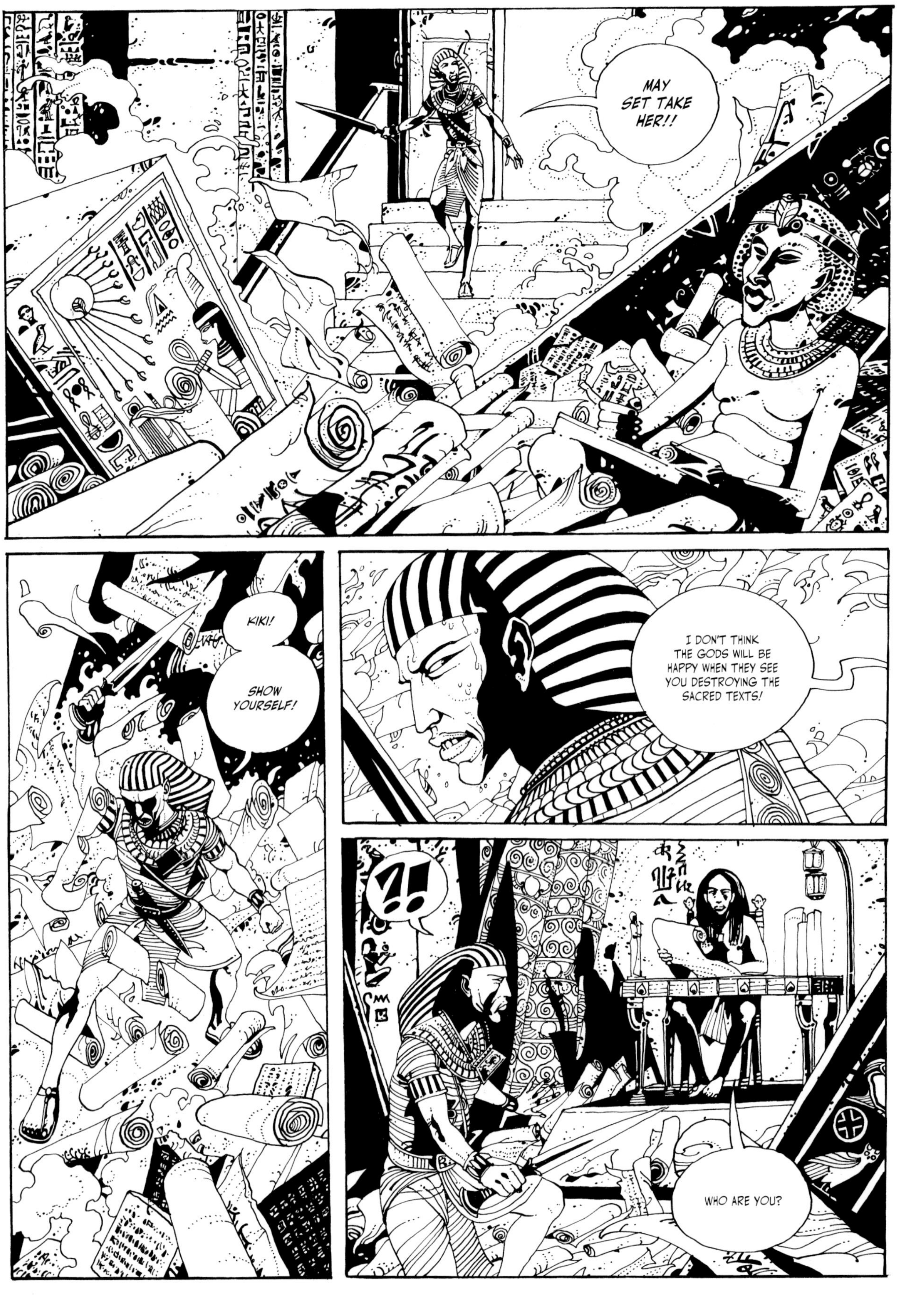
MAY SET TAKE HER!!
KIKI!
SHOW YOURSELF!
I DON'T THINK THE GODS WILL BE HAPPY WHEN THEY SEE YOU DESTROYING THE SACRED TEXTS!
?!
WHO ARE YOU?

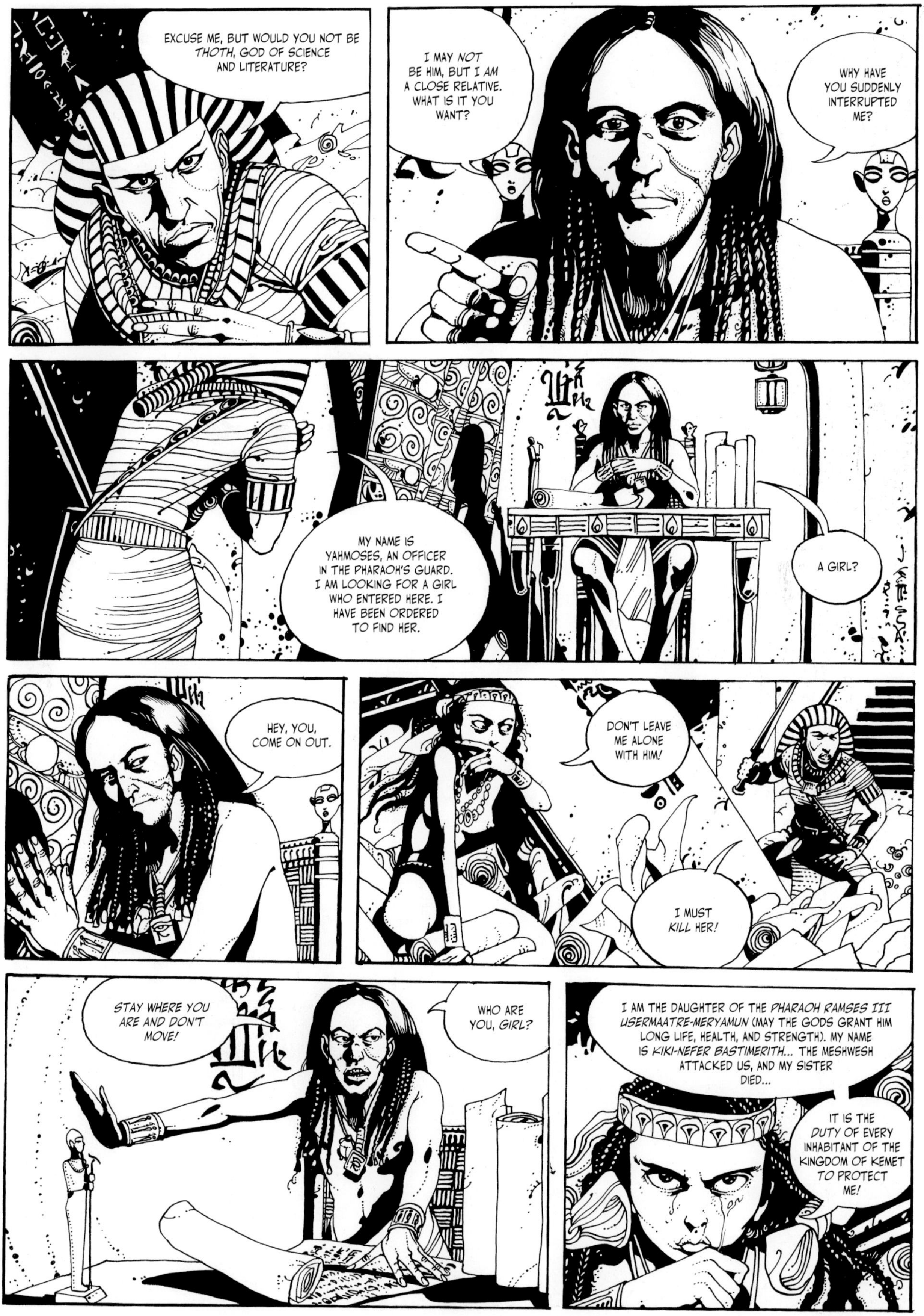
EXCUSE ME, BUT WOULD YOU NOT BE THOTH, GOD OF SCIENCE AND LITERATURE?
I MAY NOT BE HIM, BUT I AM A CLOSE RELATIVE. WHAT IS IT YOU WANT?
WHY HAVE YOU SUDDENLY INTERRUPTED ME?
MY NAME IS YAHMOSES, AN OFFICER IN THE PHARAOH'S GUARD. I AM LOOKING FOR A GIRL WHO ENTERED HERE. I HAVE BEEN ORDERED TO FIND HER.
A GIRL?
HEY, YOU, COME ON OUT.
DON'T LEAVE ME ALONE WITH HIM!
I MUST KILL HER!
STAY WHERE YOU ARE AND DON'T MOVE!
WHO ARE YOU, GIRL?
I AM THE DAUGHTER OF THE PHARAOH RAMSES III USERMAATRE-MERYAMUN (MAY THE GODS GRANT HIM LONG LIFE, HEALTH, AND STRENGTH). MY NAME IS KIKI-NEFER BASTIMERITH... THE MESHWESH ATTACKED US, AND MY SISTER DIED...
IT IS THE DUTY OF EVERY INHABITANT OF THE KINGDOM OF KEMET TO PROTECT ME!

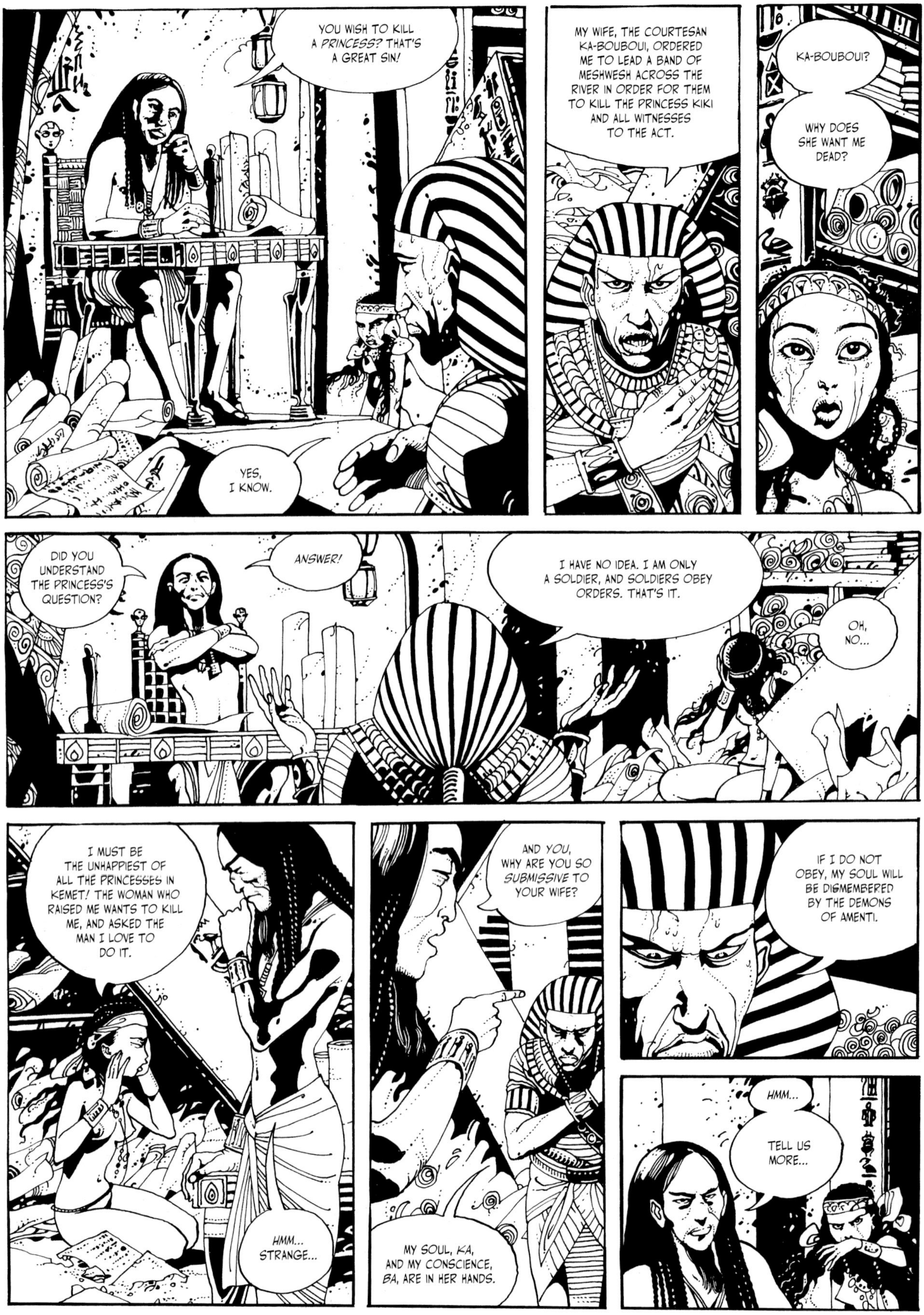
YOU WISH TO KILL A *PRINCESS?* THAT'S A GREAT SIN!
YES, I KNOW.
MY WIFE, THE COURTESAN KA-BOUBOUI, ORDERED ME TO LEAD A BAND OF MESHWESH ACROSS THE RIVER IN ORDER FOR THEM TO KILL THE PRINCESS KIKI AND ALL WITNESSES TO THE ACT.
KA-BOUBOUI?
WHY DOES SHE WANT ME DEAD?
DID YOU UNDERSTAND THE PRINCESS'S QUESTION?
ANSWER!
I HAVE NO IDEA. I AM ONLY A SOLDIER, AND SOLDIERS OBEY ORDERS. THAT'S IT.
OH, NO...
I MUST BE THE UNHAPPIEST OF ALL THE PRINCESSES IN KEMET! THE WOMAN WHO RAISED ME WANTS TO KILL ME, AND ASKED THE MAN I LOVE TO DO IT.
HMM... STRANGE...
AND *YOU,* WHY ARE YOU SO *SUBMISSIVE* TO YOUR WIFE?
MY SOUL, *KA,* AND MY CONSCIENCE, *BA,* ARE IN HER HANDS.
IF I DO NOT OBEY, MY SOUL WILL BE DISMEMBERED BY THE DEMONS OF AMENTI.
HMM...
TELL US MORE...

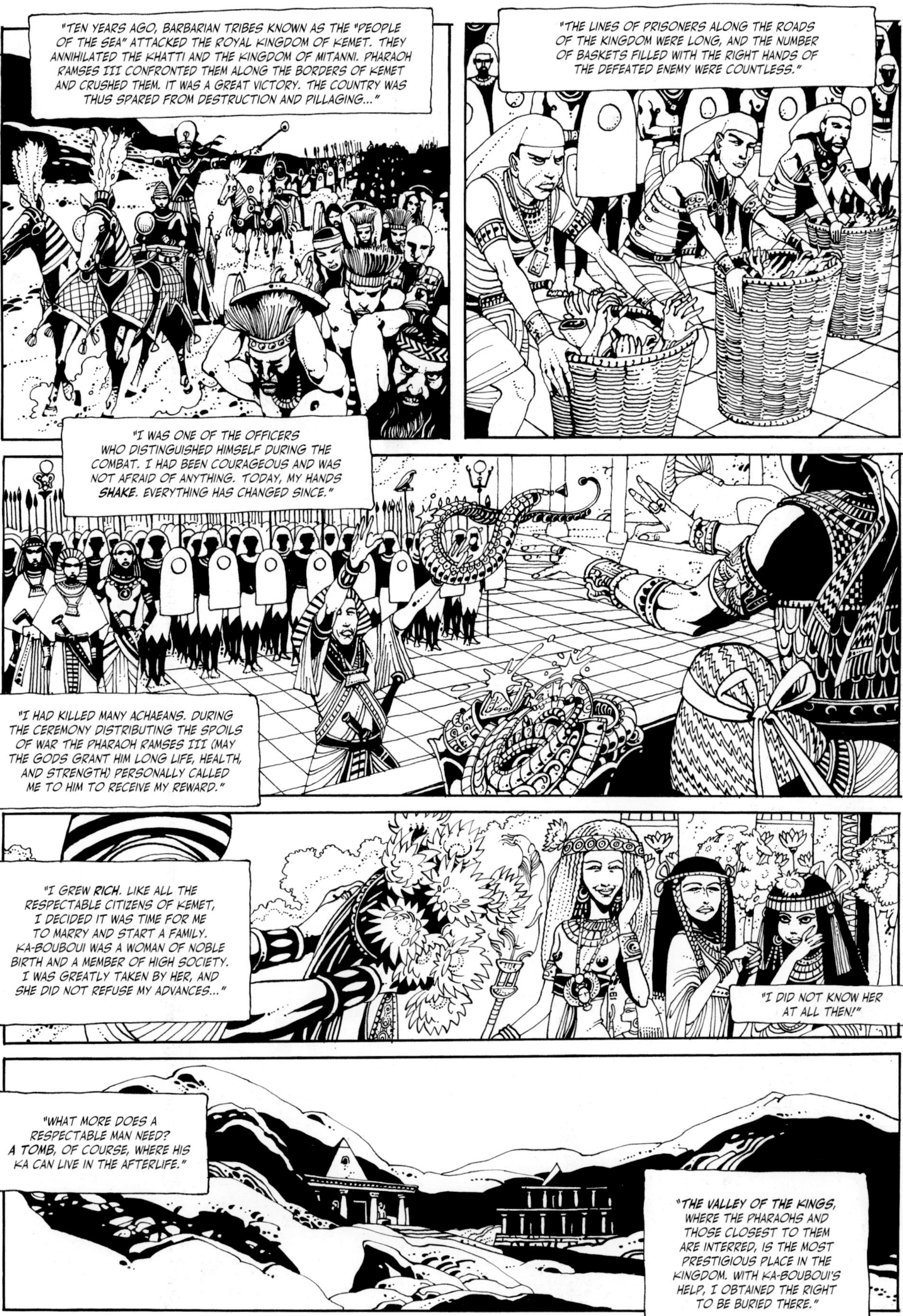
"TEN YEARS AGO, BARBARIAN TRIBES KNOWN AS THE "PEOPLE OF THE SEA" ATTACKED THE ROYAL KINGDOM OF KEMET. THEY ANNIHILATED THE KHATTI AND THE KINGDOM OF MITANNI. PHARAOH RAMSES III CONFRONTED THEM ALONG THE BORDERS OF KEMET AND CRUSHED THEM. IT WAS A GREAT VICTORY. THE COUNTRY WAS THUS SPARED FROM DESTRUCTION AND PILLAGING..."
"THE LINES OF PRISONERS ALONG THE ROADS OF THE KINGDOM WERE LONG, AND THE NUMBER OF BASKETS FILLED WITH THE RIGHT HANDS OF THE DEFEATED ENEMY WERE COUNTLESS."
"I WAS ONE OF THE OFFICERS WHO DISTINGUISHED HIMSELF DURING THE COMBAT. I HAD BEEN COURAGEOUS AND WAS NOT AFRAID OF ANYTHING. TODAY, MY HANDS **SHAKE**. EVERYTHING HAS CHANGED SINCE."
"I HAD KILLED MANY ACHAEANS. DURING THE CEREMONY DISTRIBUTING THE SPOILS OF WAR THE PHARAOH RAMSES III (MAY THE GODS GRANT HIM LONG LIFE, HEALTH, AND STRENGTH) PERSONALLY CALLED ME TO HIM TO RECEIVE MY REWARD."
"I GREW **RICH**. LIKE ALL THE RESPECTABLE CITIZENS OF KEMET, I DECIDED IT WAS TIME FOR ME TO MARRY AND START A FAMILY. KA-BOUBOUI WAS A WOMAN OF NOBLE BIRTH AND A MEMBER OF HIGH SOCIETY. I WAS GREATLY TAKEN BY HER, AND SHE DID NOT REFUSE MY ADVANCES..."
"I DID NOT KNOW HER AT ALL THEN!"
"WHAT MORE DOES A RESPECTABLE MAN NEED? **A TOMB**, OF COURSE, WHERE HIS KA CAN LIVE IN THE AFTERLIFE."
"**THE VALLEY OF THE KINGS**, WHERE THE PHARAOHS AND THOSE CLOSEST TO THEM ARE INTERRED, IS THE MOST PRESTIGIOUS PLACE IN THE KINGDOM. WITH KA-BOUBOUI'S HELP, I OBTAINED THE RIGHT TO BE BURIED THERE."

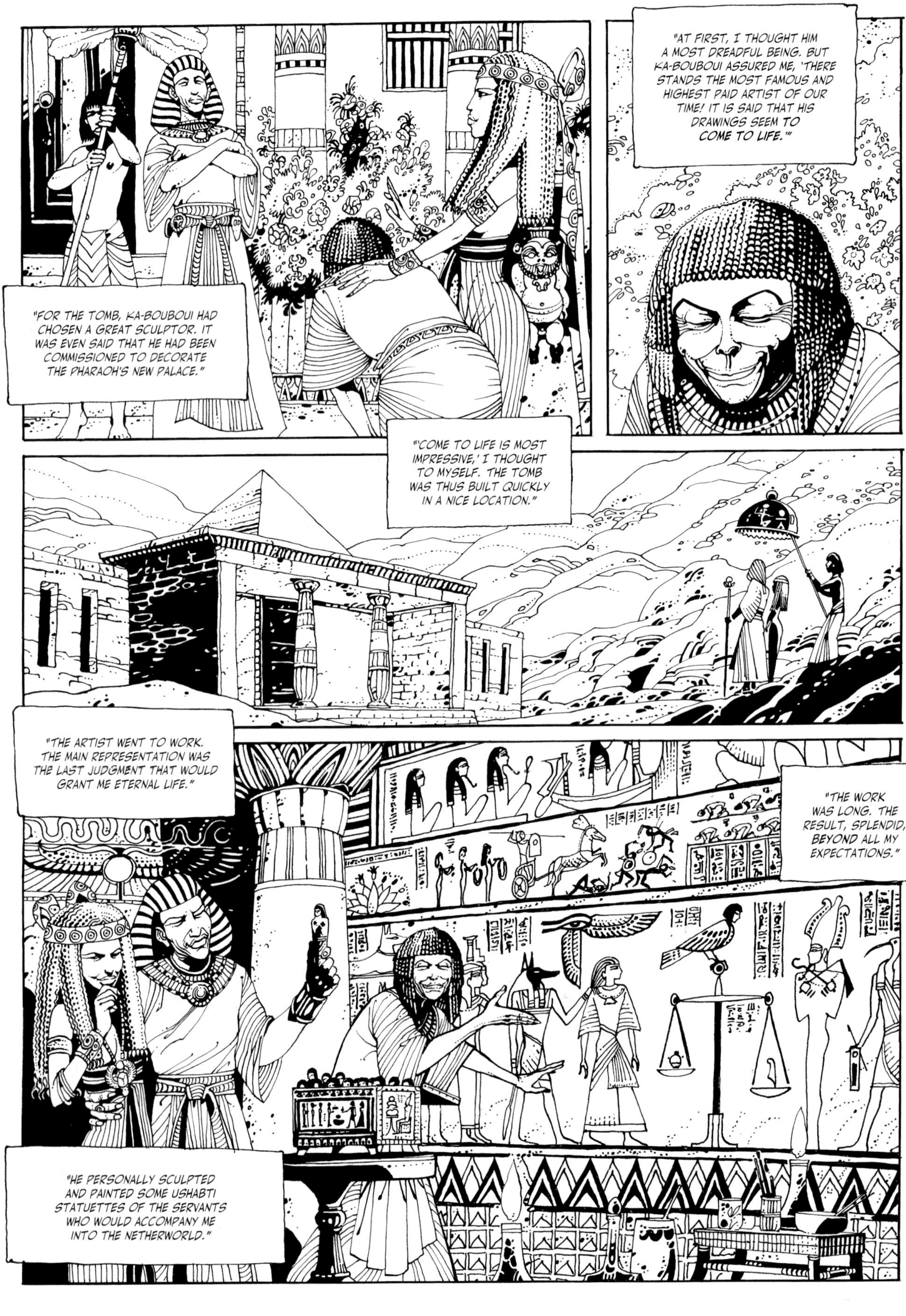
"FOR THE TOMB, KA-BOUBOUI HAD CHOSEN A GREAT SCULPTOR. IT WAS EVEN SAID THAT HE HAD BEEN COMMISSIONED TO DECORATE THE PHARAOH'S NEW PALACE."
"AT FIRST, I THOUGHT HIM A MOST DREADFUL BEING. BUT KA-BOUBOUI ASSURED ME, 'THERE STANDS THE MOST FAMOUS AND HIGHEST PAID ARTIST OF OUR TIME! IT IS SAID THAT HIS DRAWINGS SEEM TO COME TO LIFE.'"
"COME TO LIFE IS MOST IMPRESSIVE,' I THOUGHT TO MYSELF. THE TOMB WAS THUS BUILT QUICKLY IN A NICE LOCATION."
"THE ARTIST WENT TO WORK. THE MAIN REPRESENTATION WAS THE LAST JUDGMENT THAT WOULD GRANT ME ETERNAL LIFE."
"THE WORK WAS LONG. THE RESULT, SPLENDID, BEYOND ALL MY EXPECTATIONS."
"HE PERSONALLY SCULPTED AND PAINTED SOME USHABTI STATUETTES OF THE SERVANTS WHO WOULD ACCOMPANY ME INTO THE NETHERWORLD."

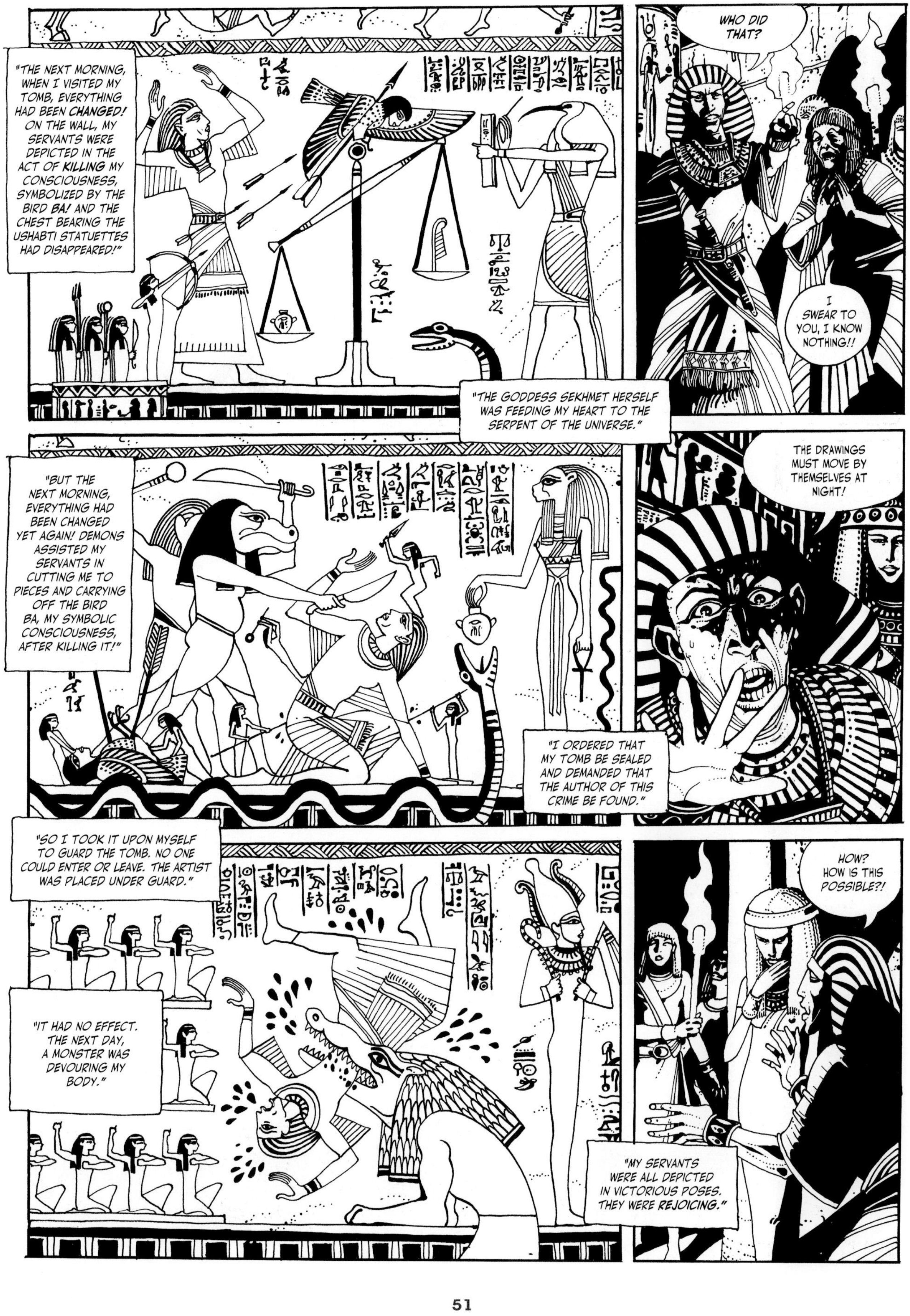
"THE NEXT MORNING, WHEN I VISITED MY TOMB, EVERYTHING HAD BEEN CHANGED! ON THE WALL, MY SERVANTS WERE DEPICTED IN THE ACT OF KILLING MY CONSCIOUSNESS, SYMBOLIZED BY THE BIRD BA! AND THE CHEST BEARING THE USHABTI STATUETTES HAD DISAPPEARED!"
"THE GODDESS SEKHMET HERSELF WAS FEEDING MY HEART TO THE SERPENT OF THE UNIVERSE."
WHO DID THAT?
I SWEAR TO YOU, I KNOW NOTHING!!
"BUT THE NEXT MORNING, EVERYTHING HAD BEEN CHANGED YET AGAIN! DEMONS ASSISTED MY SERVANTS IN CUTTING ME TO PIECES AND CARRYING OFF THE BIRD BA, MY SYMBOLIC CONSCIOUSNESS, AFTER KILLING IT!"
THE DRAWINGS MUST MOVE BY THEMSELVES AT NIGHT!
"I ORDERED THAT MY TOMB BE SEALED AND DEMANDED THAT THE AUTHOR OF THIS CRIME BE FOUND."
"SO I TOOK IT UPON MYSELF TO GUARD THE TOMB. NO ONE COULD ENTER OR LEAVE. THE ARTIST WAS PLACED UNDER GUARD."
"IT HAD NO EFFECT. THE NEXT DAY, A MONSTER WAS DEVOURING MY BODY."
HOW? HOW IS THIS POSSIBLE?!
"MY SERVANTS WERE ALL DEPICTED IN VICTORIOUS POSES. THEY WERE REJOICING."

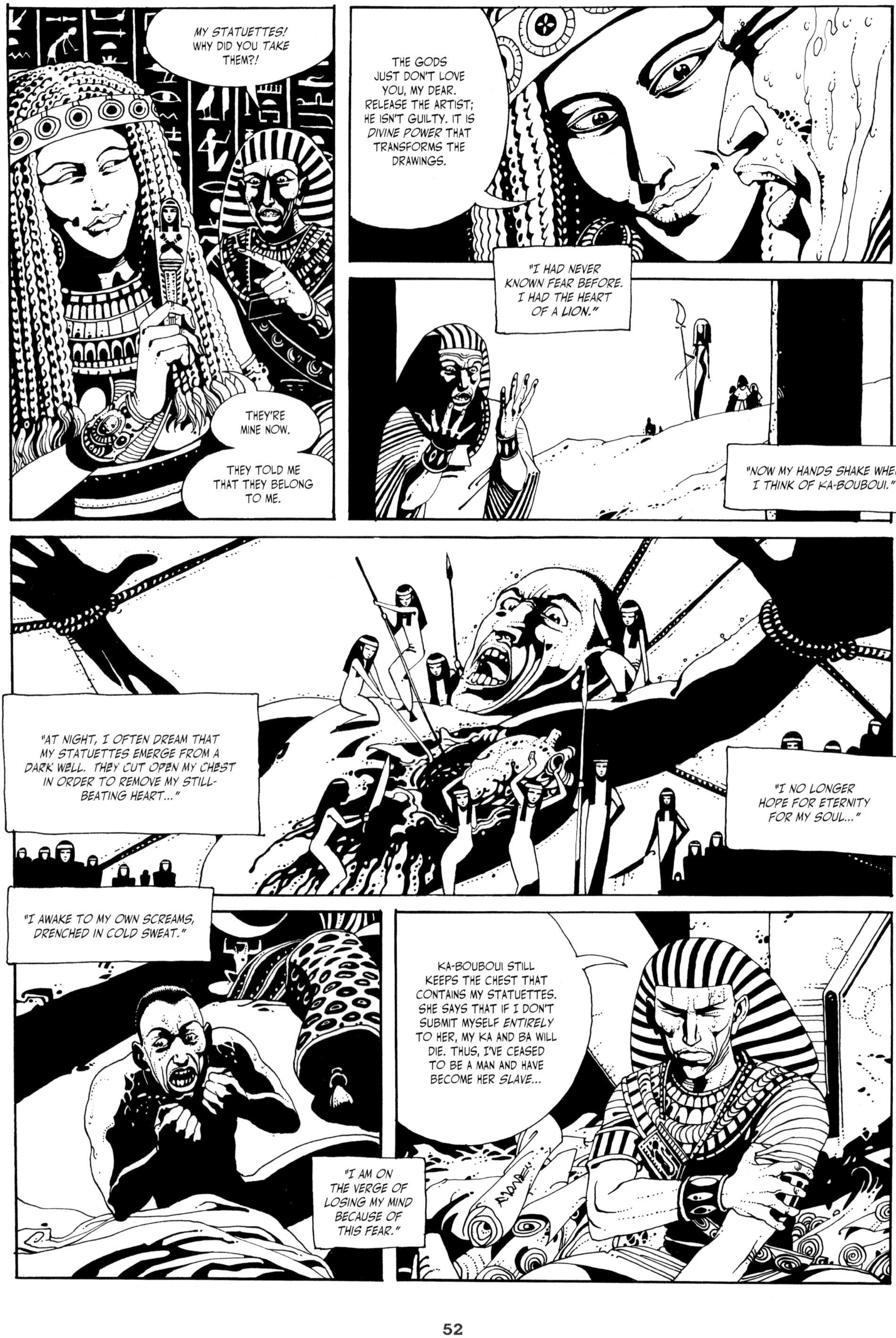
MY STATUETTES! WHY DID YOU TAKE THEM?!
THEY'RE MINE NOW.
THEY TOLD ME THAT THEY BELONG TO ME.
THE GODS JUST DON'T LOVE YOU, MY DEAR. RELEASE THE ARTIST; HE ISN'T GUILTY. IT IS DIVINE POWER THAT TRANSFORMS THE DRAWINGS.
"I HAD NEVER KNOWN FEAR BEFORE. I HAD THE HEART OF A LION."
"NOW MY HANDS SHAKE WHEN I THINK OF KA-BOUBOUI."
"AT NIGHT, I OFTEN DREAM THAT MY STATUETTES EMERGE FROM A DARK WELL. THEY CUT OPEN MY CHEST IN ORDER TO REMOVE MY STILL-BEATING HEART..."
"I NO LONGER HOPE FOR ETERNITY FOR MY SOUL..."
"I AWAKE TO MY OWN SCREAMS, DRENCHED IN COLD SWEAT."
"I AM ON THE VERGE OF LOSING MY MIND BECAUSE OF THIS FEAR."
KA-BOUBOUI STILL KEEPS THE CHEST THAT CONTAINS MY STATUETTES. SHE SAYS THAT IF I DON'T SUBMIT MYSELF ENTIRELY TO HER, MY KA AND BA WILL DIE. THUS, I'VE CEASED TO BE A MAN AND HAVE BECOME HER SLAVE...

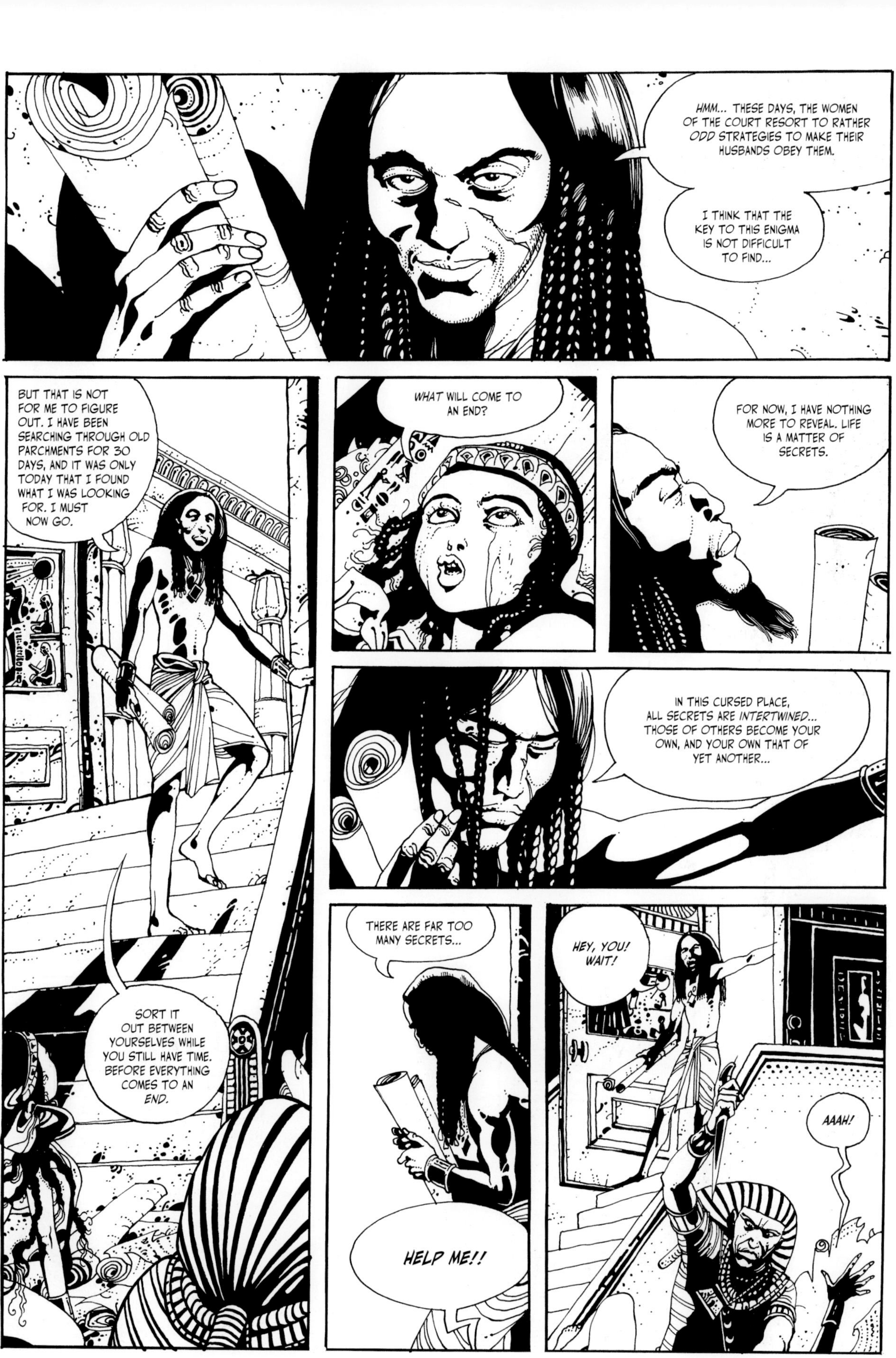

HMM... THESE DAYS, THE WOMEN OF THE COURT RESORT TO RATHER *ODD* STRATEGIES TO MAKE THEIR HUSBANDS OBEY THEM.
I THINK THAT THE KEY TO THIS ENIGMA IS NOT DIFFICULT TO FIND...
BUT THAT IS NOT FOR ME TO FIGURE OUT. I HAVE BEEN SEARCHING THROUGH OLD PARCHMENTS FOR 30 DAYS, AND IT WAS ONLY TODAY THAT I FOUND WHAT I WAS LOOKING FOR. I MUST NOW GO.
SORT IT OUT BETWEEN YOURSELVES WHILE YOU STILL HAVE TIME. BEFORE EVERYTHING COMES TO AN *END*.
WHAT WILL COME TO AN END?
FOR NOW, I HAVE NOTHING MORE TO REVEAL. LIFE IS A MATTER OF SECRETS.
IN THIS CURSED PLACE, ALL SECRETS ARE *INTERTWINED*... THOSE OF OTHERS BECOME YOUR OWN, AND YOUR OWN THAT OF YET ANOTHER...
THERE ARE FAR TOO MANY SECRETS...
HELP ME!!
HEY, YOU! WAIT!
AAAH!

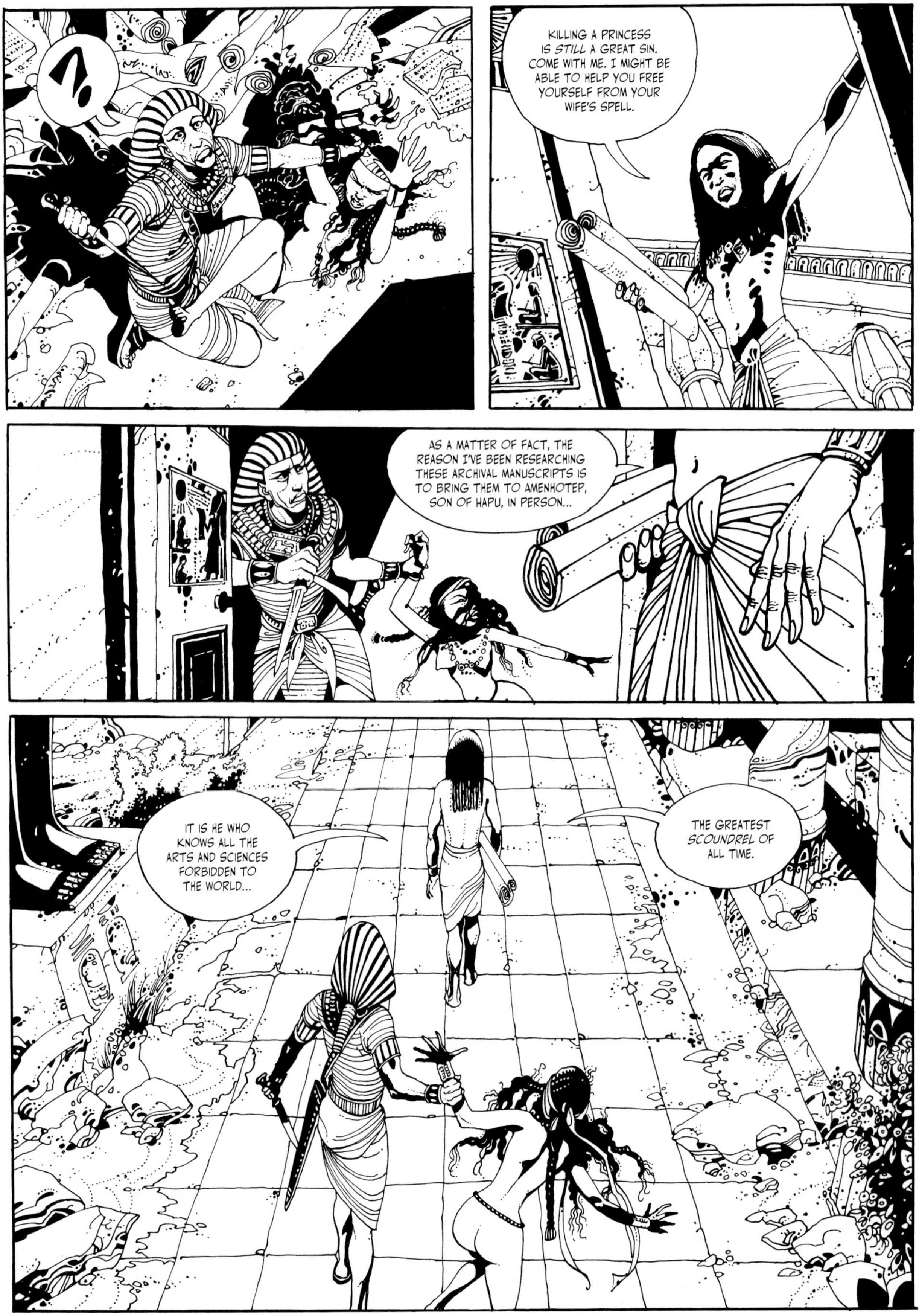
?!
KILLING A PRINCESS IS STILL A GREAT SIN. COME WITH ME. I MIGHT BE ABLE TO HELP YOU FREE YOURSELF FROM YOUR WIFE'S SPELL.
AS A MATTER OF FACT, THE REASON I'VE BEEN RESEARCHING THESE ARCHIVAL MANUSCRIPTS IS TO BRING THEM TO AMENHOTEP, SON OF HAPU, IN PERSON...
IT IS HE WHO KNOWS ALL THE ARTS AND SCIENCES FORBIDDEN TO THE WORLD...
THE GREATEST SCOUNDREL OF ALL TIME.

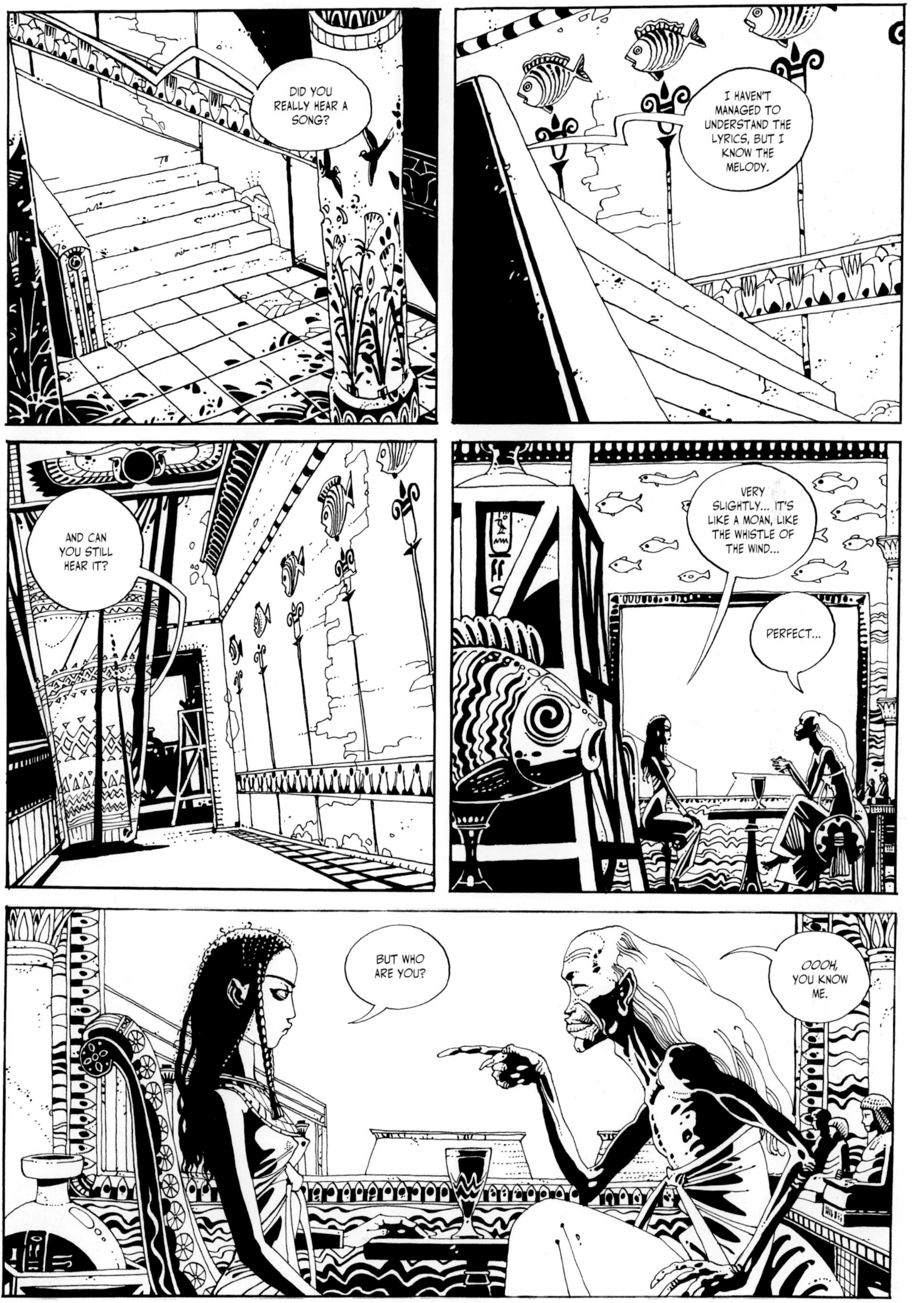
DID YOU REALLY HEAR A SONG?
I HAVEN'T MANAGED TO UNDERSTAND THE LYRICS, BUT I KNOW THE MELODY.
AND CAN YOU STILL HEAR IT?
VERY SLIGHTLY... IT'S LIKE A MOAN, LIKE THE WHISTLE OF THE WIND...
PERFECT...
BUT WHO ARE YOU?
OOOH, YOU KNOW ME.

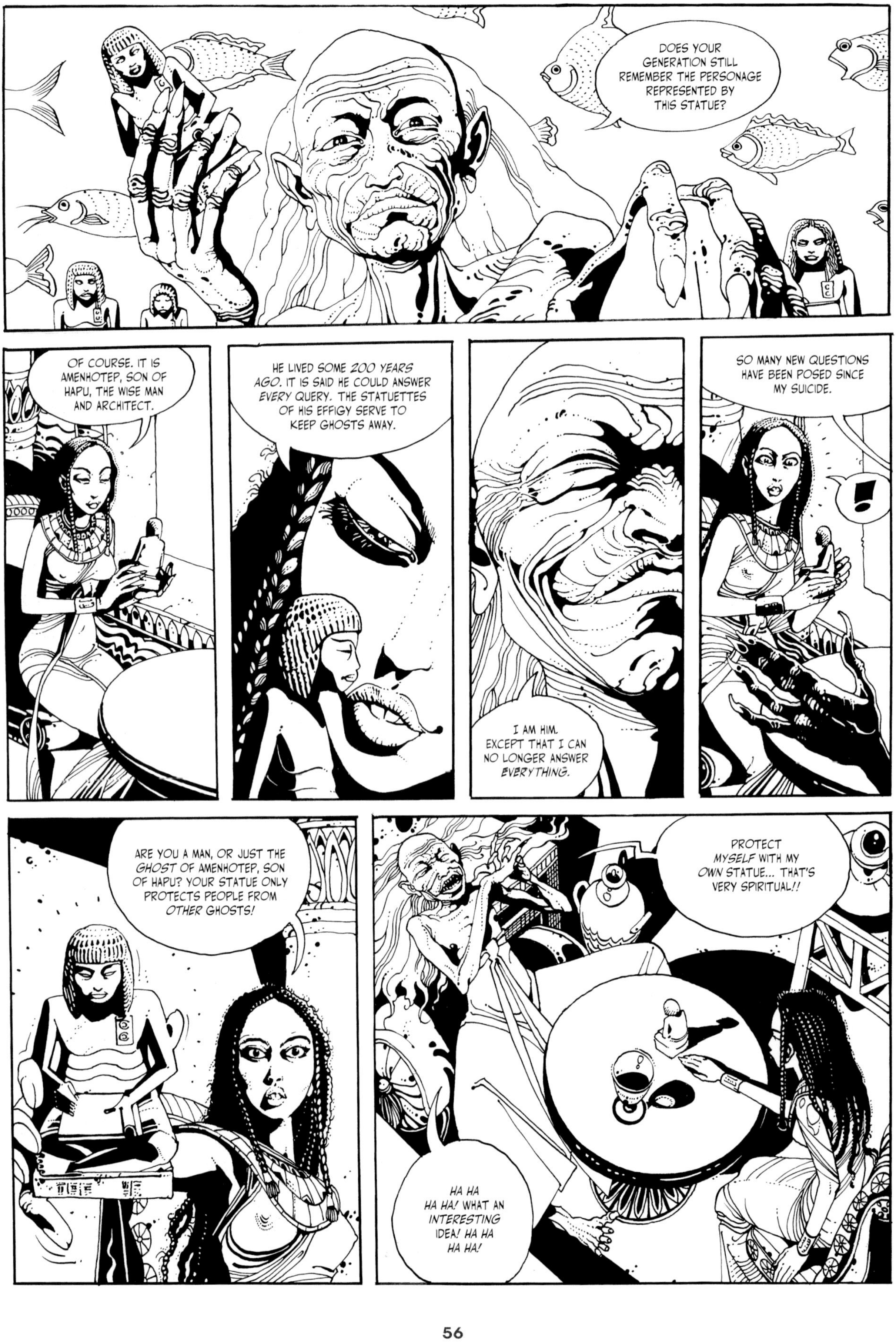
DOES YOUR GENERATION STILL REMEMBER THE PERSONAGE REPRESENTED BY THIS STATUE?
OF COURSE. IT IS AMENHOTEP, SON OF HAPU, THE WISE MAN AND ARCHITECT.
HE LIVED SOME 200 YEARS AGO. IT IS SAID HE COULD ANSWER EVERY QUERY. THE STATUETTES OF HIS EFFIGY SERVE TO KEEP GHOSTS AWAY.
I AM HIM. EXCEPT THAT I CAN NO LONGER ANSWER EVERYTHING.
SO MANY NEW QUESTIONS HAVE BEEN POSED SINCE MY SUICIDE.
!
ARE YOU A MAN, OR JUST THE GHOST OF AMENHOTEP, SON OF HAPU? YOUR STATUE ONLY PROTECTS PEOPLE FROM OTHER GHOSTS!
PROTECT MYSELF WITH MY OWN STATUE... THAT'S VERY SPIRITUAL!!
HA HA HA HA! WHAT AN INTERESTING IDEA! HA HA HA HA!

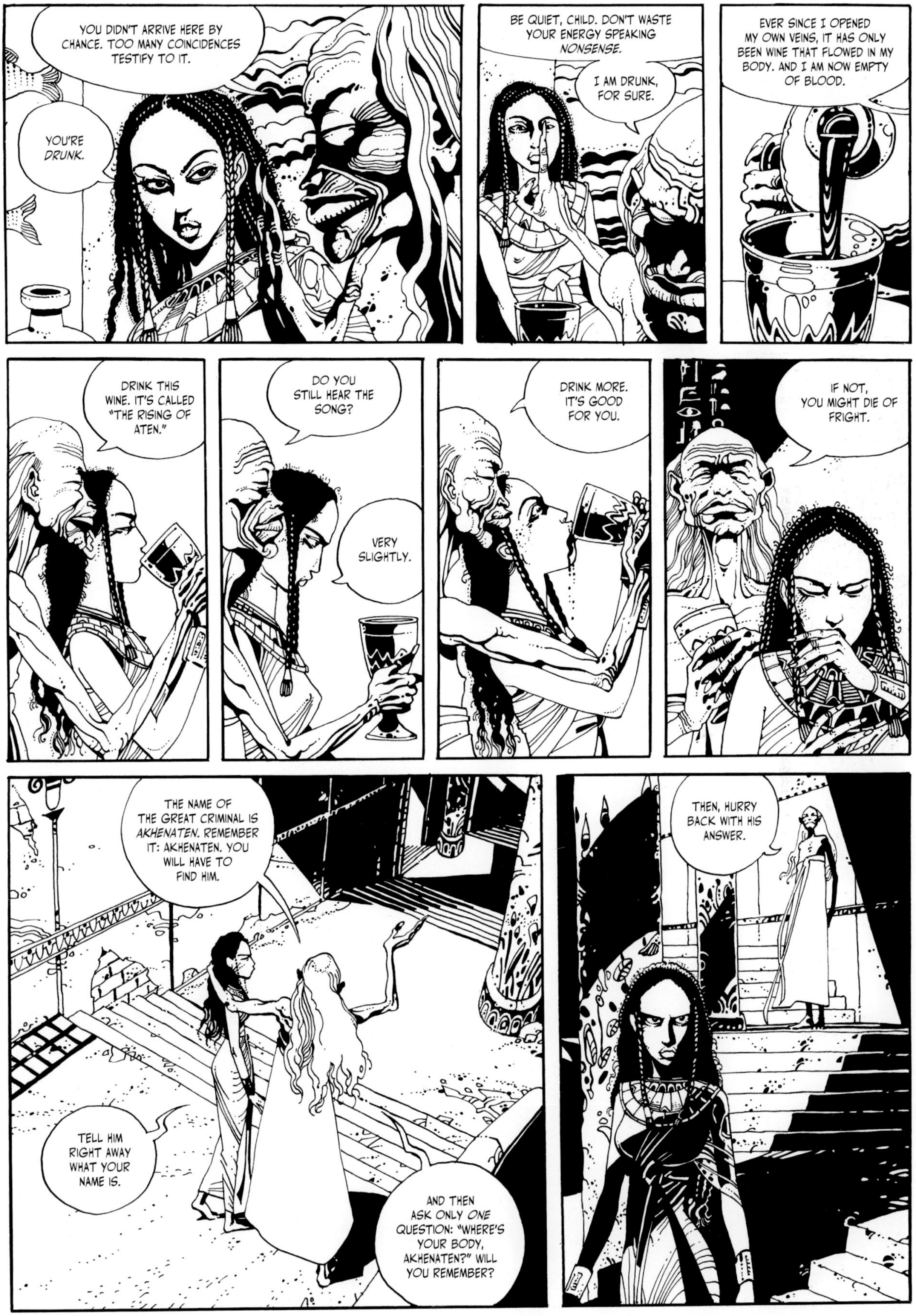
YOU DIDN'T ARRIVE HERE BY CHANCE. TOO MANY COINCIDENCES TESTIFY TO IT.
YOU'RE *DRUNK.*
BE QUIET, CHILD. DON'T WASTE YOUR ENERGY SPEAKING *NONSENSE.*
I AM DRUNK, FOR SURE.
EVER SINCE I OPENED MY OWN VEINS, IT HAS ONLY BEEN WINE THAT FLOWED IN MY BODY. AND I AM NOW EMPTY OF BLOOD.
DRINK THIS WINE. IT'S CALLED "THE RISING OF ATEN."
DO YOU STILL HEAR THE SONG?
VERY SLIGHTLY.
DRINK MORE. IT'S GOOD FOR YOU.
IF NOT, YOU MIGHT DIE OF FRIGHT.
THE NAME OF THE GREAT CRIMINAL IS *AKHENATEN.* REMEMBER IT: AKHENATEN. YOU WILL HAVE TO FIND HIM.
TELL HIM RIGHT AWAY WHAT YOUR NAME IS.
AND THEN ASK ONLY *ONE* QUESTION: "WHERE'S YOUR BODY, AKHENATEN?" WILL YOU REMEMBER?
THEN, HURRY BACK WITH HIS ANSWER.

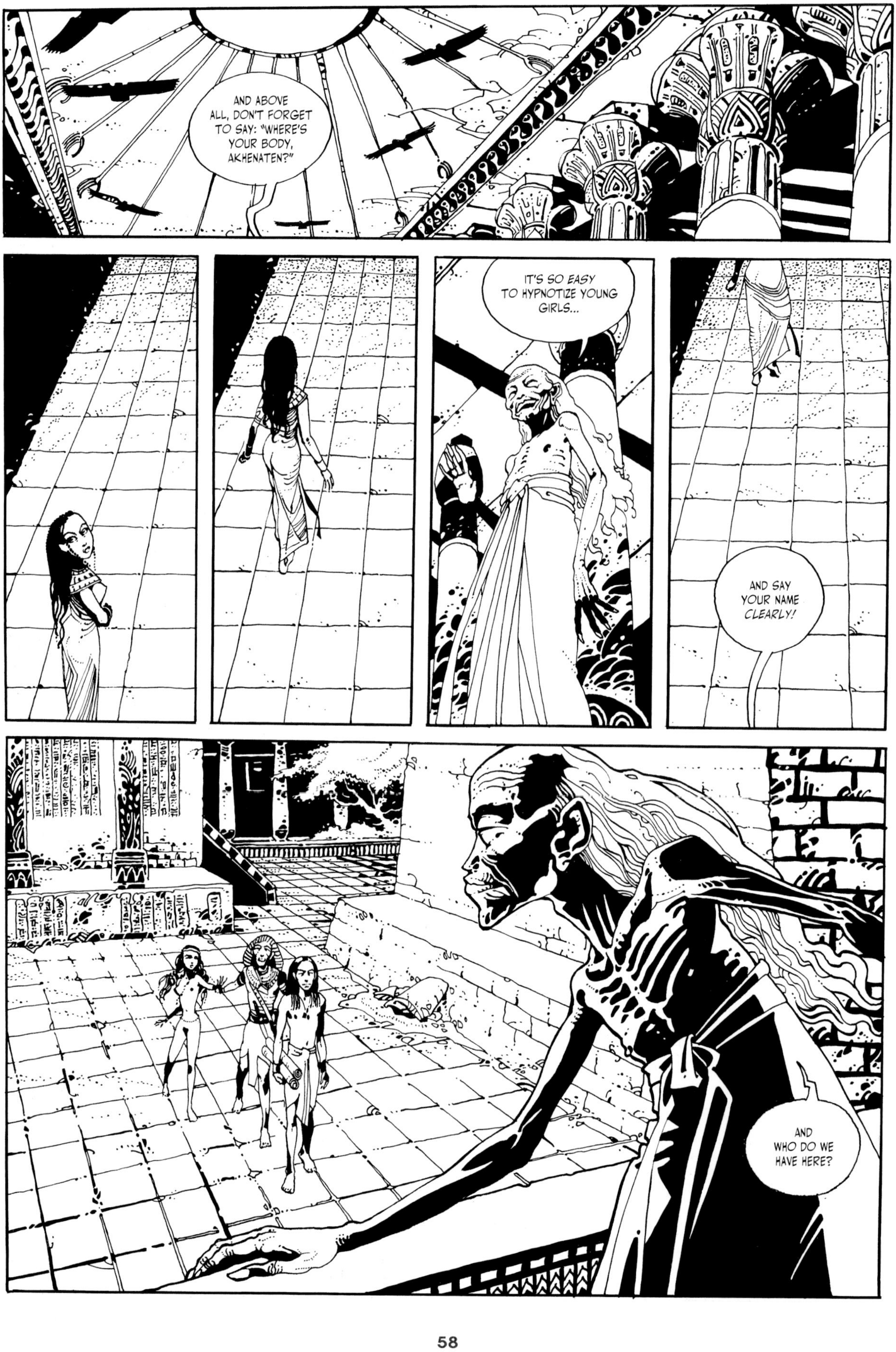
AND ABOVE ALL, DON'T FORGET TO SAY: "WHERE'S YOUR BODY, AKHENATEN?"
IT'S SO *EASY* TO HYPNOTIZE YOUNG GIRLS...
AND SAY YOUR NAME *CLEARLY!*
AND WHO DO WE HAVE HERE?

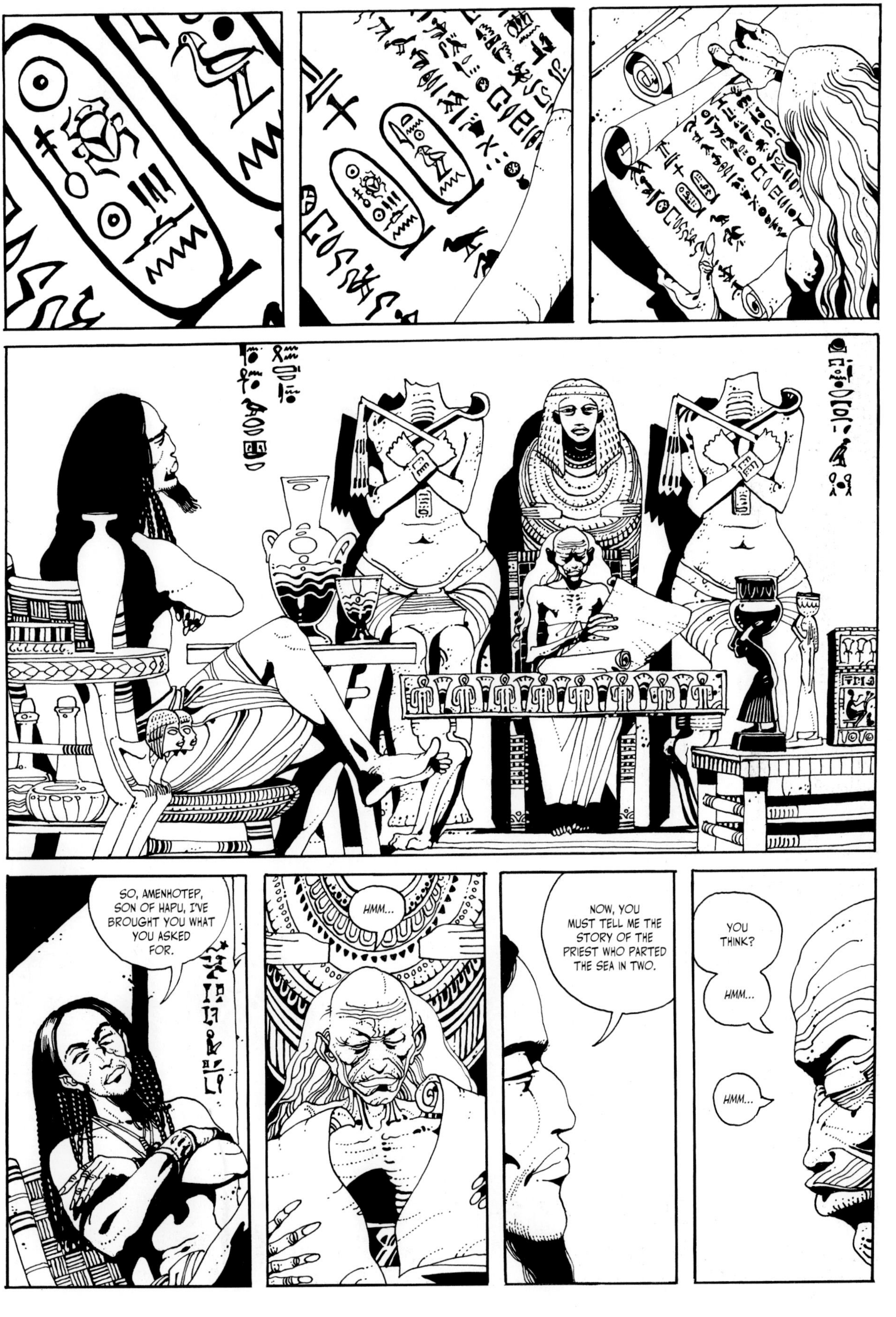
SO, AMENHOTEP, SON OF HAPU, I'VE BROUGHT YOU WHAT YOU ASKED FOR.
HMM...
NOW, YOU MUST TELL ME THE STORY OF THE PRIEST WHO PARTED THE SEA IN TWO.
YOU THINK?
HMM...
HMM...

HMM...

AND WHO ARE THESE PEOPLE WHO CAME WITH YOU?

HEY, COME IN!

I SALUTE YOU, O GREAT SAGE!

ALLOW ME TO...

WHAT...?! I WILL NOT BOW BEFORE THIS MUMMY...! I AM THE PHARAOH'S DAUGHTER.

YOU'RE ALL MAD!

THEY BURST INTO THE HALL OF ARCHIVES JUST AS I FOUND THE PAPYRUS I SOUGHT. THE GIRL CLAIMS TO BE THE CHILD OF THE PHARAOH'S WIFE. THE OFFICER WAS TRYING TO KILL HER. I THOUGHT THAT...

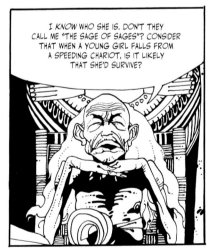

I KNOW WHO SHE IS. DON'T THEY CALL ME "THE SAGE OF SAGES"? CONSIDER THAT WHEN A YOUNG GIRL FALLS FROM A SPEEDING CHARIOT, IS IT LIKELY THAT SHE'D SURVIVE?

AND YET, SHE BEARS HARDLY ANY SCRATCHES. THEN, SHE BURSTS RIGHT INTO THE HALL WHERE YOU WERE.

MY ONLY FRIEND IN THIS WORLD, MY SARCOPHAGUS, WILL CONFIRM THESE WORDS. IT IS IMPOSSIBLE.

BUT THAT IS NOT ALL. ANOTHER GIRL FELL FROM THE SAME CHARIOT AND ALSO SURVIVED. SHE CAME TO FIND ME. AND STILL, THERE'S MORE. DO YOU KNOW HER NAME?

TITI-NEFER.

REVERSE THE TWO PARTS OF THIS NAME AND YOU WILL GET THAT OF THE GREAT CRIMINAL'S WIFE. AND MORE, SHE HEARS HIS CHANT!

I WILL THROW MYSELF TO THE CROCODILES IF THESE ARE ALL SIMPLY COINCIDENCES!

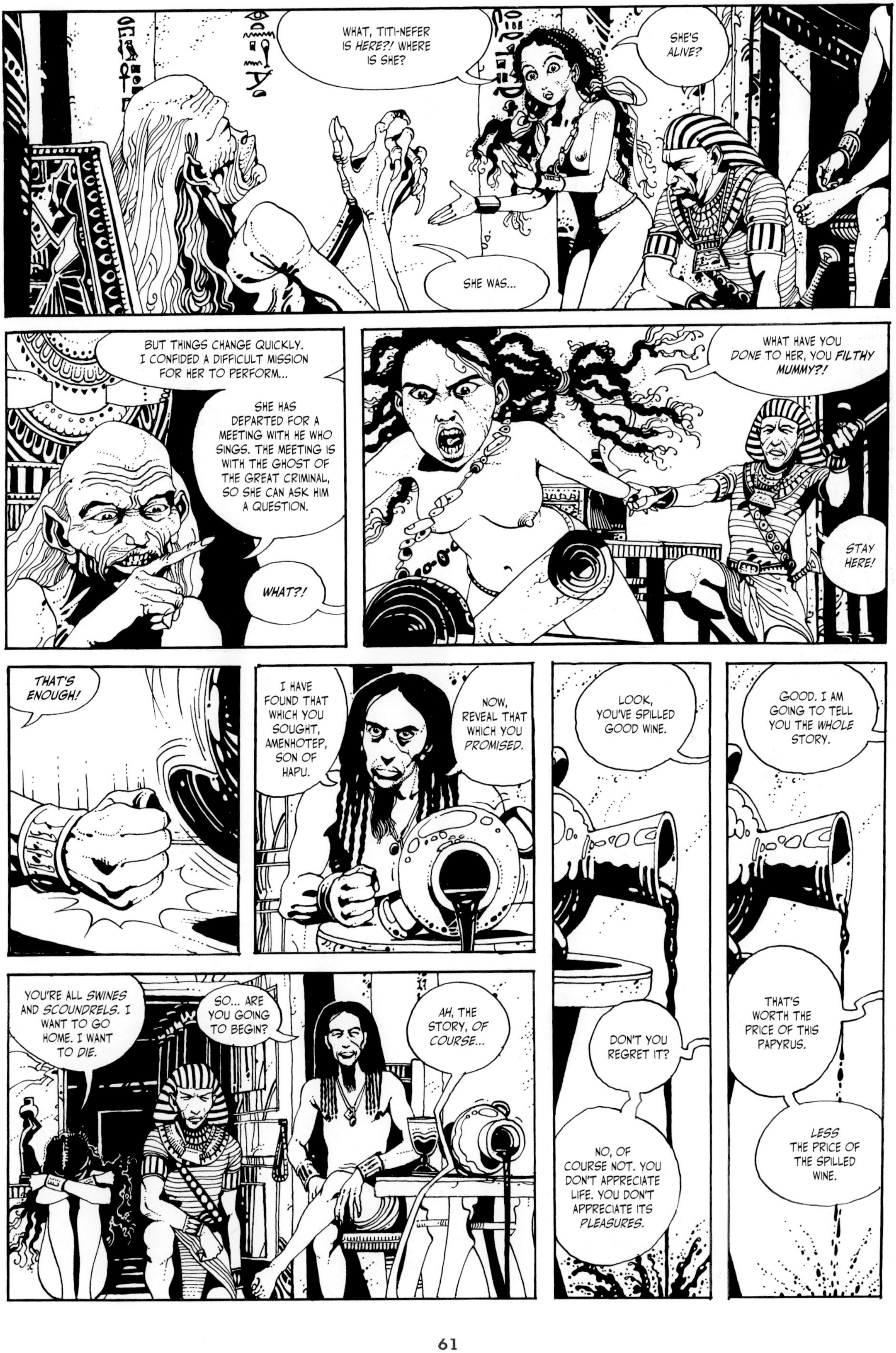
WHAT, TITI-NEFER IS HERE?! WHERE IS SHE?
SHE'S ALIVE?
SHE WAS...
BUT THINGS CHANGE QUICKLY. I CONFIDED A DIFFICULT MISSION FOR HER TO PERFORM...
SHE HAS DEPARTED FOR A MEETING WITH HE WHO SINGS. THE MEETING IS WITH THE GHOST OF THE GREAT CRIMINAL, SO SHE CAN ASK HIM A QUESTION.
WHAT?!
WHAT HAVE YOU DONE TO HER, YOU FILTHY MUMMY?!
STAY HERE!
THAT'S ENOUGH!
I HAVE FOUND THAT WHICH YOU SOUGHT, AMENHOTEP, SON OF HAPU.
NOW, REVEAL THAT WHICH YOU PROMISED.
LOOK, YOU'VE SPILLED GOOD WINE.
GOOD. I AM GOING TO TELL YOU THE WHOLE STORY.
YOU'RE ALL SWINES AND SCOUNDRELS. I WANT TO GO HOME. I WANT TO DIE.
SO... ARE YOU GOING TO BEGIN?
AH, THE STORY, OF COURSE...
DON'T YOU REGRET IT?
NO, OF COURSE NOT. YOU DON'T APPRECIATE LIFE. YOU DON'T APPRECIATE ITS PLEASURES.
THAT'S WORTH THE PRICE OF THIS PAPYRUS.
LESS THE PRICE OF THE SPILLED WINE.

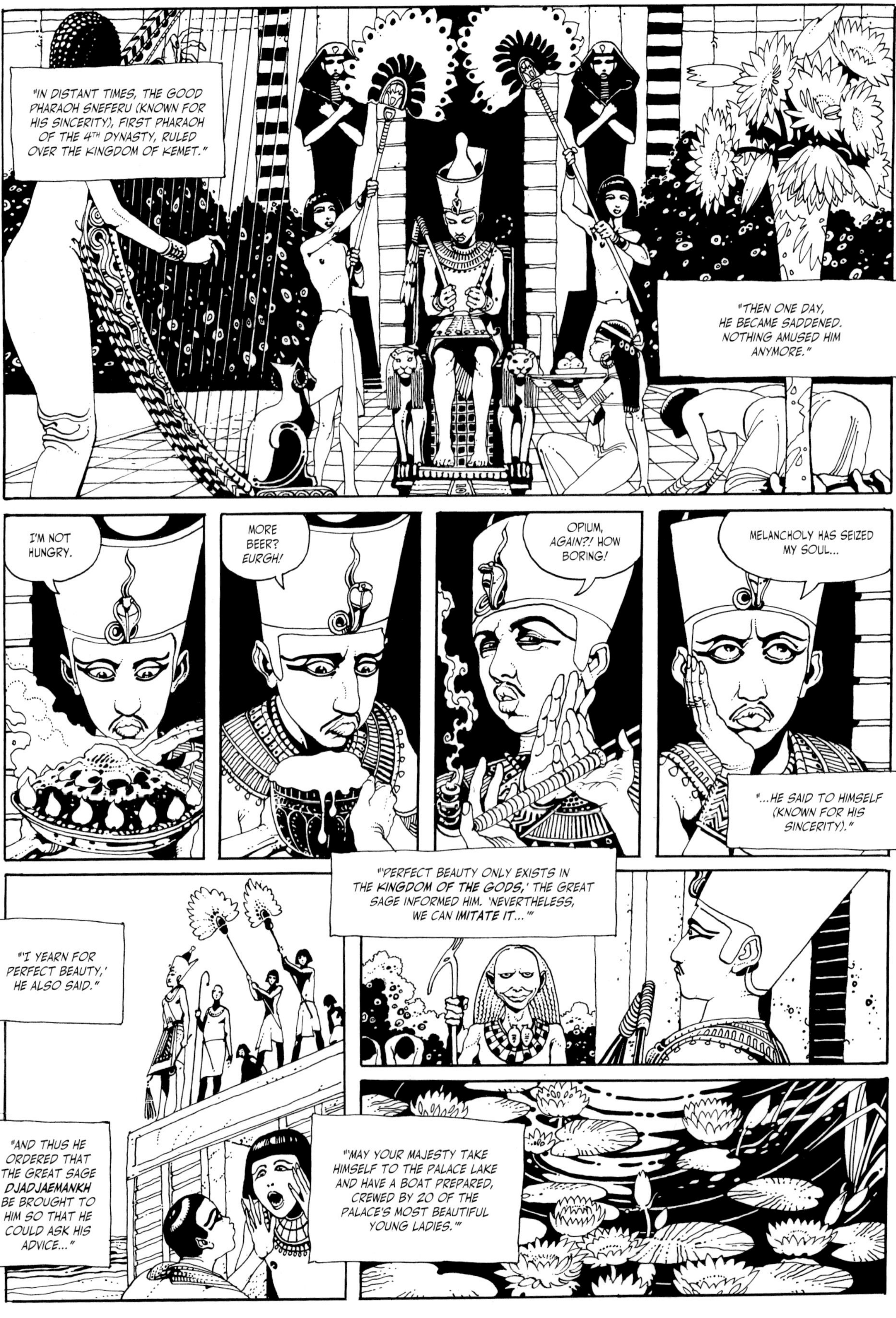
"IN DISTANT TIMES, THE GOOD PHARAOH SNEFERU (KNOWN FOR HIS SINCERITY), FIRST PHARAOH OF THE 4TH DYNASTY, RULED OVER THE KINGDOM OF KEMET."
"THEN ONE DAY, HE BECAME SADDENED. NOTHING AMUSED HIM ANYMORE."
I'M NOT HUNGRY.
MORE BEER? EURGH!
OPIUM, AGAIN?! HOW BORING!
MELANCHOLY HAS SEIZED MY SOUL...
"...HE SAID TO HIMSELF (KNOWN FOR HIS SINCERITY)."
"'I YEARN FOR PERFECT BEAUTY,' HE ALSO SAID."
"'PERFECT BEAUTY ONLY EXISTS IN THE KINGDOM OF THE GODS,' THE GREAT SAGE INFORMED HIM. 'NEVERTHELESS, WE CAN IMITATE IT...'"
"AND THUS HE ORDERED THAT THE GREAT SAGE DJADJAEMANKH BE BROUGHT TO HIM SO THAT HE COULD ASK HIS ADVICE..."
"'MAY YOUR MAJESTY TAKE HIMSELF TO THE PALACE LAKE AND HAVE A BOAT PREPARED, CREWED BY 20 OF THE PALACE'S MOST BEAUTIFUL YOUNG LADIES.'"

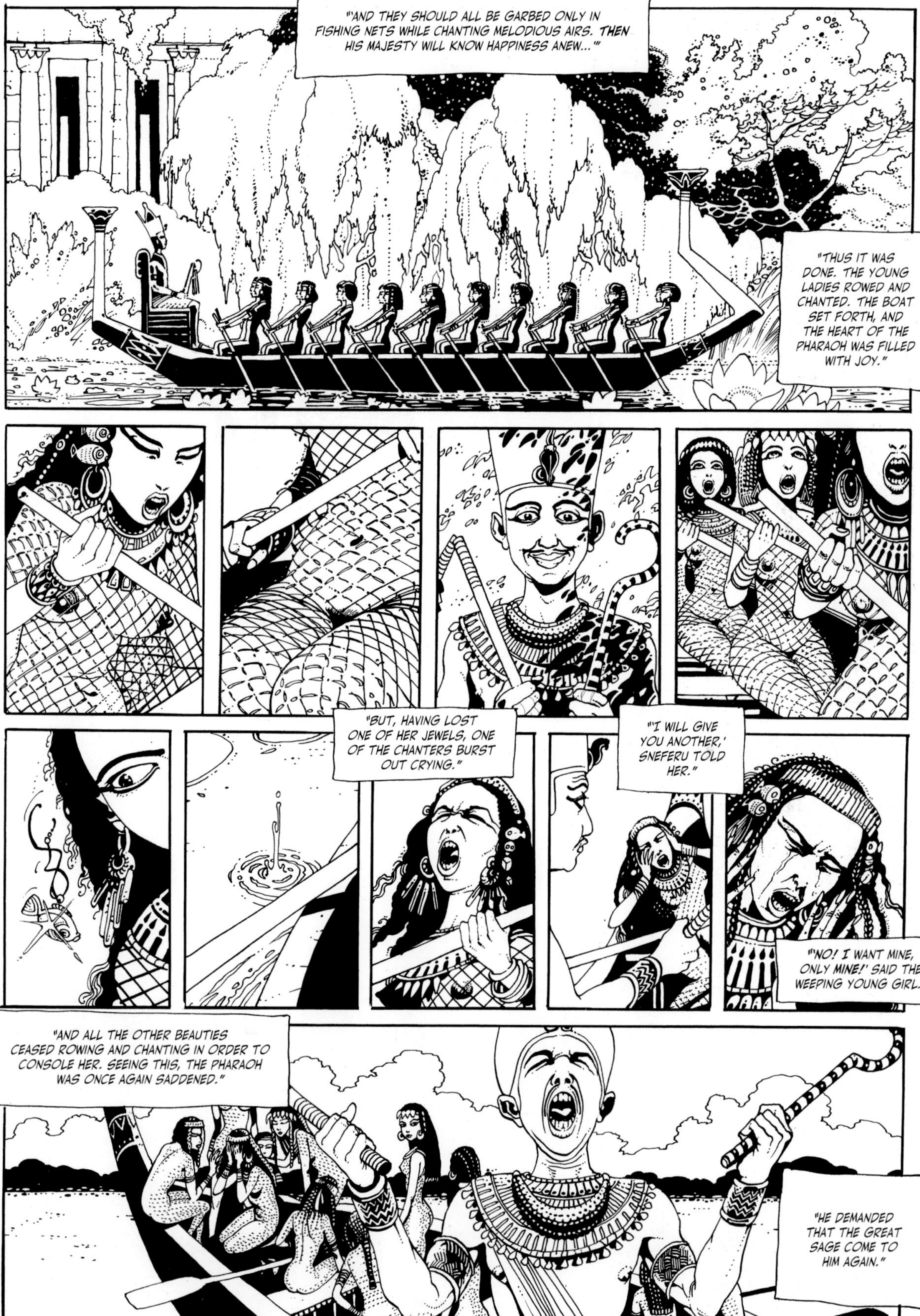
"AND THEY SHOULD ALL BE GARBED ONLY IN FISHING NETS WHILE CHANTING MELODIOUS AIRS. THEN HIS MAJESTY WILL KNOW HAPPINESS ANEW..."
"THUS IT WAS DONE. THE YOUNG LADIES ROWED AND CHANTED. THE BOAT SET FORTH, AND THE HEART OF THE PHARAOH WAS FILLED WITH JOY."
"BUT, HAVING LOST ONE OF HER JEWELS, ONE OF THE CHANTERS BURST OUT CRYING."
"'I WILL GIVE YOU ANOTHER,' SNEFERU TOLD HER."
"'NO! I WANT MINE, ONLY MINE!' SAID THE WEEPING YOUNG GIRL."
"AND ALL THE OTHER BEAUTIES CEASED ROWING AND CHANTING IN ORDER TO CONSOLE HER. SEEING THIS, THE PHARAOH WAS ONCE AGAIN SADDENED."
"HE DEMANDED THAT THE GREAT SAGE COME TO HIM AGAIN."

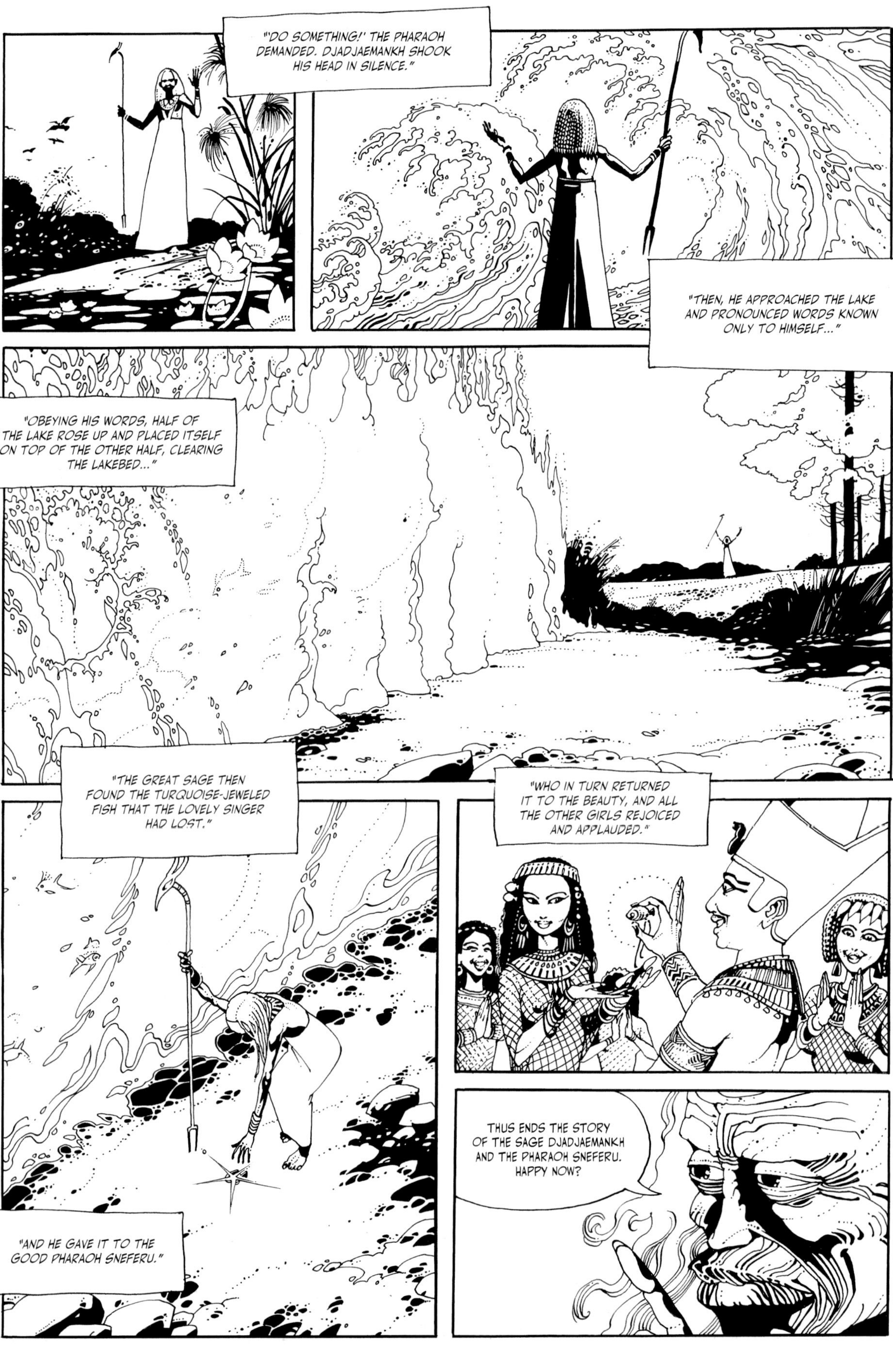

"DO SOMETHING!' THE PHARAOH DEMANDED. DJADJAEMANKH SHOOK HIS HEAD IN SILENCE."
"THEN, HE APPROACHED THE LAKE AND PRONOUNCED WORDS KNOWN ONLY TO HIMSELF..."
"OBEYING HIS WORDS, HALF OF THE LAKE ROSE UP AND PLACED ITSELF ON TOP OF THE OTHER HALF, CLEARING THE LAKEBED..."
"THE GREAT SAGE THEN FOUND THE TURQUOISE-JEWELED FISH THAT THE LOVELY SINGER HAD LOST."
"AND HE GAVE IT TO THE GOOD PHARAOH SNEFERU."
"WHO IN TURN RETURNED IT TO THE BEAUTY, AND ALL THE OTHER GIRLS REJOICED AND APPLAUDED."
THUS ENDS THE STORY OF THE SAGE DJADJAEMANKH AND THE PHARAOH SNEFERU. HAPPY NOW?

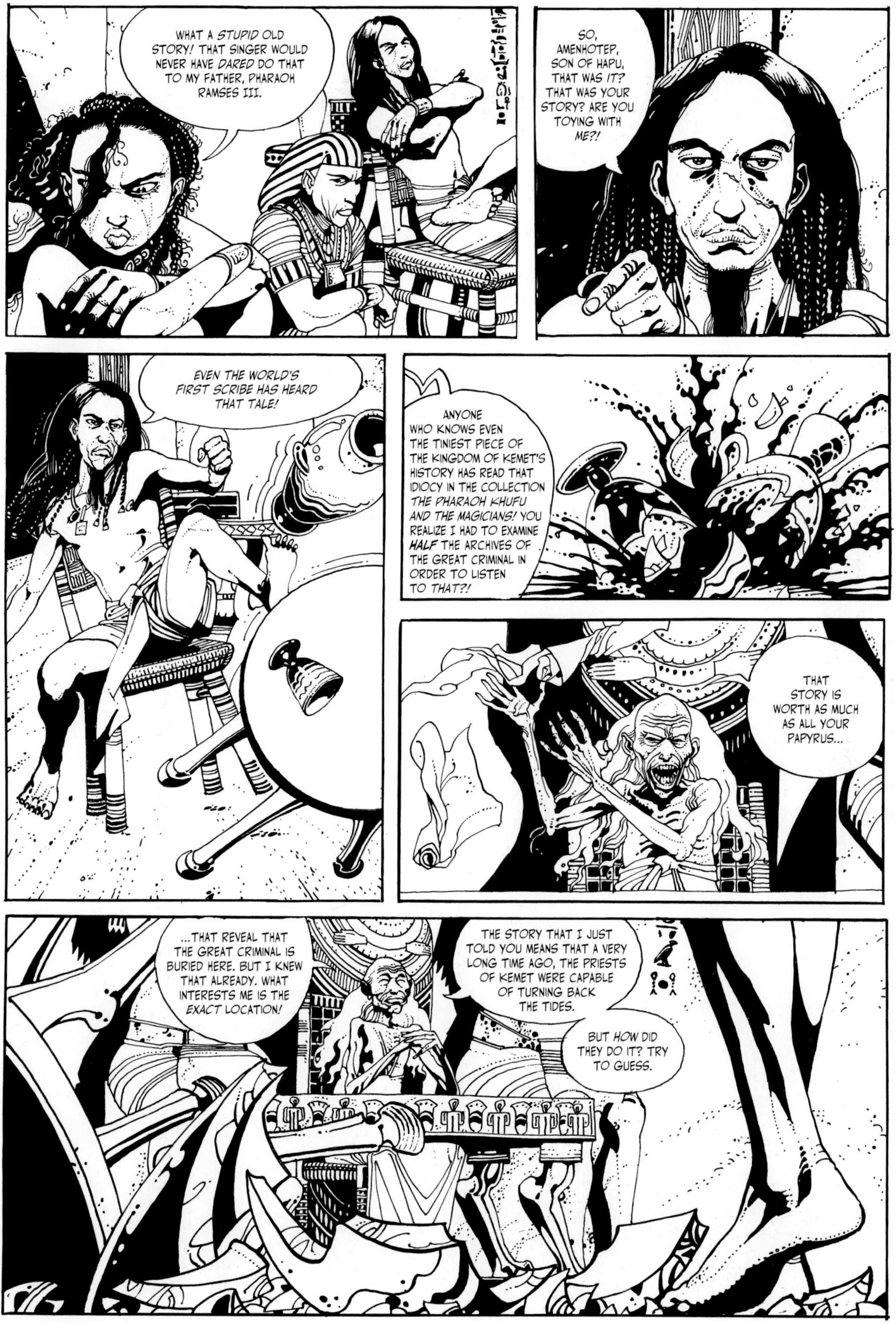
WHAT A STUPID OLD STORY! THAT SINGER WOULD NEVER HAVE DARED DO THAT TO MY FATHER, PHARAOH RAMSES III.
SO, AMENHOTEP, SON OF HAPU, THAT WAS IT? THAT WAS YOUR STORY? ARE YOU TOYING WITH ME?!
EVEN THE WORLD'S FIRST SCRIBE HAS HEARD THAT TALE!
ANYONE WHO KNOWS EVEN THE TINIEST PIECE OF THE KINGDOM OF KEMET'S HISTORY HAS READ THAT IDIOCY IN THE COLLECTION THE PHARAOH KHUFU AND THE MAGICIANS! YOU REALIZE I HAD TO EXAMINE HALF THE ARCHIVES OF THE GREAT CRIMINAL IN ORDER TO LISTEN TO THAT?!
THAT STORY IS WORTH AS MUCH AS ALL YOUR PAPYRUS...
...THAT REVEAL THAT THE GREAT CRIMINAL IS BURIED HERE. BUT I KNEW THAT ALREADY. WHAT INTERESTS ME IS THE EXACT LOCATION!
THE STORY THAT I JUST TOLD YOU MEANS THAT A VERY LONG TIME AGO, THE PRIESTS OF KEMET WERE CAPABLE OF TURNING BACK THE TIDES.
BUT HOW DID THEY DO IT? TRY TO GUESS.

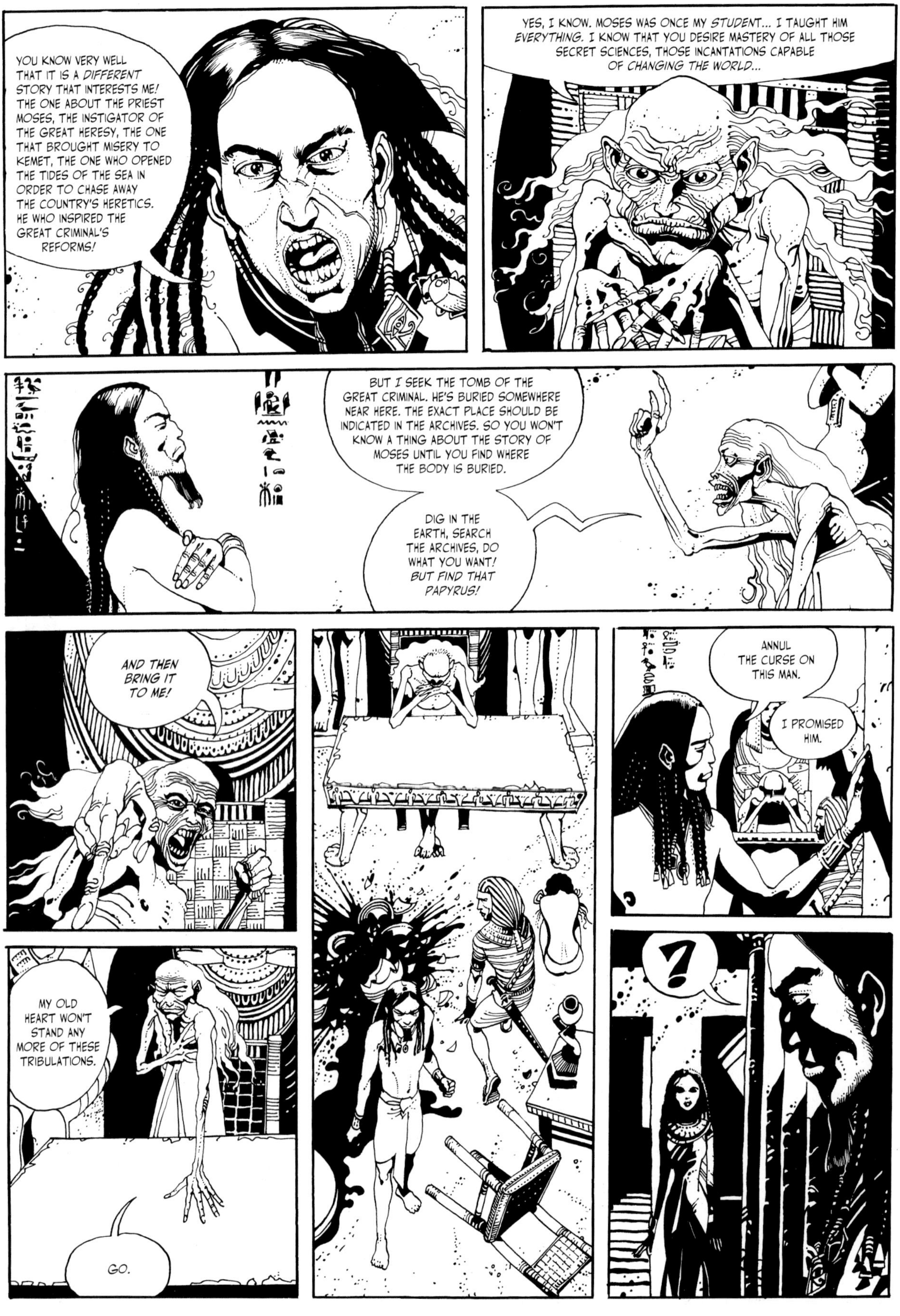

YOU KNOW VERY WELL THAT IT IS A *DIFFERENT* STORY THAT INTERESTS ME! THE ONE ABOUT THE PRIEST MOSES, THE INSTIGATOR OF THE GREAT HERESY, THE ONE THAT BROUGHT MISERY TO KEMET, THE ONE WHO OPENED THE TIDES OF THE SEA IN ORDER TO CHASE AWAY THE COUNTRY'S HERETICS. HE WHO INSPIRED THE GREAT CRIMINAL'S REFORMS!
YES, I KNOW. MOSES WAS ONCE MY *STUDENT*... I TAUGHT HIM *EVERYTHING.* I KNOW THAT YOU DESIRE MASTERY OF ALL THOSE SECRET SCIENCES, THOSE INCANTATIONS CAPABLE OF *CHANGING THE WORLD*...
BUT *I* SEEK THE TOMB OF THE GREAT CRIMINAL. HE'S BURIED SOMEWHERE NEAR HERE. THE EXACT PLACE SHOULD BE INDICATED IN THE ARCHIVES. SO YOU WON'T KNOW A THING ABOUT THE STORY OF MOSES UNTIL YOU FIND WHERE THE BODY IS BURIED.
DIG IN THE EARTH, SEARCH THE ARCHIVES, DO WHAT YOU WANT! *BUT FIND THAT PAPYRUS!*
AND THEN BRING IT TO ME!
MY OLD HEART WON'T STAND ANY MORE OF THESE TRIBULATIONS.
GO.
ANNUL THE CURSE ON THIS MAN.
I PROMISED HIM.
?

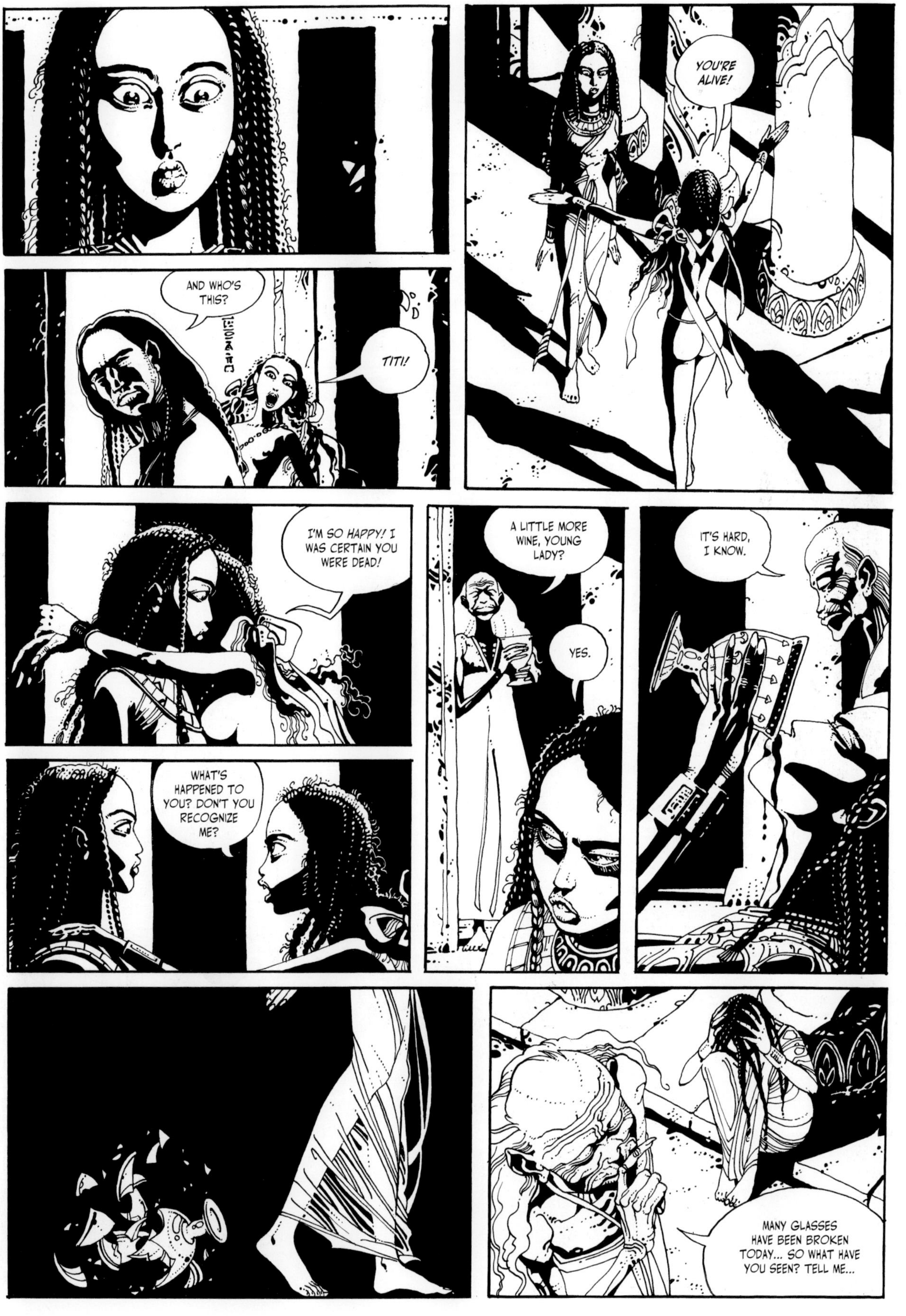
YOU'RE ALIVE!
AND WHO'S THIS?
TITI!
I'M SO HAPPY! I WAS CERTAIN YOU WERE DEAD!
WHAT'S HAPPENED TO YOU? DON'T YOU RECOGNIZE ME?
A LITTLE MORE WINE, YOUNG LADY?
YES.
IT'S HARD, I KNOW.
MANY GLASSES HAVE BEEN BROKEN TODAY... SO WHAT HAVE YOU SEEN? TELL ME...

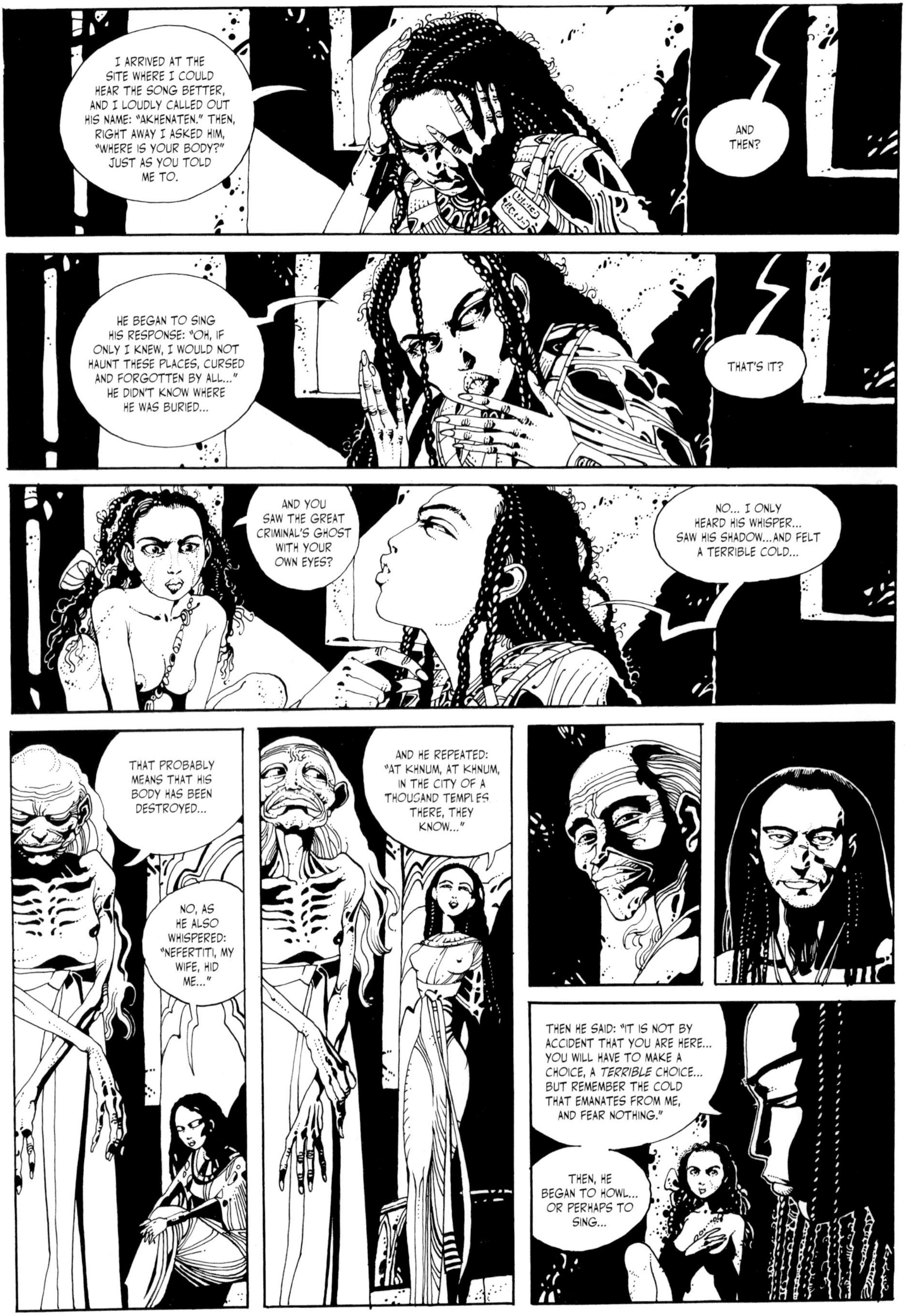
I ARRIVED AT THE SITE WHERE I COULD HEAR THE SONG BETTER, AND I LOUDLY CALLED OUT HIS NAME: "AKHENATEN." THEN, RIGHT AWAY I ASKED HIM, "WHERE IS YOUR BODY?" JUST AS YOU TOLD ME TO.
AND THEN?
HE BEGAN TO SING HIS RESPONSE: "OH, IF ONLY I KNEW, I WOULD NOT HAUNT THESE PLACES, CURSED AND FORGOTTEN BY ALL..." HE DIDN'T KNOW WHERE HE WAS BURIED...
THAT'S IT?
AND YOU SAW THE GREAT CRIMINAL'S GHOST WITH YOUR OWN EYES?
NO... I ONLY HEARD HIS WHISPER... SAW HIS SHADOW...AND FELT A TERRIBLE COLD...
THAT PROBABLY MEANS THAT HIS BODY HAS BEEN DESTROYED...
NO, AS HE ALSO WHISPERED: "NEFERTITI, MY WIFE, HID ME..."
AND HE REPEATED: "AT KHNUM, AT KHNUM, IN THE CITY OF A THOUSAND TEMPLES THERE, THEY KNOW..."
THEN HE SAID: "IT IS NOT BY ACCIDENT THAT YOU ARE HERE... YOU WILL HAVE TO MAKE A CHOICE, A *TERRIBLE* CHOICE... BUT REMEMBER THE COLD THAT EMANATES FROM ME, AND FEAR NOTHING."
THEN, HE BEGAN TO HOWL... OR PERHAPS TO SING...

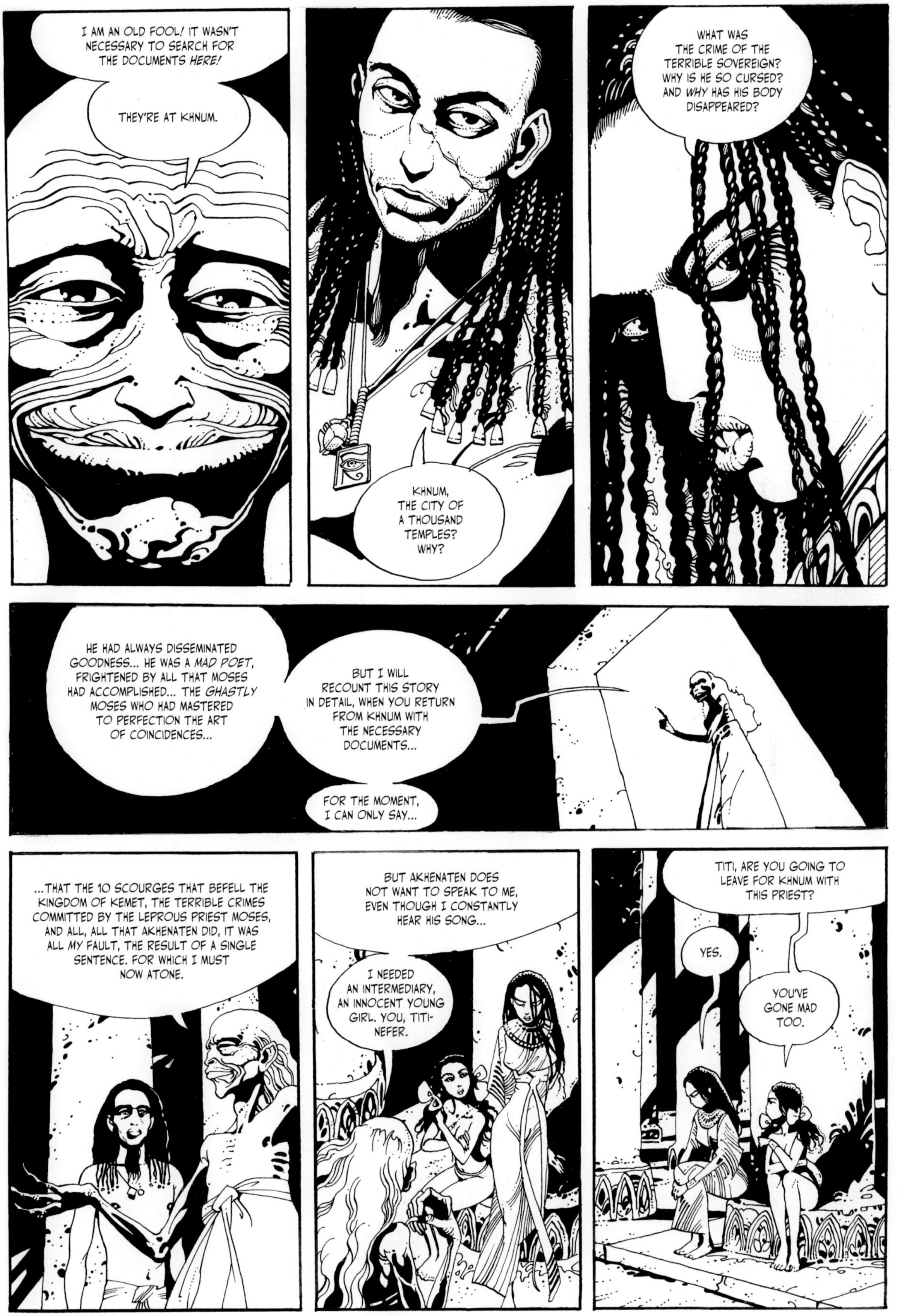
I AM AN OLD FOOL! IT WASN'T NECESSARY TO SEARCH FOR THE DOCUMENTS *HERE!*
THEY'RE AT KHNUM.
KHNUM, THE CITY OF A THOUSAND TEMPLES? WHY?
WHAT WAS THE CRIME OF THE TERRIBLE SOVEREIGN? WHY IS HE SO CURSED? AND *WHY* HAS HIS BODY DISAPPEARED?
HE HAD ALWAYS DISSEMINATED GOODNESS... HE WAS A *MAD POET*, FRIGHTENED BY ALL THAT MOSES HAD ACCOMPLISHED... THE *GHASTLY* MOSES WHO HAD MASTERED TO PERFECTION THE ART OF COINCIDENCES...
BUT I WILL RECOUNT THIS STORY IN DETAIL, WHEN YOU RETURN FROM KHNUM WITH THE NECESSARY DOCUMENTS...
FOR THE MOMENT, I CAN ONLY SAY...
...THAT THE 10 SCOURGES THAT BEFELL THE KINGDOM OF KEMET, THE TERRIBLE CRIMES COMMITTED BY THE LEPROUS PRIEST MOSES, AND ALL, ALL THAT AKHENATEN DID, IT WAS ALL MY FAULT, THE RESULT OF A SINGLE SENTENCE. FOR WHICH I MUST NOW ATONE.
BUT AKHENATEN DOES NOT WANT TO SPEAK TO ME, EVEN THOUGH I CONSTANTLY HEAR HIS SONG...
I NEEDED AN INTERMEDIARY, AN INNOCENT YOUNG GIRL. YOU, TITI-NEFER.
TITI, ARE YOU GOING TO LEAVE FOR KHNUM WITH THIS PRIEST?
YES.
YOU'VE GONE MAD TOO.

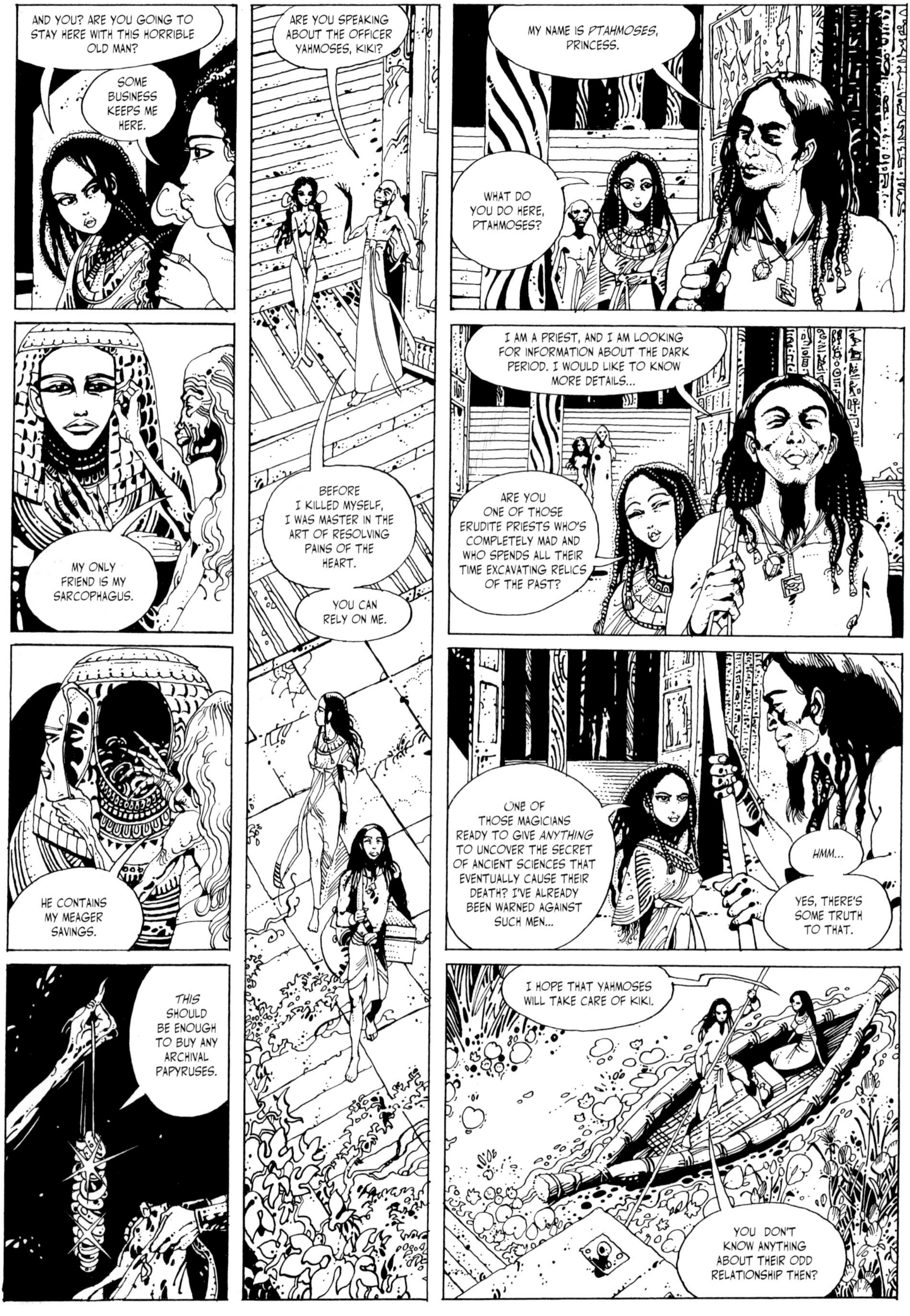
AND YOU? ARE YOU GOING TO STAY HERE WITH THIS HORRIBLE OLD MAN?
SOME BUSINESS KEEPS ME HERE.
MY ONLY FRIEND IS MY SARCOPHAGUS.
HE CONTAINS MY MEAGER SAVINGS.
THIS SHOULD BE ENOUGH TO BUY ANY ARCHIVAL PAPYRUSES.
ARE YOU SPEAKING ABOUT THE OFFICER YAHMOSES, KIKI?
BEFORE I KILLED MYSELF, I WAS MASTER IN THE ART OF RESOLVING PAINS OF THE HEART.
YOU CAN RELY ON ME.
MY NAME IS PTAHMOSES, PRINCESS.
WHAT DO YOU DO HERE, PTAHMOSES?
I AM A PRIEST, AND I AM LOOKING FOR INFORMATION ABOUT THE DARK PERIOD. I WOULD LIKE TO KNOW MORE DETAILS...
ARE YOU ONE OF THOSE ERUDITE PRIESTS WHO'S COMPLETELY MAD AND WHO SPENDS ALL THEIR TIME EXCAVATING RELICS OF THE PAST?
ONE OF THOSE MAGICIANS READY TO GIVE ANYTHING TO UNCOVER THE SECRET OF ANCIENT SCIENCES THAT EVENTUALLY CAUSE THEIR DEATH? I'VE ALREADY BEEN WARNED AGAINST SUCH MEN...
HMM...
YES, THERE'S SOME TRUTH TO THAT.
I HOPE THAT YAHMOSES WILL TAKE CARE OF KIKI.
YOU DON'T KNOW ANYTHING ABOUT THEIR ODD RELATIONSHIP THEN?

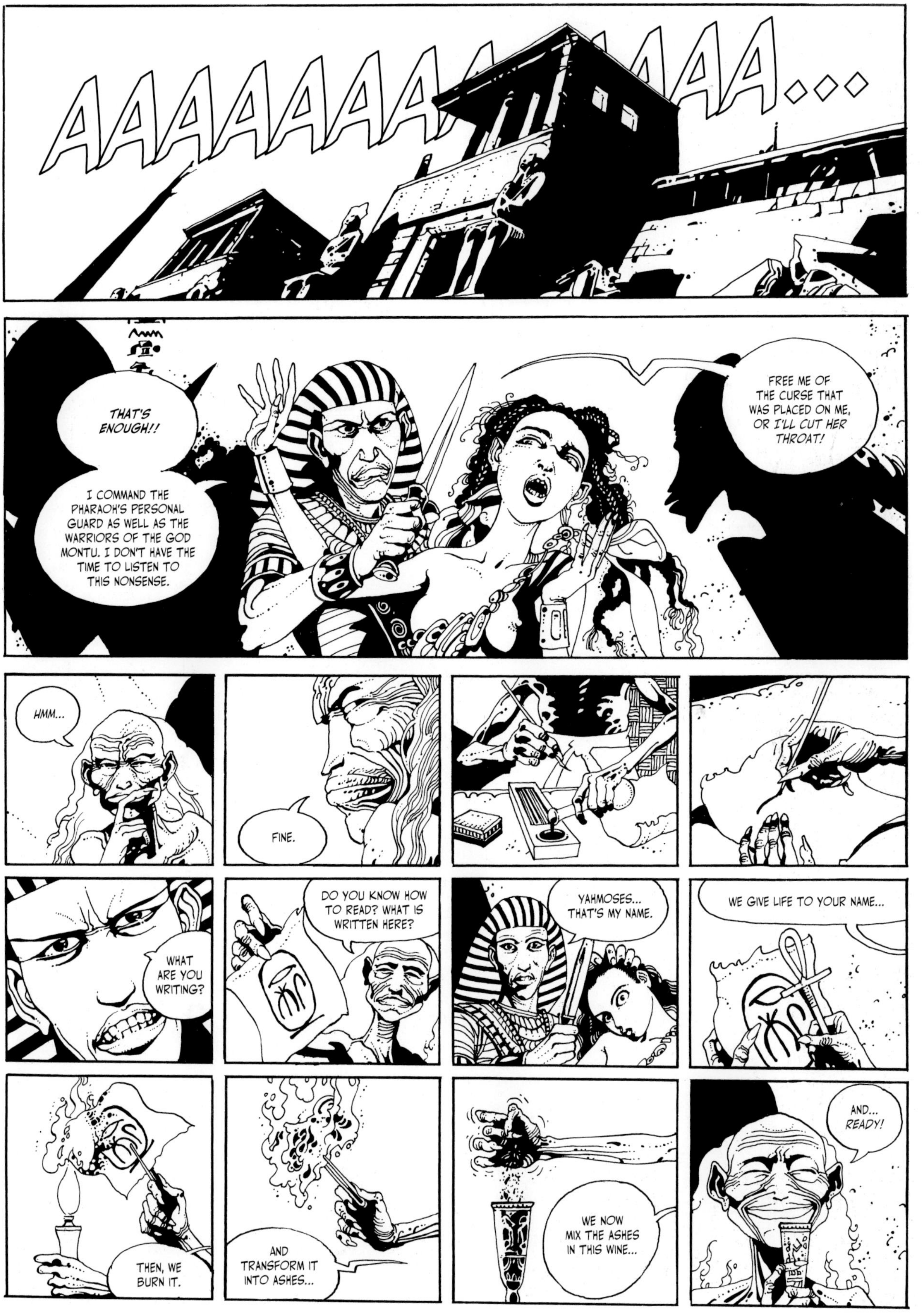
AAAAAAAAAAAA...
THAT'S ENOUGH!!
I COMMAND THE PHARAOH'S PERSONAL GUARD AS WELL AS THE WARRIORS OF THE GOD MONTU. I DON'T HAVE THE TIME TO LISTEN TO THIS NONSENSE.
FREE ME OF THE CURSE THAT WAS PLACED ON ME, OR I'LL CUT HER THROAT!
HMM...
FINE.
WHAT ARE YOU WRITING?
DO YOU KNOW HOW TO READ? WHAT IS WRITTEN HERE?
YAHMOSES... THAT'S MY NAME.
WE GIVE LIFE TO YOUR NAME...
THEN, WE BURN IT.
AND TRANSFORM IT INTO ASHES...
WE NOW MIX THE ASHES IN THIS WINE...
AND... READY!

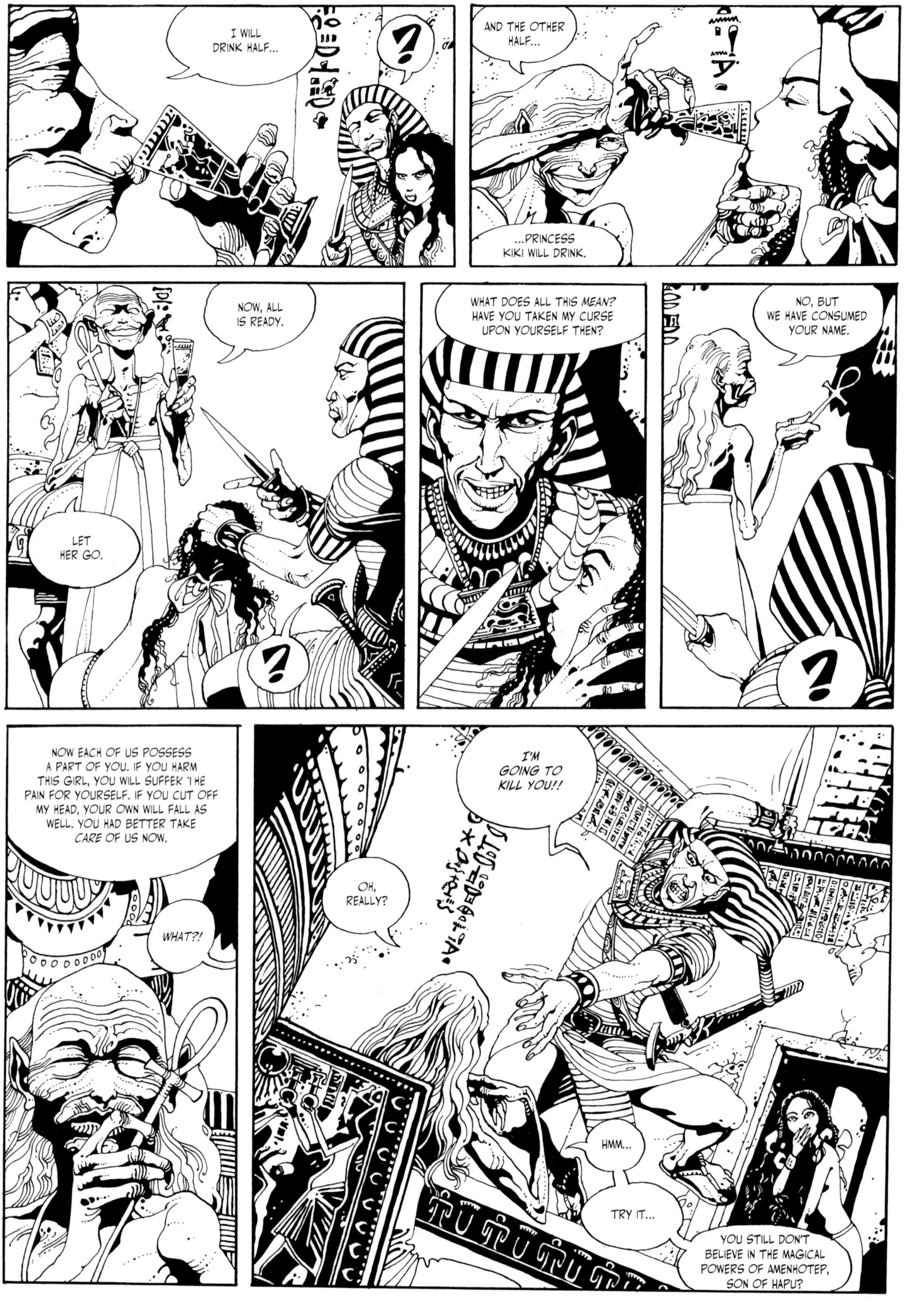
I WILL DRINK HALF...
?
AND THE OTHER HALF...
...PRINCESS KIKI WILL DRINK.
NOW, ALL IS READY.
LET HER GO.
?
WHAT DOES ALL THIS *MEAN?* HAVE YOU TAKEN MY CURSE UPON YOURSELF THEN?
NO, BUT WE HAVE CONSUMED YOUR NAME.
?
NOW EACH OF US POSSESS A PART OF YOU. IF YOU HARM THIS GIRL, YOU WILL SUFFER THE PAIN FOR YOURSELF. IF YOU CUT OFF MY HEAD, YOUR OWN WILL FALL AS WELL. YOU HAD BETTER TAKE *CARE* OF US NOW.
WHAT?!
I'M GOING TO KILL YOU!!
OH, REALLY?
HMM...
TRY IT...
YOU STILL DON'T BELIEVE IN THE MAGICAL POWERS OF AMENHOTEP, SON OF HAPU?

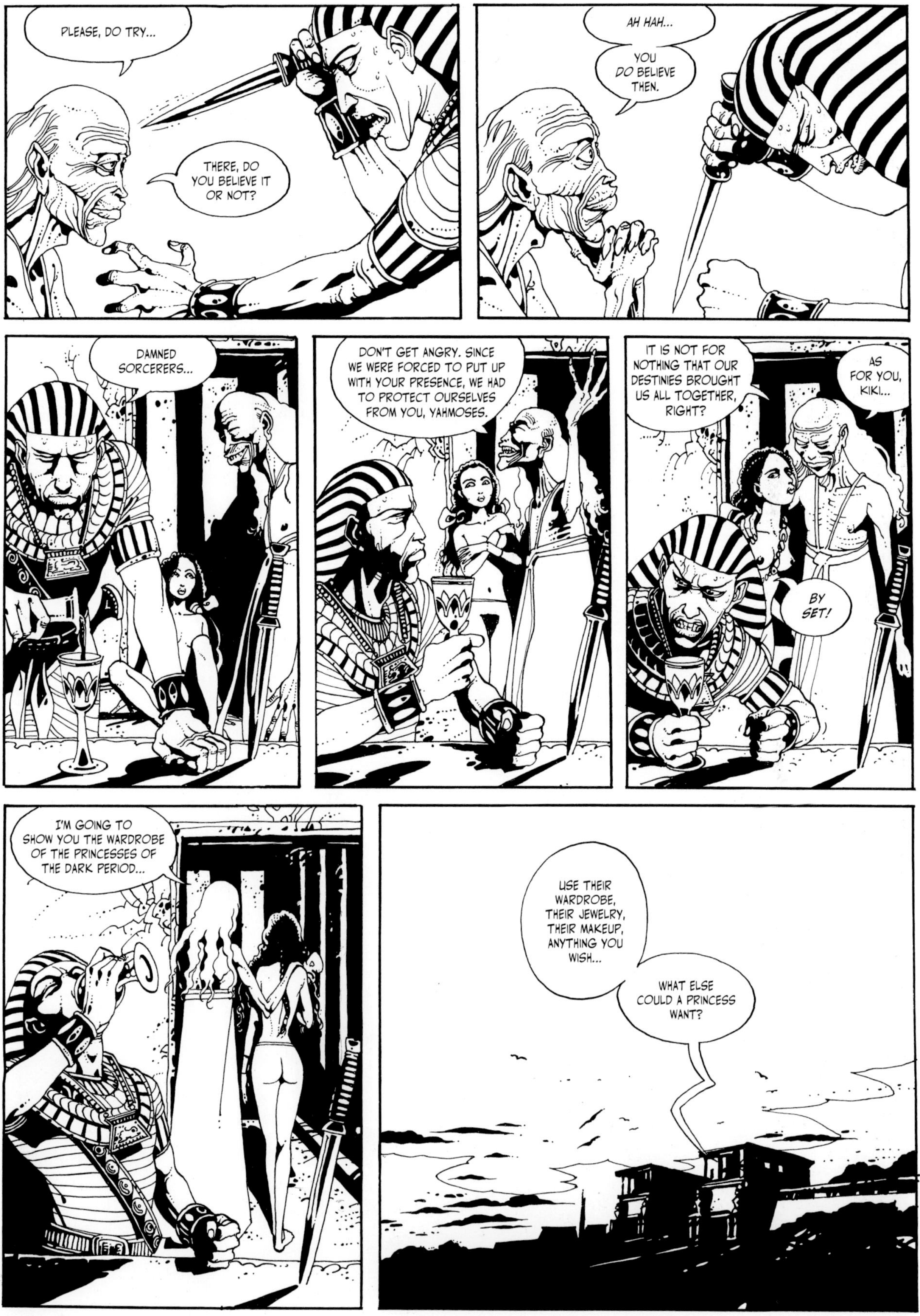
PLEASE, DO TRY...
THERE, DO YOU BELIEVE IT OR NOT?
AH HAH...
YOU DO BELIEVE THEN.
DAMNED SORCERERS...
DON'T GET ANGRY. SINCE WE WERE FORCED TO PUT UP WITH YOUR PRESENCE, WE HAD TO PROTECT OURSELVES FROM YOU, YAHMOSES.
IT IS NOT FOR NOTHING THAT OUR DESTINIES BROUGHT US ALL TOGETHER, RIGHT?
AS FOR YOU, KIKI...
BY SET!
I'M GOING TO SHOW YOU THE WARDROBE OF THE PRINCESSES OF THE DARK PERIOD...
USE THEIR WARDROBE, THEIR JEWELRY, THEIR MAKEUP, ANYTHING YOU WISH...
WHAT ELSE COULD A PRINCESS WANT?

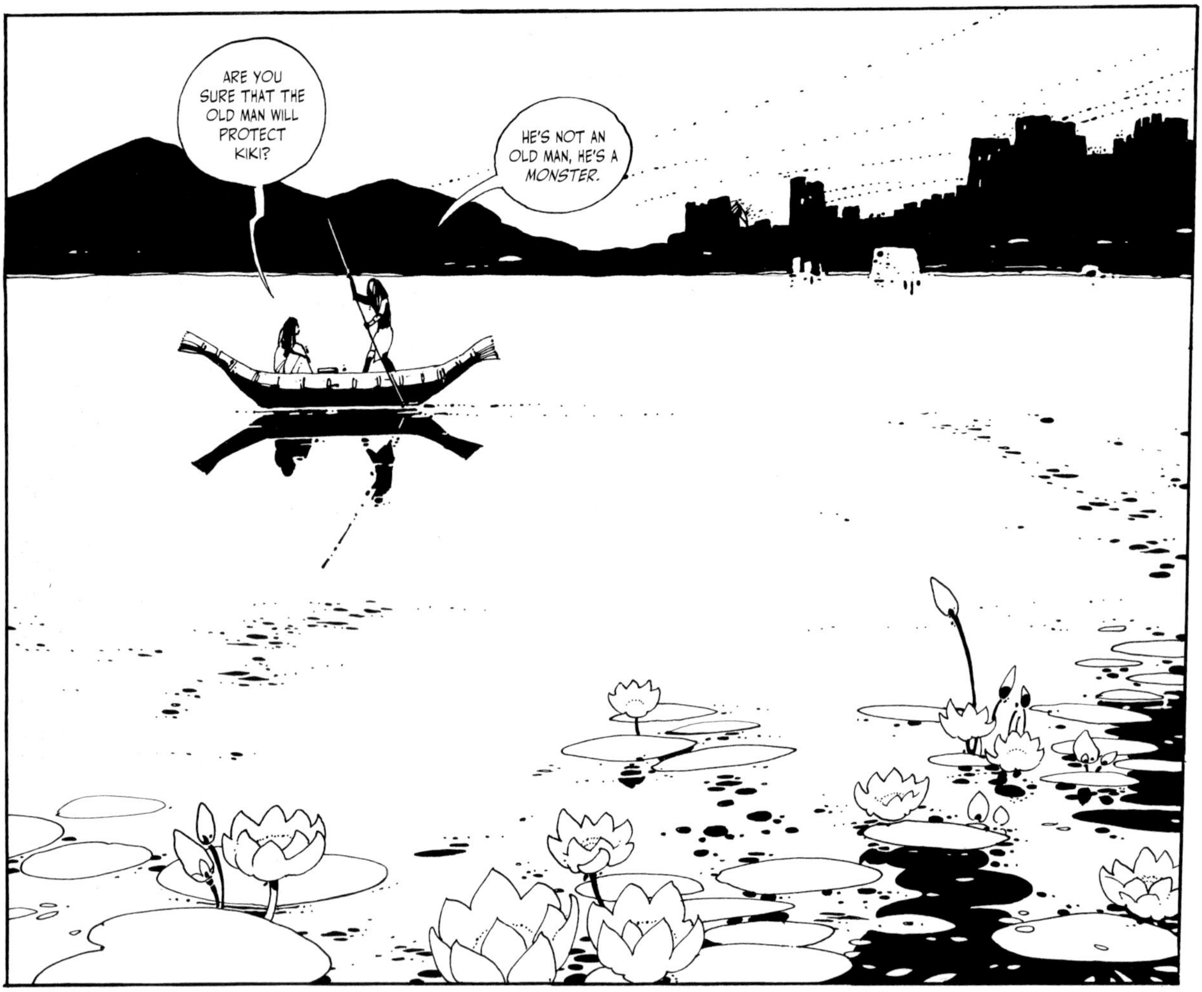
ARE YOU SURE THAT THE OLD MAN WILL PROTECT KIKI?
HE'S NOT AN OLD MAN, HE'S A *MONSTER*.

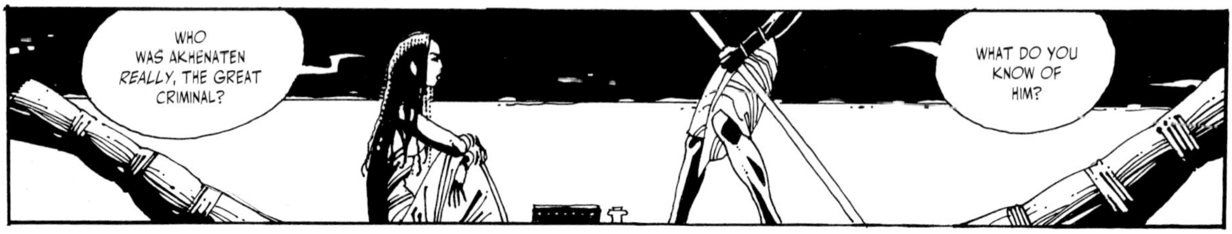
WHO WAS AKHENATEN *REALLY*, THE GREAT CRIMINAL?
WHAT DO YOU KNOW OF HIM?

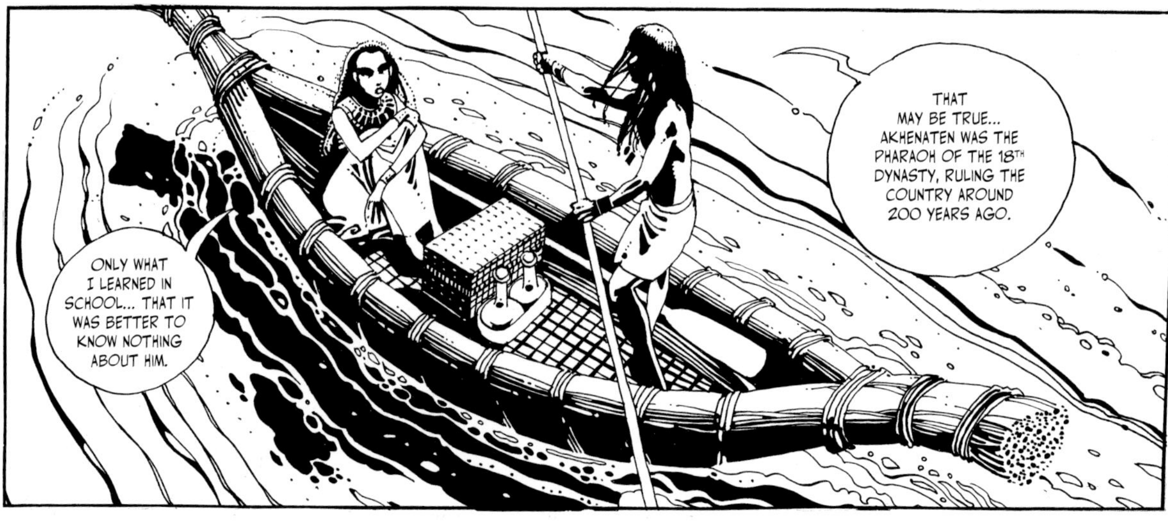
ONLY WHAT I LEARNED IN SCHOOL... THAT IT WAS BETTER TO KNOW NOTHING ABOUT HIM.
THAT MAY BE TRUE... AKHENATEN WAS THE PHARAOH OF THE 18TH DYNASTY, RULING THE COUNTRY AROUND 200 YEARS AGO.

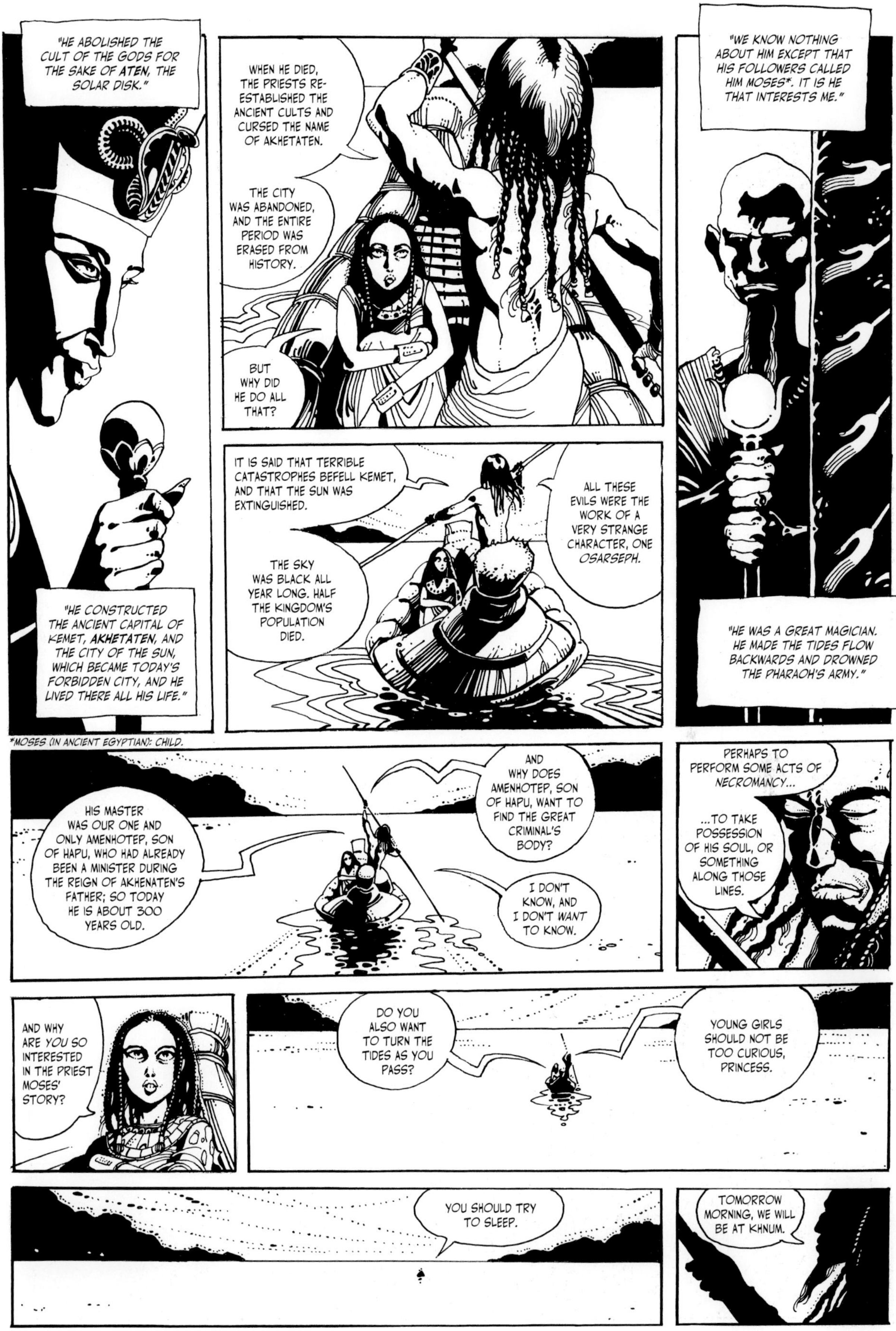
"HE ABOLISHED THE CULT OF THE GODS FOR THE SAKE OF **ATEN**, THE SOLAR DISK."
"HE CONSTRUCTED THE ANCIENT CAPITAL OF KEMET, **AKHETATEN**, AND THE CITY OF THE SUN, WHICH BECAME TODAY'S FORBIDDEN CITY, AND HE LIVED THERE ALL HIS LIFE."
WHEN HE DIED, THE PRIESTS RE-ESTABLISHED THE ANCIENT CULTS AND CURSED THE NAME OF AKHETATEN.
THE CITY WAS ABANDONED, AND THE ENTIRE PERIOD WAS ERASED FROM HISTORY.
BUT WHY DID HE DO ALL THAT?
IT IS SAID THAT TERRIBLE CATASTROPHES BEFELL KEMET, AND THAT THE SUN WAS EXTINGUISHED.
THE SKY WAS BLACK ALL YEAR LONG. HALF THE KINGDOM'S POPULATION DIED.
ALL THESE EVILS WERE THE WORK OF A VERY STRANGE CHARACTER, ONE *OSARSEPH*.
"WE KNOW NOTHING ABOUT HIM EXCEPT THAT HIS FOLLOWERS CALLED HIM MOSES*. IT IS HE THAT INTERESTS ME."
"HE WAS A GREAT MAGICIAN. HE MADE THE TIDES FLOW BACKWARDS AND DROWNED THE PHARAOH'S ARMY."
*MOSES (IN ANCIENT EGYPTIAN): CHILD.
HIS MASTER WAS OUR ONE AND ONLY AMENHOTEP, SON OF HAPU, WHO HAD ALREADY BEEN A MINISTER DURING THE REIGN OF AKHENATEN'S FATHER; SO TODAY HE IS ABOUT 300 YEARS OLD.
AND WHY DOES AMENHOTEP, SON OF HAPU, WANT TO FIND THE GREAT CRIMINAL'S BODY?
I DON'T KNOW, AND I DON'T *WANT* TO KNOW.
PERHAPS TO PERFORM SOME ACTS OF NECROMANCY...
...TO TAKE POSSESSION OF HIS SOUL, OR SOMETHING ALONG THOSE LINES.
AND WHY ARE *YOU* SO INTERESTED IN THE PRIEST MOSES' STORY?
DO YOU ALSO WANT TO TURN THE TIDES AS YOU PASS?
YOUNG GIRLS SHOULD NOT BE TOO CURIOUS, PRINCESS.
YOU SHOULD TRY TO SLEEP.
TOMORROW MORNING, WE WILL BE AT KHNUM.

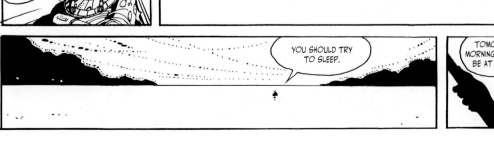

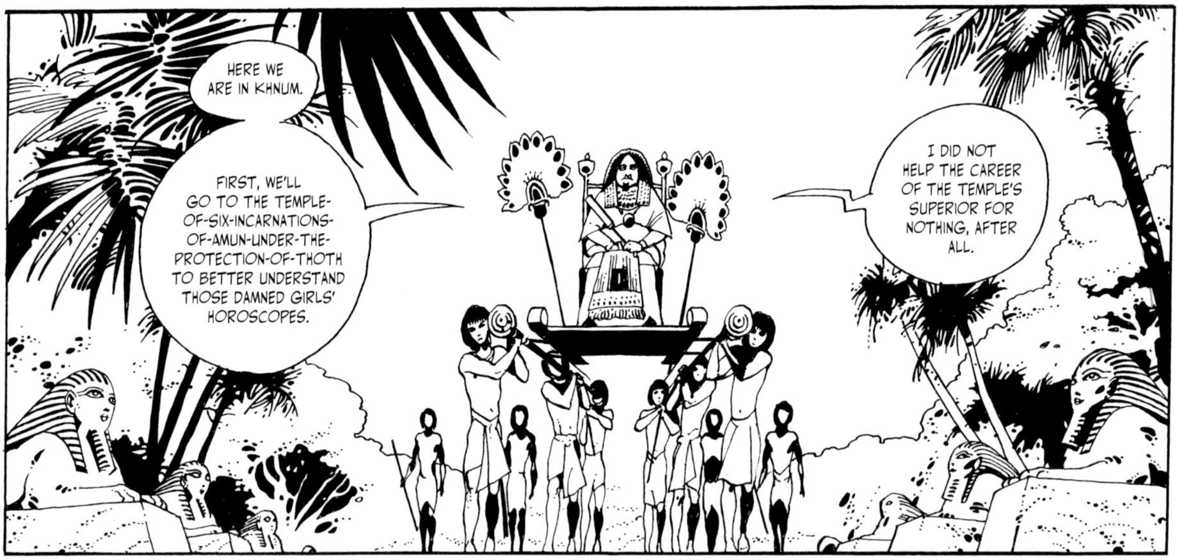
HERE WE ARE IN KHNUM.
FIRST, WE'LL GO TO THE TEMPLE-OF-SIX-INCARNATIONS-OF-AMUN-UNDER-THE-PROTECTION-OF-THOTH TO BETTER UNDERSTAND THOSE DAMNED GIRLS' HOROSCOPES.
I DID NOT HELP THE CAREER OF THE TEMPLE'S SUPERIOR FOR NOTHING, AFTER ALL.

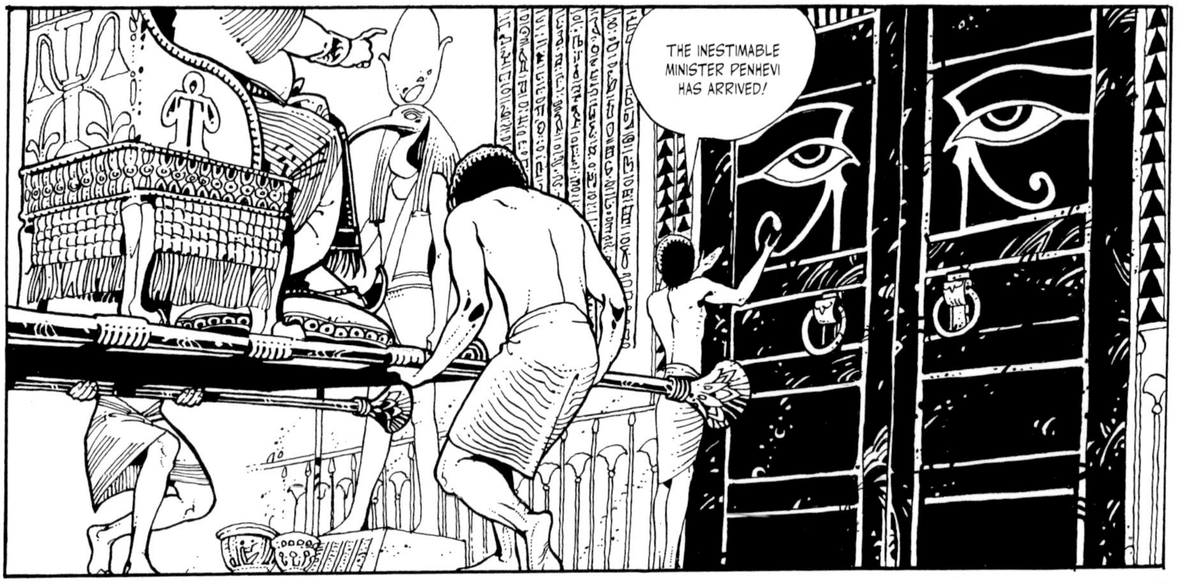
THE INESTIMABLE MINISTER PENHEVI HAS ARRIVED!

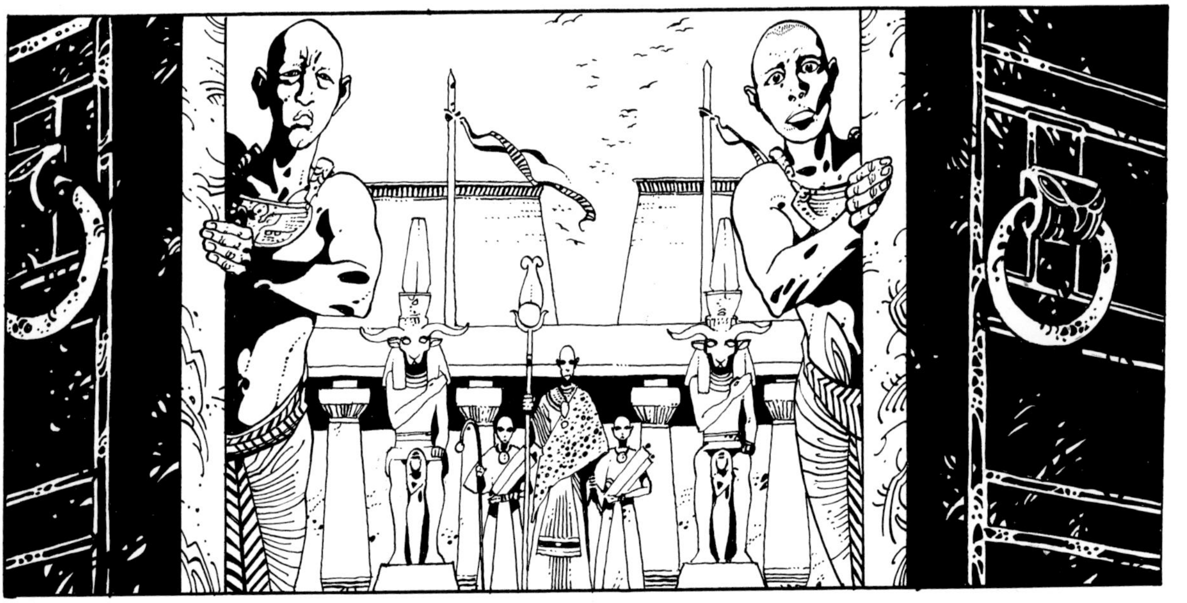

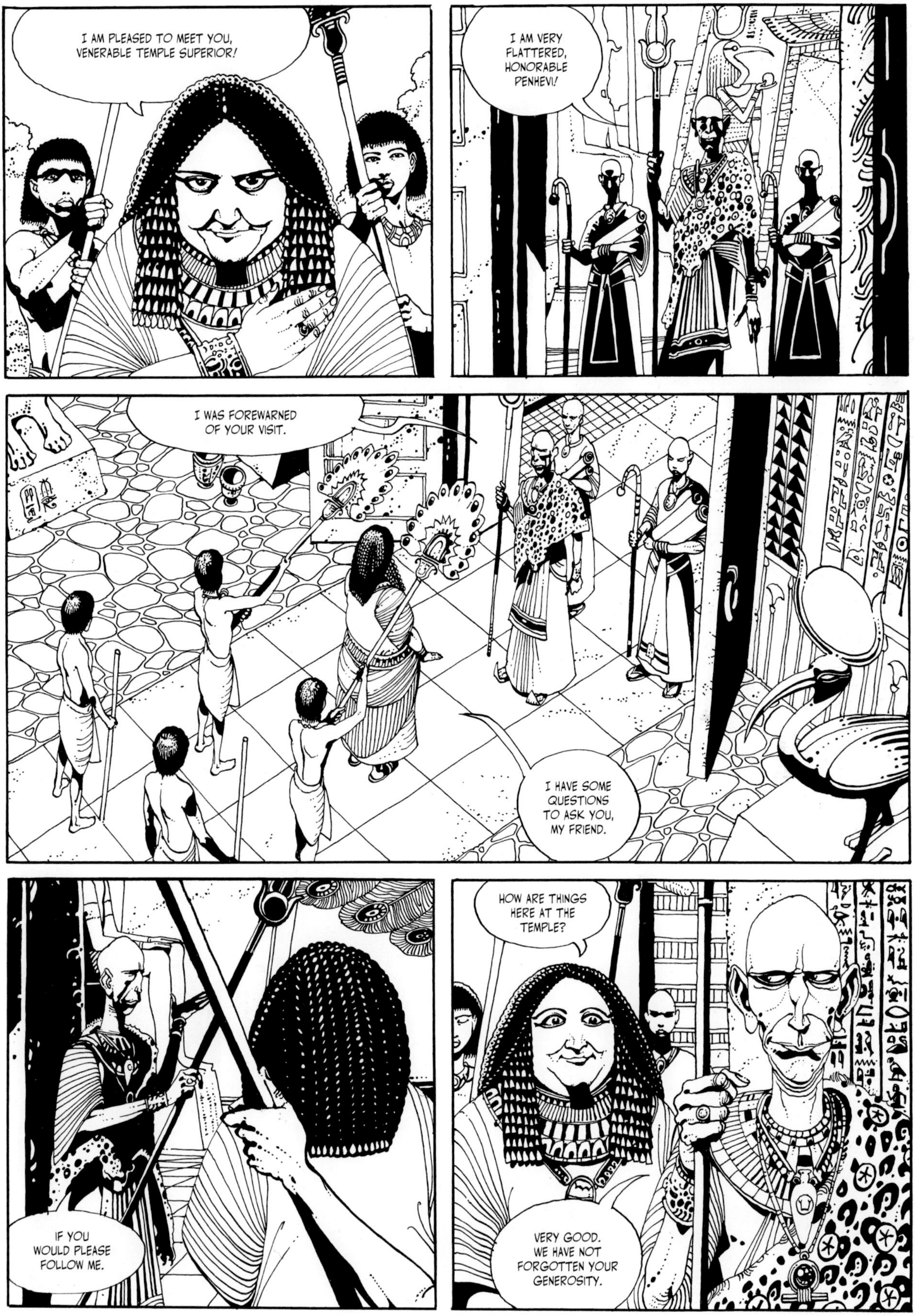
I AM PLEASED TO MEET YOU, VENERABLE TEMPLE SUPERIOR!
I AM VERY FLATTERED, HONORABLE PENHEVI!
I WAS FOREWARNED OF YOUR VISIT.
I HAVE SOME QUESTIONS TO ASK YOU, MY FRIEND.
IF YOU WOULD PLEASE FOLLOW ME.
HOW ARE THINGS HERE AT THE TEMPLE?
VERY GOOD. WE HAVE NOT FORGOTTEN YOUR GENEROSITY.

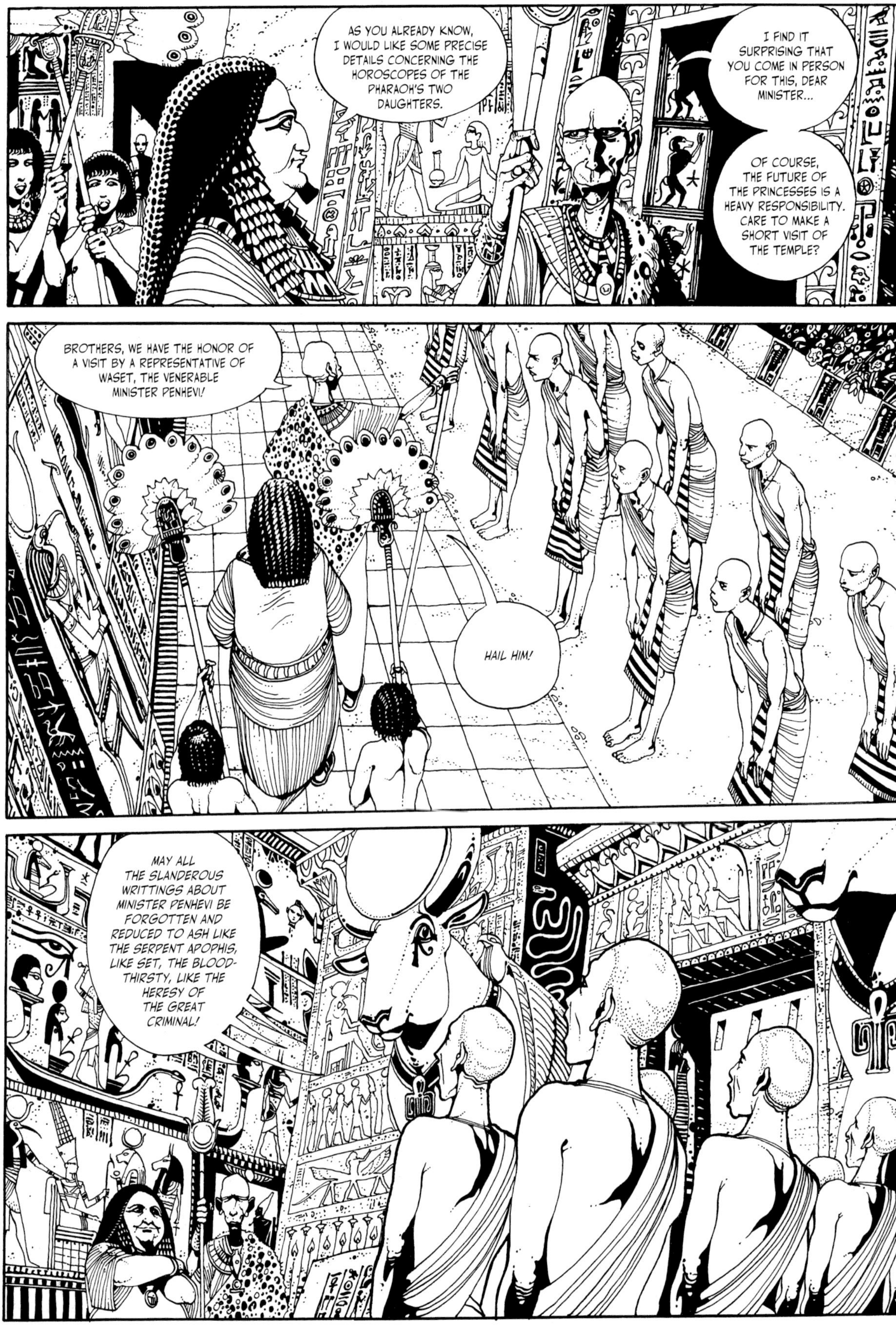
AS YOU ALREADY KNOW, I WOULD LIKE SOME PRECISE DETAILS CONCERNING THE HOROSCOPES OF THE PHARAOH'S TWO DAUGHTERS.
I FIND IT SURPRISING THAT YOU COME IN PERSON FOR THIS, DEAR MINISTER...
OF COURSE, THE FUTURE OF THE PRINCESSES IS A HEAVY RESPONSIBILITY. CARE TO MAKE A SHORT VISIT OF THE TEMPLE?
BROTHERS, WE HAVE THE HONOR OF A VISIT BY A REPRESENTATIVE OF WASET, THE VENERABLE MINISTER PENHEVI!
HAIL HIM!
MAY ALL THE SLANDEROUS WRITTINGS ABOUT MINISTER PENHEVI BE FORGOTTEN AND REDUCED TO ASH LIKE THE SERPENT APOPHIS, LIKE SET, THE BLOOD-THIRSTY, LIKE THE HERESY OF THE GREAT CRIMINAL!

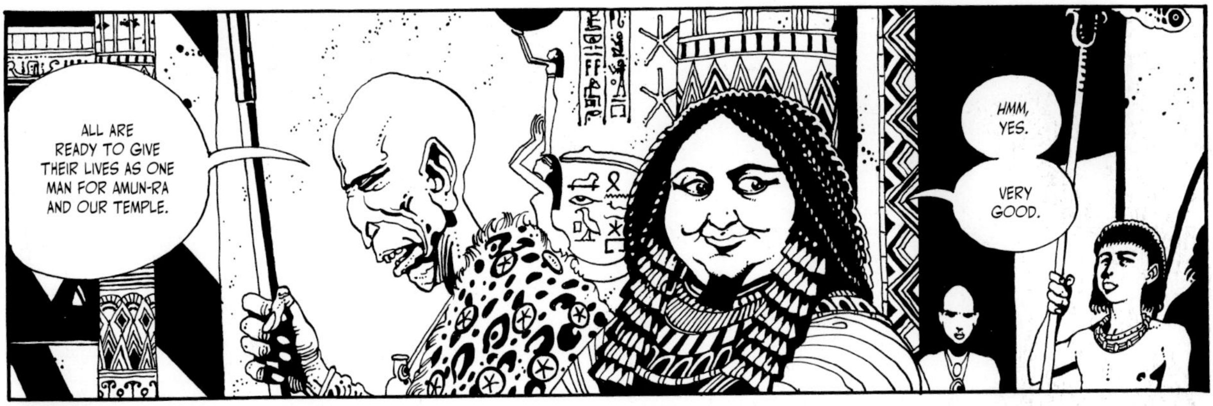
ALL ARE READY TO GIVE THEIR LIVES AS ONE MAN FOR AMUN-RA AND OUR TEMPLE.
HMM, YES.
VERY GOOD.

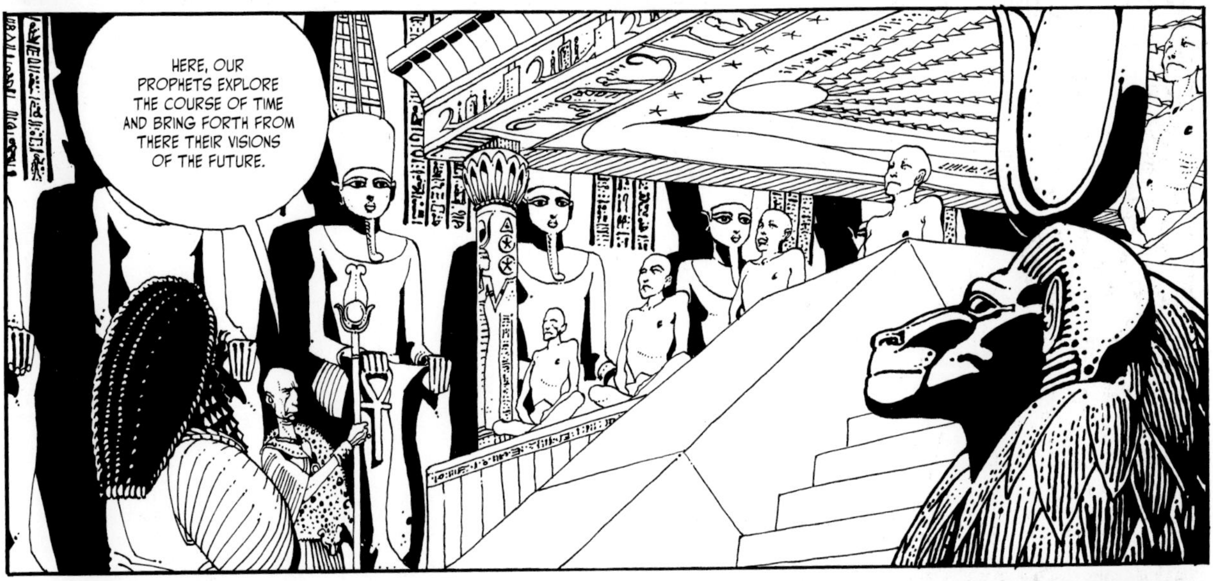
HERE, OUR PROPHETS EXPLORE THE COURSE OF TIME AND BRING FORTH FROM THERE THEIR VISIONS OF THE FUTURE.

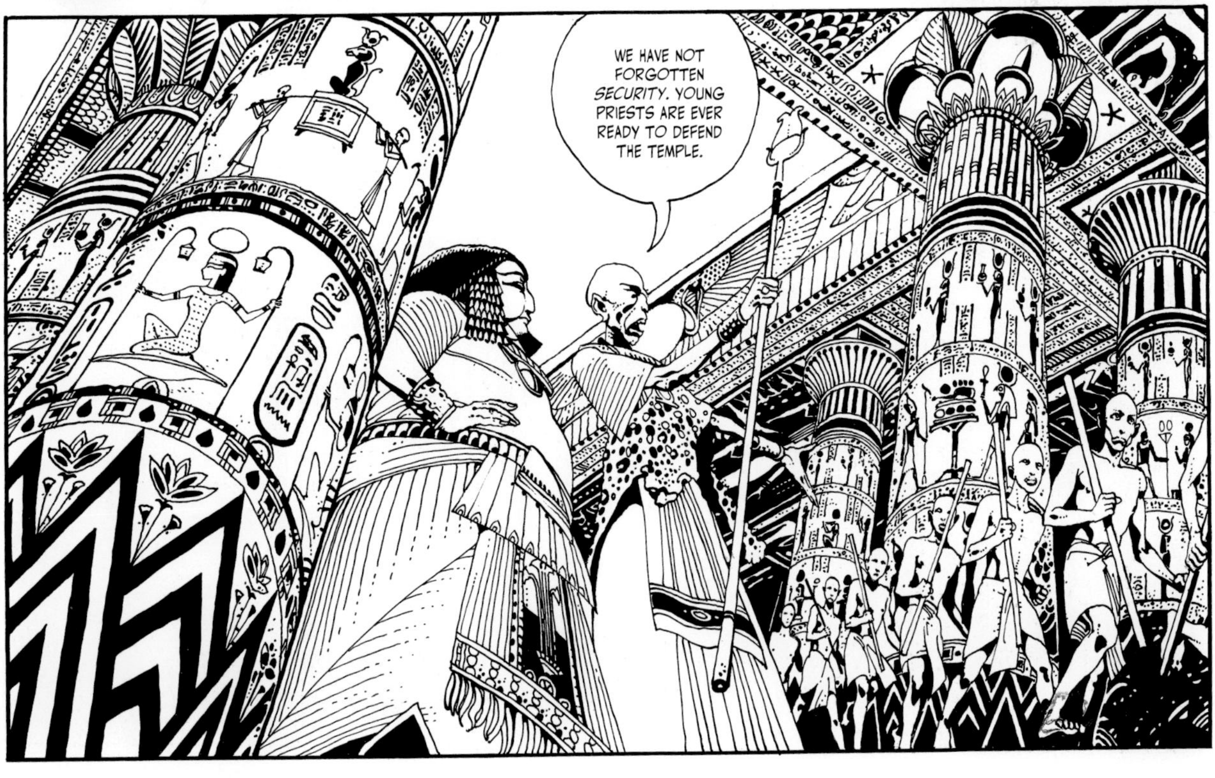
WE HAVE NOT FORGOTTEN *SECURITY*. YOUNG PRIESTS ARE EVER READY TO DEFEND THE TEMPLE.

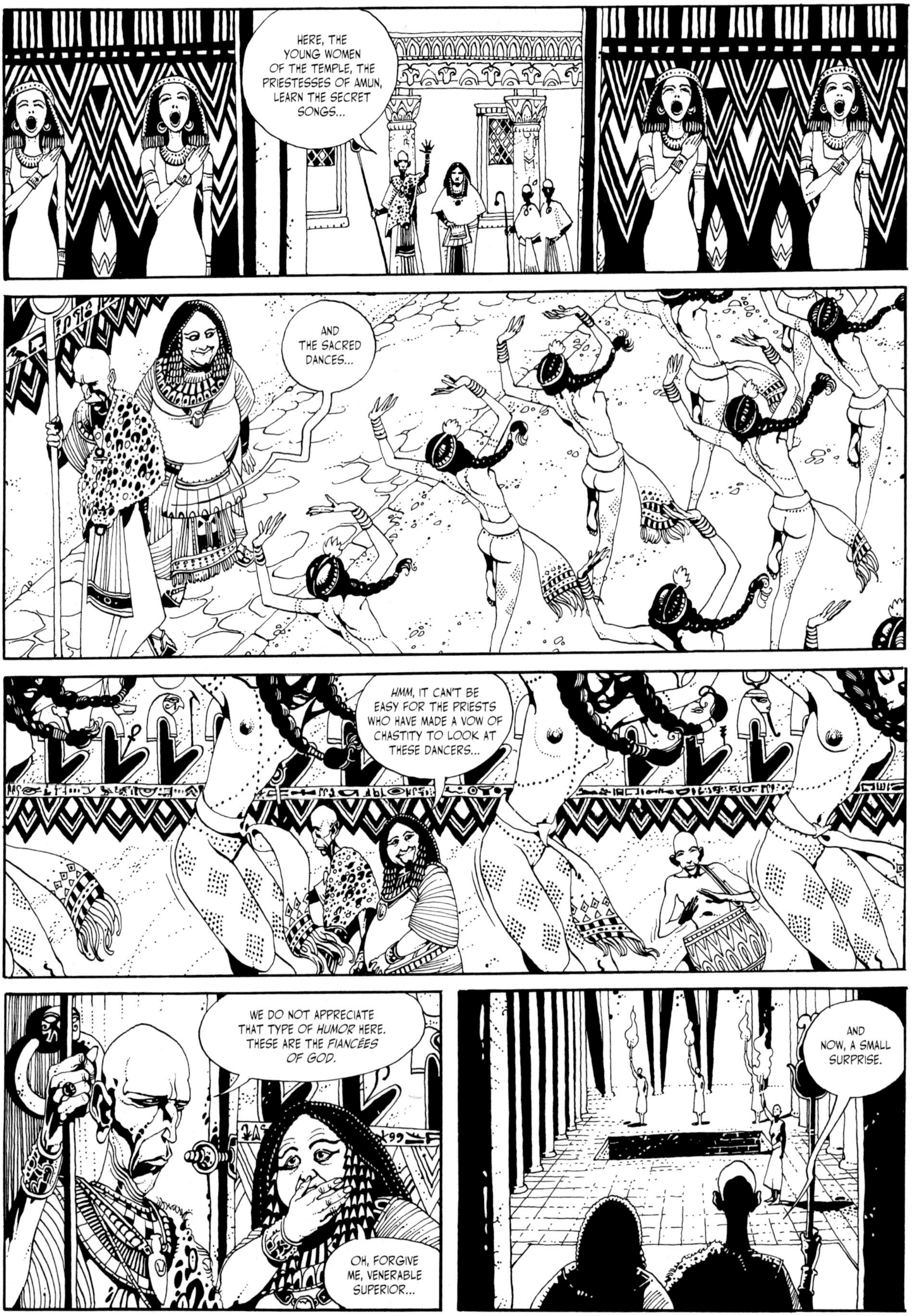
HERE, THE YOUNG WOMEN OF THE TEMPLE, THE PRIESTESSES OF AMUN, LEARN THE SECRET SONGS...
AND THE SACRED DANCES...
HMM, IT CAN'T BE EASY FOR THE PRIESTS WHO HAVE MADE A VOW OF CHASTITY TO LOOK AT THESE DANCERS...
WE DO NOT APPRECIATE THAT TYPE OF HUMOR HERE. THESE ARE THE FIANCÉES OF GOD.
OH, FORGIVE ME, VENERABLE SUPERIOR...
AND NOW, A SMALL SURPRISE.

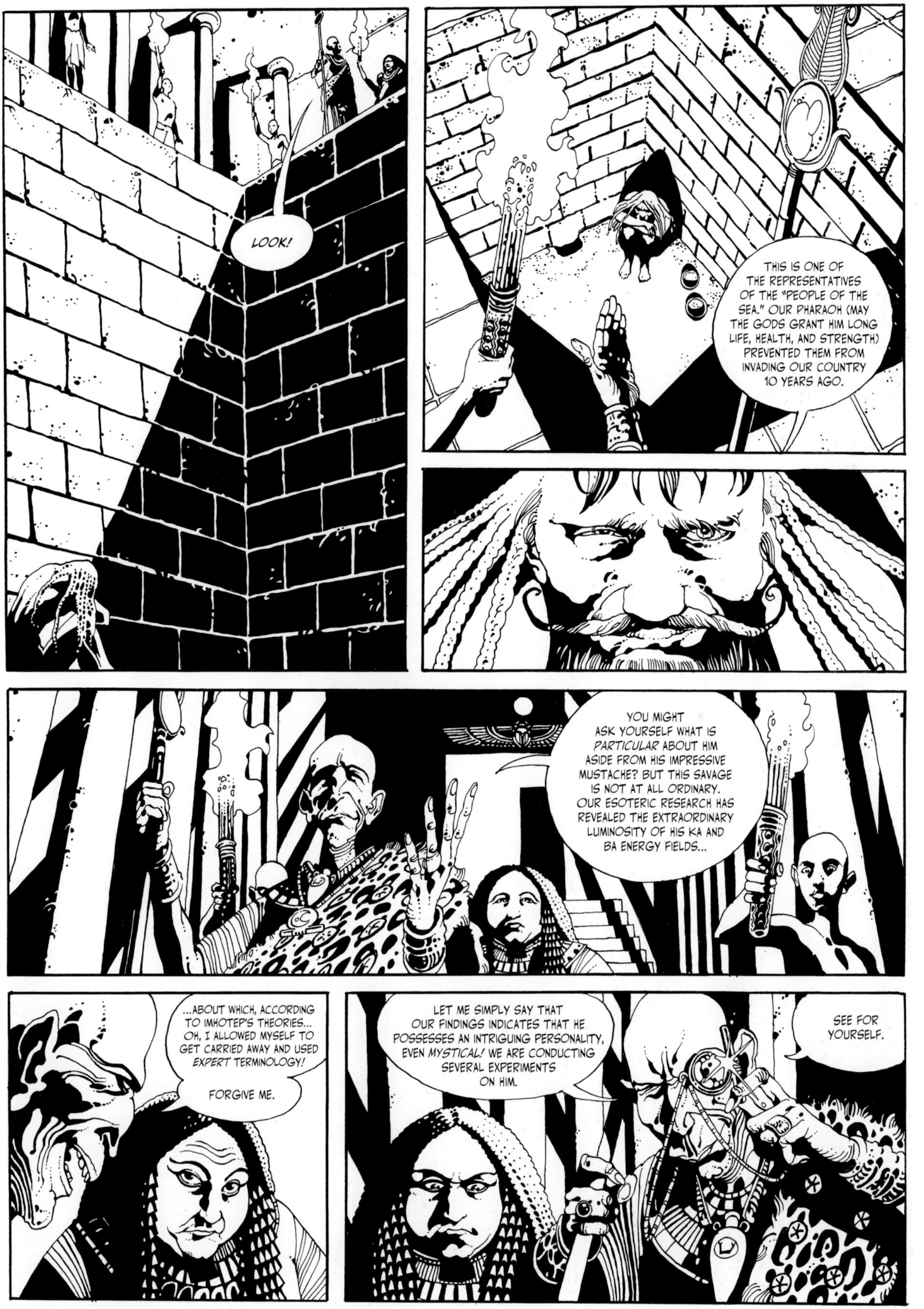
LOOK!
THIS IS ONE OF THE REPRESENTATIVES OF THE "PEOPLE OF THE SEA." OUR PHARAOH (MAY THE GODS GRANT HIM LONG LIFE, HEALTH, AND STRENGTH) PREVENTED THEM FROM INVADING OUR COUNTRY 10 YEARS AGO.
YOU MIGHT ASK YOURSELF WHAT IS *PARTICULAR* ABOUT HIM ASIDE FROM HIS IMPRESSIVE MUSTACHE? BUT THIS SAVAGE IS NOT AT ALL ORDINARY. OUR ESOTERIC RESEARCH HAS REVEALED THE EXTRAORDINARY LUMINOSITY OF HIS KA AND BA ENERGY FIELDS...
...ABOUT WHICH, ACCORDING TO IMHOTEP'S THEORIES... OH, I ALLOWED MYSELF TO GET CARRIED AWAY AND USED *EXPERT* TERMINOLOGY!
FORGIVE ME.
LET ME SIMPLY SAY THAT OUR FINDINGS INDICATES THAT HE POSSESSES AN INTRIGUING PERSONALITY, EVEN *MYSTICAL!* WE ARE CONDUCTING SEVERAL EXPERIMENTS ON HIM.
SEE FOR YOURSELF.

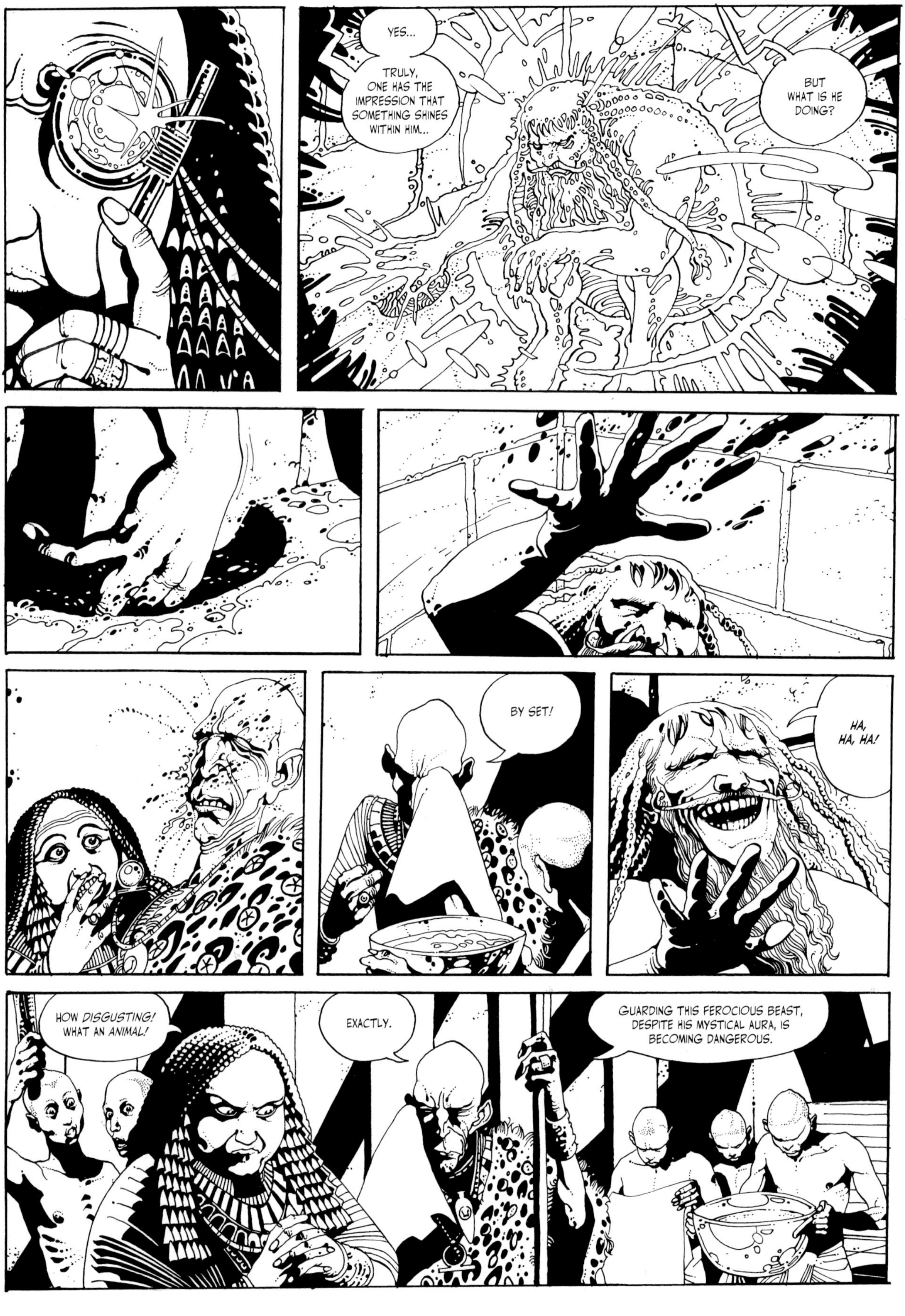
YES...
TRULY, ONE HAS THE IMPRESSION THAT SOMETHING SHINES WITHIN HIM...
BUT WHAT IS HE DOING?
BY SET!
HA, HA, HA!
HOW DISGUSTING! WHAT AN ANIMAL!
EXACTLY.
GUARDING THIS FEROCIOUS BEAST, DESPITE HIS MYSTICAL AURA, IS BECOMING DANGEROUS.

HE WILL BE PUNISHED.
I ALSO WANTED TO SHOW YOU THE HALL DEDICATED TO ASTROLOGY...
SINCE THE PURPOSE OF YOUR VISIT DEALS WITH *HOROSCOPES*...
HERE, WE CALCULATE THE DESTINY OF BEINGS WITH STARTLING PRECISION!
ONE DAY, AS AN EXPERIMENT, I ORDERED A SLAVE, WHOSE HOROSCOPE PROMISED A LONG LIFE, TO BE HANGED. AND WOULD YOU BELIEVE IT? THE ROPE *BROKE!*

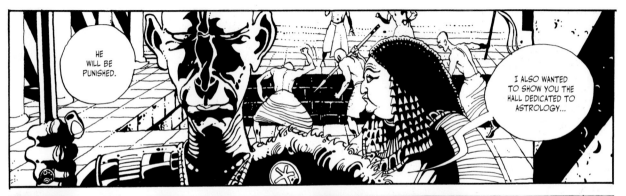

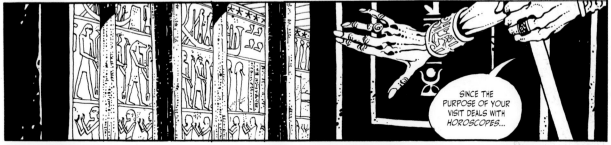

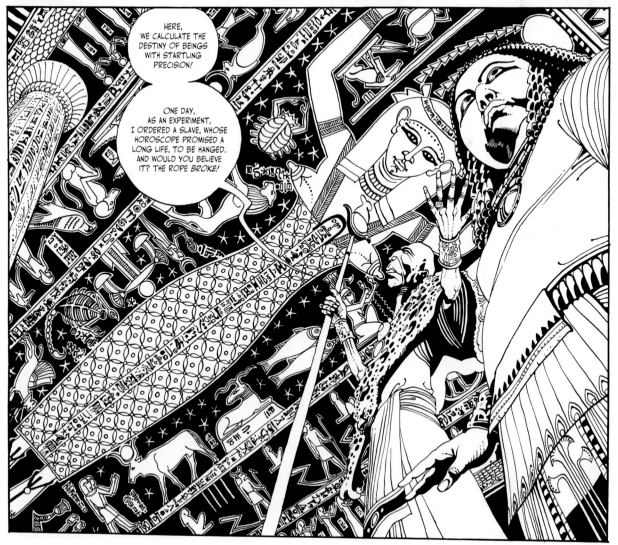

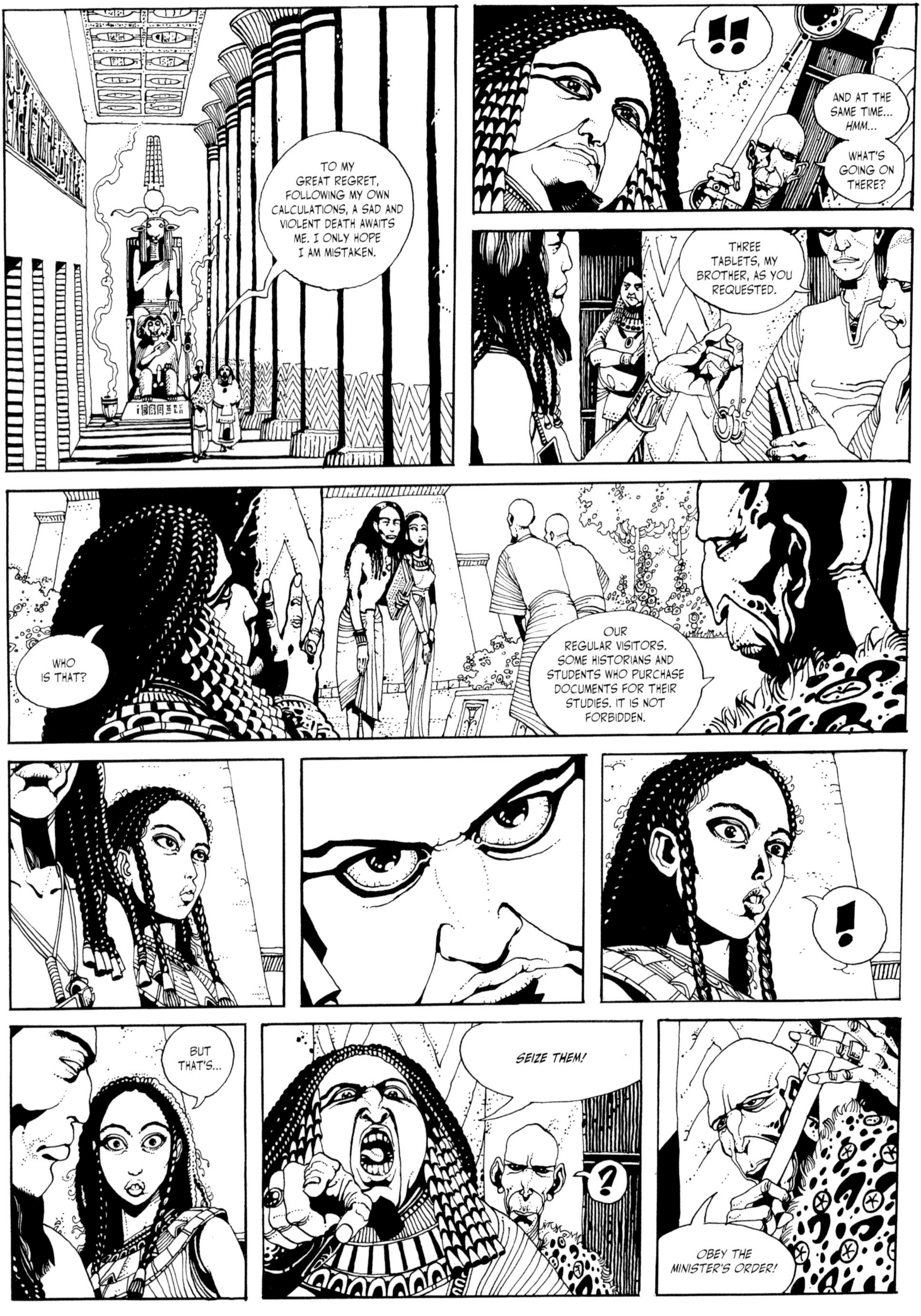
TO MY GREAT REGRET, FOLLOWING MY OWN CALCULATIONS, A SAD AND VIOLENT DEATH AWAITS ME. I ONLY HOPE I AM MISTAKEN.
!!
AND AT THE SAME TIME... HMM...
WHAT'S GOING ON THERE?
THREE TABLETS, MY BROTHER, AS YOU REQUESTED.
WHO IS THAT?
OUR REGULAR VISITORS. SOME HISTORIANS AND STUDENTS WHO PURCHASE DOCUMENTS FOR THEIR STUDIES. IT IS NOT FORBIDDEN.
!
BUT THAT'S...
SEIZE THEM!
?
OBEY THE MINISTER'S ORDER!

!
DON'T TOUCH ME!
I RECOGNIZED THEM. THEY ARE DANGEROUS CRIMINALS!
HOW DARE YOU SAY THAT? I AM THE PRINCESS TITI-NEFER!
SHE IS A MISERABLE USURPER! I DON'T KNOW WHO THIS MAN IS. SHE, ON THE OTHER HAND, MUST BE INTERROGATED!
PENHEVI, DON'T YOU RECOGNIZE ME?
HMM... I DON'T KNOW ANYTHING ABOUT THE PRINCESS, BUT HER COMPANION REMINDS ME OF SOMEONE...
IF I AM NOT MISTAKEN... WOULDN'T HE BE THE ONE...

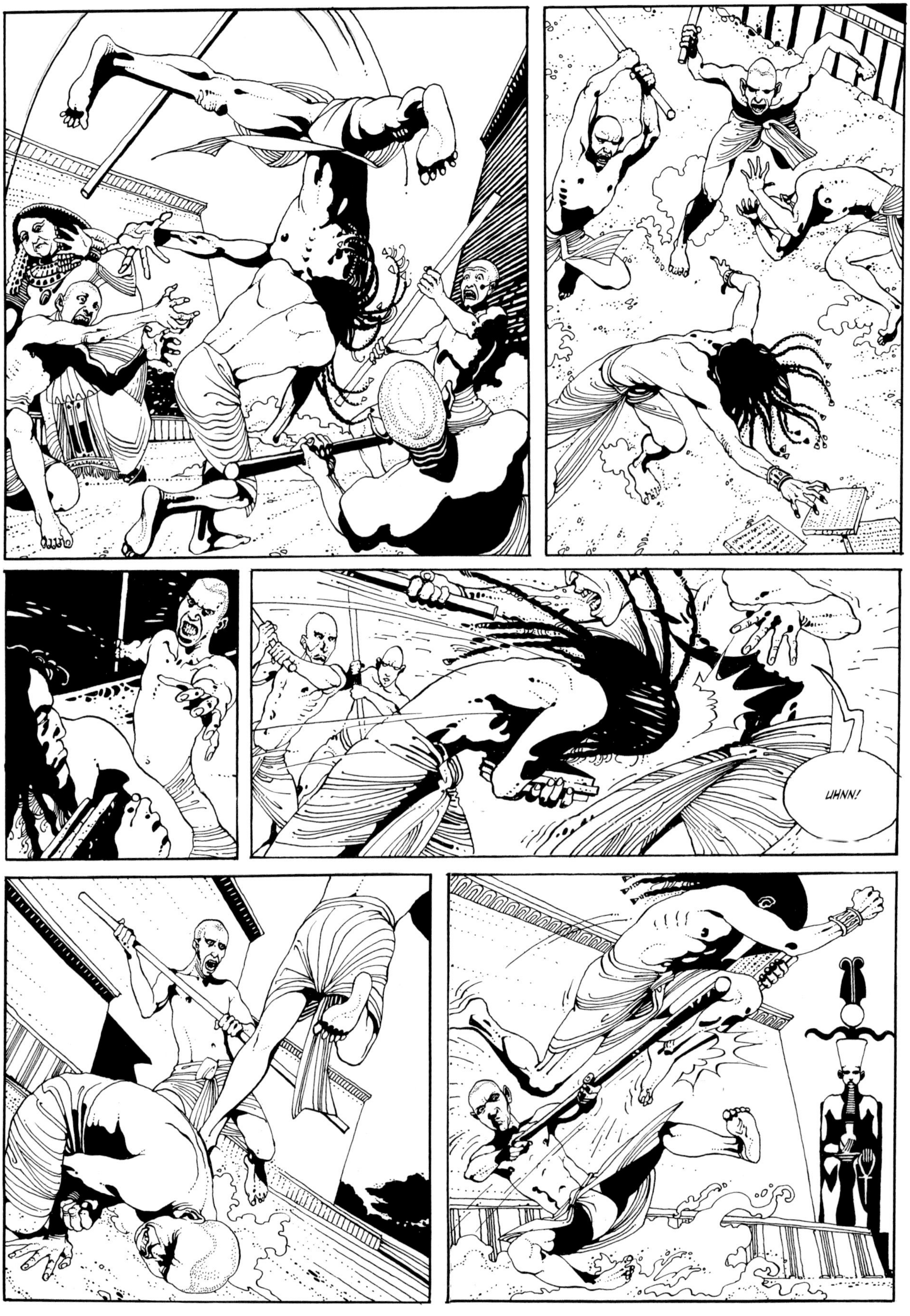
UHNN!

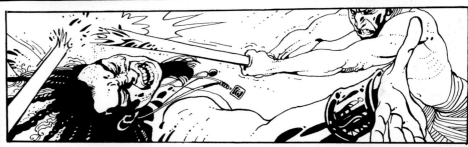

YES, NOW I AM *SURE* THAT'S HIM! THE LONG HAIR, THAT *SCAR* ON HIS FACE, I DIDN'T RECOGNIZE HIM RIGHT AWAY.

IT'S PTAHMOSES, THE PRIEST-KILLER...LET'S FIND OUT WHY HE THOUGHT OF USE TO PAY US A VISIT...

HMM... SOME TABLETS IN BABYLONIAN...ABOUT BURIALS... WHERE ABOUTS?
...AH ...IN THE FORBIDDEN CITY?
HAVE YOU THEN AN INTEREST IN THE BANNED PARTS OF HISTORY, PTAHMOSES? THIS MAN IS AN OLD STUDENT OF OUR TEMPLE. INTERROGATE HIM!
WHILE I MUST URGENTLY INTERROGATE THE GIRL!
BRING FORTH THE GIRL SO SHE MAY BE INTERROGATED BY THE VENERABLE MINISTER.
PENHEVI, YOU TRAITOR!
ARE YOU SURE THAT SHE IS NOT...UM, THE PRINCESS?
WHAT DO YOU TAKE ME FOR, VENERABLE SUPERIOR?!
WELL...IN THAT CASE, LET US MEET AGAIN FOLLOWING THE INTERROGATIONS, DEAR PENHEVI.
VERY WELL..
IT'S A STATE SECRET! A THREAT TO THE THRONE!

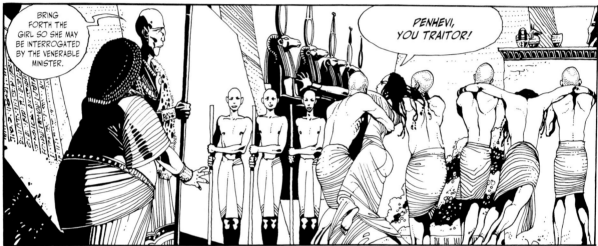

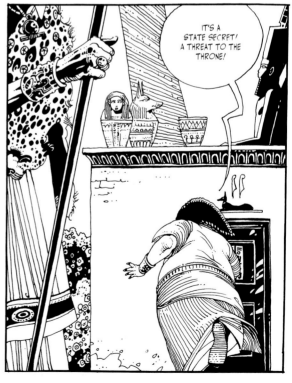

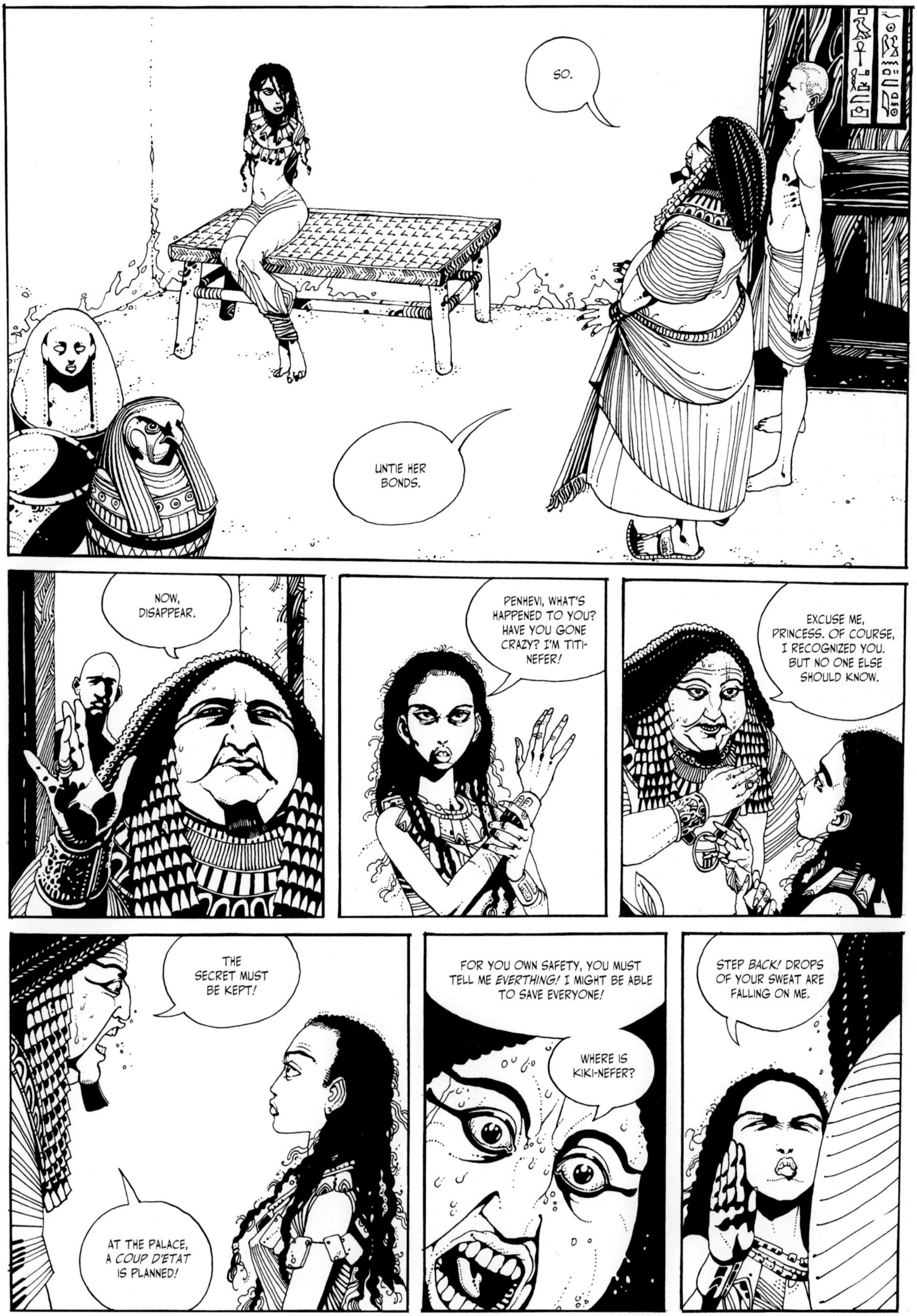
SO.
UNTIE HER BONDS.
NOW, DISAPPEAR.
PENHEVI, WHAT'S HAPPENED TO YOU? HAVE YOU GONE CRAZY? I'M TITI-NEFER!
EXCUSE ME, PRINCESS. OF COURSE, I RECOGNIZED YOU. BUT NO ONE ELSE SHOULD KNOW.
THE SECRET MUST BE KEPT!
AT THE PALACE, A *COUP D'ETAT* IS PLANNED!
FOR YOU OWN SAFETY, YOU MUST TELL ME *EVERTHING!* I MIGHT BE ABLE TO SAVE EVERYONE!
WHERE IS KIKI-NEFER?
STEP *BACK!* DROPS OF YOUR SWEAT ARE FALLING ON ME.

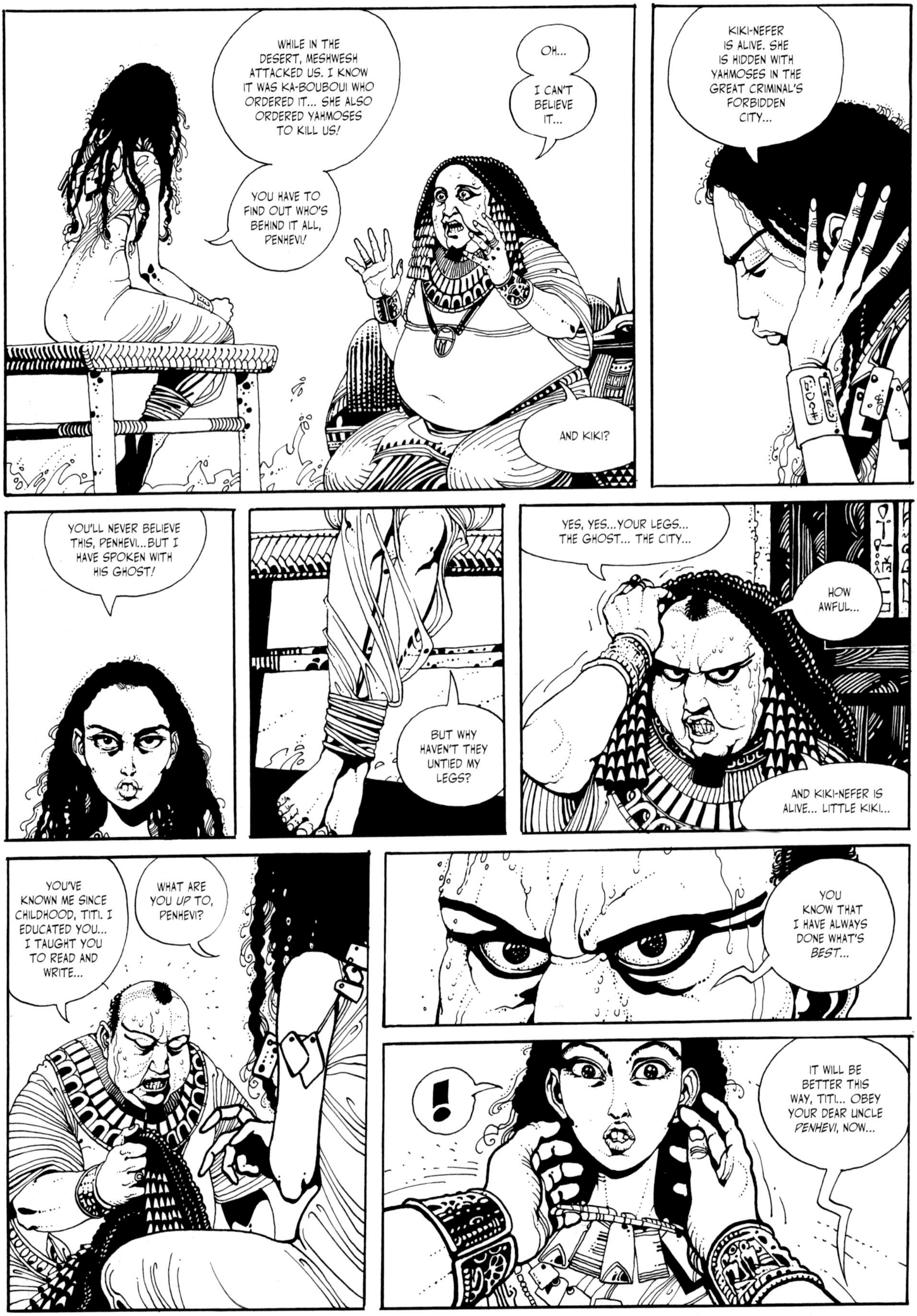
WHILE IN THE DESERT, MESHWESH ATTACKED US. I KNOW IT WAS KA-BOUBOUI WHO ORDERED IT... SHE ALSO ORDERED YAHMOSES TO KILL US!
YOU HAVE TO FIND OUT WHO'S BEHIND IT ALL, PENHEVI!
OH...
I CAN'T BELIEVE IT...
AND KIKI?
KIKI-NEFER IS ALIVE. SHE IS HIDDEN WITH YAHMOSES IN THE GREAT CRIMINAL'S FORBIDDEN CITY...
YOU'LL NEVER BELIEVE THIS, PENHEVI...BUT I HAVE SPOKEN WITH HIS GHOST!
BUT WHY HAVEN'T THEY UNTIED MY LEGS?
YES, YES...YOUR LEGS... THE GHOST... THE CITY...
HOW AWFUL...
AND KIKI-NEFER IS ALIVE... LITTLE KIKI...
YOU'VE KNOWN ME SINCE CHILDHOOD, TITI. I EDUCATED YOU... I TAUGHT YOU TO READ AND WRITE...
WHAT ARE YOU UP TO, PENHEVI?
YOU KNOW THAT I HAVE ALWAYS DONE WHAT'S *BEST*...
!
IT WILL BE BETTER THIS WAY, TITI... OBEY YOUR DEAR UNCLE *PENHEVI*, NOW...

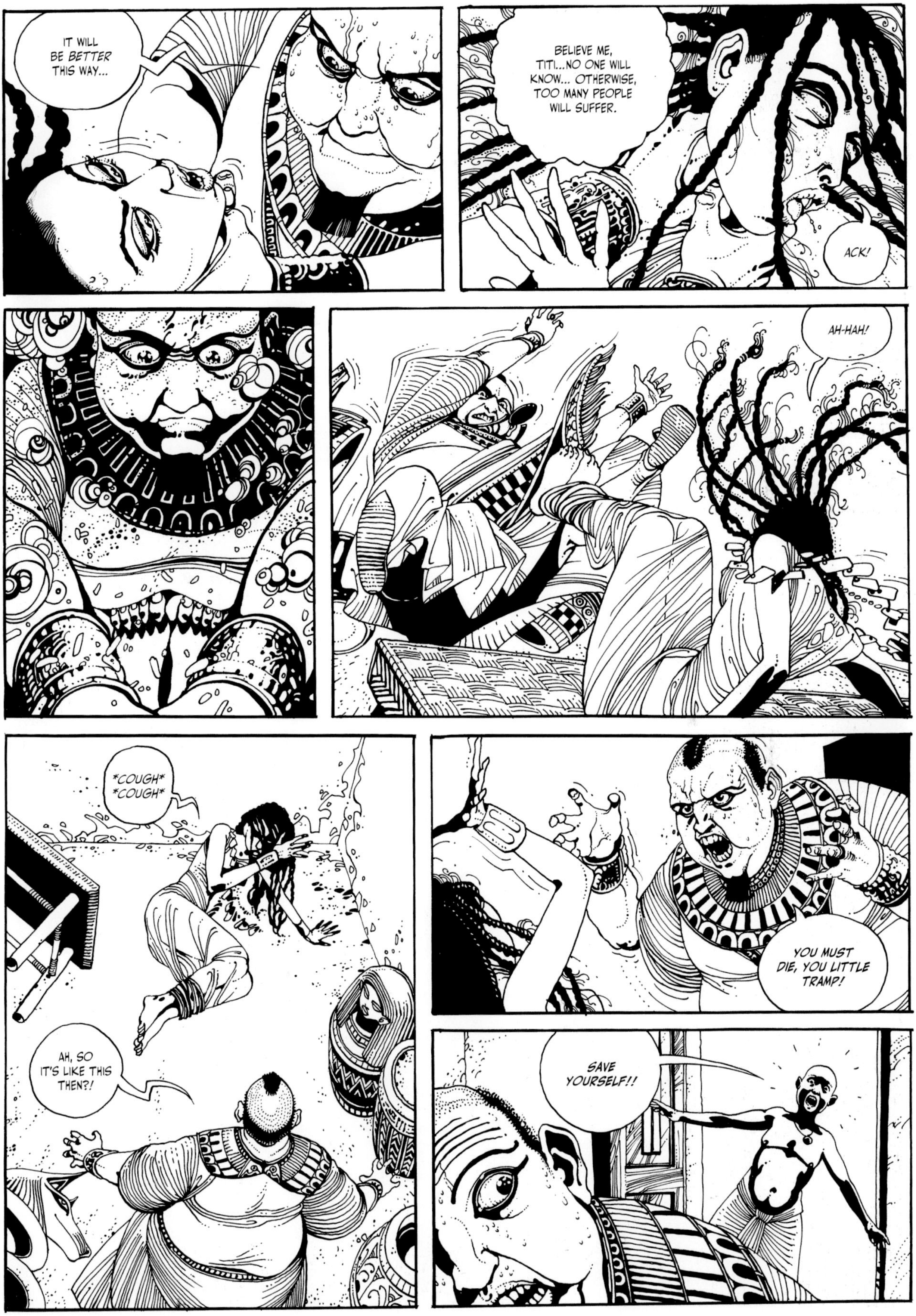
IT WILL BE BETTER THIS WAY...
BELIEVE ME, TITI...NO ONE WILL KNOW... OTHERWISE, TOO MANY PEOPLE WILL SUFFER.
ACK!
AH-HAH!
COUGH *COUGH*
AH, SO IT'S LIKE THIS THEN?!
YOU MUST DIE, YOU LITTLE TRAMP!
SAVE YOURSELF!!

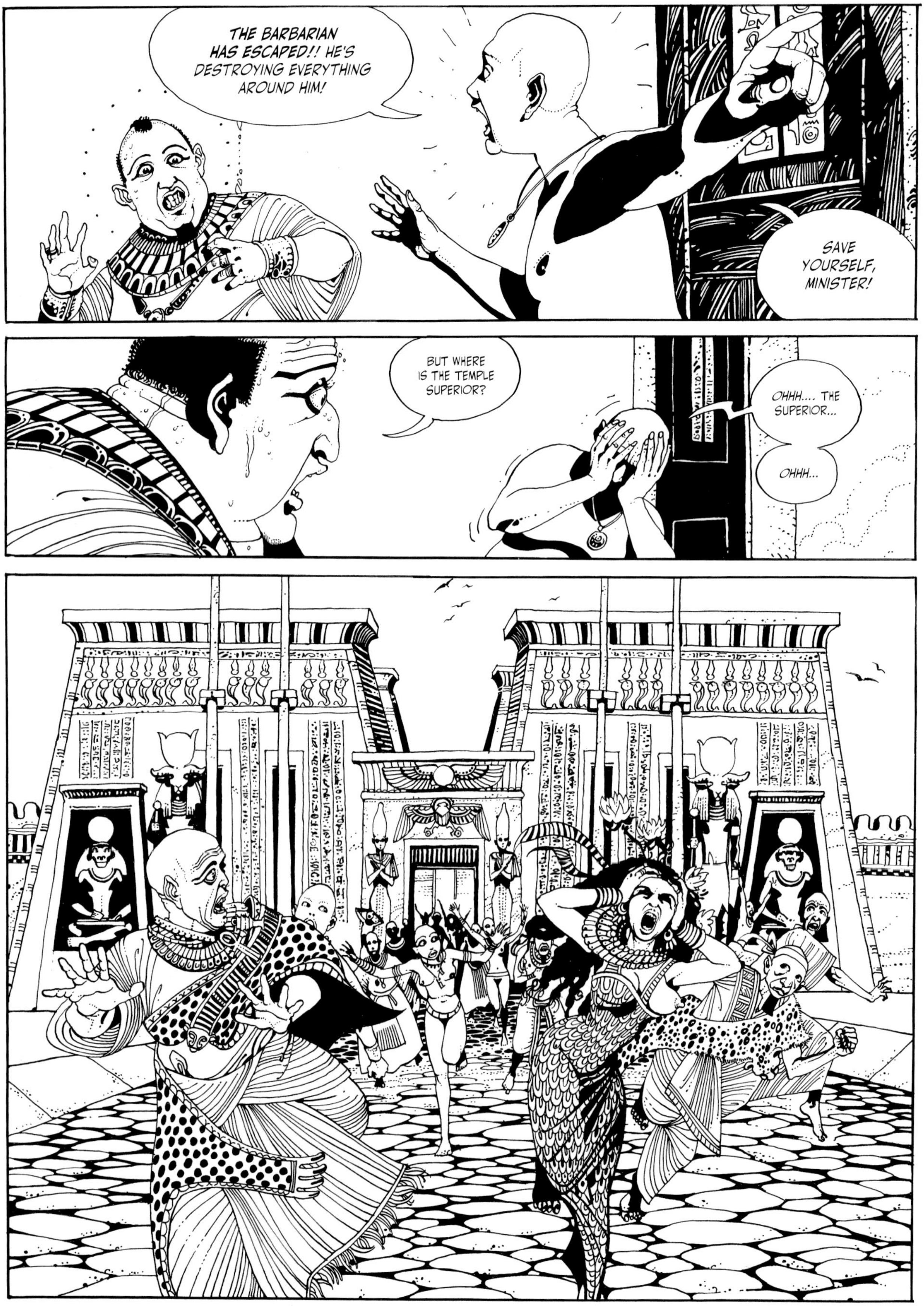
THE BARBARIAN HAS ESCAPED!! HE'S DESTROYING EVERYTHING AROUND HIM!
SAVE YOURSELF, MINISTER!
BUT WHERE IS THE TEMPLE SUPERIOR?
OHHH.... THE SUPERIOR...
OHHH...

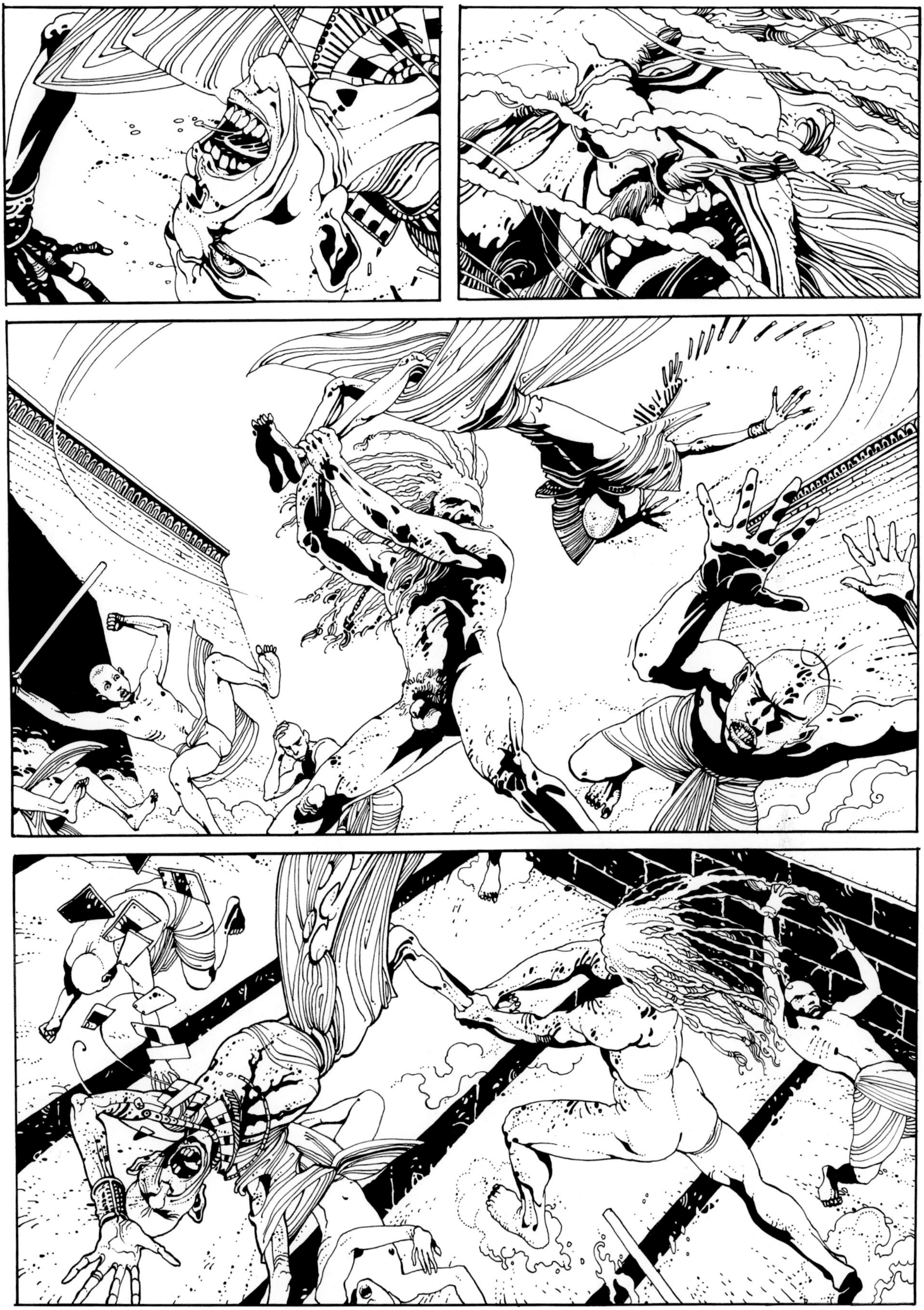

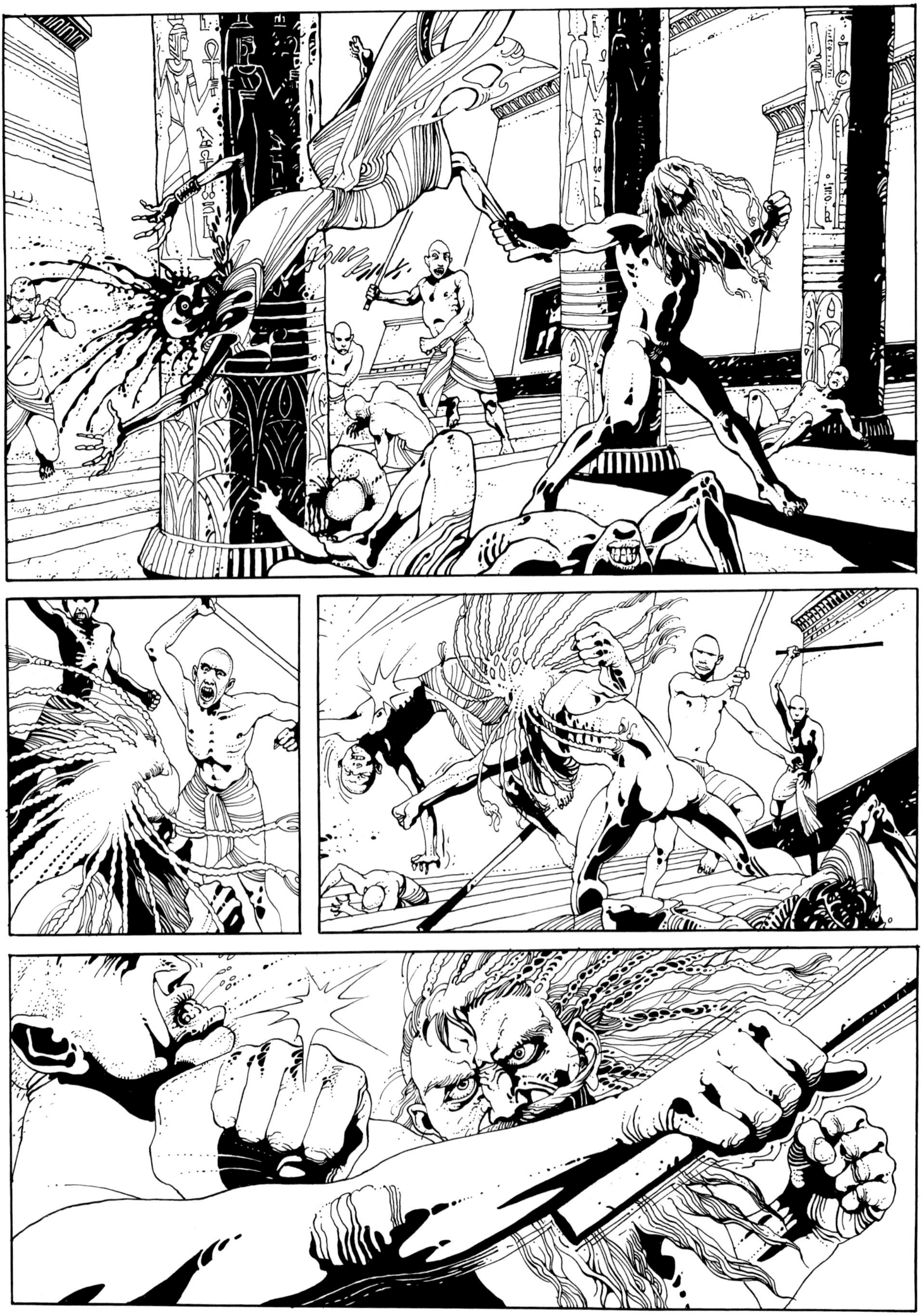

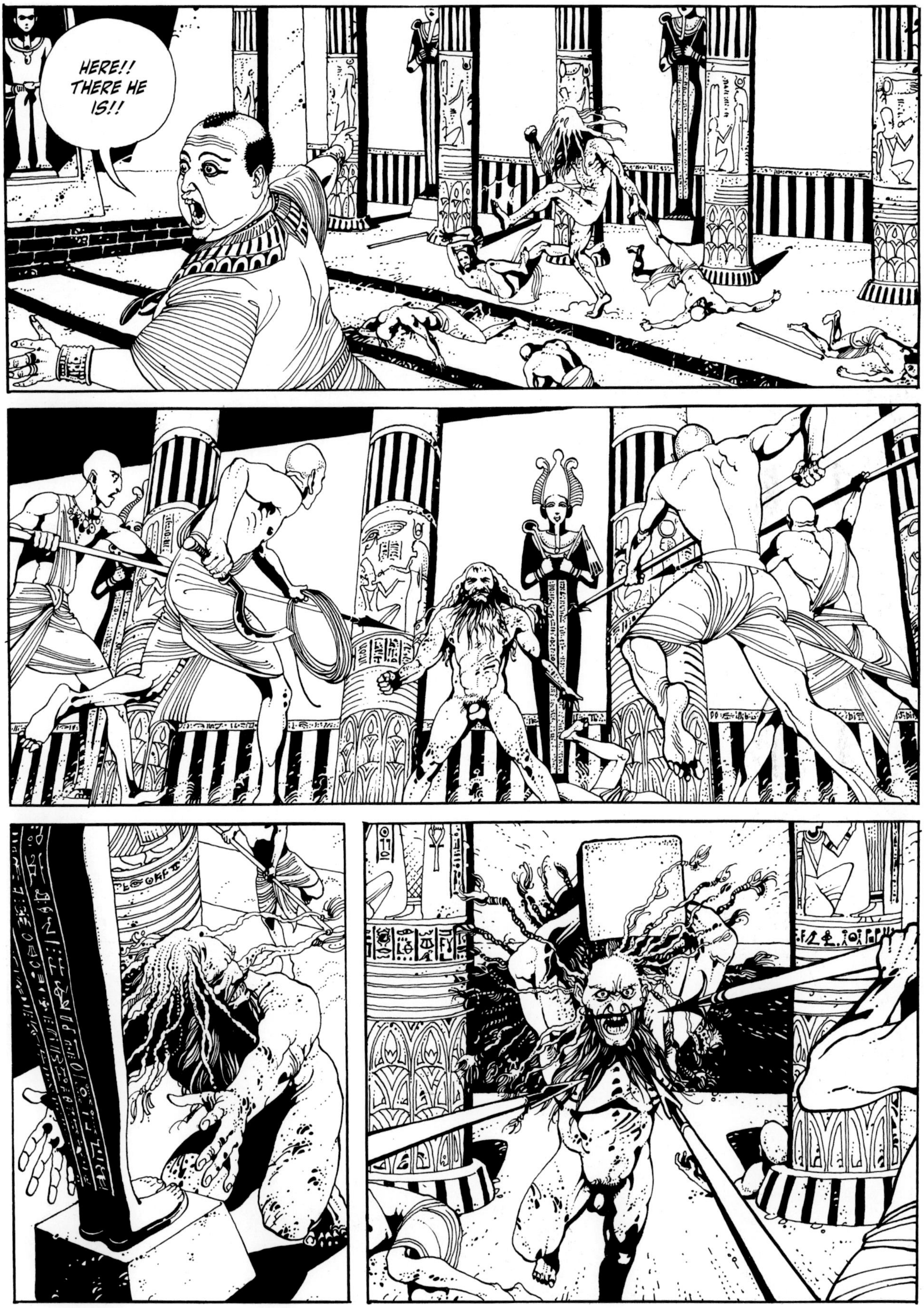
HERE!! THERE HE IS!!

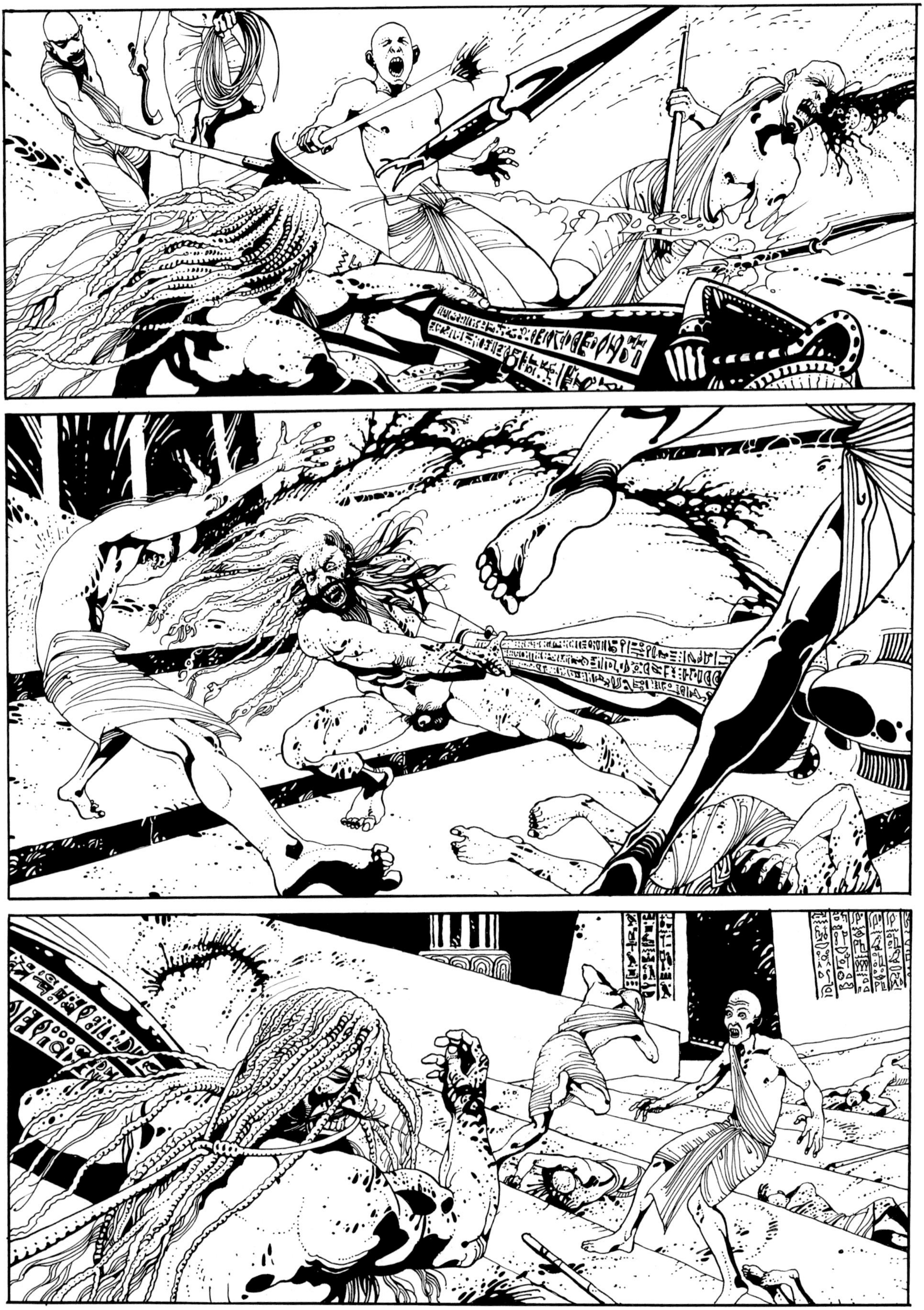

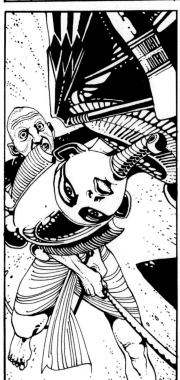

O GODS!

O
GODS!!
O
GODS!!!

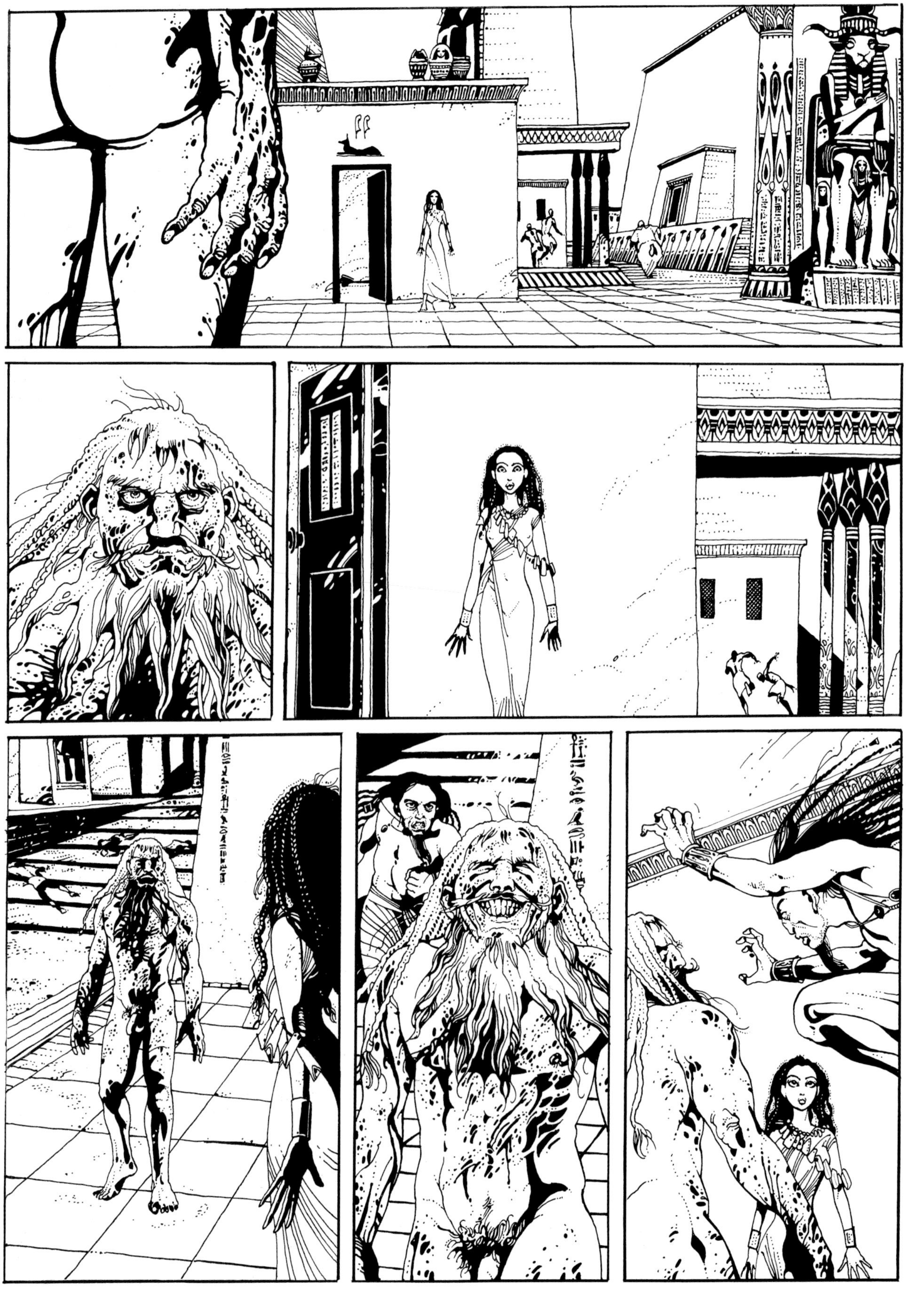

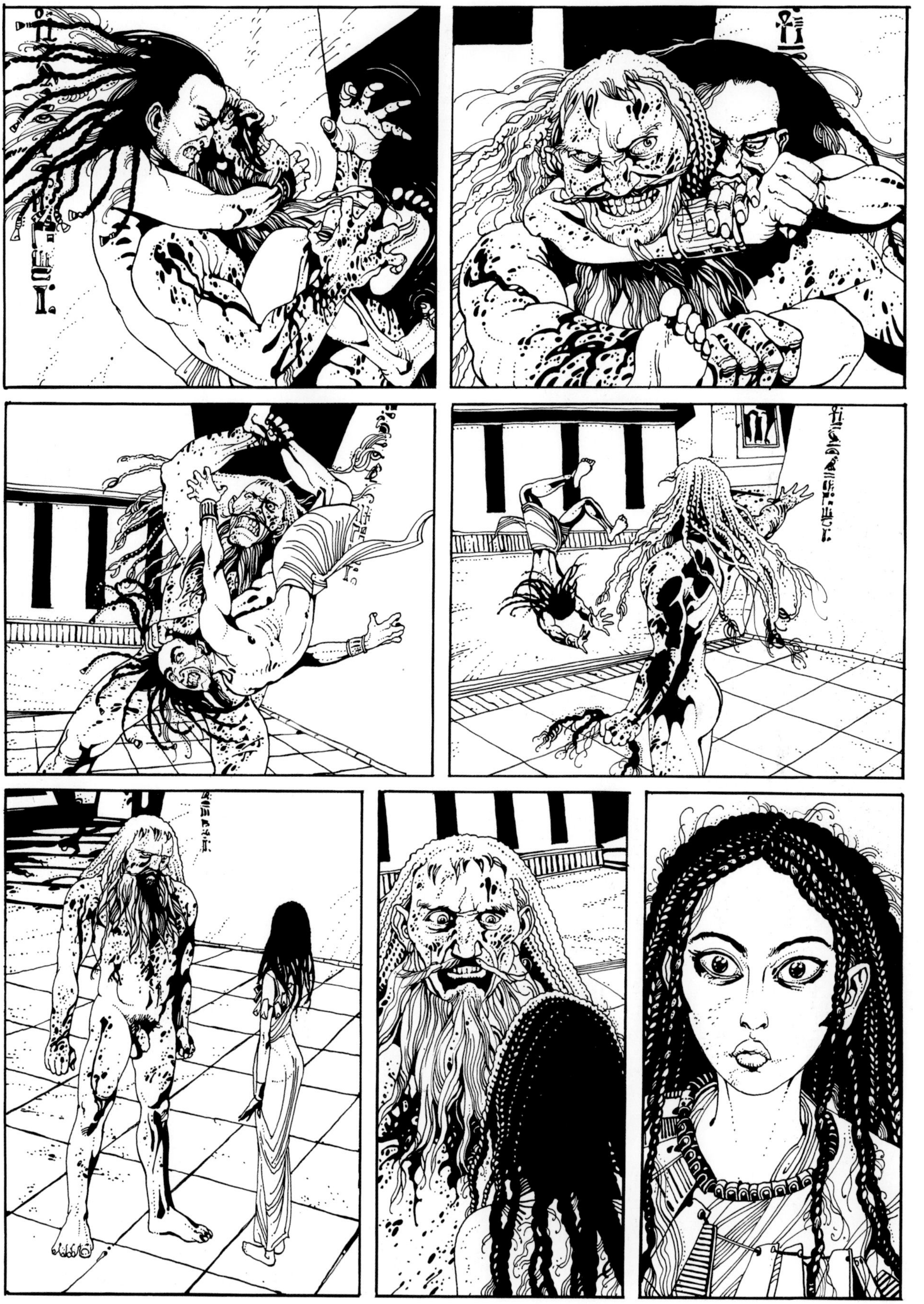

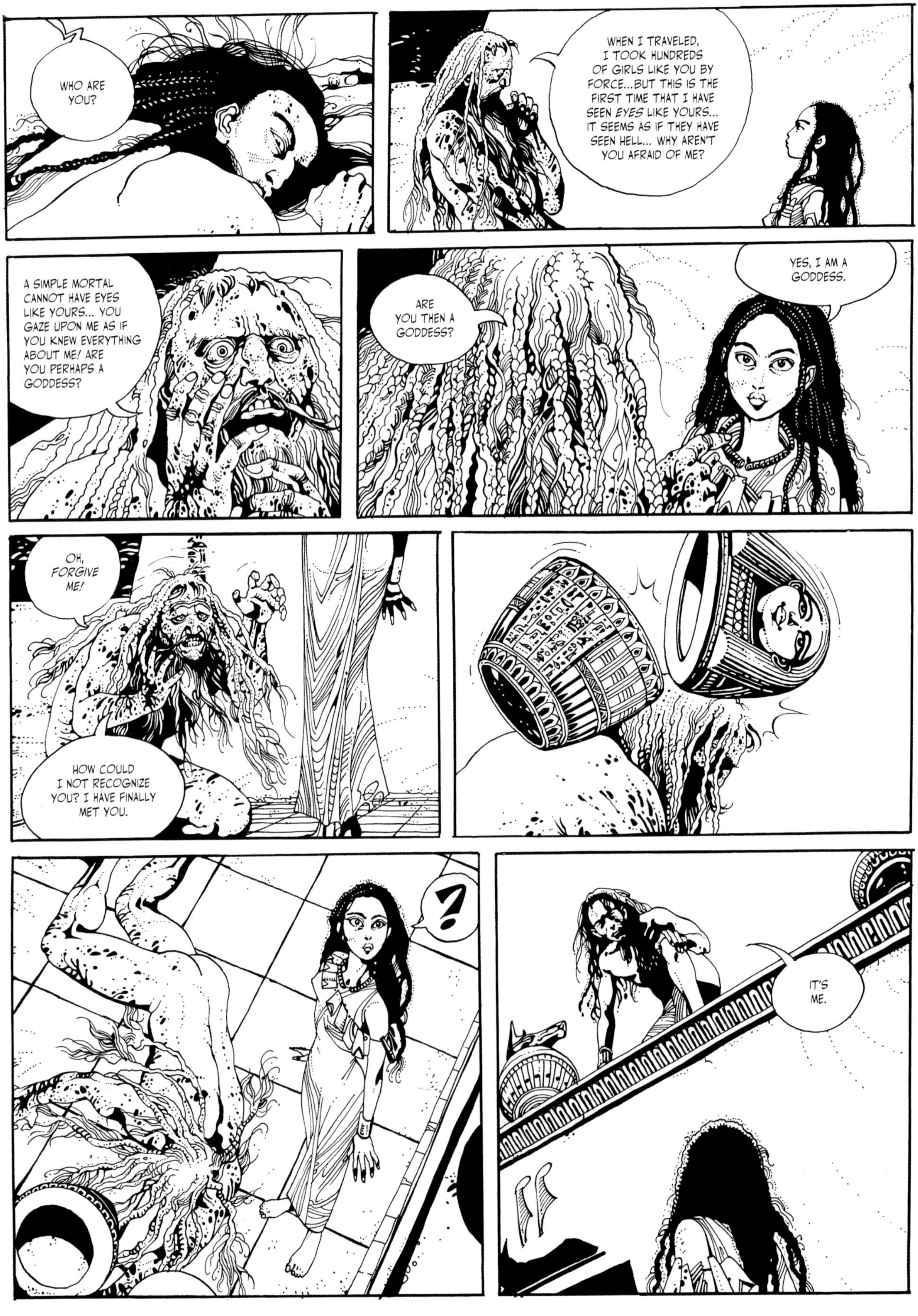
WHO ARE YOU?
WHEN I TRAVELED, I TOOK HUNDREDS OF GIRLS LIKE YOU BY FORCE...BUT THIS IS THE FIRST TIME THAT I HAVE SEEN *EYES* LIKE YOURS... IT SEEMS AS IF THEY HAVE SEEN HELL... WHY AREN'T YOU AFRAID OF ME?
A SIMPLE MORTAL CANNOT HAVE EYES LIKE YOURS... YOU GAZE UPON ME AS IF YOU KNEW EVERYTHING ABOUT ME! ARE YOU PERHAPS A GODDESS?
ARE YOU THEN A GODDESS?
YES, I AM A GODDESS.
OH, FORGIVE ME!
HOW COULD I NOT RECOGNIZE YOU? I HAVE FINALLY MET YOU.
?
IT'S ME.

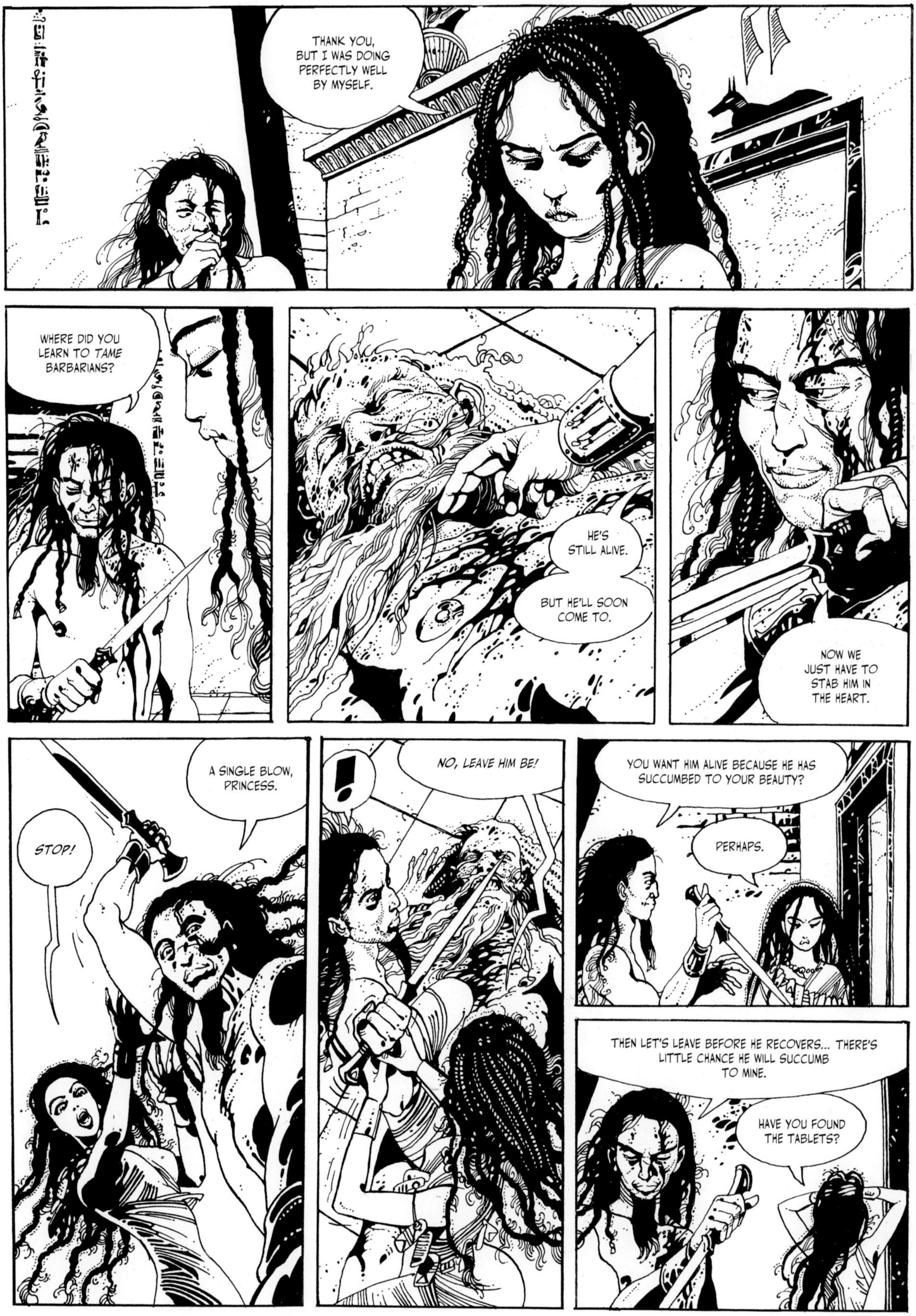
THANK YOU, BUT I WAS DOING PERFECTLY WELL BY MYSELF.
WHERE DID YOU LEARN TO *TAME* BARBARIANS?
HE'S STILL ALIVE.
BUT HE'LL SOON COME TO.
NOW WE JUST HAVE TO STAB HIM IN THE HEART.
A SINGLE BLOW, PRINCESS.
STOP!
!
NO, LEAVE HIM BE!
YOU WANT HIM ALIVE BECAUSE HE HAS SUCCUMBED TO YOUR BEAUTY?
PERHAPS.
THEN LET'S LEAVE BEFORE HE RECOVERS... THERE'S LITTLE CHANCE HE WILL SUCCUMB TO MINE.
HAVE YOU FOUND THE TABLETS?

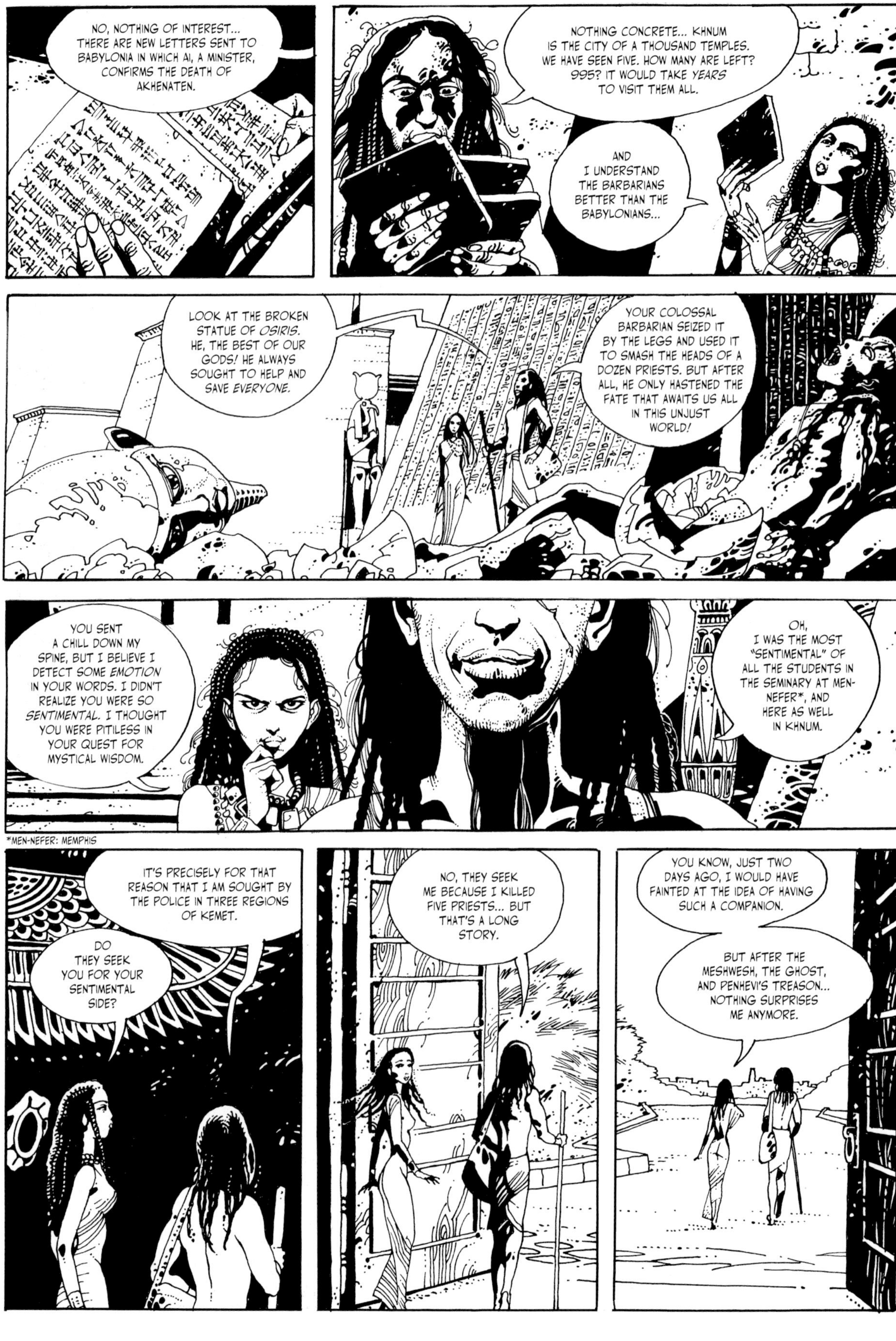
NO, NOTHING OF INTEREST... THERE ARE NEW LETTERS SENT TO BABYLONIA IN WHICH AI, A MINISTER, CONFIRMS THE DEATH OF AKHENATEN.
NOTHING CONCRETE... KHNUM IS THE CITY OF A THOUSAND TEMPLES. WE HAVE SEEN FIVE. HOW MANY ARE LEFT? 995? IT WOULD TAKE *YEARS* TO VISIT THEM ALL.
AND I UNDERSTAND THE BARBARIANS BETTER THAN THE BABYLONIANS...
LOOK AT THE BROKEN STATUE OF *OSIRIS*. HE, THE BEST OF OUR GODS! HE ALWAYS SOUGHT TO HELP AND SAVE *EVERYONE*.
YOUR COLOSSAL BARBARIAN SEIZED IT BY THE LEGS AND USED IT TO SMASH THE HEADS OF A DOZEN PRIESTS. BUT AFTER ALL, HE ONLY HASTENED THE FATE THAT AWAITS US ALL IN THIS UNJUST WORLD!
YOU SENT A CHILL DOWN MY SPINE, BUT I BELIEVE I DETECT SOME *EMOTION* IN YOUR WORDS. I DIDN'T REALIZE YOU WERE SO *SENTIMENTAL*. I THOUGHT YOU WERE PITILESS IN YOUR QUEST FOR MYSTICAL WISDOM.
OH, I WAS THE MOST "SENTIMENTAL" OF ALL THE STUDENTS IN THE SEMINARY AT MEN-NEFER*, AND HERE AS WELL IN KHNUM.
IT'S PRECISELY FOR THAT REASON THAT I AM SOUGHT BY THE POLICE IN THREE REGIONS OF KEMET.
DO THEY SEEK YOU FOR YOUR SENTIMENTAL SIDE?
NO, THEY SEEK ME BECAUSE I KILLED FIVE PRIESTS... BUT THAT'S A LONG STORY.
YOU KNOW, JUST TWO DAYS AGO, I WOULD HAVE FAINTED AT THE IDEA OF HAVING SUCH A COMPANION.
BUT AFTER THE MESHWESH, THE GHOST, AND PENHEVI'S TREASON... NOTHING SURPRISES ME ANYMORE.

*MEN-NEFER: MEMPHIS

AT THIS TIME OF YEAR, THERE ARE MANY PILGRIMS VISITING KHNUM'S SACRED PLACES. ALL THE HOTELS AND THE BROTHELS AWAIT THEM. YOU'RE NOT SCARED THAT I MIGHT DESPOIL YOU?

WE NEED A ROOM ON THE ROOF SO WE ARE NOT DISTURBED.

I CAN SEE YOU'VE COME FROM AFAR.

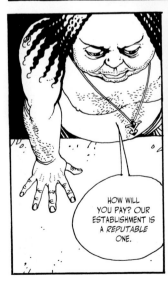

HOW WILL YOU PAY? OUR ESTABLISHMENT IS A *REPUTABLE* ONE.

WITH THESE GOLD DEBENS...

AND ALSO...

YOU PROBABLY DON'T EAT MEAT, VENERABLE PRIEST, IS THAT IT?

NOR DO WE. EVERYONE IS PIOUS IN KHNUM. IT'S WELL KNOWN.

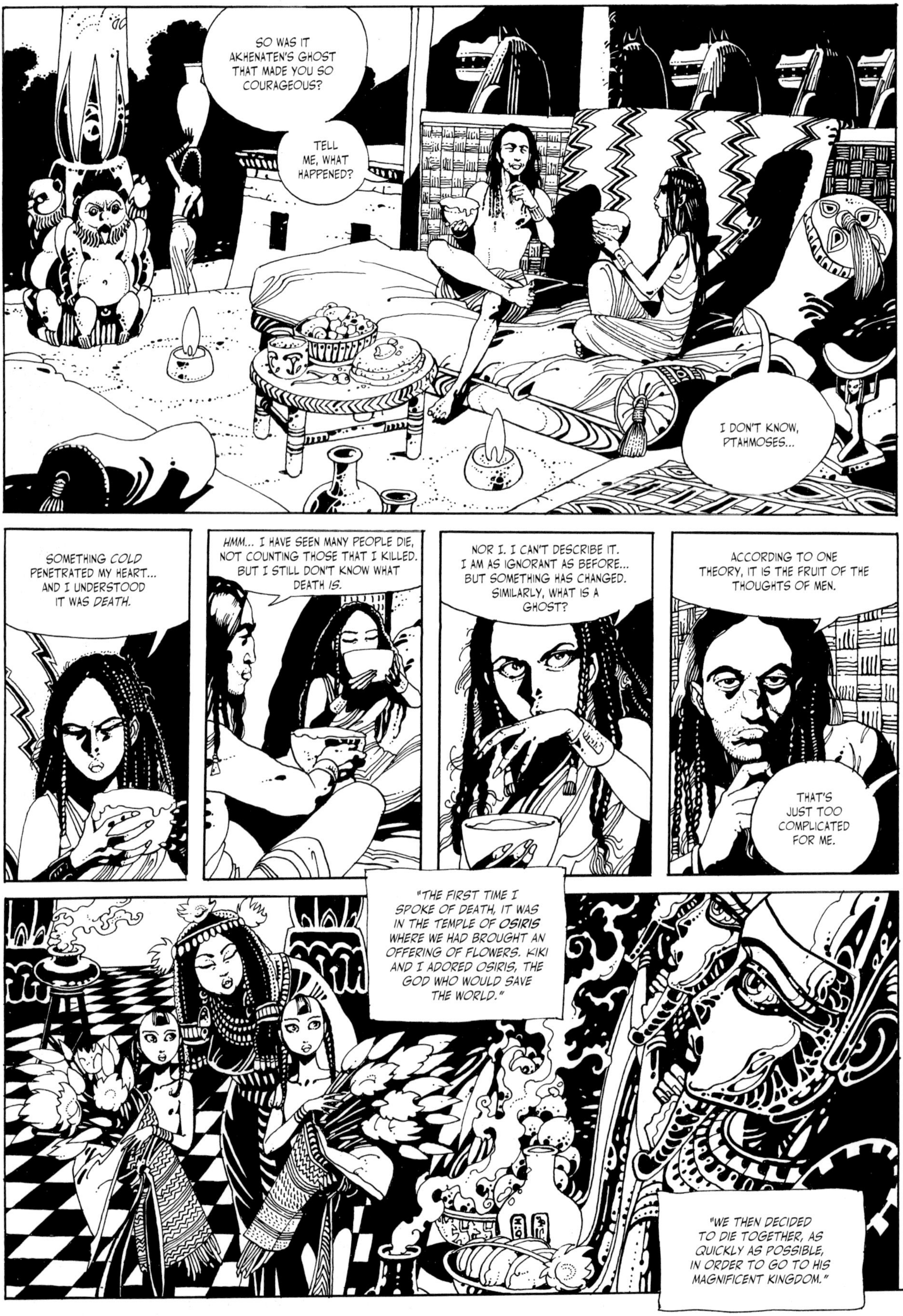
SO WAS IT AKHENATEN'S GHOST THAT MADE YOU SO COURAGEOUS?
TELL ME, WHAT HAPPENED?
I DON'T KNOW, PTAHMOSES...
SOMETHING COLD PENETRATED MY HEART... AND I UNDERSTOOD IT WAS DEATH.
HMM... I HAVE SEEN MANY PEOPLE DIE, NOT COUNTING THOSE THAT I KILLED. BUT I STILL DON'T KNOW WHAT DEATH IS.
NOR I. I CAN'T DESCRIBE IT. I AM AS IGNORANT AS BEFORE... BUT SOMETHING HAS CHANGED. SIMILARLY, WHAT IS A GHOST?
ACCORDING TO ONE THEORY, IT IS THE FRUIT OF THE THOUGHTS OF MEN.
THAT'S JUST TOO COMPLICATED FOR ME.
"THE FIRST TIME I SPOKE OF DEATH, IT WAS IN THE TEMPLE OF OSIRIS WHERE WE HAD BROUGHT AN OFFERING OF FLOWERS. KIKI AND I ADORED OSIRIS, THE GOD WHO WOULD SAVE THE WORLD."
"WE THEN DECIDED TO DIE TOGETHER, AS QUICKLY AS POSSIBLE, IN ORDER TO GO TO HIS MAGNIFICENT KINGDOM."

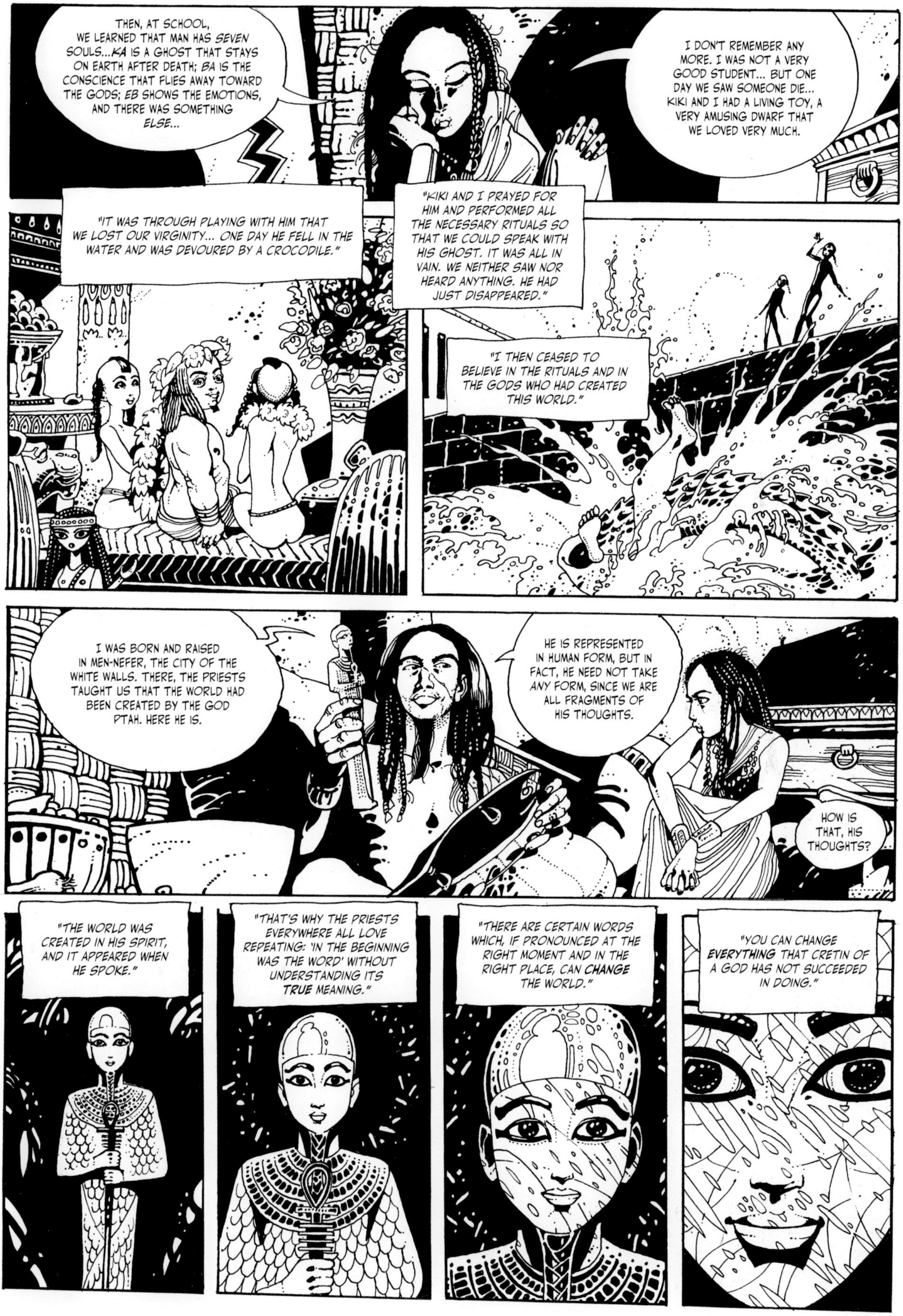
THEN, AT SCHOOL, WE LEARNED THAT MAN HAS *SEVEN* SOULS... *KA* IS A GHOST THAT STAYS ON EARTH AFTER DEATH; *BA* IS THE CONSCIENCE THAT FLIES AWAY TOWARD THE GODS; *EB* SHOWS THE EMOTIONS, AND THERE WAS SOMETHING *ELSE*...
I DON'T REMEMBER ANY MORE. I WAS NOT A VERY GOOD STUDENT... BUT ONE DAY WE SAW SOMEONE DIE... KIKI AND I HAD A LIVING TOY, A VERY AMUSING DWARF THAT WE LOVED VERY MUCH.
"IT WAS THROUGH PLAYING WITH HIM THAT WE LOST OUR VIRGINITY... ONE DAY HE FELL IN THE WATER AND WAS DEVOURED BY A CROCODILE."
"KIKI AND I PRAYED FOR HIM AND PERFORMED ALL THE NECESSARY RITUALS SO THAT WE COULD SPEAK WITH HIS GHOST. IT WAS ALL IN VAIN. WE NEITHER SAW NOR HEARD ANYTHING. HE HAD JUST DISAPPEARED."
"I THEN CEASED TO BELIEVE IN THE RITUALS AND IN THE GODS WHO HAD CREATED THIS WORLD."
I WAS BORN AND RAISED IN MEN-NEFER, THE CITY OF THE WHITE WALLS. THERE, THE PRIESTS TAUGHT US THAT THE WORLD HAD BEEN CREATED BY THE GOD PTAH. HERE HE IS.
HE IS REPRESENTED IN HUMAN FORM, BUT IN FACT, HE NEED NOT TAKE ANY FORM, SINCE WE ARE ALL FRAGMENTS OF HIS THOUGHTS.
HOW IS THAT, HIS THOUGHTS?
"THE WORLD WAS CREATED IN HIS SPIRIT, AND IT APPEARED WHEN HE SPOKE."
"THAT'S WHY THE PRIESTS EVERYWHERE ALL LOVE REPEATING: 'IN THE BEGINNING WAS THE WORD' WITHOUT UNDERSTANDING ITS **TRUE** MEANING."
"THERE ARE CERTAIN WORDS WHICH, IF PRONOUNCED AT THE RIGHT MOMENT AND IN THE RIGHT PLACE, CAN **CHANGE** THE WORLD."
"YOU CAN CHANGE **EVERYTHING** THAT CRETIN OF A GOD HAS NOT SUCCEEDED IN DOING."

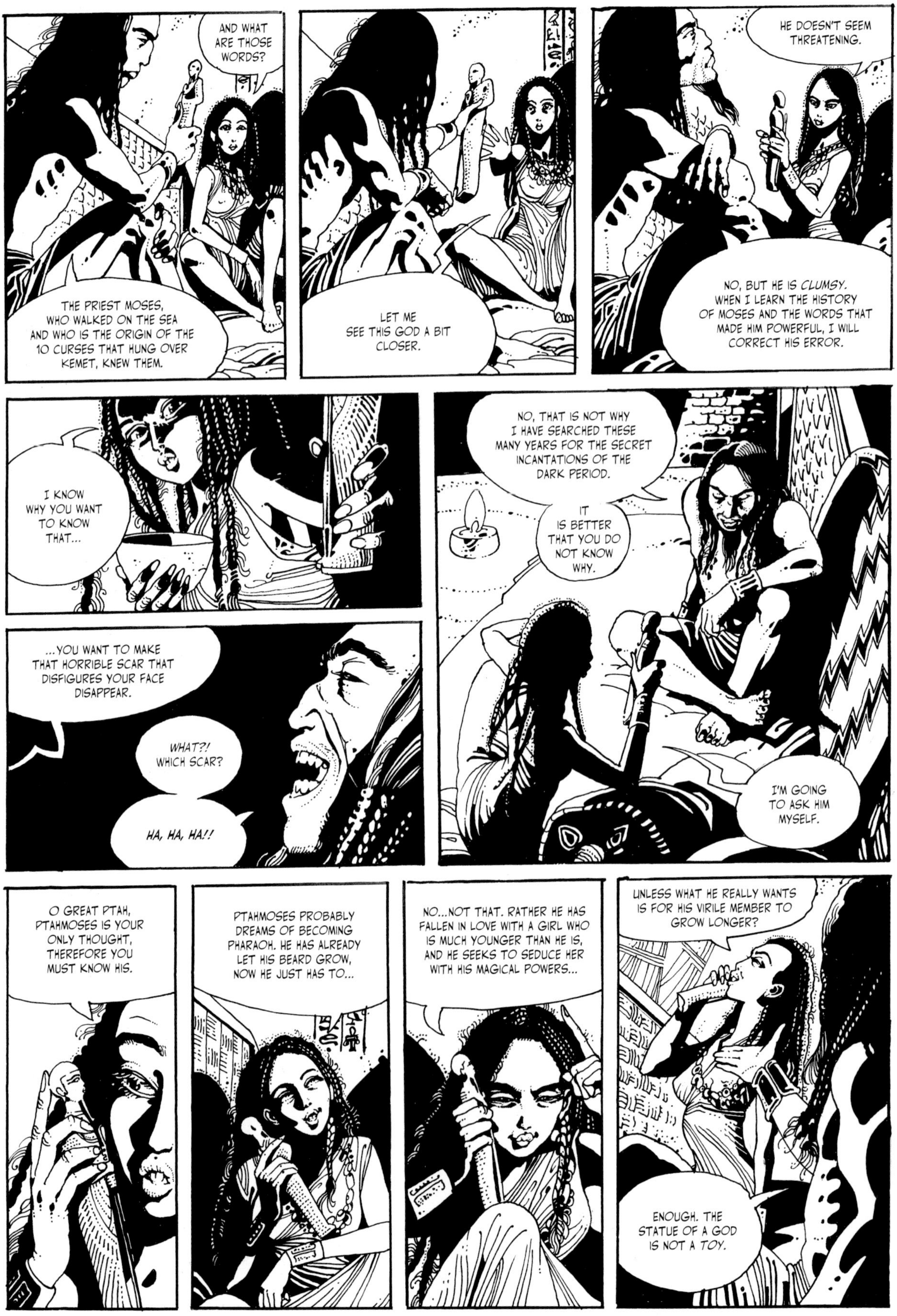
AND WHAT ARE THOSE WORDS?
THE PRIEST MOSES, WHO WALKED ON THE SEA AND WHO IS THE ORIGIN OF THE 10 CURSES THAT HUNG OVER KEMET, KNEW THEM.
LET ME SEE THIS GOD A BIT CLOSER.
HE DOESN'T SEEM THREATENING.
NO, BUT HE IS *CLUMSY*. WHEN I LEARN THE HISTORY OF MOSES AND THE WORDS THAT MADE HIM POWERFUL, I WILL CORRECT HIS ERROR.
I KNOW WHY YOU WANT TO KNOW THAT...
NO, THAT IS NOT WHY I HAVE SEARCHED THESE MANY YEARS FOR THE SECRET INCANTATIONS OF THE DARK PERIOD.
IT IS BETTER THAT YOU DO NOT KNOW WHY.
...YOU WANT TO MAKE THAT HORRIBLE SCAR THAT DISFIGURES YOUR FACE DISAPPEAR.
WHAT?! WHICH SCAR?
HA, HA, HA!!
I'M GOING TO ASK HIM MYSELF.
O GREAT PTAH, PTAHMOSES IS YOUR ONLY THOUGHT, THEREFORE YOU MUST KNOW HIS.
PTAHMOSES PROBABLY DREAMS OF BECOMING PHARAOH. HE HAS ALREADY LET HIS BEARD GROW, NOW HE JUST HAS TO...
NO...NOT THAT. RATHER HE HAS FALLEN IN LOVE WITH A GIRL WHO IS MUCH YOUNGER THAN HE IS, AND HE SEEKS TO SEDUCE HER WITH HIS MAGICAL POWERS...
UNLESS WHAT HE REALLY WANTS IS FOR HIS VIRILE MEMBER TO GROW LONGER?
ENOUGH. THE STATUE OF A GOD IS NOT A *TOY*.

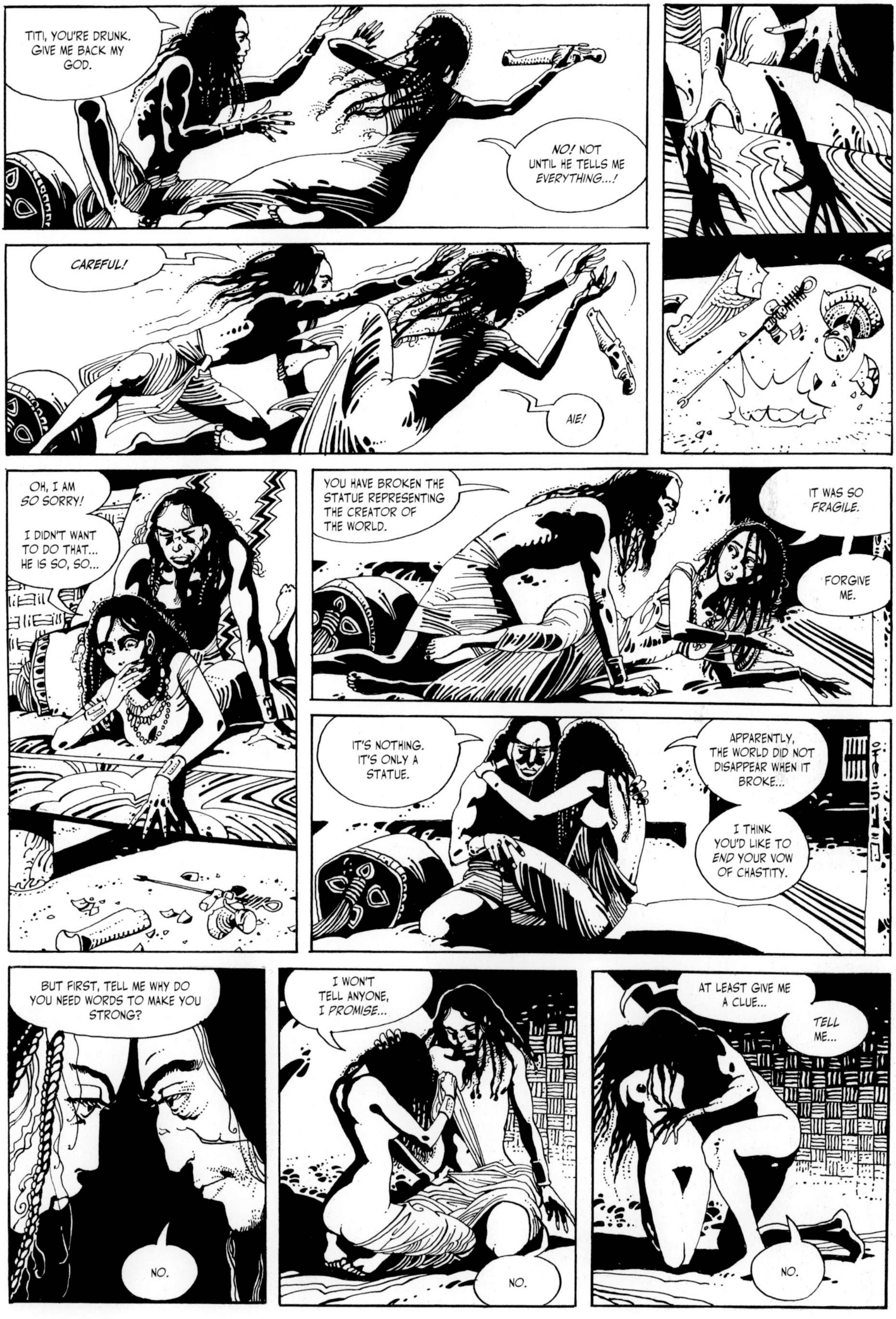
TITI, YOU'RE DRUNK. GIVE ME BACK MY GOD.
NO! NOT UNTIL HE TELLS ME EVERYTHING...!
CAREFUL!
AIE!
OH, I AM SO SORRY!
I DIDN'T WANT TO DO THAT... HE IS SO, SO...
YOU HAVE BROKEN THE STATUE REPRESENTING THE CREATOR OF THE WORLD.
IT WAS SO FRAGILE.
FORGIVE ME.
IT'S NOTHING. IT'S ONLY A STATUE.
APPARENTLY, THE WORLD DID NOT DISAPPEAR WHEN IT BROKE...
I THINK YOU'D LIKE TO END YOUR VOW OF CHASTITY.
BUT FIRST, TELL ME WHY DO YOU NEED WORDS TO MAKE YOU STRONG?
NO.
I WON'T TELL ANYONE, I PROMISE...
NO.
AT LEAST GIVE ME A CLUE...
TELL ME...
NO.

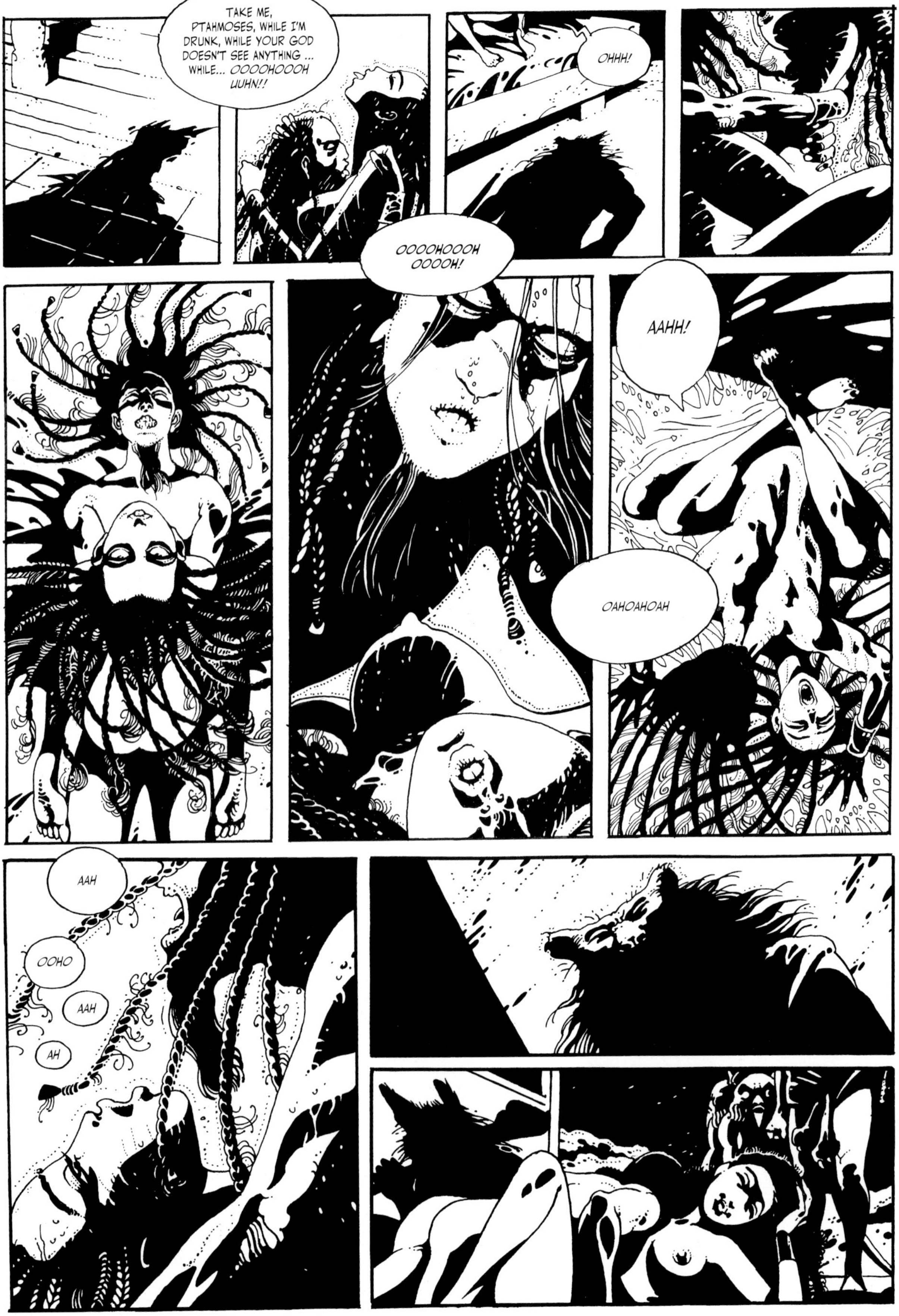
TAKE ME, PTAHMOSES, WHILE I'M DRUNK, WHILE YOUR GOD DOESN'T SEE ANYTHING ... WHILE... OOOOHOOOH UUHN!!
OHHH!
OOOOHOOOH OOOOH!
AAHH!
OAHOAHOAH
AAH
OOHO
AAH
AH

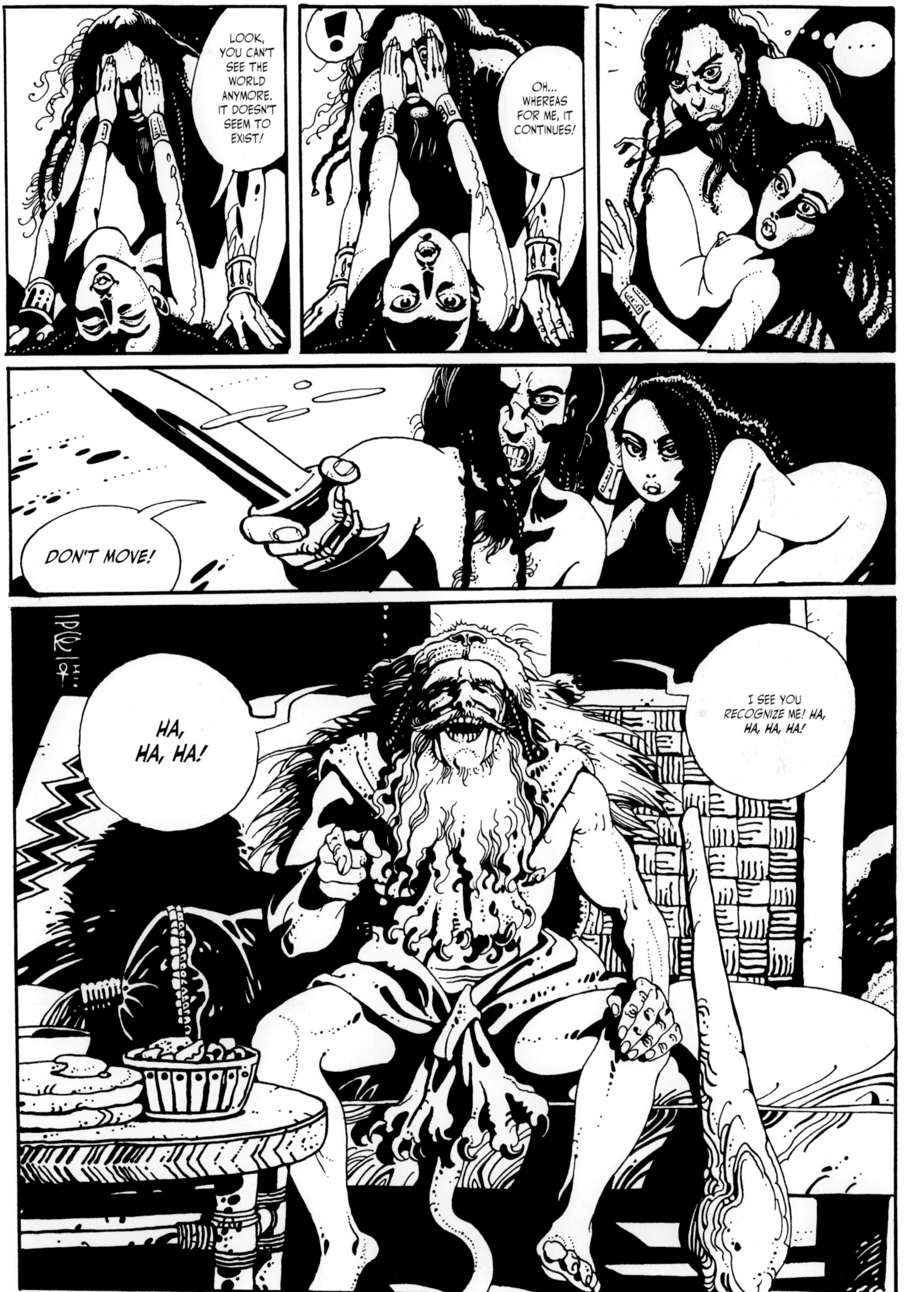
LOOK, YOU CAN'T SEE THE WORLD ANYMORE. IT DOESN'T SEEM TO EXIST!
!
OH... WHEREAS FOR ME, IT CONTINUES!
...
DON'T MOVE!
HA, HA, HA!
I SEE YOU RECOGNIZE ME! HA, HA, HA, HA!

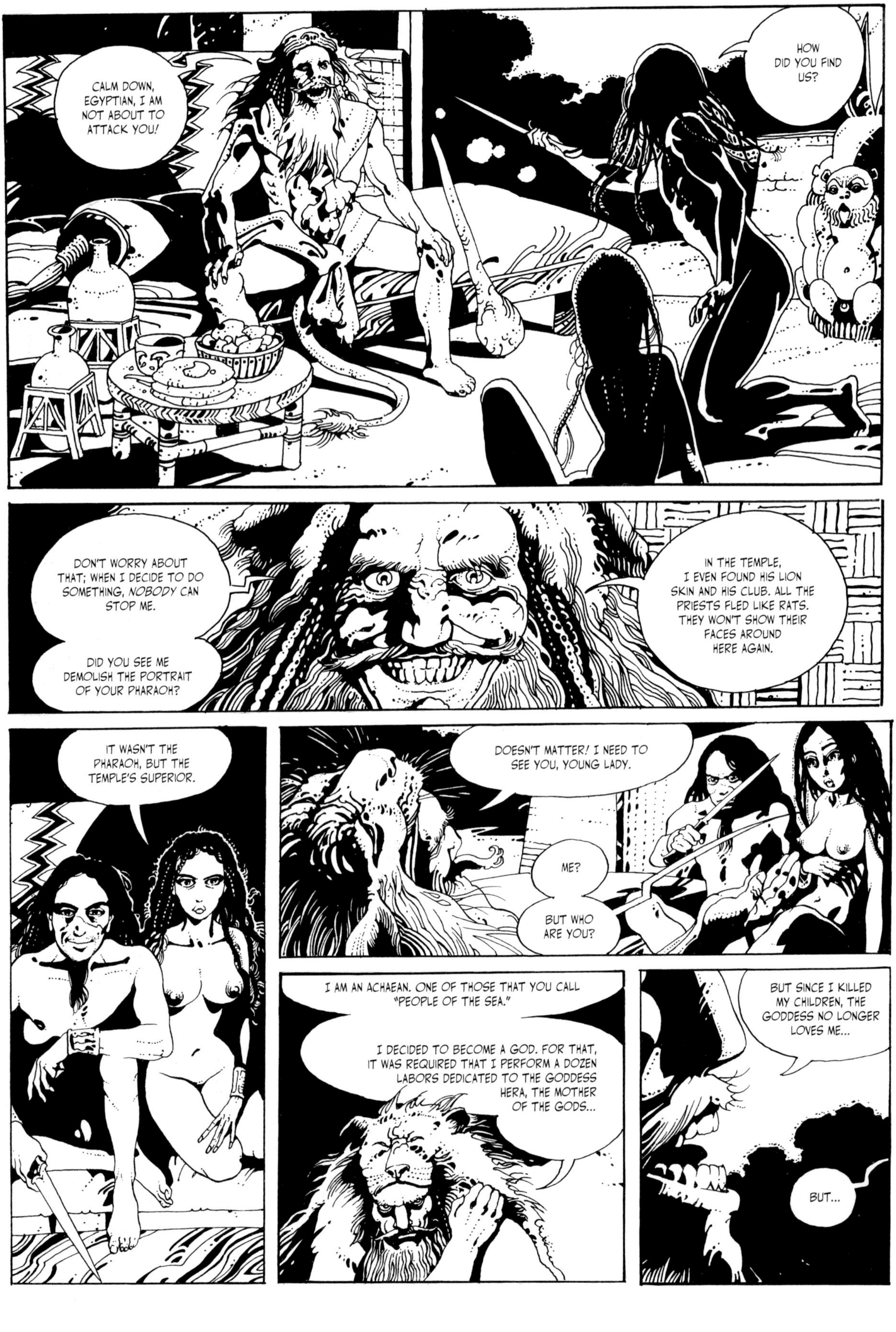
CALM DOWN, EGYPTIAN, I AM NOT ABOUT TO ATTACK YOU!
HOW DID YOU FIND US?
DON'T WORRY ABOUT THAT; WHEN I DECIDE TO DO SOMETHING, NOBODY CAN STOP ME.
DID YOU SEE ME DEMOLISH THE PORTRAIT OF YOUR PHARAOH?
IN THE TEMPLE, I EVEN FOUND HIS LION SKIN AND HIS CLUB. ALL THE PRIESTS FLED LIKE RATS. THEY WON'T SHOW THEIR FACES AROUND HERE AGAIN.
IT WASN'T THE PHARAOH, BUT THE TEMPLE'S SUPERIOR.
DOESN'T MATTER! I NEED TO SEE YOU, YOUNG LADY.
ME?
BUT WHO ARE YOU?
I AM AN ACHAEAN. ONE OF THOSE THAT YOU CALL "PEOPLE OF THE SEA."
I DECIDED TO BECOME A GOD. FOR THAT, IT WAS REQUIRED THAT I PERFORM A DOZEN LABORS DEDICATED TO THE GODDESS HERA, THE MOTHER OF THE GODS...
BUT SINCE I KILLED MY CHILDREN, THE GODDESS NO LONGER LOVES ME...
BUT...

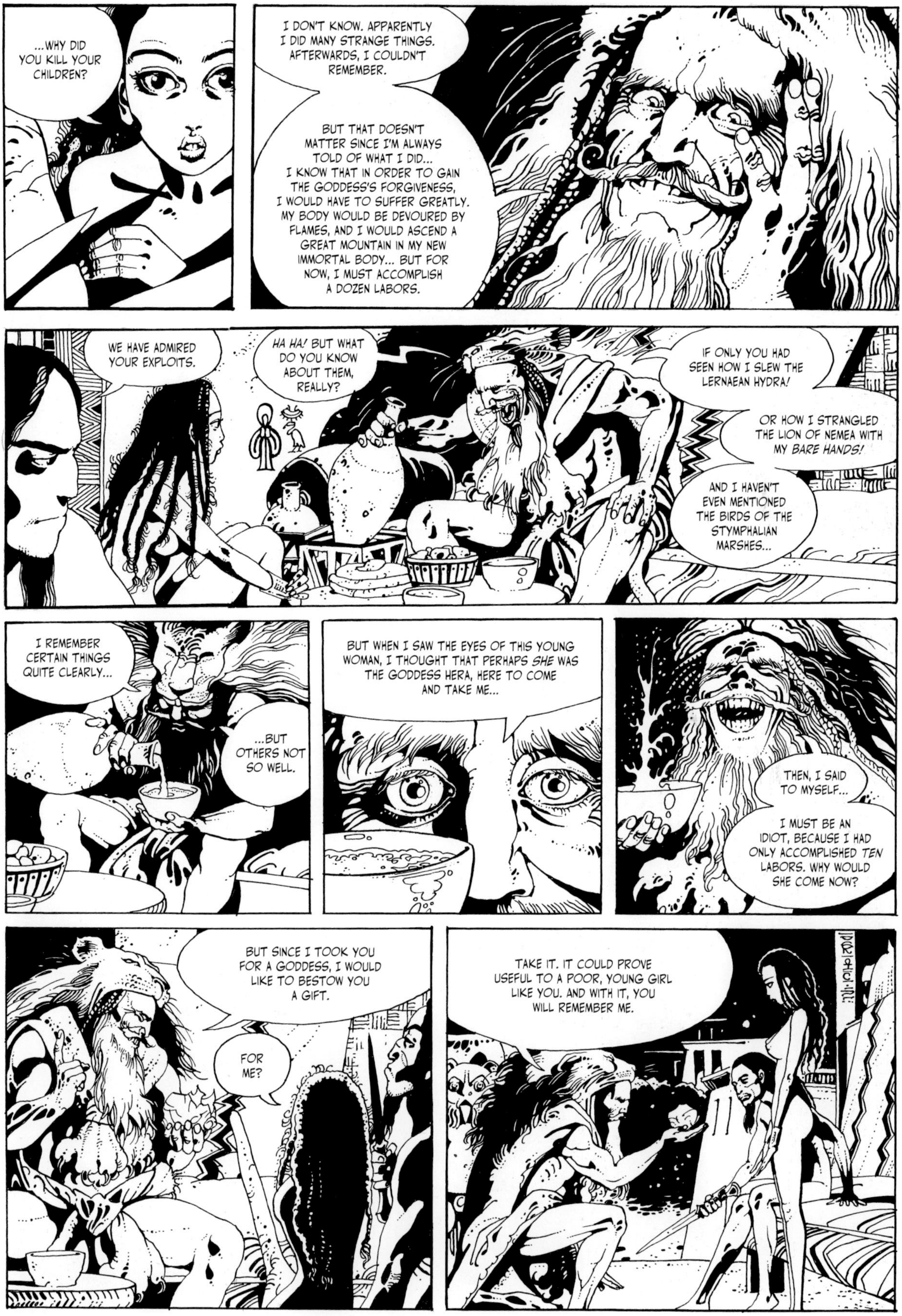
...WHY DID YOU KILL YOUR CHILDREN?
I DON'T KNOW. APPARENTLY I DID MANY STRANGE THINGS. AFTERWARDS, I COULDN'T REMEMBER.
BUT THAT DOESN'T MATTER SINCE I'M ALWAYS TOLD OF WHAT I DID... I KNOW THAT IN ORDER TO GAIN THE GODDESS'S FORGIVENESS, I WOULD HAVE TO SUFFER GREATLY. MY BODY WOULD BE DEVOURED BY FLAMES, AND I WOULD ASCEND A GREAT MOUNTAIN IN MY NEW IMMORTAL BODY... BUT FOR NOW, I MUST ACCOMPLISH A DOZEN LABORS.
WE HAVE ADMIRED YOUR EXPLOITS.
HA HA! BUT WHAT DO YOU KNOW ABOUT THEM, REALLY?
IF ONLY YOU HAD SEEN HOW I SLEW THE LERNAEAN HYDRA!
OR HOW I STRANGLED THE LION OF NEMEA WITH MY *BARE HANDS!*
AND I HAVEN'T EVEN MENTIONED THE BIRDS OF THE STYMPHALIAN MARSHES...
I REMEMBER CERTAIN THINGS QUITE CLEARLY...
...BUT OTHERS NOT SO WELL.
BUT WHEN I SAW THE EYES OF THIS YOUNG WOMAN, I THOUGHT THAT PERHAPS *SHE* WAS THE GODDESS HERA, HERE TO COME AND TAKE ME...
THEN, I SAID TO MYSELF...
I MUST BE AN IDIOT, BECAUSE I HAD ONLY ACCOMPLISHED *TEN* LABORS. WHY WOULD SHE COME NOW?
BUT SINCE I TOOK YOU FOR A GODDESS, I WOULD LIKE TO BESTOW YOU A GIFT.
FOR ME?
TAKE IT. IT COULD PROVE USEFUL TO A POOR, YOUNG GIRL LIKE YOU. AND WITH IT, YOU WILL REMEMBER ME.

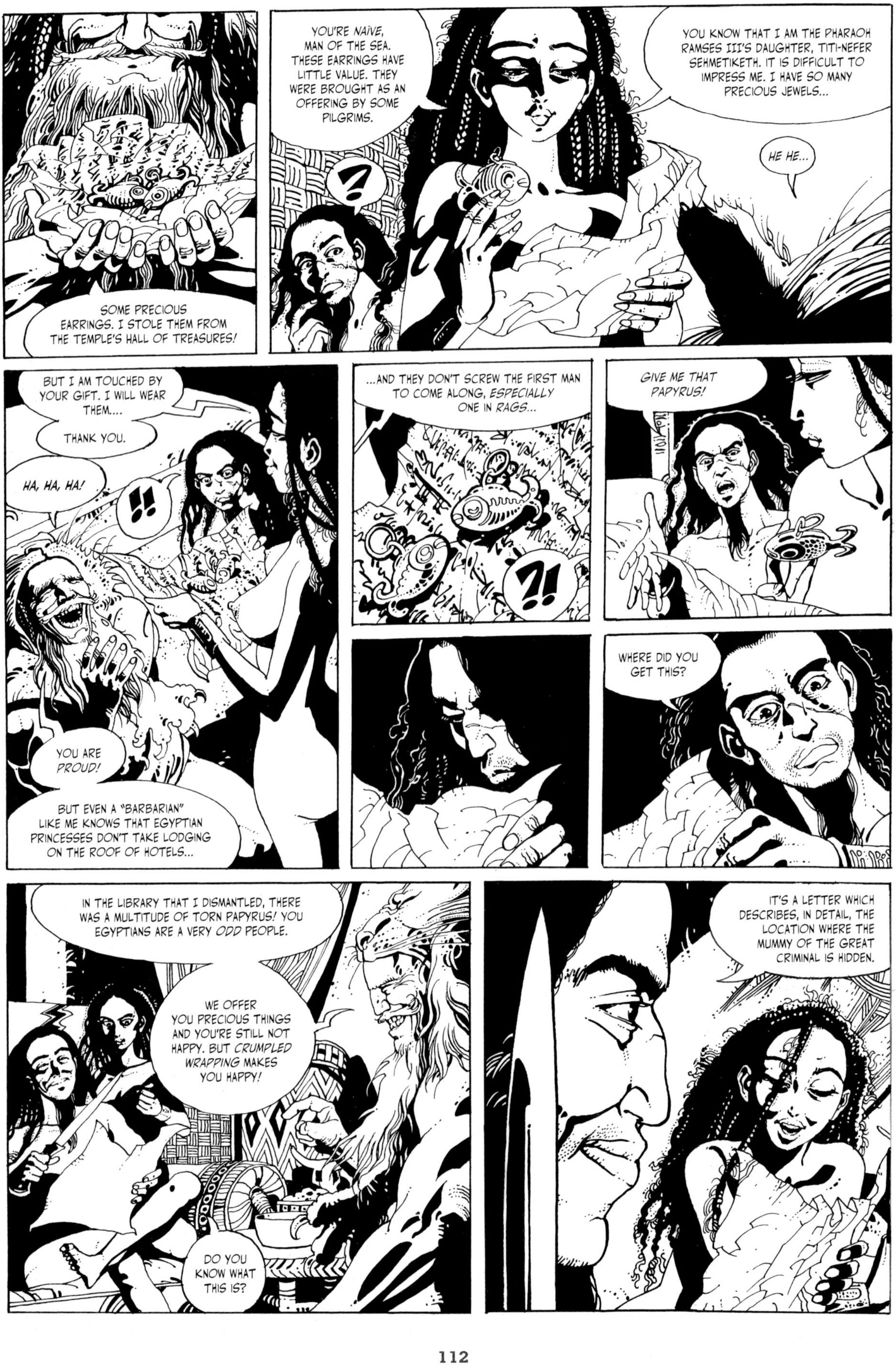
SOME PRECIOUS EARRINGS. I STOLE THEM FROM THE TEMPLE'S HALL OF TREASURES!
YOU'RE NAÏVE, MAN OF THE SEA. THESE EARRINGS HAVE LITTLE VALUE. THEY WERE BROUGHT AS AN OFFERING BY SOME PILGRIMS.
?
YOU KNOW THAT I AM THE PHARAOH RAMSES III'S DAUGHTER, TITI-NEFER SEHMETIKETH. IT IS DIFFICULT TO IMPRESS ME. I HAVE SO MANY PRECIOUS JEWELS...
HE HE...
BUT I AM TOUCHED BY YOUR GIFT. I WILL WEAR THEM....
THANK YOU.
HA, HA, HA!
!!
YOU ARE PROUD!
BUT EVEN A "BARBARIAN" LIKE ME KNOWS THAT EGYPTIAN PRINCESSES DON'T TAKE LODGING ON THE ROOF OF HOTELS...
...AND THEY DON'T SCREW THE FIRST MAN TO COME ALONG, ESPECIALLY ONE IN RAGS...
?!
GIVE ME THAT PAPYRUS!
WHERE DID YOU GET THIS?
IN THE LIBRARY THAT I DISMANTLED, THERE WAS A MULTITUDE OF TORN PAPYRUS! YOU EGYPTIANS ARE A VERY ODD PEOPLE.
WE OFFER YOU PRECIOUS THINGS AND YOU'RE STILL NOT HAPPY. BUT CRUMPLED WRAPPING MAKES YOU HAPPY!
DO YOU KNOW WHAT THIS IS?
IT'S A LETTER WHICH DESCRIBES, IN DETAIL, THE LOCATION WHERE THE MUMMY OF THE GREAT CRIMINAL IS HIDDEN.

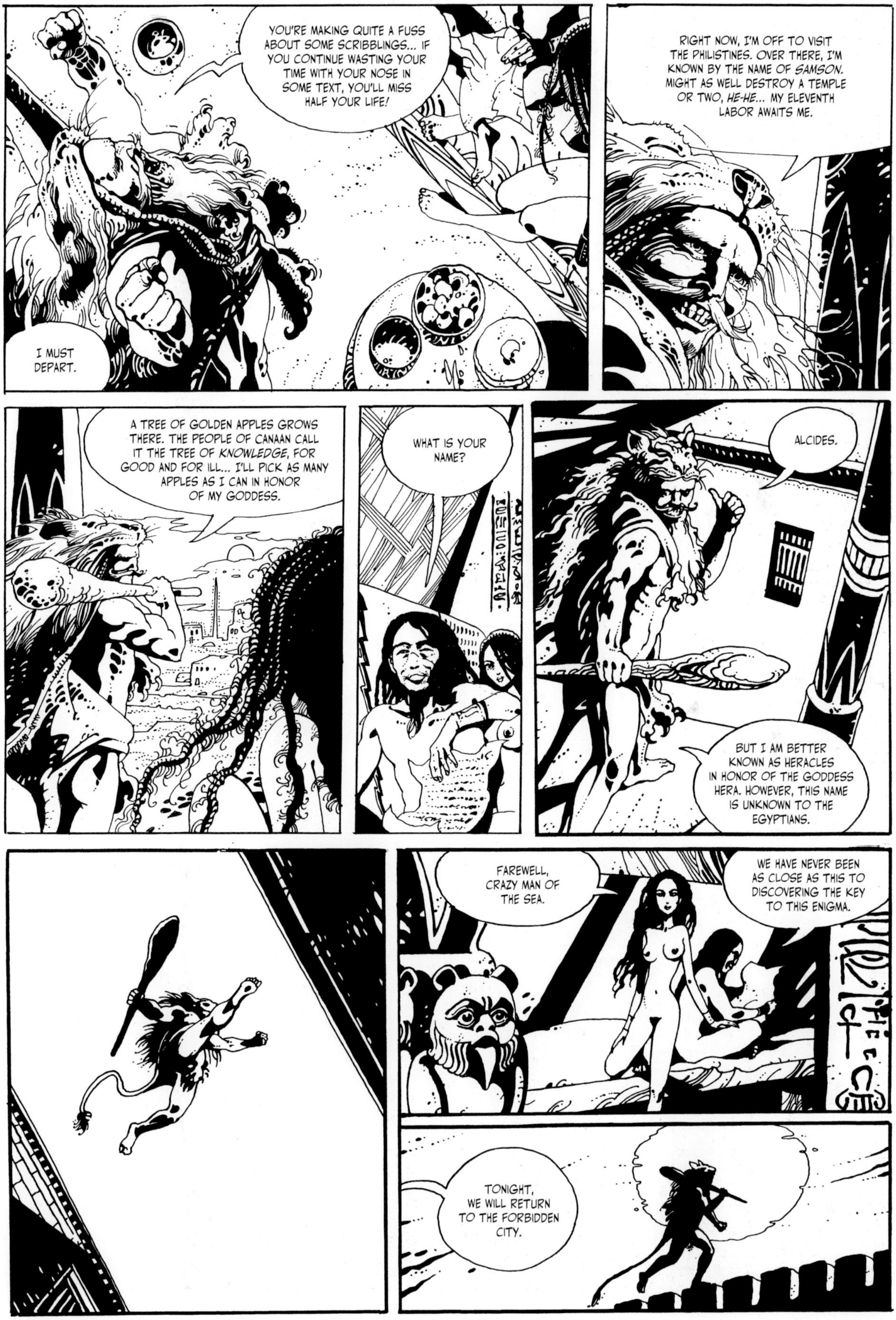
YOU'RE MAKING QUITE A FUSS ABOUT SOME SCRIBBLINGS... IF YOU CONTINUE WASTING YOUR TIME WITH YOUR NOSE IN SOME TEXT, YOU'LL MISS HALF YOUR LIFE!
I MUST DEPART.
RIGHT NOW, I'M OFF TO VISIT THE PHILISTINES. OVER THERE, I'M KNOWN BY THE NAME OF *SAMSON.* MIGHT AS WELL DESTROY A TEMPLE OR TWO, *HE-HE*... MY ELEVENTH LABOR AWAITS ME.
A TREE OF GOLDEN APPLES GROWS THERE. THE PEOPLE OF CANAAN CALL IT THE TREE OF *KNOWLEDGE*, FOR GOOD AND FOR ILL... I'LL PICK AS MANY APPLES AS I CAN IN HONOR OF MY GODDESS.
WHAT IS YOUR NAME?
ALCIDES.
BUT I AM BETTER KNOWN AS HERACLES IN HONOR OF THE GODDESS HERA. HOWEVER, THIS NAME IS UNKNOWN TO THE EGYPTIANS.
FAREWELL, CRAZY MAN OF THE SEA.
WE HAVE NEVER BEEN AS CLOSE AS THIS TO DISCOVERING THE KEY TO THIS ENIGMA.
TONIGHT, WE WILL RETURN TO THE FORBIDDEN CITY.

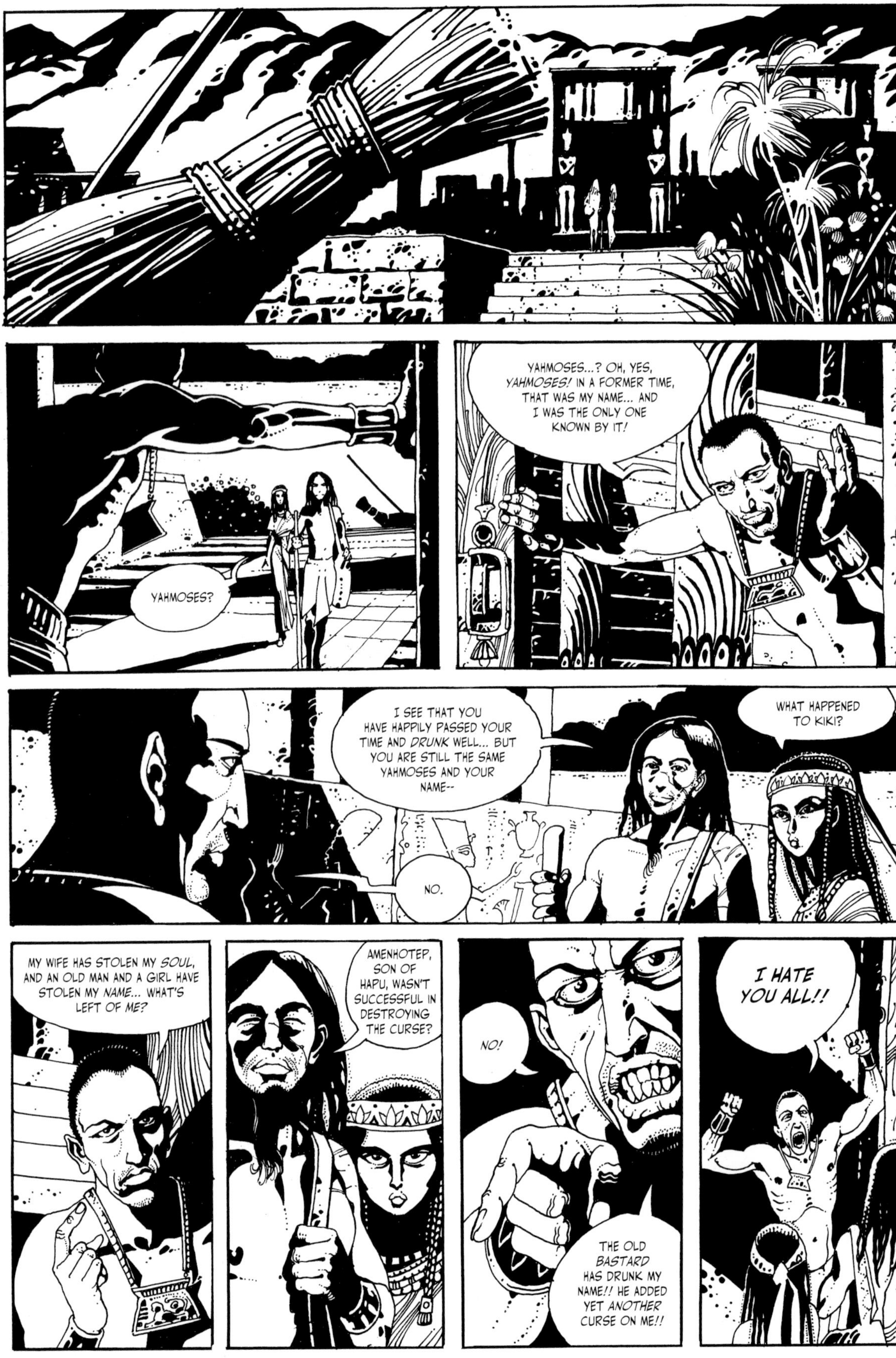
YAHMOSES?
YAHMOSES...? OH, YES, YAHMOSES! IN A FORMER TIME, THAT WAS MY NAME... AND I WAS THE ONLY ONE KNOWN BY IT!
I SEE THAT YOU HAVE HAPPILY PASSED YOUR TIME AND DRUNK WELL... BUT YOU ARE STILL THE SAME YAHMOSES AND YOUR NAME--
NO.
WHAT HAPPENED TO KIKI?
MY WIFE HAS STOLEN MY SOUL, AND AN OLD MAN AND A GIRL HAVE STOLEN MY NAME... WHAT'S LEFT OF ME?
AMENHOTEP, SON OF HAPU, WASN'T SUCCESSFUL IN DESTROYING THE CURSE?
NO!
THE OLD BASTARD HAS DRUNK MY NAME!! HE ADDED YET ANOTHER CURSE ON ME!!
I HATE YOU ALL!!

CALM YOURSELF... YOU WILL REGAIN YOUR NAME. YOU'RE STRONG. I KNOW YOU.

YOU KNOW, I WAS QUITE A GOOD WRESTLER ONCE.

STRONG?! OH YES!!

"ONE DAY I FOUGHT IN BOUTS BEFORE THE PHARAOH (MAY THE GODS GRANT HIM LONG LIFE, HEALTH, AND STRENGTH). I WAS PITTED AGAINST A GIANT BABYLONIAN!"

"HE WAS LIKE ALL BARBARIANS AND RELIED ENTIRELY ON HIS FISTS TO WIN."

"IN THE KINGDOM OF KEMET, CONTESTS REQUIRE AGILITY, AN ABILITY TO FEINT, AND TO ATTACK. ALL THAT I SHOWED HIM."

"AND YOU KNOW WHAT HAPPENED?"

I KNOW. YOU THREW HIM ON THE GROUND. EVERYONE HEARD HIS SKULL CRACK. THE PHARAOH WAS DELIGHTED.

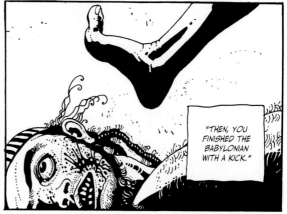

"THEN, YOU FINISHED THE BABYLONIAN WITH A KICK."

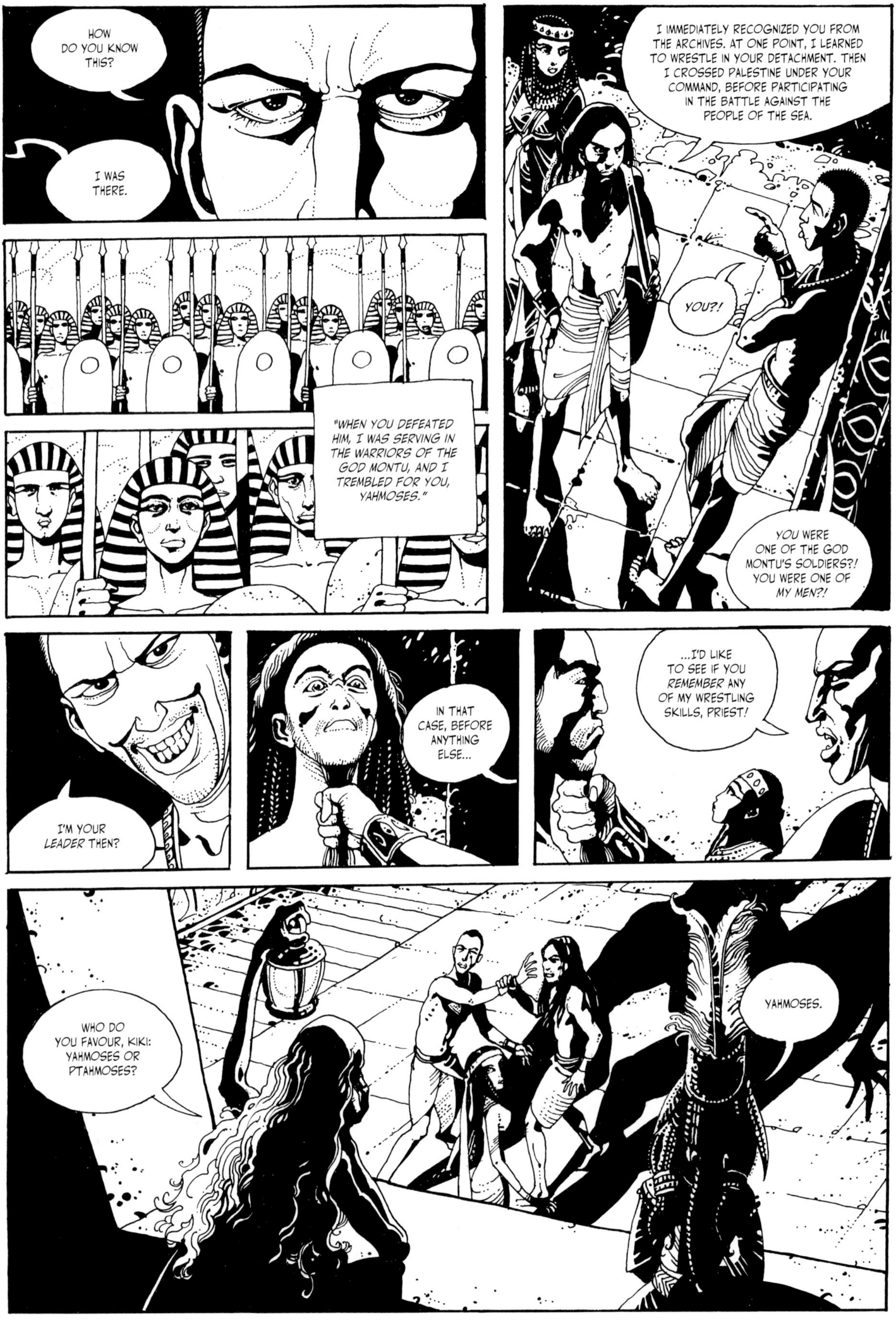
HOW DO YOU KNOW THIS?
I WAS THERE.
"WHEN YOU DEFEATED HIM, I WAS SERVING IN THE WARRIORS OF THE GOD MONTU, AND I TREMBLED FOR YOU, YAHMOSES."
I IMMEDIATELY RECOGNIZED YOU FROM THE ARCHIVES. AT ONE POINT, I LEARNED TO WRESTLE IN YOUR DETACHMENT. THEN I CROSSED PALESTINE UNDER YOUR COMMAND, BEFORE PARTICIPATING IN THE BATTLE AGAINST THE PEOPLE OF THE SEA.
YOU?!
YOU WERE ONE OF THE GOD MONTU'S SOLDIERS?! YOU WERE ONE OF MY MEN?!
I'M YOUR LEADER THEN?
IN THAT CASE, BEFORE ANYTHING ELSE...
...I'D LIKE TO SEE IF YOU REMEMBER ANY OF MY WRESTLING SKILLS, PRIEST!
WHO DO YOU FAVOUR, KIKI: YAHMOSES OR PTAHMOSES?
YAHMOSES.

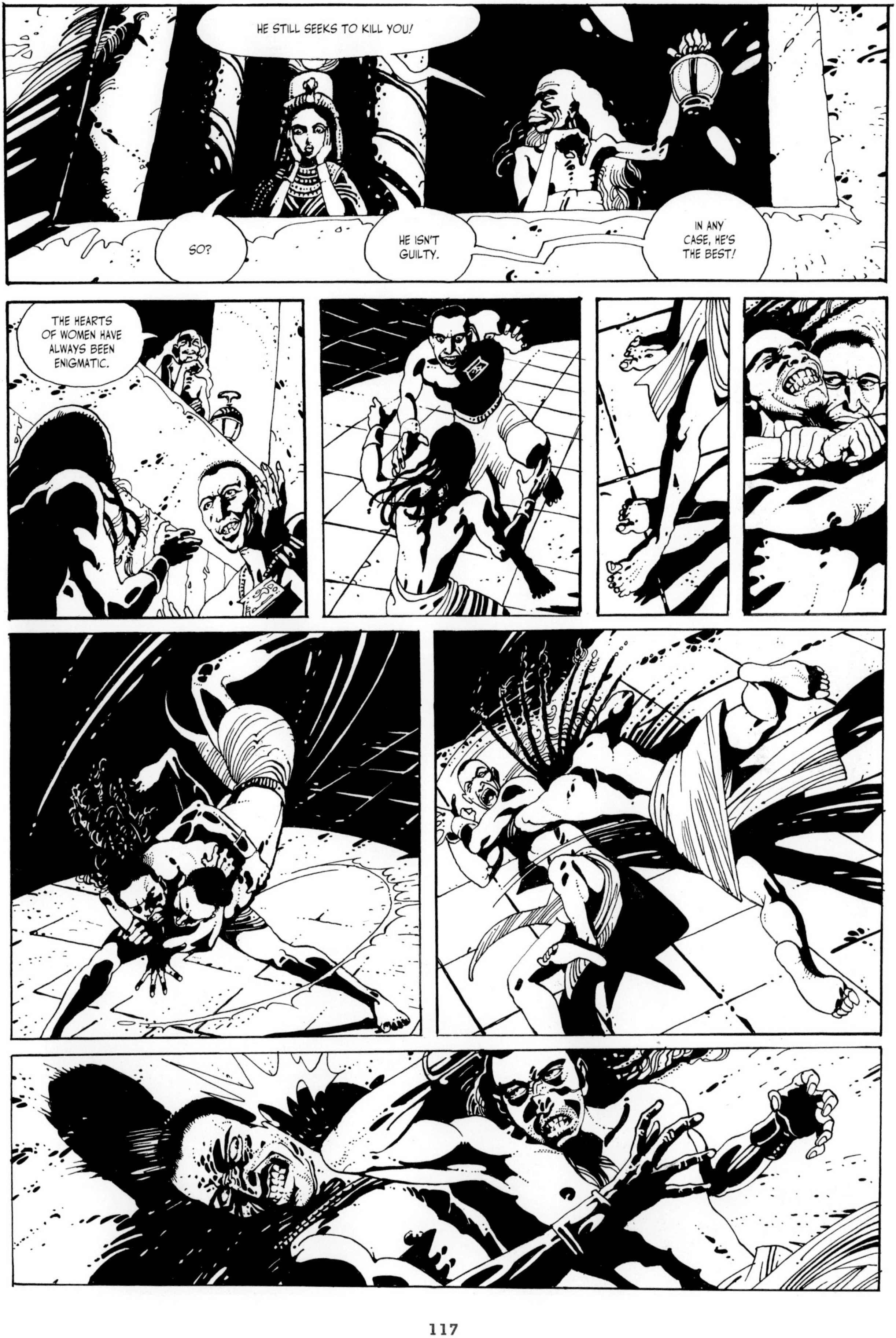
HE STILL SEEKS TO KILL YOU!
SO?
HE ISN'T GUILTY.
IN ANY CASE, HE'S THE BEST!
THE HEARTS OF WOMEN HAVE ALWAYS BEEN ENIGMATIC.

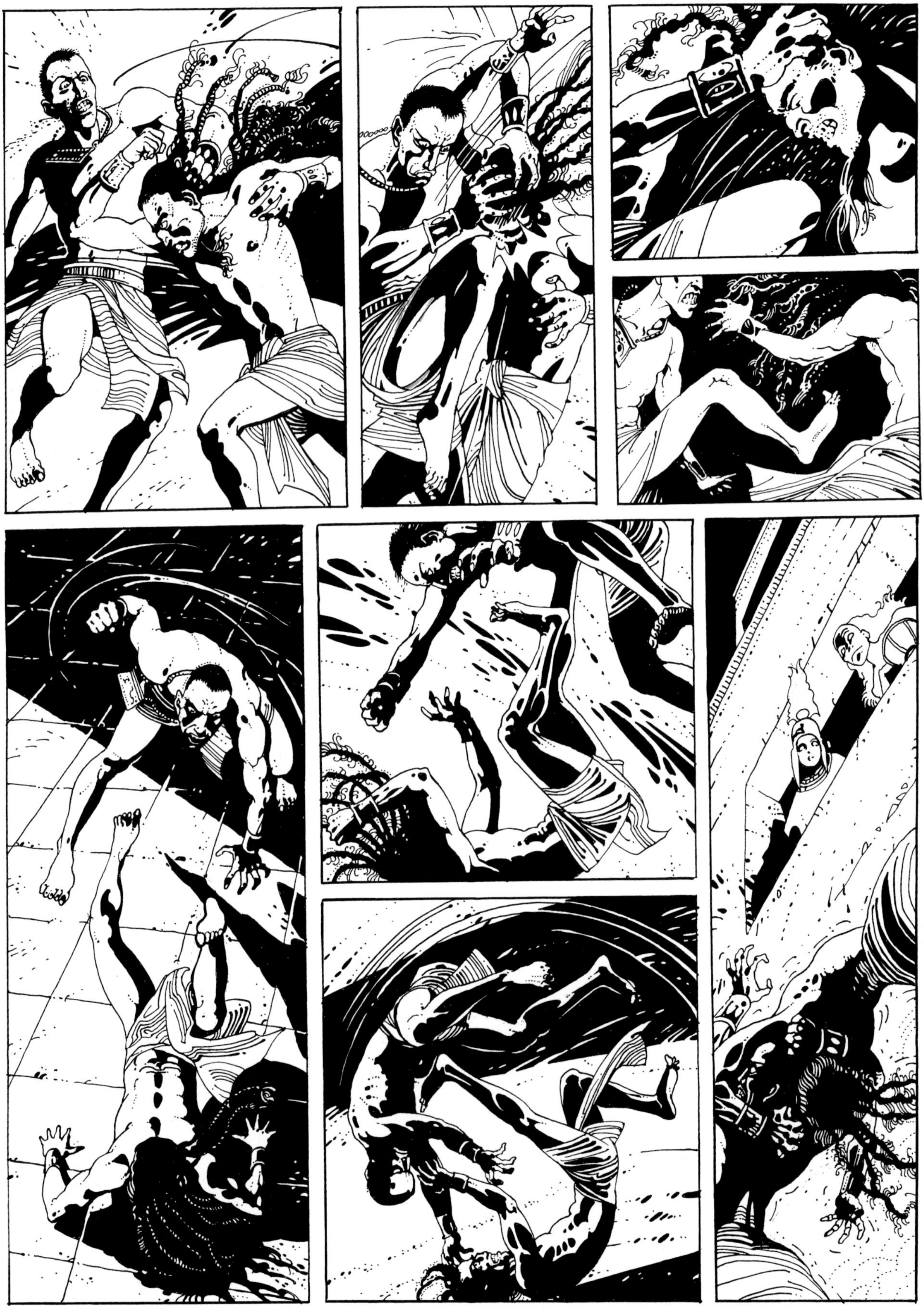

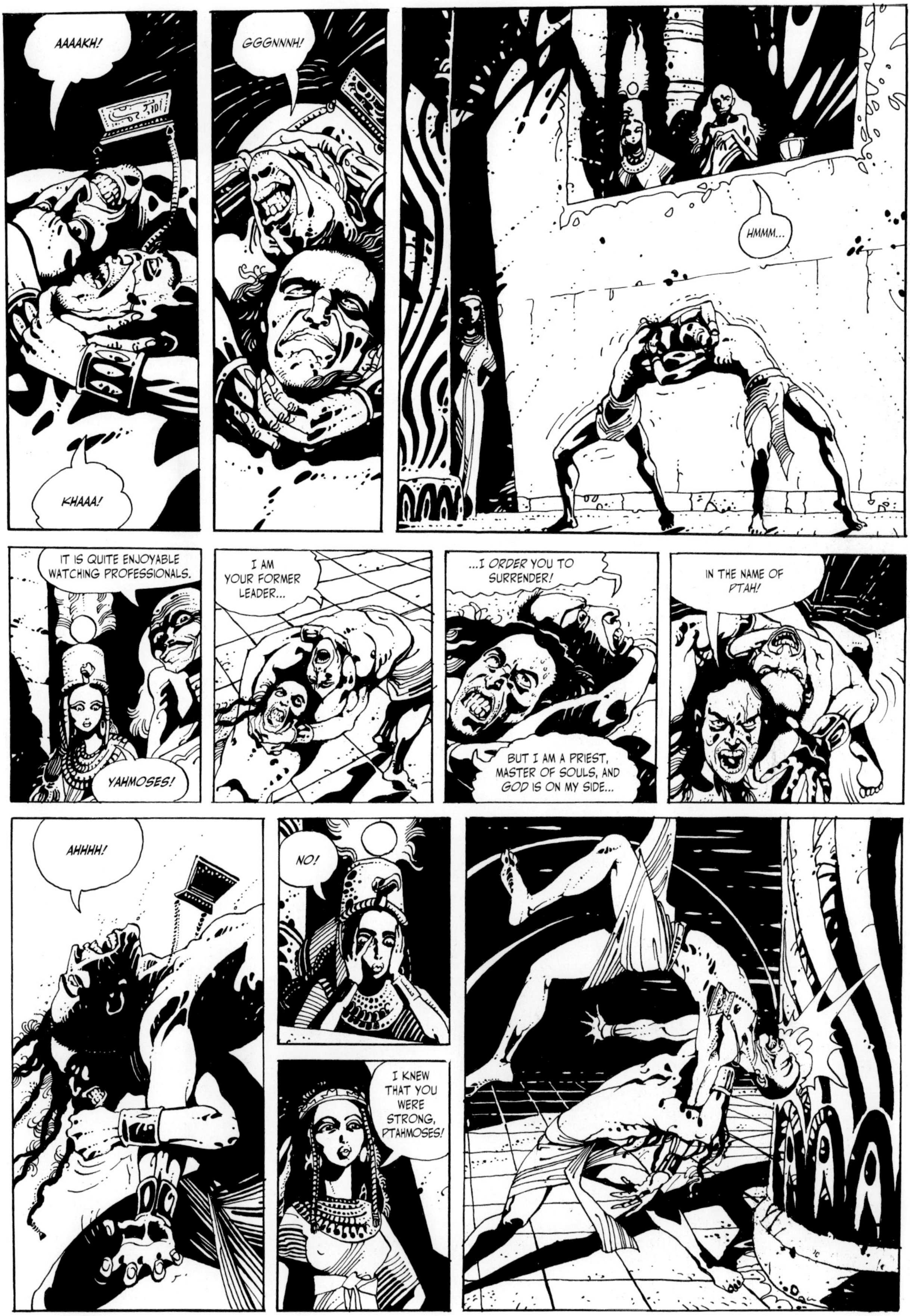

AAAAKH!
KHAAA!
GGGNNNH!
HMMM...
IT IS QUITE ENJOYABLE WATCHING PROFESSIONALS.
YAHMOSES!
I AM YOUR FORMER LEADER...
...I *ORDER* YOU TO SURRENDER!
BUT I AM A PRIEST, MASTER OF SOULS, AND *GOD* IS ON MY SIDE...
IN THE NAME OF *PTAH!*
AHHHH!
NO!
I KNEW THAT YOU WERE STRONG, PTAHMOSES!

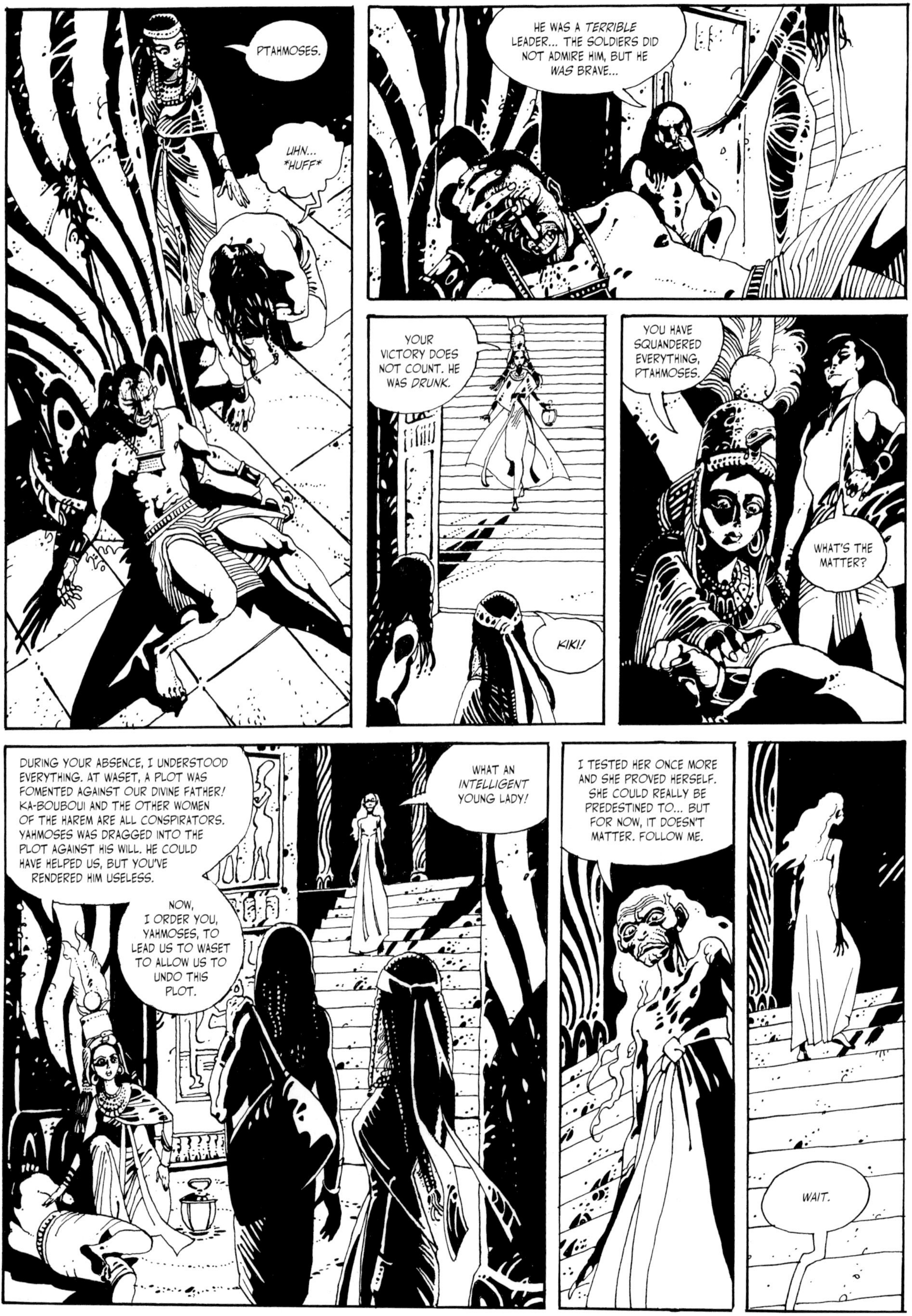
PTAHMOSES.
UHN... *HUFF*
HE WAS A TERRIBLE LEADER... THE SOLDIERS DID NOT ADMIRE HIM, BUT HE WAS BRAVE...
YOUR VICTORY DOES NOT COUNT. HE WAS DRUNK.
KIKI!
YOU HAVE SQUANDERED EVERYTHING, PTAHMOSES.
WHAT'S THE MATTER?
DURING YOUR ABSENCE, I UNDERSTOOD EVERYTHING. AT WASET, A PLOT WAS FOMENTED AGAINST OUR DIVINE FATHER! KA-BOUBOUI AND THE OTHER WOMEN OF THE HAREM ARE ALL CONSPIRATORS. YAHMOSES WAS DRAGGED INTO THE PLOT AGAINST HIS WILL. HE COULD HAVE HELPED US, BUT YOU'VE RENDERED HIM USELESS.
NOW, I ORDER YOU, YAHMOSES, TO LEAD US TO WASET TO ALLOW US TO UNDO THIS PLOT.
WHAT AN INTELLIGENT YOUNG LADY!
I TESTED HER ONCE MORE AND SHE PROVED HERSELF. SHE COULD REALLY BE PREDESTINED TO... BUT FOR NOW, IT DOESN'T MATTER. FOLLOW ME.
WAIT.

HOW DID YOU TEST ME?

WHAT ARE YOU SAYING?

YOU ARE WEARING THE CLOTHING OF A QUEEN, AREN'T YOU? THIS WAS WHAT ALLOWED ME TO SEE IF YOU HAD GOOD FORTUNE...

...OR NOT.

I DON'T UNDERSTAND. EXPLAIN IT TO ME MORE CLEARLY.

VERY WELL. I WANTED TO KNOW WHETHER DESTINY WOULD CONTINUE TO PROTECT YOU, OR IF YOU WERE ONLY THE MEANS TO BRING TITI HERE.

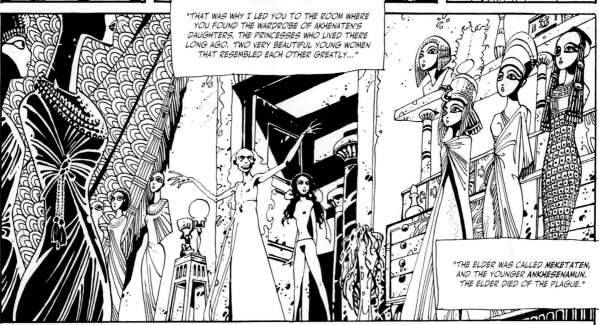

"THAT WAS WHY I LED YOU TO THE ROOM WHERE YOU FOUND THE WARDROBE OF AKHENATEN'S DAUGHTERS, THE PRINCESSES WHO LIVED THERE LONG AGO. TWO VERY BEAUTIFUL YOUNG WOMEN THAT RESEMBLED EACH OTHER GREATLY..."

"THE ELDER WAS CALLED MEKETATEN, AND THE YOUNGER ANKHESENAMUN. THE ELDER DIED OF THE PLAGUE."

"THE YOUNGER LIVED FOR A LONG TIME."

TO THE RIGHT, WERE THE CLOTHES BELONGING TO MEKETATEN. THEY ARE STILL CONTAMINATED WITH THE PLAGUE, AND NO ONE HAS TOUCHED THEM SINCE HER DEATH.

ON THE LEFT, YOU HAD THOSE OF ANKHESENAMUN, AND THEY REPRESENTED NO DANGER AT ALL. NO ONE HAS TOUCHED THEM EITHER.

"NOT SINCE THE CITY WAS ABANDONED."

I PROPOSED THAT KIKI CHOOSE THE CLOTHING SHE WOULD PREFER, AND SHE CHOSE THOSE ON THE LEFT, PROVING THAT HER DESTINY HAS PROTECTED HER. IT WAS A SIMPLE EXPERIMENT.

YOU ARE TRULY THE WICKEDEST OF SCOUNDRELS.

I WARNED YOU.

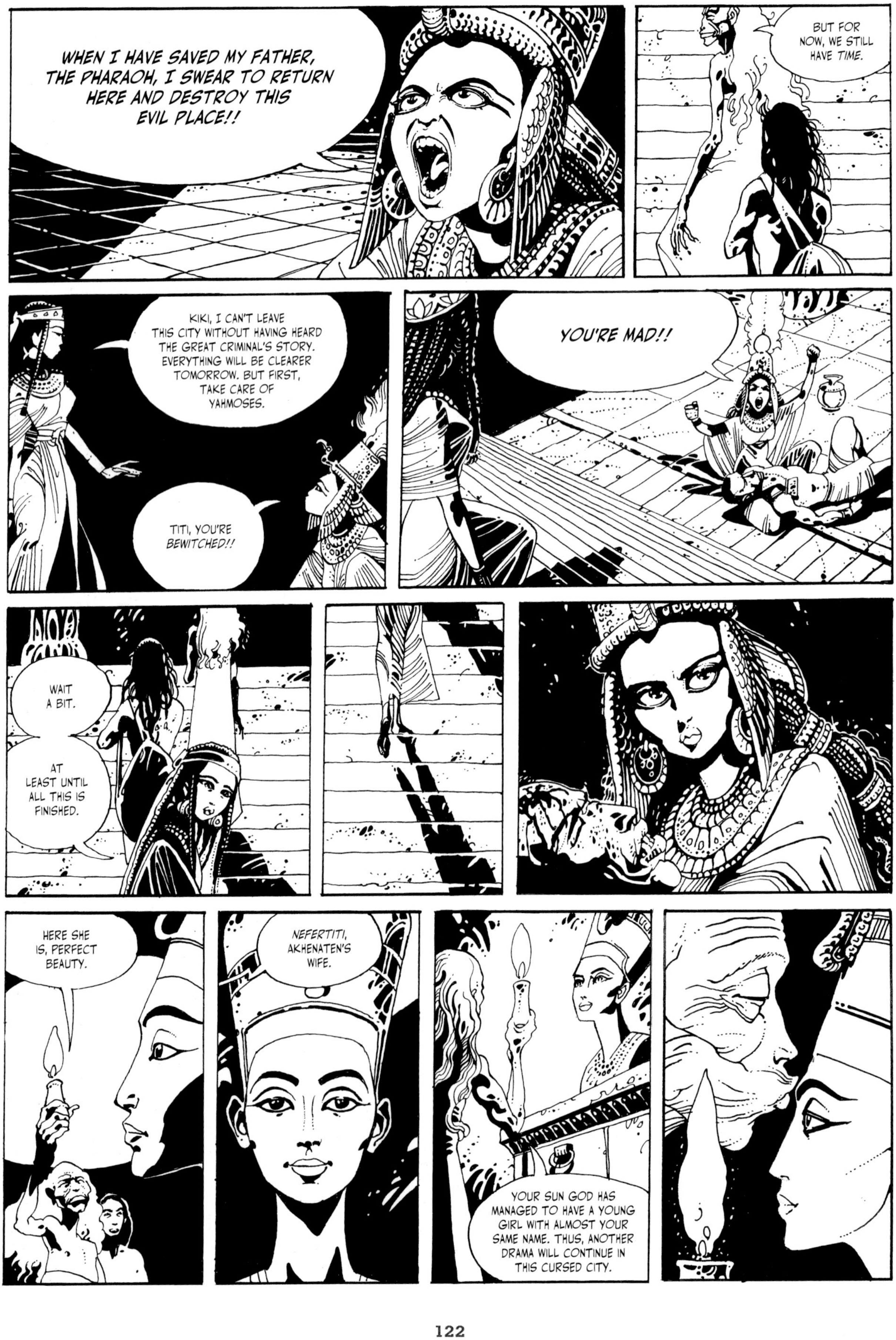
WHEN I HAVE SAVED MY FATHER, THE PHARAOH, I SWEAR TO RETURN HERE AND DESTROY THIS EVIL PLACE!!
BUT FOR NOW, WE STILL HAVE TIME.
KIKI, I CAN'T LEAVE THIS CITY WITHOUT HAVING HEARD THE GREAT CRIMINAL'S STORY. EVERYTHING WILL BE CLEARER TOMORROW. BUT FIRST, TAKE CARE OF YAHMOSES.
TITI, YOU'RE BEWITCHED!!
YOU'RE MAD!!
WAIT A BIT.
AT LEAST UNTIL ALL THIS IS FINISHED.
HERE SHE IS, PERFECT BEAUTY.
NEFERTITI, AKHENATEN'S WIFE.
YOUR SUN GOD HAS MANAGED TO HAVE A YOUNG GIRL WITH ALMOST YOUR SAME NAME. THUS, ANOTHER DRAMA WILL CONTINUE IN THIS CURSED CITY.

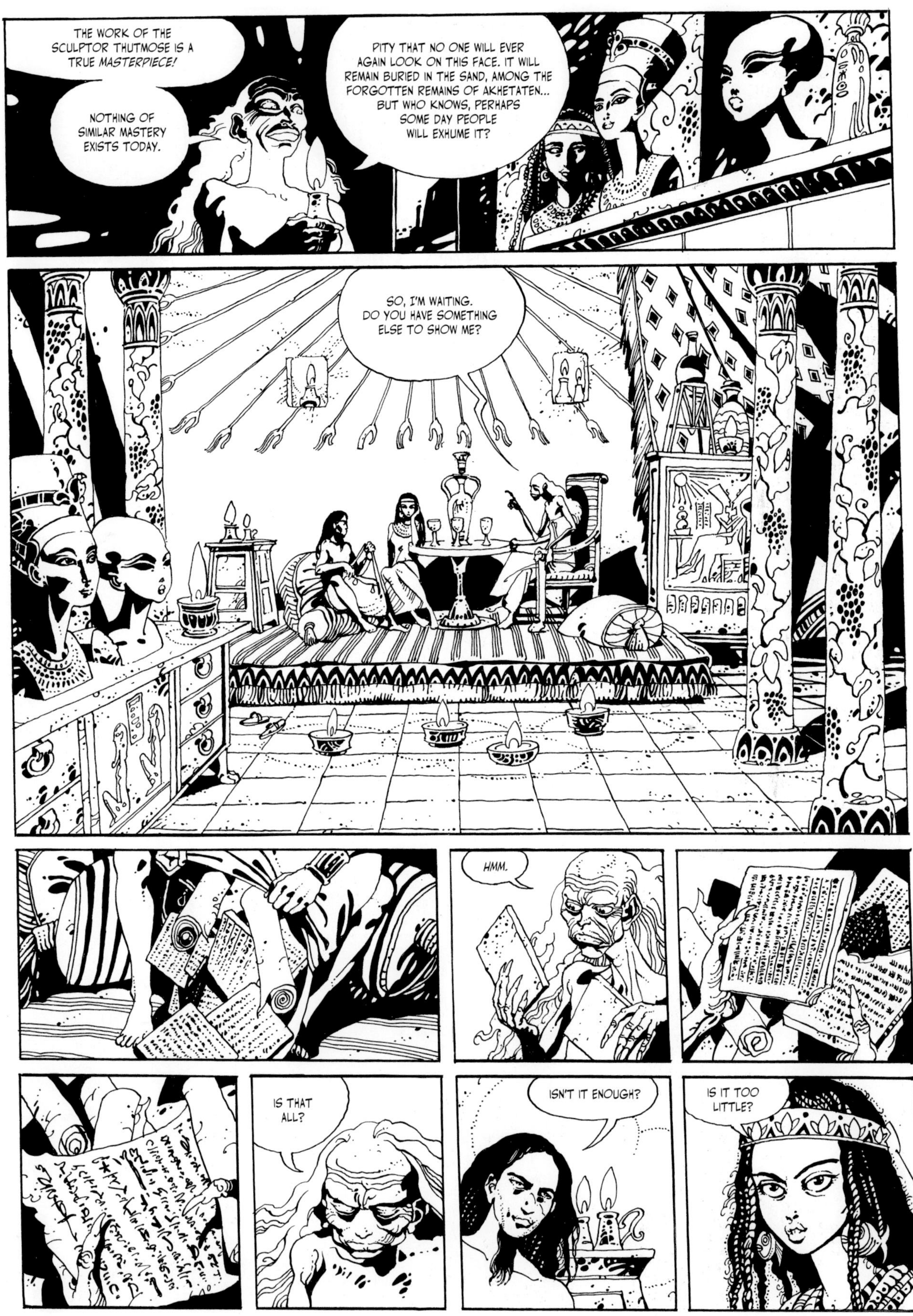
THE WORK OF THE SCULPTOR THUTMOSE IS A TRUE *MASTERPIECE!*
NOTHING OF SIMILAR MASTERY EXISTS TODAY.
PITY THAT NO ONE WILL EVER AGAIN LOOK ON THIS FACE. IT WILL REMAIN BURIED IN THE SAND, AMONG THE FORGOTTEN REMAINS OF AKHETATEN... BUT WHO KNOWS, PERHAPS SOME DAY PEOPLE WILL EXHUME IT?
SO, I'M WAITING. DO YOU HAVE SOMETHING ELSE TO SHOW ME?
HMM.
IS THAT ALL?
ISN'T IT ENOUGH?
IS IT TOO LITTLE?

IS IT POSSIBLE THAT ALL THIS BUSINESS WOULD HAVE BEEN IN VAIN?

NO.

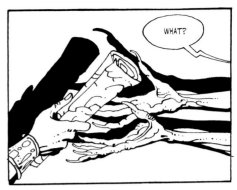

WHAT?

HMM...

IT'S...HER HANDWRITING! THE LETTER IS ADDRESSED TO MINISTER AI OF THE CITY OF KHNUM. IT'S FROM THE QUEEN AND WIDOW...

WHAT?!

IS IT THE LETTER FROM NEFERTITI?

"DEAR MASTER AND FRIEND, THERE IS NO ONE BUT YOU IN WHOM I CAN CONFIDE, THIS OLD MONKEY D'AMEHO..." THAT PART ISN'T IMPORTANT...

"I HAVE PLACED THE BODY OF MY AKHENATEN AWAY FROM HIS ENEMIES, AND I HOPE THAT YOU WILL SOON BE ABLE TO COME TO BURY IT ACCORDING TO THE PRECEPTS OF ATEN... I DON'T HAVE MUCH TIME... I HAVE HIDDEN IT..."

BY SET! THIS IS REALLY CLOSE!!

AND THE HISTORY, AMENHOTEP, SON OF HAPU? TELL US MORE OF THE HISTORY!

I AM AN OLD MAN, MORE THAN 300 YEARS OLD...AND ELDERS DO LIKE *TRADITIONS*. THE KNOWLEDGE THAT I AM GOING TO IMPART TO YOU CANNOT BE HEARD BY ANYONE EXCEPT BY A PRIEST OF THE HIGHEST ORDER. AND A PRIEST MUST SHAVE HIS HEAD. THEREFORE, INDULGE ME.

ALRIGHT... TITI-NEFER, GET DRESSED.

DON'T FORGET TO TAKE THE DRESSES FROM THE *LEFT!* AND YOU, PTAHMOSES, SHAVE YOUR SKULL.

WHY?

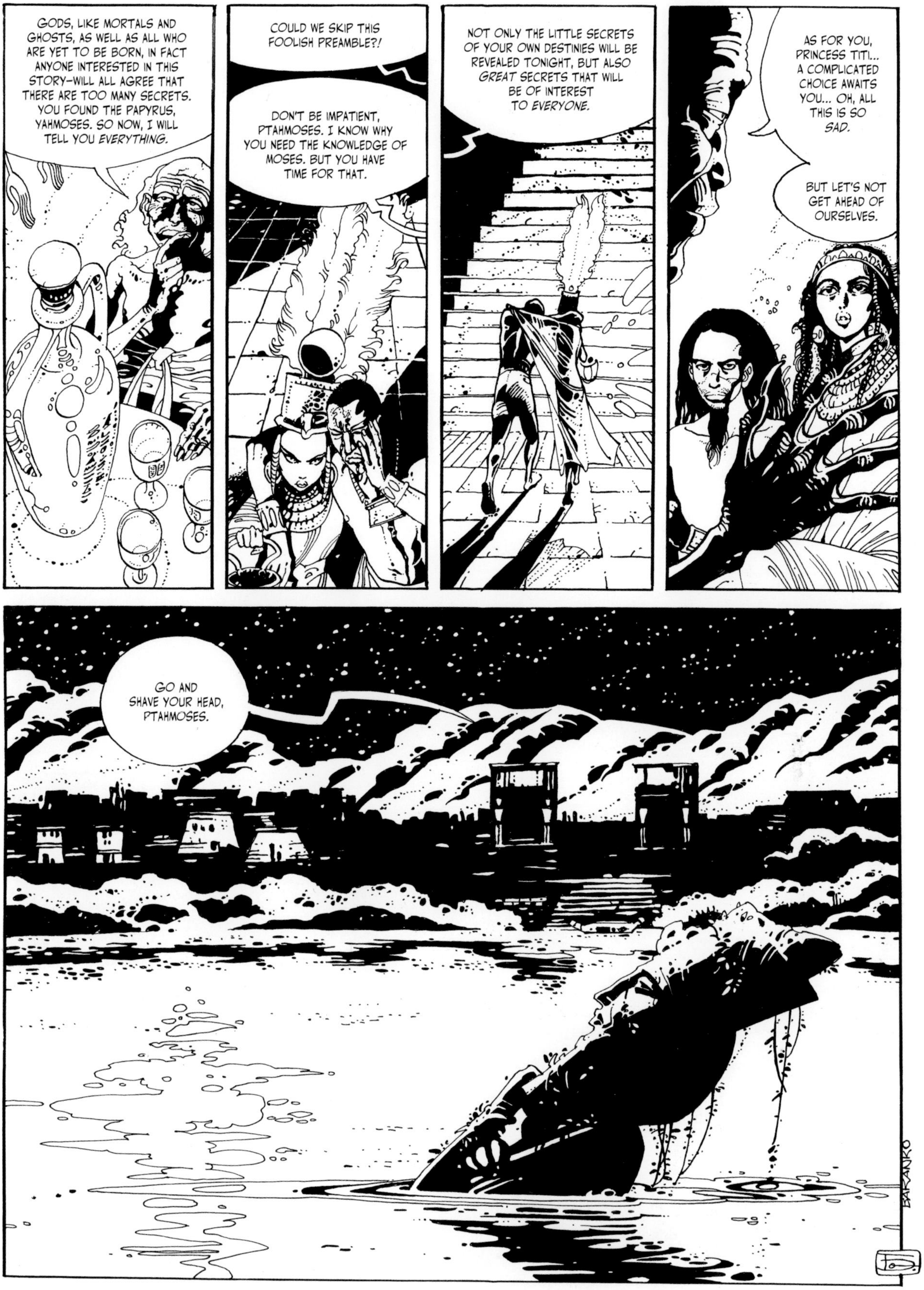
GODS, LIKE MORTALS AND GHOSTS, AS WELL AS ALL WHO ARE YET TO BE BORN, IN FACT ANYONE INTERESTED IN THIS STORY–WILL ALL AGREE THAT THERE ARE TOO MANY SECRETS. YOU FOUND THE PAPYRUS, YAHMOSES. SO NOW, I WILL TELL YOU *EVERYTHING*.
COULD WE SKIP THIS FOOLISH PREAMBLE?!
DON'T BE IMPATIENT, PTAHMOSES. I KNOW WHY YOU NEED THE KNOWLEDGE OF MOSES. BUT YOU HAVE TIME FOR THAT.
NOT ONLY THE LITTLE SECRETS OF YOUR OWN DESTINIES WILL BE REVEALED TONIGHT, BUT ALSO *GREAT* SECRETS THAT WILL BE OF INTEREST TO *EVERYONE*.
AS FOR YOU, PRINCESS TITI... A COMPLICATED CHOICE AWAITS YOU... OH, ALL THIS IS SO *SAD*.
BUT LET'S NOT GET AHEAD OF OURSELVES.
GO AND SHAVE YOUR HEAD, PTAHMOSES.
BARANKO

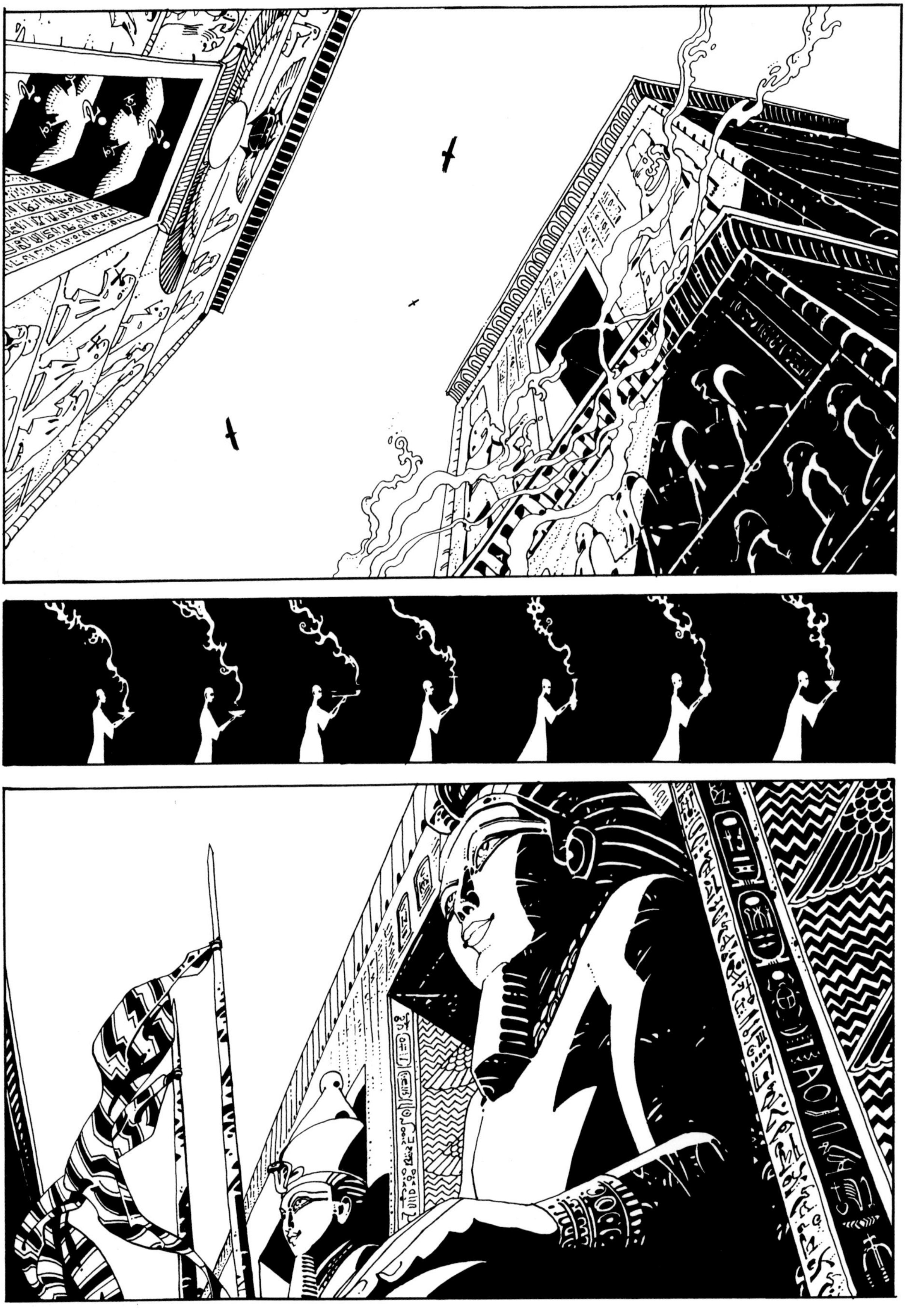

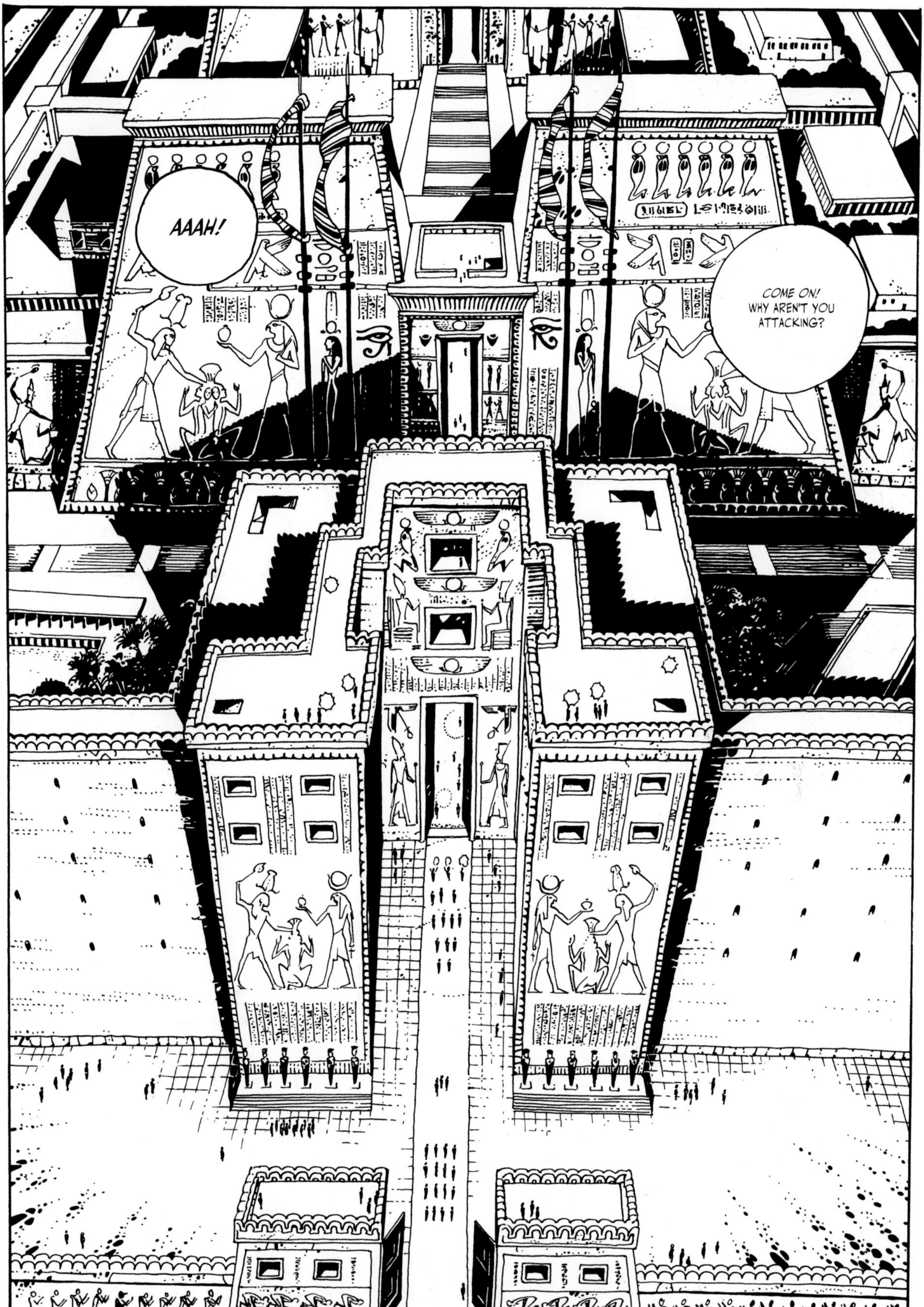
AAAH!
COME ON! WHY AREN'T YOU ATTACKING?

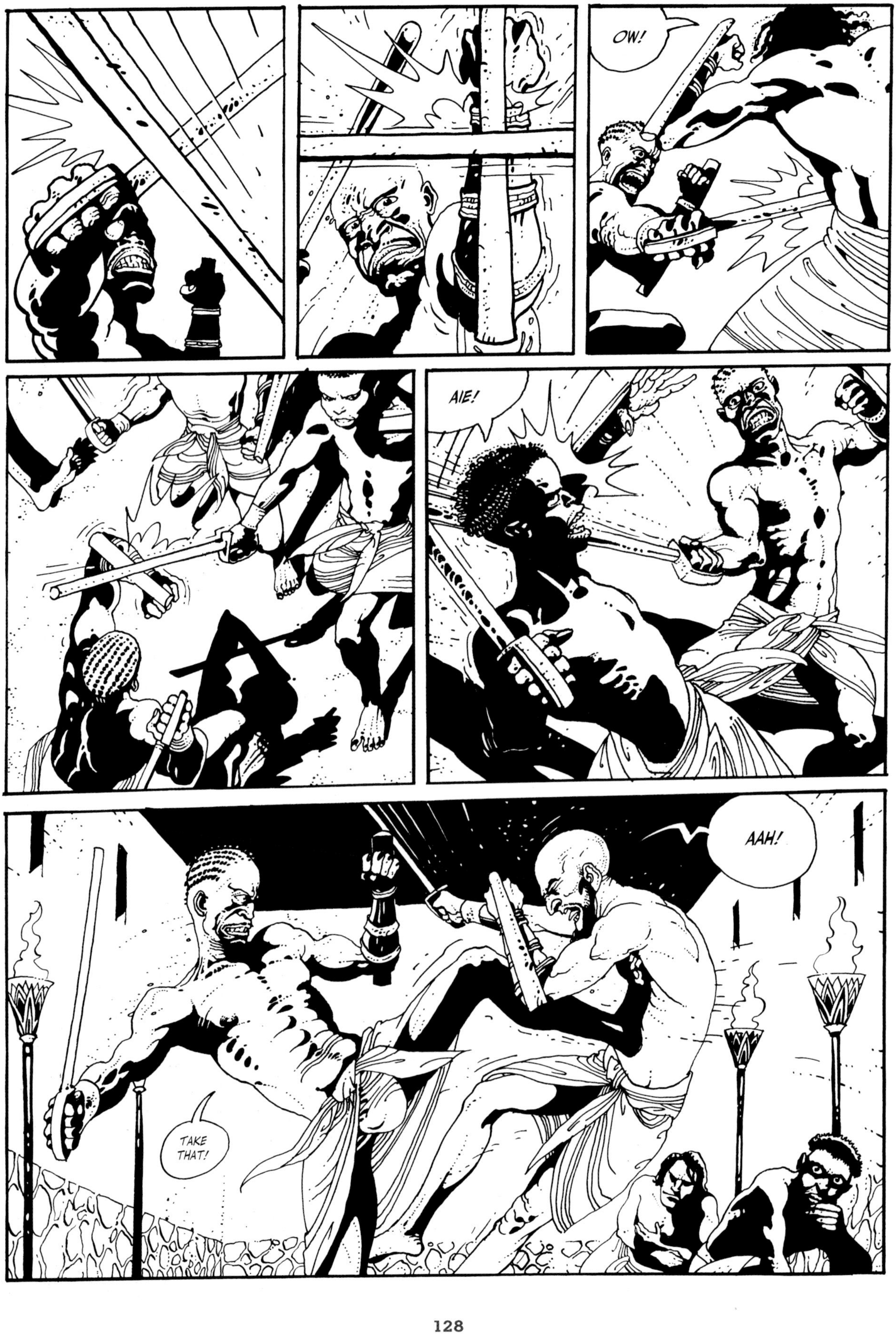
OW!
AIE!
AAH!
TAKE THAT!

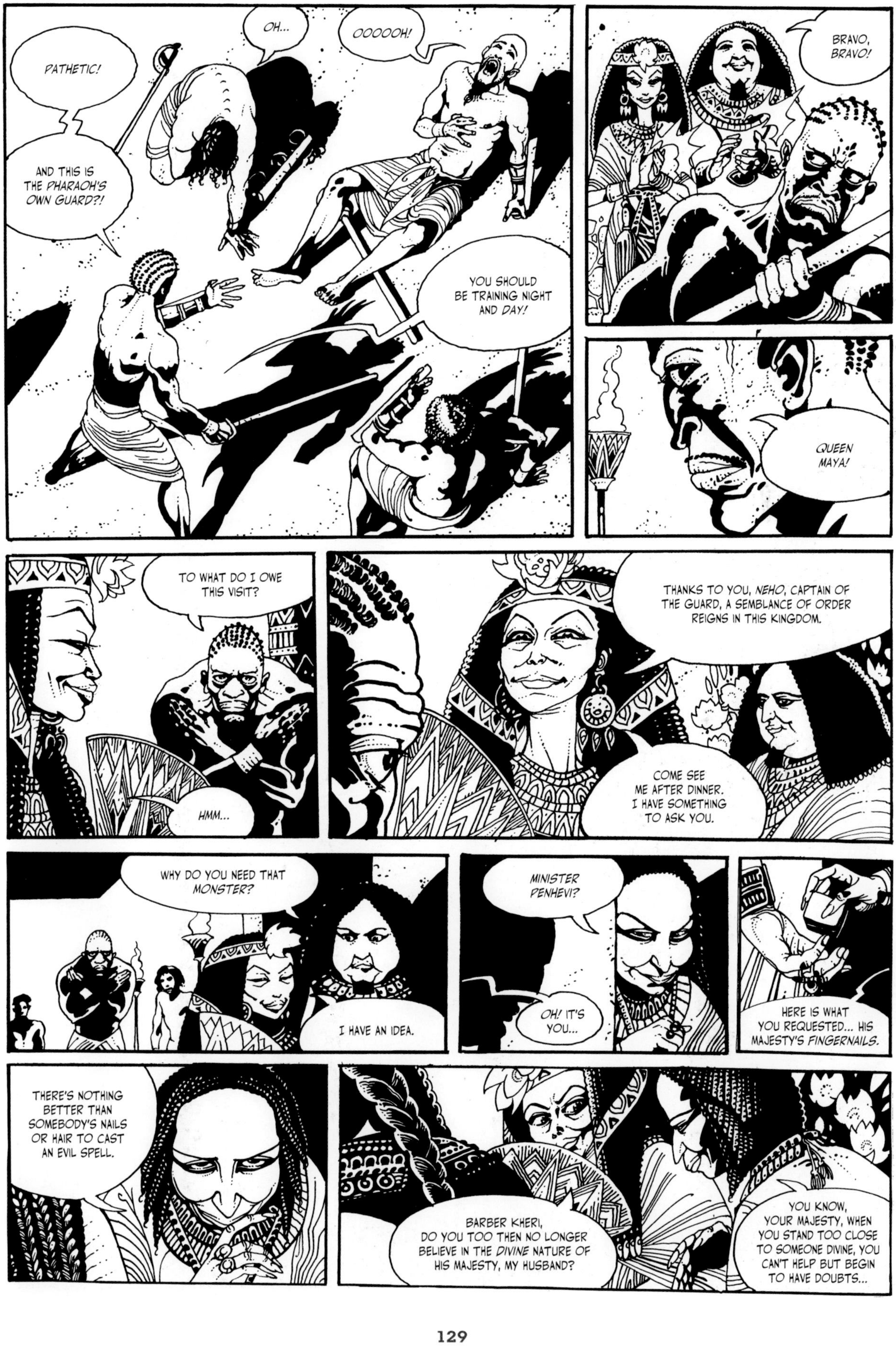
PATHETIC!
AND THIS IS THE PHARAOH'S OWN GUARD?!
OH...
OOOOOH!
YOU SHOULD BE TRAINING NIGHT AND DAY!
BRAVO, BRAVO!
QUEEN MAYA!
TO WHAT DO I OWE THIS VISIT?
HMM...
THANKS TO YOU, NEHO, CAPTAIN OF THE GUARD, A SEMBLANCE OF ORDER REIGNS IN THIS KINGDOM.
COME SEE ME AFTER DINNER. I HAVE SOMETHING TO ASK YOU.
WHY DO YOU NEED THAT MONSTER?
I HAVE AN IDEA.
MINISTER PENHEVI?
OH! IT'S YOU...
HERE IS WHAT YOU REQUESTED... HIS MAJESTY'S FINGERNAILS.
THERE'S NOTHING BETTER THAN SOMEBODY'S NAILS OR HAIR TO CAST AN EVIL SPELL.
BARBER KHERI, DO YOU TOO THEN NO LONGER BELIEVE IN THE DIVINE NATURE OF HIS MAJESTY, MY HUSBAND?
YOU KNOW, YOUR MAJESTY, WHEN YOU STAND TOO CLOSE TO SOMEONE DIVINE, YOU CAN'T HELP BUT BEGIN TO HAVE DOUBTS...

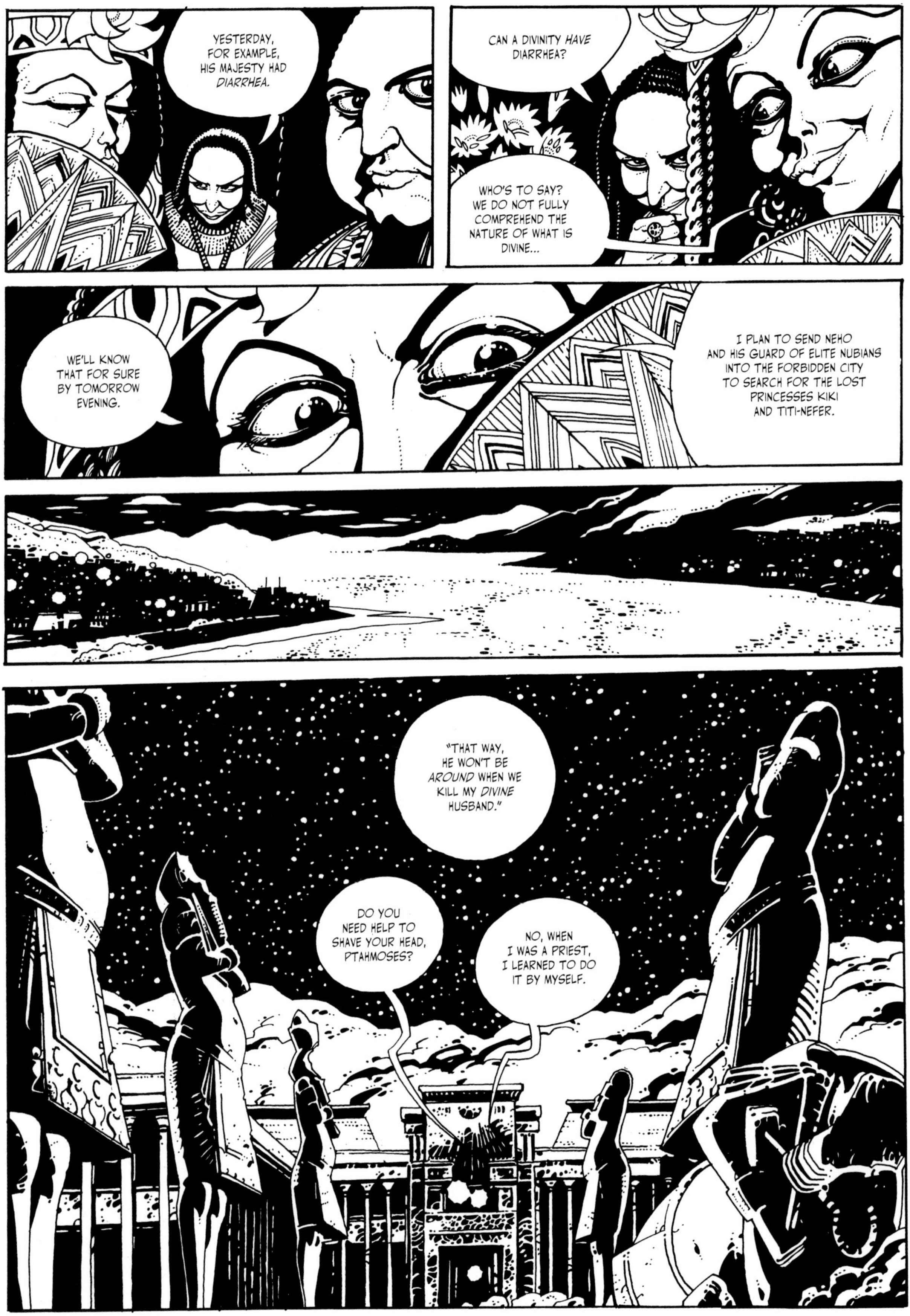
YESTERDAY, FOR EXAMPLE, HIS MAJESTY HAD DIARRHEA.
CAN A DIVINITY HAVE DIARRHEA?
WHO'S TO SAY? WE DO NOT FULLY COMPREHEND THE NATURE OF WHAT IS DIVINE...
WE'LL KNOW THAT FOR SURE BY TOMORROW EVENING.
I PLAN TO SEND NEHO AND HIS GUARD OF ELITE NUBIANS INTO THE FORBIDDEN CITY TO SEARCH FOR THE LOST PRINCESSES KIKI AND TITI-NEFER.
"THAT WAY, HE WON'T BE AROUND WHEN WE KILL MY DIVINE HUSBAND."
DO YOU NEED HELP TO SHAVE YOUR HEAD, PTAHMOSES?
NO, WHEN I WAS A PRIEST, I LEARNED TO DO IT BY MYSELF.

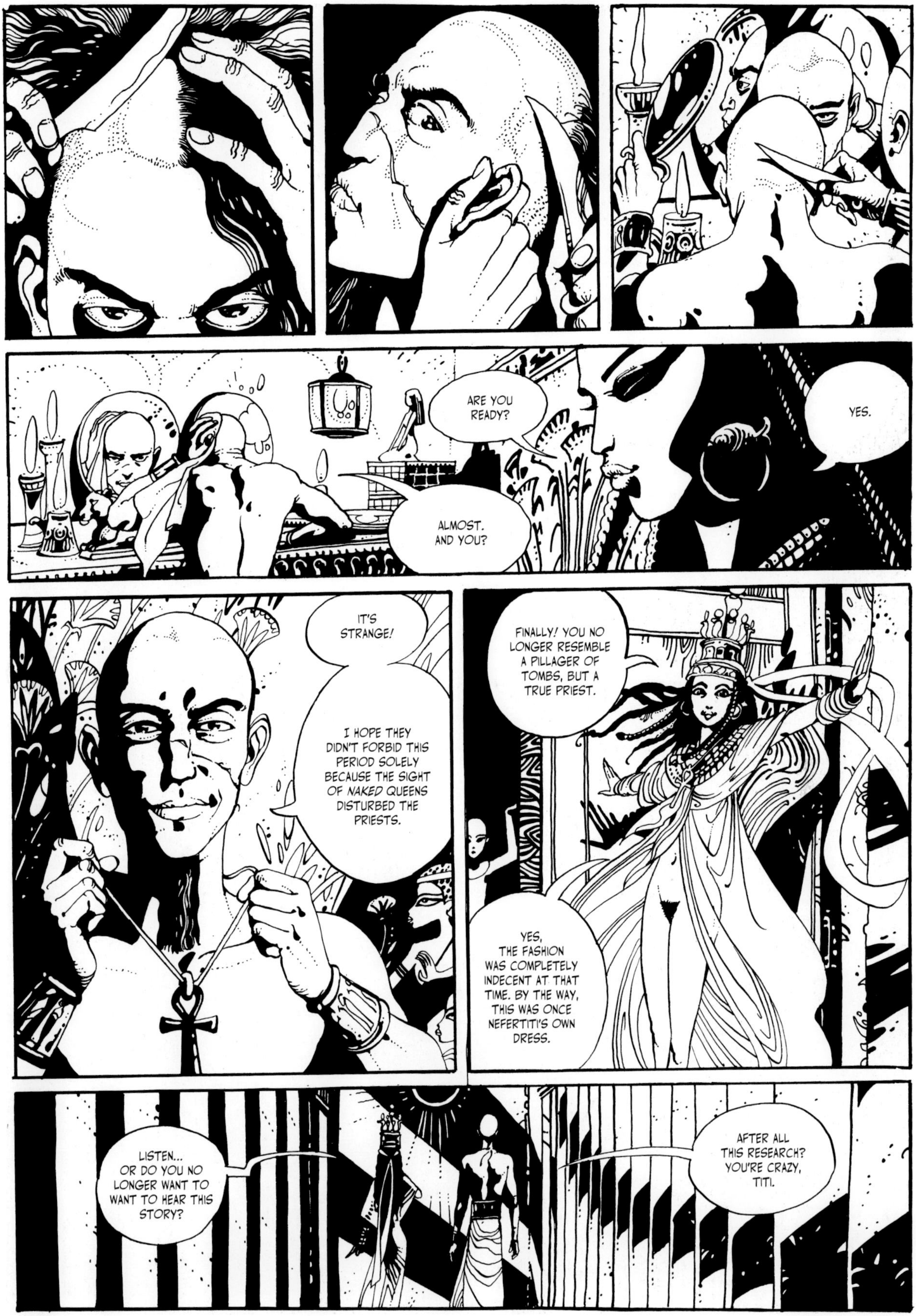
ARE YOU READY?
ALMOST. AND YOU?
YES.
IT'S STRANGE!
I HOPE THEY DIDN'T FORBID THIS PERIOD SOLELY BECAUSE THE SIGHT OF *NAKED* QUEENS DISTURBED THE PRIESTS.
FINALLY! YOU NO LONGER RESEMBLE A PILLAGER OF TOMBS, BUT A TRUE PRIEST.
YES, THE FASHION WAS COMPLETELY INDECENT AT THAT TIME. BY THE WAY, THIS WAS ONCE NEFERTITI'S OWN DRESS.
LISTEN... OR DO YOU NO LONGER WANT TO WANT TO HEAR THIS STORY?
AFTER ALL THIS RESEARCH? YOU'RE CRAZY, TITI.

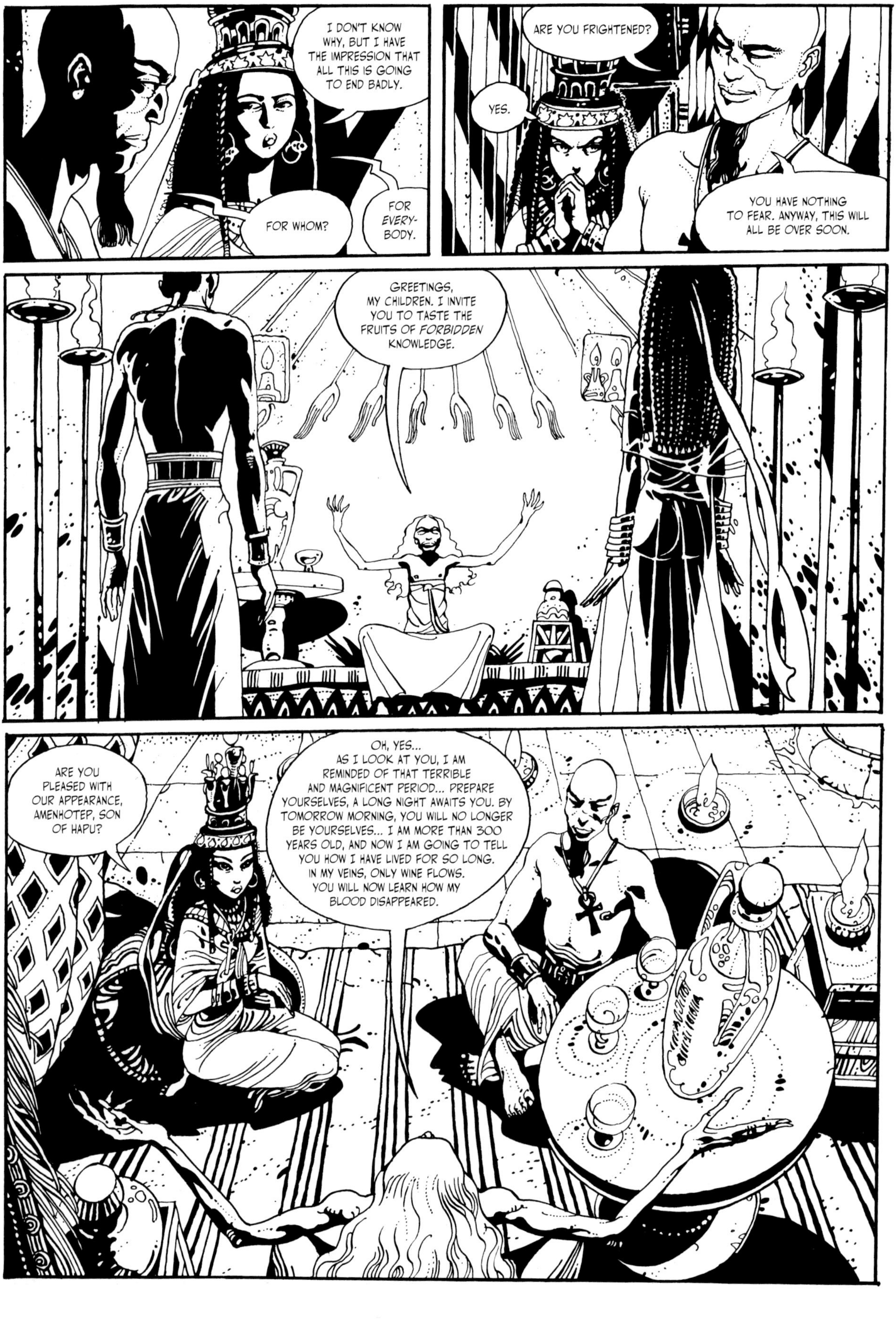

I DON'T KNOW WHY, BUT I HAVE THE IMPRESSION THAT ALL THIS IS GOING TO END BADLY.
FOR WHOM?
FOR EVERY-BODY.
ARE YOU FRIGHTENED?
YES.
YOU HAVE NOTHING TO FEAR. ANYWAY, THIS WILL ALL BE OVER SOON.
GREETINGS, MY CHILDREN. I INVITE YOU TO TASTE THE FRUITS OF *FORBIDDEN* KNOWLEDGE.
ARE YOU PLEASED WITH OUR APPEARANCE, AMENHOTEP, SON OF HAPU?
OH, YES... AS I LOOK AT YOU, I AM REMINDED OF THAT TERRIBLE AND MAGNIFICENT PERIOD... PREPARE YOURSELVES, A LONG NIGHT AWAITS YOU. BY TOMORROW MORNING, YOU WILL NO LONGER BE YOURSELVES... I AM MORE THAN 300 YEARS OLD, AND NOW I AM GOING TO TELL YOU HOW I HAVE LIVED FOR SO LONG. IN MY VEINS, ONLY WINE FLOWS. YOU WILL NOW LEARN HOW MY BLOOD DISAPPEARED.

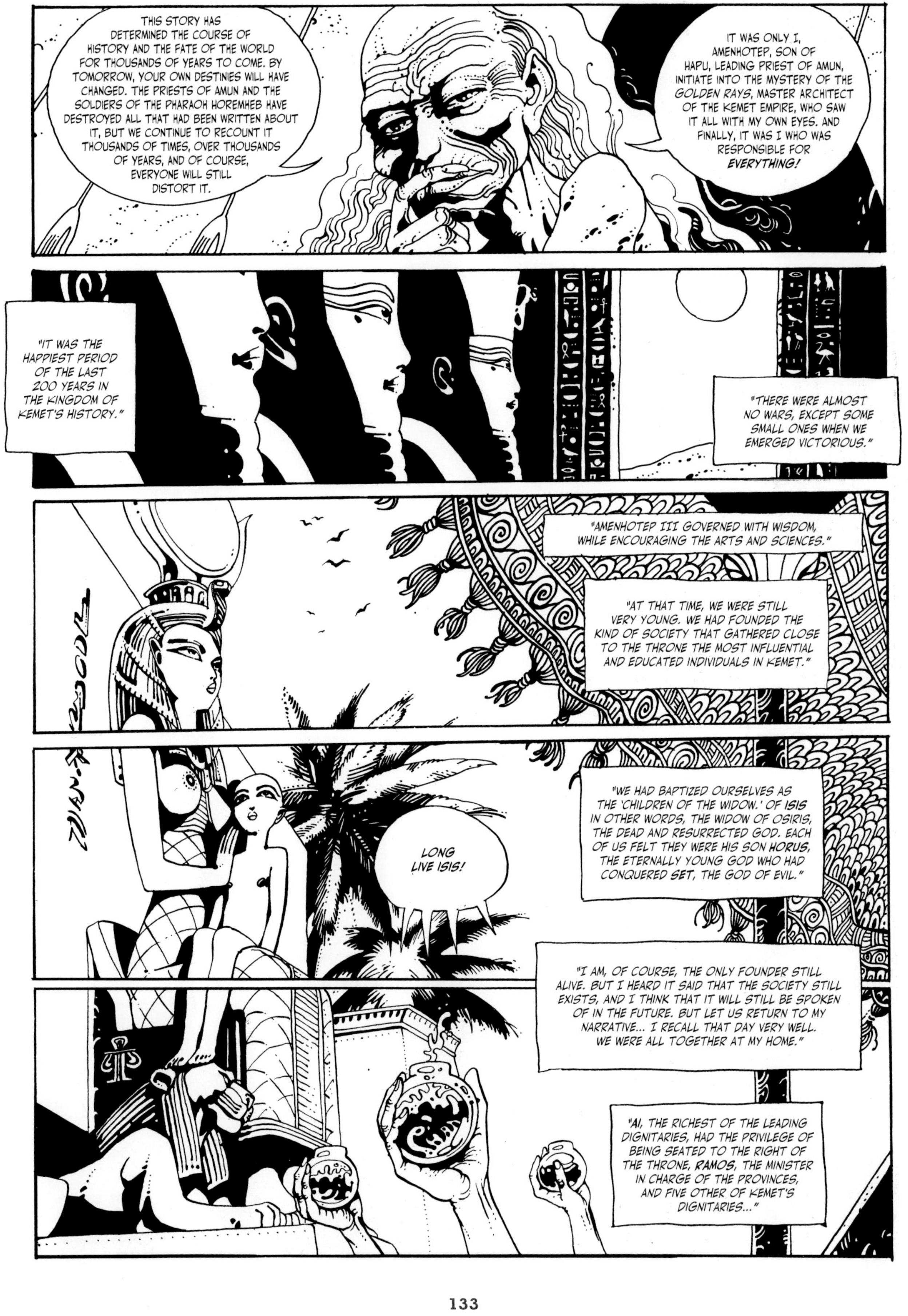
THIS STORY HAS DETERMINED THE COURSE OF HISTORY AND THE FATE OF THE WORLD FOR THOUSANDS OF YEARS TO COME. BY TOMORROW, YOUR OWN DESTINIES WILL HAVE CHANGED. THE PRIESTS OF AMUN AND THE SOLDIERS OF THE PHARAOH HOREMHEB HAVE DESTROYED ALL THAT HAD BEEN WRITTEN ABOUT IT, BUT WE CONTINUE TO RECOUNT IT THOUSANDS OF TIMES, OVER THOUSANDS OF YEARS, AND OF COURSE, EVERYONE WILL STILL DISTORT IT.
IT WAS ONLY I, AMENHOTEP, SON OF HAPU, LEADING PRIEST OF AMUN, INITIATE INTO THE MYSTERY OF THE *GOLDEN RAYS*, MASTER ARCHITECT OF THE KEMET EMPIRE, WHO SAW IT ALL WITH MY OWN EYES. AND FINALLY, IT WAS I WHO WAS RESPONSIBLE FOR ***EVERYTHING!***
"IT WAS THE HAPPIEST PERIOD OF THE LAST 200 YEARS IN THE KINGDOM OF KEMET'S HISTORY."
"THERE WERE ALMOST NO WARS, EXCEPT SOME SMALL ONES WHEN WE EMERGED VICTORIOUS."
"AMENHOTEP III GOVERNED WITH WISDOM, WHILE ENCOURAGING THE ARTS AND SCIENCES."
"AT THAT TIME, WE WERE STILL VERY YOUNG. WE HAD FOUNDED THE KIND OF SOCIETY THAT GATHERED CLOSE TO THE THRONE THE MOST INFLUENTIAL AND EDUCATED INDIVIDUALS IN KEMET."
"WE HAD BAPTIZED OURSELVES AS THE 'CHILDREN OF THE WIDOW.' OF **ISIS** IN OTHER WORDS, THE WIDOW OF OSIRIS, THE DEAD AND RESURRECTED GOD. EACH OF US FELT THEY WERE HIS SON **HORUS**, THE ETERNALLY YOUNG GOD WHO HAD CONQUERED **SET**, THE GOD OF EVIL."
LONG LIVE ISIS!
"I AM, OF COURSE, THE ONLY FOUNDER STILL ALIVE. BUT I HEARD IT SAID THAT THE SOCIETY STILL EXISTS, AND I THINK THAT IT WILL STILL BE SPOKEN OF IN THE FUTURE. BUT LET US RETURN TO MY NARRATIVE... I RECALL THAT DAY VERY WELL. WE WERE ALL TOGETHER AT MY HOME."
"**AI**, THE RICHEST OF THE LEADING DIGNITARIES, HAD THE PRIVILEGE OF BEING SEATED TO THE RIGHT OF THE THRONE, **RAMOS**, THE MINISTER IN CHARGE OF THE PROVINCES, AND FIVE OTHER OF KEMET'S DIGNITARIES..."

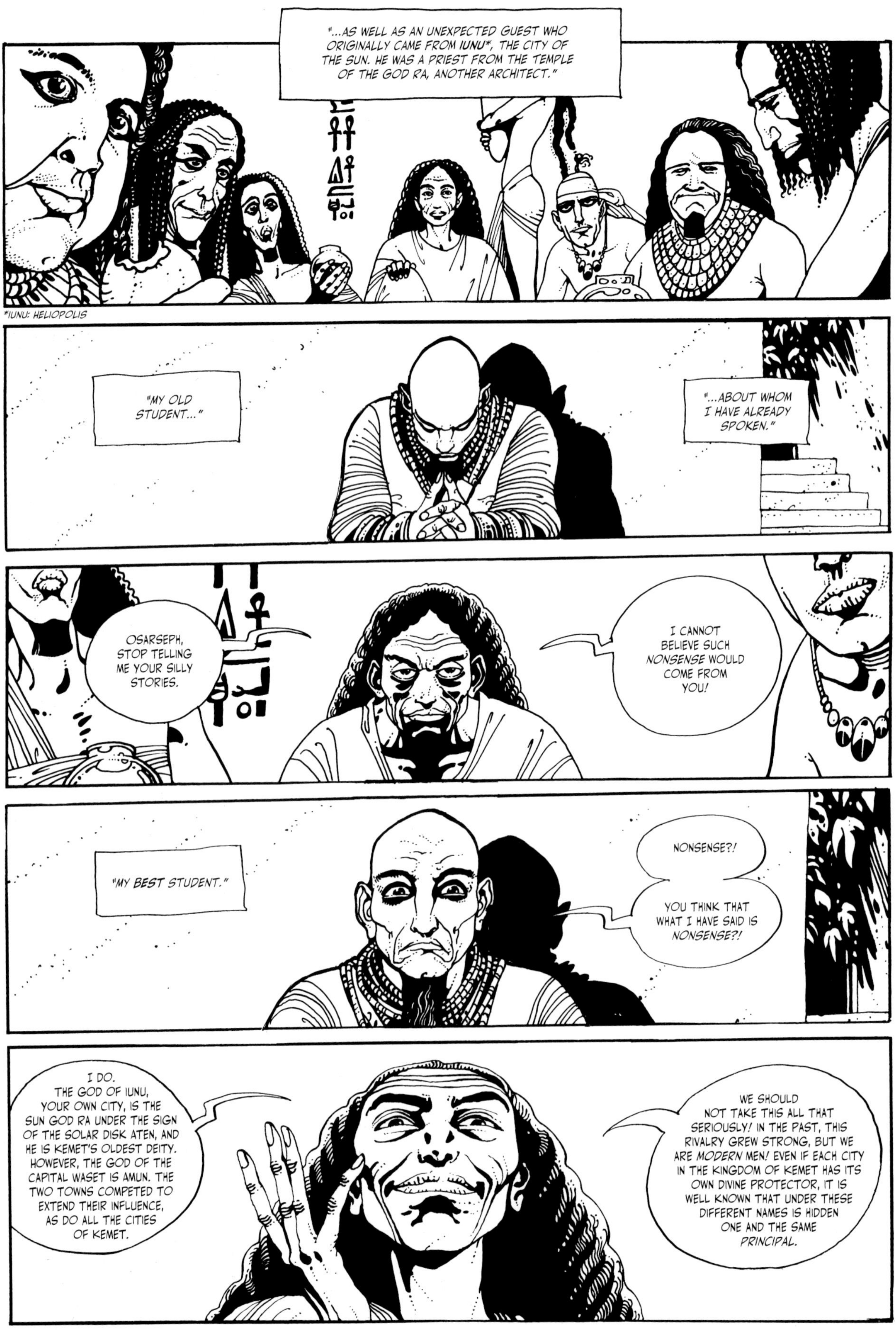
"...AS WELL AS AN UNEXPECTED GUEST WHO ORIGINALLY CAME FROM IUNU*, THE CITY OF THE SUN. HE WAS A PRIEST FROM THE TEMPLE OF THE GOD RA, ANOTHER ARCHITECT."
*IUNU: HELIOPOLIS
"MY OLD STUDENT..."
"...ABOUT WHOM I HAVE ALREADY SPOKEN."
OSARSEPH, STOP TELLING ME YOUR SILLY STORIES.
I CANNOT BELIEVE SUCH NONSENSE WOULD COME FROM YOU!
"MY BEST STUDENT."
NONSENSE?!
YOU THINK THAT WHAT I HAVE SAID IS NONSENSE?!
I DO. THE GOD OF IUNU, YOUR OWN CITY, IS THE SUN GOD RA UNDER THE SIGN OF THE SOLAR DISK ATEN, AND HE IS KEMET'S OLDEST DEITY. HOWEVER, THE GOD OF THE CAPITAL WASET IS AMUN. THE TWO TOWNS COMPETED TO EXTEND THEIR INFLUENCE, AS DO ALL THE CITIES OF KEMET.
WE SHOULD NOT TAKE THIS ALL THAT SERIOUSLY! IN THE PAST, THIS RIVALRY GREW STRONG, BUT WE ARE MODERN MEN! EVEN IF EACH CITY IN THE KINGDOM OF KEMET HAS ITS OWN DIVINE PROTECTOR, IT IS WELL KNOWN THAT UNDER THESE DIFFERENT NAMES IS HIDDEN ONE AND THE SAME PRINCIPAL.

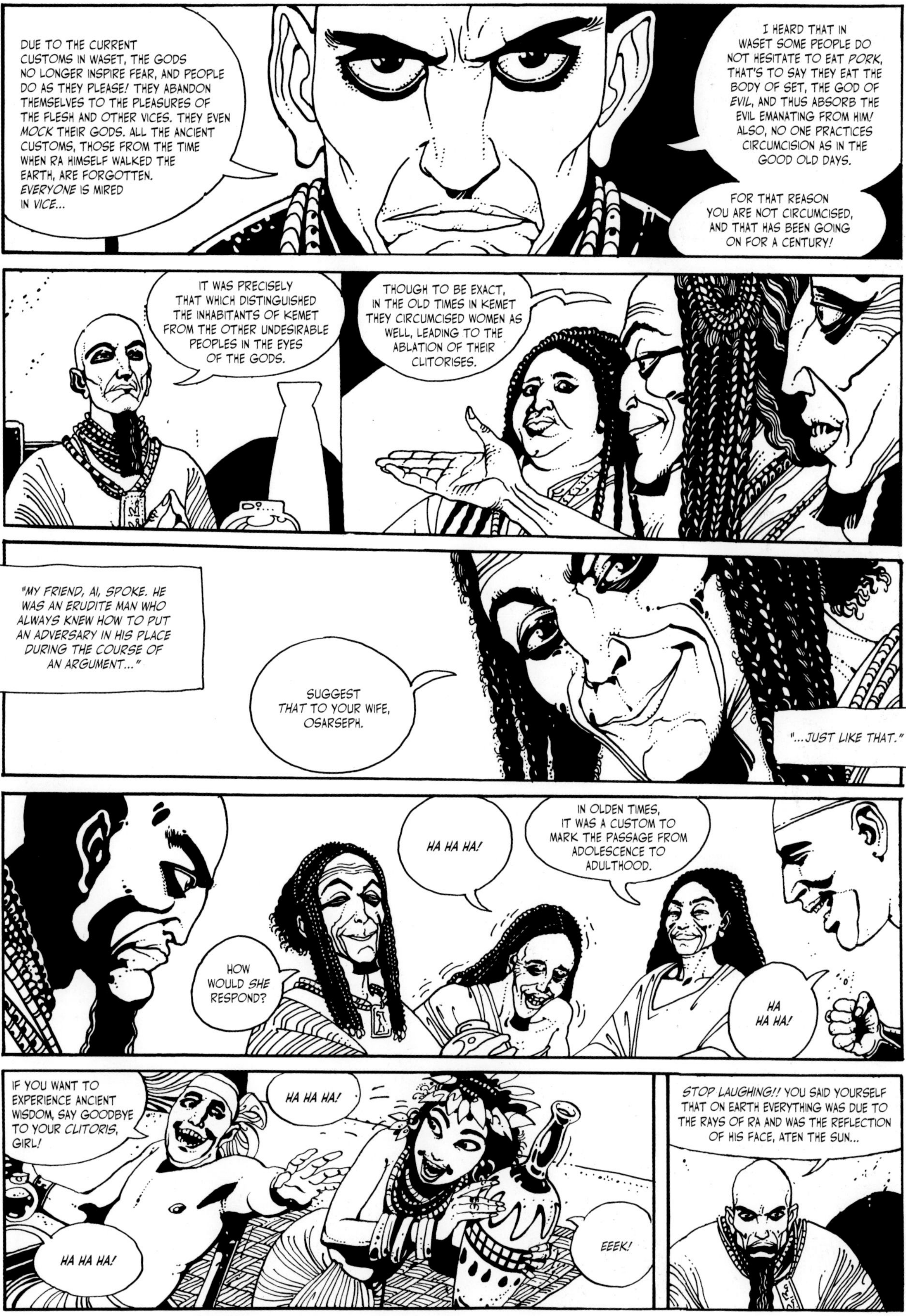
DUE TO THE CURRENT CUSTOMS IN WASET, THE GODS NO LONGER INSPIRE FEAR, AND PEOPLE DO AS THEY PLEASE! THEY ABANDON THEMSELVES TO THE PLEASURES OF THE FLESH AND OTHER VICES. THEY EVEN *MOCK* THEIR GODS. ALL THE ANCIENT CUSTOMS, THOSE FROM THE TIME WHEN RA HIMSELF WALKED THE EARTH, ARE FORGOTTEN. *EVERYONE* IS MIRED IN *VICE*...
I HEARD THAT IN WASET SOME PEOPLE DO NOT HESITATE TO EAT *PORK*, THAT'S TO SAY THEY EAT THE BODY OF SET, THE GOD OF *EVIL*, AND THUS ABSORB THE EVIL EMANATING FROM HIM! ALSO, NO ONE PRACTICES CIRCUMCISION AS IN THE GOOD OLD DAYS.
FOR THAT REASON YOU ARE NOT CIRCUMCISED, AND THAT HAS BEEN GOING ON FOR A CENTURY!
IT WAS PRECISELY THAT WHICH DISTINGUISHED THE INHABITANTS OF KEMET FROM THE OTHER UNDESIRABLE PEOPLES IN THE EYES OF THE GODS.
THOUGH TO BE EXACT, IN THE OLD TIMES IN KEMET THEY CIRCUMCISED WOMEN AS WELL, LEADING TO THE ABLATION OF THEIR CLITORISES.
"MY FRIEND, AI, SPOKE. HE WAS AN ERUDITE MAN WHO ALWAYS KNEW HOW TO PUT AN ADVERSARY IN HIS PLACE DURING THE COURSE OF AN ARGUMENT..."
SUGGEST *THAT* TO YOUR WIFE, OSARSEPH.
"...JUST LIKE THAT."
HA HA HA!
IN OLDEN TIMES, IT WAS A CUSTOM TO MARK THE PASSAGE FROM ADOLESCENCE TO ADULTHOOD.
HOW WOULD *SHE* RESPOND?
HA HA HA!
IF YOU WANT TO EXPERIENCE ANCIENT WISDOM, SAY GOODBYE TO YOUR *CLITORIS*, GIRL!
HA HA HA!
HA HA HA!
EEEK!
STOP LAUGHING!! YOU SAID YOURSELF THAT ON EARTH EVERYTHING WAS DUE TO THE RAYS OF RA AND WAS THE REFLECTION OF HIS FACE, ATEN THE SUN...

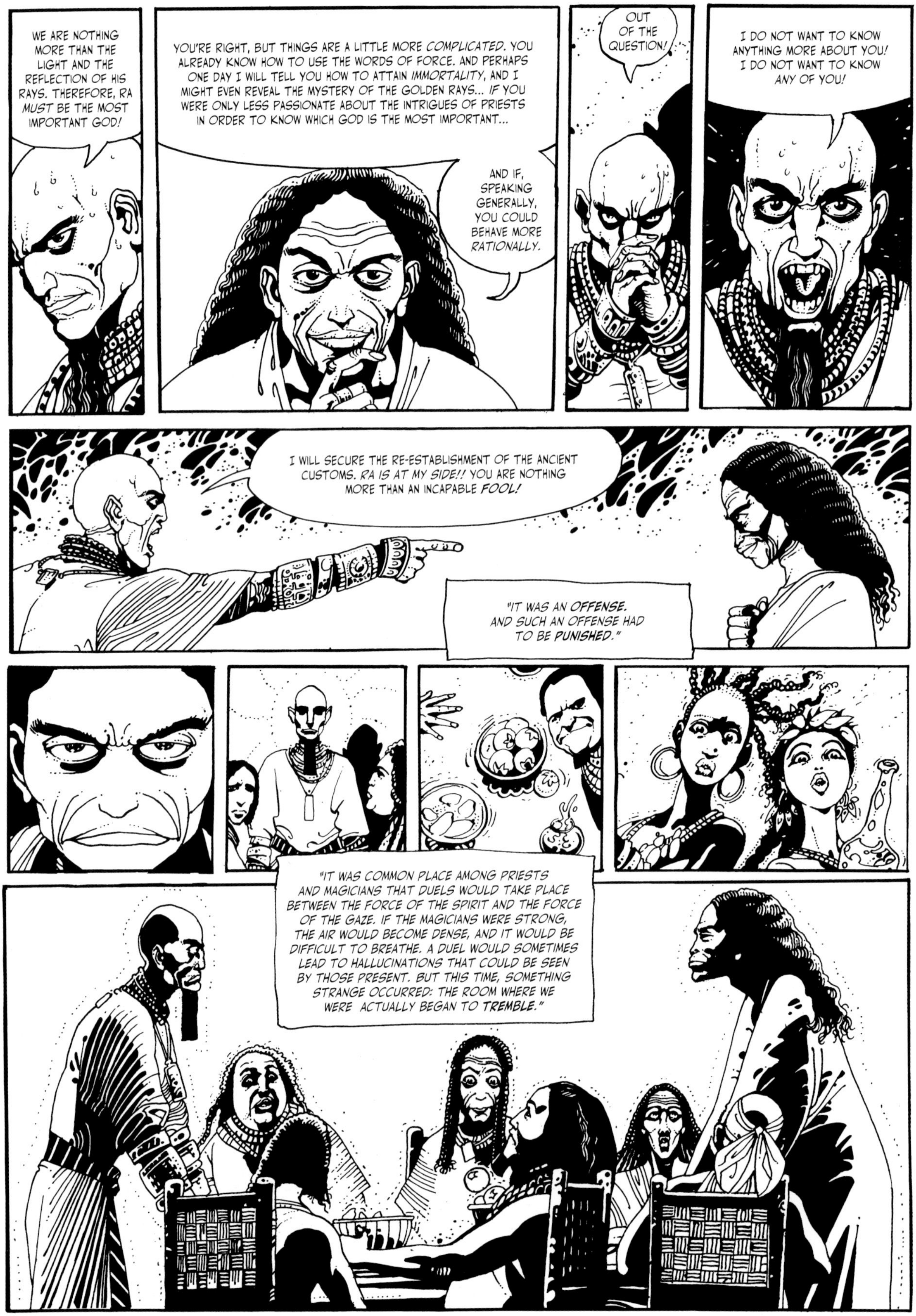
WE ARE NOTHING MORE THAN THE LIGHT AND THE REFLECTION OF HIS RAYS. THEREFORE, RA *MUST* BE THE MOST IMPORTANT GOD!
YOU'RE RIGHT, BUT THINGS ARE A LITTLE MORE *COMPLICATED*. YOU ALREADY KNOW HOW TO USE THE WORDS OF FORCE. AND PERHAPS ONE DAY I WILL TELL YOU HOW TO ATTAIN *IMMORTALITY*, AND I MIGHT EVEN REVEAL THE MYSTERY OF THE GOLDEN RAYS... *IF* YOU WERE ONLY LESS PASSIONATE ABOUT THE INTRIGUES OF PRIESTS IN ORDER TO KNOW WHICH GOD IS THE MOST IMPORTANT...
AND IF, SPEAKING GENERALLY, YOU COULD BEHAVE MORE *RATIONALLY*.
OUT OF THE QUESTION!
I DO NOT WANT TO KNOW ANYTHING MORE ABOUT YOU! I DO NOT WANT TO KNOW *ANY OF YOU!*
I WILL SECURE THE RE-ESTABLISHMENT OF THE ANCIENT CUSTOMS. *RA IS AT MY SIDE!!* YOU ARE NOTHING MORE THAN AN INCAPABLE *FOOL!*
"IT WAS AN ***OFFENSE****. AND SUCH AN OFFENSE HAD TO BE* ***PUNISHED****."*
"IT WAS COMMON PLACE AMONG PRIESTS AND MAGICIANS THAT DUELS WOULD TAKE PLACE BETWEEN THE FORCE OF THE SPIRIT AND THE FORCE OF THE GAZE. IF THE MAGICIANS WERE STRONG, THE AIR WOULD BECOME DENSE, AND IT WOULD BE DIFFICULT TO BREATHE. A DUEL WOULD SOMETIMES LEAD TO HALLUCINATIONS THAT COULD BE SEEN BY THOSE PRESENT. BUT THIS TIME, SOMETHING STRANGE OCCURRED: THE ROOM WHERE WE WERE ACTUALLY BEGAN TO ***TREMBLE****."*

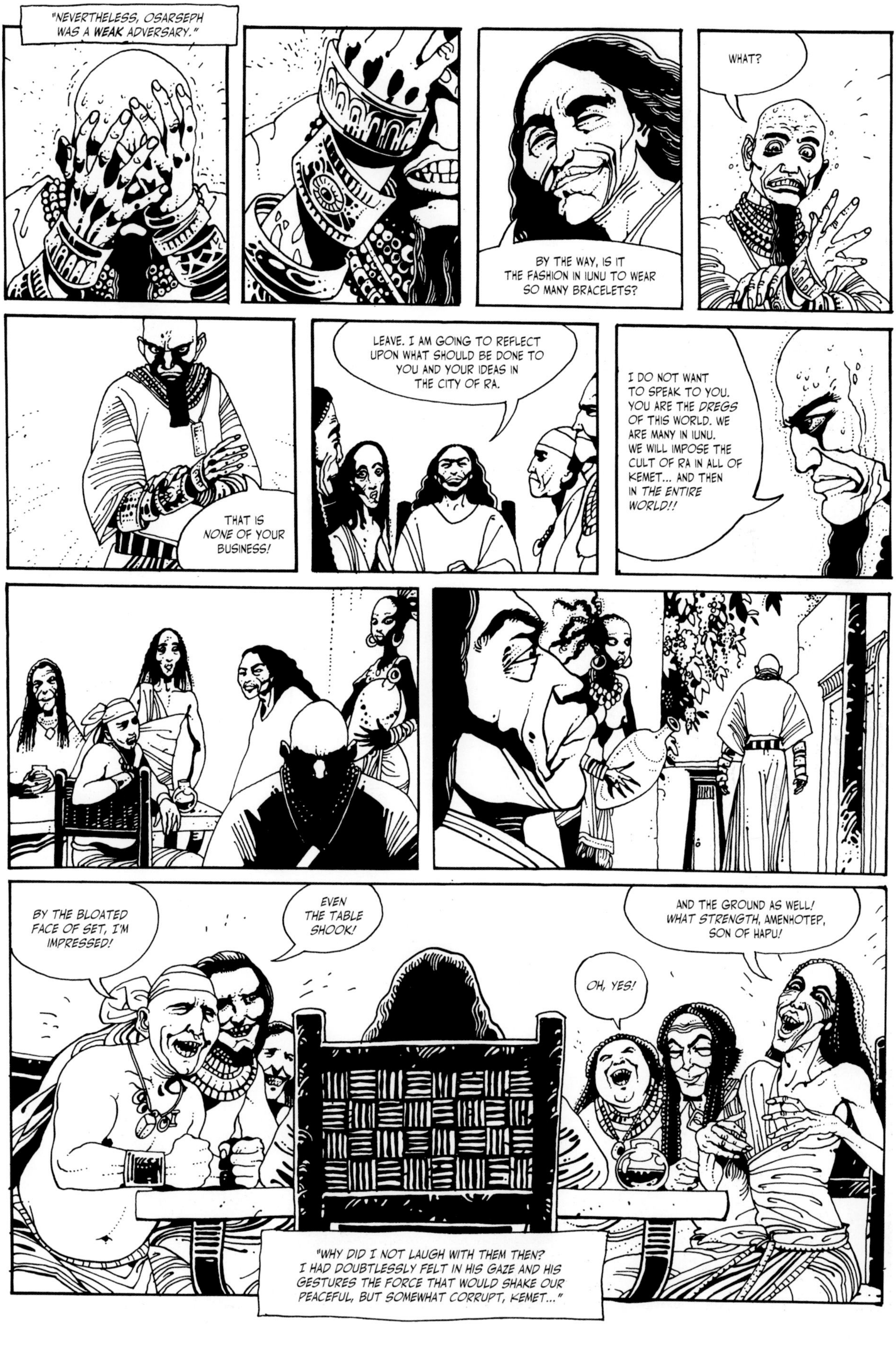

"NEVERTHELESS, OSARSEPH WAS A WEAK ADVERSARY."
BY THE WAY, IS IT THE FASHION IN IUNU TO WEAR SO MANY BRACELETS?
WHAT?
THAT IS NONE OF YOUR BUSINESS!
LEAVE. I AM GOING TO REFLECT UPON WHAT SHOULD BE DONE TO YOU AND YOUR IDEAS IN THE CITY OF RA.
I DO NOT WANT TO SPEAK TO YOU. YOU ARE THE DREGS OF THIS WORLD. WE ARE MANY IN IUNU. WE WILL IMPOSE THE CULT OF RA IN ALL OF KEMET... AND THEN IN THE ENTIRE WORLD!!
BY THE BLOATED FACE OF SET, I'M IMPRESSED!
EVEN THE TABLE SHOOK!
OH, YES!
AND THE GROUND AS WELL! WHAT STRENGTH, AMENHOTEP, SON OF HAPU!
"WHY DID I NOT LAUGH WITH THEM THEN? I HAD DOUBTLESSLY FELT IN HIS GAZE AND HIS GESTURES THE FORCE THAT WOULD SHAKE OUR PEACEFUL, BUT SOMEWHAT CORRUPT, KEMET..."

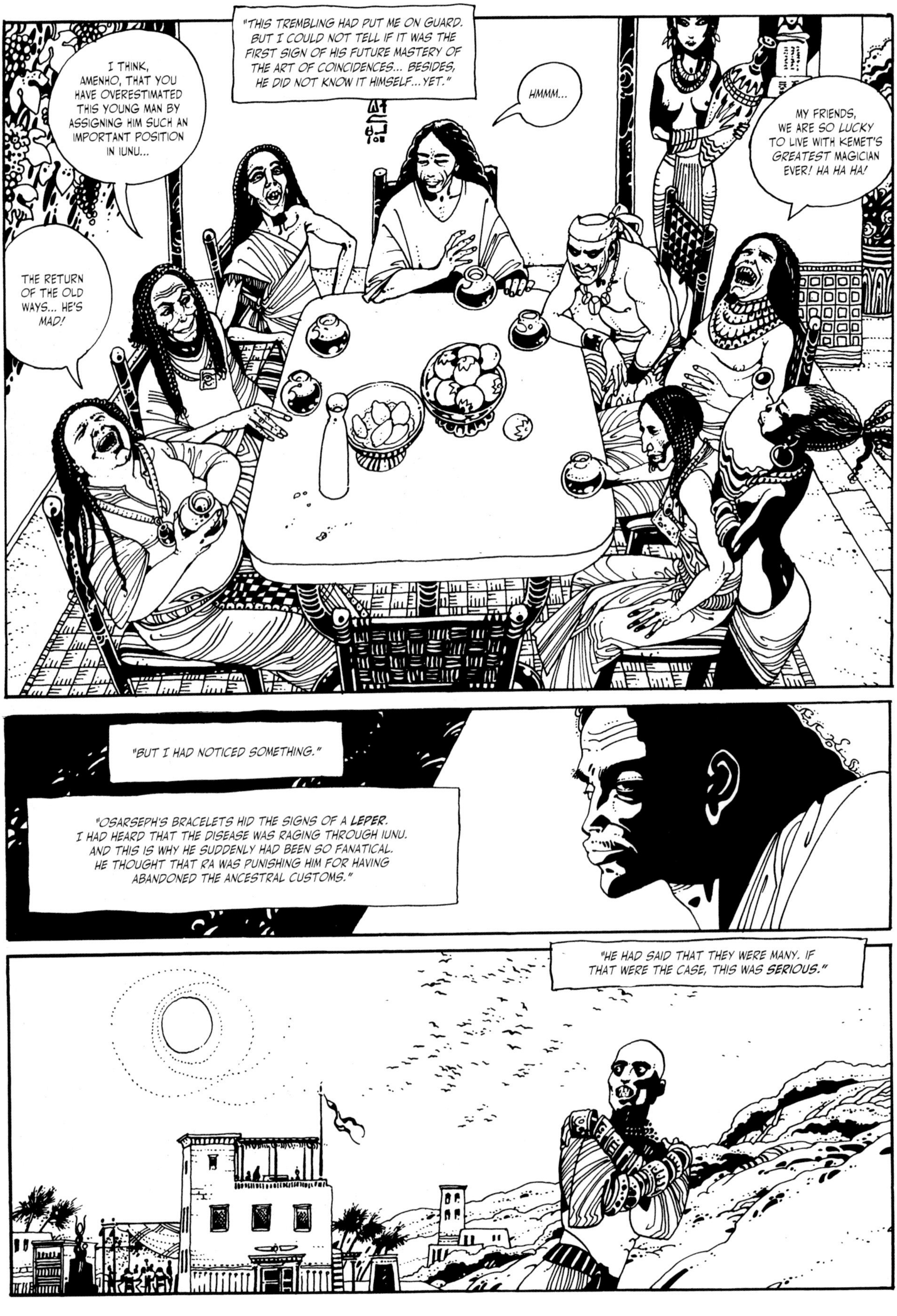
"THIS TREMBLING HAD PUT ME ON GUARD. BUT I COULD NOT TELL IF IT WAS THE FIRST SIGN OF HIS FUTURE MASTERY OF THE ART OF COINCIDENCES... BESIDES, HE DID NOT KNOW IT HIMSELF...YET."
I THINK, AMENHO, THAT YOU HAVE OVERESTIMATED THIS YOUNG MAN BY ASSIGNING HIM SUCH AN IMPORTANT POSITION IN IUNU...
THE RETURN OF THE OLD WAYS... HE'S MAD!
HMMM...
MY FRIENDS, WE ARE SO LUCKY TO LIVE WITH KEMET'S GREATEST MAGICIAN EVER! HA HA HA!
"BUT I HAD NOTICED SOMETHING."
"OSARSEPH'S BRACELETS HID THE SIGNS OF A LEPER. I HAD HEARD THAT THE DISEASE WAS RAGING THROUGH IUNU. AND THIS IS WHY HE SUDDENLY HAD BEEN SO FANATICAL. HE THOUGHT THAT RA WAS PUNISHING HIM FOR HAVING ABANDONED THE ANCESTRAL CUSTOMS."
"HE HAD SAID THAT THEY WERE MANY. IF THAT WERE THE CASE, THIS WAS SERIOUS."

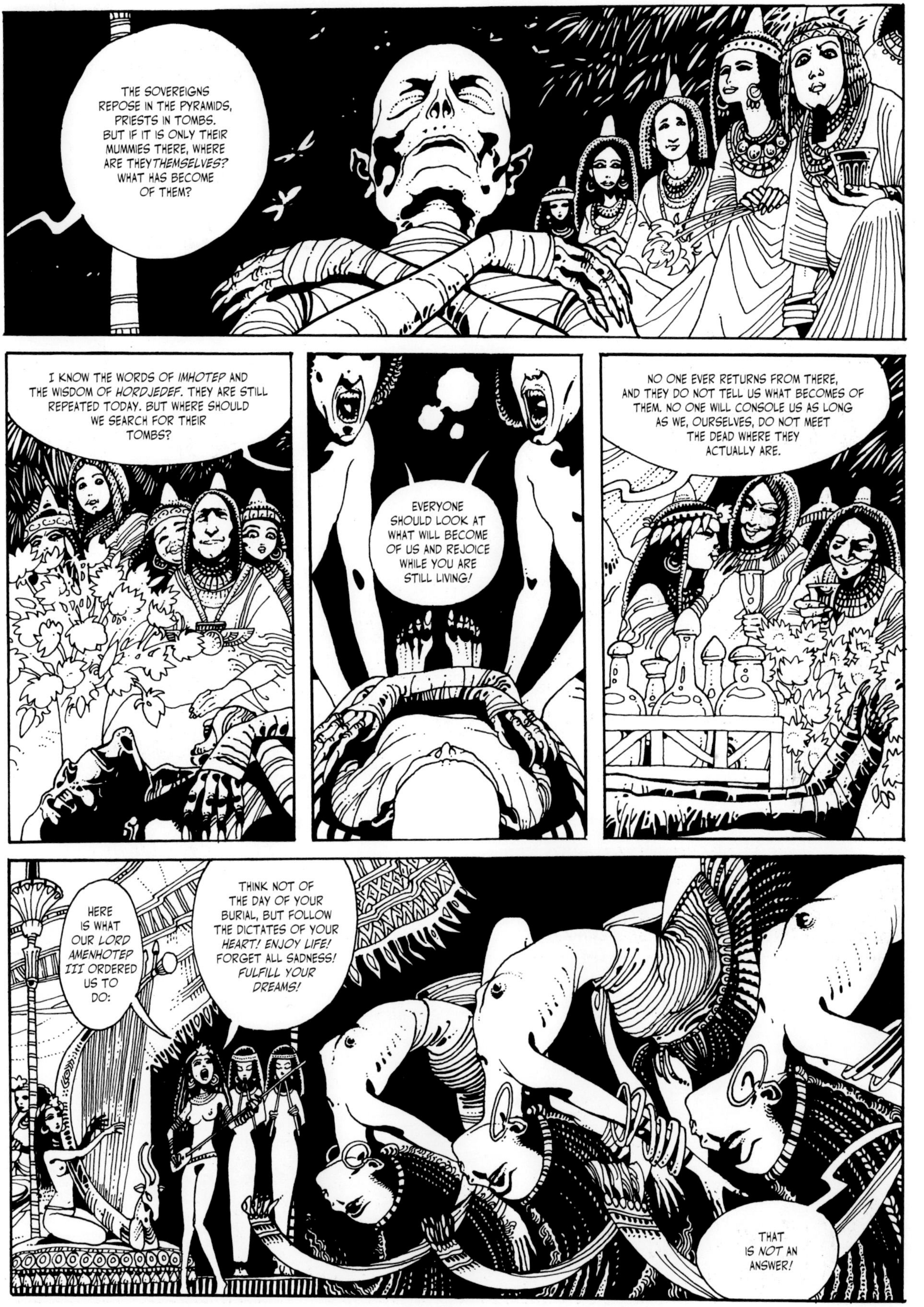
THE SOVEREIGNS REPOSE IN THE PYRAMIDS, PRIESTS IN TOMBS. BUT IF IT IS ONLY THEIR MUMMIES THERE, WHERE ARE THEY *THEMSELVES?* WHAT HAS BECOME OF THEM?
I KNOW THE WORDS OF *IMHOTEP* AND THE WISDOM OF *HORDJEDEF*. THEY ARE STILL REPEATED TODAY. BUT WHERE SHOULD WE SEARCH FOR THEIR TOMBS?
EVERYONE SHOULD LOOK AT WHAT WILL BECOME OF US AND REJOICE WHILE YOU ARE STILL LIVING!
NO ONE EVER RETURNS FROM THERE, AND THEY DO NOT TELL US WHAT BECOMES OF THEM. NO ONE WILL CONSOLE US AS LONG AS WE, OURSELVES, DO NOT MEET THE DEAD WHERE THEY ACTUALLY ARE.
HERE IS WHAT OUR *LORD AMENHOTEP III* ORDERED US TO DO:
THINK NOT OF THE DAY OF YOUR BURIAL, BUT FOLLOW THE DICTATES OF YOUR *HEART! ENJOY LIFE! FORGET ALL SADNESS! FULFILL YOUR DREAMS!*
THAT IS *NOT* AN ANSWER!

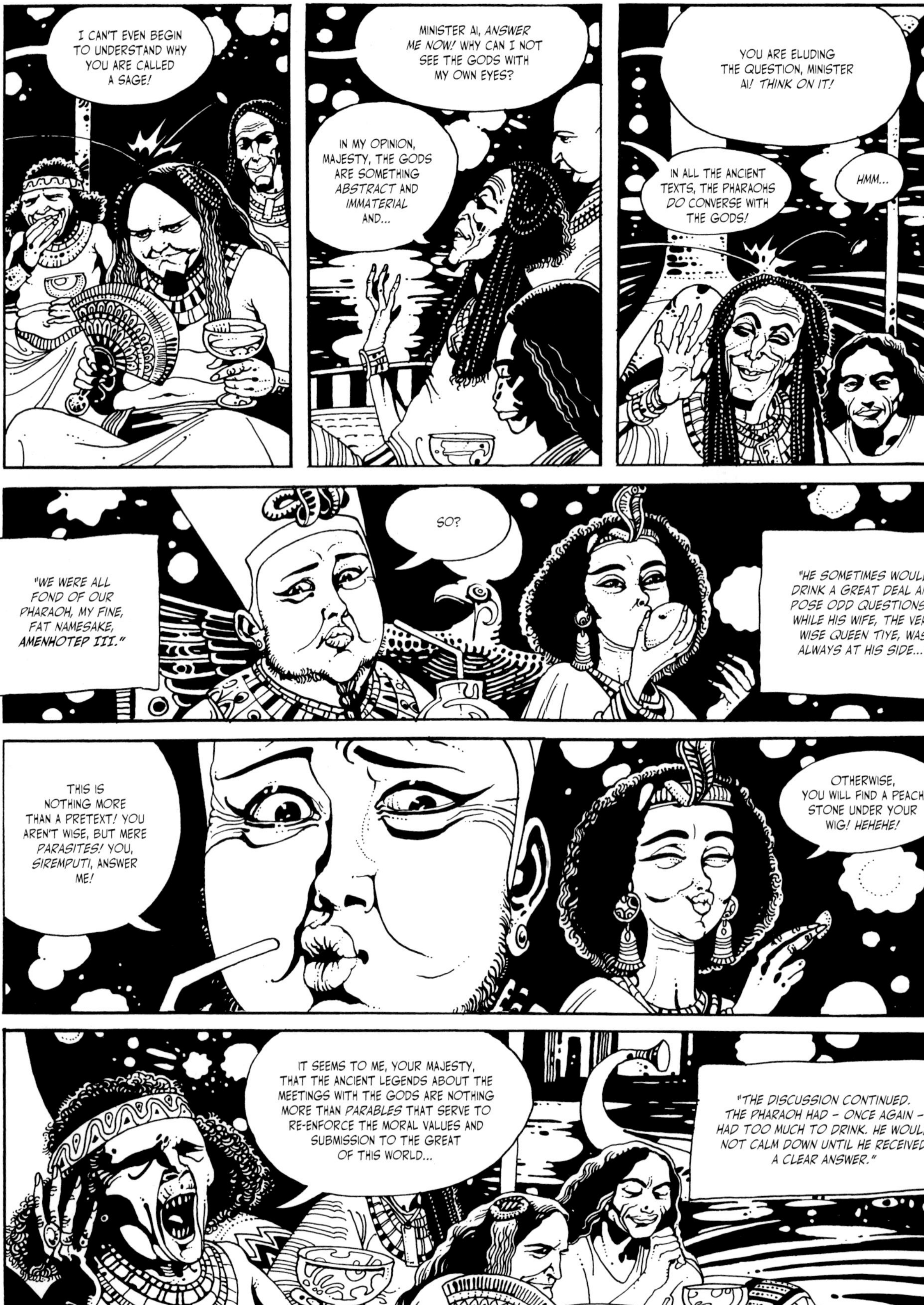
I CAN'T EVEN BEGIN TO UNDERSTAND WHY YOU ARE CALLED A SAGE!
MINISTER AI, ANSWER ME NOW! WHY CAN I NOT SEE THE GODS WITH MY OWN EYES?
IN MY OPINION, MAJESTY, THE GODS ARE SOMETHING ABSTRACT AND IMMATERIAL AND...
YOU ARE ELUDING THE QUESTION, MINISTER AI! THINK ON IT!
IN ALL THE ANCIENT TEXTS, THE PHARAOHS DO CONVERSE WITH THE GODS!
HMM...
"WE WERE ALL FOND OF OUR PHARAOH, MY FINE, FAT NAMESAKE, AMENHOTEP III."
SO?
"HE SOMETIMES WOULD DRINK A GREAT DEAL AND POSE ODD QUESTIONS... WHILE HIS WIFE, THE VERY WISE QUEEN TIYE, WAS ALWAYS AT HIS SIDE..."
THIS IS NOTHING MORE THAN A PRETEXT! YOU AREN'T WISE, BUT MERE PARASITES! YOU, SIREMPUTI, ANSWER ME!
OTHERWISE, YOU WILL FIND A PEACH STONE UNDER YOUR WIG! HEHEHE!
IT SEEMS TO ME, YOUR MAJESTY, THAT THE ANCIENT LEGENDS ABOUT THE MEETINGS WITH THE GODS ARE NOTHING MORE THAN PARABLES THAT SERVE TO RE-ENFORCE THE MORAL VALUES AND SUBMISSION TO THE GREAT OF THIS WORLD...
"THE DISCUSSION CONTINUED. THE PHARAOH HAD - ONCE AGAIN - HAD TOO MUCH TO DRINK. HE WOULD NOT CALM DOWN UNTIL HE RECEIVED A CLEAR ANSWER."

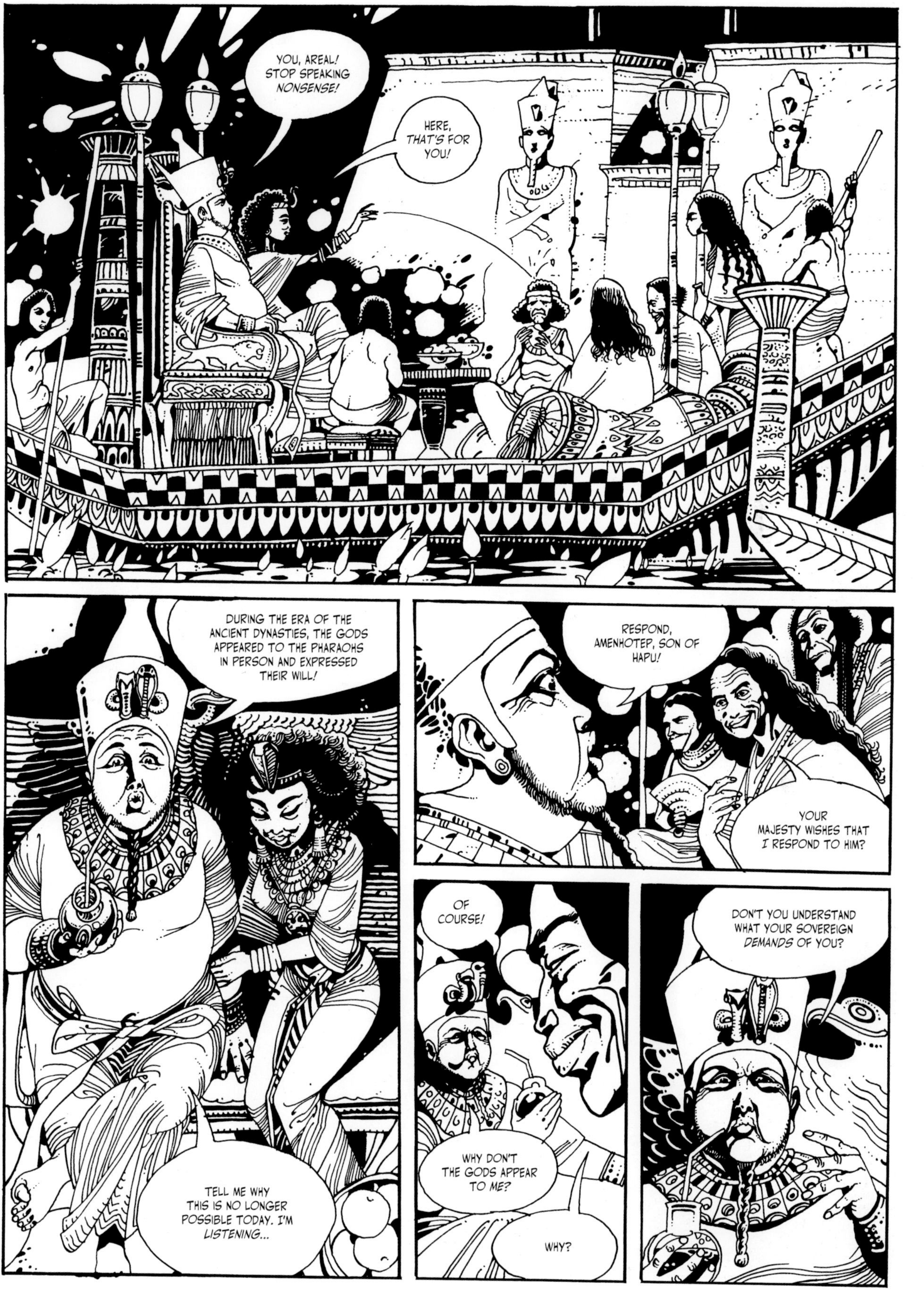
YOU, AREAL! STOP SPEAKING NONSENSE!
HERE, THAT'S FOR YOU!
DURING THE ERA OF THE ANCIENT DYNASTIES, THE GODS APPEARED TO THE PHARAOHS IN PERSON AND EXPRESSED THEIR WILL!
TELL ME WHY THIS IS NO LONGER POSSIBLE TODAY. I'M LISTENING...
RESPOND, AMENHOTEP, SON OF HAPU!
YOUR MAJESTY WISHES THAT I RESPOND TO HIM?
OF COURSE!
WHY DON'T THE GODS APPEAR TO ME?
WHY?
DON'T YOU UNDERSTAND WHAT YOUR SOVEREIGN DEMANDS OF YOU?

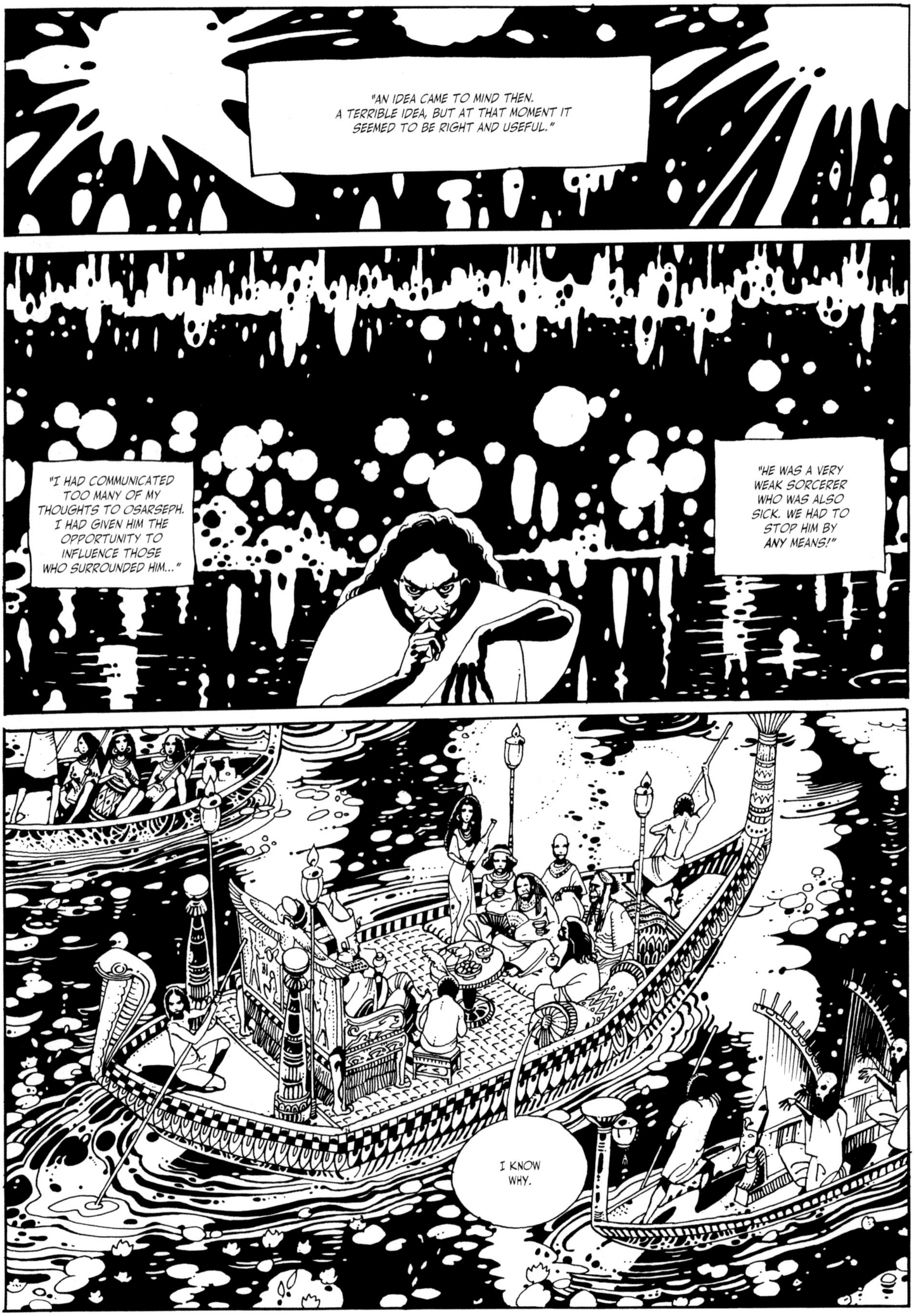
"AN IDEA CAME TO MIND THEN. A TERRIBLE IDEA, BUT AT THAT MOMENT IT SEEMED TO BE RIGHT AND USEFUL."
"I HAD COMMUNICATED TOO MANY OF MY THOUGHTS TO OSARSEPH. I HAD GIVEN HIM THE OPPORTUNITY TO INFLUENCE THOSE WHO SURROUNDED HIM..."
"HE WAS A VERY WEAK SORCERER WHO WAS ALSO SICK. WE HAD TO STOP HIM BY ANY MEANS!"
I KNOW WHY.

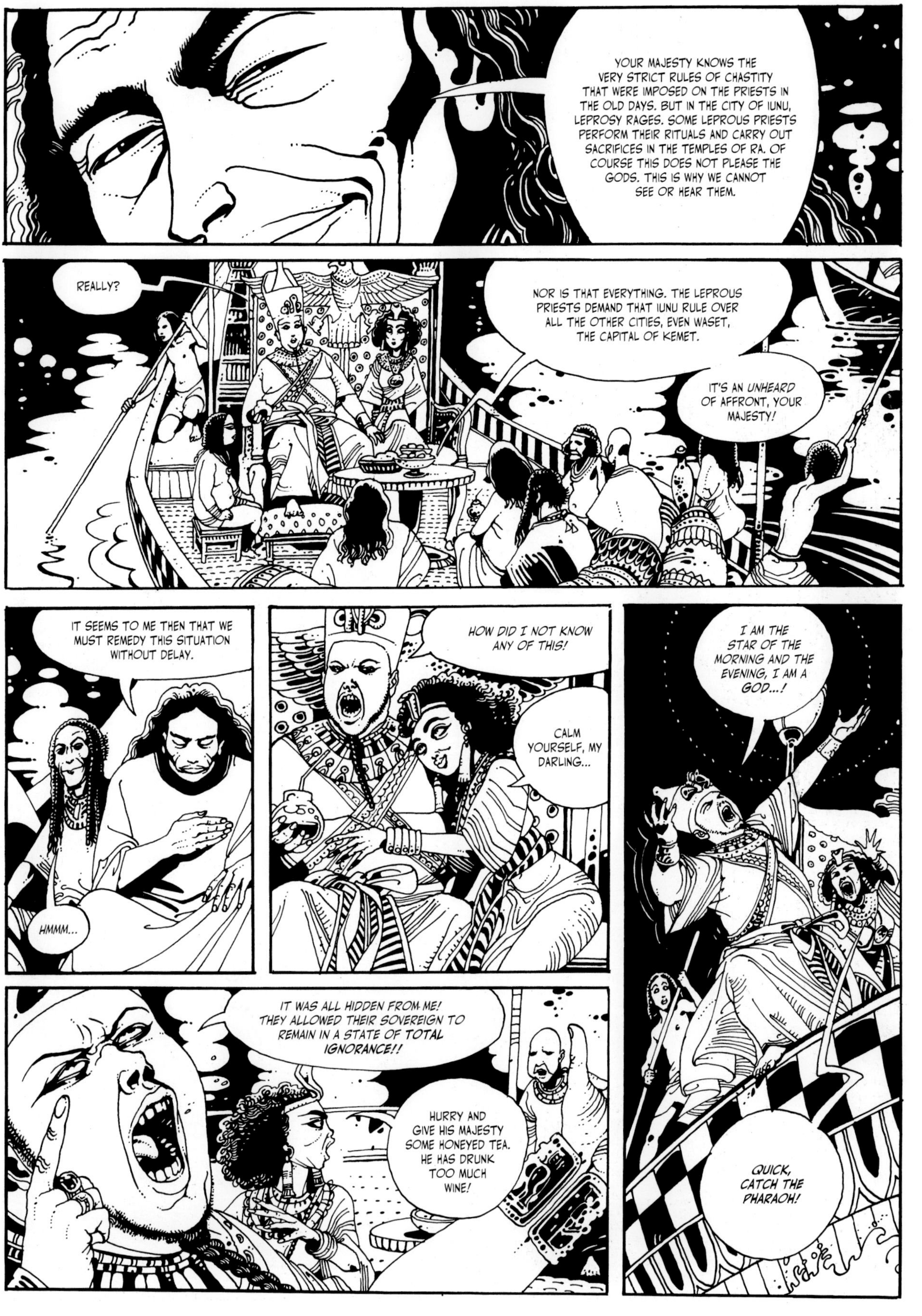
YOUR MAJESTY KNOWS THE VERY STRICT RULES OF CHASTITY THAT WERE IMPOSED ON THE PRIESTS IN THE OLD DAYS. BUT IN THE CITY OF IUNU, LEPROSY RAGES. SOME LEPROUS PRIESTS PERFORM THEIR RITUALS AND CARRY OUT SACRIFICES IN THE TEMPLES OF RA. OF COURSE THIS DOES NOT PLEASE THE GODS. THIS IS WHY WE CANNOT SEE OR HEAR THEM.
REALLY?
NOR IS THAT EVERYTHING. THE LEPROUS PRIESTS DEMAND THAT IUNU RULE OVER ALL THE OTHER CITIES, EVEN WASET, THE CAPITAL OF KEMET.
IT'S AN *UNHEARD* OF AFFRONT, YOUR MAJESTY!
IT SEEMS TO ME THEN THAT WE MUST REMEDY THIS SITUATION WITHOUT DELAY.
HMMM...
HOW DID I NOT KNOW ANY OF THIS!
CALM YOURSELF, MY DARLING...
I AM THE STAR OF THE MORNING AND THE EVENING, I AM A ***GOD...!***
IT WAS ALL HIDDEN FROM ME! THEY ALLOWED THEIR SOVEREIGN TO REMAIN IN A STATE OF ***TOTAL IGNORANCE!!***
HURRY AND GIVE HIS MAJESTY SOME HONEYED TEA. HE HAS DRUNK TOO MUCH WINE!
QUICK, CATCH THE PHARAOH!

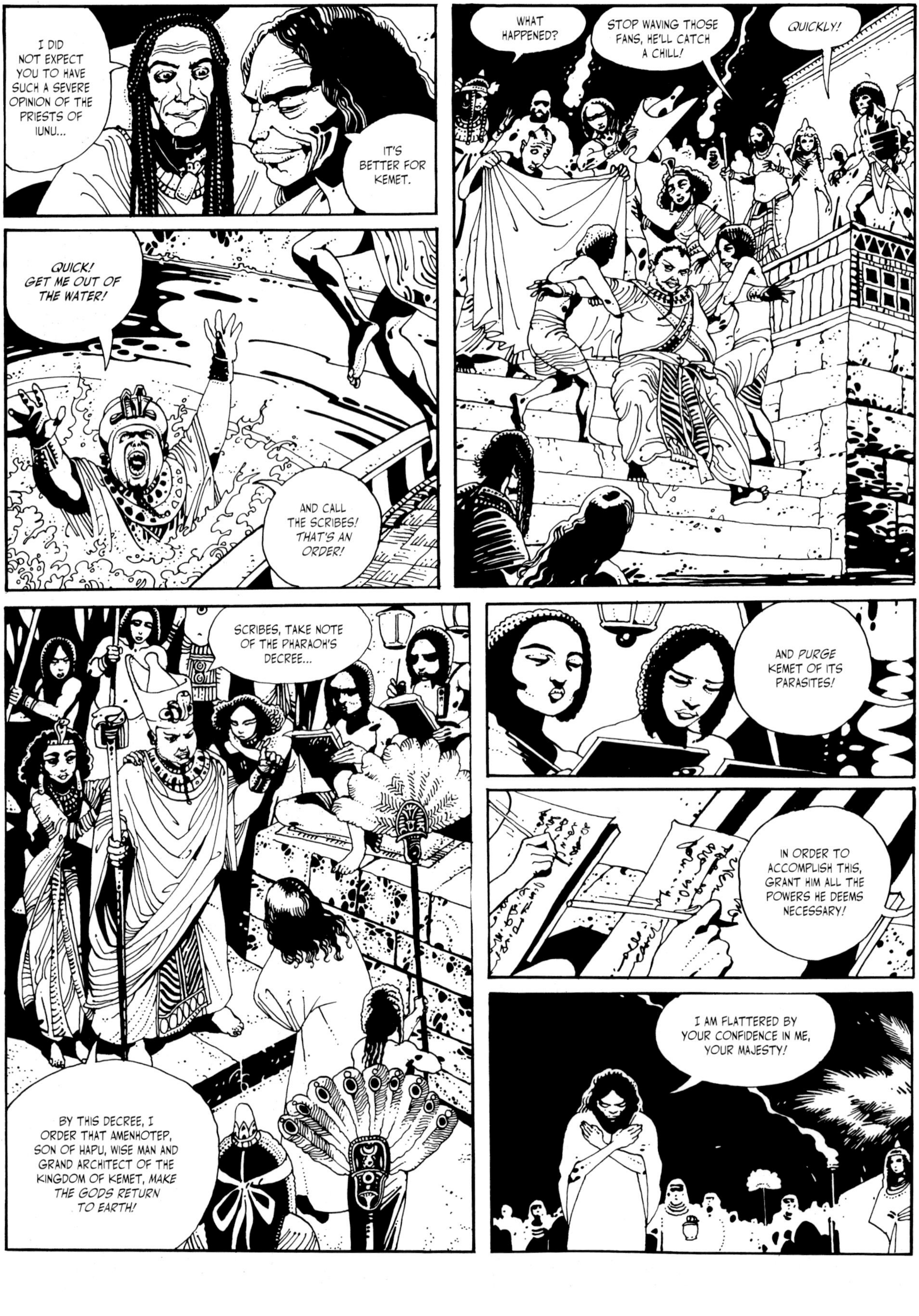
I DID NOT EXPECT YOU TO HAVE SUCH A SEVERE OPINION OF THE PRIESTS OF IUNU...
IT'S BETTER FOR KEMET.
WHAT HAPPENED?
STOP WAVING THOSE FANS, HE'LL CATCH A CHILL!
QUICKLY!
QUICK! GET ME OUT OF THE WATER!
AND CALL THE SCRIBES! THAT'S AN ORDER!
SCRIBES, TAKE NOTE OF THE PHARAOH'S DECREE...
BY THIS DECREE, I ORDER THAT AMENHOTEP, SON OF HAPU, WISE MAN AND GRAND ARCHITECT OF THE KINGDOM OF KEMET, MAKE THE GODS RETURN TO EARTH!
AND PURGE KEMET OF ITS PARASITES!
IN ORDER TO ACCOMPLISH THIS, GRANT HIM ALL THE POWERS HE DEEMS NECESSARY!
I AM FLATTERED BY YOUR CONFIDENCE IN ME, YOUR MAJESTY!

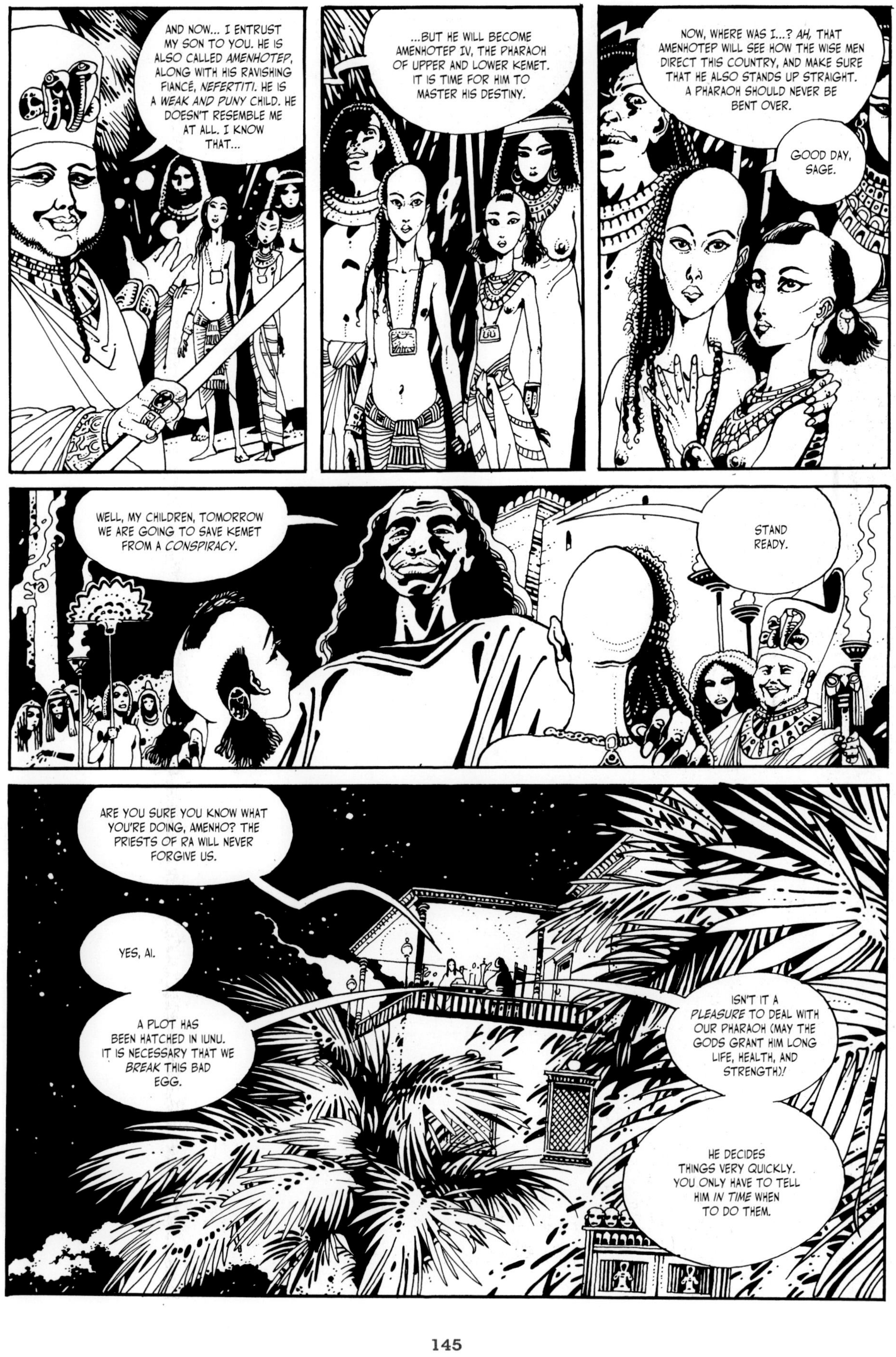
AND NOW... I ENTRUST MY SON TO YOU. HE IS ALSO CALLED *AMENHOTEP*, ALONG WITH HIS RAVISHING FIANCÉ, *NEFERTITI*. HE IS A *WEAK AND PUNY* CHILD. HE DOESN'T RESEMBLE ME AT ALL. I KNOW THAT...
...BUT HE WILL BECOME AMENHOTEP IV, THE PHARAOH OF UPPER AND LOWER KEMET. IT IS TIME FOR HIM TO MASTER HIS DESTINY.
NOW, WHERE WAS I...? *AH*, THAT AMENHOTEP WILL SEE HOW THE WISE MEN DIRECT THIS COUNTRY, AND MAKE SURE THAT HE ALSO STANDS UP STRAIGHT. A PHARAOH SHOULD NEVER BE BENT OVER.
GOOD DAY, SAGE.
WELL, MY CHILDREN, TOMORROW WE ARE GOING TO SAVE KEMET FROM A *CONSPIRACY*.
STAND READY.
ARE YOU SURE YOU KNOW WHAT YOU'RE DOING, AMENHO? THE PRIESTS OF RA WILL NEVER FORGIVE US.
YES, AI.
A PLOT HAS BEEN HATCHED IN IUNU. IT IS NECESSARY THAT WE *BREAK* THIS BAD EGG.
ISN'T IT A *PLEASURE* TO DEAL WITH OUR PHARAOH (MAY THE GODS GRANT HIM LONG LIFE, HEALTH, AND STRENGTH)!
HE DECIDES THINGS VERY QUICKLY. YOU ONLY HAVE TO TELL HIM *IN TIME* WHEN TO DO THEM.

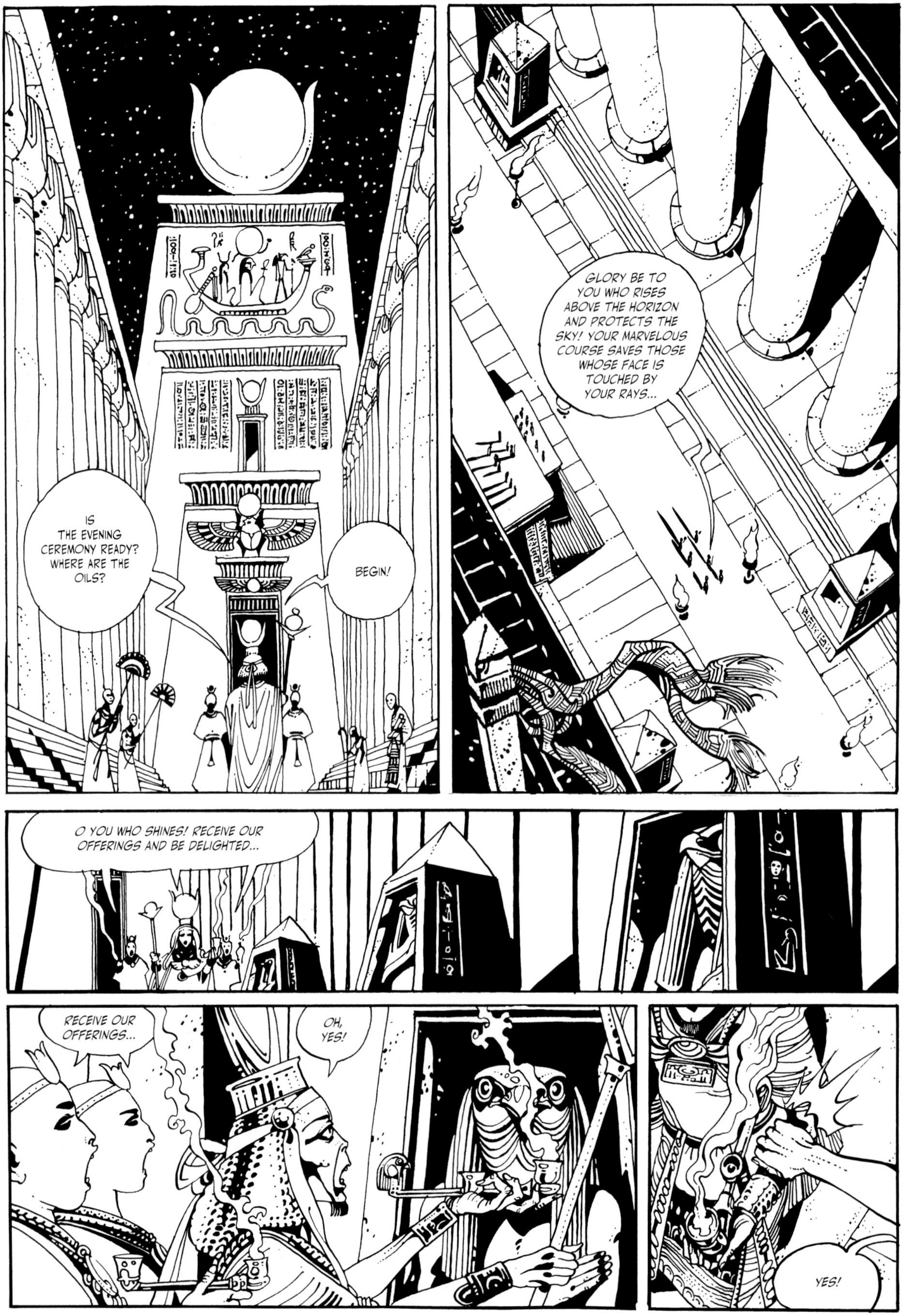
IS THE EVENING CEREMONY READY? WHERE ARE THE OILS?
BEGIN!
GLORY BE TO YOU WHO RISES ABOVE THE HORIZON AND PROTECTS THE SKY! YOUR MARVELOUS COURSE SAVES THOSE WHOSE FACE IS TOUCHED BY YOUR RAYS...
O YOU WHO SHINES! RECEIVE OUR OFFERINGS AND BE DELIGHTED...
RECEIVE OUR OFFERINGS...
OH, YES!
YES!

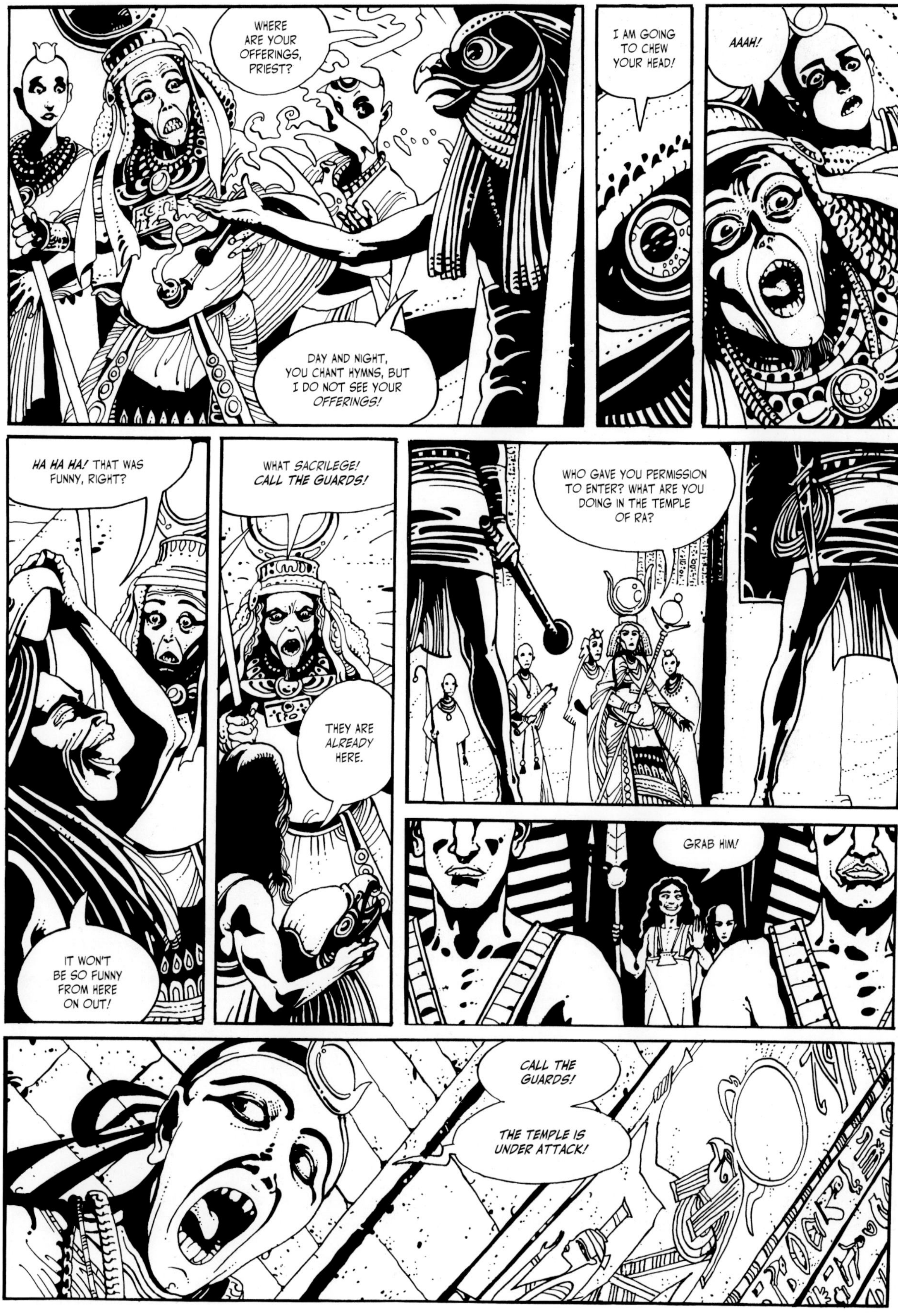
WHERE ARE YOUR OFFERINGS, PRIEST?
DAY AND NIGHT, YOU CHANT HYMNS, BUT I DO NOT SEE YOUR *OFFERINGS!*
I AM GOING TO CHEW YOUR HEAD!
AAAH!
HA HA HA! THAT WAS FUNNY, RIGHT?
IT WON'T BE SO FUNNY FROM HERE ON OUT!
WHAT *SACRILEGE!* **CALL THE GUARDS!**
THEY ARE *ALREADY* HERE.
WHO GAVE YOU PERMISSION TO ENTER? WHAT ARE YOU DOING IN THE TEMPLE OF RA?
GRAB HIM!
CALL THE GUARDS!
THE TEMPLE IS UNDER ATTACK!

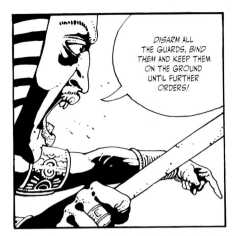

DISARM ALL THE GUARDS, *BIND THEM* AND KEEP THEM ON THE GROUND UNTIL FURTHER ORDERS!

I AM THE *GRAND PRIEST* AND THE *SUPERIOR* OF THE TEMPLE OF RA! HOW DARE YOU TREAT ME LIKE THIS?

THE GREAT MAGICIAN AND THE PROPHET OF OUR TEMPLE IS *OSARSEPH*, STUDENT OF AMENHOTEP, SON OF HAPU, WHO IS, HIMSELF, THE FRIEND AND COUNCILOR OF THE PHARAOH AMENHOTEP III (MAY THE GODS GRANT HIM LONG LIFE, HEALTH, AND STRENGTH)!

I KNOW THAT. I AM AMENHOTEP, SON OF HAPU.

IT IS YOU?!

BUT THEN, WHY...?

FIRSTLY, I DREAMT OF MEETING MY DEAR STUDENT, OSARSEPH. SECONDLY, YOU HAVE BOTH STRAYED FROM THE TEMPLE'S IDEALS BECAUSE YOU HAVE PROFANED IT WITH YOUR LEPERS...

THIRDLY, IT IS NO LONGER THE TEMPLE OF RA, BUT THE TEMPLE OF *AMUN-RA*. THIS IS A NEW TITLE IN THE THEOLOGY OF WASET. THE TWO GODS HAVE BEEN UNITED TO FORM ONE, AND THE CENTER OF THIS NEW CULT WILL BE WASET, THE CAPITAL OF THE KINGDOM OF KEMET!

THE MOST IMPORTANT SACRED OBJECTS WILL BE TRANSFERRED TO THE CAPITAL INCLUDING *BENBEN*, THE DIVINE STONE, AND RA'S BOAT OF A MILLION YEARS... ARE THERE ANY OBJECTIONS?

BUT...

BY THE WAY...

...WE MUST COUNT THE *BEAUTY SPOTS* ON YOUR FACE. ACCORDING TO THE ANCIENT LAWS REGARDING *PURITY*, DO YOU NOT HAVE *TOO MANY* FOR A PRIEST?

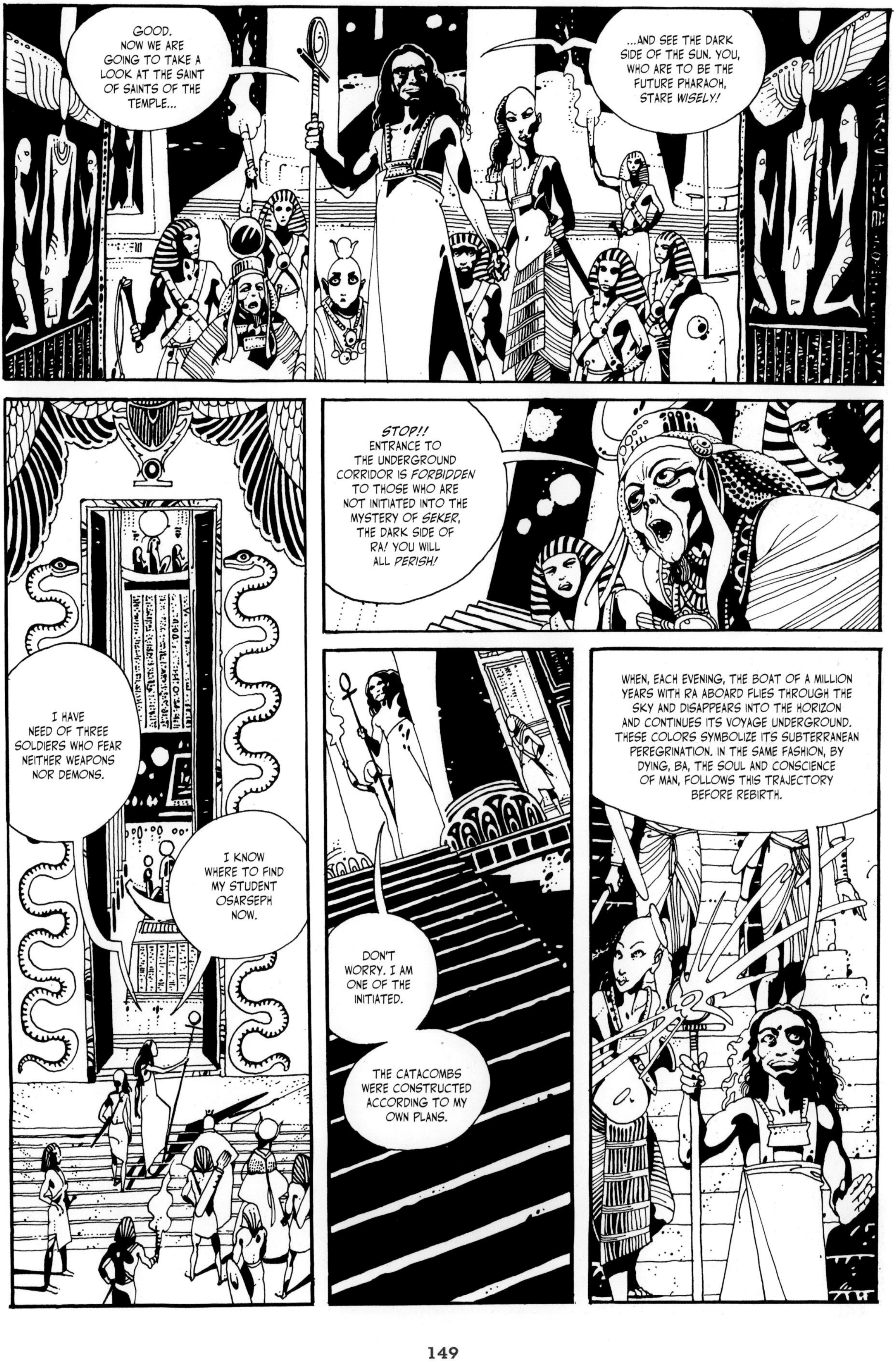
GOOD. NOW WE ARE GOING TO TAKE A LOOK AT THE SAINT OF SAINTS OF THE TEMPLE...
...AND SEE THE DARK SIDE OF THE SUN. YOU, WHO ARE TO BE THE FUTURE PHARAOH, STARE *WISELY!*
I HAVE NEED OF THREE SOLDIERS WHO FEAR NEITHER WEAPONS NOR DEMONS.
I KNOW WHERE TO FIND MY STUDENT OSARSEPH NOW.
STOP!! ENTRANCE TO THE UNDERGROUND CORRIDOR IS *FORBIDDEN* TO THOSE WHO ARE NOT INITIATED INTO THE MYSTERY OF *SEKER*, THE DARK SIDE OF RA! YOU WILL ALL *PERISH!*
DON'T WORRY. I AM ONE OF THE INITIATED.
THE CATACOMBS WERE CONSTRUCTED ACCORDING TO MY OWN PLANS.
WHEN, EACH EVENING, THE BOAT OF A MILLION YEARS WITH RA ABOARD FLIES THROUGH THE SKY AND DISAPPEARS INTO THE HORIZON AND CONTINUES ITS VOYAGE UNDERGROUND. THESE COLORS SYMBOLIZE ITS SUBTERRANEAN PEREGRINATION. IN THE SAME FASHION, BY DYING, BA, THE SOUL AND CONSCIENCE OF MAN, FOLLOWS THIS TRAJECTORY BEFORE REBIRTH.

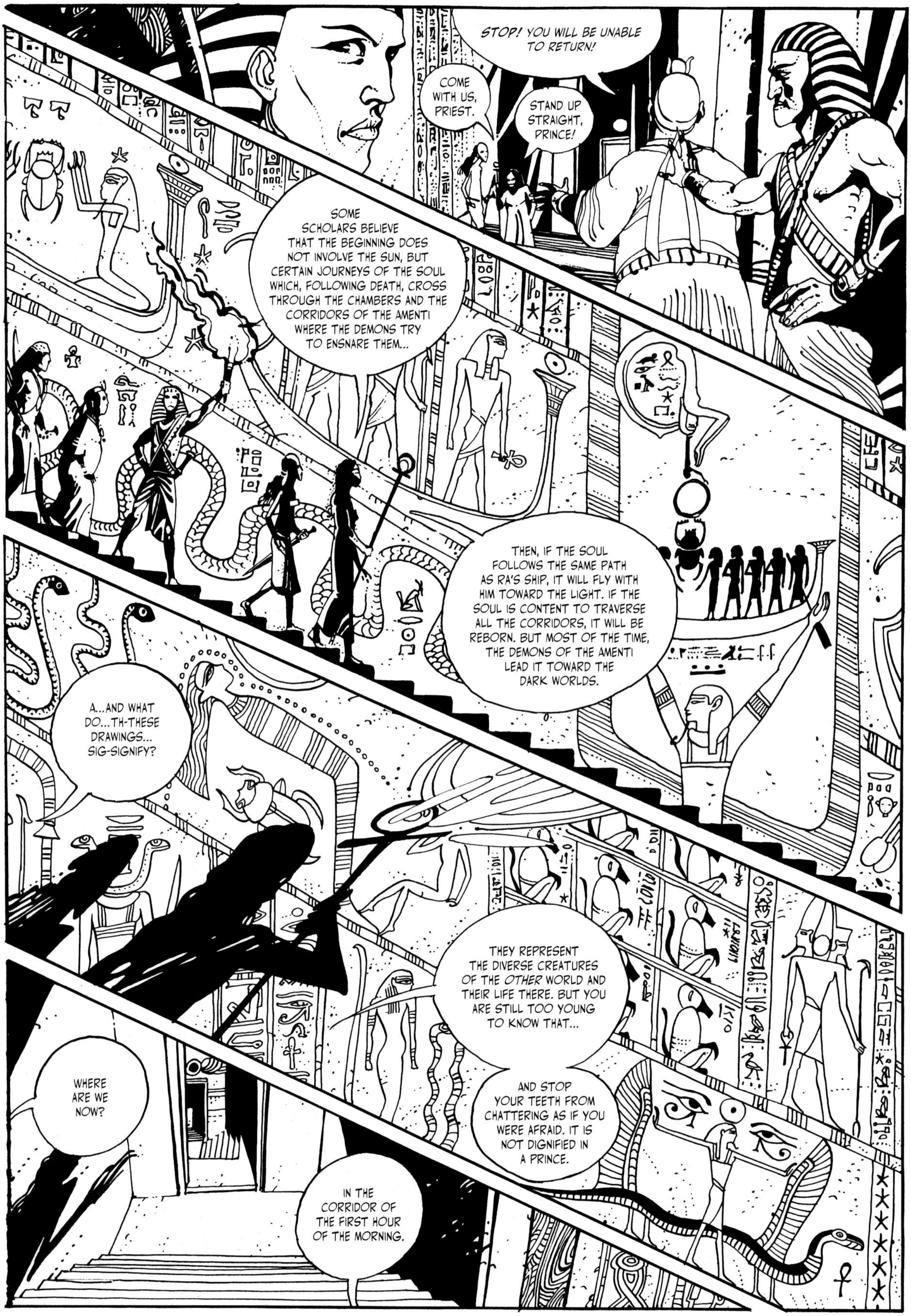
STOP! YOU WILL BE UNABLE TO RETURN!
COME WITH US, PRIEST.
STAND UP STRAIGHT, PRINCE!
SOME SCHOLARS BELIEVE THAT THE BEGINNING DOES NOT INVOLVE THE SUN, BUT CERTAIN JOURNEYS OF THE SOUL WHICH, FOLLOWING DEATH, CROSS THROUGH THE CHAMBERS AND THE CORRIDORS OF THE AMENTI WHERE THE DEMONS TRY TO ENSNARE THEM...
THEN, IF THE SOUL FOLLOWS THE SAME PATH AS RA'S SHIP, IT WILL FLY WITH HIM TOWARD THE LIGHT. IF THE SOUL IS CONTENT TO TRAVERSE ALL THE CORRIDORS, IT WILL BE REBORN. BUT MOST OF THE TIME, THE DEMONS OF THE AMENTI LEAD IT TOWARD THE DARK WORLDS.
A...AND WHAT DO...TH-THESE DRAWINGS... SIG-SIGNIFY?
THEY REPRESENT THE DIVERSE CREATURES OF THE OTHER WORLD AND THEIR LIFE THERE. BUT YOU ARE STILL TOO YOUNG TO KNOW THAT...
AND STOP YOUR TEETH FROM CHATTERING AS IF YOU WERE AFRAID. IT IS NOT DIGNIFIED IN A PRINCE.
WHERE ARE WE NOW?
IN THE CORRIDOR OF THE FIRST HOUR OF THE MORNING.

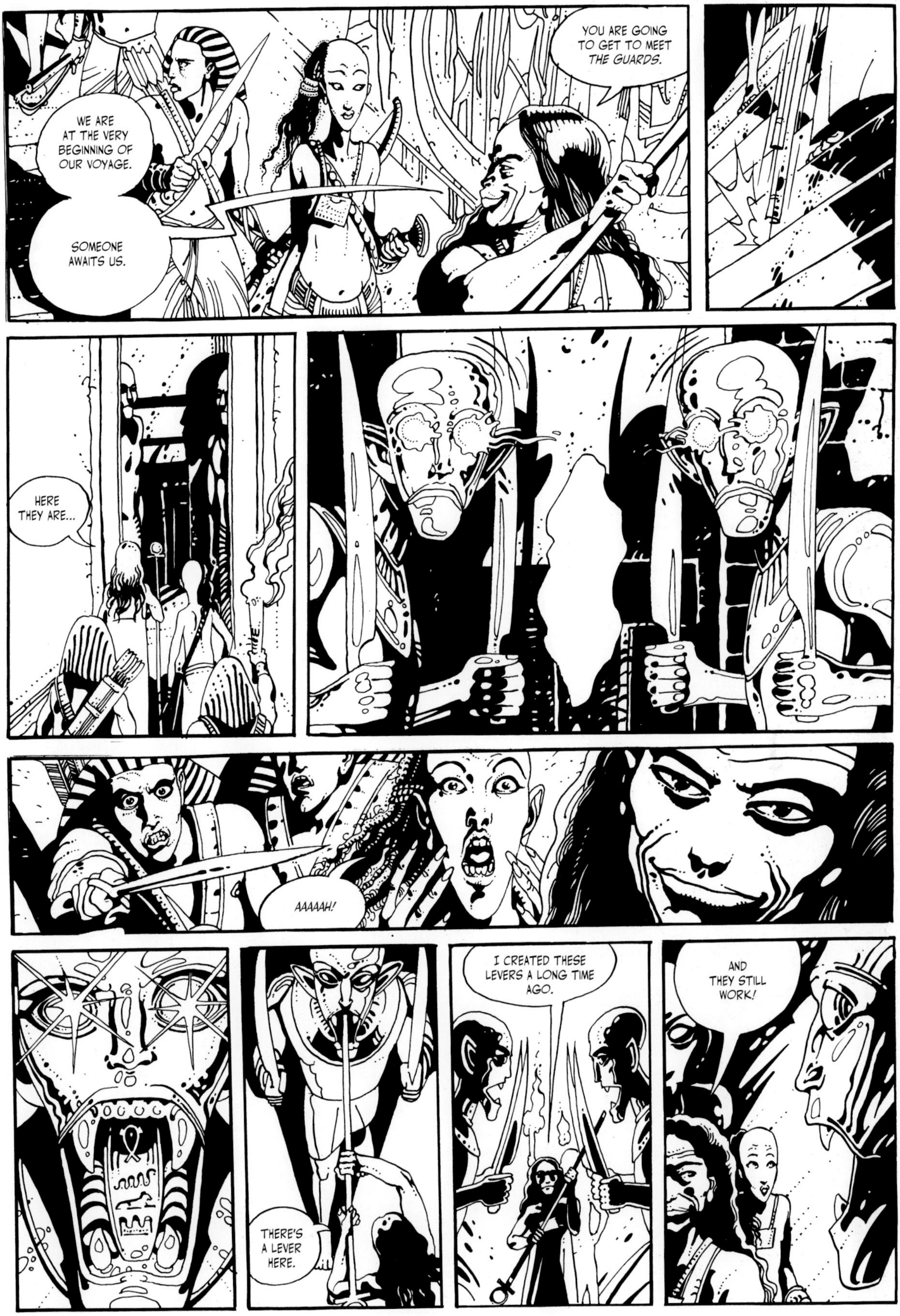

WE ARE AT THE VERY BEGINNING OF OUR VOYAGE.
SOMEONE AWAITS US.
YOU ARE GOING TO GET TO MEET *THE GUARDS.*
HERE THEY ARE...
AAAAAH!
THERE'S A LEVER HERE.
I CREATED THESE LEVERS A LONG TIME AGO.
AND THEY STILL WORK!

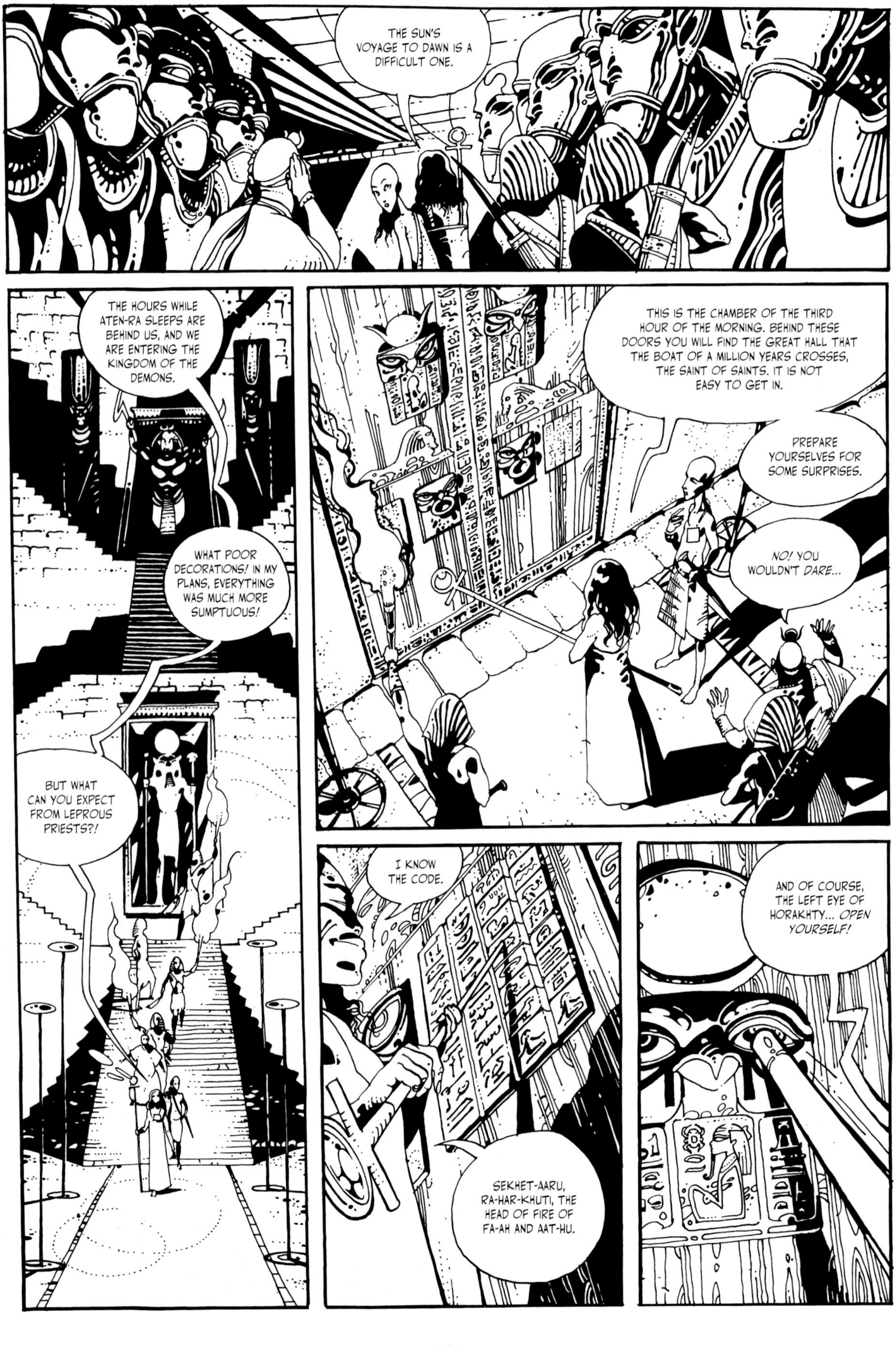
THE SUN'S VOYAGE TO DAWN IS A DIFFICULT ONE.
THE HOURS WHILE ATEN-RA SLEEPS ARE BEHIND US, AND WE ARE ENTERING THE KINGDOM OF THE DEMONS.
WHAT POOR DECORATIONS! IN MY PLANS, EVERYTHING WAS MUCH MORE SUMPTUOUS!
BUT WHAT CAN YOU EXPECT FROM LEPROUS PRIESTS?!
THIS IS THE CHAMBER OF THE THIRD HOUR OF THE MORNING. BEHIND THESE DOORS YOU WILL FIND THE GREAT HALL THAT THE BOAT OF A MILLION YEARS CROSSES, THE SAINT OF SAINTS. IT IS NOT EASY TO GET IN.
PREPARE YOURSELVES FOR SOME SURPRISES.
NO! YOU WOULDN'T *DARE*...
I KNOW THE CODE.
SEKHET-AARU, RA-HAR-KHUTI, THE HEAD OF FIRE OF FA-AH AND AAT-HU.
AND OF COURSE, THE LEFT EYE OF HORAKHTY... *OPEN YOURSELF!*

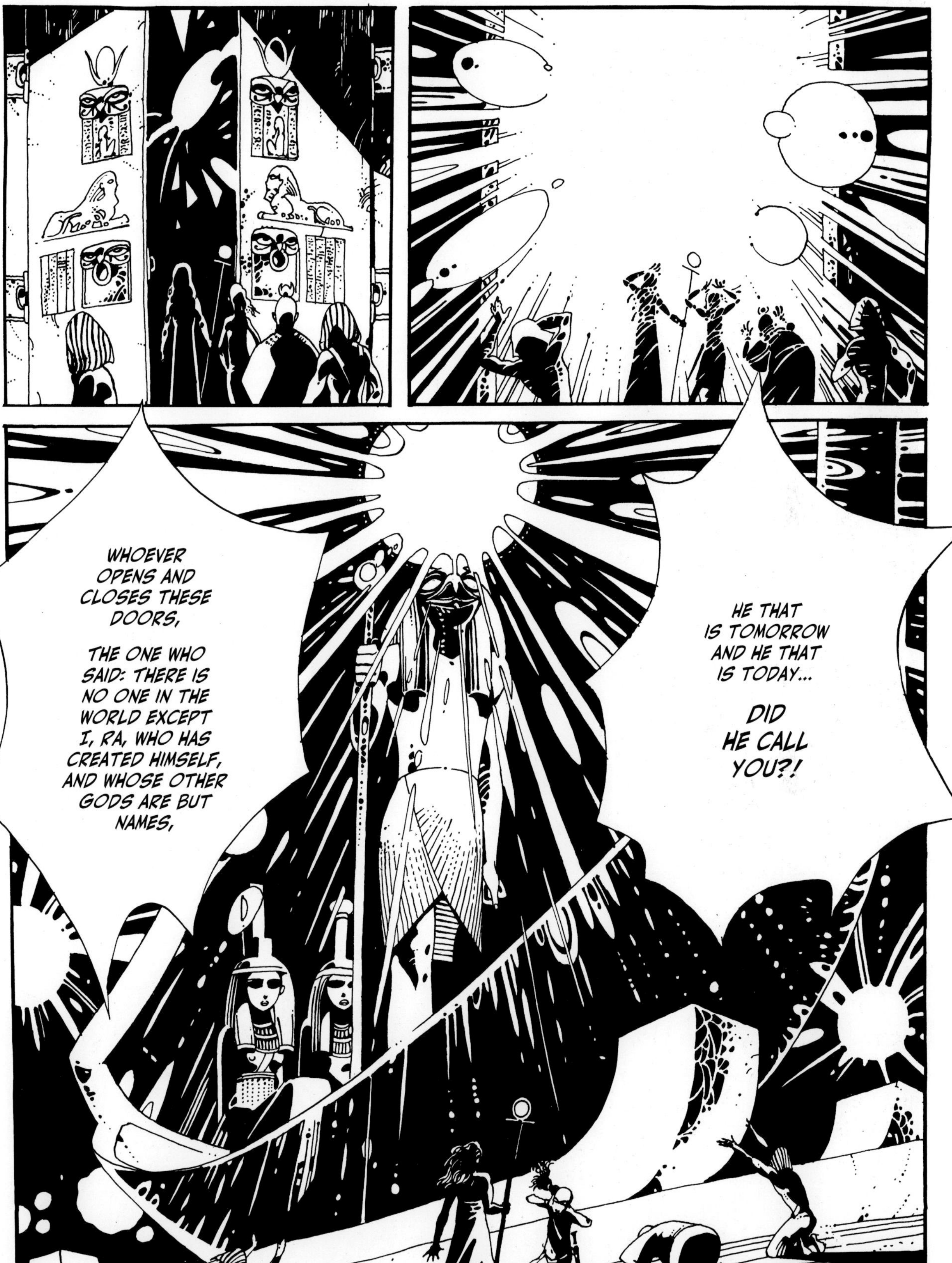
WHOEVER OPENS AND CLOSES THESE DOORS,
THE ONE WHO SAID: THERE IS NO ONE IN THE WORLD EXCEPT I, RA, WHO HAS CREATED HIMSELF, AND WHOSE OTHER GODS ARE BUT NAMES,
HE THAT IS TOMORROW AND HE THAT IS TODAY...
DID HE CALL YOU?!

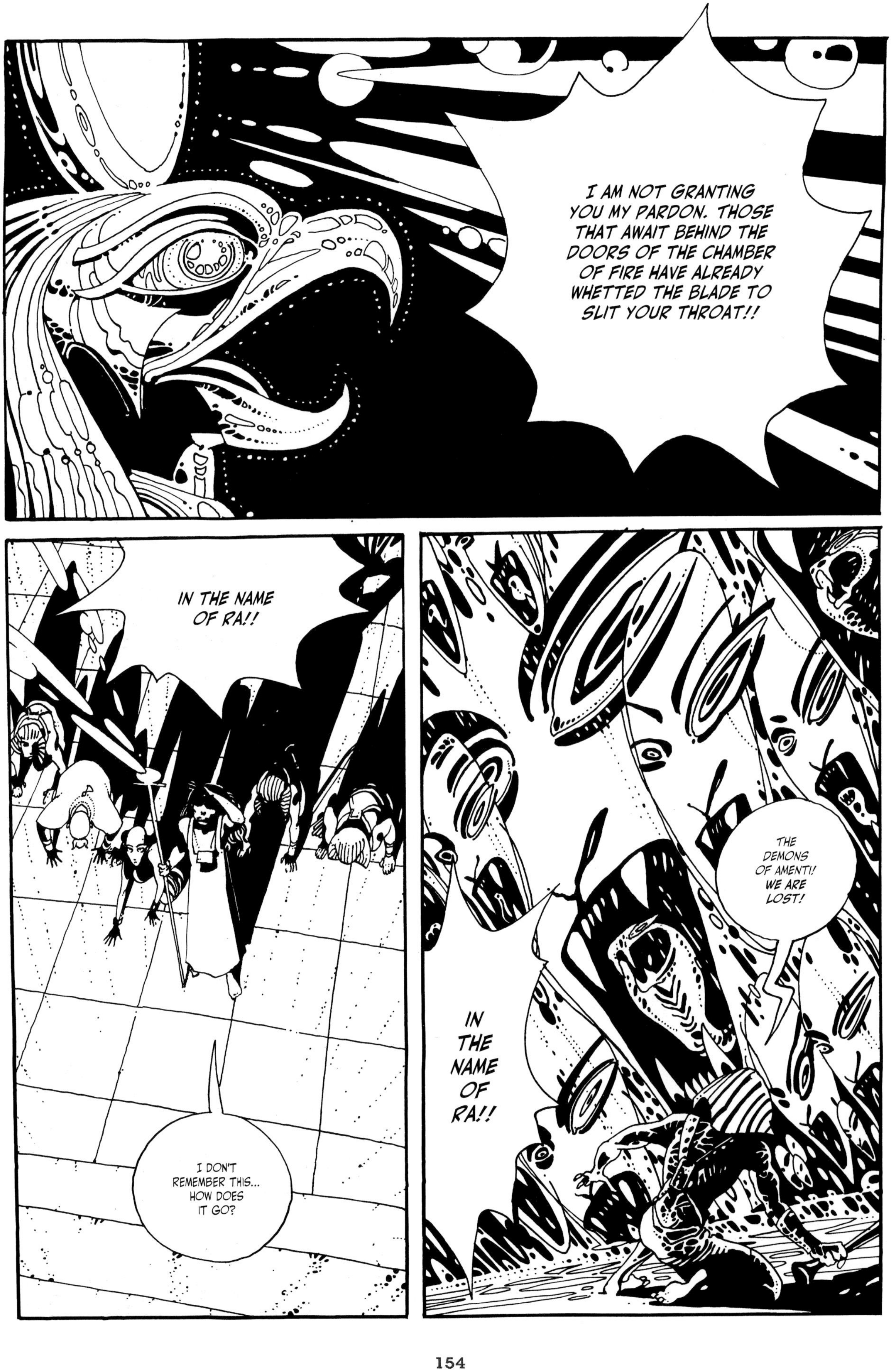
I AM NOT GRANTING YOU MY PARDON. THOSE THAT AWAIT BEHIND THE DOORS OF THE CHAMBER OF FIRE HAVE ALREADY WHETTED THE BLADE TO SLIT YOUR THROAT!!
IN THE NAME OF RA!!
I DON'T REMEMBER THIS... HOW DOES IT GO?
THE DEMONS OF AMENTI! WE ARE LOST!
IN THE NAME OF RA!!

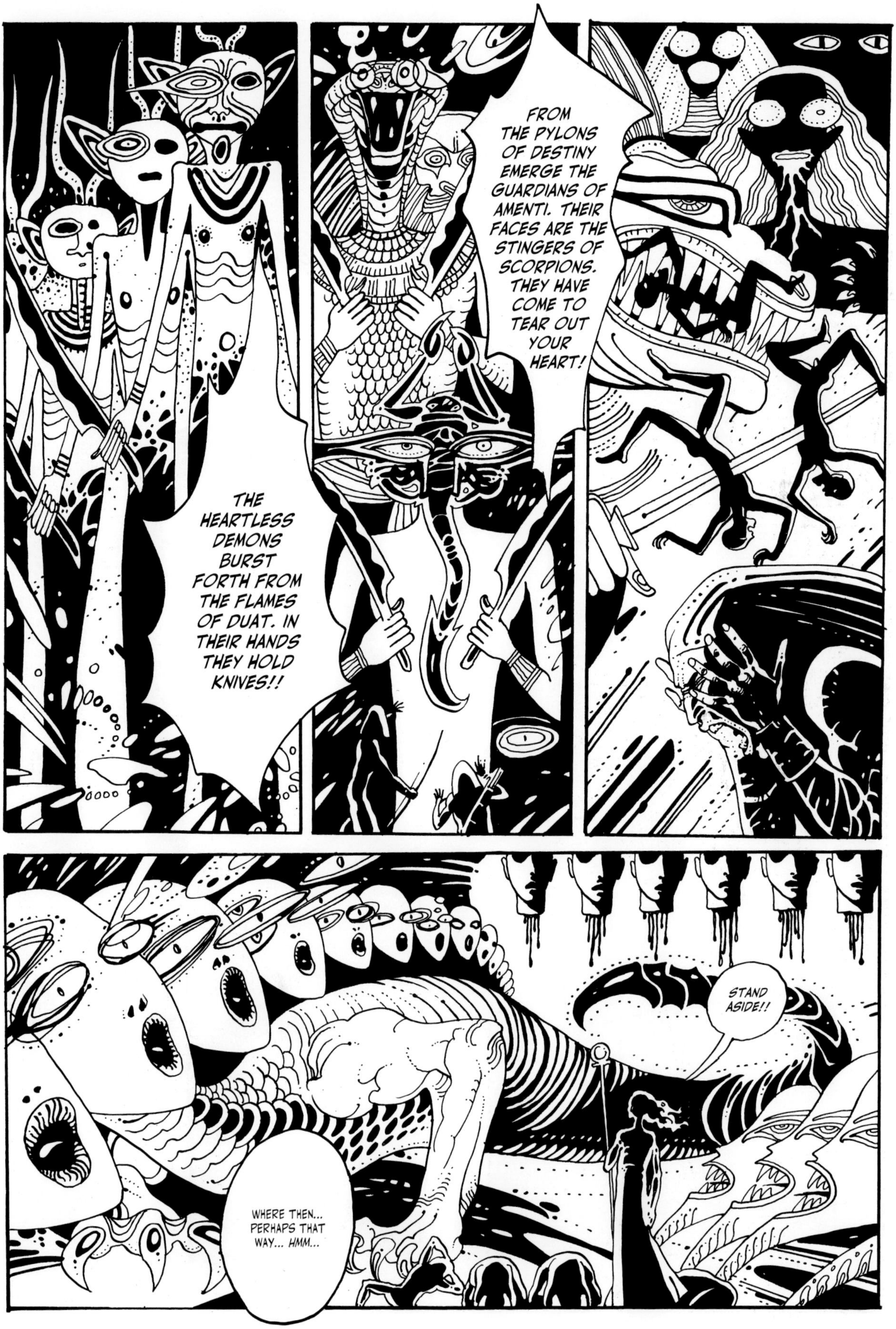
THE HEARTLESS DEMONS BURST FORTH FROM THE FLAMES OF DUAT. IN THEIR HANDS THEY HOLD KNIVES!!
FROM THE PYLONS OF DESTINY EMERGE THE GUARDIANS OF AMENTI. THEIR FACES ARE THE STINGERS OF SCORPIONS. THEY HAVE COME TO TEAR OUT YOUR HEART!
STAND ASIDE!!
WHERE THEN... PERHAPS THAT WAY... HMM...

WE HAVE FOLLOWED THE PATH OF RA'S BOAT AND WE HAVE OFFENDED HIM! WE ARE ALL GOING TO PERISH!

WHAT DO WE DO, PRIEST?

FORWARD! FOLLOW ME!

I HAVE FINALLY UNDERSTOOD.

CLIMB THE STEPS! SOME PRIESTS ARE SEATED ON HIGH. THEIR TRUMPETS SHRIEK AND CREATE VISIONS USING MIRRORS AND CRYSTALS!

MEANWHILE, I WILL PUT THINGS IN ORDER HERE...

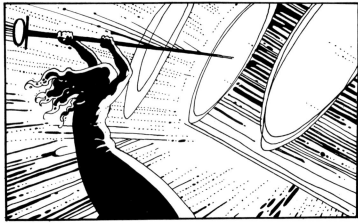

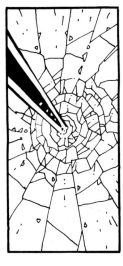

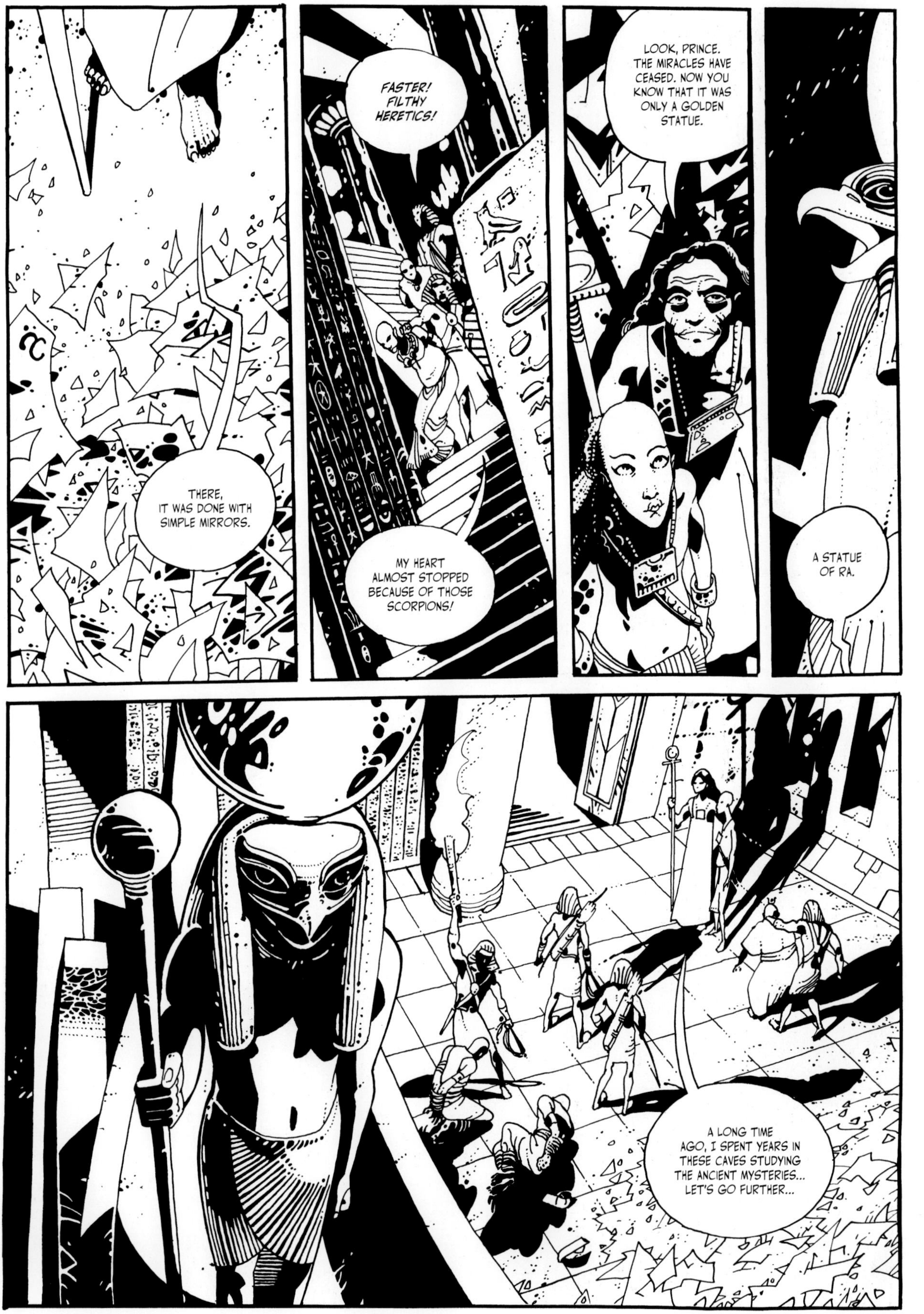
THERE, IT WAS DONE WITH SIMPLE MIRRORS.
FASTER! FILTHY HERETICS!
MY HEART ALMOST STOPPED BECAUSE OF THOSE SCORPIONS!
LOOK, PRINCE. THE MIRACLES HAVE CEASED. NOW YOU KNOW THAT IT WAS ONLY A GOLDEN STATUE.
A STATUE OF RA.
A LONG TIME AGO, I SPENT YEARS IN THESE CAVES STUDYING THE ANCIENT MYSTERIES... LET'S GO FURTHER...

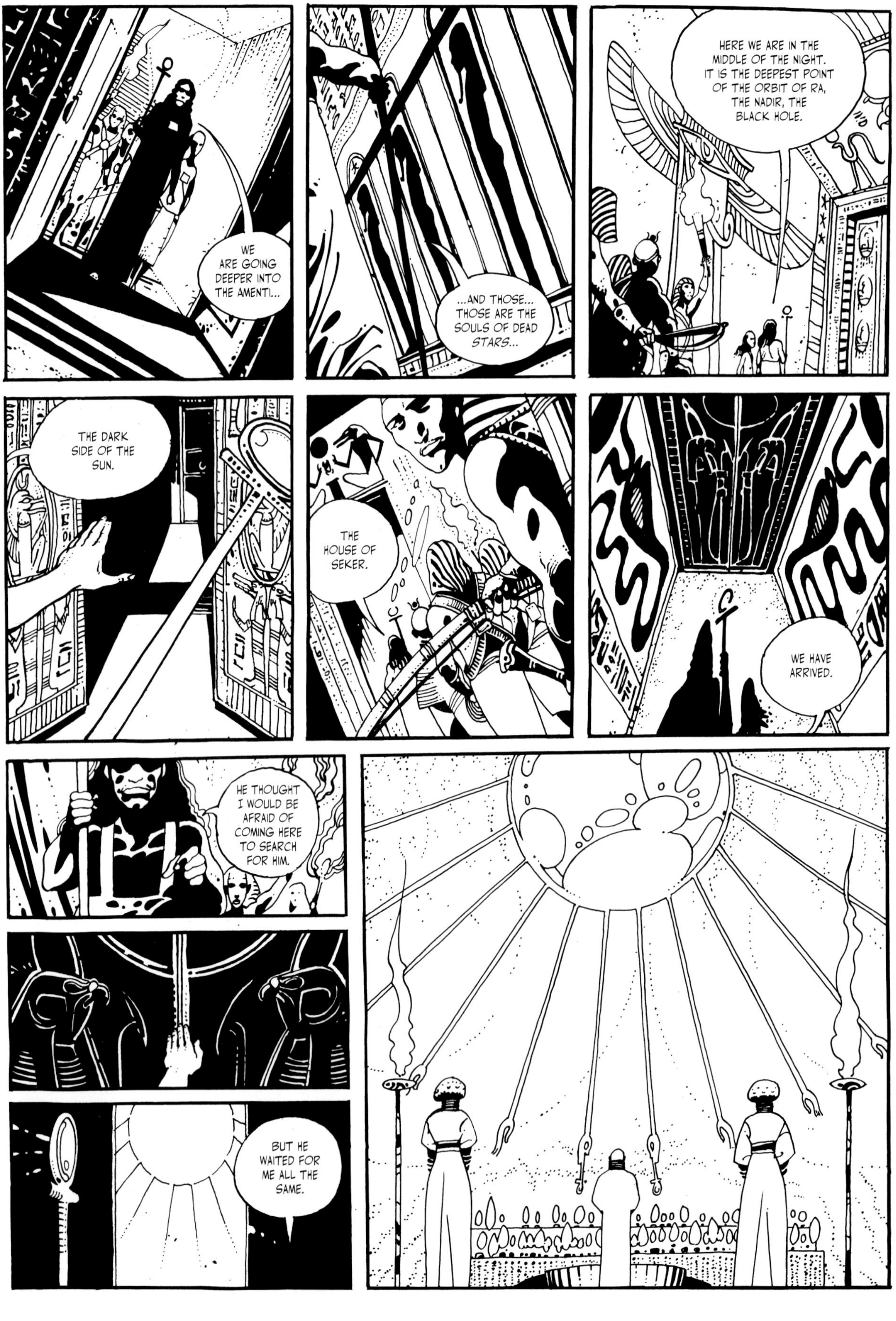
WE ARE GOING DEEPER INTO THE AMENTI...
...AND THOSE... THOSE ARE THE SOULS OF DEAD STARS...
HERE WE ARE IN THE MIDDLE OF THE NIGHT. IT IS THE DEEPEST POINT OF THE ORBIT OF RA, THE NADIR, THE BLACK HOLE.
THE DARK SIDE OF THE SUN.
THE HOUSE OF SEKER.
WE HAVE ARRIVED.
HE THOUGHT I WOULD BE AFRAID OF COMING HERE TO SEARCH FOR HIM.
BUT HE WAITED FOR ME ALL THE SAME.

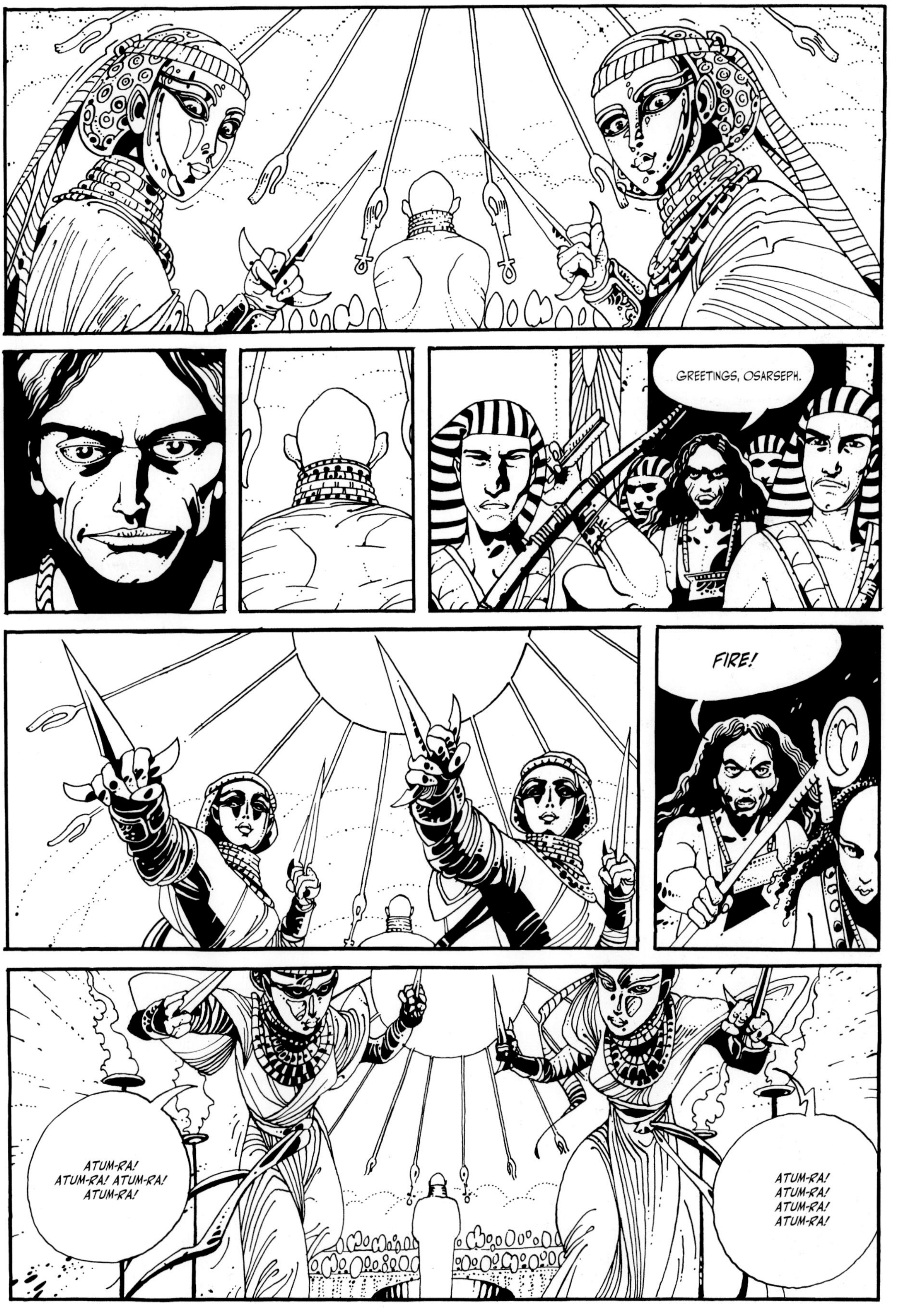
GREETINGS, OSARSEPH.
FIRE!
ATUM-RA! ATUM-RA! ATUM-RA! ATUM-RA!
ATUM-RA! ATUM-RA! ATUM-RA! ATUM-RA!

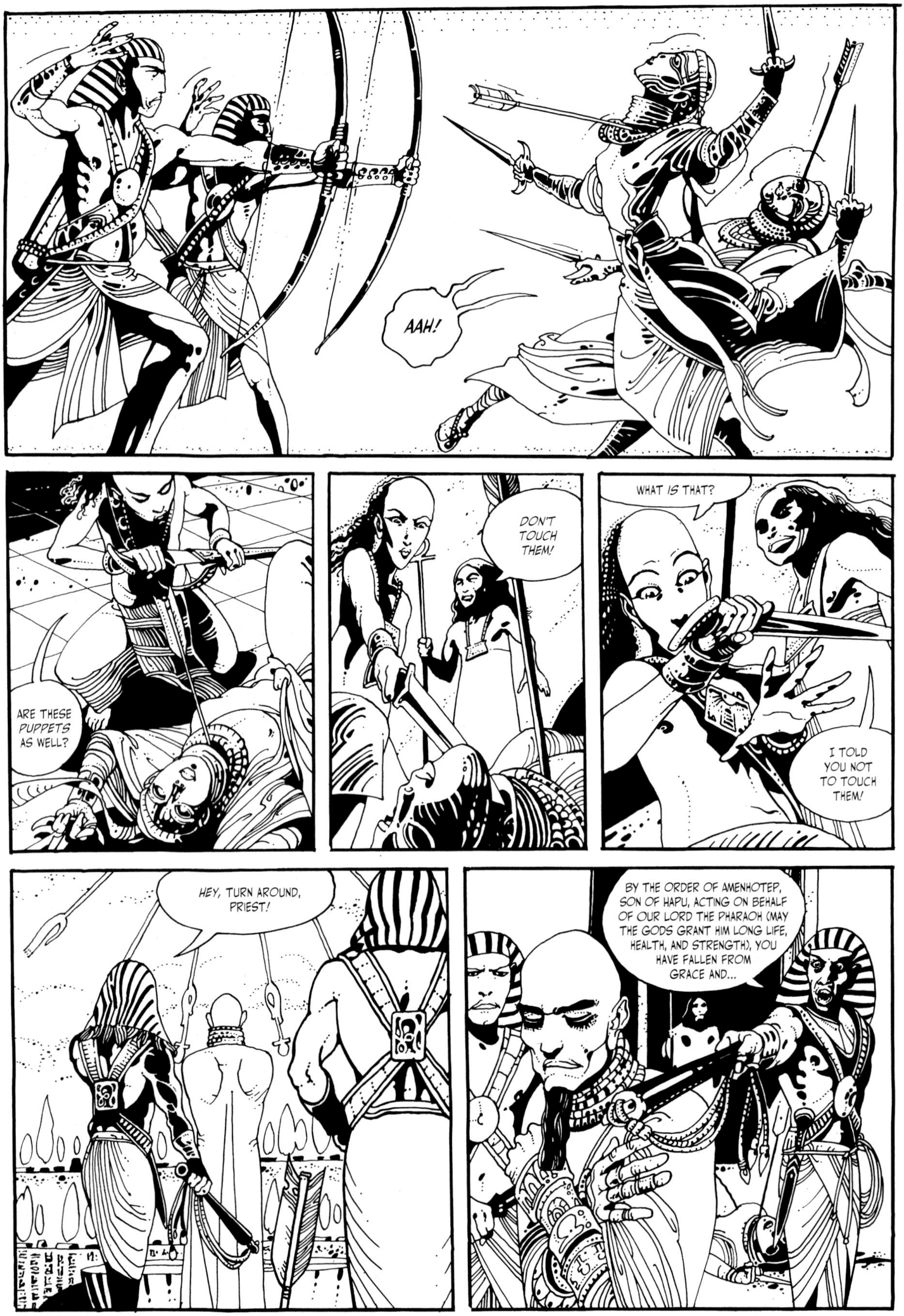
AAH!
ARE THESE PUPPETS AS WELL?
DON'T TOUCH THEM!
WHAT IS THAT?
I TOLD YOU NOT TO TOUCH THEM!
HEY, TURN AROUND, PRIEST!
BY THE ORDER OF AMENHOTEP, SON OF HAPU, ACTING ON BEHALF OF OUR LORD THE PHARAOH (MAY THE GODS GRANT HIM LONG LIFE, HEALTH, AND STRENGTH), YOU HAVE FALLEN FROM GRACE AND...

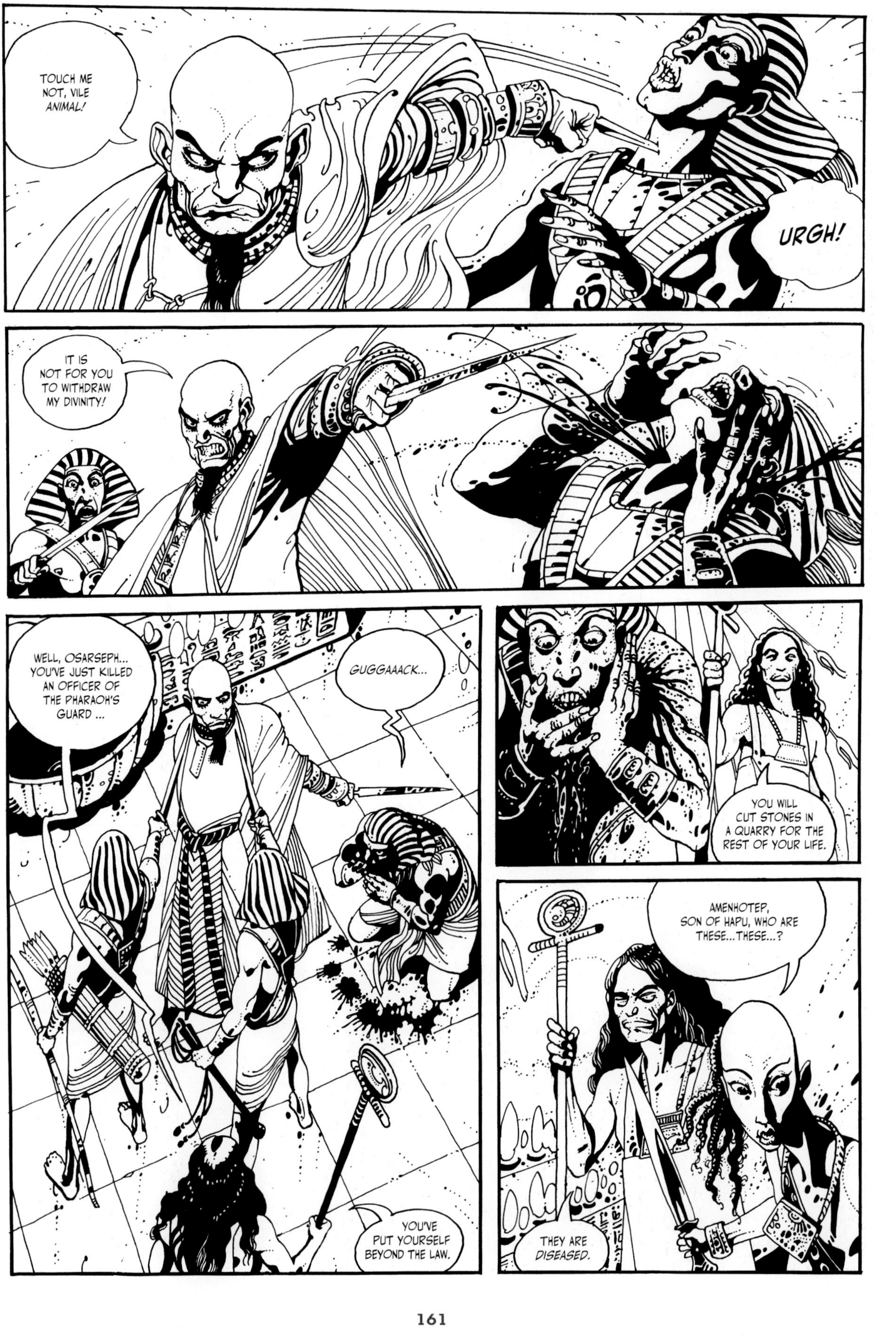
TOUCH ME NOT, VILE *ANIMAL!*
URGH!
IT IS NOT FOR YOU TO WITHDRAW MY DIVINITY!
WELL, OSARSEPH... YOU'VE JUST KILLED AN OFFICER OF THE PHARAOH'S GUARD ...
GUGGAAACK...
YOU'VE PUT YOURSELF BEYOND THE LAW.
YOU WILL CUT STONES IN A QUARRY FOR THE REST OF YOUR LIFE.
AMENHOTEP, SON OF HAPU, WHO ARE THESE...THESE...?
THEY ARE *DISEASED.*

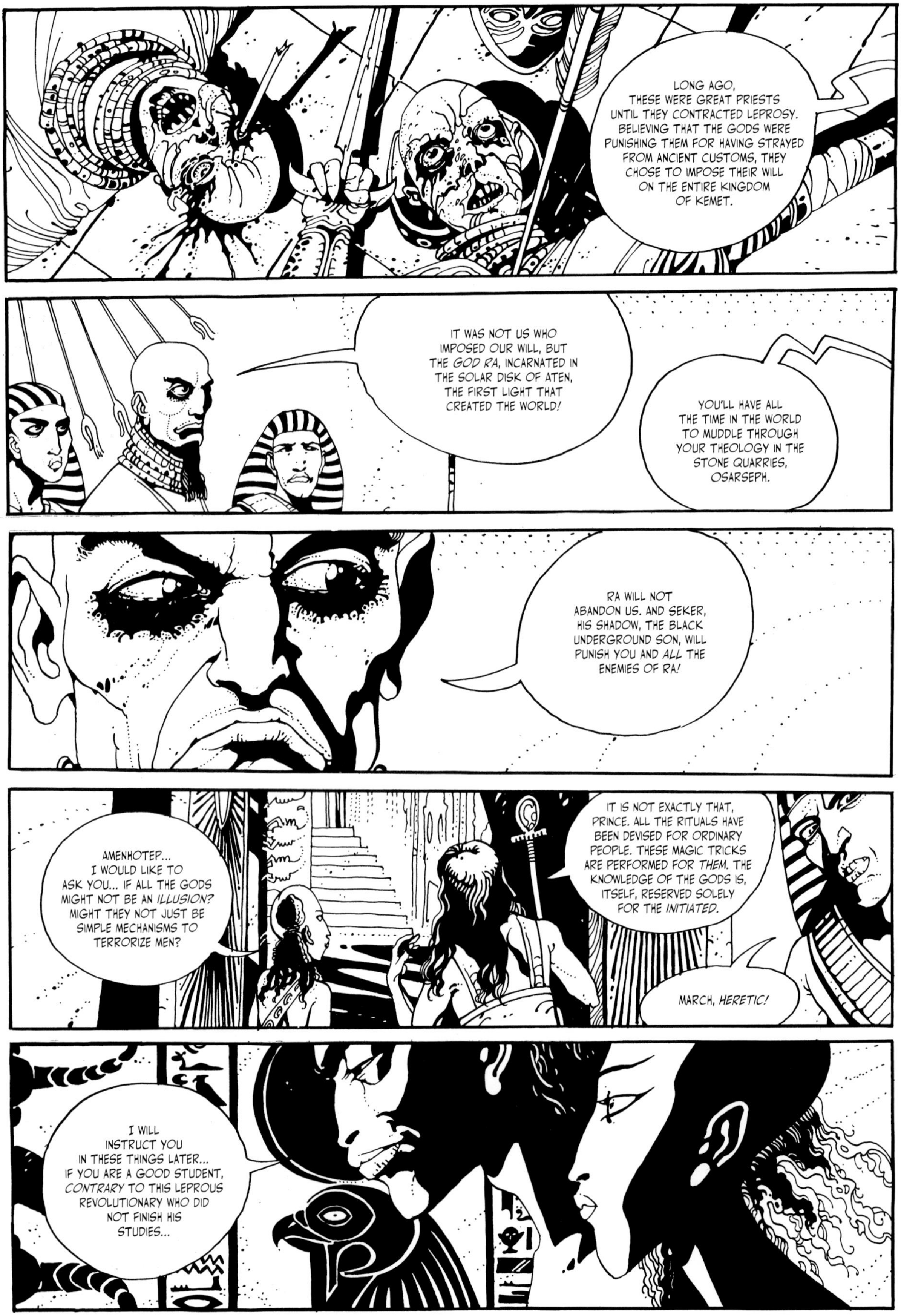
LONG AGO, THESE WERE GREAT PRIESTS UNTIL THEY CONTRACTED LEPROSY. BELIEVING THAT THE GODS WERE PUNISHING THEM FOR HAVING STRAYED FROM ANCIENT CUSTOMS, THEY CHOSE TO IMPOSE THEIR WILL ON THE ENTIRE KINGDOM OF KEMET.
IT WAS NOT US WHO IMPOSED OUR WILL, BUT THE *GOD RA*, INCARNATED IN THE SOLAR DISK OF ATEN, THE FIRST LIGHT THAT CREATED THE WORLD!
YOU'LL HAVE ALL THE TIME IN THE WORLD TO MUDDLE THROUGH YOUR THEOLOGY IN THE STONE QUARRIES, OSARSEPH.
RA WILL NOT ABANDON US. AND SEKER, HIS SHADOW, THE BLACK UNDERGROUND SON, WILL PUNISH YOU AND *ALL* THE ENEMIES OF RA!
AMENHOTEP... I WOULD LIKE TO ASK YOU... IF ALL THE GODS MIGHT NOT BE AN *ILLUSION*? MIGHT THEY NOT JUST BE SIMPLE MECHANISMS TO TERRORIZE MEN?
IT IS NOT EXACTLY THAT, PRINCE. ALL THE RITUALS HAVE BEEN DEVISED FOR ORDINARY PEOPLE. THESE MAGIC TRICKS ARE PERFORMED FOR *THEM*. THE KNOWLEDGE OF THE GODS IS, ITSELF, RESERVED SOLELY FOR THE *INITIATED*.
MARCH, *HERETIC!*
I WILL INSTRUCT YOU IN THESE THINGS LATER... IF YOU ARE A GOOD STUDENT, *CONTRARY* TO THIS LEPROUS REVOLUTIONARY WHO DID NOT FINISH HIS STUDIES...

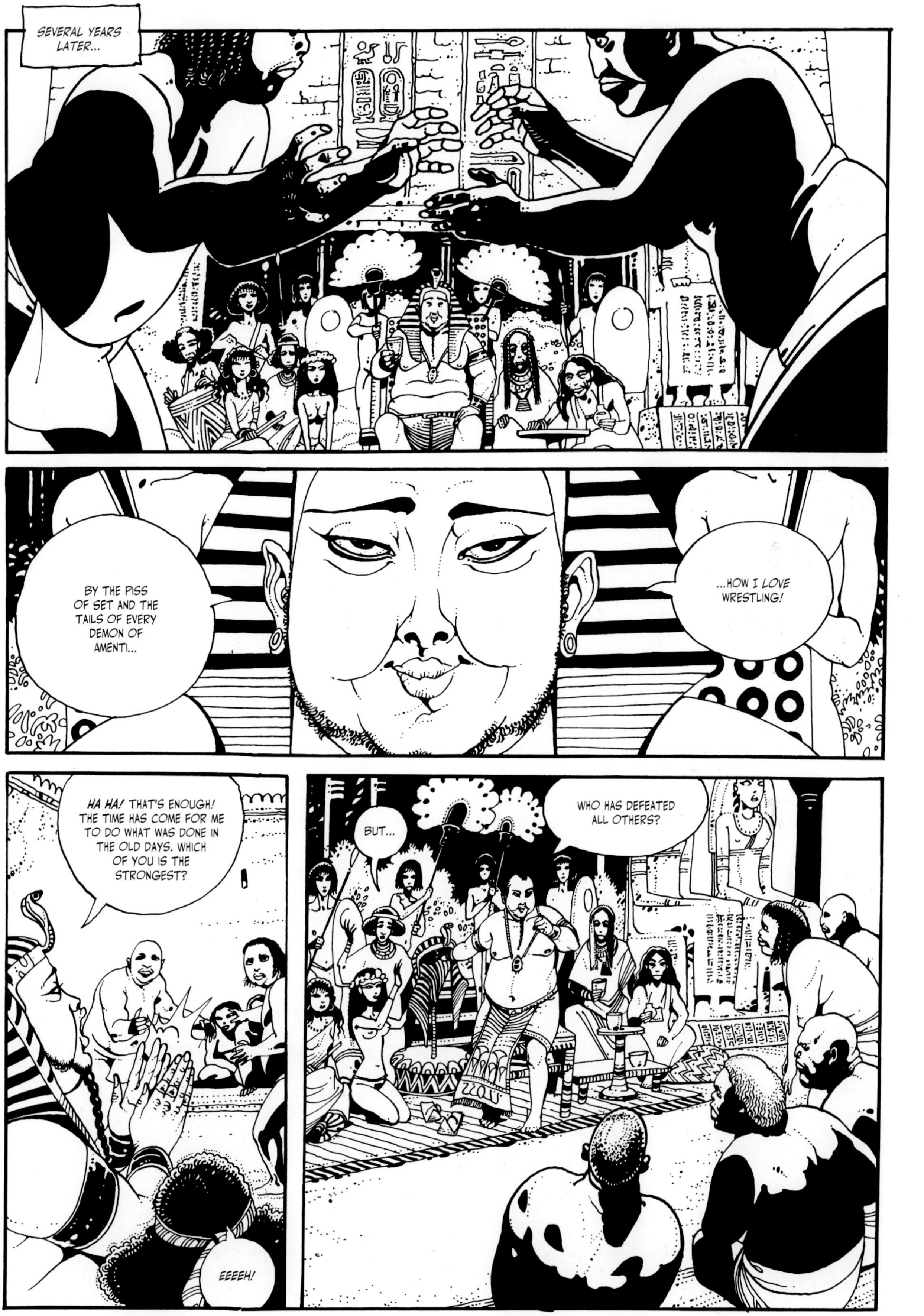
SEVERAL YEARS LATER...
BY THE PISS OF SET AND THE TAILS OF EVERY DEMON OF AMENTI...
...HOW I *LOVE* WRESTLING!
HA HA! THAT'S ENOUGH! THE TIME HAS COME FOR ME TO DO WHAT WAS DONE IN THE OLD DAYS. WHICH OF YOU IS THE STRONGEST?
EEEEH!
BUT...
WHO HAS DEFEATED ALL OTHERS?

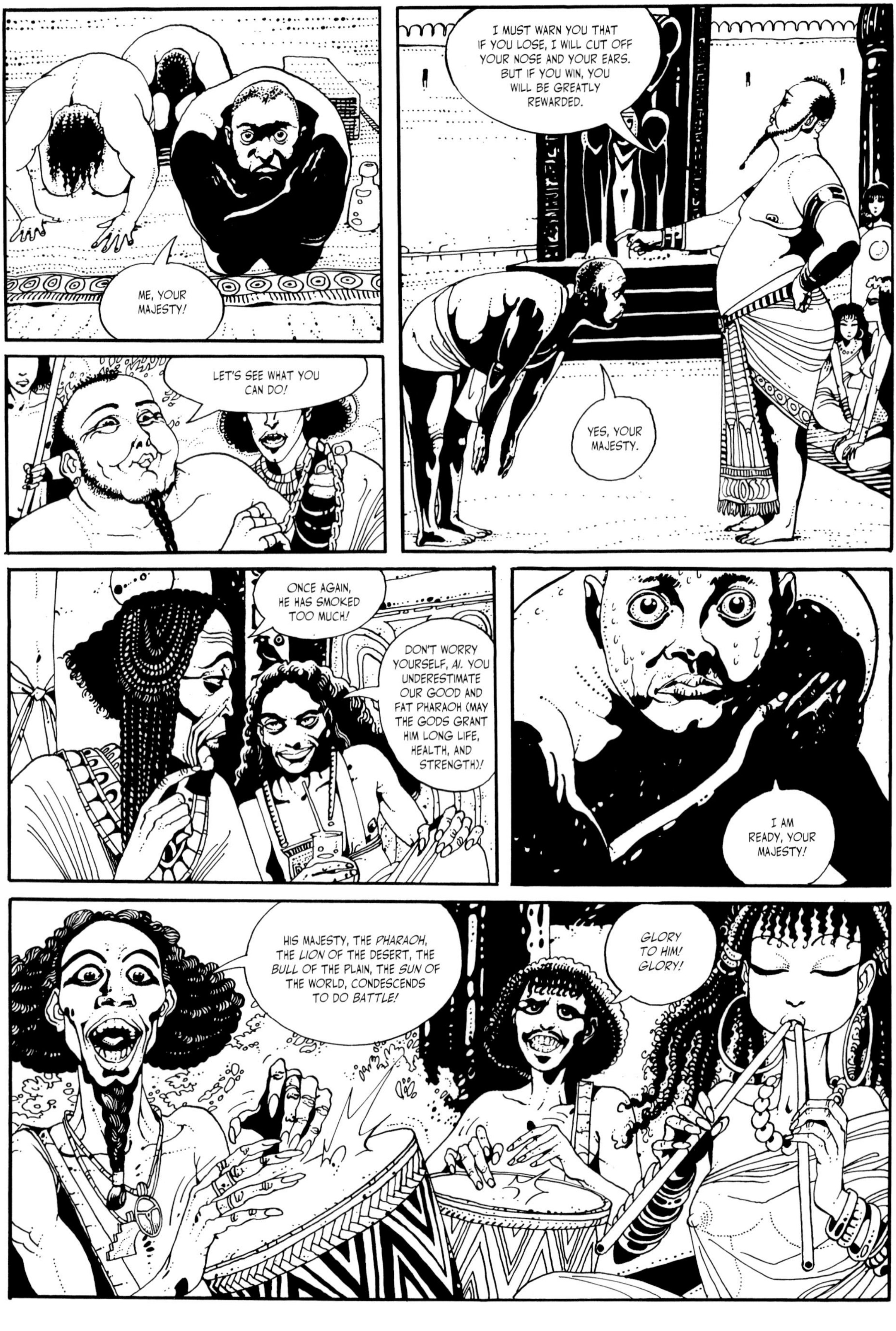
ME, YOUR MAJESTY!
I MUST WARN YOU THAT IF YOU LOSE, I WILL CUT OFF YOUR NOSE AND YOUR EARS. BUT IF YOU WIN, YOU WILL BE GREATLY REWARDED.
YES, YOUR MAJESTY.
LET'S SEE WHAT YOU CAN DO!
ONCE AGAIN, HE HAS SMOKED TOO MUCH!
DON'T WORRY YOURSELF, *AI*. YOU UNDERESTIMATE OUR GOOD AND FAT PHARAOH (MAY THE GODS GRANT HIM LONG LIFE, HEALTH, AND STRENGTH)!
I AM READY, YOUR MAJESTY!
HIS MAJESTY, THE *PHARAOH*, THE *LION* OF THE DESERT, THE *BULL* OF THE PLAIN, THE *SUN* OF THE WORLD, CONDESCENDS TO DO BATTLE!
GLORY TO HIM! GLORY!

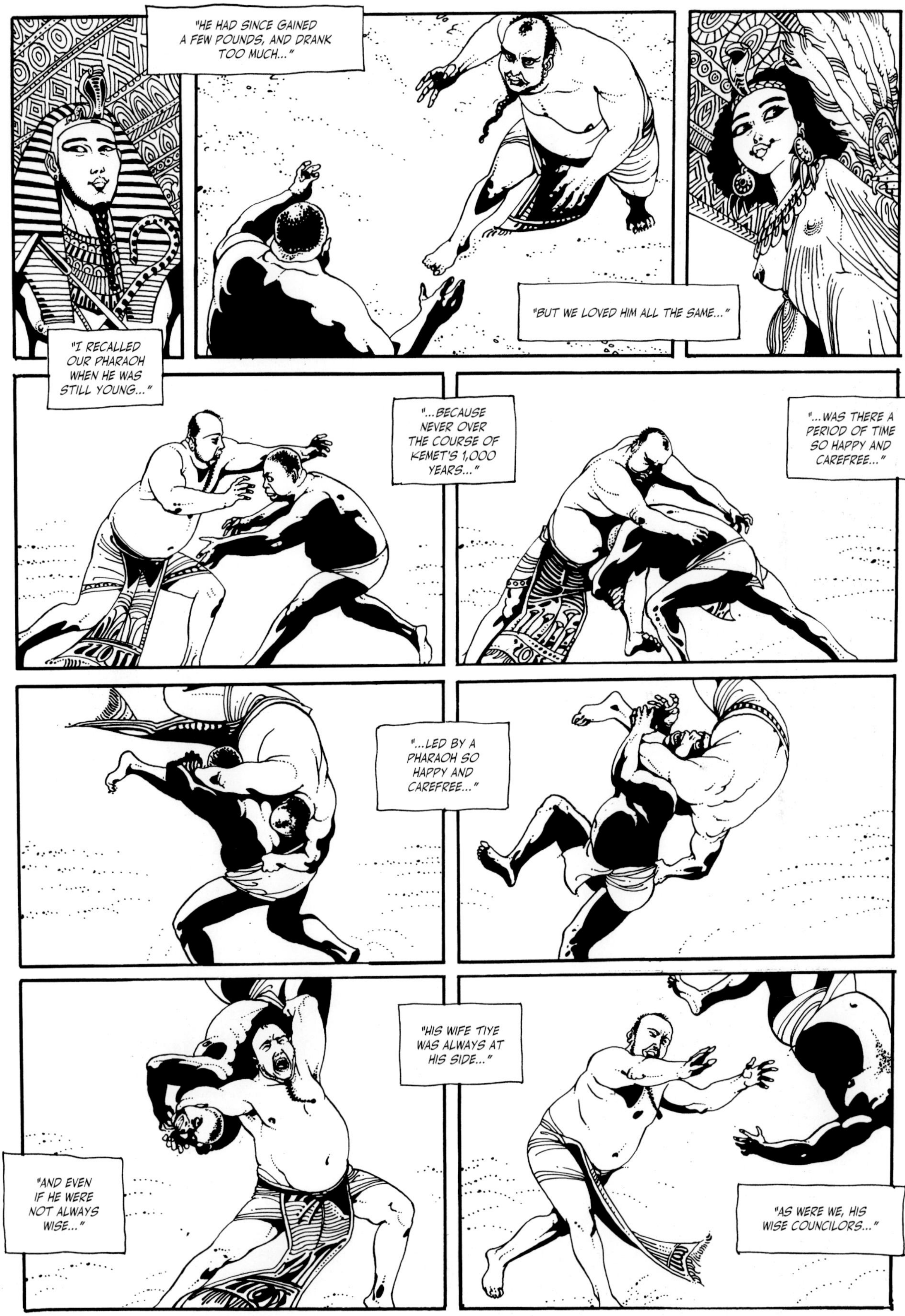
"I RECALLED OUR PHARAOH WHEN HE WAS STILL YOUNG..."
"HE HAD SINCE GAINED A FEW POUNDS, AND DRANK TOO MUCH..."
"BUT WE LOVED HIM ALL THE SAME..."
"...BECAUSE NEVER OVER THE COURSE OF KEMET'S 1,000 YEARS..."
"...WAS THERE A PERIOD OF TIME SO HAPPY AND CAREFREE..."
"...LED BY A PHARAOH SO HAPPY AND CAREFREE..."
"HIS WIFE TIYE WAS ALWAYS AT HIS SIDE..."
"AND EVEN IF HE WERE NOT ALWAYS WISE..."
"AS WERE WE, HIS WISE COUNCILORS..."

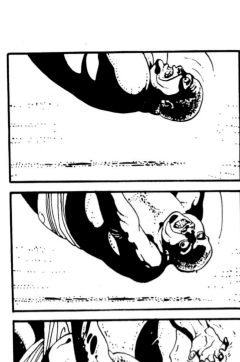

EVERYONE SAW IT! HIS MAJESTY MADE THE EARTH *QUAKE* LIKE THE GIANT HERYSHAF, LIKE THE FLYING BEHEDETI DISK OF HORUS!

HE IS A LIVING GOD!!

"HOWEVER, ONCE MORE, I DID NOT SHARE IN THEIR JOY. THESE FREQUENT QUAKES TROUBLED ME."

YOU DIDN'T ALLOW ME TO *WIN*! THIS GOLD IS YOUR REWARD!

"THERE WAS SOME- THING SLIGHTLY OFF..."

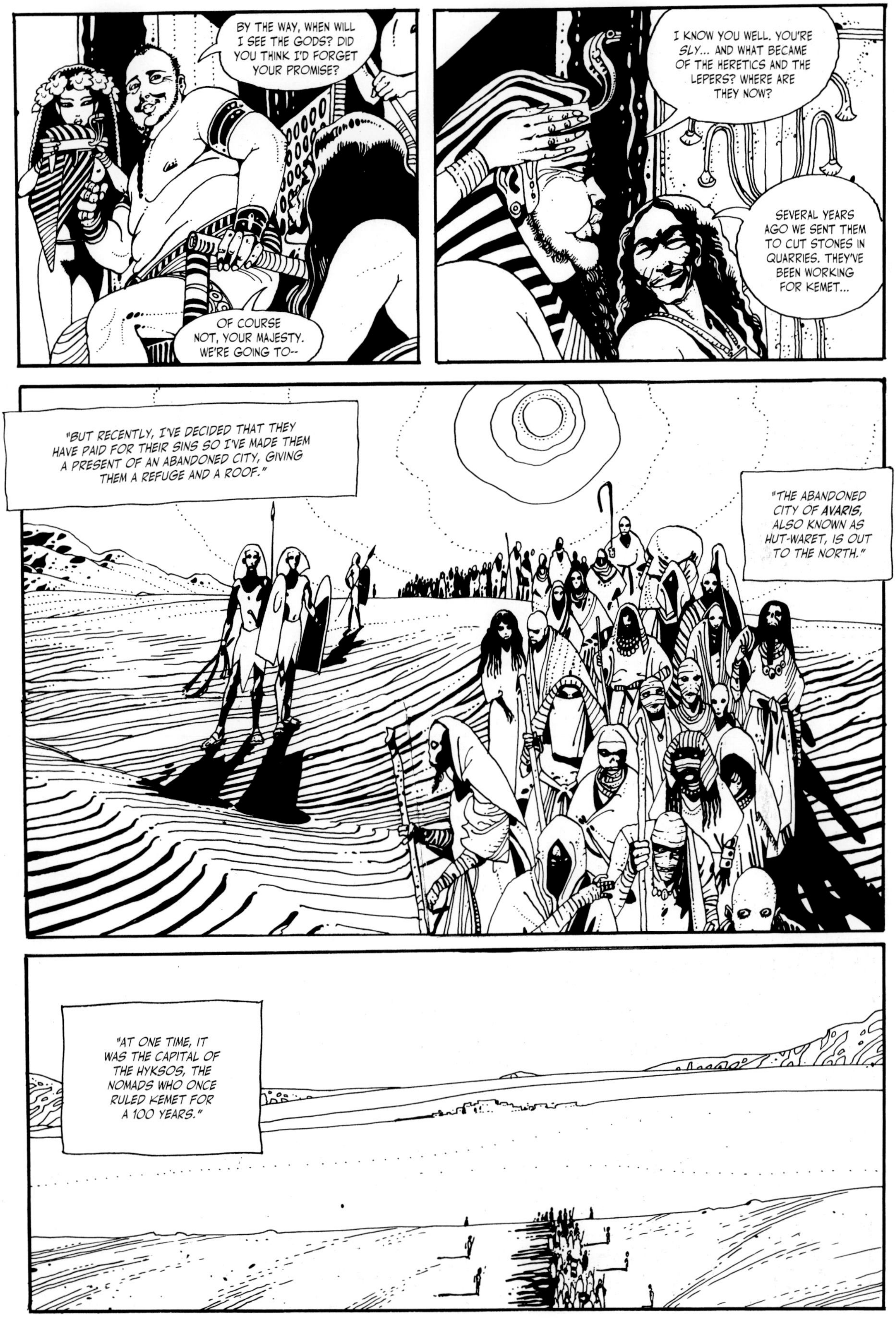

BY THE WAY, WHEN WILL I SEE THE GODS? DID YOU THINK I'D FORGET YOUR PROMISE?
OF COURSE NOT, YOUR MAJESTY. WE'RE GOING TO--
I KNOW YOU WELL. YOU'RE SLY... AND WHAT BECAME OF THE HERETICS AND THE LEPERS? WHERE ARE THEY NOW?
SEVERAL YEARS AGO WE SENT THEM TO CUT STONES IN QUARRIES. THEY'VE BEEN WORKING FOR KEMET...
"BUT RECENTLY, I'VE DECIDED THAT THEY HAVE PAID FOR THEIR SINS SO I'VE MADE THEM A PRESENT OF AN ABANDONED CITY, GIVING THEM A REFUGE AND A ROOF."
"THE ABANDONED CITY OF AVARIS, ALSO KNOWN AS HUT-WARET, IS OUT TO THE NORTH."
"AT ONE TIME, IT WAS THE CAPITAL OF THE HYKSOS, THE NOMADS WHO ONCE RULED KEMET FOR A 100 YEARS."

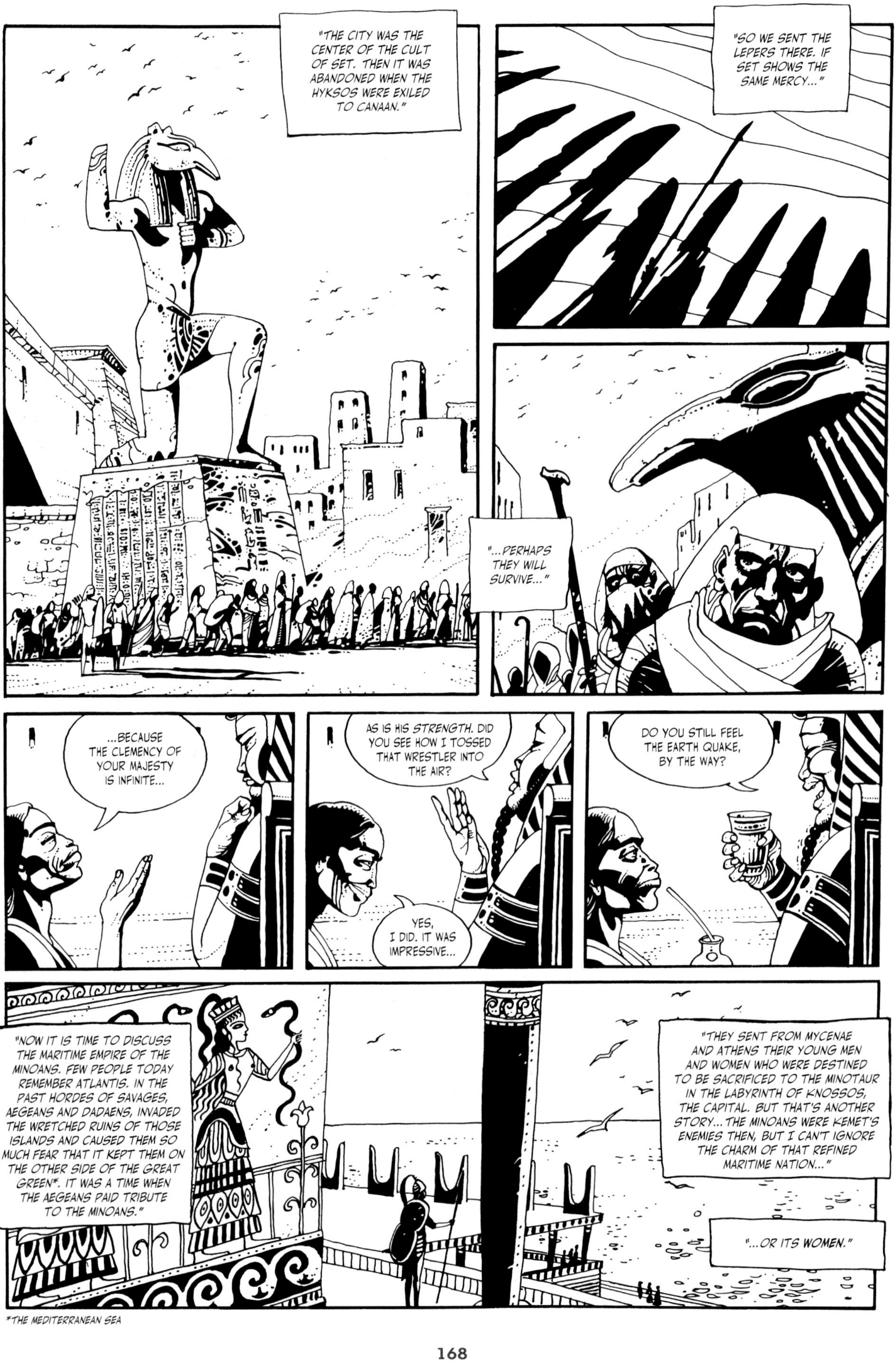
"THE CITY WAS THE CENTER OF THE CULT OF SET. THEN IT WAS ABANDONED WHEN THE HYKSOS WERE EXILED TO CANAAN."
"SO WE SENT THE LEPERS THERE. IF SET SHOWS THE SAME MERCY..."
"...PERHAPS THEY WILL SURVIVE..."
...BECAUSE THE CLEMENCY OF YOUR MAJESTY IS INFINITE...
AS IS HIS STRENGTH. DID YOU SEE HOW I TOSSED THAT WRESTLER INTO THE AIR?
YES, I DID. IT WAS IMPRESSIVE...
DO YOU STILL FEEL THE EARTH QUAKE, BY THE WAY?
"NOW IT IS TIME TO DISCUSS THE MARITIME EMPIRE OF THE MINOANS. FEW PEOPLE TODAY REMEMBER ATLANTIS. IN THE PAST HORDES OF SAVAGES, AEGEANS AND DADAENS, INVADED THE WRETCHED RUINS OF THOSE ISLANDS AND CAUSED THEM SO MUCH FEAR THAT IT KEPT THEM ON THE OTHER SIDE OF THE GREAT GREEN*. IT WAS A TIME WHEN THE AEGEANS PAID TRIBUTE TO THE MINOANS."
"THEY SENT FROM MYCENAE AND ATHENS THEIR YOUNG MEN AND WOMEN WHO WERE DESTINED TO BE SACRIFICED TO THE MINOTAUR IN THE LABYRINTH OF KNOSSOS, THE CAPITAL. BUT THAT'S ANOTHER STORY... THE MINOANS WERE KEMET'S ENEMIES THEN, BUT I CAN'T IGNORE THE CHARM OF THAT REFINED MARITIME NATION..."
"...OR ITS WOMEN."

*THE MEDITERRANEAN SEA

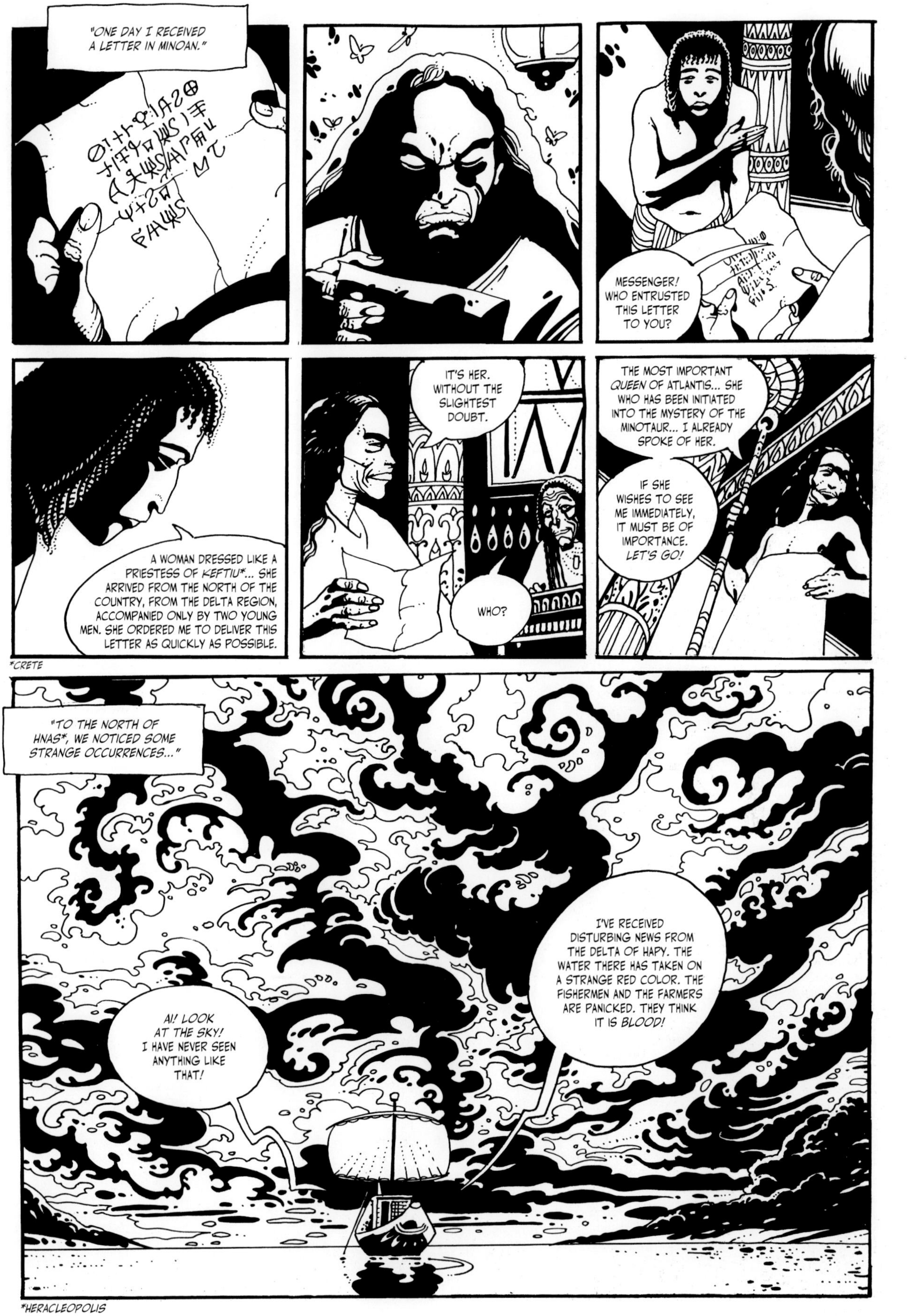
"ONE DAY I RECEIVED A LETTER IN MINOAN."
MESSENGER! WHO ENTRUSTED THIS LETTER TO YOU?
A WOMAN DRESSED LIKE A PRIESTESS OF KEFTIU*... SHE ARRIVED FROM THE NORTH OF THE COUNTRY, FROM THE DELTA REGION, ACCOMPANIED ONLY BY TWO YOUNG MEN. SHE ORDERED ME TO DELIVER THIS LETTER AS QUICKLY AS POSSIBLE.
IT'S HER. WITHOUT THE SLIGHTEST DOUBT.
WHO?
THE MOST IMPORTANT QUEEN OF ATLANTIS... SHE WHO HAS BEEN INITIATED INTO THE MYSTERY OF THE MINOTAUR... I ALREADY SPOKE OF HER.
IF SHE WISHES TO SEE ME IMMEDIATELY, IT MUST BE OF IMPORTANCE. LET'S GO!
*CRETE
"TO THE NORTH OF HNAS*, WE NOTICED SOME STRANGE OCCURRENCES..."
AI! LOOK AT THE SKY! I HAVE NEVER SEEN ANYTHING LIKE THAT!
I'VE RECEIVED DISTURBING NEWS FROM THE DELTA OF HAPY. THE WATER THERE HAS TAKEN ON A STRANGE RED COLOR. THE FISHERMEN AND THE FARMERS ARE PANICKED. THEY THINK IT IS BLOOD!
*HERACLEOPOLIS

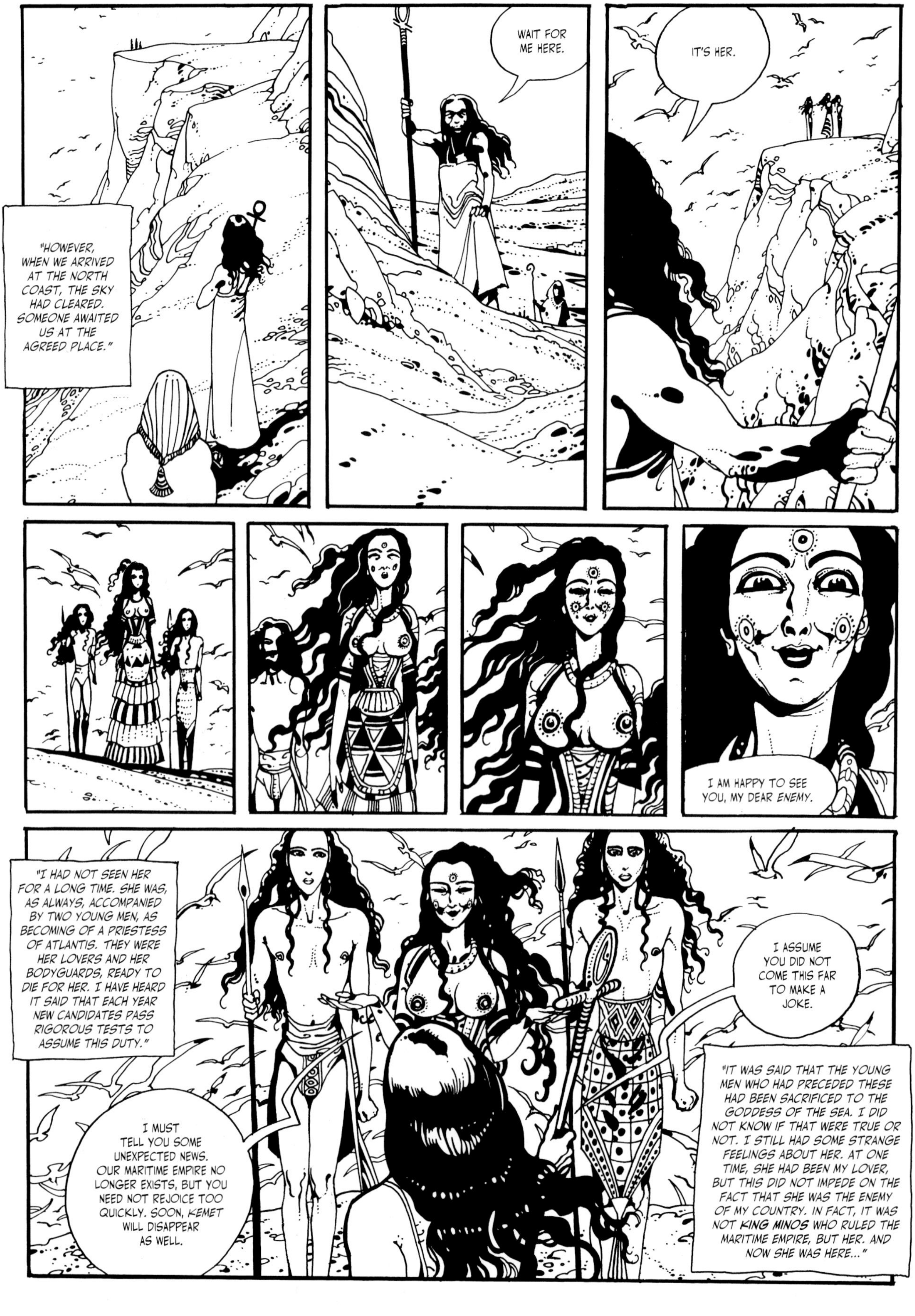
"HOWEVER, WHEN WE ARRIVED AT THE NORTH COAST, THE SKY HAD CLEARED. SOMEONE AWAITED US AT THE AGREED PLACE."
WAIT FOR ME HERE.
IT'S HER.
I AM HAPPY TO SEE YOU, MY DEAR ENEMY.
"I HAD NOT SEEN HER FOR A LONG TIME. SHE WAS, AS ALWAYS, ACCOMPANIED BY TWO YOUNG MEN, AS BECOMING OF A PRIESTESS OF ATLANTIS. THEY WERE HER LOVERS AND HER BODYGUARDS, READY TO DIE FOR HER. I HAVE HEARD IT SAID THAT EACH YEAR NEW CANDIDATES PASS RIGOROUS TESTS TO ASSUME THIS DUTY."
I ASSUME YOU DID NOT COME THIS FAR TO MAKE A JOKE.
I MUST TELL YOU SOME UNEXPECTED NEWS. OUR MARITIME EMPIRE NO LONGER EXISTS, BUT YOU NEED NOT REJOICE TOO QUICKLY. SOON, KEMET WILL DISAPPEAR AS WELL.
"IT WAS SAID THAT THE YOUNG MEN WHO HAD PRECEDED THESE HAD BEEN SACRIFICED TO THE GODDESS OF THE SEA. I DID NOT KNOW IF THAT WERE TRUE OR NOT. I STILL HAD SOME STRANGE FEELINGS ABOUT HER. AT ONE TIME, SHE HAD BEEN MY LOVER, BUT THIS DID NOT IMPEDE ON THE FACT THAT SHE WAS THE ENEMY OF MY COUNTRY. IN FACT, IT WAS NOT **KING MINOS** WHO RULED THE MARITIME EMPIRE, BUT HER. AND NOW SHE WAS HERE..."

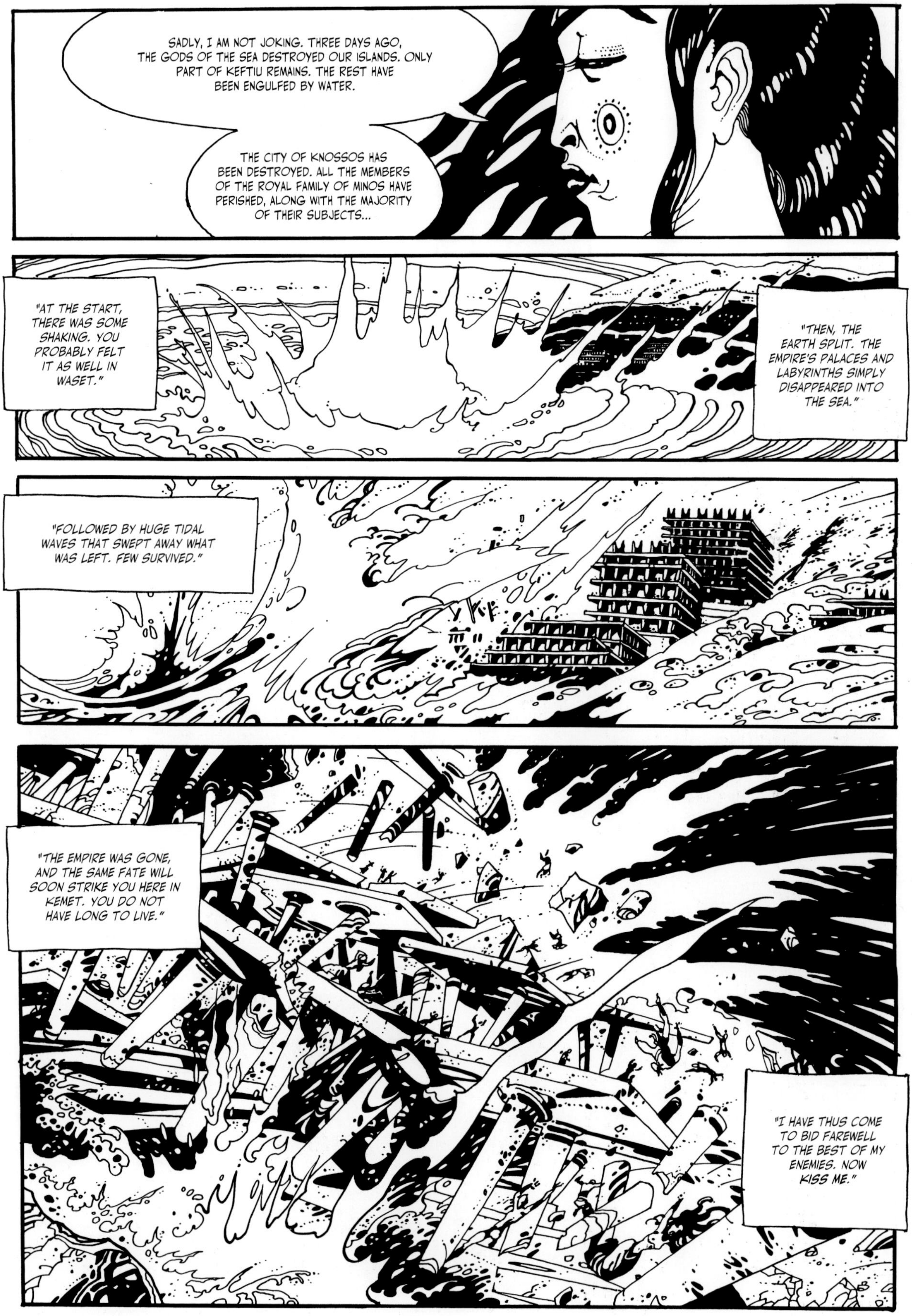
SADLY, I AM NOT JOKING. THREE DAYS AGO, THE GODS OF THE SEA DESTROYED OUR ISLANDS. ONLY PART OF KEFTIU REMAINS. THE REST HAVE BEEN ENGULFED BY WATER.
THE CITY OF KNOSSOS HAS BEEN DESTROYED. ALL THE MEMBERS OF THE ROYAL FAMILY OF MINOS HAVE PERISHED, ALONG WITH THE MAJORITY OF THEIR SUBJECTS...
"AT THE START, THERE WAS SOME SHAKING. YOU PROBABLY FELT IT AS WELL IN WASET."
"THEN, THE EARTH SPLIT. THE EMPIRE'S PALACES AND LABYRINTHS SIMPLY DISAPPEARED INTO THE SEA."
"FOLLOWED BY HUGE TIDAL WAVES THAT SWEPT AWAY WHAT WAS LEFT. FEW SURVIVED."
"THE EMPIRE WAS GONE, AND THE SAME FATE WILL SOON STRIKE YOU HERE IN KEMET. YOU DO NOT HAVE LONG TO LIVE."
"I HAVE THUS COME TO BID FAREWELL TO THE BEST OF MY ENEMIES. NOW KISS ME."

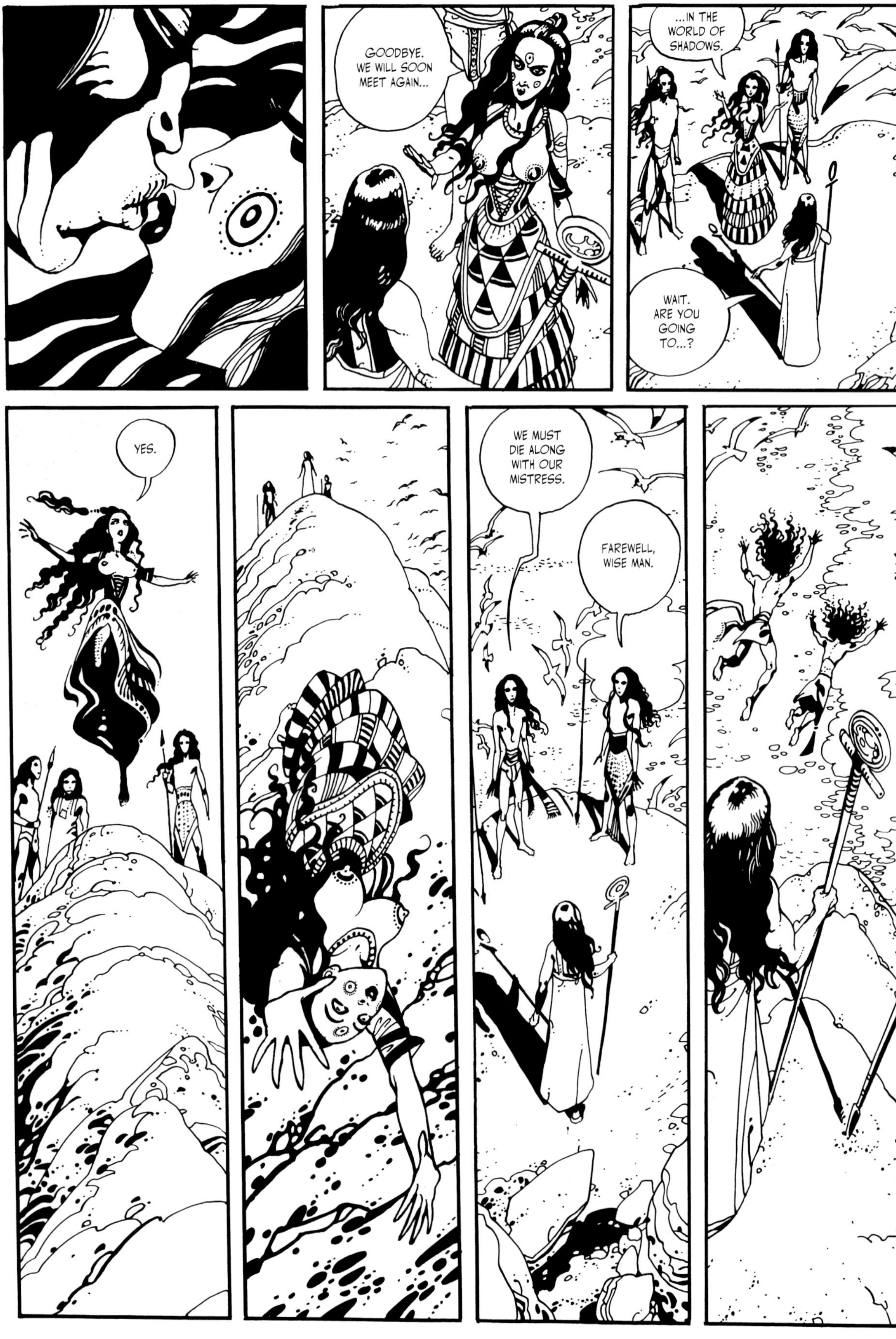
GOODBYE. WE WILL SOON MEET AGAIN...
...IN THE WORLD OF SHADOWS.
WAIT. ARE YOU GOING TO...?
YES.
WE MUST DIE ALONG WITH OUR MISTRESS.
FAREWELL, WISE MAN.

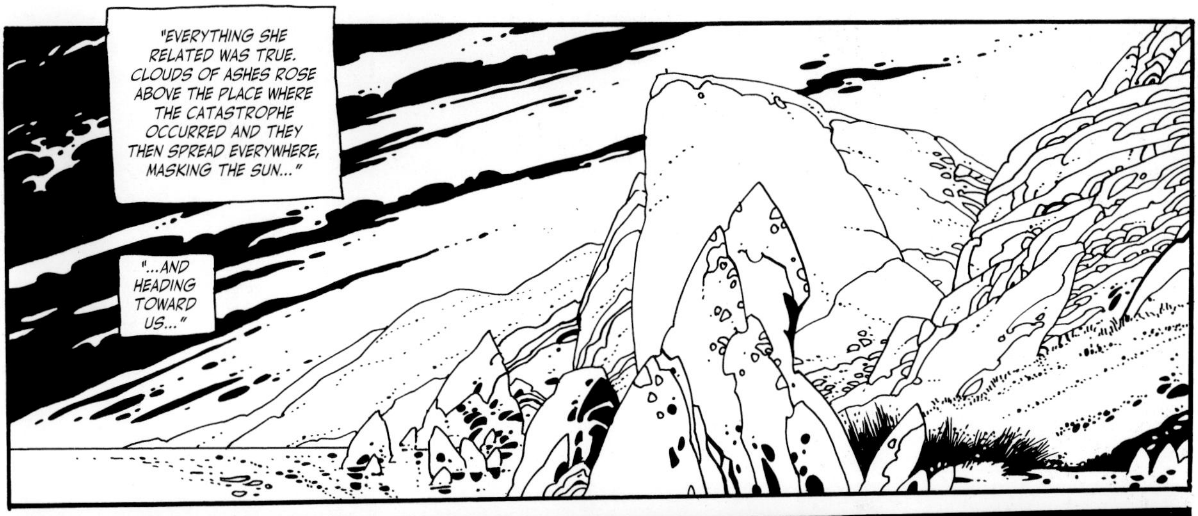
"EVERYTHING SHE RELATED WAS TRUE. CLOUDS OF ASHES ROSE ABOVE THE PLACE WHERE THE CATASTROPHE OCCURRED AND THEY THEN SPREAD EVERYWHERE, MASKING THE SUN..."
"...AND HEADING TOWARD US..."

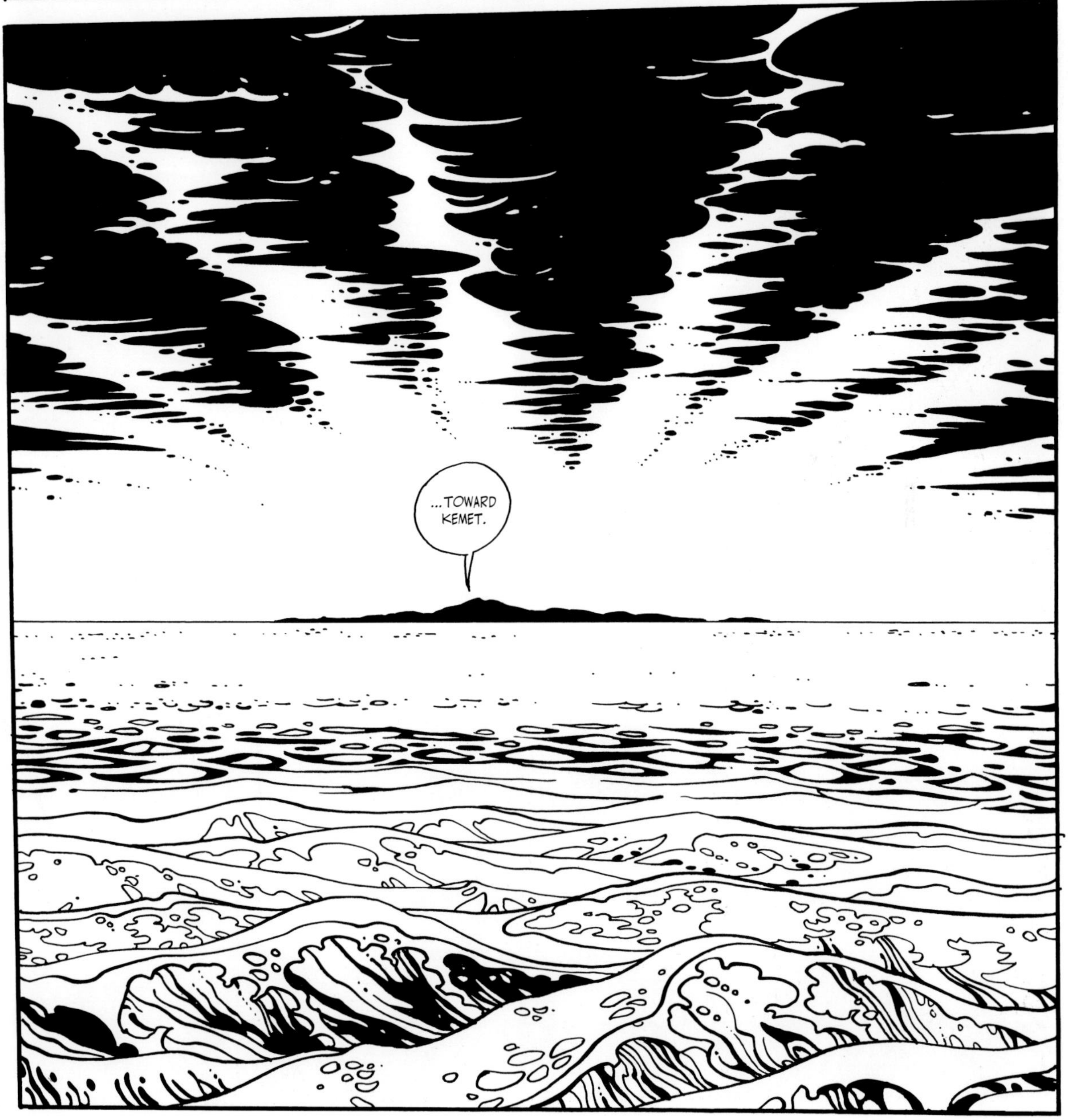
...TOWARD KEMET.

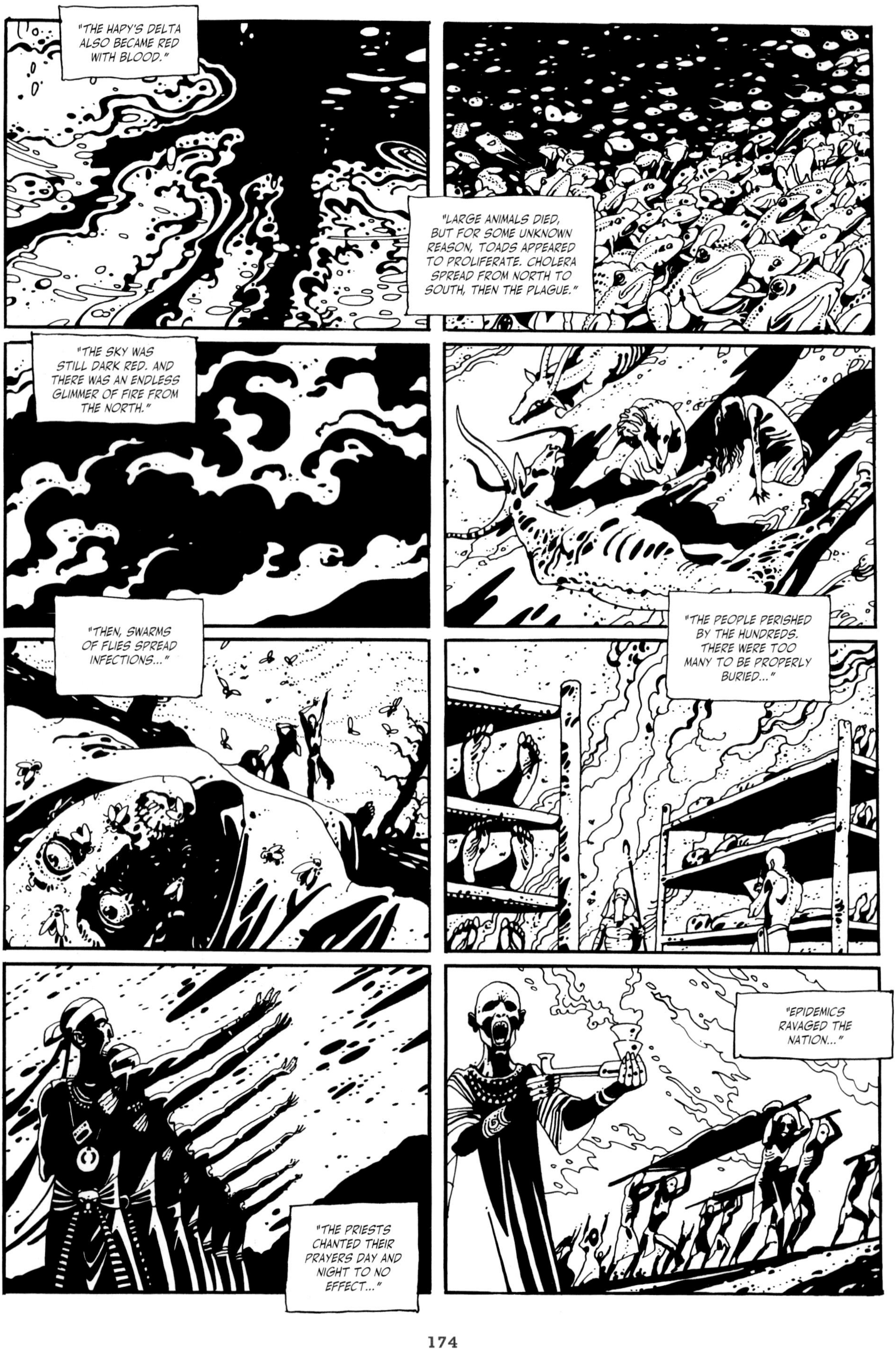
"THE HAPY'S DELTA ALSO BECAME RED WITH BLOOD."
"LARGE ANIMALS DIED, BUT FOR SOME UNKNOWN REASON, TOADS APPEARED TO PROLIFERATE. CHOLERA SPREAD FROM NORTH TO SOUTH, THEN THE PLAGUE."
"THE SKY WAS STILL DARK RED. AND THERE WAS AN ENDLESS GLIMMER OF FIRE FROM THE NORTH."
"THEN, SWARMS OF FLIES SPREAD INFECTIONS..."
"THE PEOPLE PERISHED BY THE HUNDREDS. THERE WERE TOO MANY TO BE PROPERLY BURIED..."
"THE PRIESTS CHANTED THEIR PRAYERS DAY AND NIGHT TO NO EFFECT..."
"EPIDEMICS RAVAGED THE NATION..."

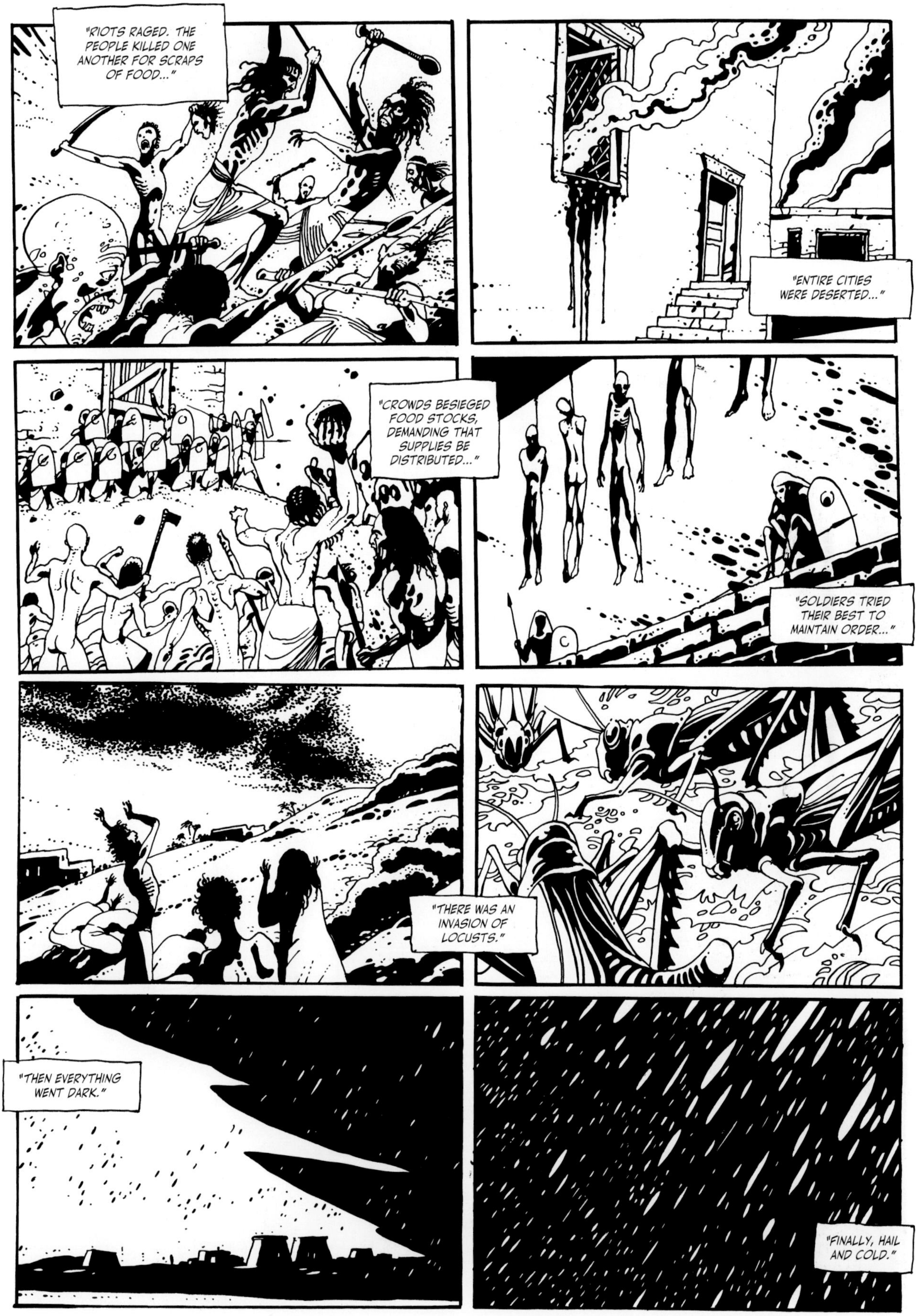
"RIOTS RAGED. THE PEOPLE KILLED ONE ANOTHER FOR SCRAPS OF FOOD..."
"ENTIRE CITIES WERE DESERTED..."
"CROWDS BESIEGED FOOD STOCKS, DEMANDING THAT SUPPLIES BE DISTRIBUTED..."
"SOLDIERS TRIED THEIR BEST TO MAINTAIN ORDER..."
"THERE WAS AN INVASION OF LOCUSTS."
"THEN EVERYTHING WENT DARK."
"FINALLY, HAIL AND COLD."

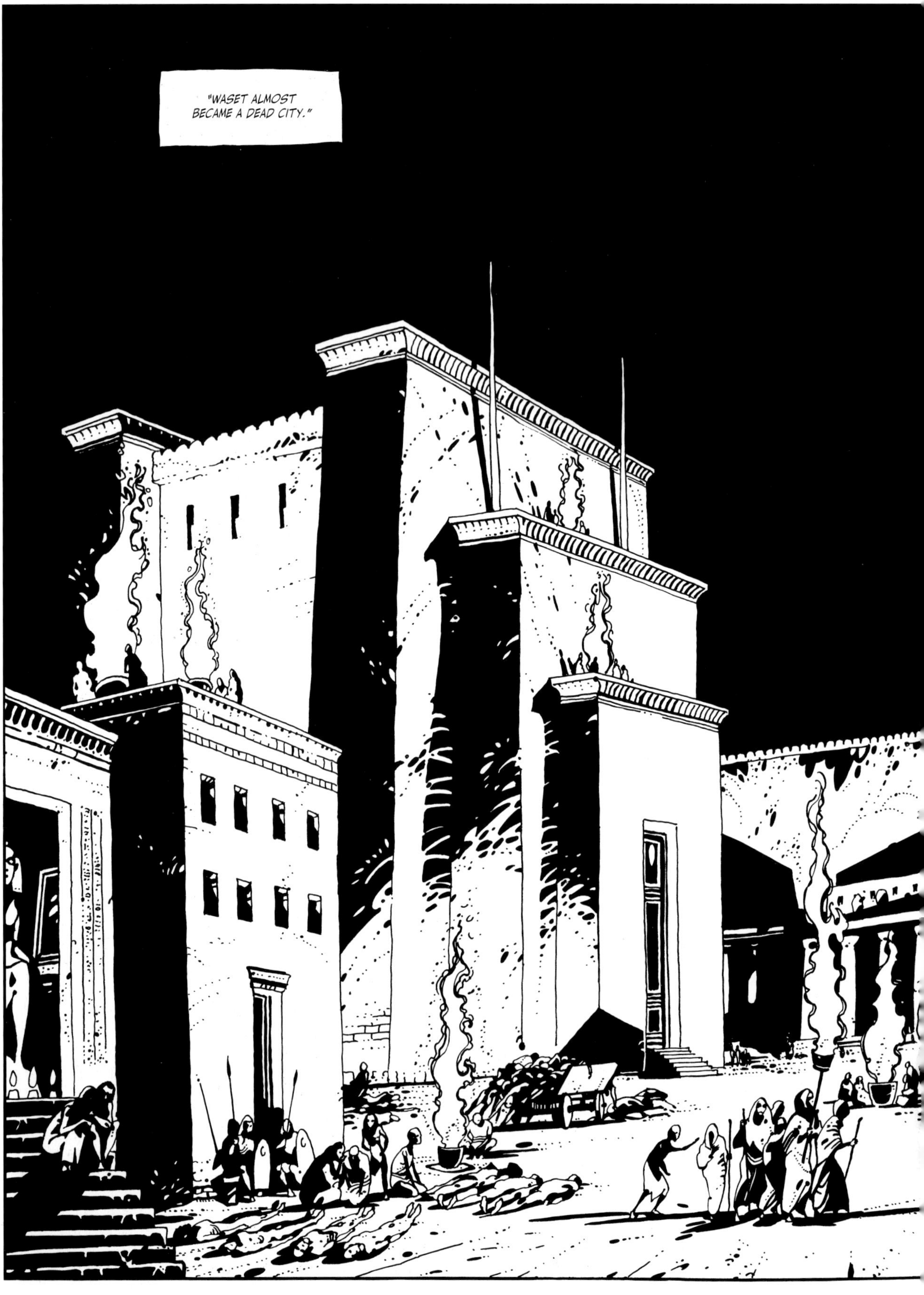
"WASET ALMOST BECAME A DEAD CITY."

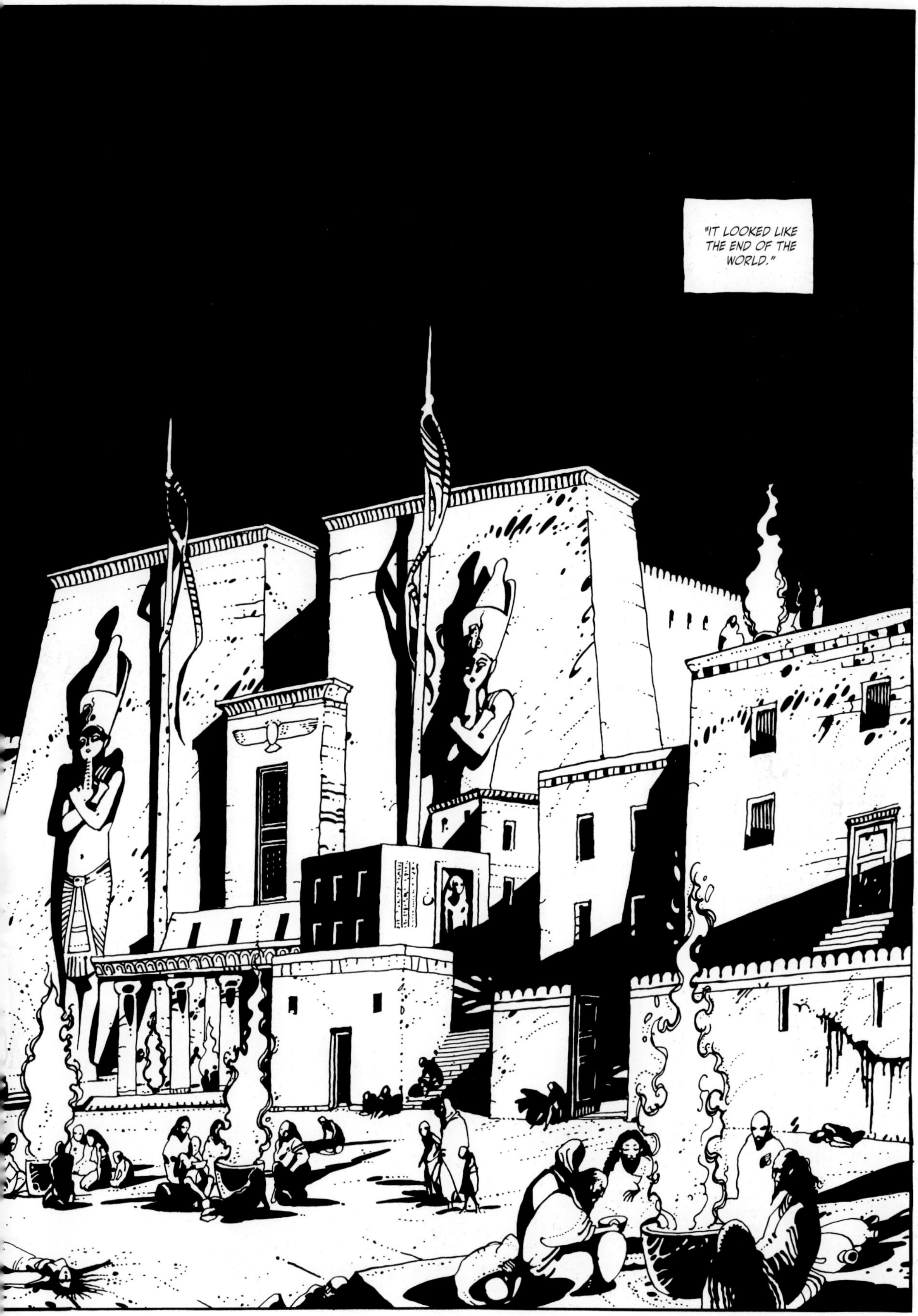
"IT LOOKED LIKE
THE END OF THE
WORLD."

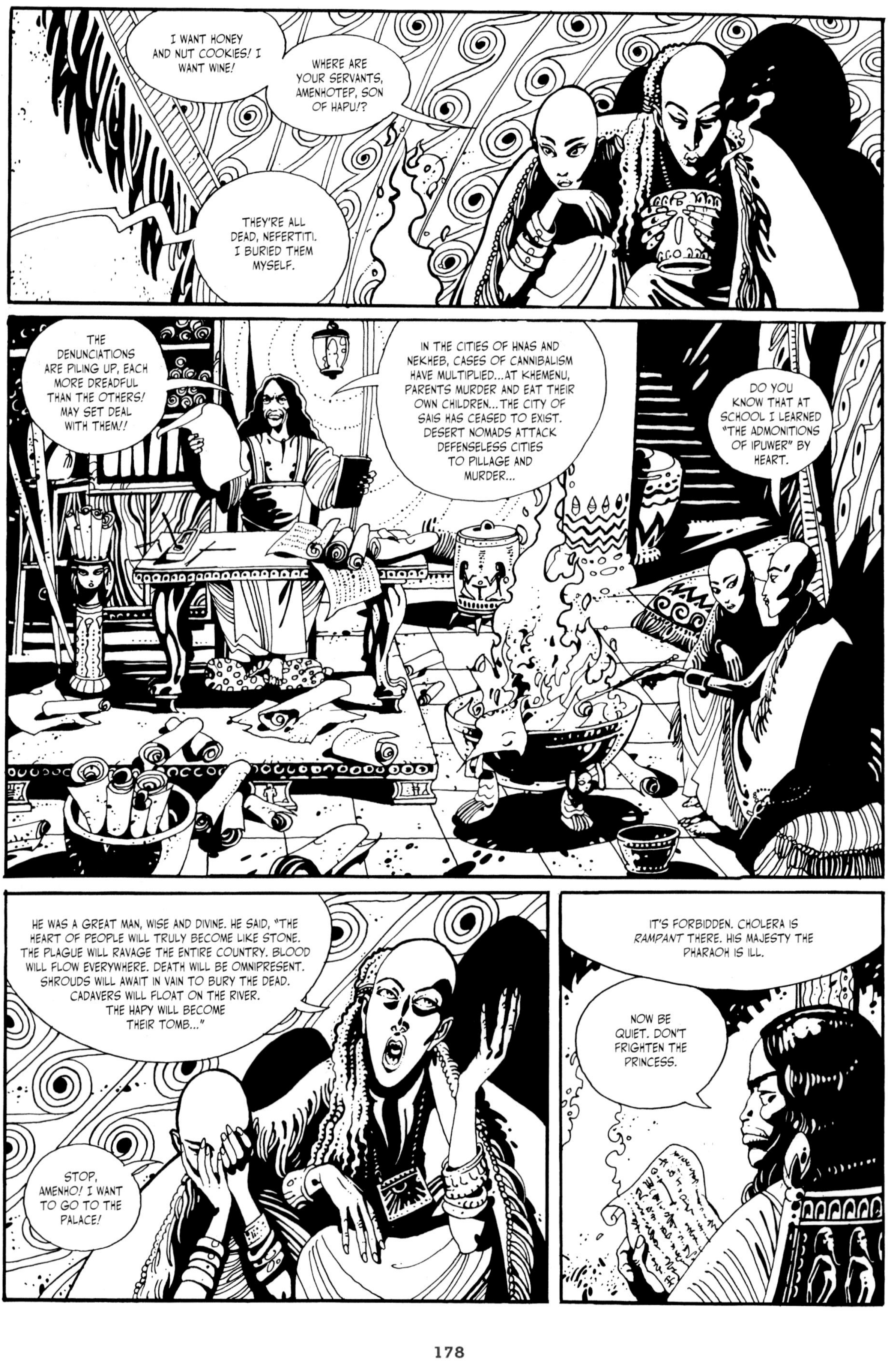
I WANT HONEY AND NUT COOKIES! I WANT WINE!
WHERE ARE YOUR SERVANTS, AMENHOTEP, SON OF HAPU!?
THEY'RE ALL DEAD, NEFERTITI. I BURIED THEM MYSELF.
THE DENUNCIATIONS ARE PILING UP, EACH MORE DREADFUL THAN THE OTHERS! MAY SET DEAL WITH THEM!!
IN THE CITIES OF HNAS AND NEKHEB, CASES OF CANNIBALISM HAVE MULTIPLIED...AT KHEMENU, PARENTS MURDER AND EAT THEIR OWN CHILDREN...THE CITY OF SAIS HAS CEASED TO EXIST. DESERT NOMADS ATTACK DEFENSELESS CITIES TO PILLAGE AND MURDER...
DO YOU KNOW THAT AT SCHOOL I LEARNED "THE ADMONITIONS OF IPUWER" BY HEART.
HE WAS A GREAT MAN, WISE AND DIVINE. HE SAID, "THE HEART OF PEOPLE WILL TRULY BECOME LIKE STONE. THE PLAGUE WILL RAVAGE THE ENTIRE COUNTRY. BLOOD WILL FLOW EVERYWHERE. DEATH WILL BE OMNIPRESENT. SHROUDS WILL AWAIT IN VAIN TO BURY THE DEAD. CADAVERS WILL FLOAT ON THE RIVER. THE HAPY WILL BECOME THEIR TOMB..."
STOP, AMENHO! I WANT TO GO TO THE PALACE!
IT'S FORBIDDEN. CHOLERA IS *RAMPANT* THERE. HIS MAJESTY THE PHARAOH IS ILL.
NOW BE QUIET. DON'T FRIGHTEN THE PRINCESS.

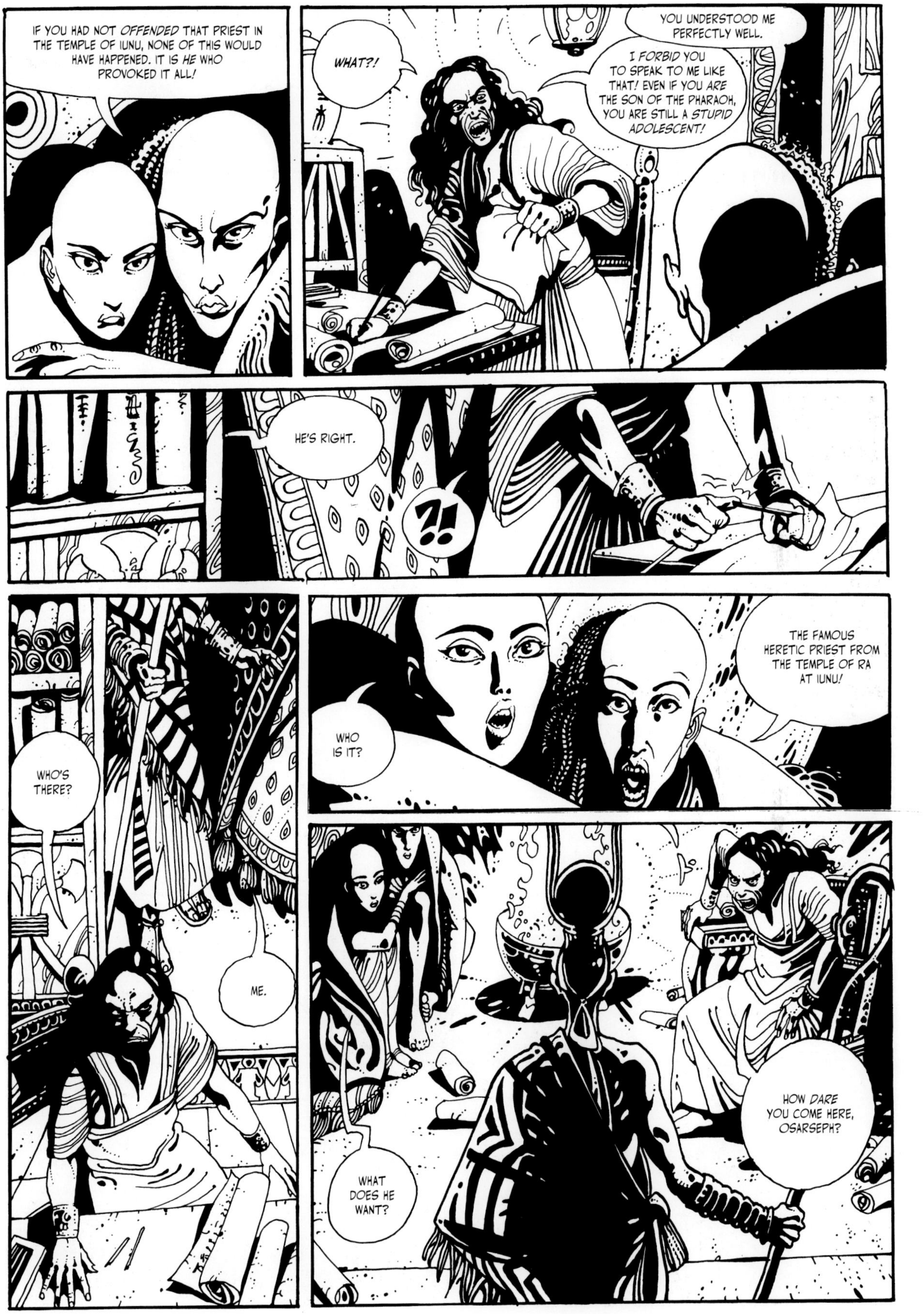
IF YOU HAD NOT *OFFENDED* THAT PRIEST IN THE TEMPLE OF IUNU, NONE OF THIS WOULD HAVE HAPPENED. IT IS *HE* WHO PROVOKED IT ALL!
WHAT?!
YOU UNDERSTOOD ME PERFECTLY WELL.
I *FORBID* YOU TO SPEAK TO ME LIKE THAT! EVEN IF YOU *ARE* THE SON OF THE PHARAOH, YOU ARE STILL A *STUPID ADOLESCENT!*
HE'S RIGHT.
?!
WHO'S THERE?
ME.
WHO IS IT?
THE FAMOUS HERETIC PRIEST FROM THE TEMPLE OF RA AT IUNU!
WHAT DOES HE WANT?
HOW *DARE* YOU COME HERE, OSARSEPH?

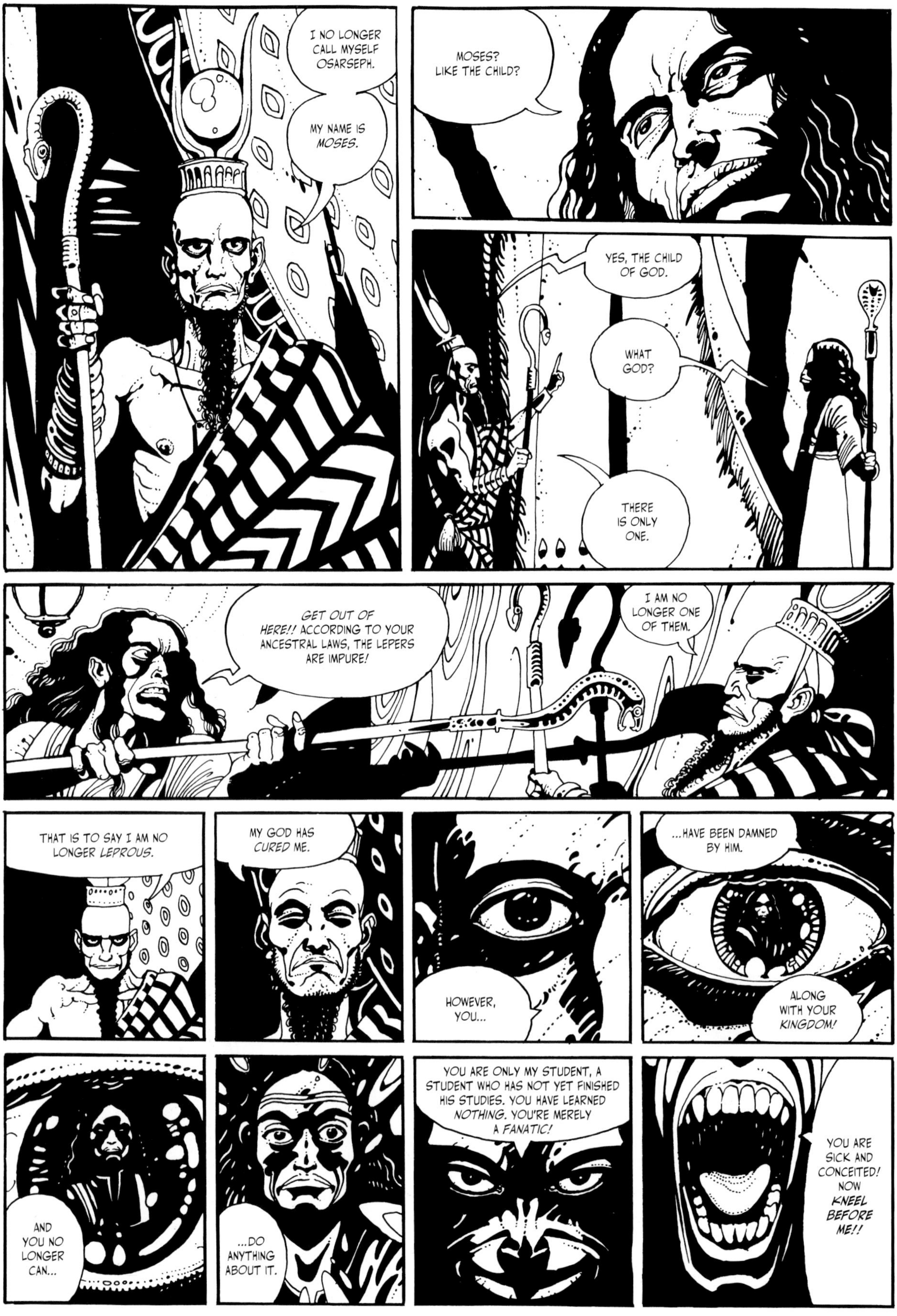
I NO LONGER CALL MYSELF OSARSEPH.
MY NAME IS *MOSES*.
MOSES? LIKE THE CHILD?
YES, THE CHILD OF GOD.
WHAT GOD?
THERE IS ONLY ONE.
GET OUT OF HERE!! ACCORDING TO YOUR ANCESTRAL LAWS, THE LEPERS ARE IMPURE!
I AM NO LONGER ONE OF THEM.
THAT IS TO SAY I AM NO LONGER *LEPROUS*.
MY GOD HAS *CURED* ME.
HOWEVER, YOU...
...HAVE BEEN DAMNED BY HIM.
ALONG WITH YOUR *KINGDOM!*
AND YOU NO LONGER CAN...
...DO ANYTHING ABOUT IT.
YOU ARE ONLY MY STUDENT, A STUDENT WHO HAS NOT YET FINISHED HIS STUDIES. YOU HAVE LEARNED *NOTHING*. YOU'RE MERELY A *FANATIC!*
YOU ARE SICK AND CONCEITED! NOW ***KNEEL BEFORE ME!!***

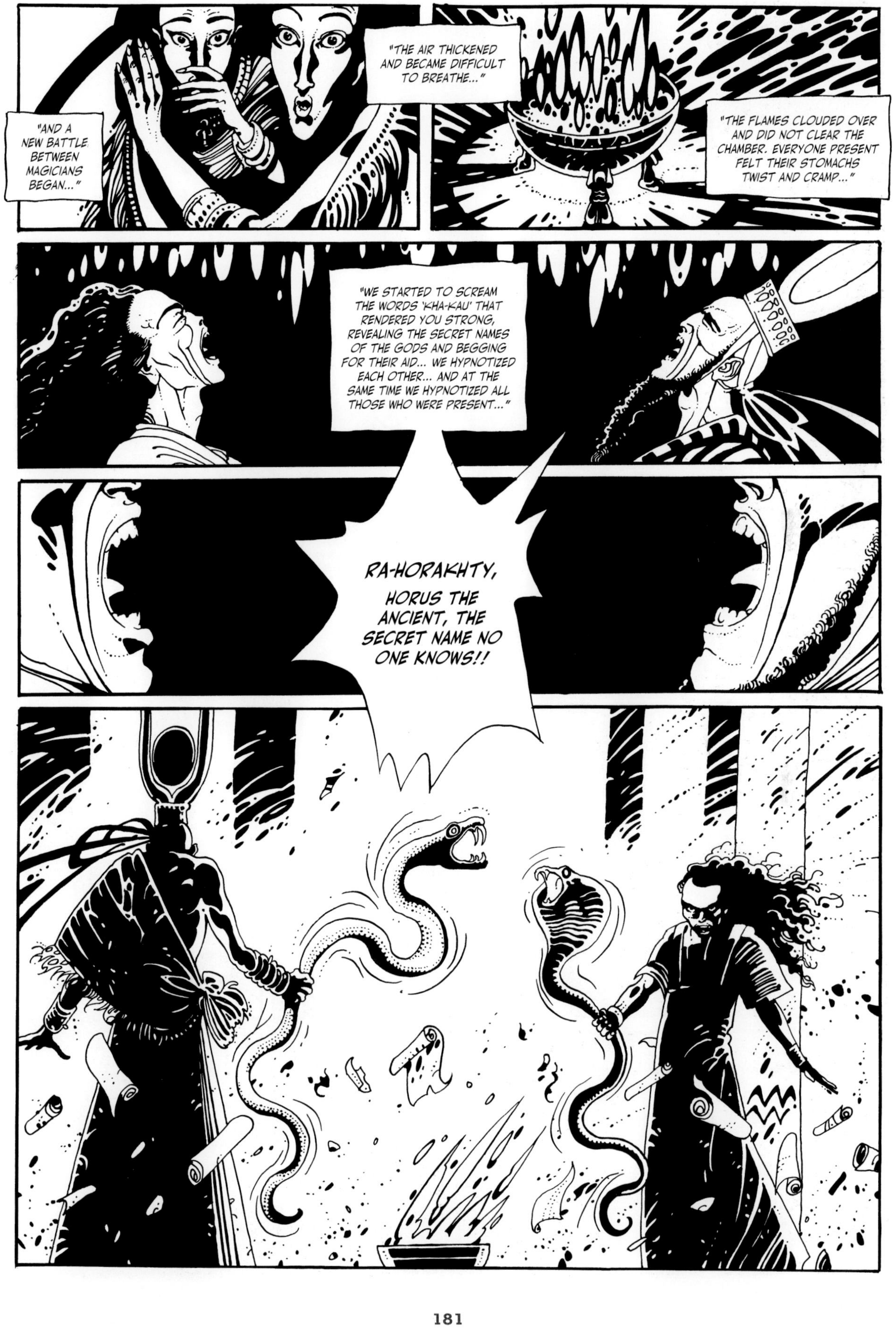
"AND A NEW BATTLE BETWEEN MAGICIANS BEGAN..."
"THE AIR THICKENED AND BECAME DIFFICULT TO BREATHE..."
"THE FLAMES CLOUDED OVER AND DID NOT CLEAR THE CHAMBER. EVERYONE PRESENT FELT THEIR STOMACHS TWIST AND CRAMP..."
"WE STARTED TO SCREAM THE WORDS 'KHA-KAU' THAT RENDERED YOU STRONG, REVEALING THE SECRET NAMES OF THE GODS AND BEGGING FOR THEIR AID... WE HYPNOTIZED EACH OTHER... AND AT THE SAME TIME WE HYPNOTIZED ALL THOSE WHO WERE PRESENT..."
RA-HORAKHTY, HORUS THE ANCIENT, THE SECRET NAME NO ONE KNOWS!!

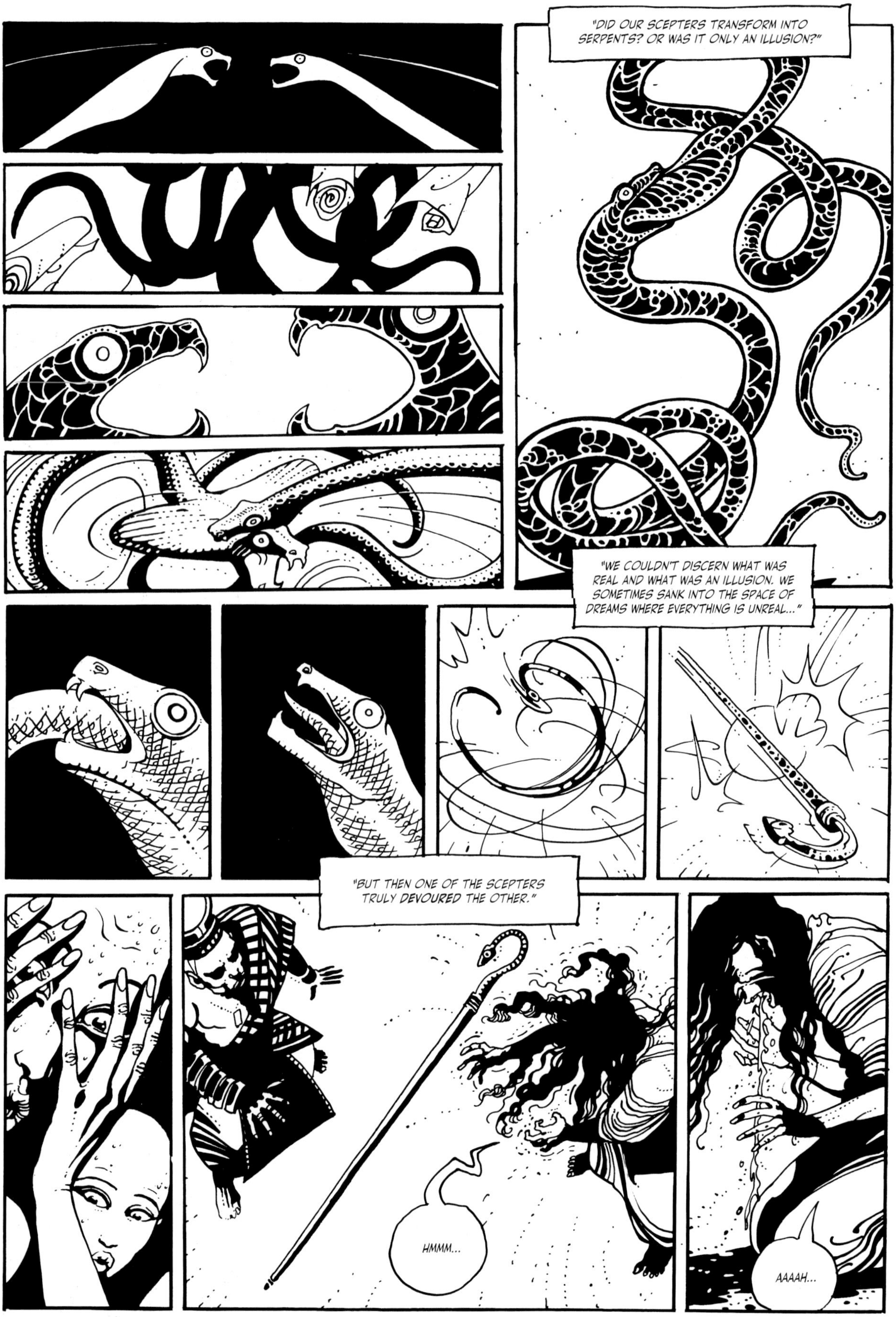
"DID OUR SCEPTERS TRANSFORM INTO SERPENTS? OR WAS IT ONLY AN ILLUSION?"
"WE COULDN'T DISCERN WHAT WAS REAL AND WHAT WAS AN ILLUSION. WE SOMETIMES SANK INTO THE SPACE OF DREAMS WHERE EVERYTHING IS UNREAL..."
"BUT THEN ONE OF THE SCEPTERS TRULY DEVOURED THE OTHER."
HMMM...
AAAAH...

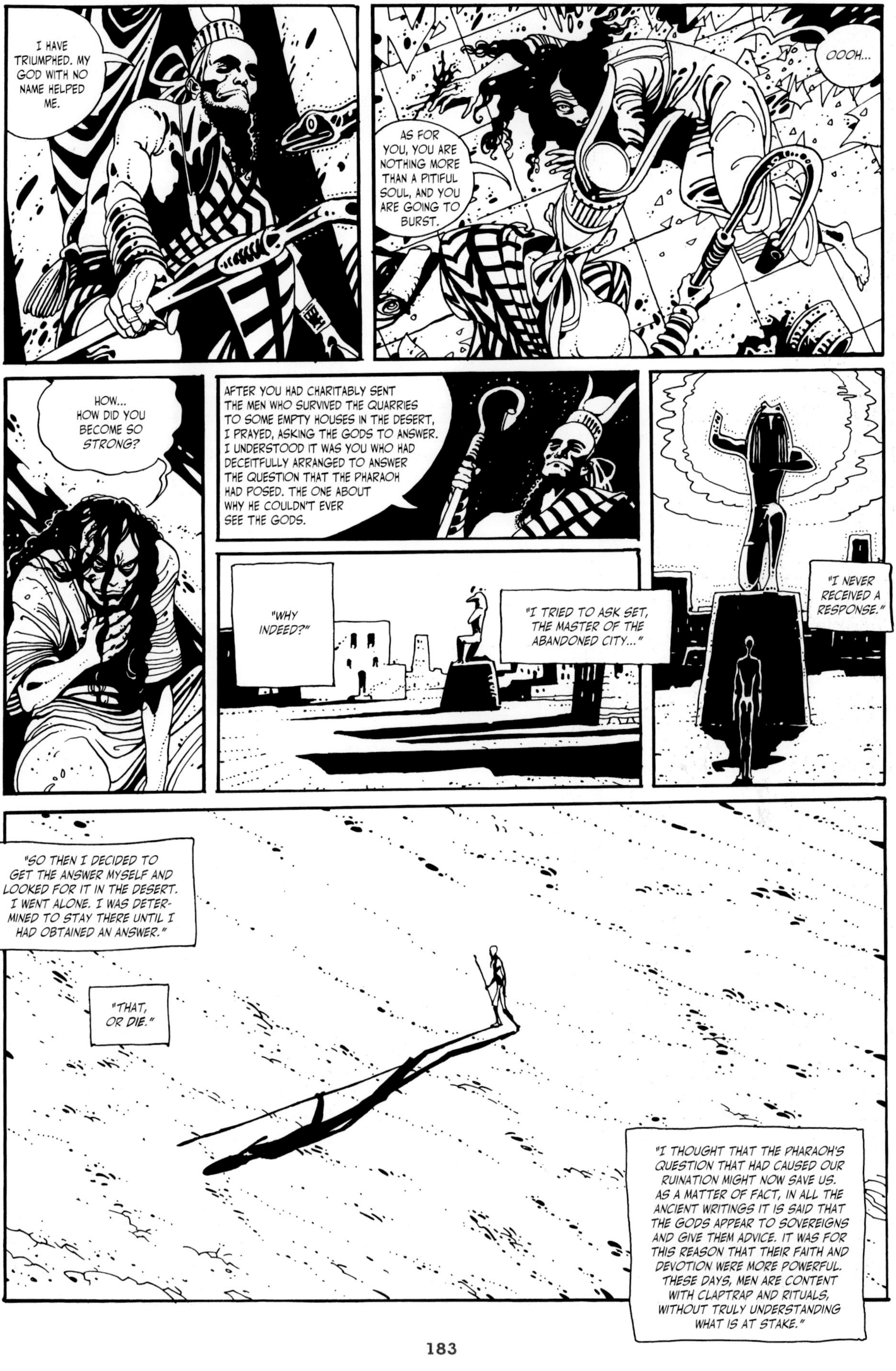

I HAVE TRIUMPHED. MY GOD WITH NO NAME HELPED ME.
OOOH...
AS FOR YOU, YOU ARE NOTHING MORE THAN A PITIFUL SOUL, AND YOU ARE GOING TO BURST.
HOW... HOW DID YOU BECOME SO STRONG?
AFTER YOU HAD CHARITABLY SENT THE MEN WHO SURVIVED THE QUARRIES TO SOME EMPTY HOUSES IN THE DESERT, I PRAYED, ASKING THE GODS TO ANSWER. I UNDERSTOOD IT WAS YOU WHO HAD DECEITFULLY ARRANGED TO ANSWER THE QUESTION THAT THE PHARAOH HAD POSED. THE ONE ABOUT WHY HE COULDN'T EVER SEE THE GODS.
"WHY INDEED?"
"I TRIED TO ASK SET, THE MASTER OF THE ABANDONED CITY..."
"I NEVER RECEIVED A RESPONSE."
"SO THEN I DECIDED TO GET THE ANSWER MYSELF AND LOOKED FOR IT IN THE DESERT. I WENT ALONE. I WAS DETERMINED TO STAY THERE UNTIL I HAD OBTAINED AN ANSWER."
"THAT, OR DIE."
"I THOUGHT THAT THE PHARAOH'S QUESTION THAT HAD CAUSED OUR RUINATION MIGHT NOW SAVE US. AS A MATTER OF FACT, IN ALL THE ANCIENT WRITINGS IT IS SAID THAT THE GODS APPEAR TO SOVEREIGNS AND GIVE THEM ADVICE. IT WAS FOR THIS REASON THAT THEIR FAITH AND DEVOTION WERE MORE POWERFUL. THESE DAYS, MEN ARE CONTENT WITH CLAPTRAP AND RITUALS, WITHOUT TRULY UNDERSTANDING WHAT IS AT STAKE."

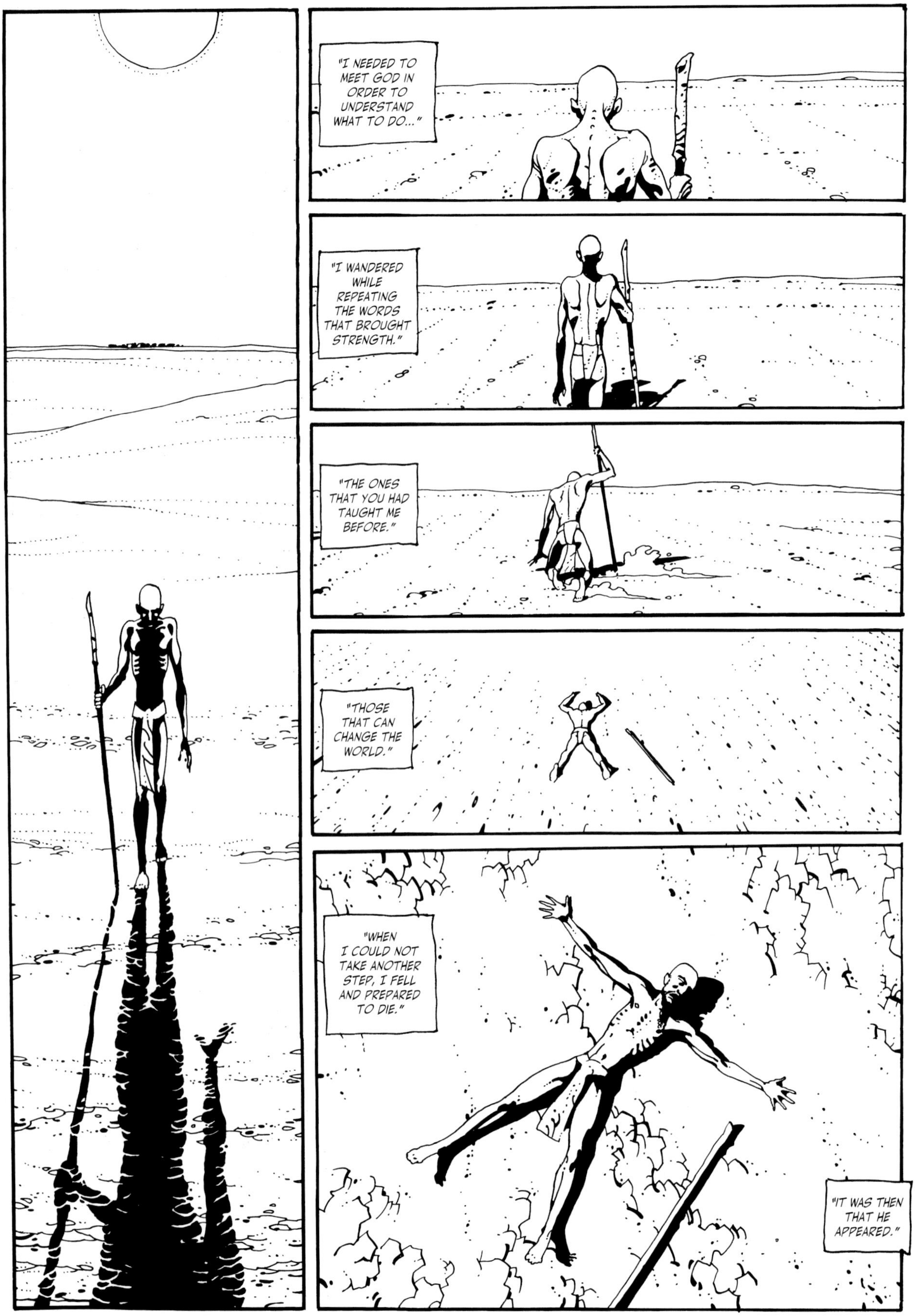
"I NEEDED TO MEET GOD IN ORDER TO UNDERSTAND WHAT TO DO..."
"I WANDERED WHILE REPEATING THE WORDS THAT BROUGHT STRENGTH."
"THE ONES THAT YOU HAD TAUGHT ME BEFORE."
"THOSE THAT CAN CHANGE THE WORLD."
"WHEN I COULD NOT TAKE ANOTHER STEP, I FELL AND PREPARED TO DIE."
"IT WAS THEN THAT HE APPEARED."

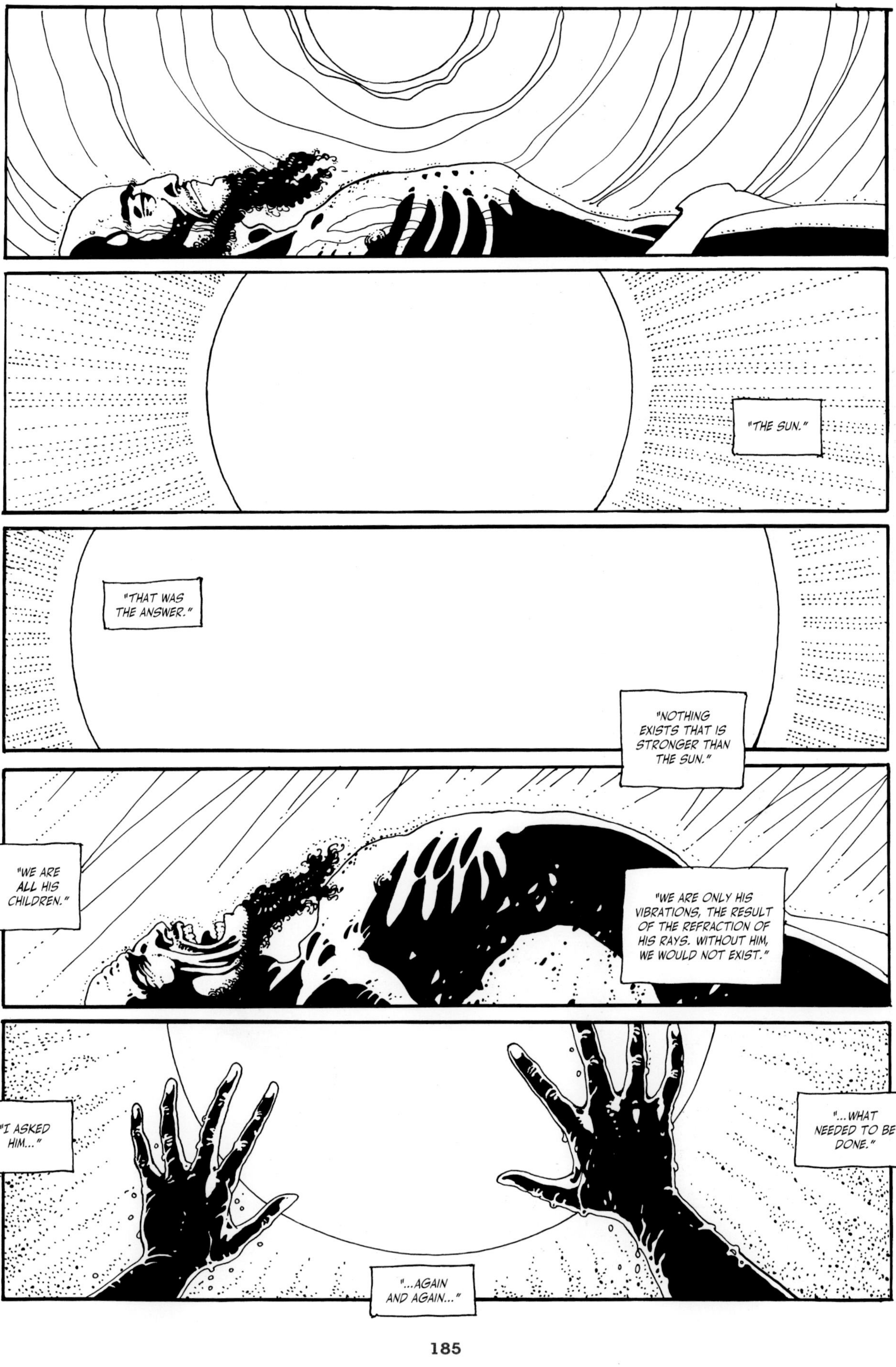
"THE SUN."
"THAT WAS THE ANSWER."
"NOTHING EXISTS THAT IS STRONGER THAN THE SUN."
"WE ARE ALL HIS CHILDREN."
"WE ARE ONLY HIS VIBRATIONS, THE RESULT OF THE REFRACTION OF HIS RAYS. WITHOUT HIM, WE WOULD NOT EXIST."
"I ASKED HIM..."
"...AGAIN AND AGAIN..."
"...WHAT NEEDED TO BE DONE."

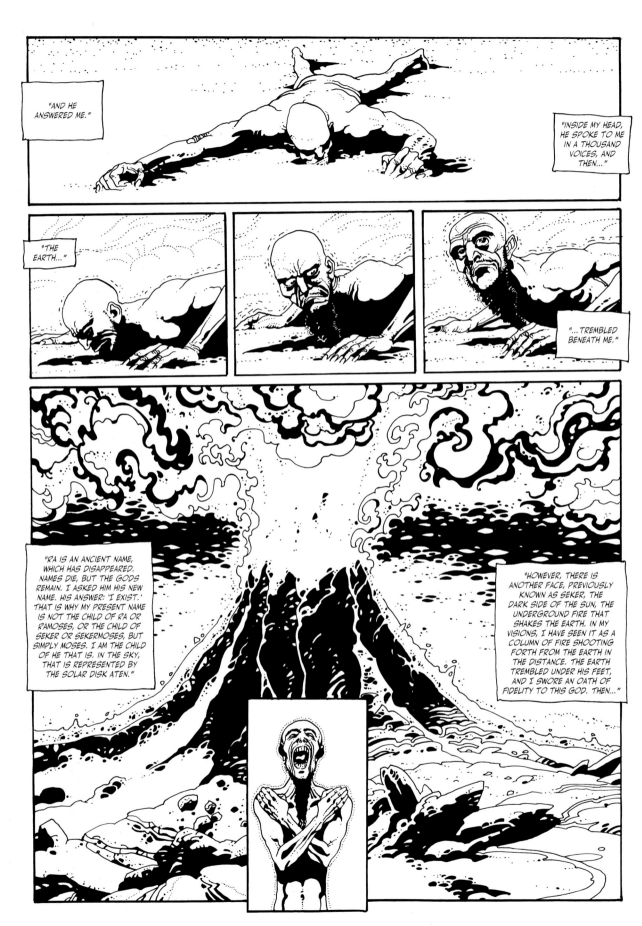

"AND HE ANSWERED ME."

"INSIDE MY HEAD, HE SPOKE TO ME IN A THOUSAND VOICES, AND THEN..."

"THE EARTH..."

"...TREMBLED BENEATH ME."

"RA IS AN ANCIENT NAME, WHICH HAS DISAPPEARED. NAMES DIE, BUT THE GODS REMAIN. I ASKED HIM HIS NEW NAME. HIS ANSWER: 'I EXIST.' THAT IS WHY MY PRESENT NAME IS NOT THE CHILD OF RA OR RAMOSES, OR THE CHILD OF SEKER OR SEKERMOSES, BUT SIMPLY MOSES. I AM THE CHILD OF HE THAT IS. IN THE SKY, THAT IS REPRESENTED BY THE SOLAR DISK ATEN."

"HOWEVER, THERE IS ANOTHER FACE, PREVIOUSLY KNOWN AS SEKER, THE DARK SIDE OF THE SUN, THE UNDERGROUND FIRE THAT SHAKES THE EARTH. IN MY VISIONS, I HAVE SEEN IT AS A COLUMN OF FIRE SHOOTING FORTH FROM THE EARTH IN THE DISTANCE. THE EARTH TREMBLED UNDER HIS FEET, AND I SWORE AN OATH OF FIDELITY TO THIS GOD. THEN..."

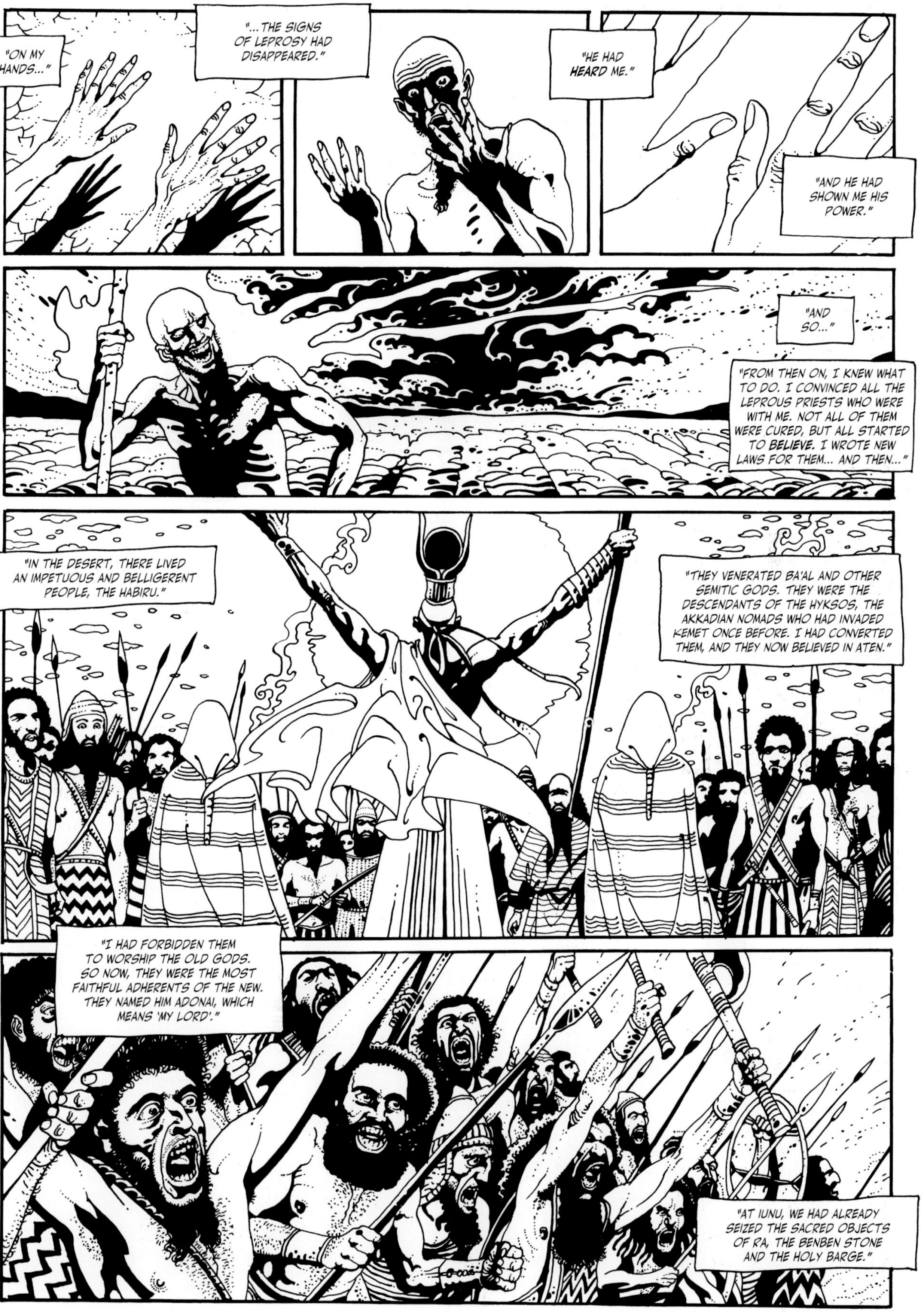

"ON MY HANDS..."
"...THE SIGNS OF LEPROSY HAD DISAPPEARED."
"HE HAD HEARD ME."
"AND HE HAD SHOWN ME HIS POWER."
"AND SO..."
"FROM THEN ON, I KNEW WHAT TO DO. I CONVINCED ALL THE LEPROUS PRIESTS WHO WERE WITH ME. NOT ALL OF THEM WERE CURED, BUT ALL STARTED TO BELIEVE. I WROTE NEW LAWS FOR THEM... AND THEN..."
"IN THE DESERT, THERE LIVED AN IMPETUOUS AND BELLIGERENT PEOPLE, THE HABIRU."
"THEY VENERATED BA'AL AND OTHER SEMITIC GODS. THEY WERE THE DESCENDANTS OF THE HYKSOS, THE AKKADIAN NOMADS WHO HAD INVADED KEMET ONCE BEFORE. I HAD CONVERTED THEM, AND THEY NOW BELIEVED IN ATEN."
"I HAD FORBIDDEN THEM TO WORSHIP THE OLD GODS. SO NOW, THEY WERE THE MOST FAITHFUL ADHERENTS OF THE NEW. THEY NAMED HIM ADONAI, WHICH MEANS 'MY LORD'."
"AT IUNU, WE HAD ALREADY SEIZED THE SACRED OBJECTS OF RA, THE BENBEN STONE AND THE HOLY BARGE."

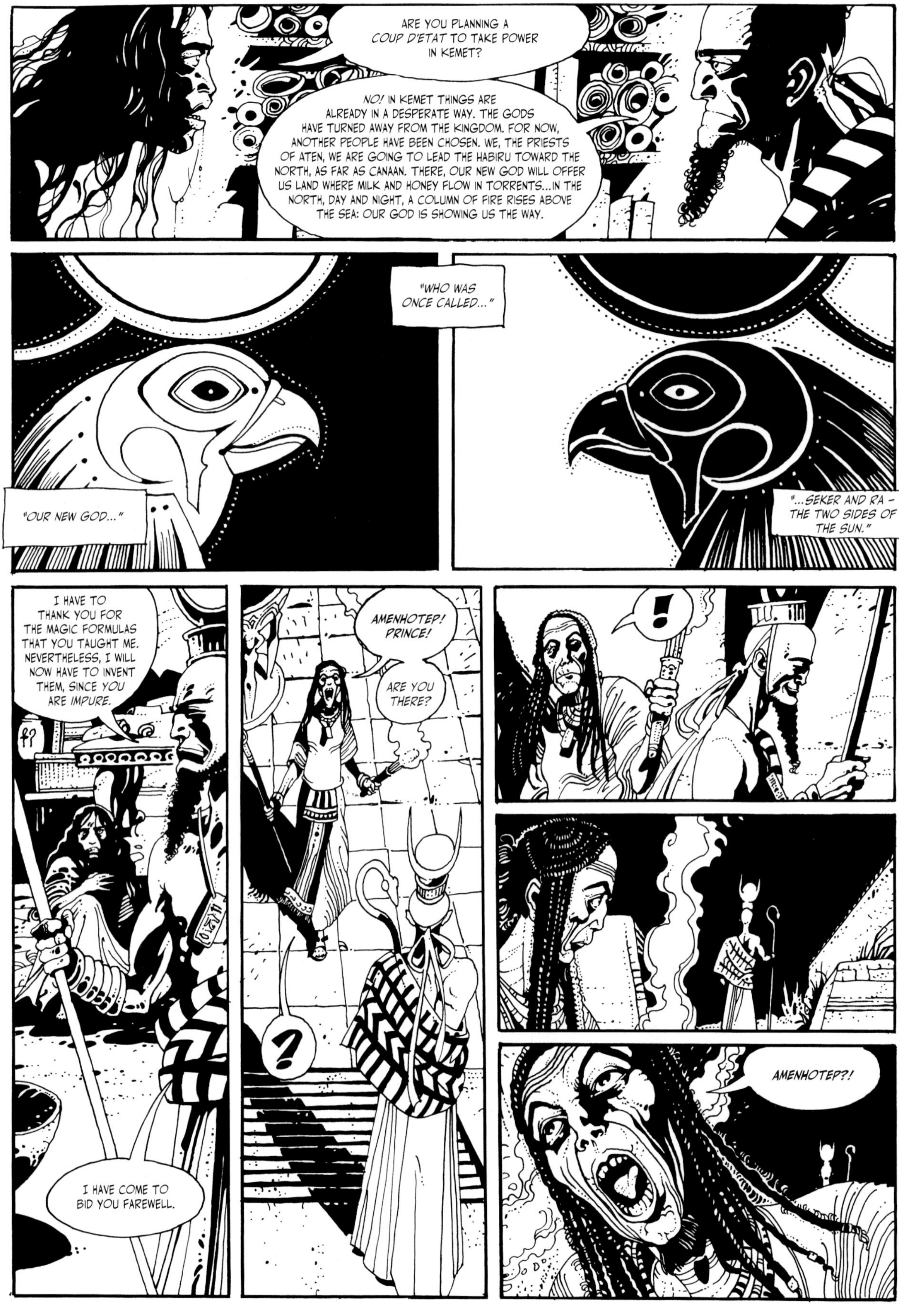

ARE YOU PLANNING A COUP D'ETAT TO TAKE POWER IN KEMET?
NO! IN KEMET THINGS ARE ALREADY IN A DESPERATE WAY. THE GODS HAVE TURNED AWAY FROM THE KINGDOM. FOR NOW, ANOTHER PEOPLE HAVE BEEN CHOSEN. WE, THE PRIESTS OF ATEN, WE ARE GOING TO LEAD THE HABIRU TOWARD THE NORTH, AS FAR AS CANAAN. THERE, OUR NEW GOD WILL OFFER US LAND WHERE MILK AND HONEY FLOW IN TORRENTS...IN THE NORTH, DAY AND NIGHT, A COLUMN OF FIRE RISES ABOVE THE SEA: OUR GOD IS SHOWING US THE WAY.
"OUR NEW GOD..."
"WHO WAS ONCE CALLED..."
"...SEKER AND RA - THE TWO SIDES OF THE SUN."
I HAVE TO THANK YOU FOR THE MAGIC FORMULAS THAT YOU TAUGHT ME. NEVERTHELESS, I WILL NOW HAVE TO INVENT THEM, SINCE YOU ARE IMPURE.
I HAVE COME TO BID YOU FAREWELL.
AMENHOTEP! PRINCE!
ARE YOU THERE?
?
!
AMENHOTEP?!

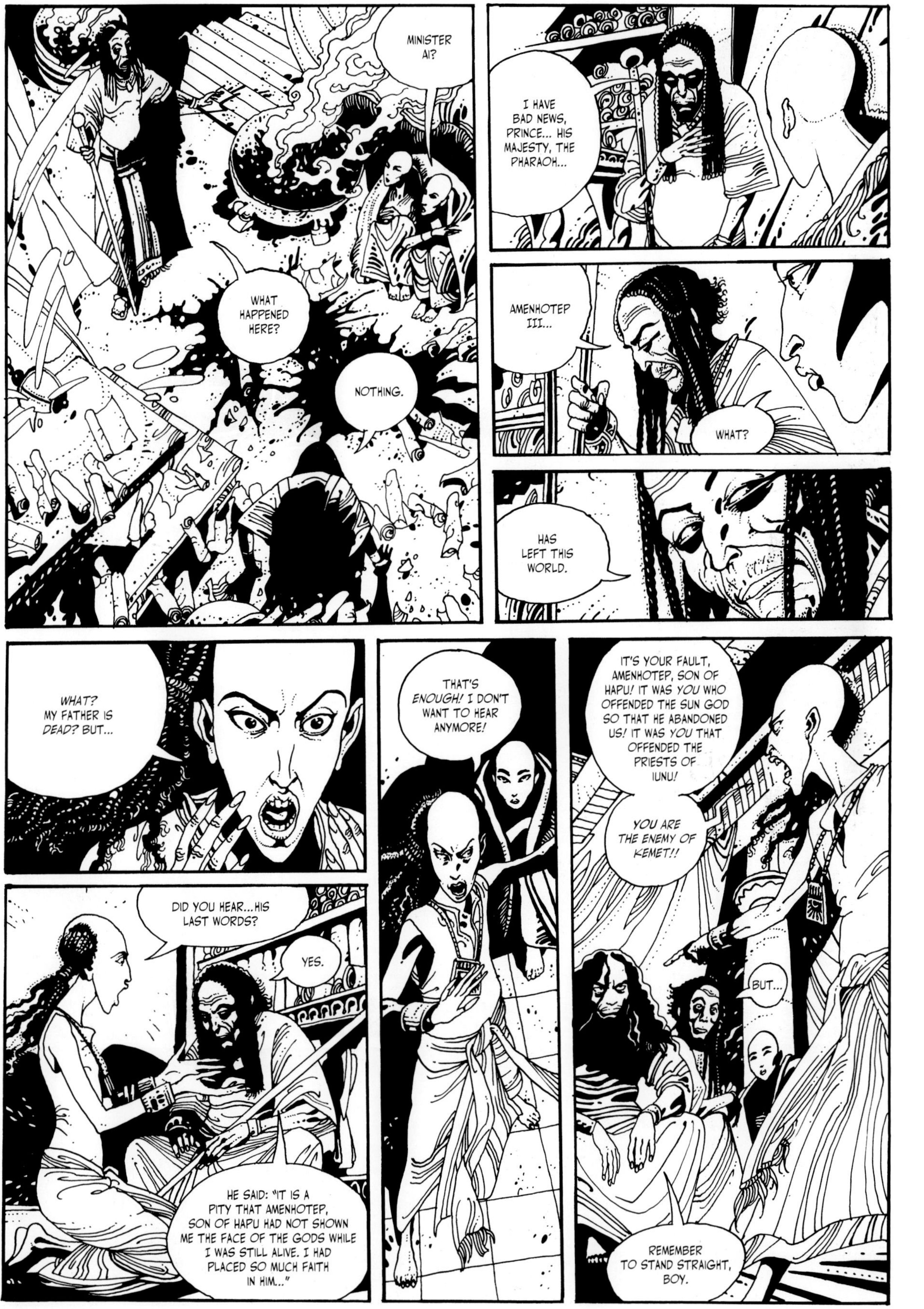
MINISTER AI?
WHAT HAPPENED HERE?
NOTHING.
I HAVE BAD NEWS, PRINCE... HIS MAJESTY, THE PHARAOH...
AMENHOTEP III...
WHAT?
HAS LEFT THIS WORLD.
WHAT? MY FATHER IS *DEAD?* BUT...
DID YOU HEAR...HIS LAST WORDS?
YES.
HE SAID: "IT IS A PITY THAT AMENHOTEP, SON OF HAPU HAD NOT SHOWN ME THE FACE OF THE GODS WHILE I WAS STILL ALIVE. I HAD PLACED SO MUCH FAITH IN HIM..."
THAT'S *ENOUGH!* I DON'T WANT TO HEAR ANYMORE!
IT'S YOUR FAULT, AMENHOTEP, SON OF HAPU! IT WAS *YOU* WHO OFFENDED THE SUN GOD SO THAT HE ABANDONED US! IT WAS *YOU* THAT OFFENDED THE PRIESTS OF IUNU!
YOU ARE THE ENEMY OF KEMET!!
BUT...
REMEMBER TO STAND STRAIGHT, BOY.

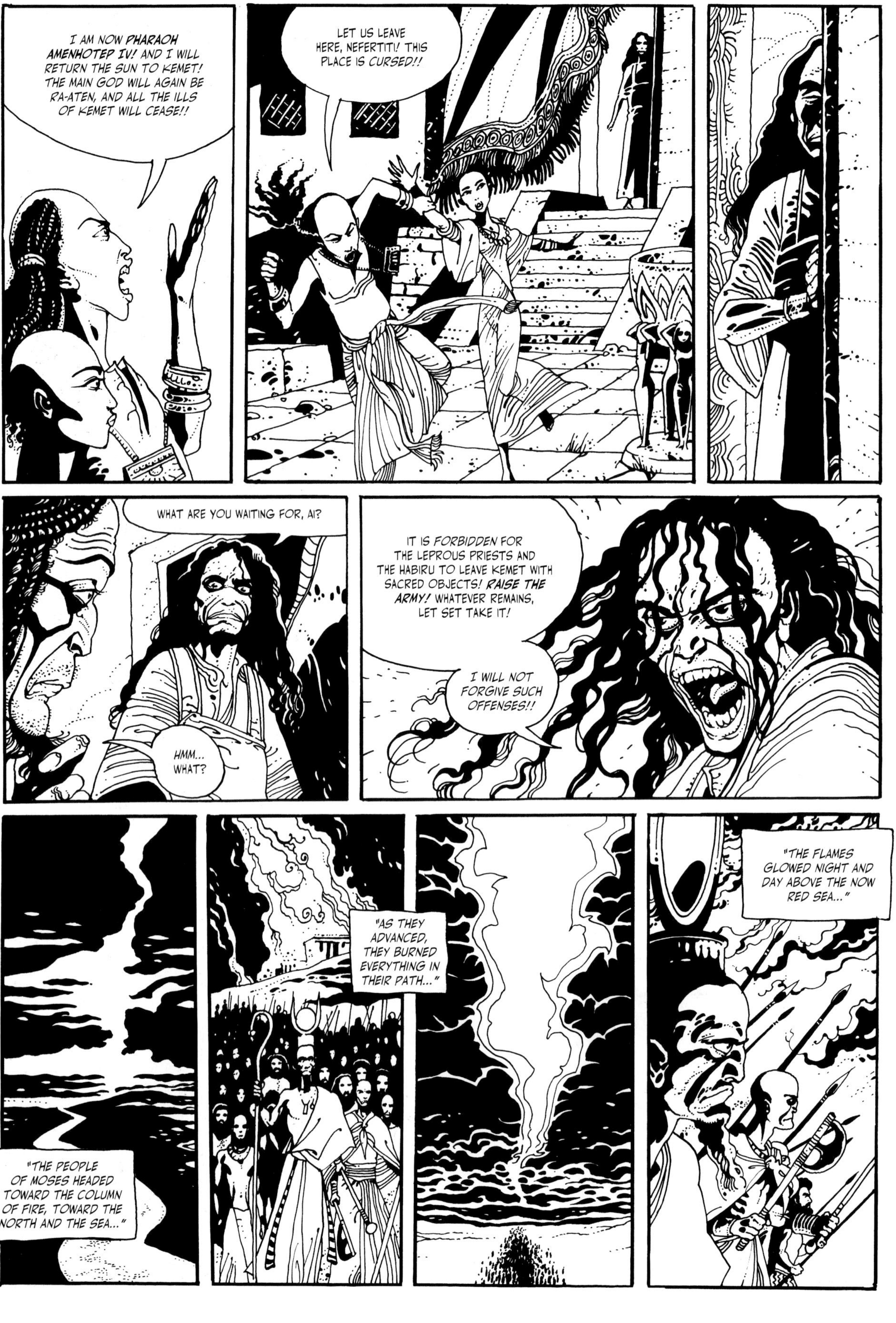

I AM NOW PHARAOH AMENHOTEP IV! AND I WILL RETURN THE SUN TO KEMET! THE MAIN GOD WILL AGAIN BE RA-ATEN, AND ALL THE ILLS OF KEMET WILL CEASE!!
LET US LEAVE HERE, NEFERTITI! THIS PLACE IS CURSED!!
WHAT ARE YOU WAITING FOR, AI?
HMM... WHAT?
IT IS FORBIDDEN FOR THE LEPROUS PRIESTS AND THE HABIRU TO LEAVE KEMET WITH SACRED OBJECTS! RAISE THE ARMY! WHATEVER REMAINS, LET SET TAKE IT!
I WILL NOT FORGIVE SUCH OFFENSES!!
"THE PEOPLE OF MOSES HEADED TOWARD THE COLUMN OF FIRE, TOWARD THE NORTH AND THE SEA..."
"AS THEY ADVANCED, THEY BURNED EVERYTHING IN THEIR PATH..."
"THE FLAMES GLOWED NIGHT AND DAY ABOVE THE NOW RED SEA..."

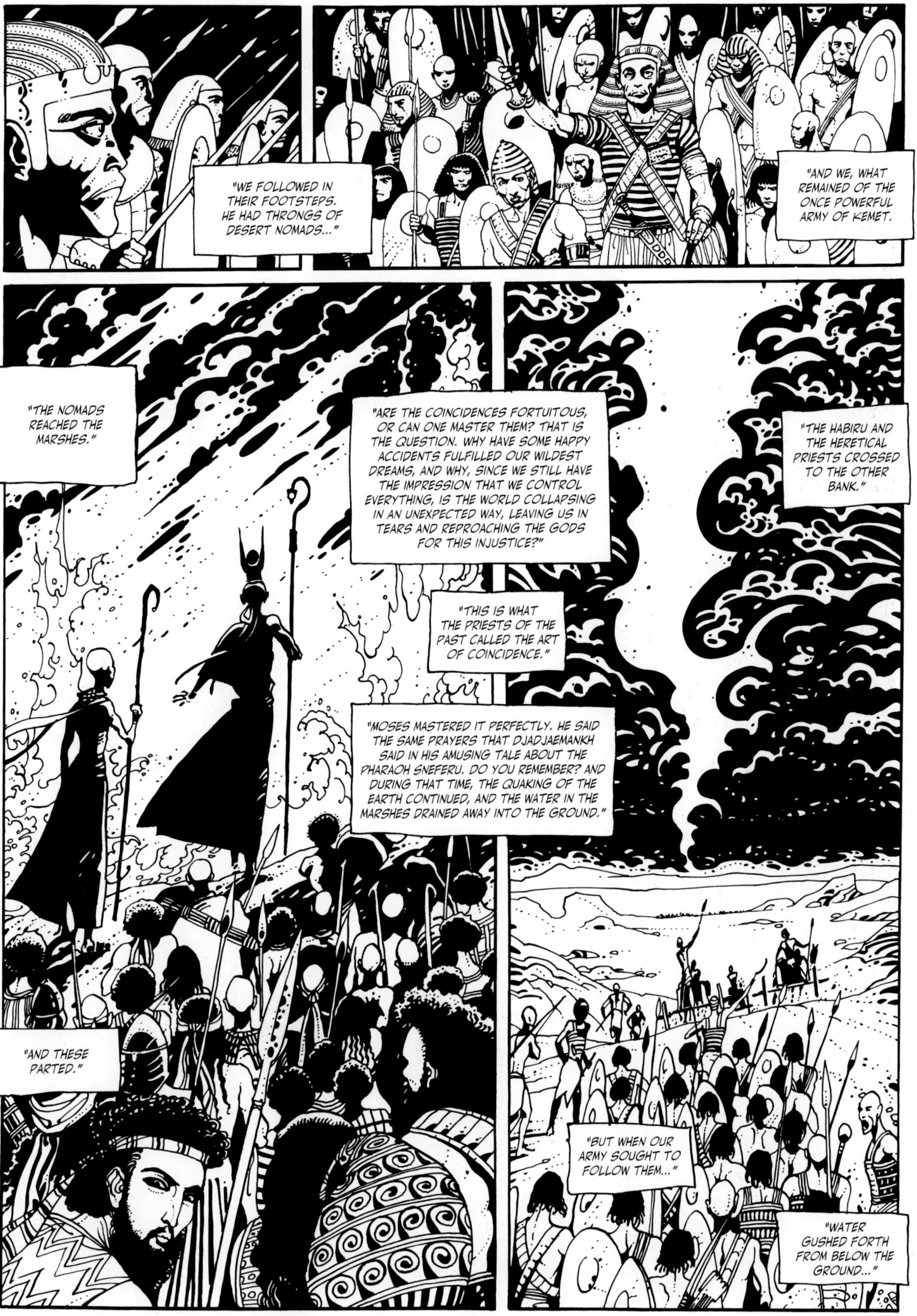
"WE FOLLOWED IN THEIR FOOTSTEPS. HE HAD THRONGS OF DESERT NOMADS..."
"AND WE, WHAT REMAINED OF THE ONCE POWERFUL ARMY OF KEMET.
"THE NOMADS REACHED THE MARSHES."
"ARE THE COINCIDENCES FORTUITOUS, OR CAN ONE MASTER THEM? THAT IS THE QUESTION. WHY HAVE SOME HAPPY ACCIDENTS FULFILLED OUR WILDEST DREAMS, AND WHY, SINCE WE STILL HAVE THE IMPRESSION THAT WE CONTROL EVERYTHING, IS THE WORLD COLLAPSING IN AN UNEXPECTED WAY, LEAVING US IN TEARS AND REPROACHING THE GODS FOR THIS INJUSTICE?"
"THIS IS WHAT THE PRIESTS OF THE PAST CALLED THE ART OF COINCIDENCE."
"MOSES MASTERED IT PERFECTLY. HE SAID THE SAME PRAYERS THAT DJADJAEMANKH SAID IN HIS AMUSING TALE ABOUT THE PHARAOH SNEFERU. DO YOU REMEMBER? AND DURING THAT TIME, THE QUAKING OF THE EARTH CONTINUED, AND THE WATER IN THE MARSHES DRAINED AWAY INTO THE GROUND."
"AND THESE PARTED."
"THE HABIRU AND THE HERETICAL PRIESTS CROSSED TO THE OTHER BANK."
"BUT WHEN OUR ARMY SOUGHT TO FOLLOW THEM..."
"WATER GUSHED FORTH FROM BELOW THE GROUND..."

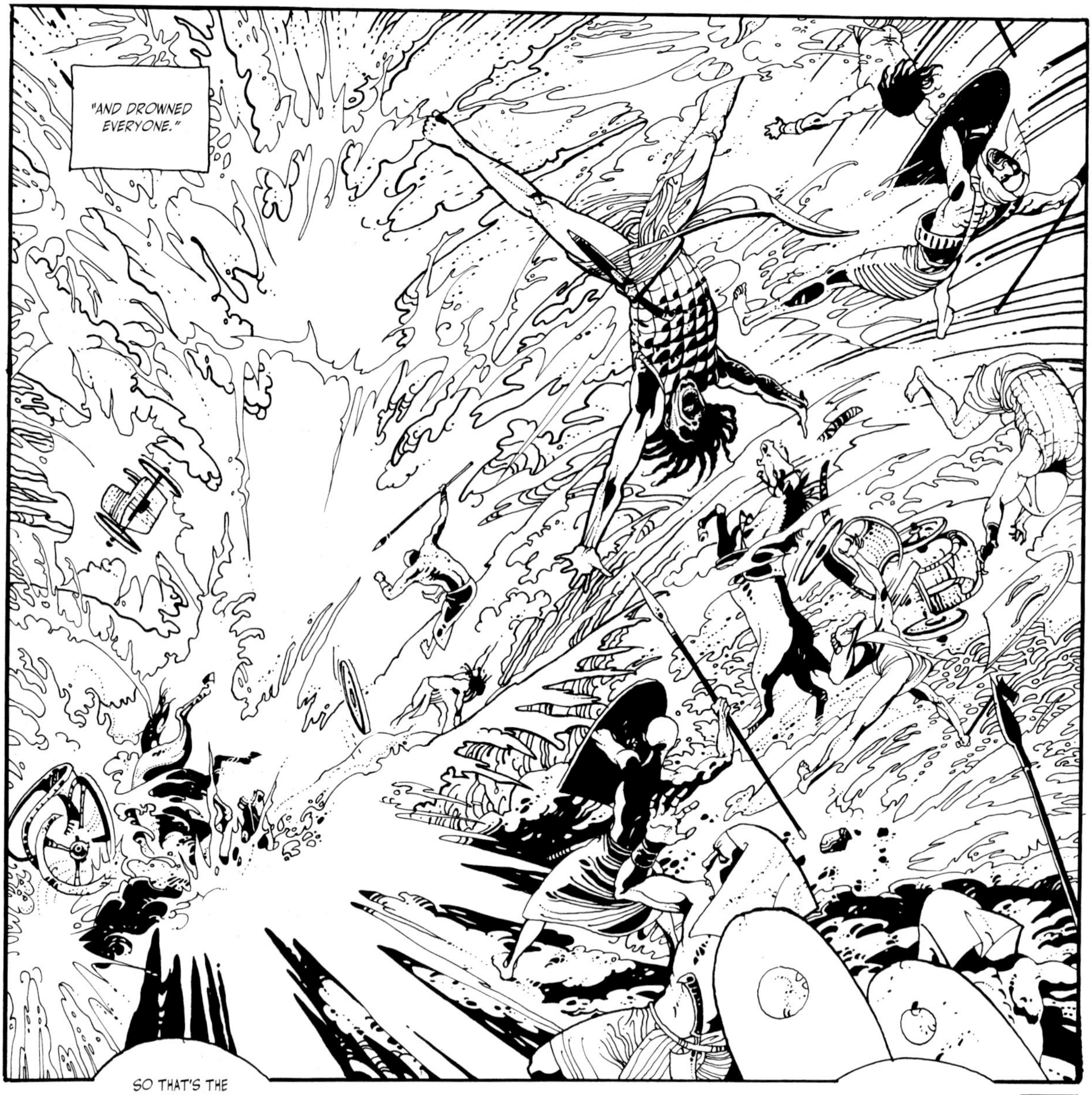
"AND DROWNED EVERYONE."

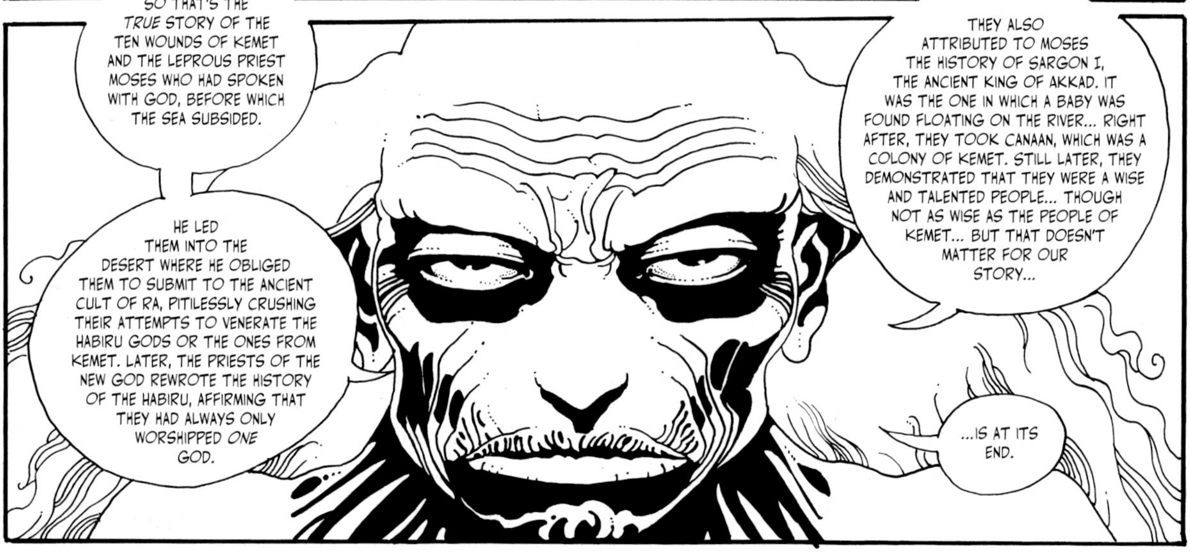
SO THAT'S THE *TRUE* STORY OF THE TEN WOUNDS OF KEMET AND THE LEPROUS PRIEST MOSES WHO HAD SPOKEN WITH GOD, BEFORE WHICH THE SEA SUBSIDED.
HE LED THEM INTO THE DESERT WHERE HE OBLIGED THEM TO SUBMIT TO THE ANCIENT CULT OF RA, PITILESSLY CRUSHING THEIR ATTEMPTS TO VENERATE THE HABIRU GODS OR THE ONES FROM KEMET. LATER, THE PRIESTS OF THE NEW GOD REWROTE THE HISTORY OF THE HABIRU, AFFIRMING THAT THEY HAD ALWAYS ONLY WORSHIPPED *ONE* GOD.
THEY ALSO ATTRIBUTED TO MOSES THE HISTORY OF SARGON I, THE ANCIENT KING OF AKKAD. IT WAS THE ONE IN WHICH A BABY WAS FOUND FLOATING ON THE RIVER... RIGHT AFTER, THEY TOOK CANAAN, WHICH WAS A COLONY OF KEMET. STILL LATER, THEY DEMONSTRATED THAT THEY WERE A WISE AND TALENTED PEOPLE... THOUGH NOT AS WISE AS THE PEOPLE OF KEMET... BUT THAT DOESN'T MATTER FOR OUR STORY...
...IS AT ITS END.

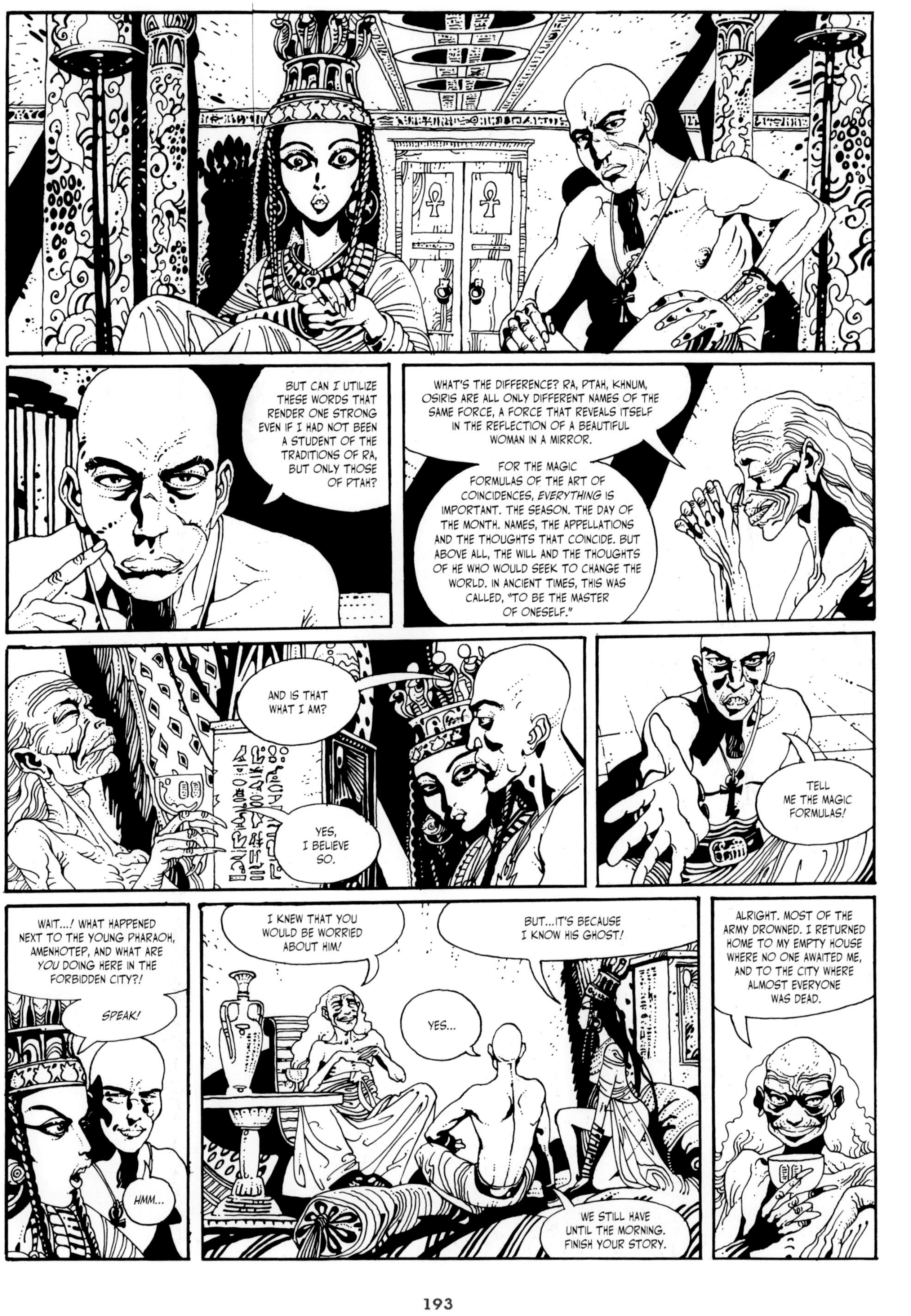

BUT CAN I UTILIZE THESE WORDS THAT RENDER ONE STRONG EVEN IF I HAD NOT BEEN A STUDENT OF THE TRADITIONS OF RA, BUT ONLY THOSE OF PTAH?
WHAT'S THE DIFFERENCE? RA, PTAH, KHNUM, OSIRIS ARE ALL ONLY DIFFERENT NAMES OF THE SAME FORCE, A FORCE THAT REVEALS ITSELF IN THE REFLECTION OF A BEAUTIFUL WOMAN IN A MIRROR.
FOR THE MAGIC FORMULAS OF THE ART OF COINCIDENCES, *EVERYTHING* IS IMPORTANT. THE SEASON. THE DAY OF THE MONTH. NAMES, THE APPELLATIONS AND THE THOUGHTS THAT COINCIDE. BUT ABOVE ALL, THE WILL AND THE THOUGHTS OF HE WHO WOULD SEEK TO CHANGE THE WORLD. IN ANCIENT TIMES, THIS WAS CALLED, "TO BE THE MASTER OF ONESELF."
AND IS THAT WHAT I AM?
YES, I BELIEVE SO.
TELL ME THE MAGIC FORMULAS!
WAIT...! WHAT HAPPENED NEXT TO THE YOUNG PHARAOH, AMENHOTEP, AND WHAT ARE *YOU* DOING HERE IN THE FORBIDDEN CITY?!
SPEAK!
HMM...
I KNEW THAT YOU WOULD BE WORRIED ABOUT HIM!
BUT...IT'S BECAUSE I KNOW HIS GHOST!
YES...
WE STILL HAVE UNTIL THE MORNING. FINISH YOUR STORY.
ALRIGHT. MOST OF THE ARMY DROWNED. I RETURNED HOME TO MY EMPTY HOUSE WHERE NO ONE AWAITED ME, AND TO THE CITY WHERE ALMOST EVERYONE WAS DEAD.

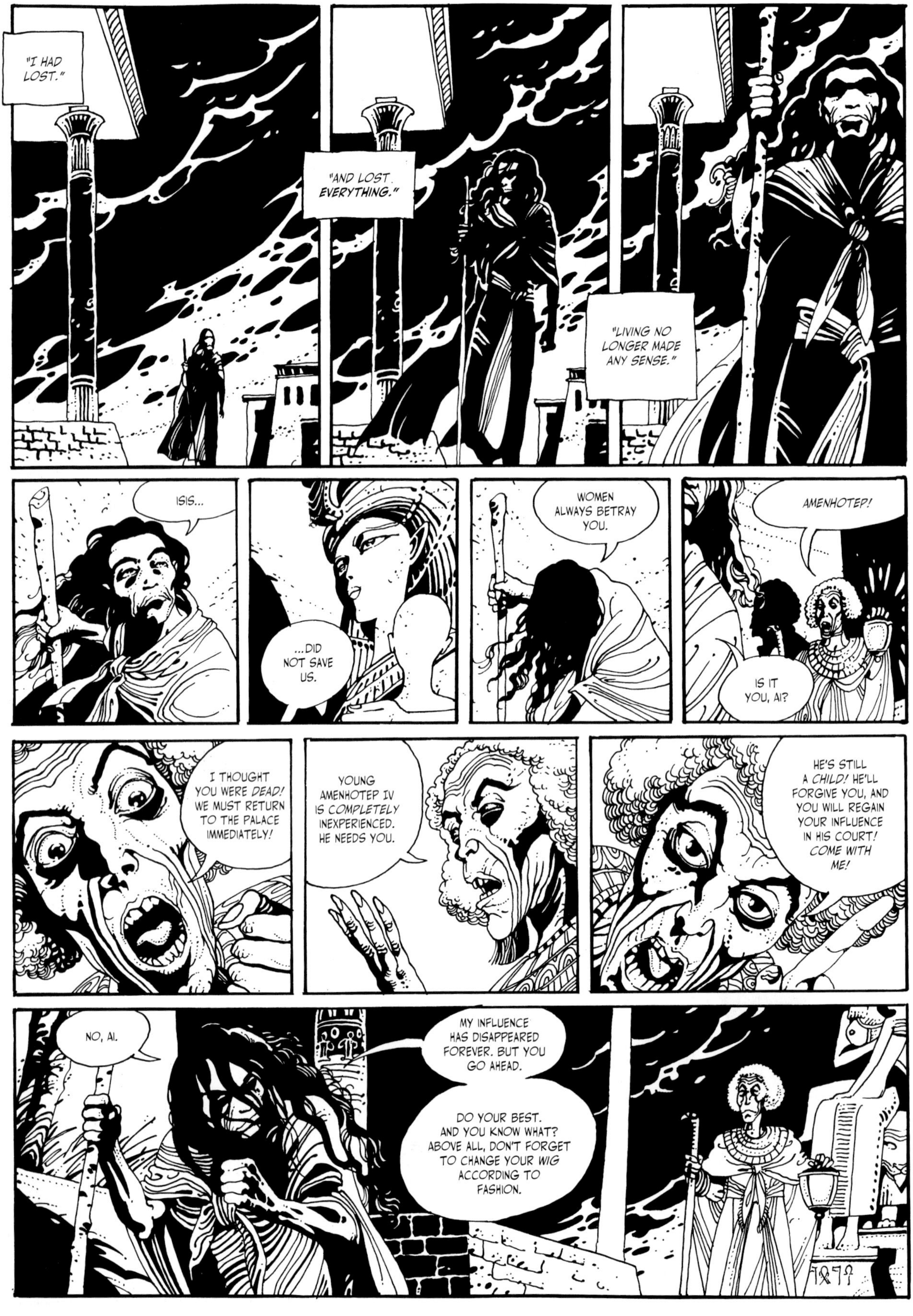
"I HAD LOST."
"AND LOST EVERYTHING."
"LIVING NO LONGER MADE ANY SENSE."
ISIS...
...DID NOT SAVE US.
WOMEN ALWAYS BETRAY YOU.
AMENHOTEP!
IS IT YOU, AI?
I THOUGHT YOU WERE DEAD! WE MUST RETURN TO THE PALACE IMMEDIATELY!
YOUNG AMENHOTEP IV IS COMPLETELY INEXPERIENCED. HE NEEDS YOU.
HE'S STILL A CHILD! HE'LL FORGIVE YOU, AND YOU WILL REGAIN YOUR INFLUENCE IN HIS COURT! COME WITH ME!
NO, AI.
MY INFLUENCE HAS DISAPPEARED FOREVER. BUT YOU GO AHEAD.
DO YOUR BEST. AND YOU KNOW WHAT? ABOVE ALL, DON'T FORGET TO CHANGE YOUR WIG ACCORDING TO FASHION.

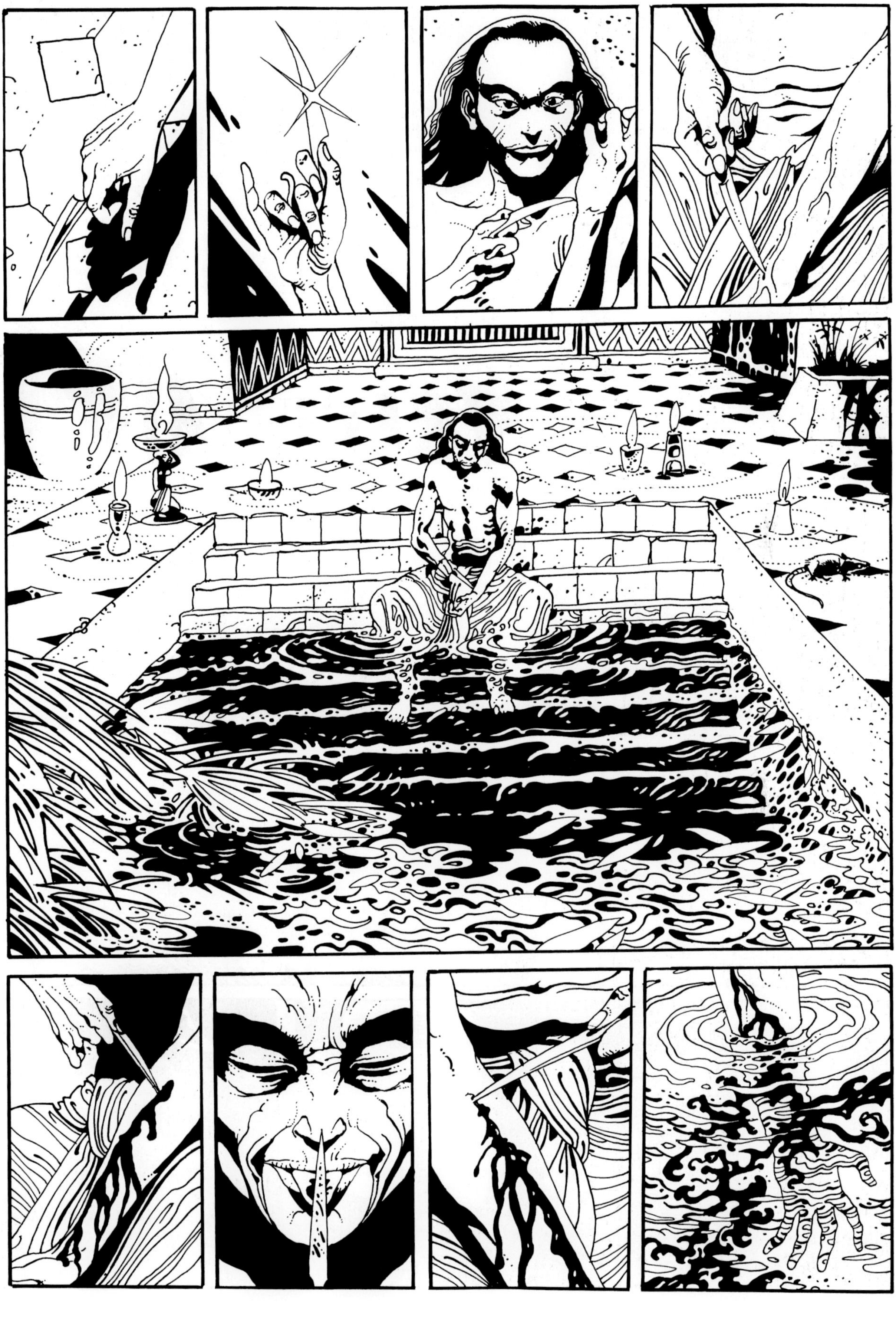

"BUT I WAS NOT DEAD."

"I LOST CONSCIOUSNESS, AND I SAW THE EYE OF HORUS THE ANCIENT...WHO STARED AT ME FROM HIS SPARKLING DARKNESS... YES, IT'S STILL JUST ANOTHER NAME FOR THE SAME IMMENSE FORCE. AND JUST THEN, I HAD RETURNED."

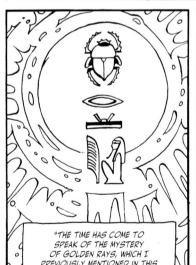

"THE TIME HAS COME TO SPEAK OF THE MYSTERY OF GOLDEN RAYS, WHICH I PREVIOUSLY MENTIONED IN THIS STORY. DURING OLDEN TIMES, THE MAGICIANS OF KEMET HAD DISCOVERED THE MEANS OF PROLONGING LIFE, RENDERING IT ESSENTIALLY ETERNAL. THIS SECRET KNOWLEDGE WAS TAUGHT IN THE SCHOOLS ATTENDED BY PRIESTS IN DIFFERENT CITIES. THE METHOD WAS SIMPLE, BUT RARE WERE THOSE WHO OBTAINED ANY RESULTS."

"IT WAS NECESSARY TO GRADUALLY DIMINISH THE QUANTITY OF ONE'S NOURISHMENT. WITH THE GOAL OF CEASING TO EAT OR DRINK ANYTHING BUT WATER. IN PLACE OF THIS SUSTENANCE, ONE WAS NOURISHED BY THE SUN'S RAYS. THIS WAS DONE BY SITTING UNDER THE SUN AT SPECIFIC HOURS DURING THE DAY, REPEATING CERTAIN PHRASES AND MEDITATING. AFTER A FEW DAYS IN DREAD OF STARVATION AND THE LOSS OF WEIGHT, ONE EXPERIENCED VISIONS..."

"THEN THE SUN CREATED DEEP INSIDE THE BODY A SORT OF IMMORTAL DOUBLE, WHICH PREVENTED THE CORPORAL ENVELOPE FROM DYING. THE PRIEST THAT ATTAINED THIS STATE WAS CALLED A SAHU. OF COURSE, I ASSIDUOUSLY FOLLOWED THESE PRECEPTS OF THE MYSTERY OF THE GOLDEN RAYS OVER MANY YEARS."

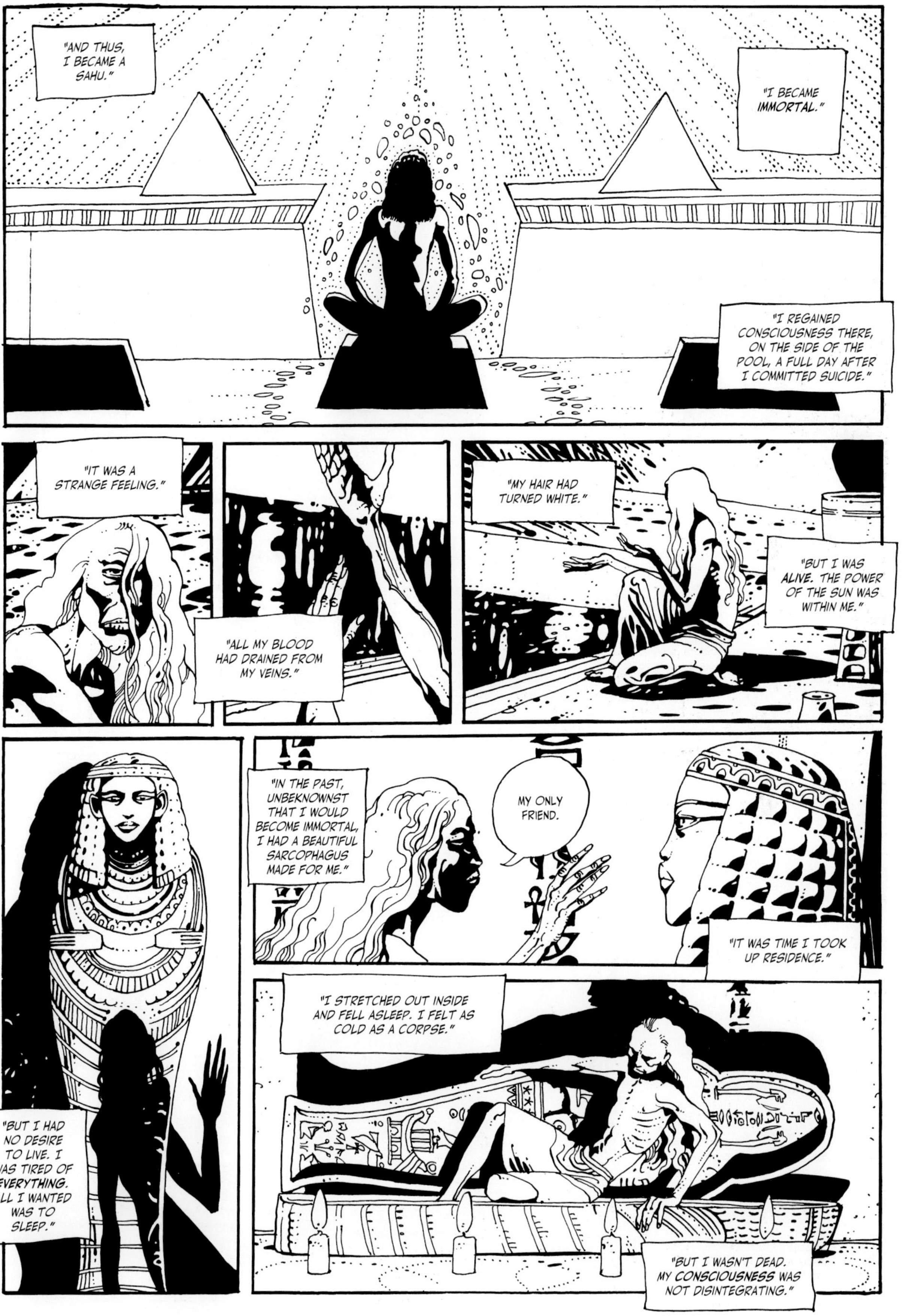
"AND THUS, I BECAME A SAHU."
"I BECAME IMMORTAL."
"I REGAINED CONSCIOUSNESS THERE, ON THE SIDE OF THE POOL, A FULL DAY AFTER I COMMITTED SUICIDE."
"IT WAS A STRANGE FEELING."
"ALL MY BLOOD HAD DRAINED FROM MY VEINS."
"MY HAIR HAD TURNED WHITE."
"BUT I WAS ALIVE. THE POWER OF THE SUN WAS WITHIN ME."
"BUT I HAD NO DESIRE TO LIVE. I WAS TIRED OF EVERYTHING. ALL I WANTED WAS TO SLEEP."
"IN THE PAST, UNBEKNOWNST THAT I WOULD BECOME IMMORTAL, I HAD A BEAUTIFUL SARCOPHAGUS MADE FOR ME."
MY ONLY FRIEND.
"IT WAS TIME I TOOK UP RESIDENCE."
"I STRETCHED OUT INSIDE AND FELL ASLEEP. I FELT AS COLD AS A CORPSE."
"BUT I WASN'T DEAD. MY CONSCIOUSNESS WAS NOT DISINTEGRATING."

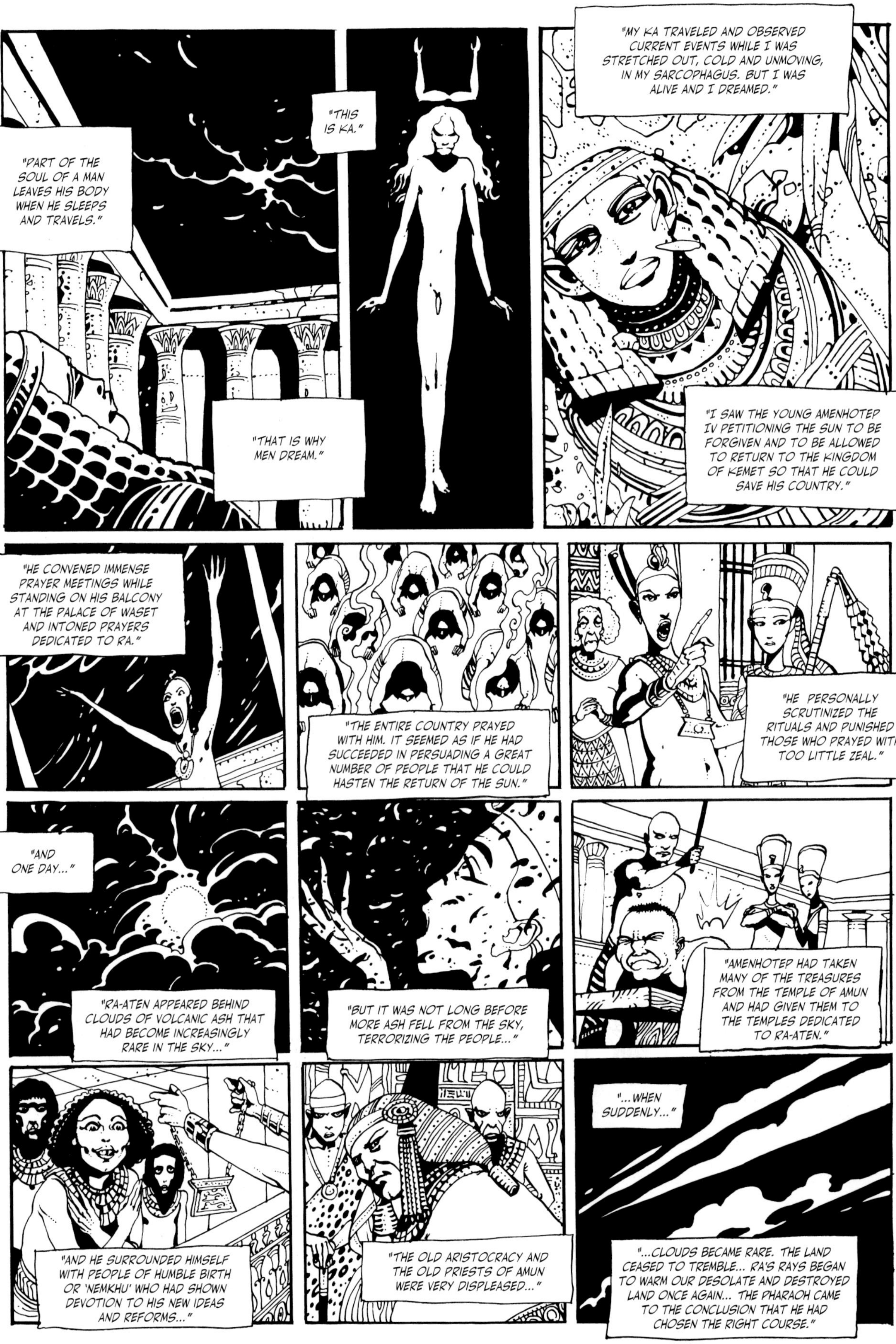
"PART OF THE SOUL OF A MAN LEAVES HIS BODY WHEN HE SLEEPS AND TRAVELS."
"THIS IS KA."
"THAT IS WHY MEN DREAM."
"MY KA TRAVELED AND OBSERVED CURRENT EVENTS WHILE I WAS STRETCHED OUT, COLD AND UNMOVING, IN MY SARCOPHAGUS. BUT I WAS ALIVE AND I DREAMED."
"I SAW THE YOUNG AMENHOTEP IV PETITIONING THE SUN TO BE FORGIVEN AND TO BE ALLOWED TO RETURN TO THE KINGDOM OF KEMET SO THAT HE COULD SAVE HIS COUNTRY."
"HE CONVENED IMMENSE PRAYER MEETINGS WHILE STANDING ON HIS BALCONY AT THE PALACE OF WASET AND INTONED PRAYERS DEDICATED TO RA."
"THE ENTIRE COUNTRY PRAYED WITH HIM. IT SEEMED AS IF HE HAD SUCCEEDED IN PERSUADING A GREAT NUMBER OF PEOPLE THAT HE COULD HASTEN THE RETURN OF THE SUN."
"HE PERSONALLY SCRUTINIZED THE RITUALS AND PUNISHED THOSE WHO PRAYED WITH TOO LITTLE ZEAL."
"AND ONE DAY..."
"RA-ATEN APPEARED BEHIND CLOUDS OF VOLCANIC ASH THAT HAD BECOME INCREASINGLY RARE IN THE SKY..."
"BUT IT WAS NOT LONG BEFORE MORE ASH FELL FROM THE SKY, TERRORIZING THE PEOPLE..."
"AMENHOTEP HAD TAKEN MANY OF THE TREASURES FROM THE TEMPLE OF AMUN AND HAD GIVEN THEM TO THE TEMPLES DEDICATED TO RA-ATEN."
"AND HE SURROUNDED HIMSELF WITH PEOPLE OF HUMBLE BIRTH OR 'NEMKHU' WHO HAD SHOWN DEVOTION TO HIS NEW IDEAS AND REFORMS..."
"THE OLD ARISTOCRACY AND THE OLD PRIESTS OF AMUN WERE VERY DISPLEASED..."
"...WHEN SUDDENLY..."
"...CLOUDS BECAME RARE. THE LAND CEASED TO TREMBLE... RA'S RAYS BEGAN TO WARM OUR DESOLATE AND DESTROYED LAND ONCE AGAIN... THE PHARAOH CAME TO THE CONCLUSION THAT HE HAD CHOSEN THE RIGHT COURSE."

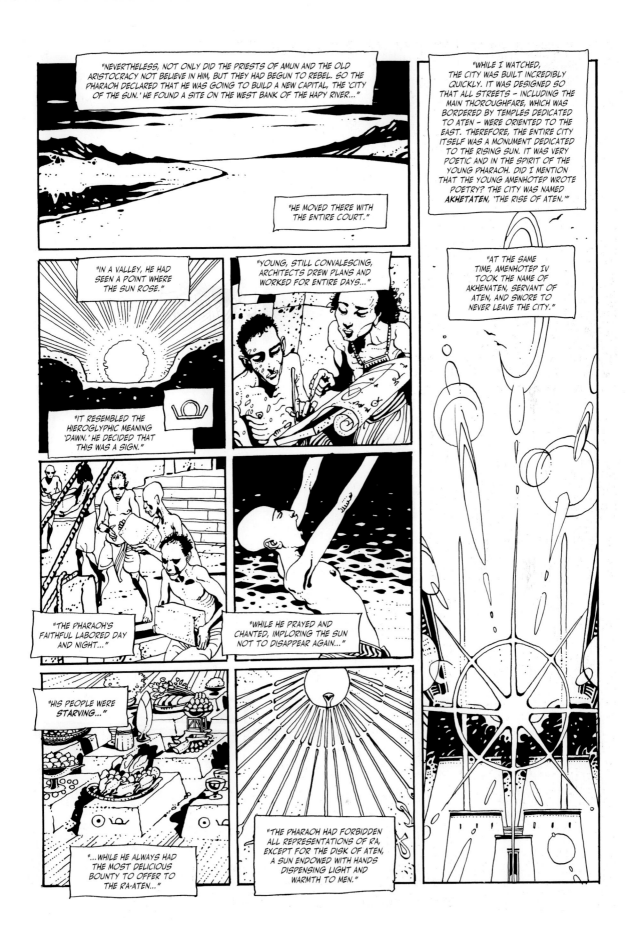

"NEVERTHELESS, NOT ONLY DID THE PRIESTS OF AMUN AND THE OLD ARISTOCRACY NOT BELIEVE IN HIM, BUT THEY HAD BEGUN TO REBEL. SO THE PHARAOH DECLARED THAT HE WAS GOING TO BUILD A NEW CAPITAL, THE 'CITY OF THE SUN.' HE FOUND A SITE ON THE WEST BANK OF THE HAPY RIVER..."

"HE MOVED THERE WITH THE ENTIRE COURT."

"WHILE I WATCHED, THE CITY WAS BUILT INCREDIBLY QUICKLY. IT WAS DESIGNED SO THAT ALL STREETS – INCLUDING THE MAIN THOROUGHFARE, WHICH WAS BORDERED BY TEMPLES DEDICATED TO ATEN – WERE ORIENTED TO THE EAST. THEREFORE, THE ENTIRE CITY ITSELF WAS A MONUMENT DEDICATED TO THE RISING SUN. IT WAS VERY POETIC AND IN THE SPIRIT OF THE YOUNG PHARAOH. DID I MENTION THAT THE YOUNG AMENHOTEP WROTE POETRY? THE CITY WAS NAMED AKHETATEN, 'THE RISE OF ATEN.'"

"IN A VALLEY, HE HAD SEEN A POINT WHERE THE SUN ROSE."

"IT RESEMBLED THE HIEROGLYPHIC MEANING 'DAWN.' HE DECIDED THAT THIS WAS A SIGN."

"YOUNG, STILL CONVALESCING, ARCHITECTS DREW PLANS AND WORKED FOR ENTIRE DAYS..."

"AT THE SAME TIME, AMENHOTEP IV TOOK THE NAME OF AKHENATEN, SERVANT OF ATEN, AND SWORE TO NEVER LEAVE THE CITY."

"THE PHARAOH'S FAITHFUL LABORED DAY AND NIGHT..."

"WHILE HE PRAYED AND CHANTED, IMPLORING THE SUN NOT TO DISAPPEAR AGAIN..."

"HIS PEOPLE WERE STARVING..."

"...WHILE HE ALWAYS HAD THE MOST DELICIOUS BOUNTY TO OFFER TO THE RA-ATEN..."

"THE PHARAOH HAD FORBIDDEN ALL REPRESENTATIONS OF RA, EXCEPT FOR THE DISK OF ATEN, A SUN ENDOWED WITH HANDS DISPENSING LIGHT AND WARMTH TO MEN."

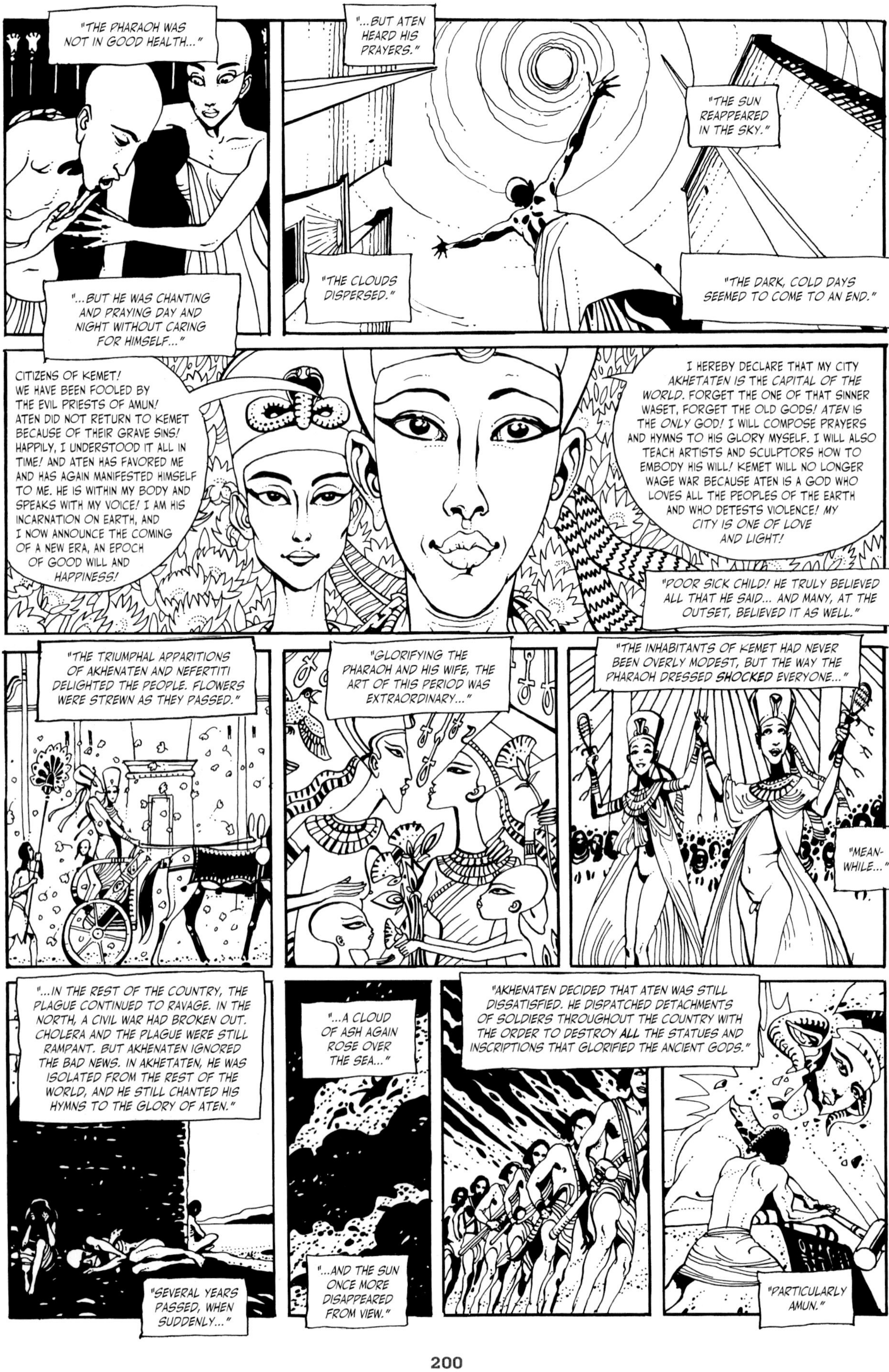

"THE PHARAOH WAS NOT IN GOOD HEALTH..."
"...BUT HE WAS CHANTING AND PRAYING DAY AND NIGHT WITHOUT CARING FOR HIMSELF..."
"...BUT ATEN HEARD HIS PRAYERS."
"THE SUN REAPPEARED IN THE SKY."
"THE CLOUDS DISPERSED."
"THE DARK, COLD DAYS SEEMED TO COME TO AN END."
CITIZENS OF KEMET! WE HAVE BEEN FOOLED BY THE EVIL PRIESTS OF AMUN! ATEN DID NOT RETURN TO KEMET BECAUSE OF THEIR GRAVE SINS! HAPPILY, I UNDERSTOOD IT ALL IN TIME! AND ATEN HAS FAVORED ME AND HAS AGAIN MANIFESTED HIMSELF TO ME. HE IS WITHIN MY BODY AND SPEAKS WITH MY VOICE! I AM HIS INCARNATION ON EARTH, AND I NOW ANNOUNCE THE COMING OF A NEW ERA, AN EPOCH OF GOOD WILL AND HAPPINESS!
I HEREBY DECLARE THAT MY CITY AKHETATEN IS THE CAPITAL OF THE WORLD. FORGET THE ONE OF THAT SINNER WASET, FORGET THE OLD GODS! ATEN IS THE *ONLY* GOD! I WILL COMPOSE PRAYERS AND HYMNS TO HIS GLORY MYSELF. I WILL ALSO TEACH ARTISTS AND SCULPTORS HOW TO EMBODY HIS WILL! KEMET WILL NO LONGER WAGE WAR BECAUSE ATEN IS A GOD WHO LOVES ALL THE PEOPLES OF THE EARTH AND WHO DETESTS VIOLENCE! MY CITY IS ONE OF LOVE AND LIGHT!
"POOR SICK CHILD! HE TRULY BELIEVED ALL THAT HE SAID... AND MANY, AT THE OUTSET, BELIEVED IT AS WELL."
"THE TRIUMPHAL APPARITIONS OF AKHENATEN AND NEFERTITI DELIGHTED THE PEOPLE. FLOWERS WERE STREWN AS THEY PASSED."
"GLORIFYING THE PHARAOH AND HIS WIFE, THE ART OF THIS PERIOD WAS EXTRAORDINARY..."
"THE INHABITANTS OF KEMET HAD NEVER BEEN OVERLY MODEST, BUT THE WAY THE PHARAOH DRESSED **SHOCKED** EVERYONE..."
"MEAN-WHILE..."
"...IN THE REST OF THE COUNTRY, THE PLAGUE CONTINUED TO RAVAGE. IN THE NORTH, A CIVIL WAR HAD BROKEN OUT. CHOLERA AND THE PLAGUE WERE STILL RAMPANT. BUT AKHENATEN IGNORED THE BAD NEWS. IN AKHETATEN, HE WAS ISOLATED FROM THE REST OF THE WORLD, AND HE STILL CHANTED HIS HYMNS TO THE GLORY OF ATEN."
"SEVERAL YEARS PASSED, WHEN SUDDENLY..."
"...A CLOUD OF ASH AGAIN ROSE OVER THE SEA..."
"...AND THE SUN ONCE MORE DISAPPEARED FROM VIEW."
"AKHENATEN DECIDED THAT ATEN WAS STILL DISSATISFIED. HE DISPATCHED DETACHMENTS OF SOLDIERS THROUGHOUT THE COUNTRY WITH THE ORDER TO DESTROY **ALL** THE STATUES AND INSCRIPTIONS THAT GLORIFIED THE ANCIENT GODS."
"PARTICULARLY AMUN."

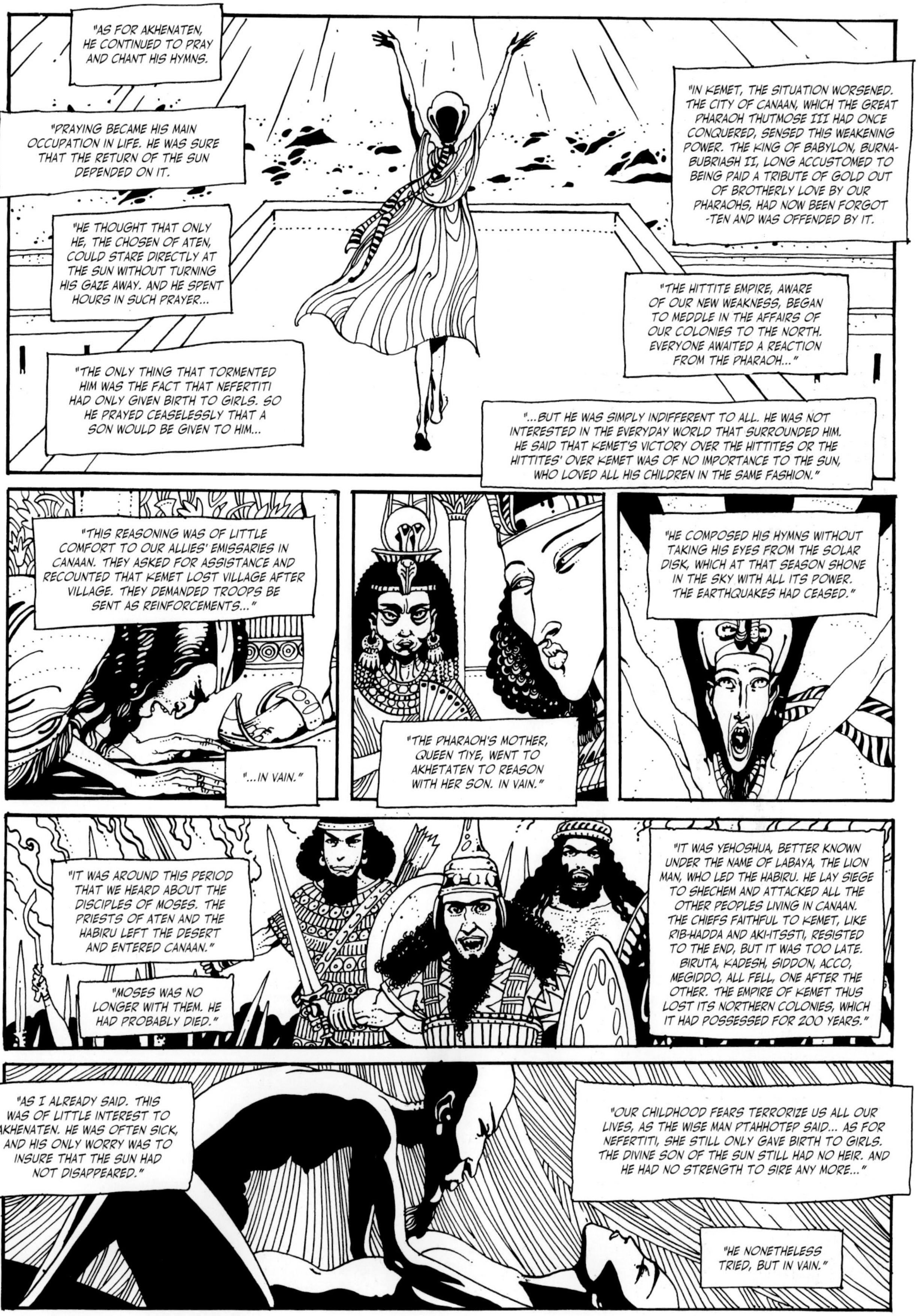
"AS FOR AKHENATEN, HE CONTINUED TO PRAY AND CHANT HIS HYMNS.
"PRAYING BECAME HIS MAIN OCCUPATION IN LIFE. HE WAS SURE THAT THE RETURN OF THE SUN DEPENDED ON IT.
"HE THOUGHT THAT ONLY HE, THE CHOSEN OF ATEN, COULD STARE DIRECTLY AT THE SUN WITHOUT TURNING HIS GAZE AWAY. AND HE SPENT HOURS IN SUCH PRAYER...
"THE ONLY THING THAT TORMENTED HIM WAS THE FACT THAT NEFERTITI HAD ONLY GIVEN BIRTH TO GIRLS. SO HE PRAYED CEASELESSLY THAT A SON WOULD BE GIVEN TO HIM...
"IN KEMET, THE SITUATION WORSENED. THE CITY OF CANAAN, WHICH THE GREAT PHARAOH THUTMOSE III HAD ONCE CONQUERED, SENSED THIS WEAKENING POWER. THE KING OF BABYLON, BURNA-BUBRIASH II, LONG ACCUSTOMED TO BEING PAID A TRIBUTE OF GOLD OUT OF BROTHERLY LOVE BY OUR PHARAOHS, HAD NOW BEEN FORGOT-TEN AND WAS OFFENDED BY IT.
"THE HITTITE EMPIRE, AWARE OF OUR NEW WEAKNESS, BEGAN TO MEDDLE IN THE AFFAIRS OF OUR COLONIES TO THE NORTH. EVERYONE AWAITED A REACTION FROM THE PHARAOH..."
"...BUT HE WAS SIMPLY INDIFFERENT TO ALL. HE WAS NOT INTERESTED IN THE EVERYDAY WORLD THAT SURROUNDED HIM. HE SAID THAT KEMET'S VICTORY OVER THE HITTITES OR THE HITTITES' OVER KEMET WAS OF NO IMPORTANCE TO THE SUN, WHO LOVED ALL HIS CHILDREN IN THE SAME FASHION."
"THIS REASONING WAS OF LITTLE COMFORT TO OUR ALLIES' EMISSARIES IN CANAAN. THEY ASKED FOR ASSISTANCE AND RECOUNTED THAT KEMET LOST VILLAGE AFTER VILLAGE. THEY DEMANDED TROOPS BE SENT AS REINFORCEMENTS..."
"...IN VAIN."
"THE PHARAOH'S MOTHER, QUEEN TIYE, WENT TO AKHETATEN TO REASON WITH HER SON. IN VAIN."
"HE COMPOSED HIS HYMNS WITHOUT TAKING HIS EYES FROM THE SOLAR DISK, WHICH AT THAT SEASON SHONE IN THE SKY WITH ALL ITS POWER. THE EARTHQUAKES HAD CEASED."
"IT WAS AROUND THIS PERIOD THAT WE HEARD ABOUT THE DISCIPLES OF MOSES. THE PRIESTS OF ATEN AND THE HABIRU LEFT THE DESERT AND ENTERED CANAAN."
"MOSES WAS NO LONGER WITH THEM. HE HAD PROBABLY DIED."
"IT WAS YEHOSHUA, BETTER KNOWN UNDER THE NAME OF LABAYA, THE LION MAN, WHO LED THE HABIRU. HE LAY SIEGE TO SHECHEM AND ATTACKED ALL THE OTHER PEOPLES LIVING IN CANAAN. THE CHIEFS FAITHFUL TO KEMET, LIKE RIB-HADDA AND AKI-ITSSTI, RESISTED TO THE END, BUT IT WAS TOO LATE. BIRUTA, KADESH, SIDDON, ACCO, MEGIDDO, ALL FELL, ONE AFTER THE OTHER. THE EMPIRE OF KEMET THUS LOST ITS NORTHERN COLONIES, WHICH IT HAD POSSESSED FOR 200 YEARS."
"AS I ALREADY SAID. THIS WAS OF LITTLE INTEREST TO AKHENATEN. HE WAS OFTEN SICK, AND HIS ONLY WORRY WAS TO INSURE THAT THE SUN HAD NOT DISAPPEARED."
"OUR CHILDHOOD FEARS TERRORIZE US ALL OUR LIVES, AS THE WISE MAN PTAHHOTEP SAID... AS FOR NEFERTITI, SHE STILL ONLY GAVE BIRTH TO GIRLS. THE DIVINE SON OF THE SUN STILL HAD NO HEIR. AND HE HAD NO STRENGTH TO SIRE ANY MORE..."
"HE NONETHELESS TRIED, BUT IN VAIN."

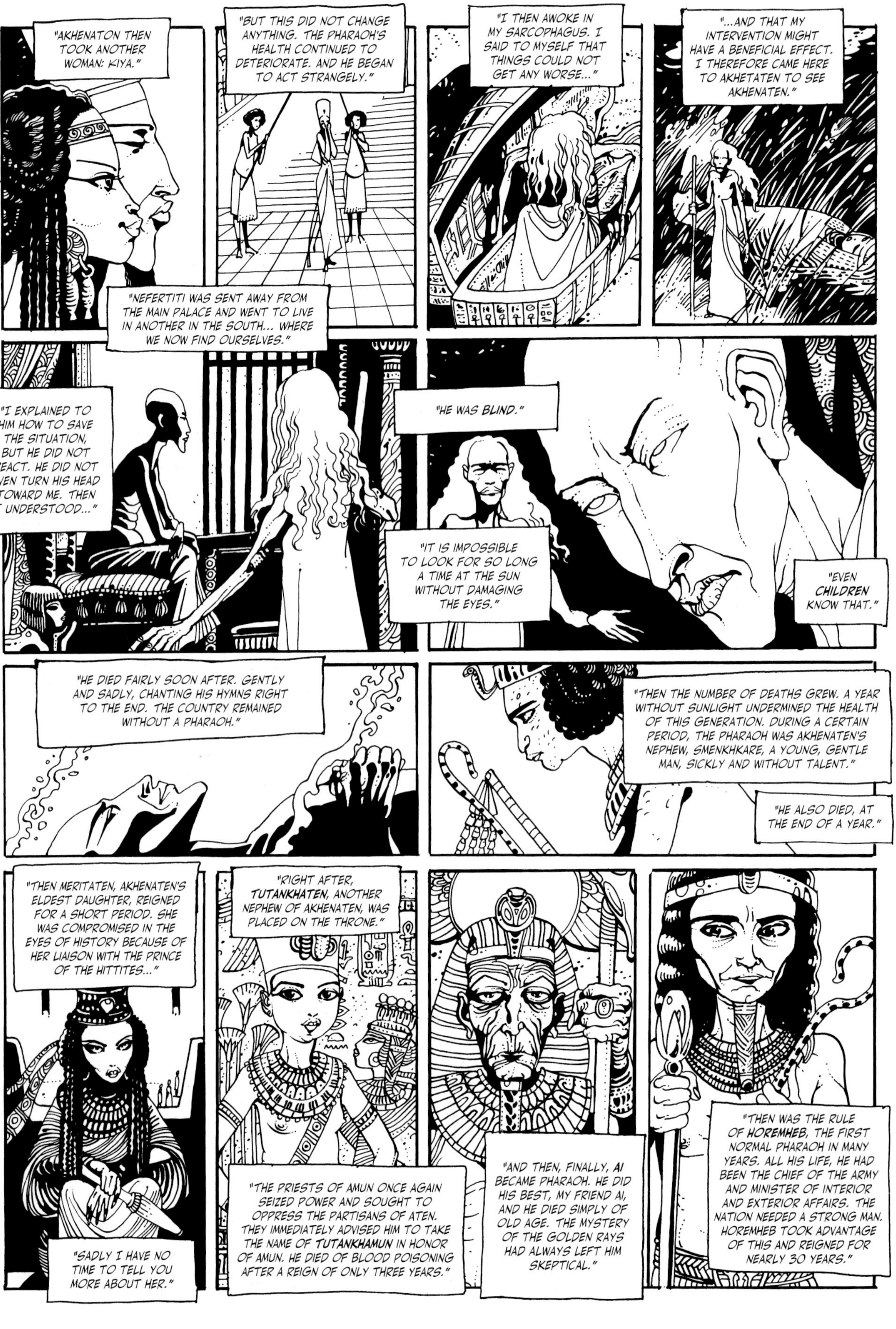
"AKHENATON THEN TOOK ANOTHER WOMAN: KIYA."
"NEFERTITI WAS SENT AWAY FROM THE MAIN PALACE AND WENT TO LIVE IN ANOTHER IN THE SOUTH... WHERE WE NOW FIND OURSELVES."
"BUT THIS DID NOT CHANGE ANYTHING. THE PHARAOH'S HEALTH CONTINUED TO DETERIORATE. AND HE BEGAN TO ACT STRANGELY."
"I THEN AWOKE IN MY SARCOPHAGUS. I SAID TO MYSELF THAT THINGS COULD NOT GET ANY WORSE..."
"...AND THAT MY INTERVENTION MIGHT HAVE A BENEFICIAL EFFECT. I THEREFORE CAME HERE TO AKHETATEN TO SEE AKHENATEN."
"I EXPLAINED TO HIM HOW TO SAVE THE SITUATION, BUT HE DID NOT REACT. HE DID NOT EVEN TURN HIS HEAD TOWARD ME. THEN I UNDERSTOOD..."
"HE WAS BLIND."
"IT IS IMPOSSIBLE TO LOOK FOR SO LONG A TIME AT THE SUN WITHOUT DAMAGING THE EYES."
"EVEN CHILDREN KNOW THAT."
"HE DIED FAIRLY SOON AFTER. GENTLY AND SADLY, CHANTING HIS HYMNS RIGHT TO THE END. THE COUNTRY REMAINED WITHOUT A PHARAOH."
"THEN THE NUMBER OF DEATHS GREW. A YEAR WITHOUT SUNLIGHT UNDERMINED THE HEALTH OF THIS GENERATION. DURING A CERTAIN PERIOD, THE PHARAOH WAS AKHENATEN'S NEPHEW, SMENKHKARE, A YOUNG, GENTLE MAN, SICKLY AND WITHOUT TALENT."
"HE ALSO DIED, AT THE END OF A YEAR."
"THEN MERITATEN, AKHENATEN'S ELDEST DAUGHTER, REIGNED FOR A SHORT PERIOD. SHE WAS COMPROMISED IN THE EYES OF HISTORY BECAUSE OF HER LIAISON WITH THE PRINCE OF THE HITTITES..."
"SADLY I HAVE NO TIME TO TELL YOU MORE ABOUT HER."
"RIGHT AFTER, TUTANKHATEN, ANOTHER NEPHEW OF AKHENATEN, WAS PLACED ON THE THRONE."
"THE PRIESTS OF AMUN ONCE AGAIN SEIZED POWER AND SOUGHT TO OPPRESS THE PARTISANS OF ATEN. THEY IMMEDIATELY ADVISED HIM TO TAKE THE NAME OF TUTANKHAMUN IN HONOR OF AMUN. HE DIED OF BLOOD POISONING AFTER A REIGN OF ONLY THREE YEARS."
"AND THEN, FINALLY, AI BECAME PHARAOH. HE DID HIS BEST, MY FRIEND AI, AND HE DIED SIMPLY OF OLD AGE. THE MYSTERY OF THE GOLDEN RAYS HAD ALWAYS LEFT HIM SKEPTICAL."
"THEN WAS THE RULE OF HOREMHEB, THE FIRST NORMAL PHARAOH IN MANY YEARS. ALL HIS LIFE, HE HAD BEEN THE CHIEF OF THE ARMY AND MINISTER OF INTERIOR AND EXTERIOR AFFAIRS. THE NATION NEEDED A STRONG MAN. HOREMHEB TOOK ADVANTAGE OF THIS AND REIGNED FOR NEARLY 30 YEARS."

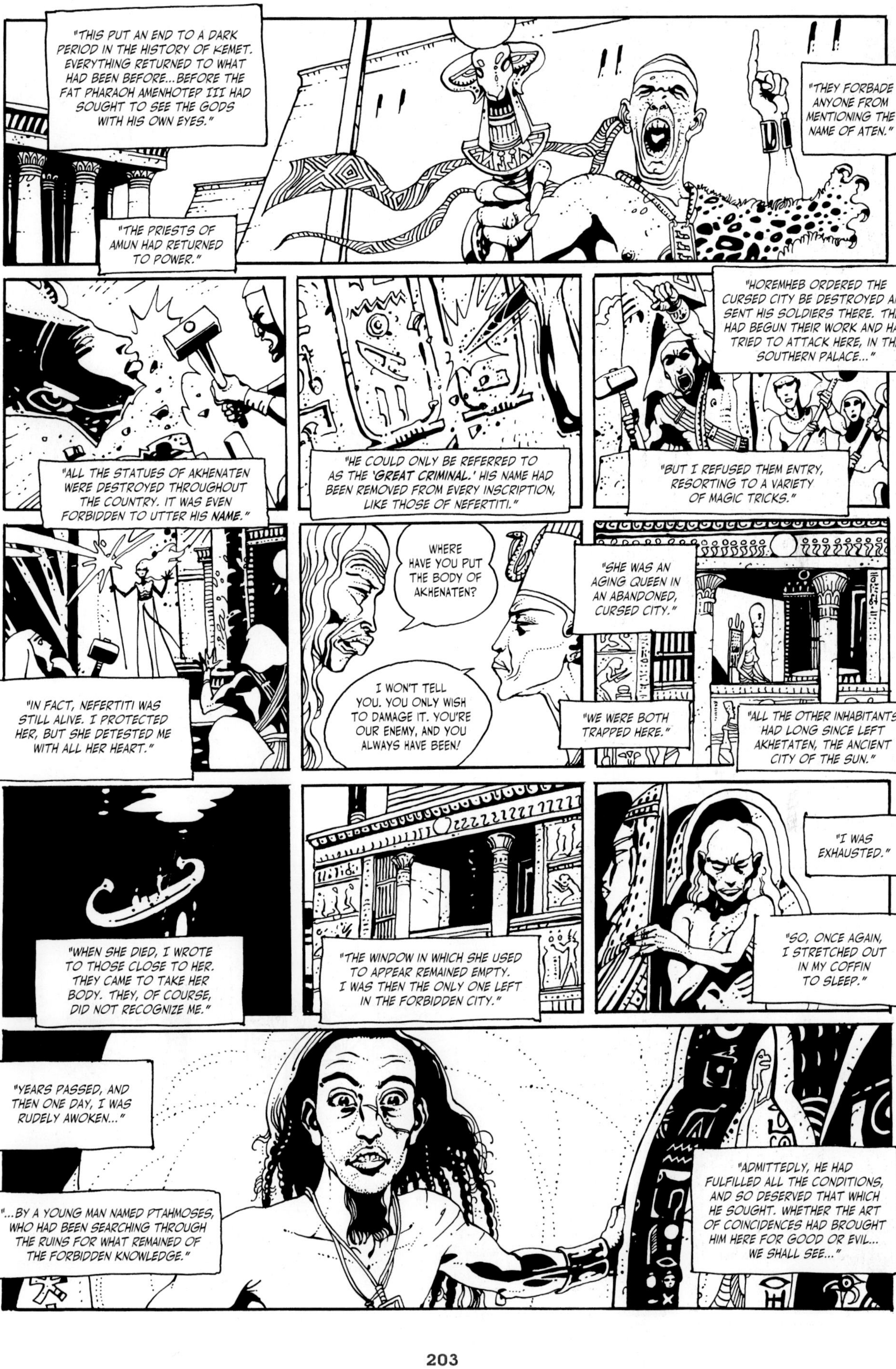
"THIS PUT AN END TO A DARK PERIOD IN THE HISTORY OF KEMET. EVERYTHING RETURNED TO WHAT HAD BEEN BEFORE...BEFORE THE FAT PHARAOH AMENHOTEP III HAD SOUGHT TO SEE THE GODS WITH HIS OWN EYES."
"THE PRIESTS OF AMUN HAD RETURNED TO POWER."
"THEY FORBADE ANYONE FROM MENTIONING THE NAME OF ATEN."
"ALL THE STATUES OF AKHENATEN WERE DESTROYED THROUGHOUT THE COUNTRY. IT WAS EVEN FORBIDDEN TO UTTER HIS NAME."
"HE COULD ONLY BE REFERRED TO AS THE 'GREAT CRIMINAL.' HIS NAME HAD BEEN REMOVED FROM EVERY INSCRIPTION, LIKE THOSE OF NEFERTITI."
"HOREMHEB ORDERED THE CURSED CITY BE DESTROYED AND SENT HIS SOLDIERS THERE. THEY HAD BEGUN THEIR WORK AND HAD TRIED TO ATTACK HERE, IN THE SOUTHERN PALACE..."
"BUT I REFUSED THEM ENTRY, RESORTING TO A VARIETY OF MAGIC TRICKS."
"IN FACT, NEFERTITI WAS STILL ALIVE. I PROTECTED HER, BUT SHE DETESTED ME WITH ALL HER HEART."
WHERE HAVE YOU PUT THE BODY OF AKHENATEN?
I WON'T TELL YOU. YOU ONLY WISH TO DAMAGE IT. YOU'RE OUR ENEMY, AND YOU ALWAYS HAVE BEEN!
"SHE WAS AN AGING QUEEN IN AN ABANDONED, CURSED CITY."
"WE WERE BOTH TRAPPED HERE."
"ALL THE OTHER INHABITANTS HAD LONG SINCE LEFT AKHETATEN, THE ANCIENT CITY OF THE SUN."
"WHEN SHE DIED, I WROTE TO THOSE CLOSE TO HER. THEY CAME TO TAKE HER BODY. THEY, OF COURSE, DID NOT RECOGNIZE ME."
"THE WINDOW IN WHICH SHE USED TO APPEAR REMAINED EMPTY. I WAS THEN THE ONLY ONE LEFT IN THE FORBIDDEN CITY."
"I WAS EXHAUSTED."
"SO, ONCE AGAIN, I STRETCHED OUT IN MY COFFIN TO SLEEP."
"YEARS PASSED, AND THEN ONE DAY, I WAS RUDELY AWOKEN..."
"...BY A YOUNG MAN NAMED PTAHMOSES, WHO HAD BEEN SEARCHING THROUGH THE RUINS FOR WHAT REMAINED OF THE FORBIDDEN KNOWLEDGE."
"ADMITTEDLY, HE HAD FULFILLED ALL THE CONDITIONS, AND SO DESERVED THAT WHICH HE SOUGHT. WHETHER THE ART OF COINCIDENCES HAD BROUGHT HIM HERE FOR GOOD OR EVIL... WE SHALL SEE..."

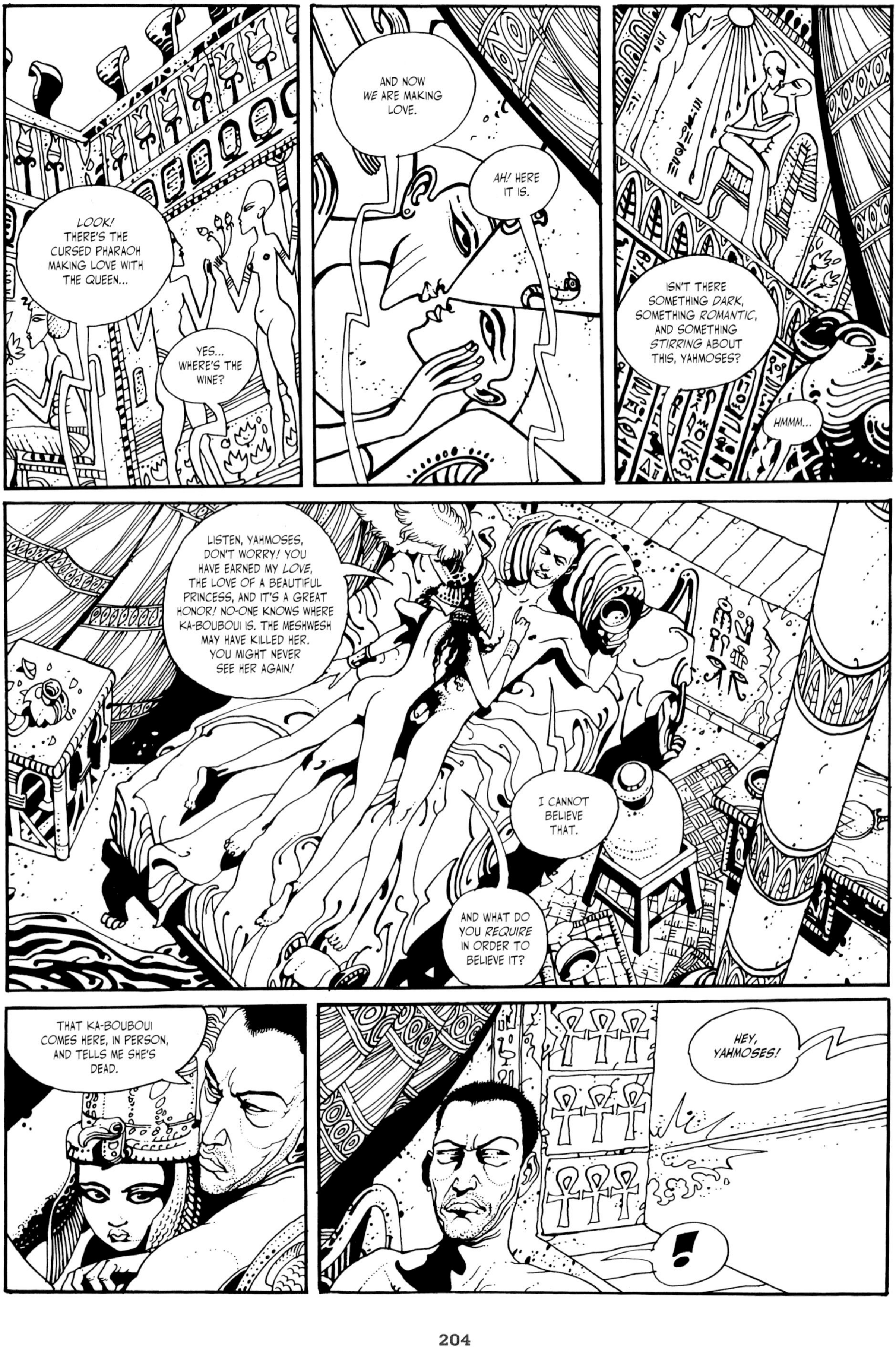
LOOK! THERE'S THE CURSED PHARAOH MAKING LOVE WITH THE QUEEN...
YES... WHERE'S THE WINE?
AND NOW WE ARE MAKING LOVE.
AH! HERE IT IS.
ISN'T THERE SOMETHING DARK, SOMETHING ROMANTIC, AND SOMETHING STIRRING ABOUT THIS, YAHMOSES?
HMMM...
LISTEN, YAHMOSES, DON'T WORRY! YOU HAVE EARNED MY LOVE, THE LOVE OF A BEAUTIFUL PRINCESS, AND IT'S A GREAT HONOR! NO-ONE KNOWS WHERE KA-BOUBOUI IS. THE MESHWESH MAY HAVE KILLED HER. YOU MIGHT NEVER SEE HER AGAIN!
I CANNOT BELIEVE THAT.
AND WHAT DO YOU REQUIRE IN ORDER TO BELIEVE IT?
THAT KA-BOUBOUI COMES HERE, IN PERSON, AND TELLS ME SHE'S DEAD.
HEY, YAHMOSES!
!

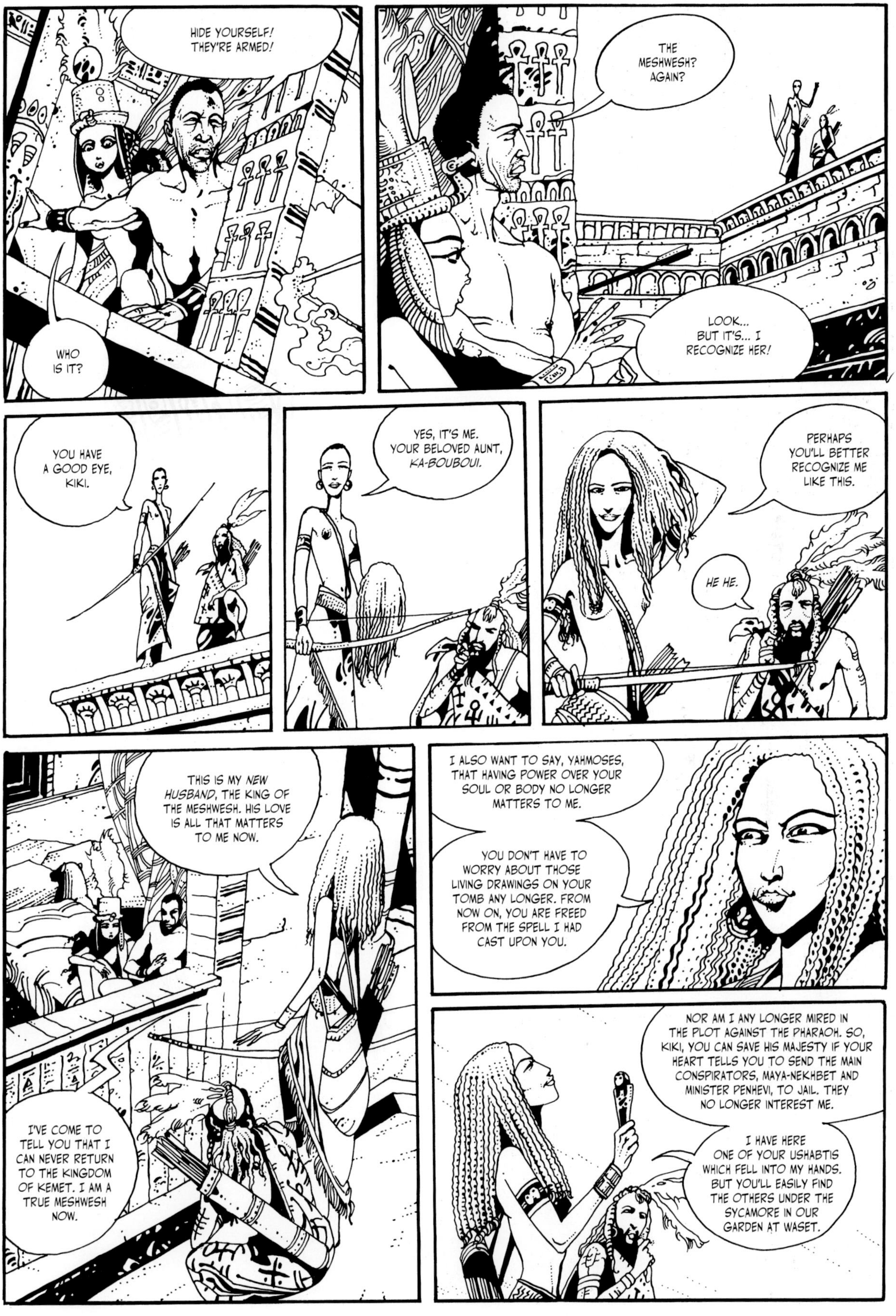
HIDE YOURSELF! THEY'RE ARMED!
WHO IS IT?
THE MESHWESH? AGAIN?
LOOK... BUT IT'S... I RECOGNIZE HER!
YOU HAVE A GOOD EYE, KIKI.
YES, IT'S ME. YOUR BELOVED AUNT, *KA-BOUBOUI.*
PERHAPS YOU'LL BETTER RECOGNIZE ME LIKE THIS.
HE HE.
THIS IS MY *NEW HUSBAND*, THE KING OF THE MESHWESH. HIS LOVE IS ALL THAT MATTERS TO ME NOW.
I'VE COME TO TELL YOU THAT I CAN NEVER RETURN TO THE KINGDOM OF KEMET. I AM A TRUE MESHWESH NOW.
I ALSO WANT TO SAY, YAHMOSES, THAT HAVING POWER OVER YOUR SOUL OR BODY NO LONGER MATTERS TO ME.
YOU DON'T HAVE TO WORRY ABOUT THOSE LIVING DRAWINGS ON YOUR TOMB ANY LONGER. FROM NOW ON, YOU ARE FREED FROM THE SPELL I HAD CAST UPON YOU.
NOR AM I ANY LONGER MIRED IN THE PLOT AGAINST THE PHARAOH. SO, KIKI, YOU CAN SAVE HIS MAJESTY IF YOUR HEART TELLS YOU TO SEND THE MAIN CONSPIRATORS, MAYA-NEKHBET AND MINISTER PENHEVI, TO JAIL. THEY NO LONGER INTEREST ME.
I HAVE HERE ONE OF YOUR USHABTIS WHICH FELL INTO MY HANDS. BUT YOU'LL EASILY FIND THE OTHERS UNDER THE SYCAMORE IN OUR GARDEN AT WASET.

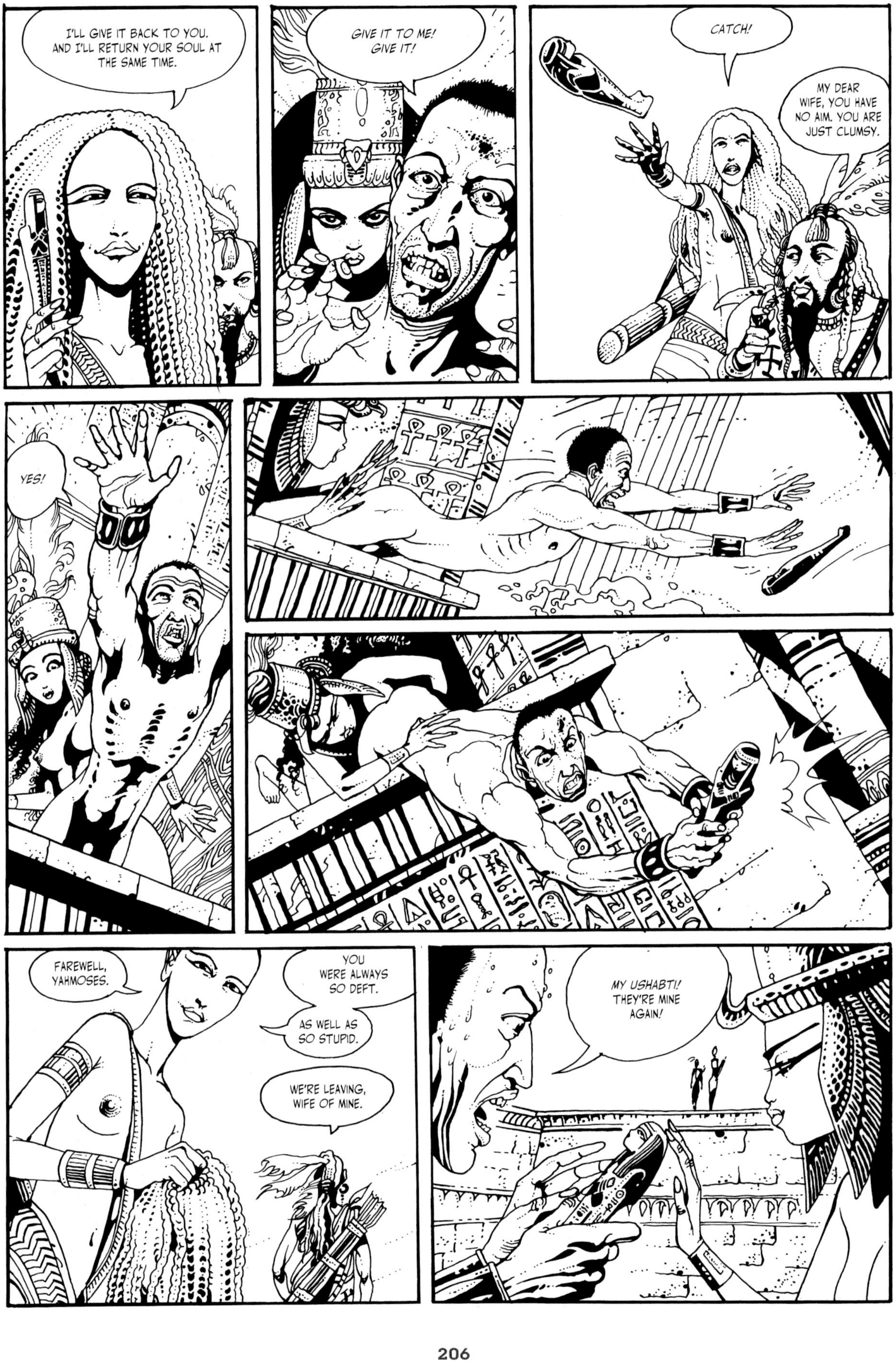
I'LL GIVE IT BACK TO YOU. AND I'LL RETURN YOUR SOUL AT THE SAME TIME.
GIVE IT TO ME! GIVE IT!
CATCH!
MY DEAR WIFE, YOU HAVE NO AIM. YOU ARE JUST CLUMSY.
YES!
FAREWELL, YAHMOSES.
YOU WERE ALWAYS SO DEFT.
AS WELL AS SO STUPID.
WE'RE LEAVING, WIFE OF MINE.
MY USHABTI! THEY'RE MINE AGAIN!

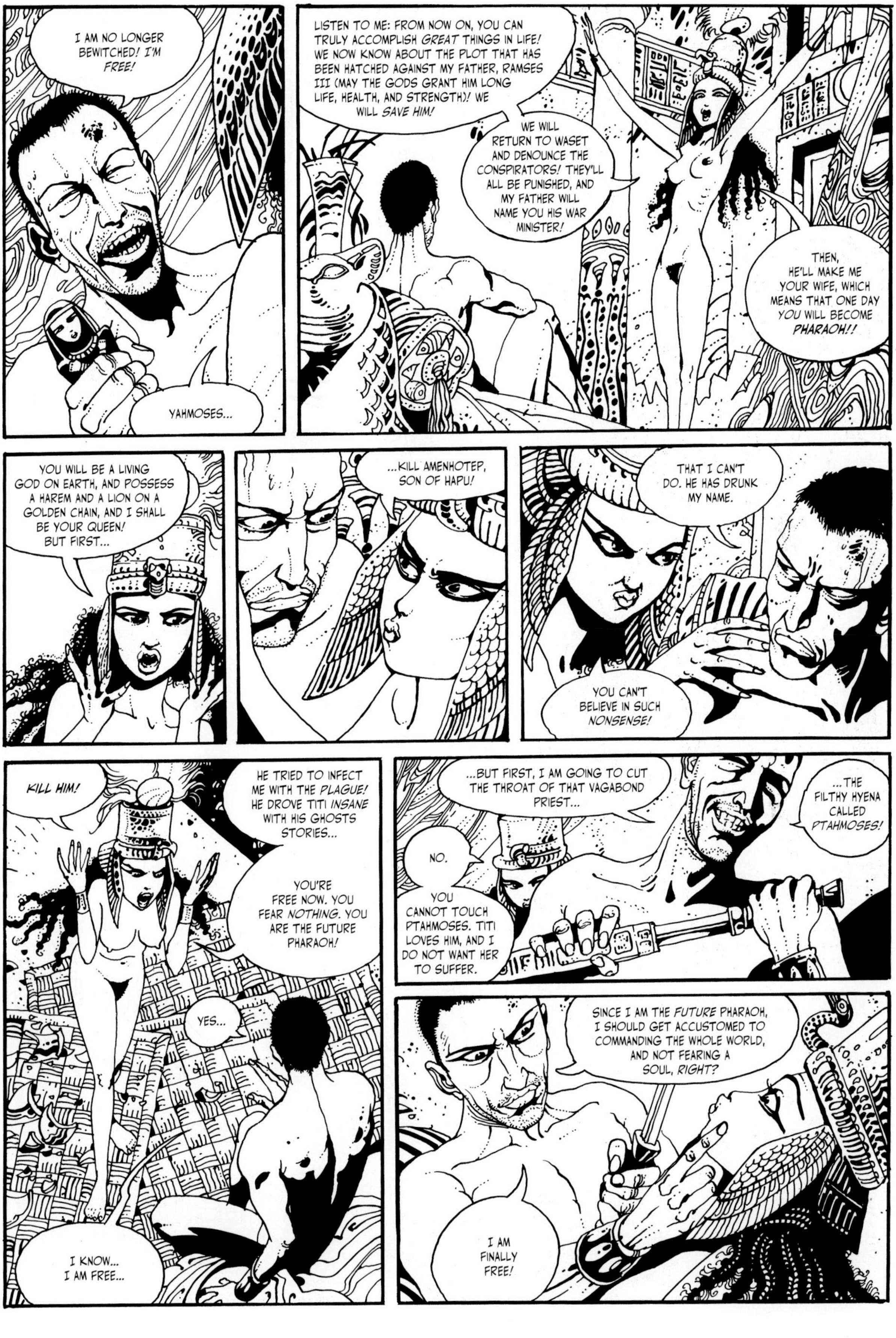
I AM NO LONGER BEWITCHED! I'M FREE!
YAHMOSES...
LISTEN TO ME: FROM NOW ON, YOU CAN TRULY ACCOMPLISH GREAT THINGS IN LIFE! WE NOW KNOW ABOUT THE PLOT THAT HAS BEEN HATCHED AGAINST MY FATHER, RAMSES III (MAY THE GODS GRANT HIM LONG LIFE, HEALTH, AND STRENGTH)! WE WILL SAVE HIM!
WE WILL RETURN TO WASET AND DENOUNCE THE CONSPIRATORS! THEY'LL ALL BE PUNISHED, AND MY FATHER WILL NAME YOU HIS WAR MINISTER!
THEN, HE'LL MAKE ME YOUR WIFE, WHICH MEANS THAT ONE DAY YOU WILL BECOME PHARAOH!!
YOU WILL BE A LIVING GOD ON EARTH, AND POSSESS A HAREM AND A LION ON A GOLDEN CHAIN, AND I SHALL BE YOUR QUEEN! BUT FIRST...
...KILL AMENHOTEP, SON OF HAPU!
THAT I CAN'T DO. HE HAS DRUNK MY NAME.
YOU CAN'T BELIEVE IN SUCH NONSENSE!
KILL HIM!
HE TRIED TO INFECT ME WITH THE PLAGUE! HE DROVE TITI INSANE WITH HIS GHOSTS STORIES...
YOU'RE FREE NOW. YOU FEAR NOTHING. YOU ARE THE FUTURE PHARAOH!
YES...
I KNOW... I AM FREE...
...BUT FIRST, I AM GOING TO CUT THE THROAT OF THAT VAGABOND PRIEST...
...THE FILTHY HYENA CALLED PTAHMOSES!
NO.
YOU CANNOT TOUCH PTAHMOSES. TITI LOVES HIM, AND I DO NOT WANT HER TO SUFFER.
SINCE I AM THE FUTURE PHARAOH, I SHOULD GET ACCUSTOMED TO COMMANDING THE WHOLE WORLD, AND NOT FEARING A SOUL, RIGHT?
I AM FINALLY FREE!

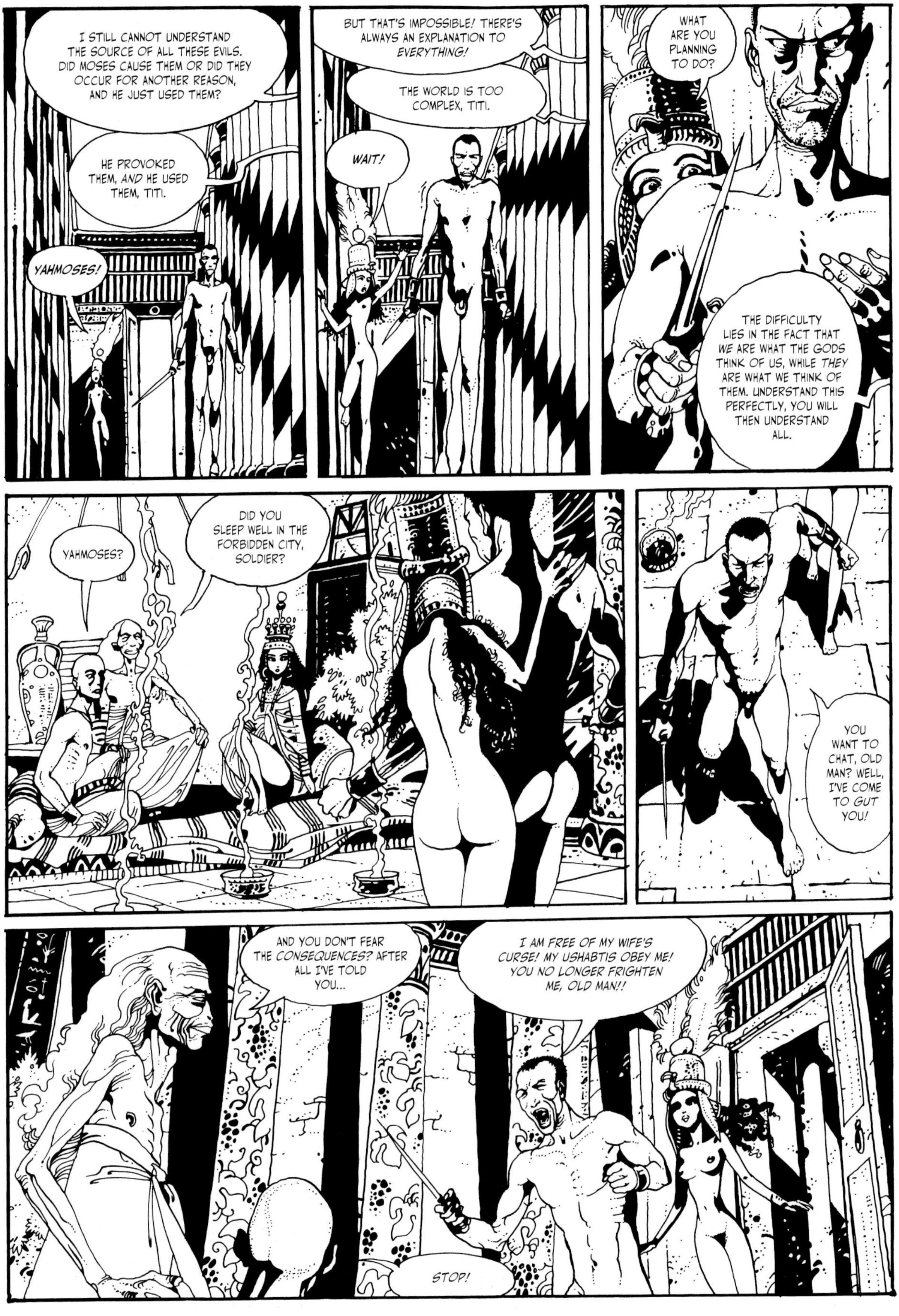
I STILL CANNOT UNDERSTAND THE SOURCE OF ALL THESE EVILS. DID MOSES CAUSE THEM OR DID THEY OCCUR FOR ANOTHER REASON, AND HE JUST USED THEM?
HE PROVOKED THEM, *AND* HE USED THEM, TITI.
YAHMOSES!
BUT THAT'S IMPOSSIBLE! THERE'S ALWAYS AN EXPLANATION TO *EVERYTHING!*
THE WORLD IS TOO COMPLEX, TITI.
WAIT!
WHAT ARE YOU PLANNING TO DO?
THE DIFFICULTY LIES IN THE FACT THAT *WE* ARE WHAT THE GODS THINK OF US, WHILE *THEY* ARE WHAT WE THINK OF THEM. UNDERSTAND THIS PERFECTLY, YOU WILL THEN UNDERSTAND ALL.
YAHMOSES?
DID YOU SLEEP WELL IN THE FORBIDDEN CITY, SOLDIER?
YOU WANT TO CHAT, OLD MAN? WELL, I'VE COME TO *GUT* YOU!
AND YOU DON'T FEAR THE *CONSEQUENCES?* AFTER ALL I'VE TOLD YOU...
I AM FREE OF MY WIFE'S CURSE! MY USHABTIS OBEY ME! YOU NO LONGER FRIGHTEN ME, OLD MAN!!
STOP!

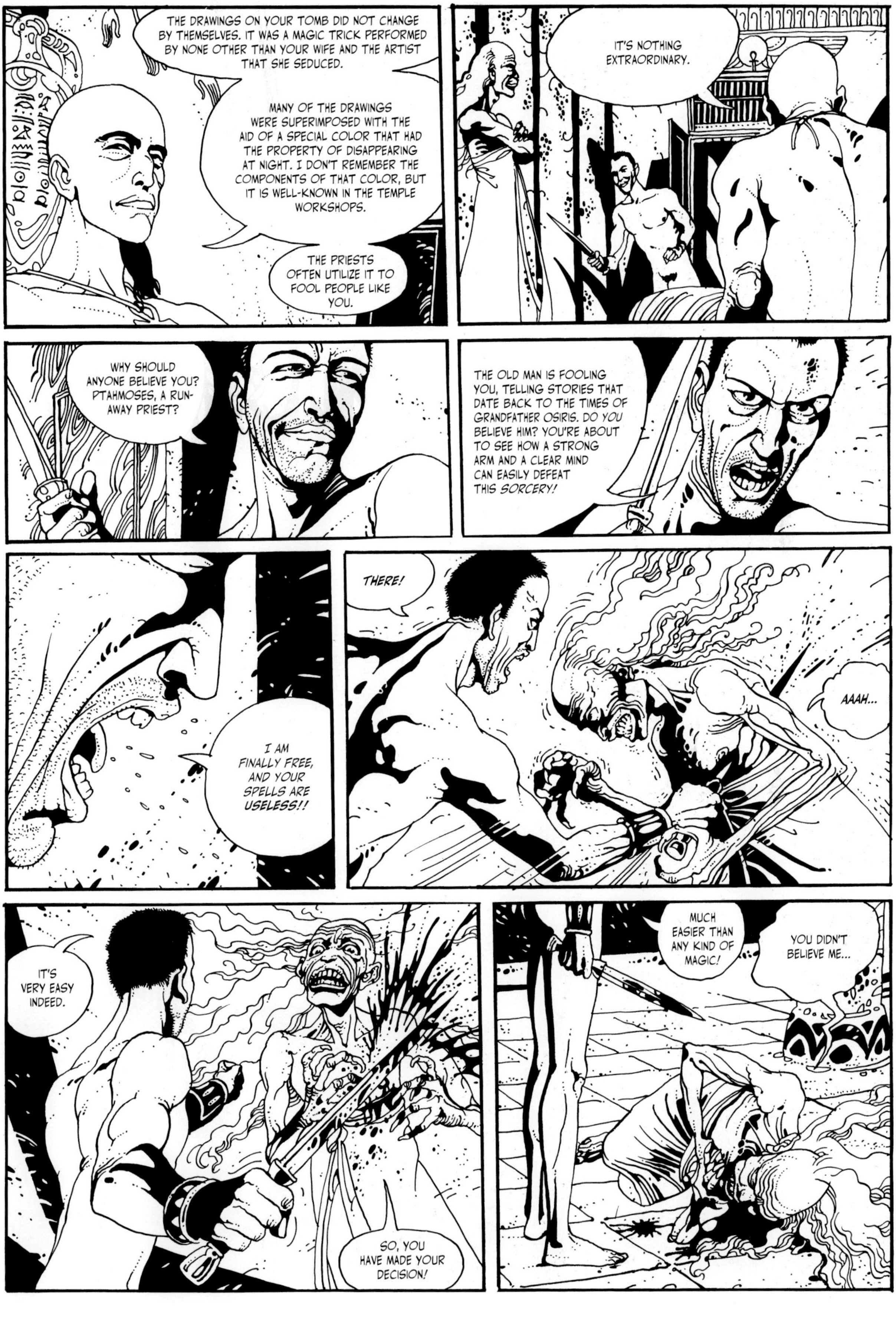
THE DRAWINGS ON YOUR TOMB DID NOT CHANGE BY THEMSELVES. IT WAS A MAGIC TRICK PERFORMED BY NONE OTHER THAN YOUR WIFE AND THE ARTIST THAT SHE SEDUCED.
MANY OF THE DRAWINGS WERE SUPERIMPOSED WITH THE AID OF A SPECIAL COLOR THAT HAD THE PROPERTY OF DISAPPEARING AT NIGHT. I DON'T REMEMBER THE COMPONENTS OF THAT COLOR, BUT IT IS WELL-KNOWN IN THE TEMPLE WORKSHOPS.
THE PRIESTS OFTEN UTILIZE IT TO FOOL PEOPLE LIKE YOU.
IT'S NOTHING EXTRAORDINARY.
WHY SHOULD ANYONE BELIEVE YOU? PTAHMOSES, A RUN-AWAY PRIEST?
THE OLD MAN IS FOOLING YOU, TELLING STORIES THAT DATE BACK TO THE TIMES OF GRANDFATHER OSIRIS. DO YOU BELIEVE HIM? YOU'RE ABOUT TO SEE HOW A STRONG ARM AND A CLEAR MIND CAN EASILY DEFEAT THIS SORCERY!
I AM FINALLY FREE, AND YOUR SPELLS ARE USELESS!!
THERE!
AAAH...
IT'S VERY EASY INDEED.
SO, YOU HAVE MADE YOUR DECISION!
MUCH EASIER THAN ANY KIND OF MAGIC!
YOU DIDN'T BELIEVE ME...

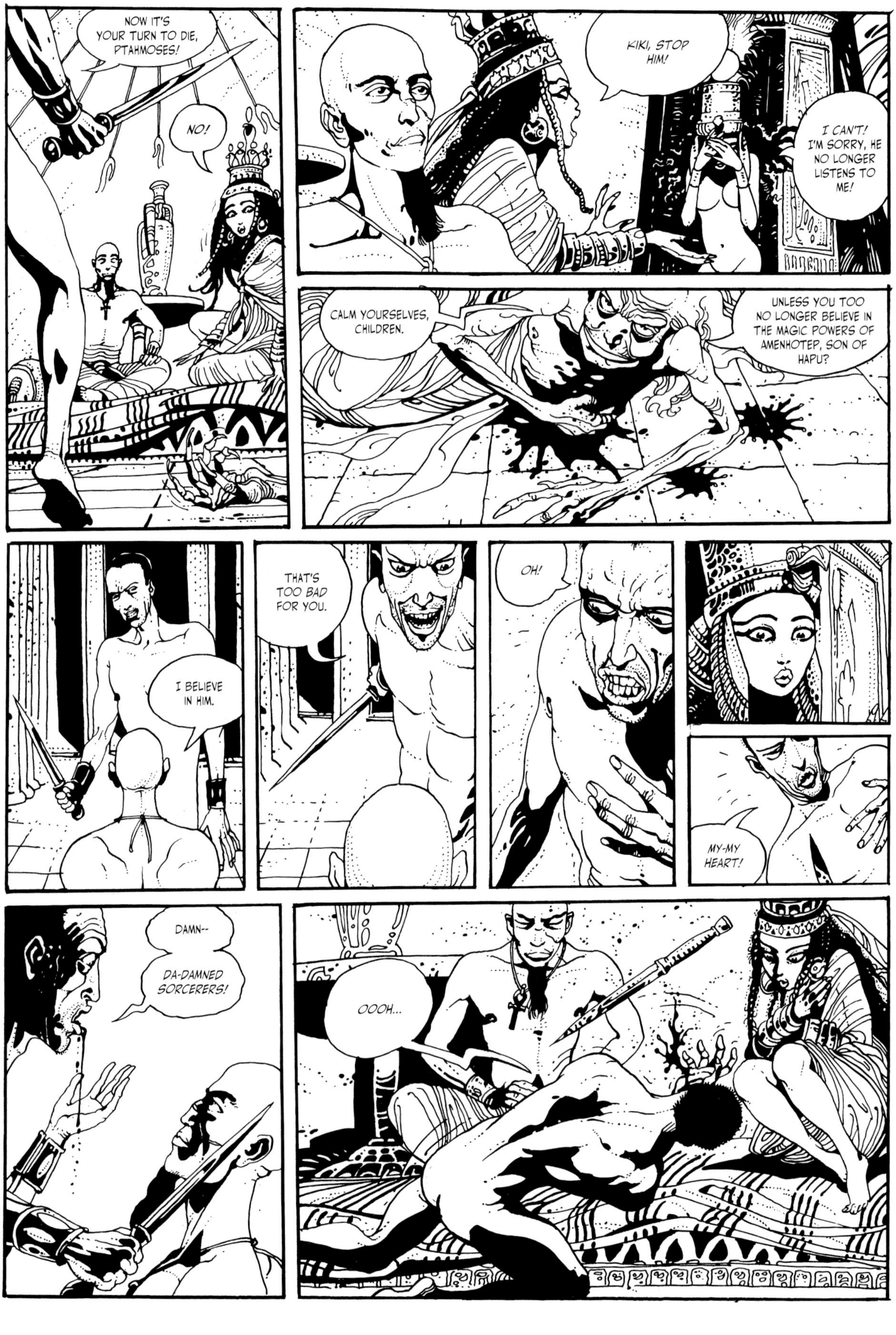
NOW IT'S YOUR TURN TO DIE, PTAHMOSES!
NO!
KIKI, STOP HIM!
I CAN'T! I'M SORRY, HE NO LONGER LISTENS TO ME!
CALM YOURSELVES, CHILDREN.
UNLESS YOU TOO NO LONGER BELIEVE IN THE MAGIC POWERS OF AMENHOTEP, SON OF HAPU?
I BELIEVE IN HIM.
THAT'S TOO BAD FOR YOU.
OH!
MY-MY HEART!
DAMN--
DA-DAMNED SORCERERS!
OOOH...

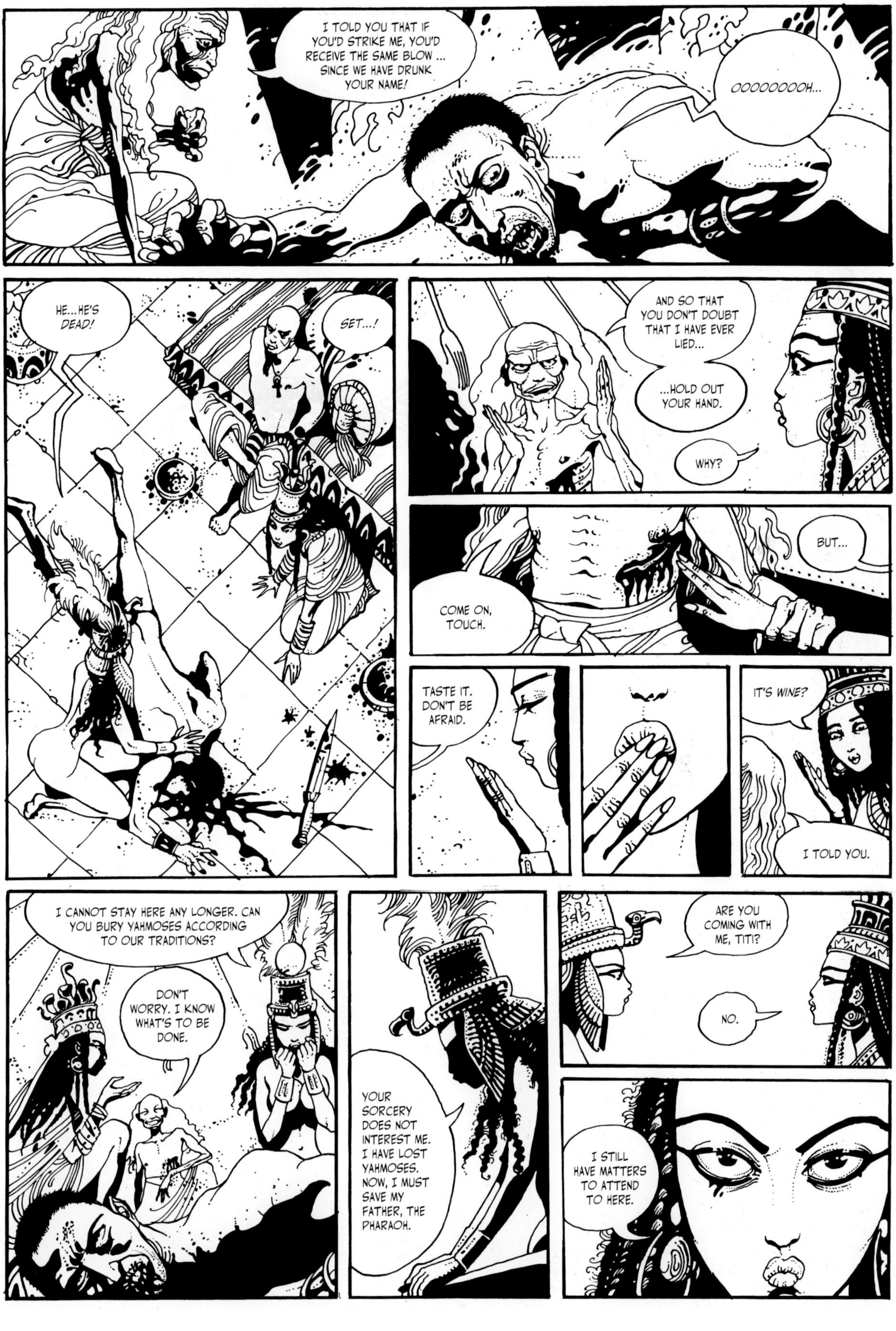
I TOLD YOU THAT IF YOU'D STRIKE ME, YOU'D RECEIVE THE SAME BLOW ... SINCE WE HAVE DRUNK YOUR NAME!
OOOOOOOOH...
HE...HE'S *DEAD!*
SET...!
AND SO THAT YOU DON'T DOUBT THAT I HAVE EVER LIED...
...HOLD OUT YOUR HAND.
WHY?
BUT...
COME ON, TOUCH.
TASTE IT. DON'T BE AFRAID.
IT'S *WINE?*
I TOLD YOU.
I CANNOT STAY HERE ANY LONGER. CAN YOU BURY YAHMOSES ACCORDING TO OUR TRADITIONS?
DON'T WORRY. I KNOW WHAT'S TO BE DONE.
YOUR SORCERY DOES NOT INTEREST ME. I HAVE LOST YAHMOSES. NOW, I MUST SAVE MY FATHER, THE PHARAOH.
ARE YOU COMING WITH ME, TITI?
NO.
I STILL HAVE MATTERS TO ATTEND TO HERE.

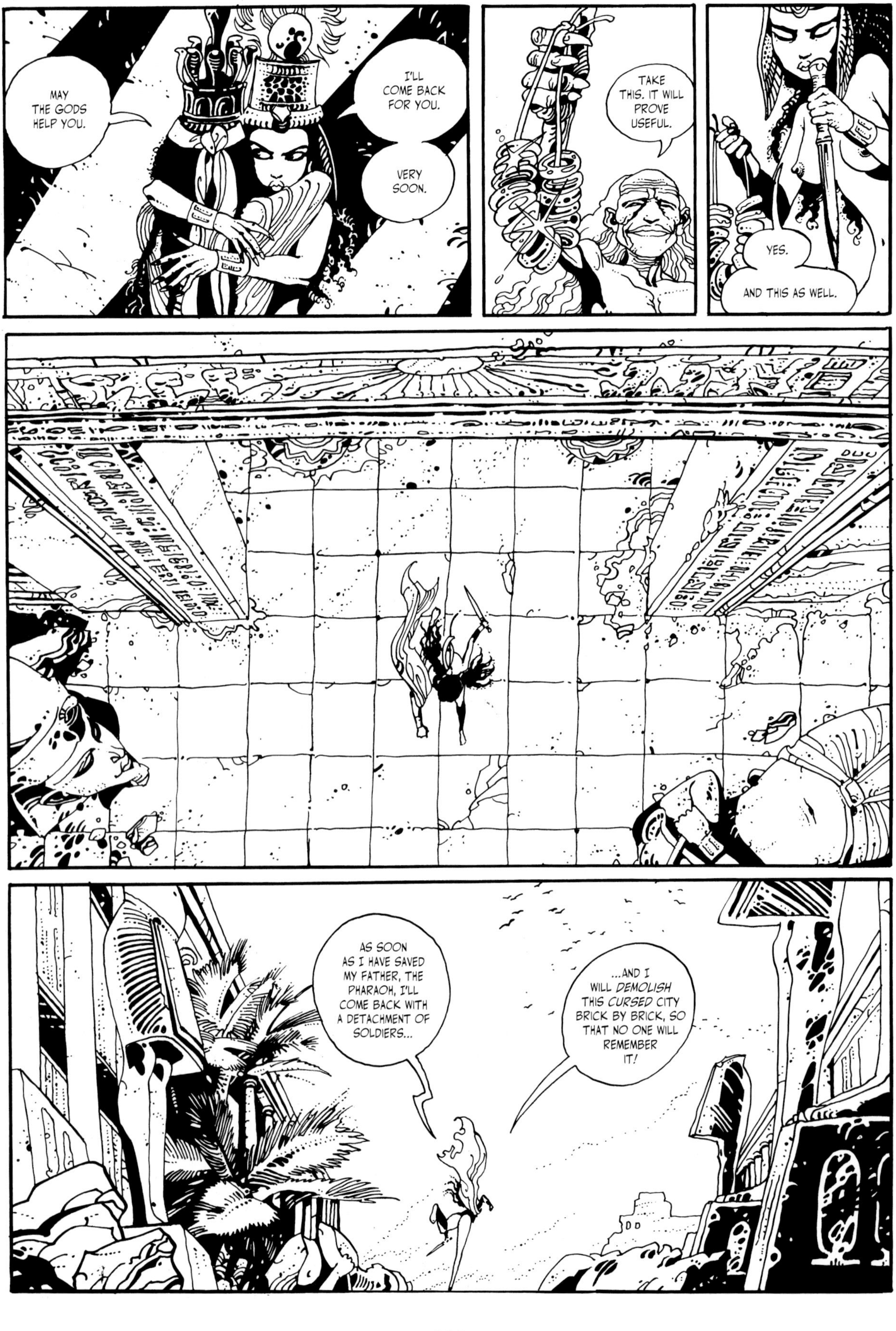
MAY THE GODS HELP YOU.
I'LL COME BACK FOR YOU.
VERY SOON.
TAKE THIS. IT WILL PROVE USEFUL.
YES.
AND THIS AS WELL.
AS SOON AS I HAVE SAVED MY FATHER, THE PHARAOH, I'LL COME BACK WITH A DETACHMENT OF SOLDIERS...
...AND I WILL *DEMOLISH* THIS *CURSED* CITY BRICK BY BRICK, SO THAT NO ONE WILL REMEMBER IT!

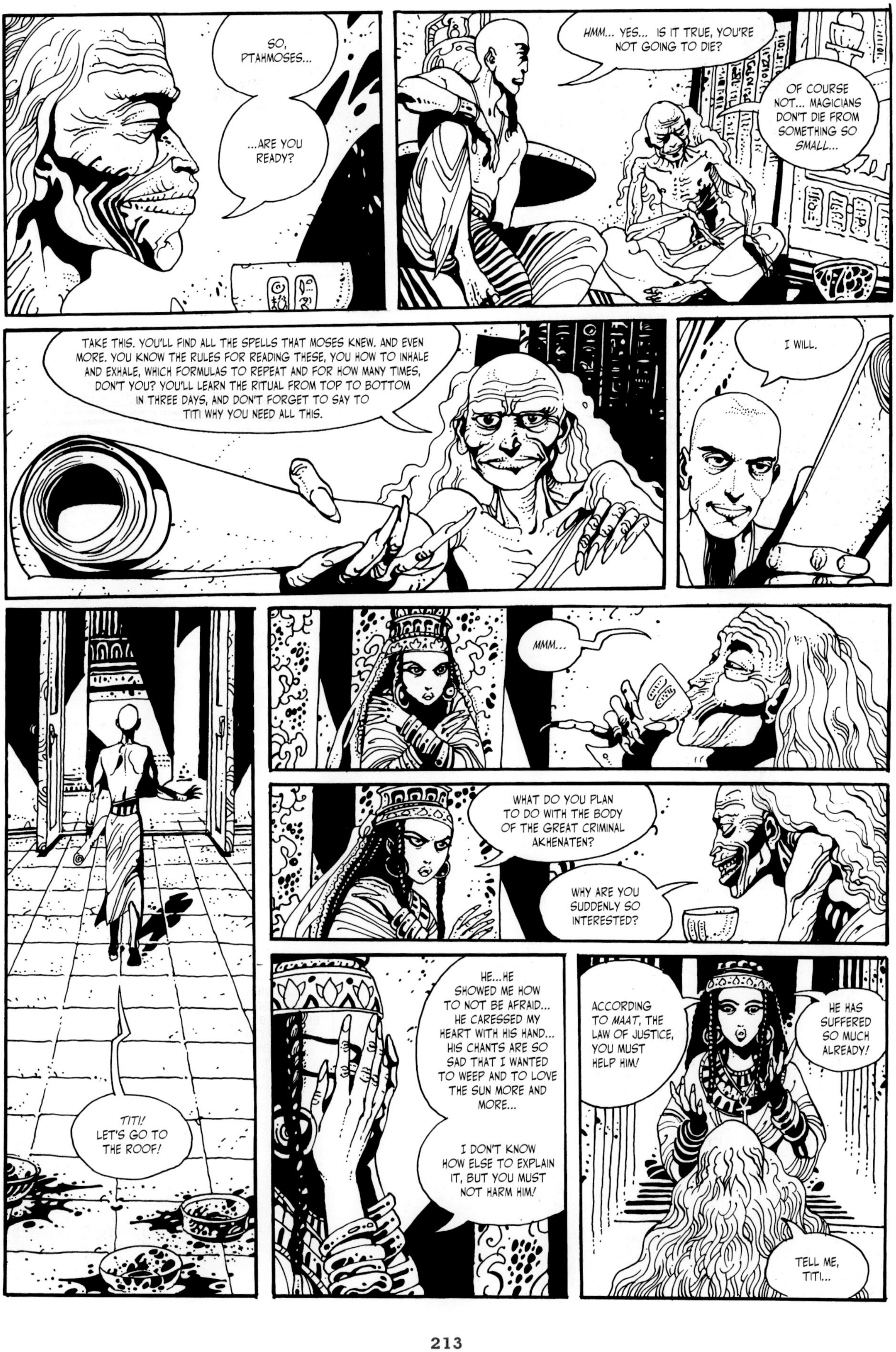
SO, PTAHMOSES...
...ARE YOU READY?
HMM... YES... IS IT TRUE, YOU'RE NOT GOING TO DIE?
OF COURSE NOT... MAGICIANS DON'T DIE FROM SOMETHING SO SMALL...
TAKE THIS. YOU'LL FIND ALL THE SPELLS THAT MOSES KNEW. AND EVEN MORE. YOU KNOW THE RULES FOR READING THESE, YOU HOW TO INHALE AND EXHALE, WHICH FORMULAS TO REPEAT AND FOR HOW MANY TIMES, DON'T YOU? YOU'LL LEARN THE RITUAL FROM TOP TO BOTTOM IN THREE DAYS, AND DON'T FORGET TO SAY TO TITI WHY YOU NEED ALL THIS.
I WILL.
TITI! LET'S GO TO THE ROOF!
MMM...
WHAT DO YOU PLAN TO DO WITH THE BODY OF THE GREAT CRIMINAL AKHENATEN?
WHY ARE YOU SUDDENLY SO INTERESTED?
HE...HE SHOWED ME HOW TO NOT BE AFRAID... HE CARESSED MY HEART WITH HIS HAND... HIS CHANTS ARE SO SAD THAT I WANTED TO WEEP AND TO LOVE THE SUN MORE AND MORE...
I DON'T KNOW HOW ELSE TO EXPLAIN IT, BUT YOU MUST NOT HARM HIM!
TELL ME, TITI...
ACCORDING TO MAAT, THE LAW OF JUSTICE, YOU MUST HELP HIM!
HE HAS SUFFERED SO MUCH ALREADY!

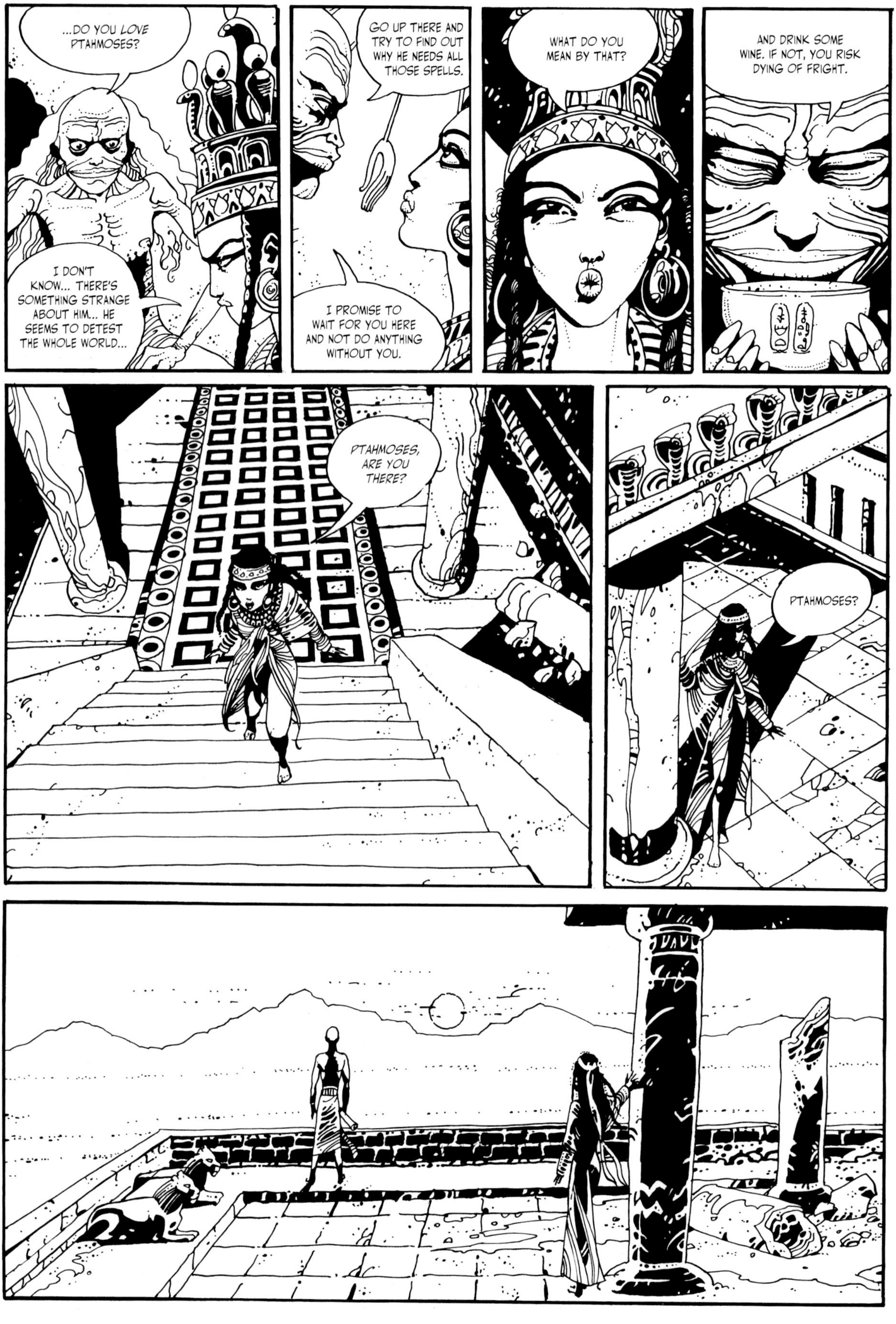
...DO YOU LOVE PTAHMOSES?
I DON'T KNOW... THERE'S SOMETHING STRANGE ABOUT HIM... HE SEEMS TO DETEST THE WHOLE WORLD...
GO UP THERE AND TRY TO FIND OUT WHY HE NEEDS ALL THOSE SPELLS.
I PROMISE TO WAIT FOR YOU HERE AND NOT DO ANYTHING WITHOUT YOU.
WHAT DO YOU MEAN BY THAT?
AND DRINK SOME WINE. IF NOT, YOU RISK DYING OF FRIGHT.
PTAHMOSES, ARE YOU THERE?
PTAHMOSES?

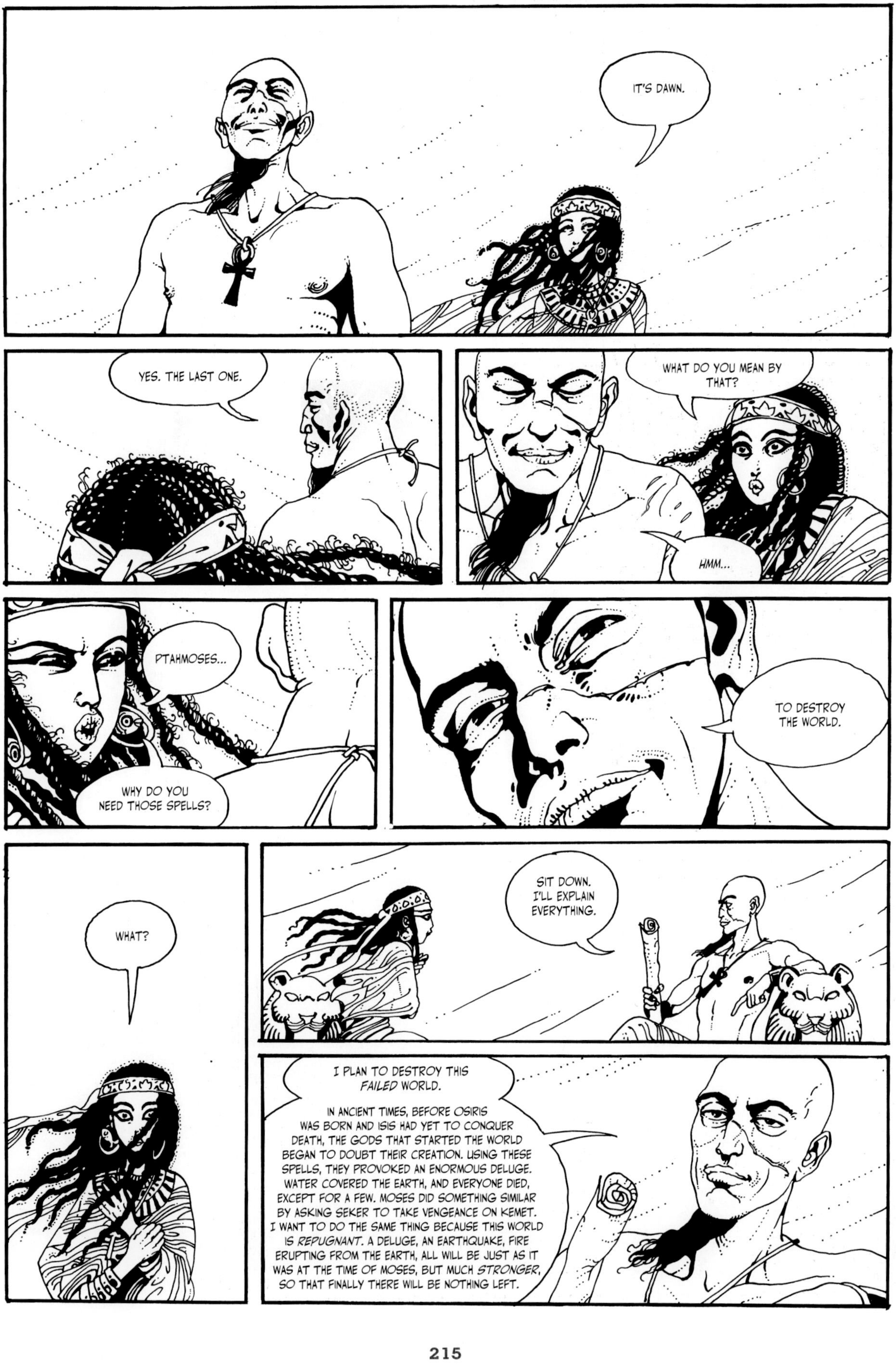

IT'S DAWN.
YES. THE LAST ONE.
WHAT DO YOU MEAN BY THAT?
HMM...
PTAHMOSES...
WHY DO YOU NEED THOSE SPELLS?
TO DESTROY THE WORLD.
WHAT?
SIT DOWN. I'LL EXPLAIN EVERYTHING.
I PLAN TO DESTROY THIS *FAILED* WORLD.
IN ANCIENT TIMES, BEFORE OSIRIS WAS BORN AND ISIS HAD YET TO CONQUER DEATH, THE GODS THAT STARTED THE WORLD BEGAN TO DOUBT THEIR CREATION. USING THESE SPELLS, THEY PROVOKED AN ENORMOUS DELUGE. WATER COVERED THE EARTH, AND EVERYONE DIED, EXCEPT FOR A FEW. MOSES DID SOMETHING SIMILAR BY ASKING SEKER TO TAKE VENGEANCE ON KEMET. I WANT TO DO THE SAME THING BECAUSE THIS WORLD IS *REPUGNANT*. A DELUGE, AN EARTHQUAKE, FIRE ERUPTING FROM THE EARTH, ALL WILL BE JUST AS IT WAS AT THE TIME OF MOSES, BUT MUCH *STRONGER*, SO THAT FINALLY THERE WILL BE NOTHING LEFT.

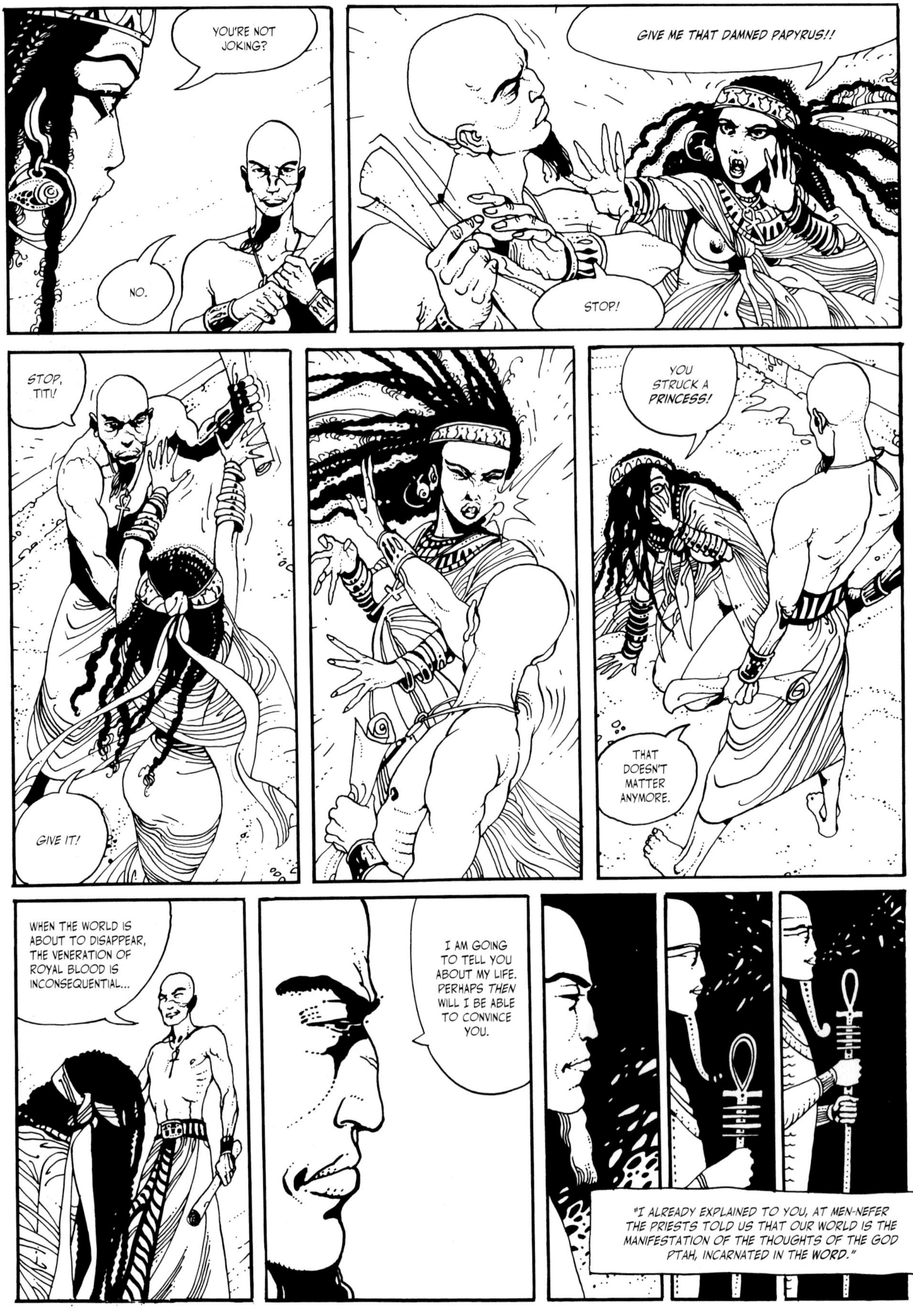

YOU'RE NOT JOKING?
NO.
GIVE ME THAT DAMNED PAPYRUS!!
STOP!
STOP, TITI!
GIVE IT!
YOU STRUCK A PRINCESS!
THAT DOESN'T MATTER ANYMORE.
WHEN THE WORLD IS ABOUT TO DISAPPEAR, THE VENERATION OF ROYAL BLOOD IS INCONSEQUENTIAL...
I AM GOING TO TELL YOU ABOUT MY LIFE. PERHAPS THEN WILL I BE ABLE TO CONVINCE YOU.
"I ALREADY EXPLAINED TO YOU, AT MEN-NEFER THE PRIESTS TOLD US THAT OUR WORLD IS THE MANIFESTATION OF THE THOUGHTS OF THE GOD PTAH, INCARNATED IN THE WORD."

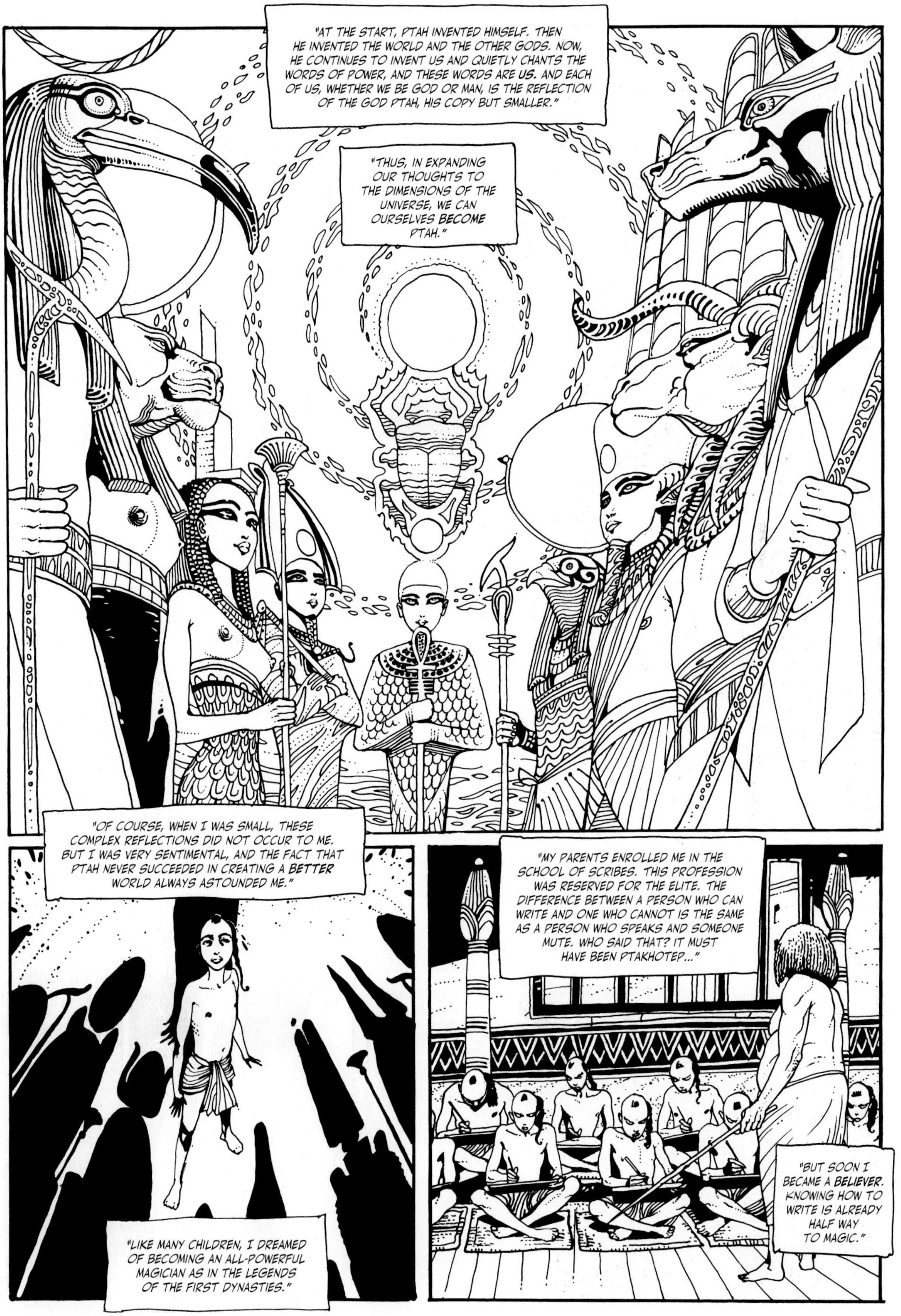
"AT THE START, PTAH INVENTED HIMSELF. THEN HE INVENTED THE WORLD AND THE OTHER GODS. NOW, HE CONTINUES TO INVENT US AND QUIETLY CHANTS THE WORDS OF POWER, AND THESE WORDS ARE **US.** AND EACH OF US, WHETHER WE BE GOD OR MAN, IS THE REFLECTION OF THE GOD PTAH, HIS COPY BUT SMALLER."
"THUS, IN EXPANDING OUR THOUGHTS TO THE DIMENSIONS OF THE UNIVERSE, WE CAN OURSELVES **BECOME** PTAH."
"OF COURSE, WHEN I WAS SMALL, THESE COMPLEX REFLECTIONS DID NOT OCCUR TO ME. BUT I WAS VERY SENTIMENTAL, AND THE FACT THAT PTAH NEVER SUCCEEDED IN CREATING A **BETTER** WORLD ALWAYS ASTOUNDED ME."
"LIKE MANY CHILDREN, I DREAMED OF BECOMING AN ALL-POWERFUL MAGICIAN AS IN THE LEGENDS OF THE FIRST DYNASTIES."
"MY PARENTS ENROLLED ME IN THE SCHOOL OF SCRIBES. THIS PROFESSION WAS RESERVED FOR THE ELITE. THE DIFFERENCE BETWEEN A PERSON WHO CAN WRITE AND ONE WHO CANNOT IS THE SAME AS A PERSON WHO SPEAKS AND SOMEONE MUTE. WHO SAID THAT? IT MUST HAVE BEEN PTAKHOTEP..."
"BUT SOON I BECAME A **BELIEVER.** KNOWING HOW TO WRITE IS ALREADY HALF WAY TO MAGIC."

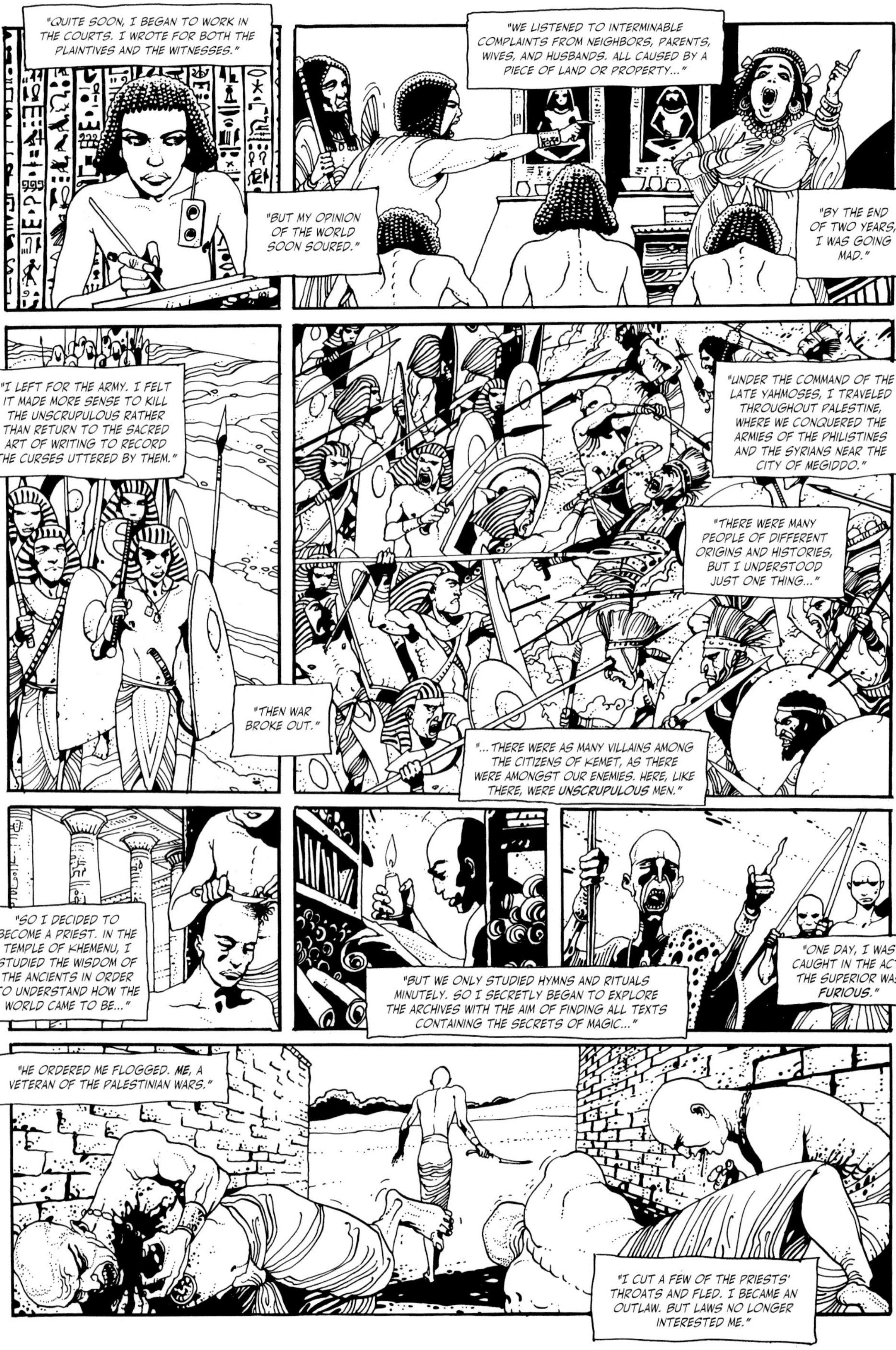
"QUITE SOON, I BEGAN TO WORK IN THE COURTS. I WROTE FOR BOTH THE PLAINTIVES AND THE WITNESSES."
"WE LISTENED TO INTERMINABLE COMPLAINTS FROM NEIGHBORS, PARENTS, WIVES, AND HUSBANDS. ALL CAUSED BY A PIECE OF LAND OR PROPERTY..."
"BUT MY OPINION OF THE WORLD SOON SOURED."
"BY THE END OF TWO YEARS, I WAS GOING MAD."
"I LEFT FOR THE ARMY. I FELT IT MADE MORE SENSE TO KILL THE UNSCRUPULOUS RATHER THAN RETURN TO THE SACRED ART OF WRITING TO RECORD THE CURSES UTTERED BY THEM."
"THEN WAR BROKE OUT."
"UNDER THE COMMAND OF THE LATE YAHMOSES, I TRAVELED THROUGHOUT PALESTINE, WHERE WE CONQUERED THE ARMIES OF THE PHILISTINES AND THE SYRIANS NEAR THE CITY OF MEGIDDO."
"THERE WERE MANY PEOPLE OF DIFFERENT ORIGINS AND HISTORIES, BUT I UNDERSTOOD JUST ONE THING..."
"...THERE WERE AS MANY VILLAINS AMONG THE CITIZENS OF KEMET, AS THERE WERE AMONGST OUR ENEMIES. HERE, LIKE THERE, WERE *UNSCRUPULOUS* MEN."
"SO I DECIDED TO BECOME A PRIEST. IN THE TEMPLE OF KHEMENU, I STUDIED THE WISDOM OF THE ANCIENTS IN ORDER TO UNDERSTAND HOW THE WORLD CAME TO BE..."
"BUT WE ONLY STUDIED HYMNS AND RITUALS MINUTELY. SO I SECRETLY BEGAN TO EXPLORE THE ARCHIVES WITH THE AIM OF FINDING ALL TEXTS CONTAINING THE SECRETS OF MAGIC..."
"ONE DAY, I WAS CAUGHT IN THE ACT. THE SUPERIOR WAS *FURIOUS*."
"HE ORDERED ME FLOGGED. *ME*, A VETERAN OF THE PALESTINIAN WARS."
"I CUT A FEW OF THE PRIESTS' THROATS AND FLED. I BECAME AN OUTLAW. BUT LAWS NO LONGER INTERESTED ME."

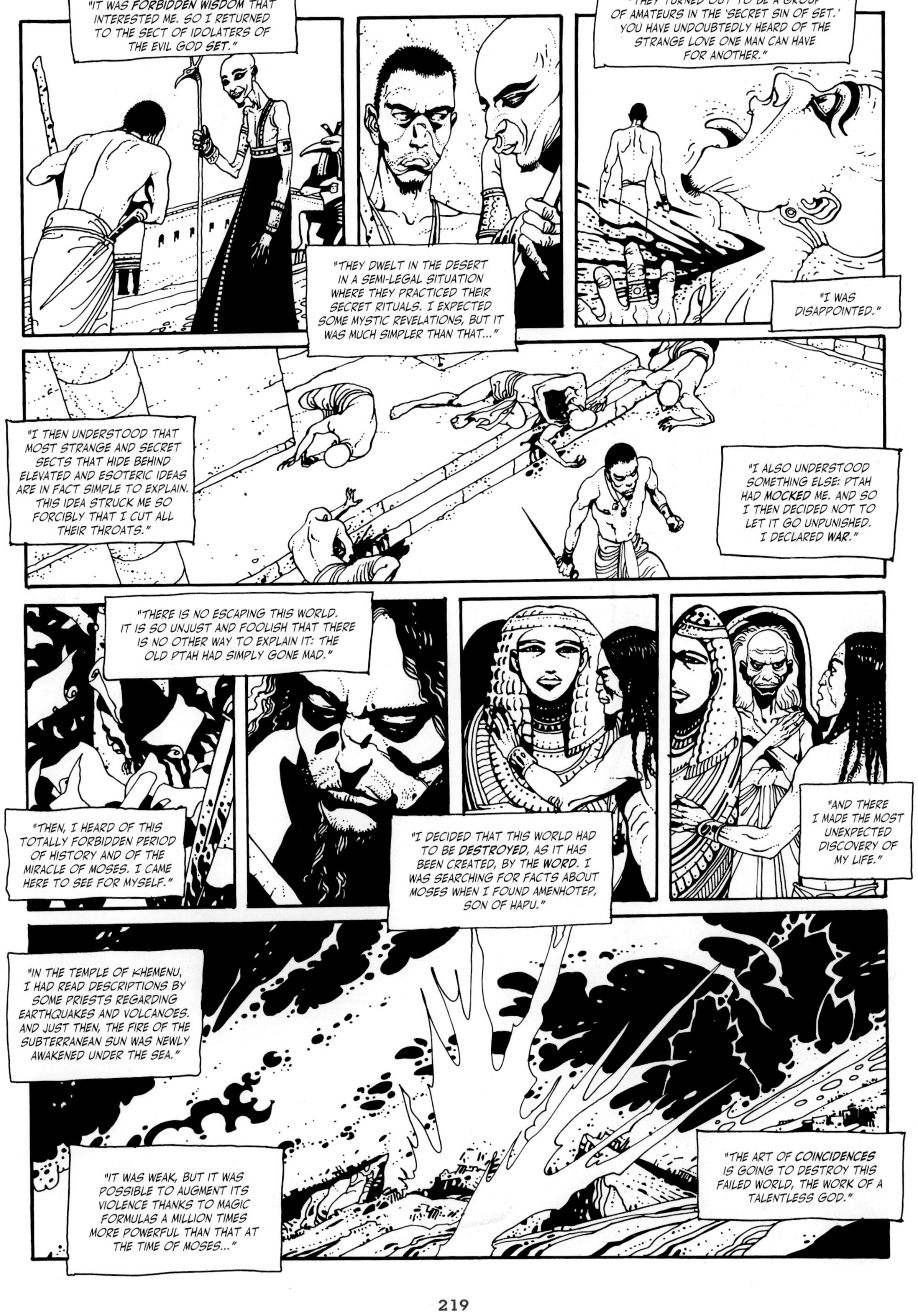
"IT WAS FORBIDDEN WISDOM THAT INTERESTED ME. SO I RETURNED TO THE SECT OF IDOLATERS OF THE EVIL GOD SET."
"THEY DWELT IN THE DESERT IN A SEMI-LEGAL SITUATION WHERE THEY PRACTICED THEIR SECRET RITUALS. I EXPECTED SOME MYSTIC REVELATIONS, BUT IT WAS MUCH SIMPLER THAN THAT..."
"THEY TURNED OUT TO BE A GROUP OF AMATEURS IN THE 'SECRET SIN OF SET.' YOU HAVE UNDOUBTEDLY HEARD OF THE STRANGE LOVE ONE MAN CAN HAVE FOR ANOTHER."
"I WAS DISAPPOINTED."
"I THEN UNDERSTOOD THAT MOST STRANGE AND SECRET SECTS THAT HIDE BEHIND ELEVATED AND ESOTERIC IDEAS ARE IN FACT SIMPLE TO EXPLAIN. THIS IDEA STRUCK ME SO FORCIBLY THAT I CUT ALL THEIR THROATS."
"I ALSO UNDERSTOOD SOMETHING ELSE: PTAH HAD MOCKED ME. AND SO I THEN DECIDED NOT TO LET IT GO UNPUNISHED. I DECLARED WAR."
"THERE IS NO ESCAPING THIS WORLD. IT IS SO UNJUST AND FOOLISH THAT THERE IS NO OTHER WAY TO EXPLAIN IT: THE OLD PTAH HAD SIMPLY GONE MAD."
"THEN, I HEARD OF THIS TOTALLY FORBIDDEN PERIOD OF HISTORY AND OF THE MIRACLE OF MOSES. I CAME HERE TO SEE FOR MYSELF."
"I DECIDED THAT THIS WORLD HAD TO BE DESTROYED, AS IT HAS BEEN CREATED, BY THE WORD. I WAS SEARCHING FOR FACTS ABOUT MOSES WHEN I FOUND AMENHOTEP, SON OF HAPU."
"AND THERE I MADE THE MOST UNEXPECTED DISCOVERY OF MY LIFE."
"IN THE TEMPLE OF KHEMENU, I HAD READ DESCRIPTIONS BY SOME PRIESTS REGARDING EARTHQUAKES AND VOLCANOES. AND JUST THEN, THE FIRE OF THE SUBTERRANEAN SUN WAS NEWLY AWAKENED UNDER THE SEA."
"IT WAS WEAK, BUT IT WAS POSSIBLE TO AUGMENT ITS VIOLENCE THANKS TO MAGIC FORMULAS A MILLION TIMES MORE POWERFUL THAN THAT AT THE TIME OF MOSES..."
"THE ART OF COINCIDENCES IS GOING TO DESTROY THIS FAILED WORLD, THE WORK OF A TALENTLESS GOD."

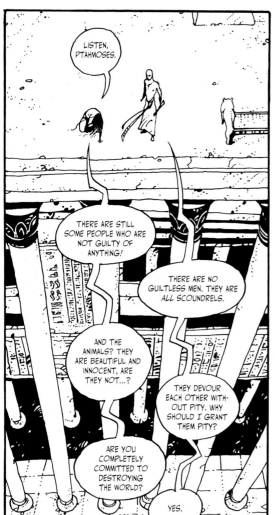

LISTEN, PTAHMOSES.

THERE ARE STILL SOME PEOPLE WHO ARE NOT GUILTY OF ANYTHING!

THERE ARE NO GUILTLESS MEN. THEY ARE ALL SCOUNDRELS.

AND THE ANIMALS? THEY ARE BEAUTIFUL AND INNOCENT, ARE THEY NOT...?

THEY DEVOUR EACH OTHER WITHOUT PITY. WHY SHOULD I GRANT THEM PITY?

ARE YOU COMPLETELY COMMITTED TO DESTROYING THE WORLD?

YES.

YOU... YOU ARE CRAZY!

DON'T CRY. WE'RE NOT GOING TO DIE.

LISTEN...

...THE WIFE OF PTAH IS THE GODDESS SEKHMET. AND, YOUR SECOND NAME IS SEHMETIKETH. THAT ISN'T JUST A SIMPLE COINCIDENCE. I WILL BE THE NEW PTAH, AND YOU THE NEW SEKHMET. WE WILL CREATE A NEW AND BETTER WORLD FROM NOTHINGNESS...

DO YOU FEEL THE WIND? IT IS THE WORLD PREPARING TO DIE.

LISTEN TO THE FORCE OF THE WORD!

I AM YESTERDAY, TODAY, AND TOMORROW. I AM THE DIVINE AND SECRET SOUL WHO CREATED THE GODS AND GAVE HEAVENLY NURTURE TO THE INHABITANTS OF THE DUAT, OF THE AMENTI, AND THE SKIES. I AM THE FLAME OF THE EAST, OWNER OF THE TWO BLINDING FACES. WHO AM I? I AM ATISHEF THE INFINITE WHO WILL CONVOKE ALL THE CREATURES WHO LIVE IN THE HEAD OF GOD. THEY HAVE MILLIONS OF NAMES, AND I KNOW THEM ALL. THEY ARE: SHENTET, NEKHBET, SATET...

PTAHMOSES...

...CAN I KISS YOU ONE LAST TIME... BEFORE IT ALL ENDS?

I AM PLEASED TO HEAR THAT YOU HAVE ACCEPTED THE IDEA, TITI...

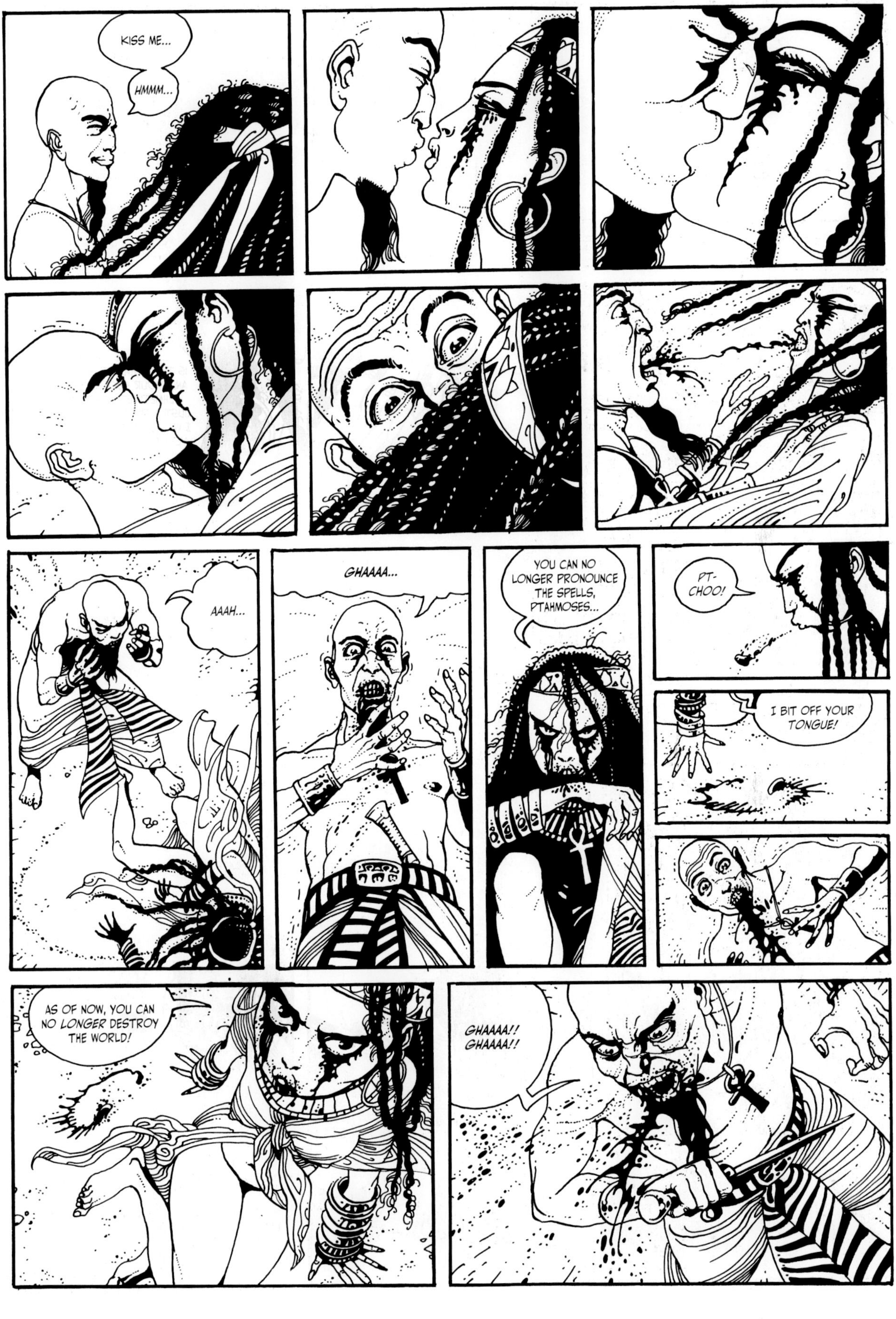
KISS ME...
HMMM...
AAAH...
GHAAAA...
YOU CAN NO LONGER PRONOUNCE THE SPELLS, PTAHMOSES...
PT-CHOO!
I BIT OFF YOUR TONGUE!
AS OF NOW, YOU CAN NO LONGER DESTROY THE WORLD!
GHAAAA!! GHAAAA!!

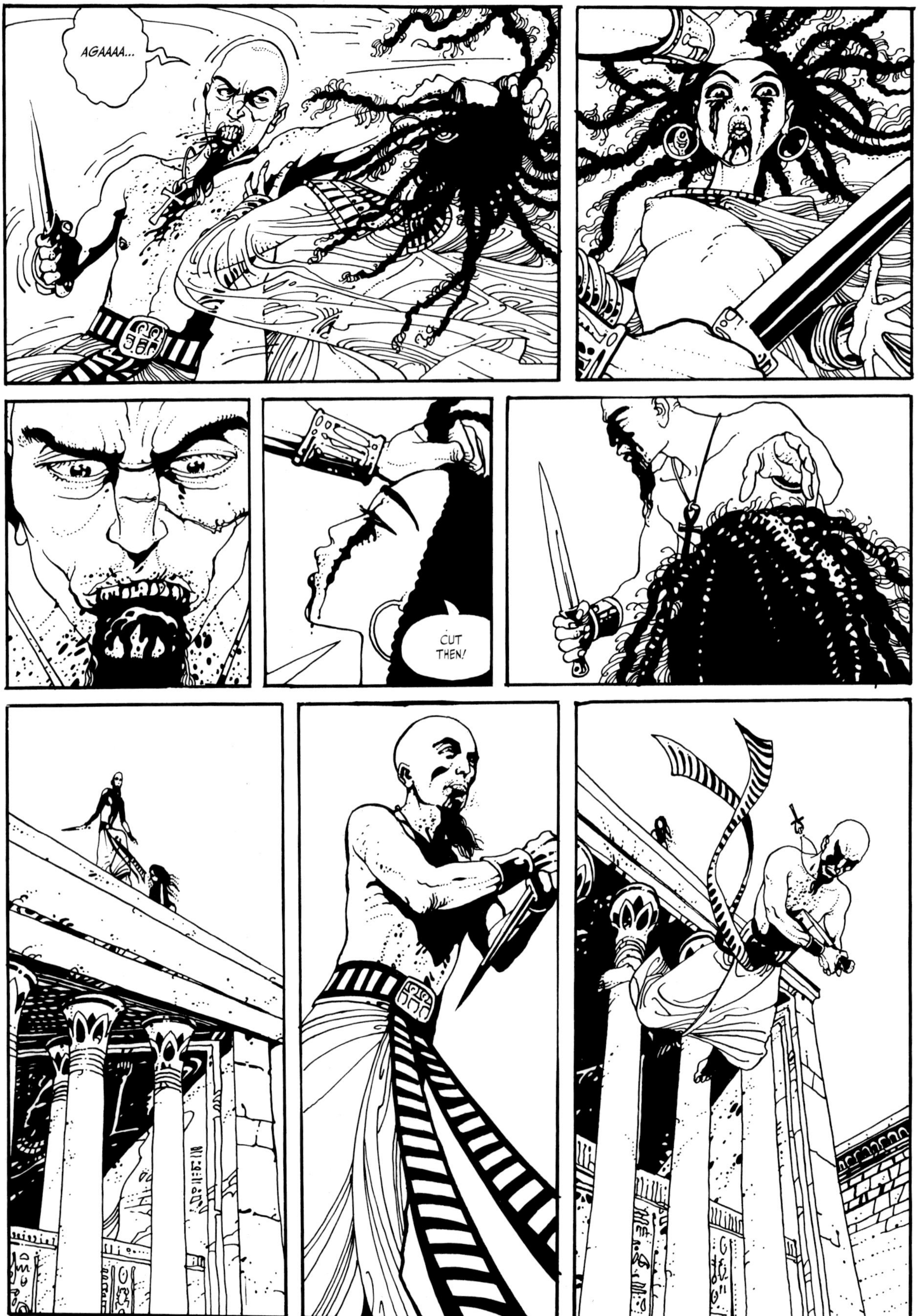
AGAAAA...
CUT THEN!

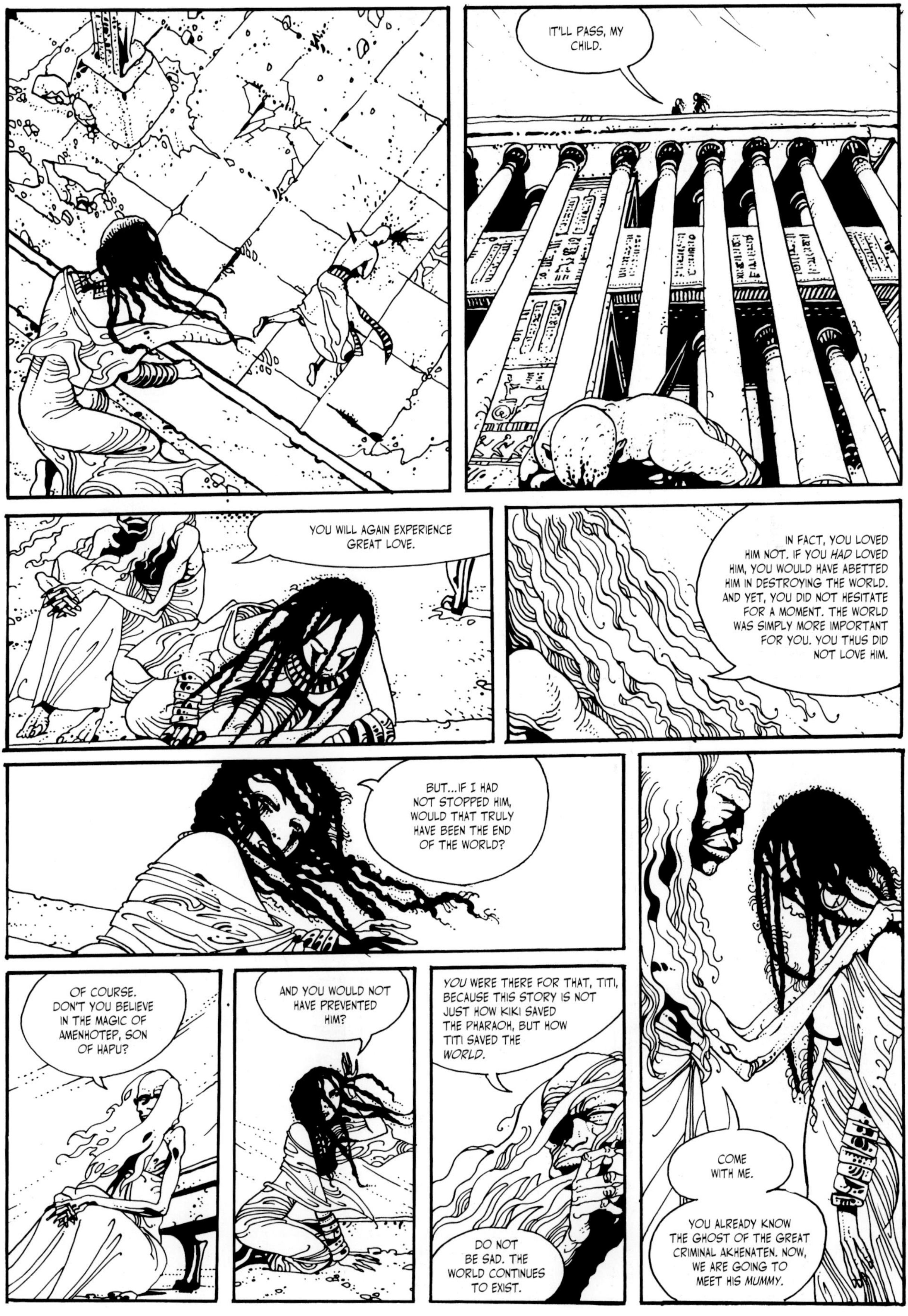
IT'LL PASS, MY CHILD.
YOU WILL AGAIN EXPERIENCE GREAT LOVE.
IN FACT, YOU LOVED HIM NOT. IF YOU *HAD* LOVED HIM, YOU WOULD HAVE ABETTED HIM IN DESTROYING THE WORLD. AND YET, YOU DID NOT HESITATE FOR A MOMENT. THE WORLD WAS SIMPLY MORE IMPORTANT FOR YOU. YOU THUS DID NOT LOVE HIM.
BUT...IF I HAD NOT STOPPED HIM, WOULD THAT TRULY HAVE BEEN THE END OF THE WORLD?
OF COURSE. DON'T YOU BELIEVE IN THE MAGIC OF AMENHOTEP, SON OF HAPU?
AND YOU WOULD NOT HAVE PREVENTED HIM?
YOU WERE THERE FOR THAT, TITI, BECAUSE THIS STORY IS NOT JUST HOW KIKI SAVED THE PHARAOH, BUT HOW TITI SAVED THE *WORLD*.
DO NOT BE SAD. THE WORLD CONTINUES TO EXIST.
COME WITH ME.
YOU ALREADY KNOW THE GHOST OF THE GREAT CRIMINAL AKHENATEN. NOW, WE ARE GOING TO MEET HIS *MUMMY*.

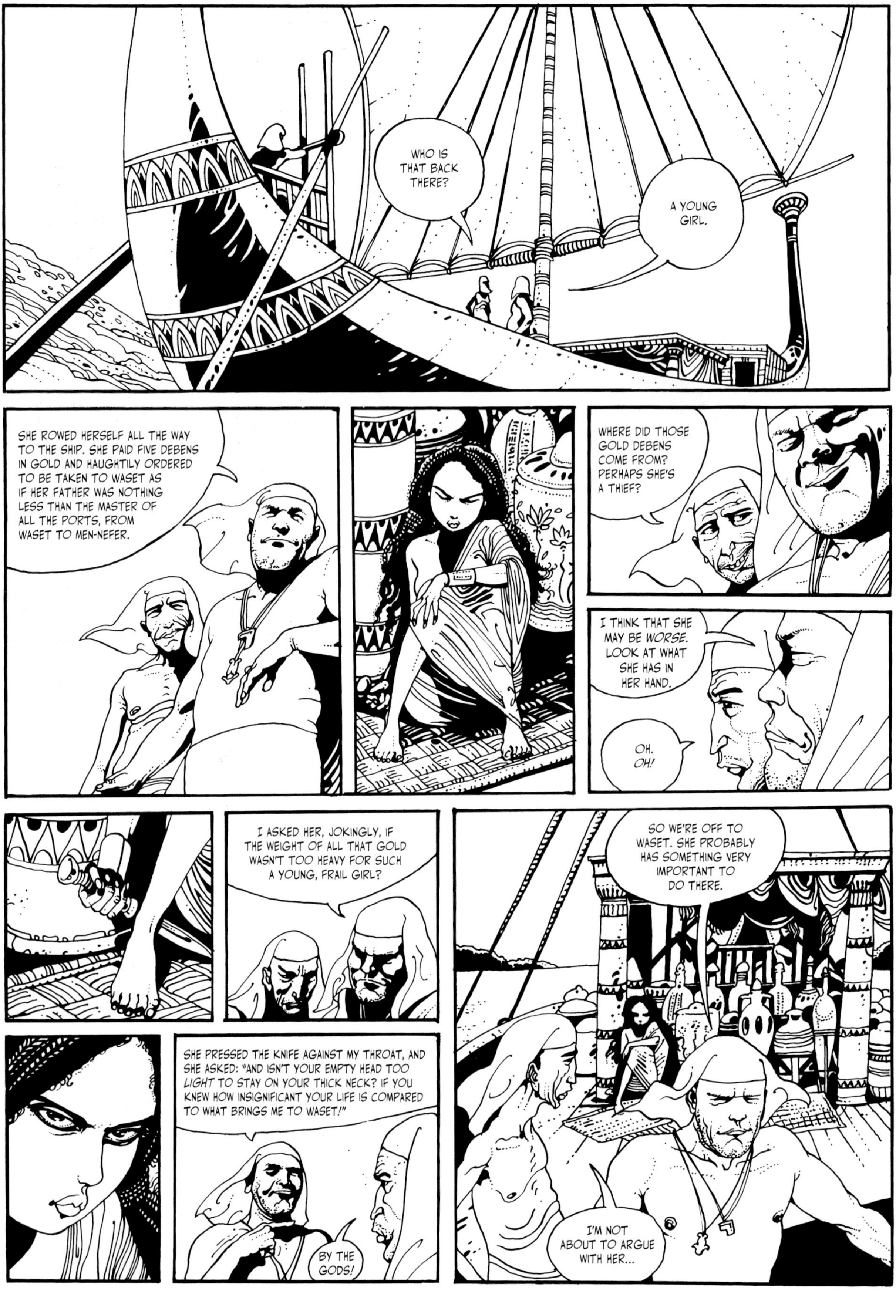
WHO IS THAT BACK THERE?
A YOUNG GIRL.
SHE ROWED HERSELF ALL THE WAY TO THE SHIP. SHE PAID FIVE DEBENS IN GOLD AND HAUGHTILY ORDERED TO BE TAKEN TO WASET AS IF HER FATHER WAS NOTHING LESS THAN THE MASTER OF ALL THE PORTS, FROM WASET TO MEN-NEFER.
WHERE DID THOSE GOLD DEBENS COME FROM? PERHAPS SHE'S A THIEF?
I THINK THAT SHE MAY BE *WORSE*. LOOK AT WHAT SHE HAS IN HER HAND.
OH. *OH!*
I ASKED HER, JOKINGLY, IF THE WEIGHT OF ALL THAT GOLD WASN'T TOO HEAVY FOR SUCH A YOUNG, FRAIL GIRL?
SO WE'RE OFF TO WASET. SHE PROBABLY HAS SOMETHING VERY IMPORTANT TO DO THERE.
I'M NOT ABOUT TO ARGUE WITH HER...
SHE PRESSED THE KNIFE AGAINST MY THROAT, AND SHE ASKED: "AND ISN'T YOUR EMPTY HEAD TOO *LIGHT* TO STAY ON YOUR THICK NECK? IF YOU KNEW HOW INSIGNIFICANT YOUR LIFE IS COMPARED TO WHAT BRINGS ME TO WASET!"
BY THE *GODS!*

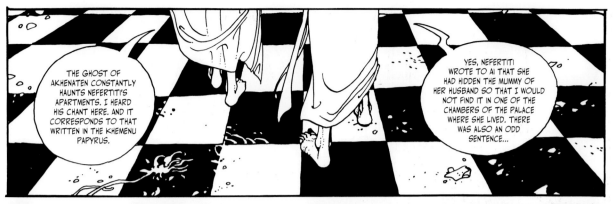

THE GHOST OF AKHENATEN CONSTANTLY HAUNTS NEFERTITI'S APARTMENTS. I HEARD HIS CHANT HERE. AND IT CORRESPONDS TO THAT WRITTEN IN THE KHEMENU PAPYRUS.

YES, NEFERTITI WROTE TO AI THAT SHE HAD HIDDEN THE MUMMY OF HER HUSBAND SO THAT I WOULD NOT FIND IT IN ONE OF THE CHAMBERS OF THE PALACE WHERE SHE LIVED. THERE WAS ALSO AN ODD SENTENCE...

YES, QUITE ODD...

IT IS SAID THAT HER LIVING FLESH COVERS THE DEAD BODY OF AKHENATEN, AND THAT SHE PRESERVED IT UNTIL HIS FRIENDS COULD FIND IT AND PERFORM THE APPROPRIATE RITUALS...

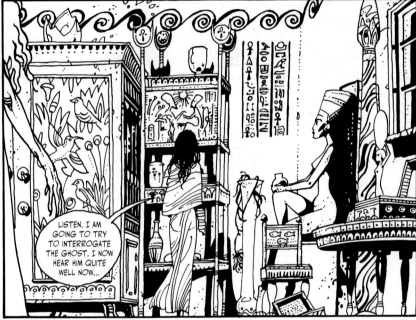

LISTEN. I AM GOING TO TRY TO INTERROGATE THE GHOST. I NOW HEAR HIM QUITE WELL NOW...

IS HE IN THE CHEST?

NO.

BEHIND THE CURTAINS?

NO.

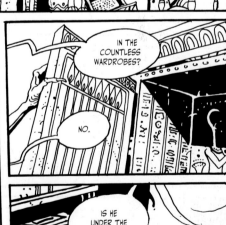

IN THE COUNTLESS WARDROBES?

NO.

IS HE UNDER THE FLOOR?

NO.

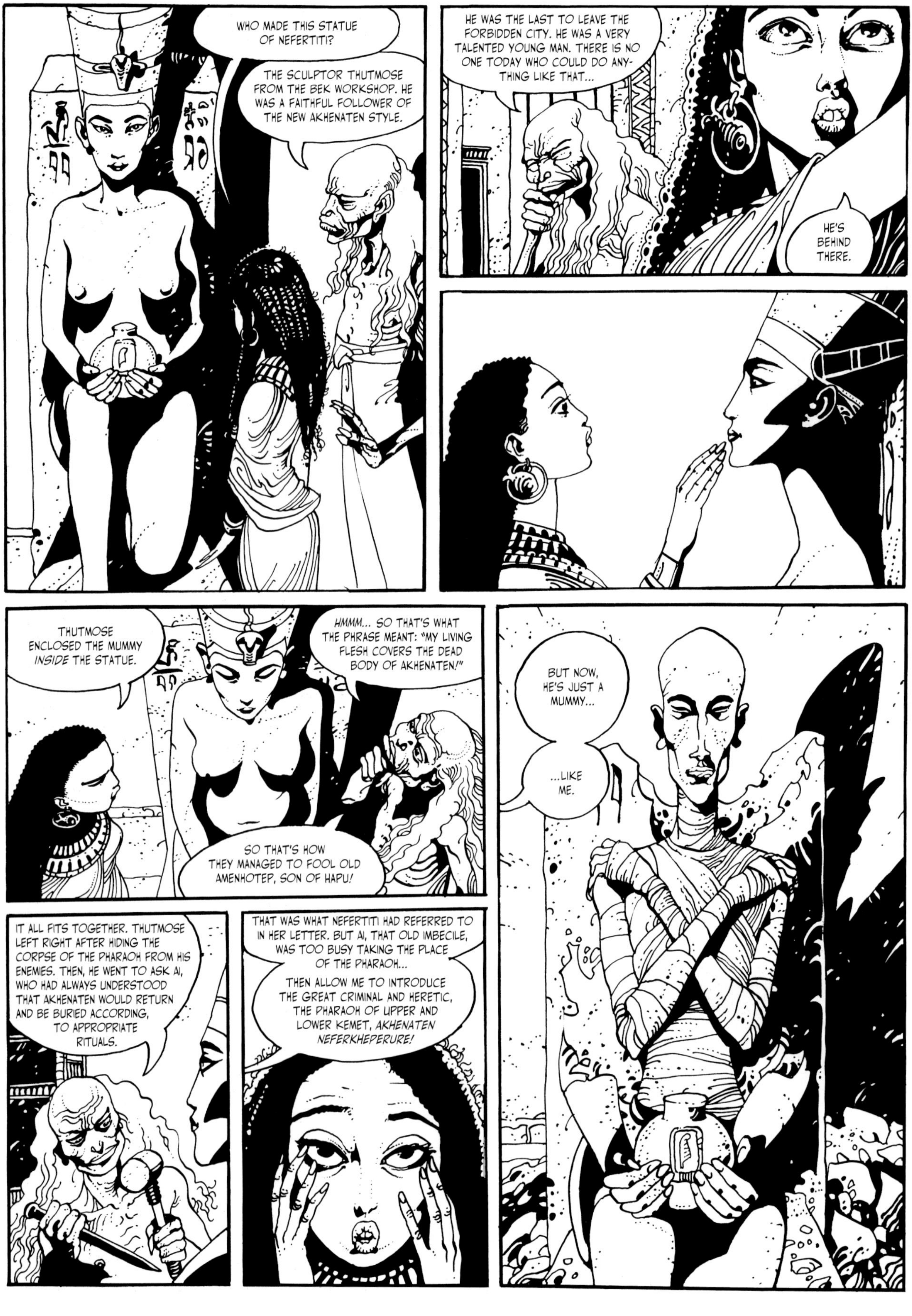
WHO MADE THIS STATUE OF NEFERTITI?
THE SCULPTOR THUTMOSE FROM THE BEK WORKSHOP. HE WAS A FAITHFUL FOLLOWER OF THE NEW AKHENATEN STYLE.
HE WAS THE LAST TO LEAVE THE FORBIDDEN CITY. HE WAS A VERY TALENTED YOUNG MAN. THERE IS NO ONE TODAY WHO COULD DO ANYTHING LIKE THAT...
HE'S BEHIND THERE.
THUTMOSE ENCLOSED THE MUMMY *INSIDE* THE STATUE.
HMMM... SO THAT'S WHAT THE PHRASE MEANT: "MY LIVING FLESH COVERS THE DEAD BODY OF AKHENATEN!"
SO THAT'S HOW THEY MANAGED TO FOOL OLD AMENHOTEP, SON OF HAPU!
BUT NOW, HE'S JUST A MUMMY...
...LIKE ME.
IT ALL FITS TOGETHER. THUTMOSE LEFT RIGHT AFTER HIDING THE CORPSE OF THE PHARAOH FROM HIS ENEMIES. THEN, HE WENT TO ASK AI, WHO HAD ALWAYS UNDERSTOOD THAT AKHENATEN WOULD RETURN AND BE BURIED ACCORDING, TO APPROPRIATE RITUALS.
THAT WAS WHAT NEFERTITI HAD REFERRED TO IN HER LETTER. BUT AI, THAT OLD IMBECILE, WAS TOO BUSY TAKING THE PLACE OF THE PHARAOH...
THEN ALLOW ME TO INTRODUCE THE GREAT CRIMINAL AND HERETIC, THE PHARAOH OF UPPER AND LOWER KEMET, *AKHENATEN NEFERKHEPERURE!*

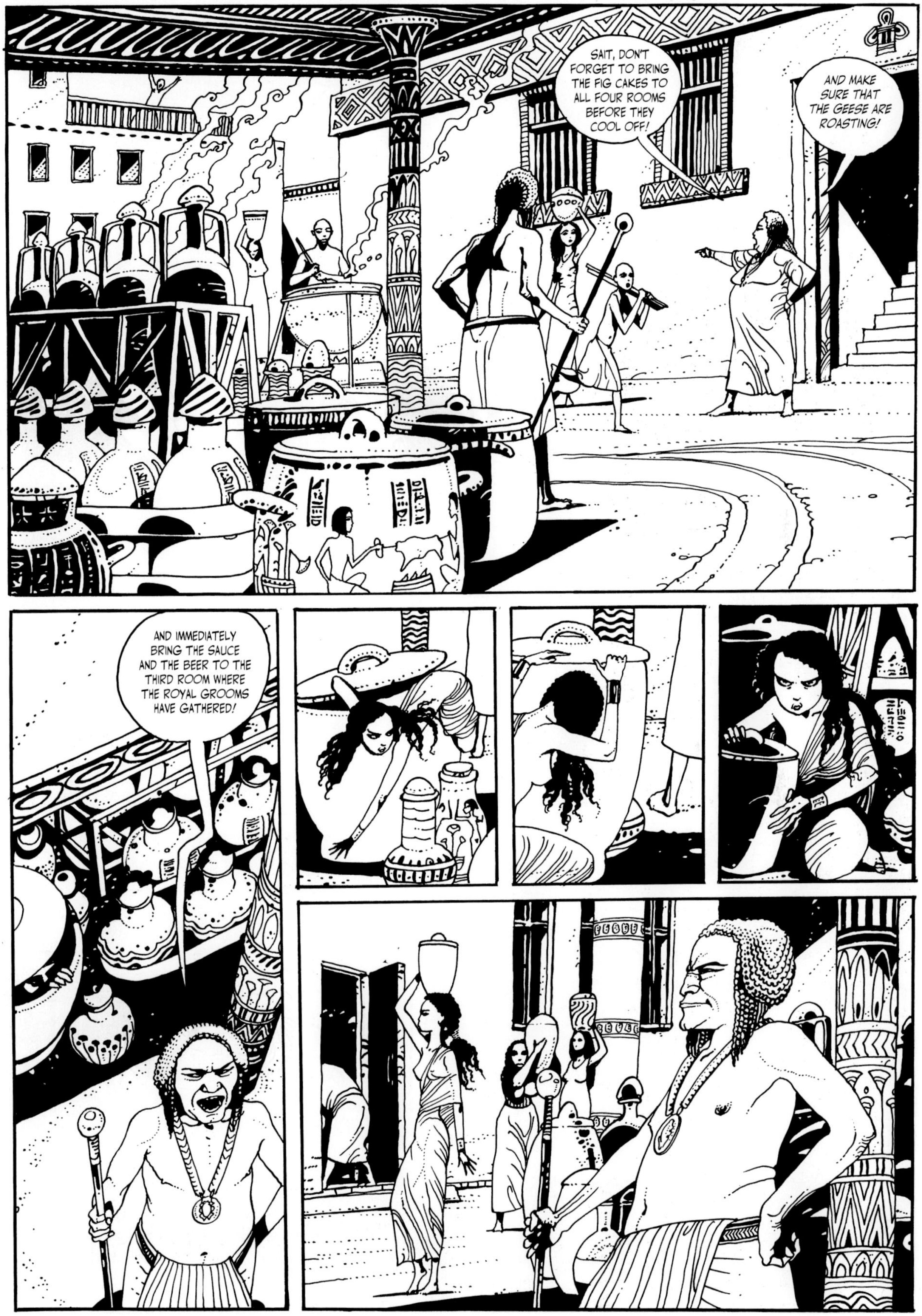
SAIT, DON'T FORGET TO BRING THE FIG CAKES TO ALL FOUR ROOMS BEFORE THEY COOL OFF!
AND MAKE SURE THAT THE GEESE ARE ROASTING!
AND IMMEDIATELY BRING THE SAUCE AND THE BEER TO THE THIRD ROOM WHERE THE ROYAL GROOMS HAVE GATHERED!

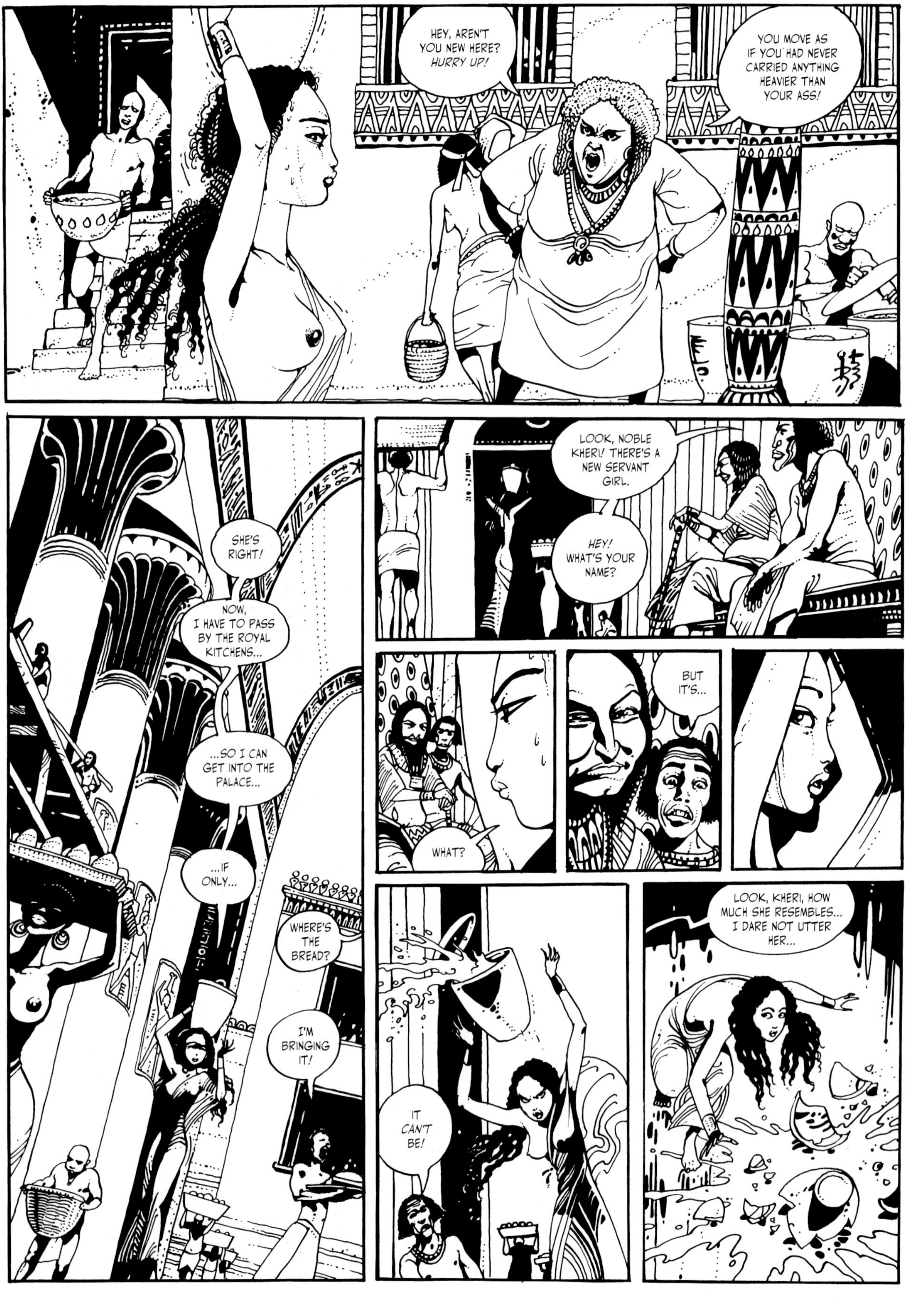
HEY, AREN'T YOU NEW HERE? *HURRY UP!*
YOU MOVE AS IF YOU HAD NEVER CARRIED ANYTHING HEAVIER THAN YOUR ASS!
SHE'S RIGHT!
NOW, I HAVE TO PASS BY THE ROYAL KITCHENS...
...SO I CAN GET INTO THE PALACE...
...IF ONLY...
WHERE'S THE BREAD?
I'M BRINGING IT!
LOOK, NOBLE KHERI! THERE'S A NEW SERVANT GIRL.
HEY! WHAT'S YOUR NAME?
WHAT?
BUT IT'S...
IT CAN'T BE!
LOOK, KHERI, HOW MUCH SHE RESEMBLES... I DARE NOT UTTER HER...

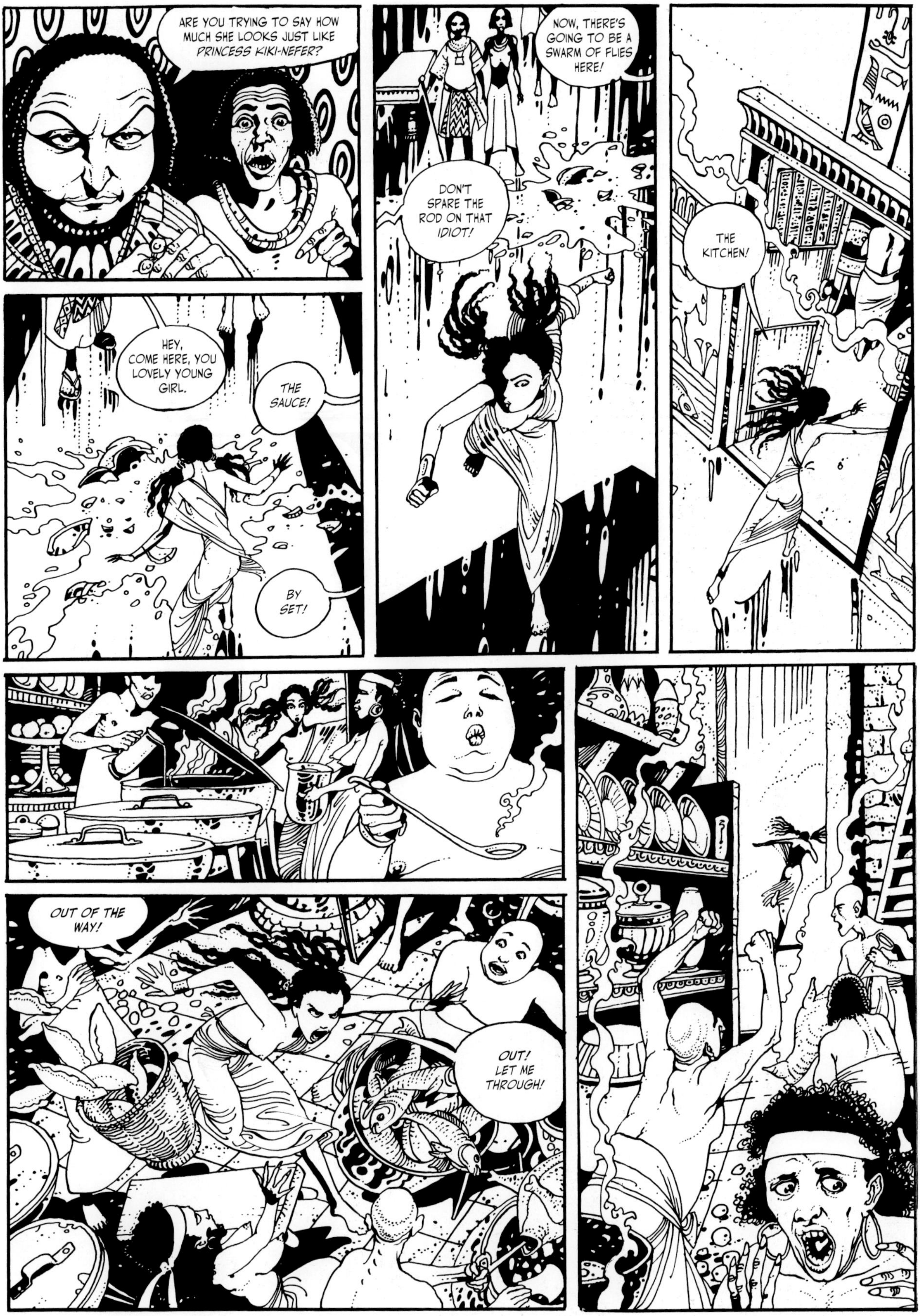
ARE YOU TRYING TO SAY HOW MUCH SHE LOOKS JUST LIKE *PRINCESS KIKI-NEFER?*
NOW, THERE'S GOING TO BE A SWARM OF FLIES HERE!
DON'T SPARE THE ROD ON THAT *IDIOT!*
THE KITCHEN!
HEY, COME HERE, YOU LOVELY YOUNG GIRL.
THE SAUCE!
BY SET!
OUT OF THE WAY!
OUT! LET ME THROUGH!

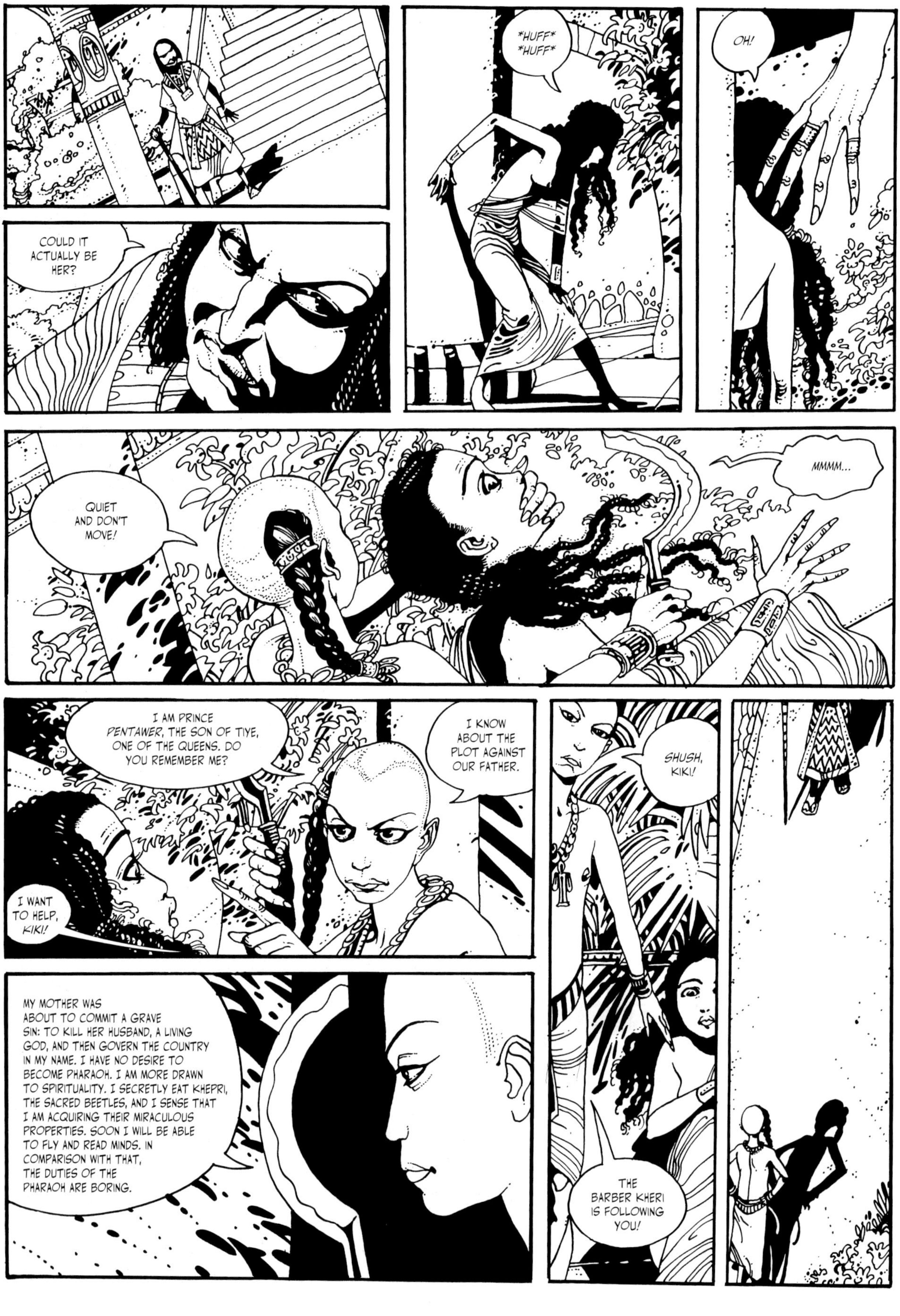
HUFF
HUFF
OH!
COULD IT ACTUALLY BE HER?
QUIET AND DON'T MOVE!
MMMM...
I AM PRINCE PENTAWER, THE SON OF TIYE, ONE OF THE QUEENS. DO YOU REMEMBER ME?
I KNOW ABOUT THE PLOT AGAINST OUR FATHER.
I WANT TO HELP, KIKI!
SHUSH, KIKI!
MY MOTHER WAS ABOUT TO COMMIT A GRAVE SIN: TO KILL HER HUSBAND, A LIVING GOD, AND THEN GOVERN THE COUNTRY IN MY NAME. I HAVE NO DESIRE TO BECOME PHARAOH. I AM MORE DRAWN TO SPIRITUALITY. I SECRETLY EAT KHEPRI, THE SACRED BEETLES, AND I SENSE THAT I AM ACQUIRING THEIR MIRACULOUS PROPERTIES. SOON I WILL BE ABLE TO FLY AND READ MINDS. IN COMPARISON WITH THAT, THE DUTIES OF THE PHARAOH ARE BORING.
THE BARBER KHERI IS FOLLOWING YOU!

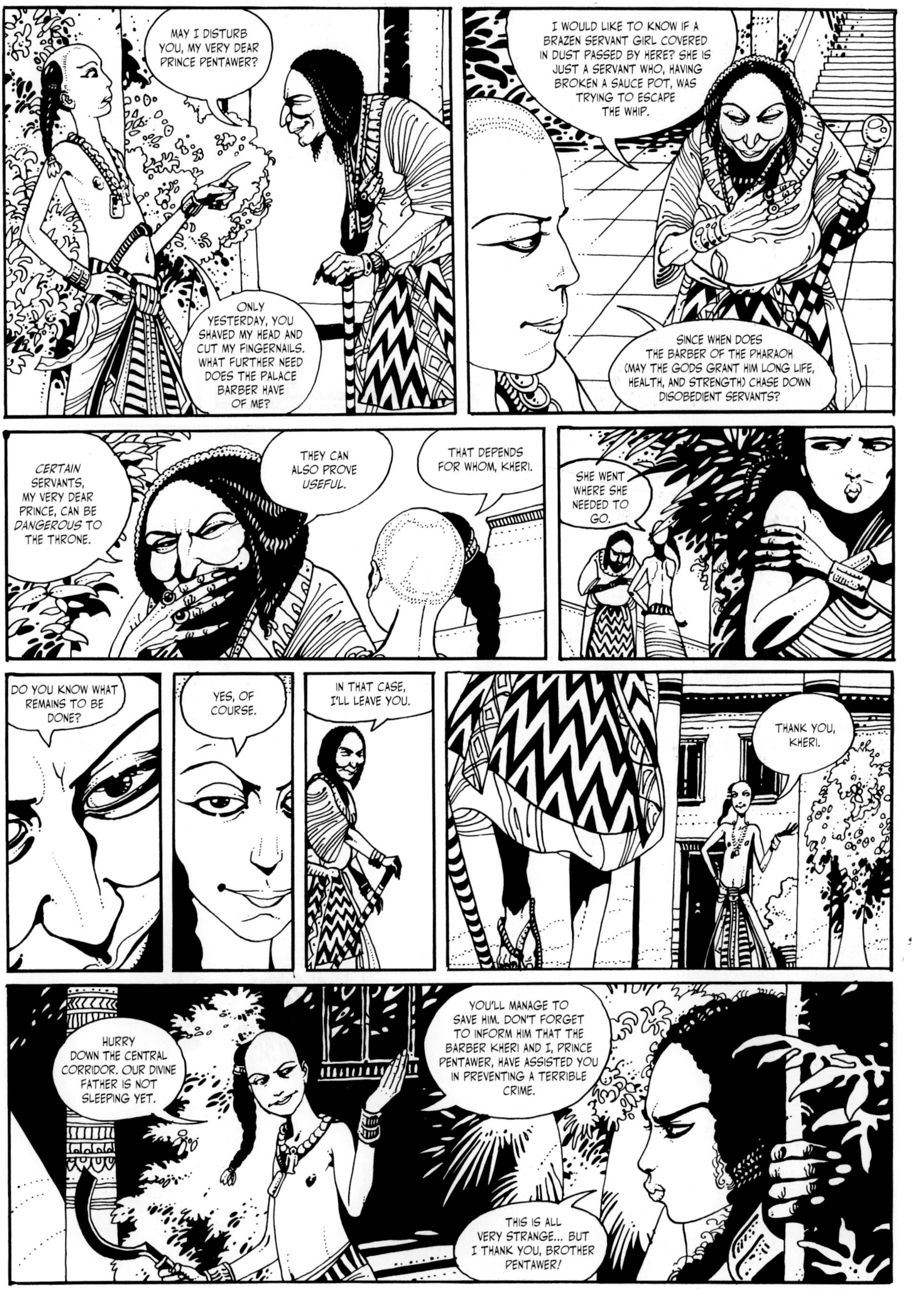
MAY I DISTURB YOU, MY VERY DEAR PRINCE PENTAWER?
ONLY YESTERDAY, YOU SHAVED MY HEAD AND CUT MY FINGERNAILS. WHAT FURTHER NEED DOES THE PALACE BARBER HAVE OF ME?
I WOULD LIKE TO KNOW IF A BRAZEN SERVANT GIRL COVERED IN DUST PASSED BY HERE? SHE IS JUST A SERVANT WHO, HAVING BROKEN A SAUCE POT, WAS TRYING TO ESCAPE THE WHIP.
SINCE WHEN DOES THE BARBER OF THE PHARAOH (MAY THE GODS GRANT HIM LONG LIFE, HEALTH, AND STRENGTH) CHASE DOWN DISOBEDIENT SERVANTS?
CERTAIN SERVANTS, MY VERY DEAR PRINCE, CAN BE *DANGEROUS* TO THE THRONE.
THEY CAN ALSO PROVE *USEFUL*.
THAT DEPENDS FOR WHOM, KHERI.
SHE WENT WHERE SHE NEEDED TO GO.
DO YOU KNOW WHAT REMAINS TO BE DONE?
YES, OF COURSE.
IN THAT CASE, I'LL LEAVE YOU.
THANK YOU, KHERI.
HURRY DOWN THE CENTRAL CORRIDOR. OUR DIVINE FATHER IS NOT SLEEPING YET.
YOU'LL MANAGE TO SAVE HIM. DON'T FORGET TO INFORM HIM THAT THE BARBER KHERI AND I, PRINCE PENTAWER, HAVE ASSISTED YOU IN PREVENTING A TERRIBLE CRIME.
THIS IS ALL VERY STRANGE... BUT I THANK YOU, BROTHER PENTAWER!

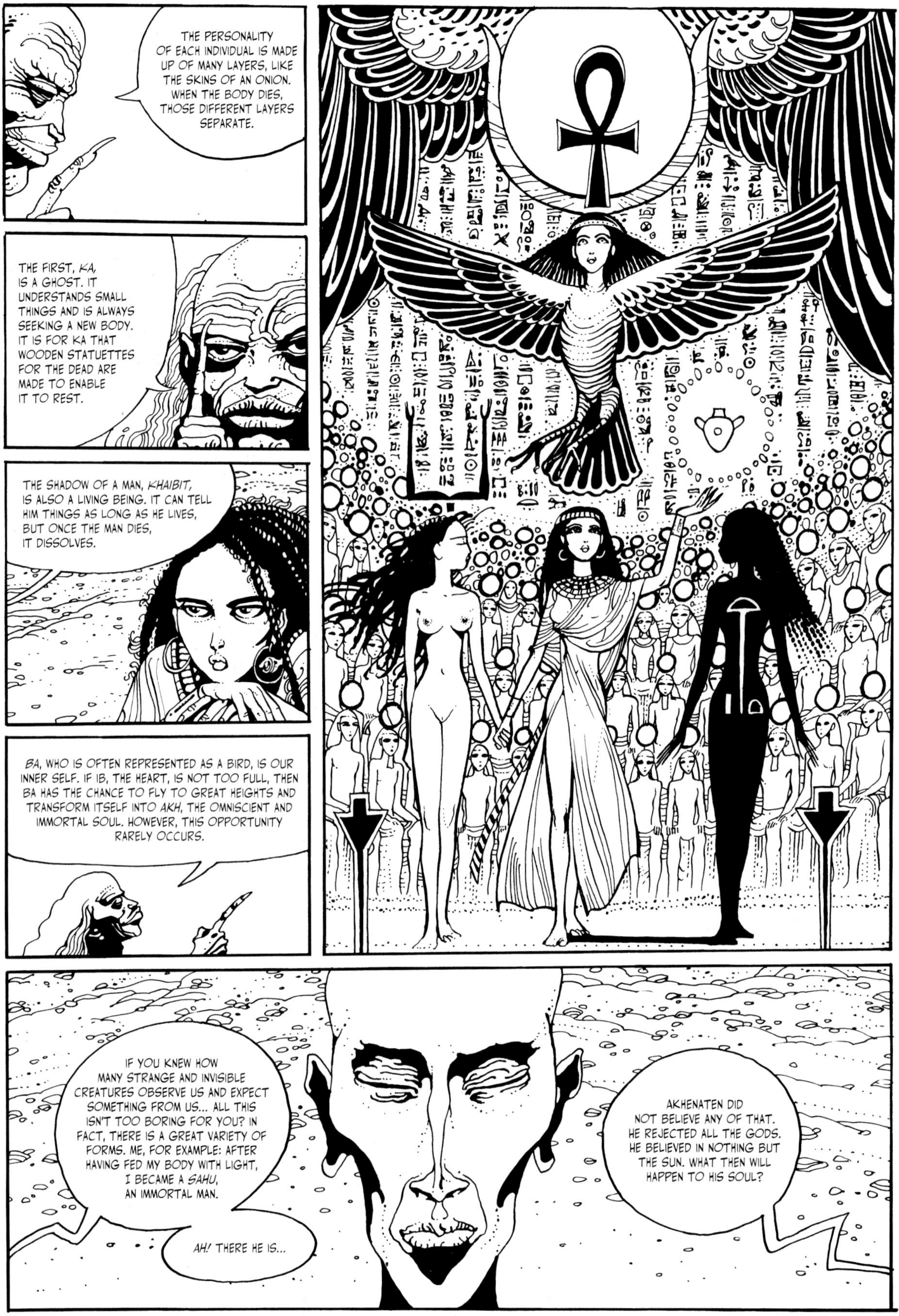
THE PERSONALITY OF EACH INDIVIDUAL IS MADE UP OF MANY LAYERS, LIKE THE SKINS OF AN ONION. WHEN THE BODY DIES, THOSE DIFFERENT LAYERS SEPARATE.
THE FIRST, *KA*, IS A GHOST. IT UNDERSTANDS SMALL THINGS AND IS ALWAYS SEEKING A NEW BODY. IT IS FOR KA THAT WOODEN STATUETTES FOR THE DEAD ARE MADE TO ENABLE IT TO REST.
THE SHADOW OF A MAN, *KHAIBIT*, IS ALSO A LIVING BEING. IT CAN TELL HIM THINGS AS LONG AS HE LIVES, BUT ONCE THE MAN DIES, IT DISSOLVES.
BA, WHO IS OFTEN REPRESENTED AS A BIRD, IS OUR INNER SELF. IF IB, THE HEART, IS NOT TOO FULL, THEN BA HAS THE CHANCE TO FLY TO GREAT HEIGHTS AND TRANSFORM ITSELF INTO *AKH*, THE OMNISCIENT AND IMMORTAL SOUL. HOWEVER, THIS OPPORTUNITY RARELY OCCURS.
IF YOU KNEW HOW MANY STRANGE AND INVISIBLE CREATURES OBSERVE US AND EXPECT SOMETHING FROM US... ALL THIS ISN'T TOO BORING FOR YOU? IN FACT, THERE IS A GREAT VARIETY OF FORMS. ME, FOR EXAMPLE: AFTER HAVING FED MY BODY WITH LIGHT, I BECAME A *SAHU*, AN IMMORTAL MAN.
AH! THERE HE IS...
AKHENATEN DID NOT BELIEVE ANY OF THAT. HE REJECTED ALL THE GODS. HE BELIEVED IN NOTHING BUT THE SUN. WHAT THEN WILL HAPPEN TO HIS SOUL?

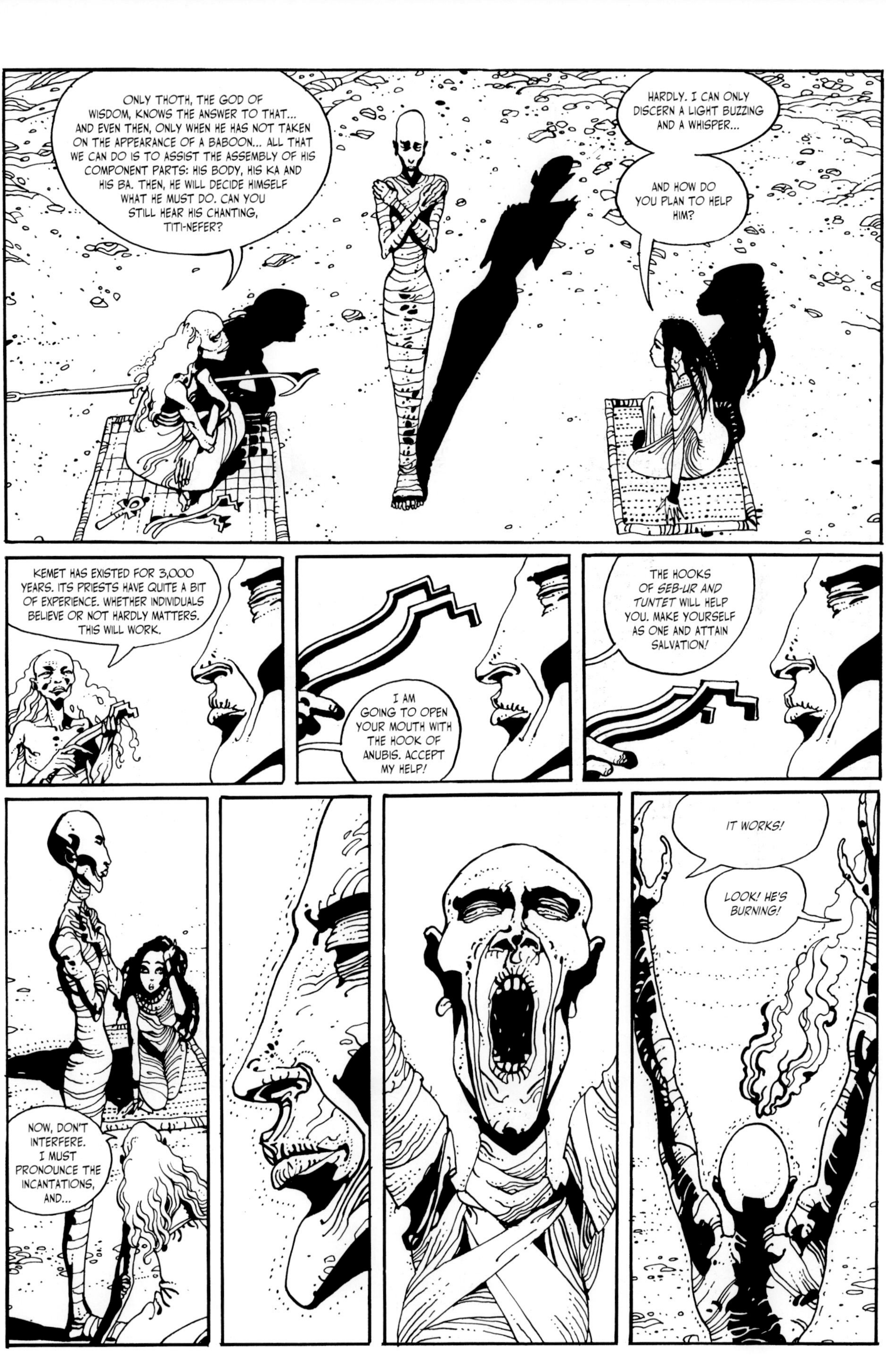
ONLY THOTH, THE GOD OF WISDOM, KNOWS THE ANSWER TO THAT... AND EVEN THEN, ONLY WHEN HE HAS NOT TAKEN ON THE APPEARANCE OF A BABOON... ALL THAT WE CAN DO IS TO ASSIST THE ASSEMBLY OF HIS COMPONENT PARTS: HIS BODY, HIS KA AND HIS BA. THEN, HE WILL DECIDE HIMSELF WHAT HE MUST DO. CAN YOU STILL HEAR HIS CHANTING, TITI-NEFER?
HARDLY. I CAN ONLY DISCERN A LIGHT BUZZING AND A WHISPER...
AND HOW DO YOU PLAN TO HELP HIM?
KEMET HAS EXISTED FOR 3,000 YEARS. ITS PRIESTS HAVE QUITE A BIT OF EXPERIENCE. WHETHER INDIVIDUALS BELIEVE OR NOT HARDLY MATTERS. THIS WILL WORK.
I AM GOING TO OPEN YOUR MOUTH WITH THE HOOK OF ANUBIS. ACCEPT MY HELP!
THE HOOKS OF *SEB-UR* AND *TUNTET* WILL HELP YOU. MAKE YOURSELF AS ONE AND ATTAIN SALVATION!
NOW, DON'T INTERFERE. I MUST PRONOUNCE THE INCANTATIONS, AND...
IT WORKS!
LOOK! HE'S BURNING!

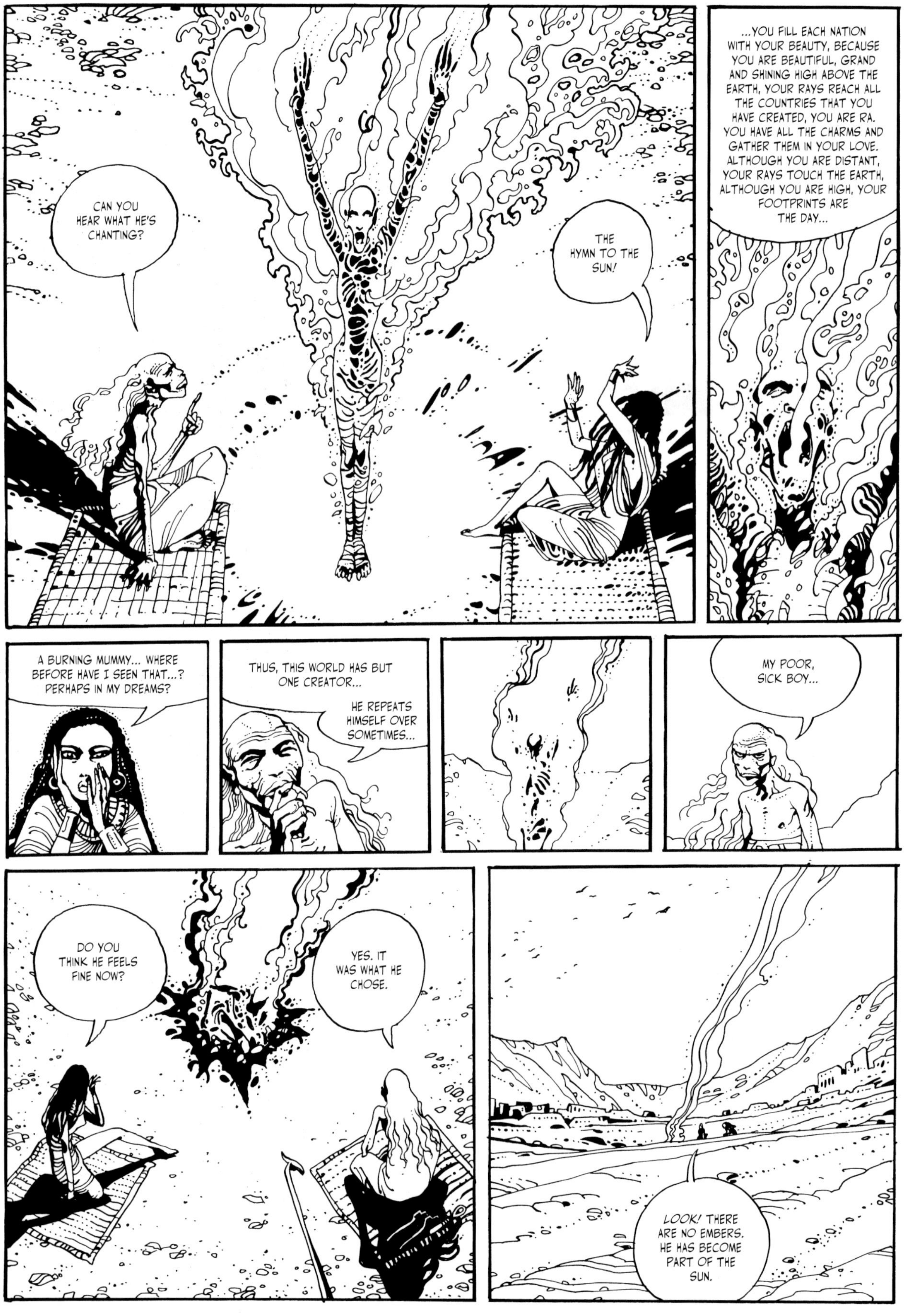
CAN YOU HEAR WHAT HE'S CHANTING?
THE HYMN TO THE SUN!
...YOU FILL EACH NATION WITH YOUR BEAUTY, BECAUSE YOU ARE BEAUTIFUL, GRAND AND SHINING HIGH ABOVE THE EARTH, YOUR RAYS REACH ALL THE COUNTRIES THAT YOU HAVE CREATED, YOU ARE RA. YOU HAVE ALL THE CHARMS AND GATHER THEM IN YOUR LOVE. ALTHOUGH YOU ARE DISTANT, YOUR RAYS TOUCH THE EARTH, ALTHOUGH YOU ARE HIGH, YOUR FOOTPRINTS ARE THE DAY...
A BURNING MUMMY... WHERE BEFORE HAVE I SEEN THAT...? PERHAPS IN MY DREAMS?
THUS, THIS WORLD HAS BUT ONE CREATOR...
HE REPEATS HIMSELF OVER SOMETIMES...
MY POOR, SICK BOY...
DO YOU THINK HE FEELS FINE NOW?
YES. IT WAS WHAT HE CHOSE.
LOOK! THERE ARE NO EMBERS. HE HAS BECOME PART OF THE SUN.

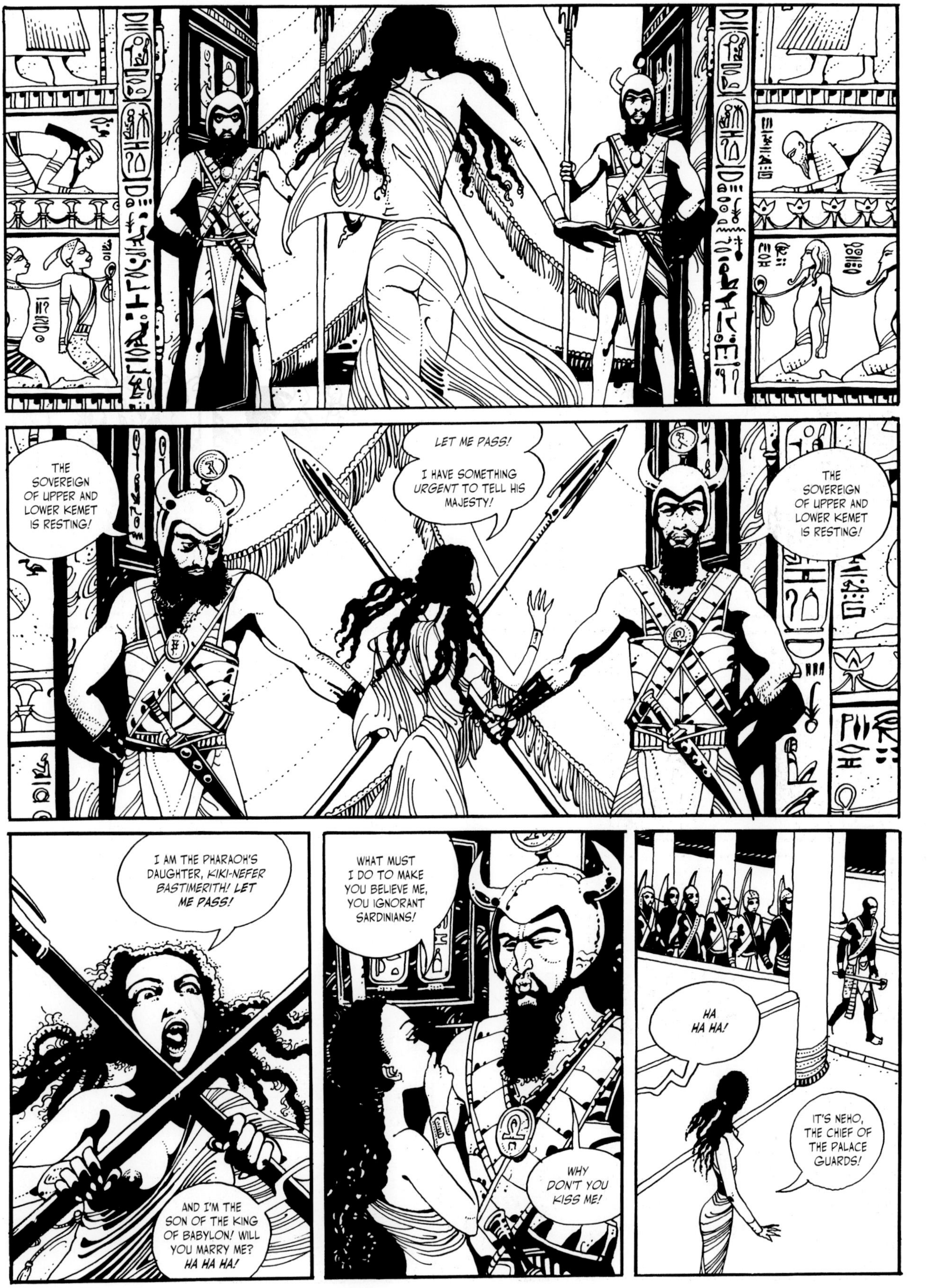
THE SOVEREIGN OF UPPER AND LOWER KEMET IS RESTING!
LET ME PASS!
I HAVE SOMETHING URGENT TO TELL HIS MAJESTY!
THE SOVEREIGN OF UPPER AND LOWER KEMET IS RESTING!
I AM THE PHARAOH'S DAUGHTER, KIKI-NEFER BASTIMERITH! LET ME PASS!
AND I'M THE SON OF THE KING OF BABYLON! WILL YOU MARRY ME? HA HA HA!
WHAT MUST I DO TO MAKE YOU BELIEVE ME, YOU IGNORANT SARDINIANS!
WHY DON'T YOU KISS ME!
HA HA HA!
IT'S NEHO, THE CHIEF OF THE PALACE GUARDS!

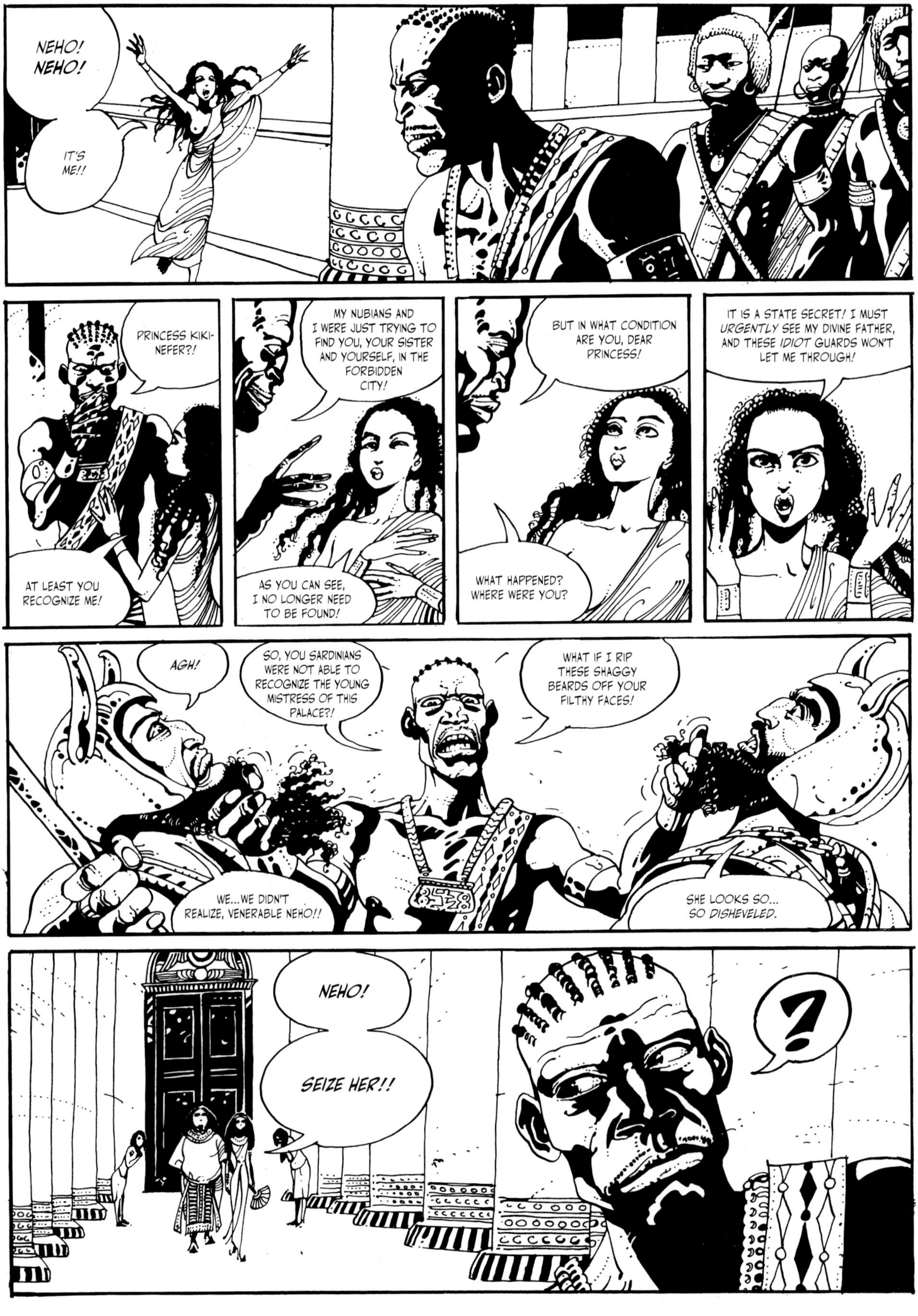
NEHO! NEHO!
IT'S ME!!
PRINCESS KIKI-NEFER?!
AT LEAST YOU RECOGNIZE ME!
MY NUBIANS AND I WERE JUST TRYING TO FIND YOU, YOUR SISTER AND YOURSELF, IN THE FORBIDDEN CITY!
AS YOU CAN SEE, I NO LONGER NEED TO BE FOUND!
BUT IN WHAT CONDITION ARE YOU, DEAR PRINCESS!
WHAT HAPPENED? WHERE WERE YOU?
IT IS A STATE SECRET! I MUST URGENTLY SEE MY DIVINE FATHER, AND THESE IDIOT GUARDS WON'T LET ME THROUGH!
AGH!
SO, YOU SARDINIANS WERE NOT ABLE TO RECOGNIZE THE YOUNG MISTRESS OF THIS PALACE?!
WHAT IF I RIP THESE SHAGGY BEARDS OFF YOUR FILTHY FACES!
WE...WE DIDN'T REALIZE, VENERABLE NEHO!!
SHE LOOKS SO... SO DISHEVELED.
NEHO!
SEIZE HER!!
?

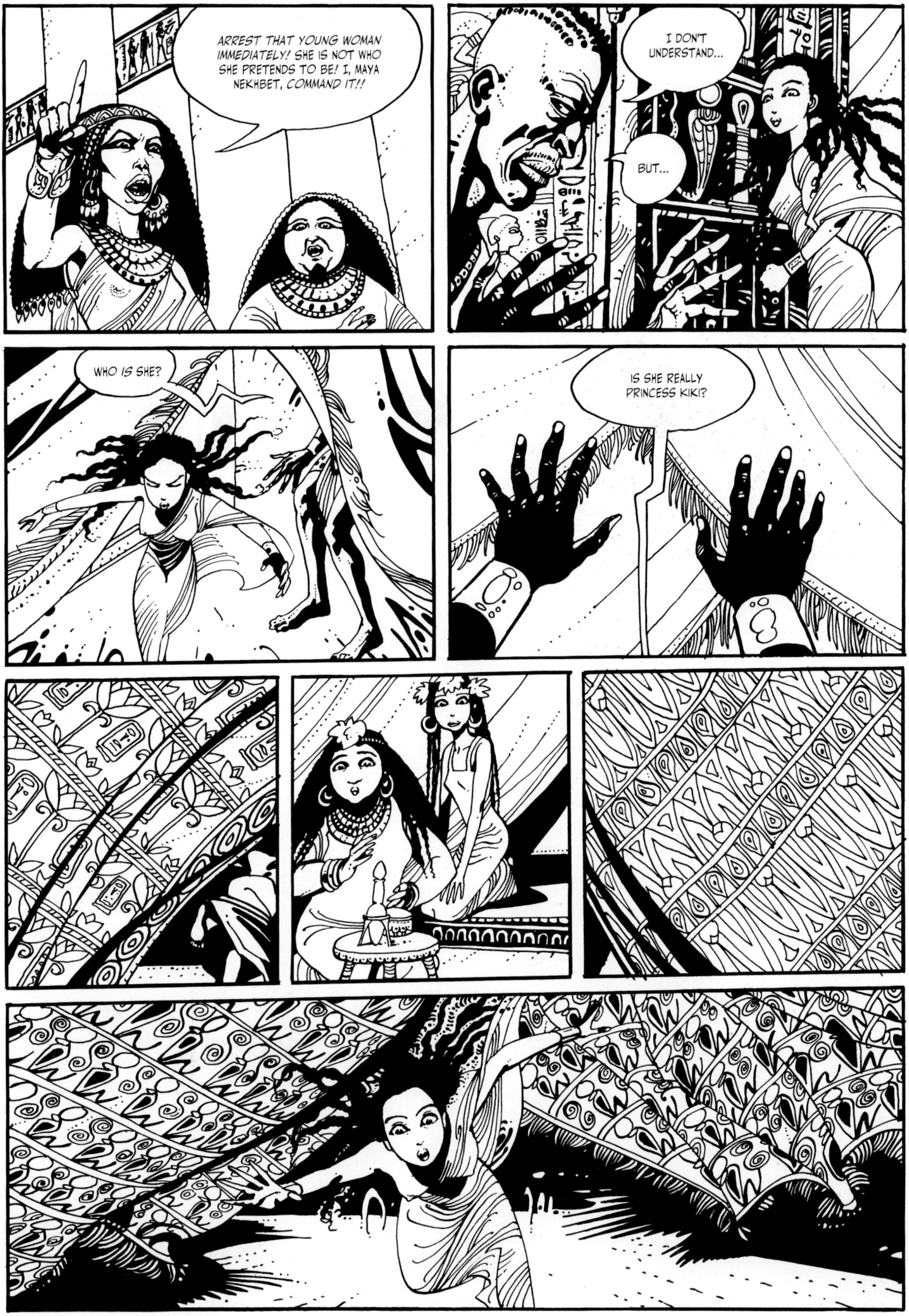
ARREST THAT YOUNG WOMAN IMMEDIATELY! SHE IS NOT WHO SHE PRETENDS TO BE! I, MAYA NEKHBET, COMMAND IT!!
I DON'T UNDERSTAND...
BUT...
WHO IS SHE?
IS SHE REALLY PRINCESS KIKI?

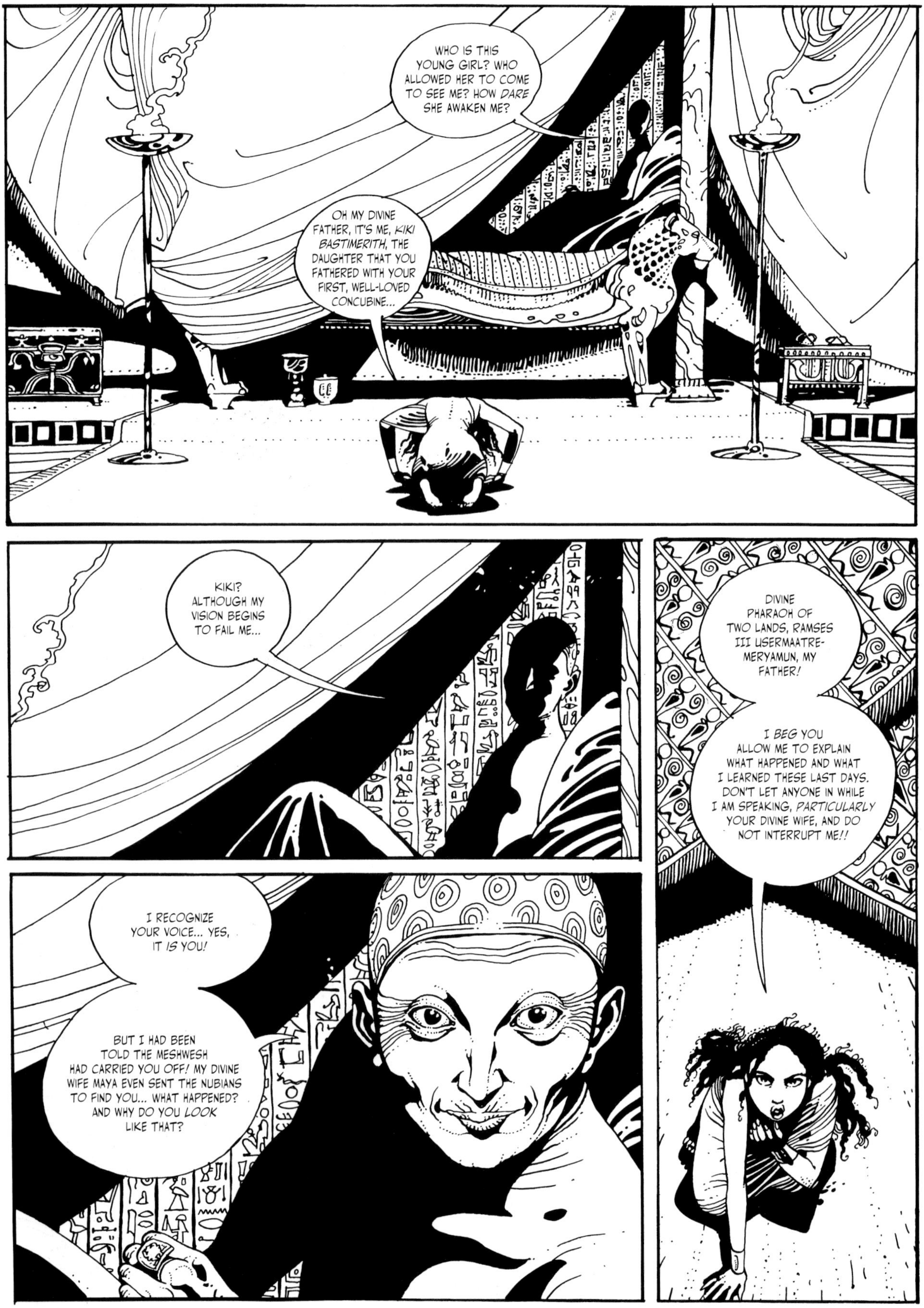
WHO IS THIS YOUNG GIRL? WHO ALLOWED HER TO COME TO SEE ME? HOW *DARE* SHE AWAKEN ME?
OH MY DIVINE FATHER, IT'S ME, *KIKI BASTIMERITH*, THE DAUGHTER THAT YOU FATHERED WITH YOUR FIRST, WELL-LOVED CONCUBINE...
KIKI? ALTHOUGH MY VISION BEGINS TO FAIL ME...
I RECOGNIZE YOUR VOICE... YES, IT *IS* YOU!
BUT I HAD BEEN TOLD THE MESHWESH HAD CARRIED YOU OFF! MY DIVINE WIFE MAYA EVEN SENT THE NUBIANS TO FIND YOU... WHAT HAPPENED? AND WHY DO YOU *LOOK* LIKE THAT?
DIVINE PHARAOH OF TWO LANDS, RAMSES III USERMAATRE-MERYAMUN, MY FATHER!
I *BEG* YOU ALLOW ME TO EXPLAIN WHAT HAPPENED AND WHAT I LEARNED THESE LAST DAYS. DON'T LET ANYONE IN WHILE I AM SPEAKING, *PARTICULARLY* YOUR DIVINE WIFE, AND DO NOT INTERRUPT ME!!

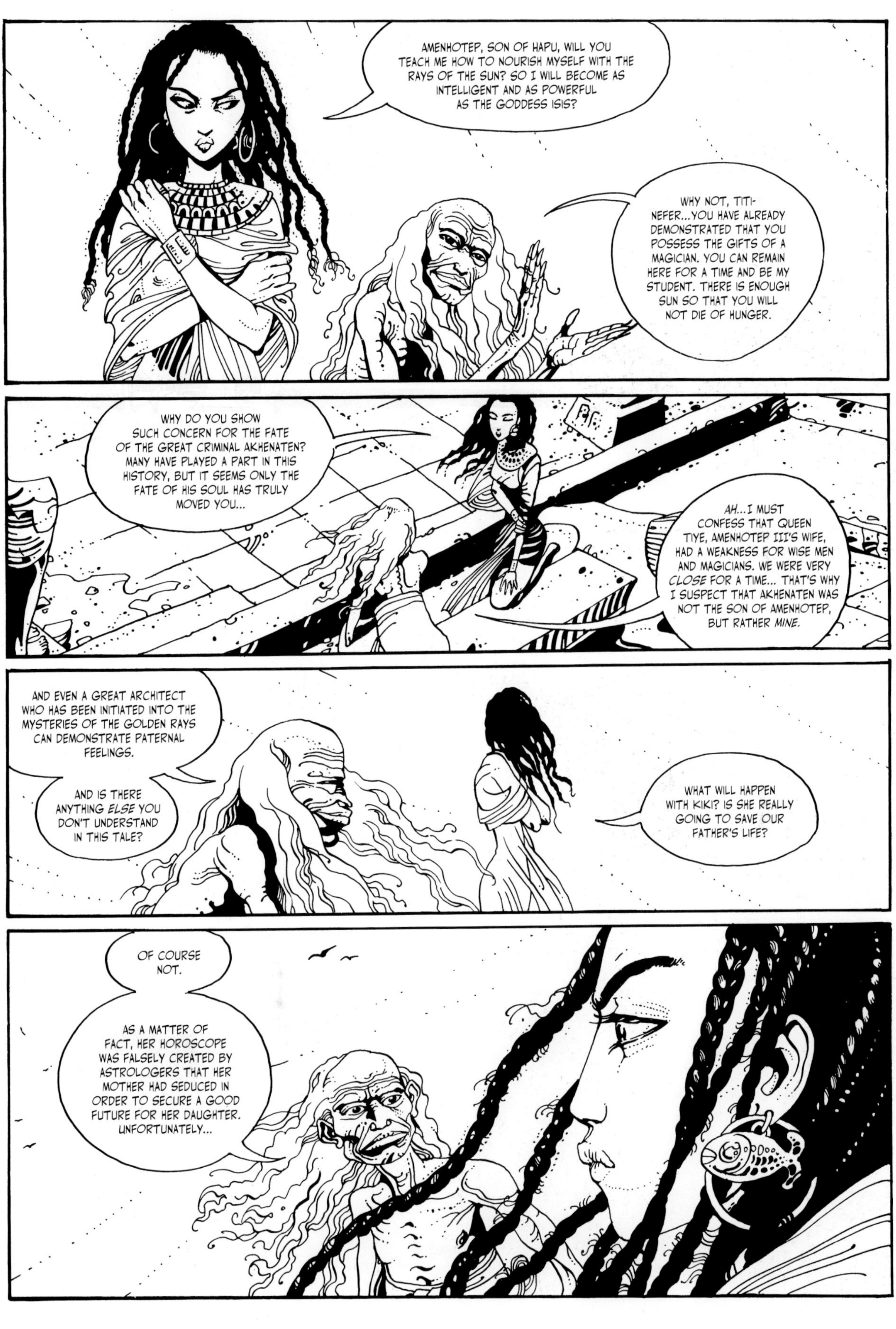
AMENHOTEP, SON OF HAPU, WILL YOU TEACH ME HOW TO NOURISH MYSELF WITH THE RAYS OF THE SUN? SO I WILL BECOME AS INTELLIGENT AND AS POWERFUL AS THE GODDESS ISIS?
WHY NOT, TITI-NEFER...YOU HAVE ALREADY DEMONSTRATED THAT YOU POSSESS THE GIFTS OF A MAGICIAN. YOU CAN REMAIN HERE FOR A TIME AND BE MY STUDENT. THERE IS ENOUGH SUN SO THAT YOU WILL NOT DIE OF HUNGER.
WHY DO YOU SHOW SUCH CONCERN FOR THE FATE OF THE GREAT CRIMINAL AKHENATEN? MANY HAVE PLAYED A PART IN THIS HISTORY, BUT IT SEEMS ONLY THE FATE OF HIS SOUL HAS TRULY MOVED YOU...
AH...I MUST CONFESS THAT QUEEN TIYE, AMENHOTEP III'S WIFE, HAD A WEAKNESS FOR WISE MEN AND MAGICIANS. WE WERE VERY *CLOSE* FOR A TIME... THAT'S WHY I SUSPECT THAT AKHENATEN WAS NOT THE SON OF AMENHOTEP, BUT RATHER *MINE*.
AND EVEN A GREAT ARCHITECT WHO HAS BEEN INITIATED INTO THE MYSTERIES OF THE GOLDEN RAYS CAN DEMONSTRATE PATERNAL FEELINGS.
AND IS THERE ANYTHING *ELSE* YOU DON'T UNDERSTAND IN THIS TALE?
WHAT WILL HAPPEN WITH KIKI? IS SHE REALLY GOING TO SAVE OUR FATHER'S LIFE?
OF COURSE NOT.
AS A MATTER OF FACT, HER HOROSCOPE WAS FALSELY CREATED BY ASTROLOGERS THAT HER MOTHER HAD SEDUCED IN ORDER TO SECURE A GOOD FUTURE FOR HER DAUGHTER. UNFORTUNATELY...

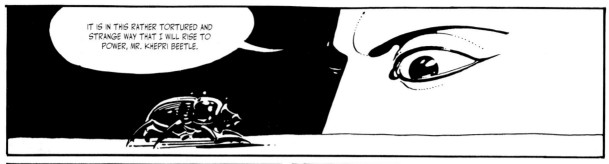

IT IS IN THIS RATHER TORTURED AND STRANGE WAY THAT I WILL RISE TO POWER, MR. KHEPRI BEETLE.

YOU MIGHT WONDER WHY I ALLOWED KIKI-NEFER TO ESCAPE?

WHY I HELPED HER TO UNRAVEL THE PLOT AGAINST MY FATHER?

SIMPLY BECAUSE IT WAS THE ONE THAT MY MOTHER AND PENHEVI HAD PLANNED, WHILE KHERI AND I HAD PLANNED ANOTHER!

KILLING MY FATHER MAKES NO SENSE. HE'LL NEVER LIVE MORE THAN 30 OR 40 DAYS BECAUSE SOME TIME AGO, KHERI THE BARBER MIXED ARSENIC IN HIS OINTMENTS AND HIS SOAPS. MY CRUEL MOTHER WANTED TO MAKE ME A MARIONETTE AND GOVERN IN MY NAME. SHE NEVER LET ME SAY ANYTHING! SHE WOULDN'T ALLOW ME TO EAT ANY SACRED BEETLES, AND IN GENERAL, TREATED ME LIKE AN IDIOT! SHE NEVER UNDERSTOOD THE HIGH ASPIRATIONS IN MY SOUL!

BUT ALL THAT DOES NOT MATTER!

KHERI HIMSELF WANTED TO REVEAL THE PLOT AT THE LAST MINUTE. KIKI ARRIVED RIGHT ON TIME TO SERVE AS MY WITNESS. MY MOTHER AND PENHEVI WILL BE PUNISHED, BUT THEN MY FATHER WILL DIE. KHERI AND I WILL THEN GOVERN KEMET. HE WILL ATTEND TO ALL THE BORING OBLIGATIONS WHILE I CONTINUE MY ESOTERIC RESEARCH.

SOME SECRET WRITINGS BY UNAS, ABOUT EATING REPRESENTATIONS OF ALL THE GODS AND THEREBY BECOMING ONE, WERE PRESERVED IN THE TEMPLES OF KHEMENU. MY MOTHER HAD FORBIDDEN ME TO READ THEM. I HEARD THAT SHE WAS TELLING PENHEVI THAT I WAS A CRAZY, MISGUIDED CHILD, BUT THAT I COULD BE USEFUL BECAUSE I WOULD NOT INTERFERE IN WHAT SHE WOULD DO WHEN SHE REIGNED. BUT KHERI AND I HAVE PROVEN CLEVERER THAN SHE IMAGINED! I WILL BECOME A GOD AND NOBODY CAN STOP ME!

HA HA HA HA HA!

AND IT'S THE WISE BARBER KHERI WHO SCHEMED THE WHOLE THING!

NOW, YOU KNOW IT ALL.

MMM...

I MUST EAT YOU SO THAT YOU NEVER BETRAY ME. YOU WILL BE THE LAST KHEPRI THAT I WILL ABSORB. FROM NOW ON, I AM GOING TO EAT SCORPIONS IN ORDER TO APPROPRIATE THE QUALITIES OF THE SCORPION GODDESS SERKET.

AND THAT'S THAT!

240

EPILOGUE

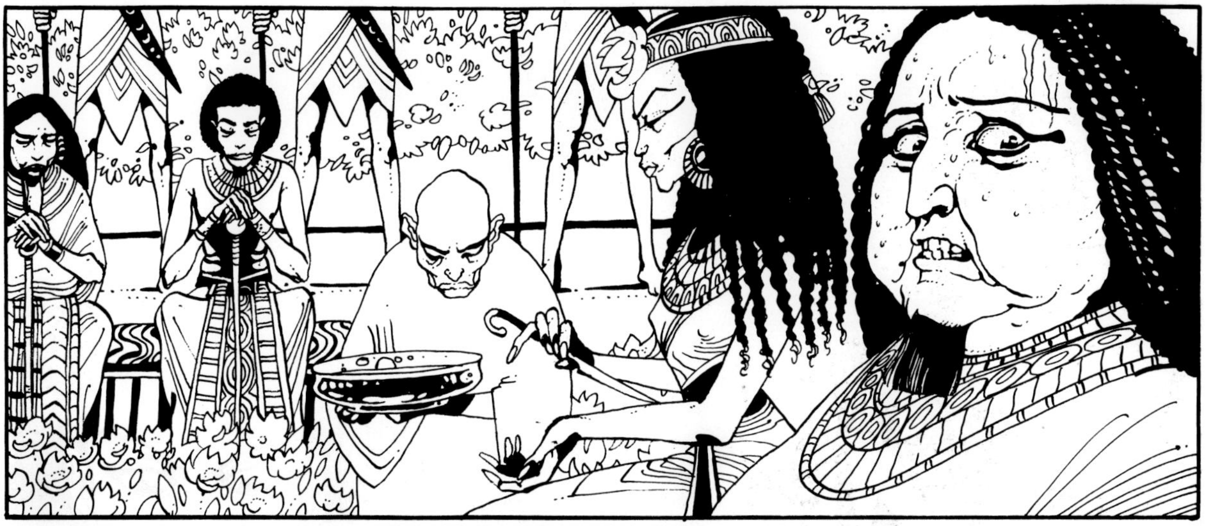

THE PLOT WAS DISCOVERED. MAYA NEKHBET AND PENHEVI WERE CAPTURED AND AFTER A LONG TRIAL, THEY WERE ORDERED TO COMMIT SUICIDE.

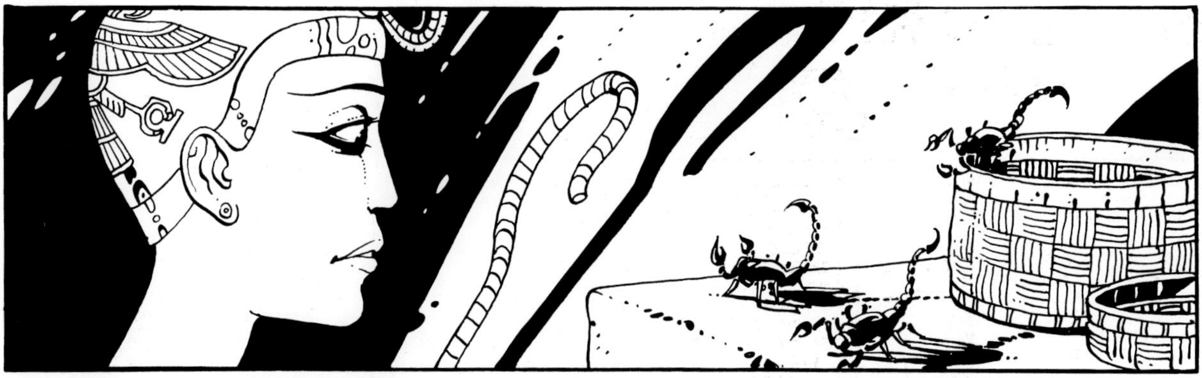

THE PHARAOH RAMSES III DIED 30 DAYS AFTER THE PLOT HAD BEEN THWARTED. SHORTLY THEREAFTER, PRINCE PENTAWER BECAME PHARAOH. THERE IS NO MENTION OF HIS REIGN. BRIEFLY INTO HIS REIGN HE TRIED TO EAT A LIVE SCORPION, WHICH STUNG HIM AND CAUSED HIS DEATH.

TITI-NEFER LIVED FOR A PERIOD OF TIME IN THE FORBIDDEN CITY OF AKHETATEN. SHE STUDIED THE MYSTERIES OF THE RAYS OF THE SUN. WHEN KIKI-NEFER FINALLY CAME TO FIND HER, SHE HAD ALREADY DEPARTED. NO ONE KNOWS WHAT BECAME OF HER.

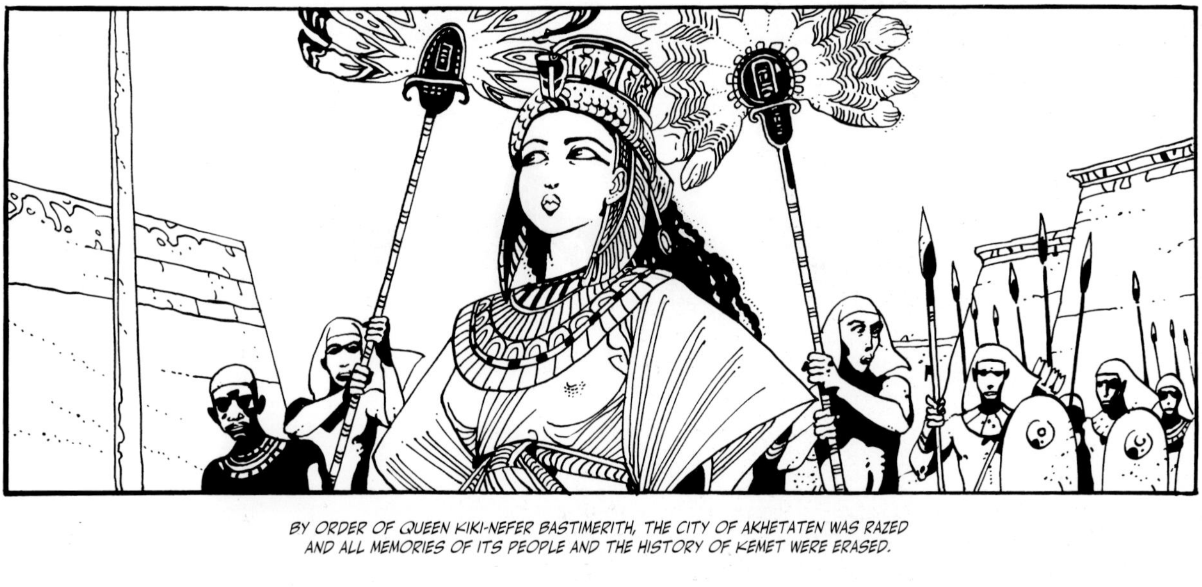

BY ORDER OF QUEEN KIKI-NEFER BASTIMERITH, THE CITY OF AKHETATEN WAS RAZED AND ALL MEMORIES OF ITS PEOPLE AND THE HISTORY OF KEMET WERE ERASED.

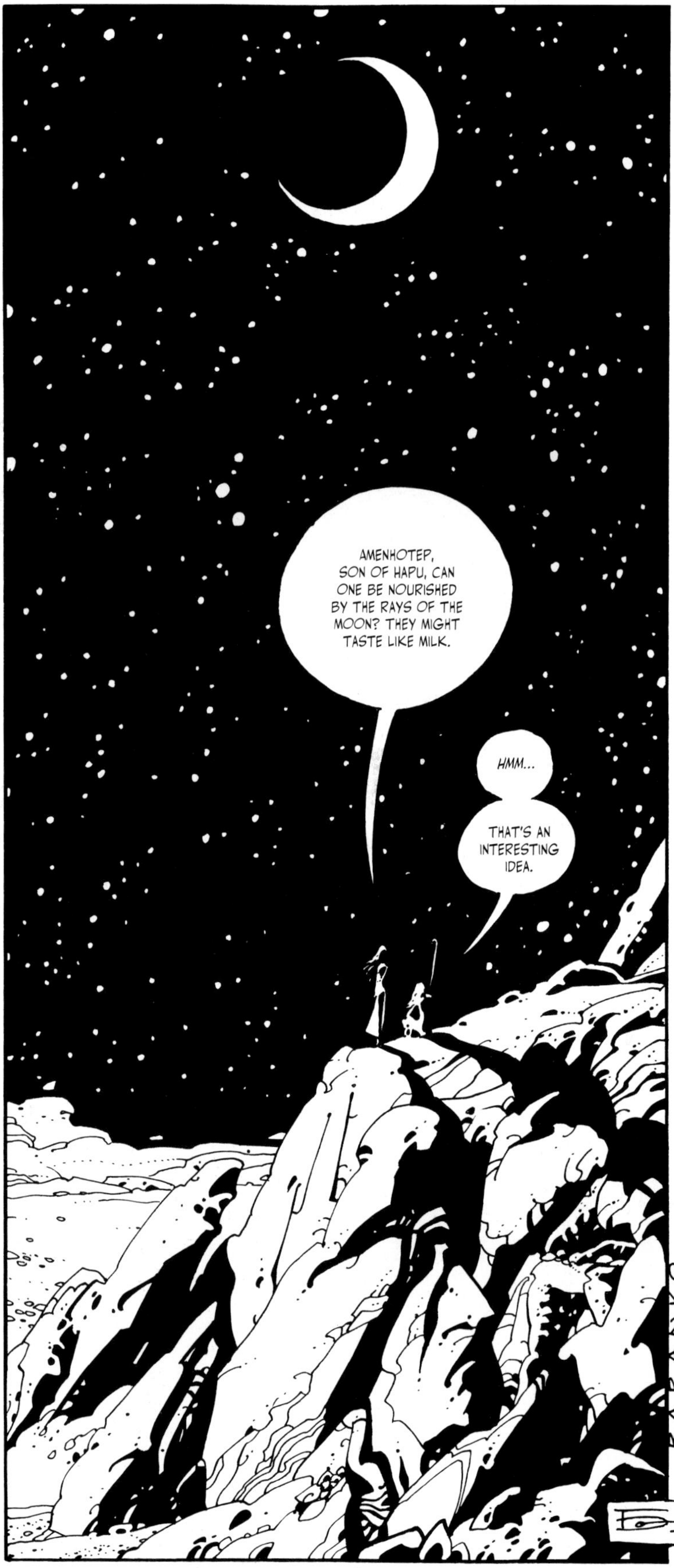
AMENHOTEP, SON OF HAPU, CAN ONE BE NOURISHED BY THE RAYS OF THE MOON? THEY MIGHT TASTE LIKE MILK.
HMM...
THAT'S AN INTERESTING IDEA.
BARANKO

THE END.

AFTERWORD

And if we were to delve into the darkness?

It was an unexpected letter from Humanoids that stirred my curiosity about one of their authors, the Ukrainian Igor Baranko. A tireless traveler and explorer of various worlds, he is not one to hesitate to choose truly unique themes to explore in his writing and drawing, as his past work testifies. His excursions have now led him to an ever-wider universe, that of Ancient Egypt.

But don't expect to discover a serene and peaceful Egypt here. Baranko has chosen to highlight the dark side of that world, so it's no accident that he chose to describe the destiny of two Egyptian princesses during the reign of Ramses III (1186-1155 BCE). This later ruler is often considered as the last great pharaoh before the inevitable, and steady, decline of the great kingdom.

But Egypt was not alone in the world back then. Fearsome predators, the "People of the Sea," a coalition formed by Aegeans, citizens from Sardis, and other ethnicities attempted to overcome "the land beloved by gods" and seize its riches. At the end of a ferocious naval battle, Ramses III succeeded in repelling the invaders, but was confronted with an internal political plot, at the state's highest level, that planned to assassinate him. The conspirators were identified and punished, receiving one of the period's worst punishments — having one's identity changed, for eternity, from a positive meaning to a negative, such as "light loves me" to "light hates me."

Baranko's art deftly illustrates this troubled epoch, and its continuous convulsions. He touches on one of the major chapters of Egyptology, the Akhenaten and Nefertiti period — a time riddled with controversy that continues to this day. For some, Akhenaten was a visionary, a precursor to monotheism; for others, he was mentally disturbed and a terrible pharaoh.

From Ancient Egyptians' point of view Akhenaten was certainly not an ideal ruler, and his mystical experiences did not leave positive impressions. During the latter Ramses era, he was referred to as "the great criminal," because he had separated from the Theban spiritual tradition where the individual was seen as integral to the multitude. Baranko examines this philosophy and highlights its anguished — some would say evil — characteristics.

And then there are the women; omnipresent, beautiful, ugly, magicians, seductresses, strong-willed, and power-hungry… Since the beginning of the Pharaonic civilization, women have played a primordial role. They could be rulers, temple superiors, doctors, writers; and Baranko has created here, in the titular princesses, some heroines with truly indomitable spirit.

Their guide is none other than Isis, "the great magician," the goddess who overcame death, and magic is most definitely at the center of Baranko's story. "Magic" is a word that today is relatively meaningless, valueless, and confused with cheap tricks and stage illusions. But in Ancient Egypt, magic, or *heka*, was the ability to turn the unfortunate incidents of destiny and to share communion with the light, and the magician-in-chief was the Pharaoh himself, charged with deflecting the dark forces threatening his country and people.

Baranko's storytelling and illustrations are impregnated with this magic and its many facets, especially through the sinister character of Amenhotep, son of Hapu. Here most Egyptologists will be taken aback. This genius – who was the right hand of the Pharaoh Amenhotep III, one of the great monarchs of the 18th Dynasty – was regarded by the Ancient Egyptians as a very wise man. As a rare honor, statues depicting him as a thoughtful, seated scribe were erected in the immense temple at Karnak where they would receive the prayers of humans and transmit them to the gods. A shining being, blessed with exceptional knowledge, a magician capable of curing the ill, Amenhotep, son of Hapu was worshipped, and his good name was preserved over centuries; he was even associated with the famous builder, Imhotep, who constructed the step pyramid at Saqqara. Thus, the wizened wizard-like appearance given him by Baranko is far from reality.

The text portrays some evil characters who used dangerous powers that the pharaonic state fought against and condemned. It explores the idea that man is not a rational being, trapped in a universe filled with invisible powers; some creative, others destructive. Thanks to "the formulas relating to the transformation to light," the wise men of ancient Egypt were capable of creating harmony between the spiritual and the material worlds that they called Maat, which controlled both the direction of the state and the idea of all coherent creation.

Baranko is an artist of space. While following his characters, we jump, fight, and penetrate some meticulously described places, and we end up, it seems to me, by crossing the darkness formed by passions and powerful magic in order to

reach the light which is initially so difficult to perceive. Could this light be the writing that the ancient Egyptians called the "words of God"?

Baranko invites us to travel through the startling events of Egypt in the Ramses era that clearly fascinated him. He has created a link between this world and himself, and while his art is occasionally violent, sometimes caricatural, it always points to the original road that deserves to be followed. And after all, didn't the Egyptians invent the comic strip in the first place?

— Christian Jacq

Christian Jacq is a French Egyptologist and author of over 35 books, including the international bestselling *Ramses* quintet. He has a doctorate in Egyptian Studies from the Sorbonne and co-founded the Ramses Institute, which is dedicated to creating a photographic description of Egypt for the preservation of endangered archaeological sites.

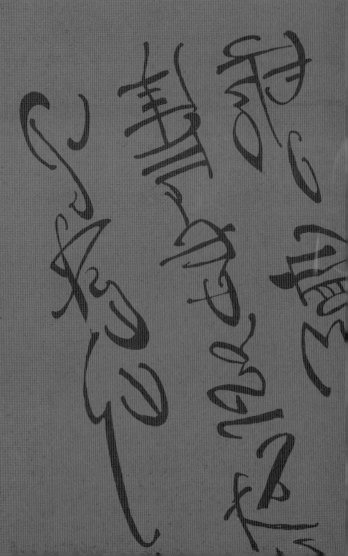